Other Five Star Titles
by Barbara Haynie:

The Terrain of Paradise

Falling Through the Cracks

Falling Through the Cracks

Barbara Haynie

Five Star • Waterville, Maine

First Edition
First Printing: September 2005

Published in 2005 in conjunction with Tekno Books.

Set in 11 pt. Plantin by Liana M. Walker.

Printed in the United States on permanent paper.

Library of Congress Cataloging-in-Publication Data

Haynie, Barbara, 1947–
    Falling through the cracks / by Barbara Haynie.
        p. cm.
    ISBN 1-59414-384-6 (hc : alk. paper)
    1. Young women—Fiction. 2. Women travelers—Fiction.
3. Americans—Mexico—Fiction. 4. Suicidal behavior—
Fiction. 5. Ecoterrorism—Fiction. 6. Mexico—Fiction.
7. Twins—Fiction. I. Title.
PS3608.A97F35 2005
    813´.6—dc22   2005013383

Dedication

For Tanja, three Jennifers, and Rags

The Rules of Scrabble®:
Blank tiles may be used as any letter desired.

One

You never see defining moments coming, do you?

I think they say that about bullets, too.

I'm losing heart.

I can feel it leaking away, lying here listening for a thunk or ping of water moving through pipes. The only trickle, though, is my own nerve leaking out.

Th-thump, th-thump, my heart goes, almost like there's more than one inside there, like an echo. And off in the distance is another beat as regular and reassuring as my own heart, because somewhere out there is the surf.

The thing is, I'm no good at waiting—my imagination always runs away with me, and the dark is only making things worse, too. Way off in the distance music is playing somewhere and then someone laughs far off, a kind of happy-lonely sound when you're surrounded by foreigners. And then this sudden clacking up close, maybe even on the screen, makes me jump.

"Blai-air?" I say, my voice also beating a weak two-time. I say it real quietly, like someone might overhear, which is certainly a possibility through these thin walls. Blair's snore doesn't skip a note, though. He's busy regenerating, now that he's spilled his seed.

Up on the ceiling the decay is like a map of a place that

never was. I shift around, trying to find a comfortable position, but the mattress seems stuffed with ill intentions. It's thin and lumpy and smells like sour mildew. Dreading whatever might be crawling around under the bed, I swing my legs over the side and slide into my sandals, which are right there where I left them, thank God.

I feel my way over in the dark to where my dress is lying across the chair. When I pick it up, it's all limp, like it fainted, and feels clammy shimmying into it. Opening and closing the door as quietly as possible, I just happen to notice a gap under it wide enough for any number of uninvited creatures to enter anytime they want.

Outside, weak light seeps from the bare bulbs over the doorways. The sound of my sandals scraping the sidewalk sets off a dog's barking, which triggers a chorus of answers throughout the whole goddamned area. The air is so thick and moist the lobby swims up all at once at me like through a fog, the light filtering through tinged green by all the potted plants plus the unrestrained use of aqua-colored tile. What with that fiberglass encased sailfish arching across the wall, I could almost be standing in an aquarium. A greenish glare spotlights the shiny tile countertop. Up until now, this counter has always contained a young man, but not now. Now, it's like an empty zoo exhibit missing the animal.

I stand there waiting. I shove the hair out of my face, and it feels like there's glue in it. The sweat is trickling down from both my armpits, one side running faster than the other, like a minuet, or maybe a fugue. I'm really not good at waiting at all. So I stand there working my heels in and out of my sandals, and the leather feels gummy against my skin, and the back of my knees stick together. It's even worse between my legs, though. On the counter, a little silver bell sits there begging to be rung, so I ring it. While I'm turning in place to look at the curious décor, all at once my position in the universe strikes me as paltry and pathetic. All I've got is my poor body, and it's tired and reeking. It's just not adequate. But I guess I have my imagination, too.

The thing is, Lily, I don't really know how I ended up down here. All I know is, one day Blair puts on one of those big, insincere smiles of his and says, "Let's go to Mexico, Iris!"

So I ask him, "Kind of sudden, isn't it?"

I mean, him and Cal making up their minds one night to spend a whole summer in some blank spot on the map just because, "It has great surf."

What's the tearing hurry? I wanted to know.

"Come on, Iris, are you in or out?"

In or out.

Blair's always in whole-hog, up to his neck, anyway. But then, that's part of the attraction, isn't it?

It's not like I felt like I couldn't leave Arcata, or anything. But it's not like I couldn't wait to leave either. I'm Blair's opposite there. I can't seem to take the plunge.

Since when did we let Cal start leading us around, anyway?

Still, again, it's not like I had to just drop everything in Arcata, because there was hardly anything to drop. It did clean out my entire life's savings, though, such as it was.

There was no one to say goodbye to, not really. I'd already done that when I left Colorado—said adios to everyone who mattered. Not unless you want to count the people living with us in Arcata. They certainly were an interesting bunch, but they weren't all that hard to leave, not really. Not like Colorado.

Anyway, now that I'm here, I have to say this isn't ex-

actly for the faint of heart. I think it would be easier if you were either really oblivious or really rash, which is why Blair is in there sleeping like a baby.

Meanwhile, here I am, standing here reeking. Feeling about as culture-shocked as a baby must when it makes its grand entrance into the wide world. I guess that's about what I've done, too, in a way—sheltered me.

I mean, it's all so utterly different down here. The rules still apply, though, don't they? People all want the same things deep down, I bet. One big human family, and all that. That sounds good. Anyway, I guess I'll find out.

The thing is, I'm just no good at waiting, especially in the dark.

"Iris!" I can hear Mama calling, "Iris! Lily! Time for bed. Chop-chop!" Sleepyheads, Dad called us. "You're asleep on your feet. Better get to bed."

I want to. I really do. It's just . . .
I'm standing here reeking.
Honestly.
I don't know when I started explaining things to Lily in my head. I didn't even realize I was doing it for a long time.

Just take a look at this dump! All I want is to ask the hotel clerk why the hell *there's* still *no hot water, but I can't even do that because I don't know any swear words in Spanish yet. Well, I mean, everybody knows "pinche."*

I wouldn't actually swear, anyway. Mama always told us you catch more flies with honey than vinegar.

I would have to think of flies, wouldn't I?

Besides, I don't know how to say "still" in Spanish either.

When I turn back to the counter, the man stands there before me, like magic.

"Oh!" It takes me a moment to shift gears into Spanish. *"Buena Noche!"* I say, polite as all get-out.

The man behind the counter is practically delicate, with a mustache as fine as mink, which defeats its purpose by making him look even more boyish. Him with these perfectly innocent eyes to go with his immature body and pathetic mustache—who could swear at such a specimen, anyway? Then again . . .

So all I'm able to ask him in my lousy Spanish is, "Please, *señor,* why is there no hot water?"

What I'm trying to find out is why the water from my shower hasn't become hot in the hour and forty-five minutes since he promised me the boiler had been turned on. Especially since hot water is the only luxury his crummy hotel promises.

I happen to know he speaks English. Blair managed to ask him when we checked in, *"Habla usted Ingles?"* and he flashed us this brilliant smile. "Of course. I went to university in Athens, Georgia."

But for some asinine reason I keep thinking I really ought to uphold my end of multiculturalism, so I keep torturing this poor language that deserves better. Like his mustache, I'm defeating my own purpose, because I hate offending people. I really do.

I'm also not usually so persistent, but in the steaming night air of San Vaciò, I'm desperate for a hot shower. *Desperado.* I need to wash away the plane trip and the bus ride, the baggage hassle, the agoraphobia, the xenophobia, and the shock of the room's squalor, to say nothing of the gaminess of hot sex (I mean that literally, as in sweaty, slippery, sticky, suffocating). To say nothing also of whatever is sharing that mattress with us. That other phobia, arachno-. I know a hot shower would make a huge difference. I can stand almost anything as long as I can have a hot shower.

I've turned on the tap every five minutes, watching with morose fascination as the water splashes into the toilet, because the entire tiny bathroom is the shower stall. (Spanish lesson *numero uno:* "Where is the bathroom?") Each time I turn it on, I try to convince myself the temperature's a teeny bit warmer, but it's not.

Now here I am, back at the front desk, hoping the young *señor* won't notice the smell of wet chicken feathers wafting up from beneath my limp dress. I apply my sweetest smile, which I admit can't compare with his for charm or guile—or beauty, for that matter.

"Wait just a few more minutes and try again, please, and I'm sure it will be hot," he tells me. And who could doubt those eyes?

I turn to leave, then undo the turn.

"Por favor," I ask him, "how do you say 'still' in Spanish?"

"Tranquilo," he answers, looking confused.

When I think about it, though, that can't be right . . . as if anything could ever just be simple or straightforward . . .

"No. Not that kind of still. Not like 'quiet.' I mean 'still,' as in 'not yet.' "

"Ahhh. You mean *todavia.*"

"Todavia, todavia. All right, thank you. Really. Thanks so much. *Muchas gracias.* "

There's no way I'm asking him how to say "hell." To hell with that.

I go back to the room, hope and faith *still* intact, and stretch out gingerly on the ratty bed next to snoring Blair to wait another fifteen minutes. *Lily, with her lily-white room, wouldn't she just love this?* If Mexico is going to grow on me, I wish it would hurry up and start. Then I start really listening to the night sounds, thrilled and repelled by the foreignness of it all, until finally, drugged by exhaustion, my disgust for the room slowly melts away and I become permeable, accepting, embracing.

Rotating slowly, step-by-step in place to avoid the toilet, beaten by a stream of water that's refreshingly robust and not *frigid*, after all, I tell myself that a cold shower makes sense in this climate, anyway. And it does.

Adaptation, not language, is my forte.

Huh, Lily?

I don't know what was wrong with me last night. I'm lousy in the dark.

Everything always seems better in daylight, don't you agree? I think you're the one who told me that in the first place.

El Colon Hotel, especially. Look how beautiful it is! It's a whole different world out here in the dining room, such a quantum leap in fortune it's hard to believe the two rooms can possibly be connected. This room is wonderful, and really pink. I mean, pink! As pink as the lobby is aqua. It's an airy, gleaming statement of pinkness, with sweating coral walls and a radiant pink-and-white checkered marble floor. Attached to the floor is a human, also dressed in pink, swaying across with a mop pressed wetly against its surface, like a kiss. The grandness of the Colon's dining room in this flea-bitten backwater strikes me as slightly surreal, which I like very much (always a tad attracted to a tinge of perversity). Unlike our horrid hotel room, the dining room has been lovingly maintained, one could even say curated, if there were such a word (but, being a Scrabble player, I happen to know there's not).

Not a breath of air is stirring. Hummingbirds zip in and

out among the flowers, suspended mid-air in the heavy ozone, defying gravity and breaking sound barriers to sip nectar. Ordinary little miracles.

"Oh look," I tell Blair, delighted to recognize among the ragged plants running wild in El Colon's garden species from my greenhouse work back in Arcata: bougainvillea, ti plants, helliconia, tuberose, a pomegranate tree, bird-of-paradise.

"It's like a little Garden of Eden!"

"Sure, Iris. Very exciting."

I don't care what he thinks, though. They're my atmosphere, ozone, and tropical allotrope, same as for the hummingbirds.

What is it that makes them so different from those cold-blooded plants back home, eh Lil'? "Flamboyance. Perfume. Scandal. That's what," she tells me. Sure, by now, she answers me too.

Blair can be very enthusiastic about things when he wants to be, but it has to come spontaneously from him—it's not something I can talk him into. He looks happy now, though. Maybe not exactly enthusiastic, but happy. He has one of those faces that can't hide anything, anyway. Him and his gloomy eyes. His face is deceptively wholesome, though—all-American in some way. Trout-speckled skin with this roan hair that sticks up like a cockscomb most of the time, and a beard that amounts to little more than peach fuzz. Still, there's something that betrays all that wholesomeness. There's something of the pirate about him, a quick, nervous look in his eyes, like something slightly dangerous is always rumbling deep inside, something he can't completely cover up. The veins always stand out in his hands.

He's cut himself shaving again, like always, and has this little piece of tissue stuck to the mole on his chin. A dot of red has bled into the center of it, so it's like a tiny hibiscus flower blooms there every morning.

16

A fountain coated in algae spills water near our table. Doves fly in and out, their wings clapping noisily, landing on the rim to drink. Sometimes the hummingbirds have to change course to miss them; otherwise, it would be like an ultra-light running into a jetliner.

I think I read somewhere that hummingbirds are the only birds that can fly backwards. *"Chuparrosa,"* the Mexicans call them, and if you roll the R's to get the sound right, it's really beautiful and sort of sounds like their flight.

Near the fountain, I notice a rotund mouse running nimbly up and down the stem of a shrub, biting off seedpods and leaping into the underbrush below to eat them. And it strikes me that, fat as it is, it's probably pregnant, and it also strikes me that it could probably easily fit under the door to our room.

The graceful man-boy concierge of last night approaches now as our waiter.

My armpits feel fresh and wonderful.

"Good morning," he says.

"Buenos dias."

Boy, that sounds bad! Us and our crummy accents.

"Did you sleep well?"

"Si, si. Claro. Muy bien." Not exactly true. Fear of bugs, ghastly mattress, cold shower.

No mention is made of the hot water. Of course, there isn't, never was, and never will be any hot water at the Colon.

"And what would you like for breakfast?"

There's also never a menu at the Colon, only the miracle that whatever you order appears in this middle-of-nowhere. So there are miracles beyond hot water at the Colon that weren't promised but come unexpectedly, like revelations, like loaves and fishes.

Already affected by Mexico's exotica, Blair seems a

17

slightly different person. Or, for all I know, maybe it's just the tip of the iceberg of a huge difference. For one thing, he's less self-assured, which is definitely good, maybe even another miracle.

Once the food arrives, we dig in and he says, "I thought we'd try to find Cal first thing, if that's okay with you," his voice submissive, verging on conciliatory, even.

He lifts my wrist and rotates it to kiss the underside. I try to smile, but even I can tell it's a failure.

"I don't know," I tell him. "Maybe we should find a better place to stay first. I don't think we can stay here. I mean, sure, the dining room is great, but our room . . ." I hate being such a coward. I happen to know for a fact there are people staying in hammocks down at the beach who are way worse off than we are, sleeping down there, bitten by sand flies, shitting behind the rocks. As a matter of fact, that's probably where Cal's staying.

And the people seem so nice here at the Colon.

Even so, "Let's find a better place," I tell him.

It's not always easy getting through to Blair, but this time he seems to hear me. I guess maybe he can tell I'm losing heart here.

"Okay, baby. We could take a walk on the beach and discuss it. We could walk down to the surf break. We'll probably run into Cal down there anyway. How would that be?" he asks, all deferential.

That could mean he's taking my feelings into consideration, or it could mean his original suggestion just trumped mine. You can't always tell who wins and who loses in these things, can you?

Our waiter interrupts meekly with the *cuenta*. Blair counts out the money, then looks up, smiling expansively.

"*Como se llama?*" he says, very friendly.

"My name is Leonardo, Leonardo Perez, but my friends in the U.S., they call me Leo." *Lay-O.*

"Well, this is a great place, Leo." *Lay-O.*

"I am happy you like it, *señor.*"

"Call me Blair, please. And this is Iris."

"Eye-res?"

"It's a flower," I tell him. Yes, and with a most un-cold-blooded flamboyance itself, I, of all people, should remember. An Iris, that temperate northerner, is about as garish and fragrant as it gets, every bit as flamboyant as any tropical orchid. I try pronouncing it Eer-r-r-rees, loosening up my tongue to roll the R, guessing the word might be the same in both languages.

"Oh, jes, Eer-r-r-rees. *Flor de lis.*"

Now that is beautiful. *"Flor de lis."* Lyrical. So the man-boy is not only a concierge and waiter, but also a poet. Or maybe it's just the language. Or maybe it's just my imagination.

I think I could love this country.

Blair turns in his chair to take in the entire room.

"It's very fancy, this room, especially the floor."

Leo's face radiates pride. "The floor, jes, Italian marble."

It doesn't make sense to me. Granted, summer is off-season, which might explain why we're the only clientele, but beyond that, it doesn't make any sense in this setting at all, for all time.

Leo, like Blair, can evidently read my mind. I really must work on my transparency.

"The Colon was once a casino, you know," he explains.

For some reason, this fact impacts Blair. "A casino! Here? In San Vaciò?"

"Si. Sure," says Leo. "San Vaciò, it wasn't always so small, so, *como se dice,* 'laid-back.' This was a busy place long ago."

19

Let me just say, Lily, that is pretty much impossible to imagine.

Nobody brought me. I came.

Blair's not bankrolling me. I work summers in a garden center in Arcata and fill in part-time at the food co-op during school. Plus, my parents wire funds from Colorado to supplement their care packages. I guess they figure the home videos, news clippings, photos of the dog, pressed flowers, new underwear, home-baked cookies, recordings of Lily's music, and even one round piece of my horse's manure once (nothing fresh, of course, a dry turd, a joke, sealed in a Zip-Loc bag)—aren't enough. They want me to be homesick, though they claim it's all for my pleasure and comfort. They want me dependent because they're afraid I'll never come home again. Thomas Wolfe and all that.

Blair sold his car to come down here, so he's flush, but for me, this trip is taking every dollar I've ever scrimped and saved.

I may be just tagging along, but I have my own reasons.

"Sure you do. If anyone has, Iris, it's you."

I'm not just making up that Lily's this agreeable, because she is. She's always been like that.

After *desayuno*, Blair and I pass along the beach, which happens to be shaped exactly like a toenail paring. At each corner of the toe, rock outcroppings dribble off into little dotted lines of white-caked islands. All white, the islands look like lit-up light bulbs, right down to insects buzzing around them, which are actually seabirds. Ankle-deep in morning sea mist, we wade through surfline like the lace of the ocean's slip. A mad little flurry of shorebirds flees ahead of us on blurred legs, advancing in step with us, always keeping a certain distance until we eventually pass, then slowing and standing one-legged, tilting their eyes into the clear shallows. Way out at sea, parallel to the shore, two unending lines of seabirds migrate in opposite directions just above the swells, like black-and-white beads strung on abacus rods.

(Except there's a minimum of nine strands on an abacus rod. I read that once on a board-game card.)

The coconut palms wave us along the way they always do, like we're important personages or something, until we end up at an overgrown hibiscus hedge. Big hedges and walls—things like that invite trespass, or at least snooping, so naturally I can't help but look. On the other side is a compound cleared of all vegetation except one huge ficus tree, stranded there strangled in lianas, ankle-deep in its own crunchy leaf litter. In the center of the compound, poised as delicately on stilts as the shorebirds, are three white stucco buildings with thatched hair and thatched eyebrows over each door, facing the sea. They look animated, like they're playing musical chairs around the monstrous tree, while, behind them, the compound disappears into a coconut plantation, like the whole thing is trying to slink off into the jungle.

Something about the compound makes me feel awfully sad to be excluded. It would be beautiful to belong here, but we don't. I can tell Blair sort of does and doesn't feel like lingering, too.

"Look," I tell him, "over there. Don't those two buildings over there look empty?" I sound overly optimistic, even to myself.

My feet drag little scuffmarks in the sand, *swish-swish,* when we leave, and I can't help glancing back. Blair takes hold of my hand, then slips his arm around my waist and leans in to smooch my neck. Sometimes I wish he weren't so good-looking. Sometimes I wish he wouldn't always look at me the way he does, with those eyes of his, all hungry and heated, almost angry, like that; those gypsy eyes stuffing you with their feelings. I don't know why I say that, because he can be awfully sweet, too.

As we drift on down the beach, I can't seem to wake up completely. Maybe it's the hazy atmosphere, or the sea's rhythm, or maybe I'm just feeling detached because everything is so foreign. Whatever it is, I feel like I can't quite get a grip on anything. The beach unspools before us like silk cloth. The sand squishes underfoot and the little combers fling up on the beach with a vengeance. Everything feels slippery, like I'm struggling to make headway. In my dreams, I'm always falling and things are always slipping away just beyond my reach.

"Let's ask about those huts, okay?" I say.

"Sure, baby. Whatever you want."

"I'm serious," I say.

Blair wraps himself around me. "I will. I mean it. I just want you to be happy down here."

I said he could be sweet. And right then, I swear, he practically drops me like a hot potato when Cal comes catapulting straight at us, mostly naked, dripping wet, knees and elbows all akimbo, the beach nearly bowing under his impact. He and Blair grab at each other, half-greeting, half-wrestling, like gladiators or prodigal sons, whichever. Gee, Cal has filled out down here. He carries it well, though. I'm not saying anything. It's just he's this big puppy of a guy. A lazy, playful, complete ass, Cal is Blair's alter ego, a person who shudders at the thought of hard work. I could be wrong, but I judge him one of those harmless types determined to lounge safely through life.

"Oh, sorry, Iris. I didn't see you there," he says finally, grinning like a crocodile. He gives me a ridiculously chaste kiss, followed by a bone-crunching hug which I tolerate in the cause of good sportsmanship, although I'm not certain why I enslave myself to these credos—multiculturalism, good sportsmanship, and so on.

I like Cal. Well, okay; I have mixed feelings about him. I did like that Cal was quiet in comparison to the rest of the group up in Arcata. I never thought Cal was a matter of "still waters run deep," though—I thought he was into it up to his eyebrows up there, just for the fun of it. I always thought Cal was kind of an idiot, not an ideologue.

And he still is. The lout hangs on to me longer than he should, until Blair has to forcibly pull me away. *Pwok!* Like un-sticking a plunger or something. I've decided there is no way on earth short of radical feminism to avoid this type of thing when you're a woman in your twenties, even when you're not all that good-looking.

"Stop!" I tell Cal, and not particularly nicely, either. "Leave off, pest!"

"*Allo, avez vous du beurre?* Sorry, Iris, *ma petite.* Have I insulted you?"

Cal and his ridiculous schoolboy French . . . He sprinkles it randomly into otherwise relatively normal conversations, and, the thing is, I don't know how he does it, considering he claims to have slept his entire way through language lab.

"*Depechez vous avec la civière!*" ("Hurry with the stretcher!") is one of his priceless gems, and "*Je m'ai casser ma jambe!*" ("I've broken my leg!"). Too bad he didn't study Spanish instead.

The truth is, though, I like male irreverence. I actually like both of them. It's just that I reserve the right to refuse service to any individual, etcetera, etcetera.

"You're a real gem," I tell him. Then, feeling I may have

overreacted, I inform Cal, "Criticism is the sincerest form of flattery."

He has snuggled in again. "You amaze me, Iris. How long did it take you to dream that up?"

Blair swoops in and wraps his arms around my chest possessively.

Cal shrugs it off. "So, where are you two staying?" he asks, his voice gone rather stale.

"At the Colon," Blair answers.

"The big splurge, uh?"

"Yeah, right. How about you?"

"I'm down here on the beach."

So . . . just as I thought.

I let Blair do all the talking. I know a showdown when I see it, anyway, so I break away and amble toward the water. The sea is shining like varnish, too bright to bear looking at, but inland, dark, heavy clouds are creeping down the sides of the mountains. A breeze comes soughing from their direction, running its cool fingers along the bumps of my spine bones, lifting my skirt and hair briefly like a miraculous levitation, but then it dies before I can even close my eyes and face into it. And, I don't know, I don't exactly like it, so I turn and go back to Blair and Cal.

Cal reaches out for me, wrapping his meaty fingers around my arm up near my armpit, awfully close to things he shouldn't be touching, which seems to motivate Blair.

"You know those huts back toward the Colon?" he asks Cal.

"You mean with the big hedge around them?" Cal says.

"Who lives there?"

"Sorry, *mon ami.*"

When I pull away, obviously disappointed, Cal tries to salvage his answer.

24

"I mean, I haven't actually met him, or anything, but I've seen the guy."

I finally speak up. "Who is he?"

"Some American, retiree or something, living there alone. He doesn't come out much, but I've seen him wandering along the beach a couple of times. Scraggly, unfriendly type fella."

"What's he do with the two vacant huts, then?" Blair says.

Cal shrugs. "*Je ne sais quoi.* Search me. Maybe he's saving them for Quetzalcoatl."

He shuffles around in the sand. I don't know how he does it. Somehow Cal manages to be lazy and antsy at the same time.

"You coming out today?" he asks Blair. He means the surf.

Blair gives me a look. There are a number of things in this look he gives me.

"Nah, not today."

A big wave crashes through.

Cal looks past us. "*Merde!*" he groans, obviously wanting to beat it, dying to be out in the waves.

"Well, look," Blair says, also looking fairly miserable, "I'll see you tomorrow, okay? You got my board? Bring my board tomorrow, okay?"

"Halloo!" Blair hollers, with one loud knock on the doorsill for extra measure, then shades his eyes and peeks through the screen of the hut. "Ahoy, in there!

"Shit! Just our luck, I suppose he's croaked or something," he mutters. I know he's just taking care of business for my sake, so he's probably actually relieved no one's home.

Then, just as we're ready to split, "Come in . . ." emerges

25

from the dark tunnel, the quavering words floating out without apparent origin.

I go in cautiously, registering subliminally the delay of the slamming screen which signals Blair has stepped in behind me. Dappled light filters through the airy, shaded, wood-scented interior of what I can only describe as a Crusoe-esque house, but with all the modern conveniences. Something about it really does feel just like a tree house. Someone has settled in comfortably, maybe too comfortably, leaving a flotsam of general dross throughout, but the place shrugs it off, immune to human carelessness. In fact, everything about it is as wonderful as our room at the Colon is squalid.

A man is sitting there on the porch, *tranquilo* as a statue, not bothering to rise with us confronting him. He looks stuck there, sagging, sagging into the sagging cushion of his wicker chair (no doubt once red, but faded now to the color of a cow's tongue), looking for all the world like the chair is trying to swallow him whole. He's older than we are, but, beyond that, it's hard to tell. I can't help but start with the guesswork, though. Stowaway, heathen, Viking? Pilgrim, refugee, poet? I collate all the possibilities and come up with sandman, although there could be traces of all those others in there too. But I settle on sandman, because that's how he strikes me: his skin and hair, even his eyes, all the color of yellowish sand. He's hooked one of his fingers up over the top of his muzzle like he has something to hide in there. The light catches the fingernail, and it looks flat and hard and gold-colored, like old mother-of-pearl. The waves crash on the beach, tolling the seconds. We have definitely interrupted his solitude. Somehow he acknowledges me without any gesture, yet I feel like our fingertips have touched, and the sensation lifts my hair, just as the breeze had.

"Wow! Isn't this great, Ire?"

We just stand there like idiots, like naughty school children in a principal's office. I wonder what he thinks of us, how we look to him. What's on the list he's collating? We just dragged in off the beach. We probably should have cleaned up first. I have the impression we're very non-threatening, though—and you certainly have to consider things like that when there's a generation gap involved.

"Hey, well, let me introduce ourselves," Blair finally says. When he does, he botches it so badly that Henry, Henry Whitman, the man disappearing into his chair, begins rattling with phlegmy chuckles, keeping them hidden behind that hand, though.

"A-hum, sorry," he says, scraping his throat clear and finally moving that hand of his, wiping his eyes with the back of it.

Blair finally finds the gumption to say, "Look, we hate to bother you, but, the thing is, we're wondering if you would possibly consider renting us one of your empty huts," direct as always.

Henry shifts uncomfortably and clears his throat again, "Ah . . . well . . . I don't know . . ." His eyes drop and he begins picking carefully at lint on the cushion, the hand like a bird's talons now. ". . . I don't think . . . I really don't . . . a-hum."

Then, while he stammers and wanders all over the place through a litany of lame excuses, I happen to notice a Scrabble board in the clutter next to his chair.

"Oh," I say perkily. Then I tone it down, making my voice into a perfect monotone. "I play Scrabble."

He stops mid-word to look me over more closely, his gaze dwelling on my pierced eyebrow, eyeballing the beaded ring dangling there, which I try to hold perfectly still. An uncomfortably long time passes before he speaks again. I've got my

27

fingers on both hands crossed behind my back.

"How long did you say you were planning to stay?"

"Three months," Blair volunteers too quickly.

The man crimps his lips and looks away, then rubs his grainy hand over his mouth, his facial expression as blank as sand. Picking a crumb up off the top of the Scrabble box with the pad of his finger, he dabs it onto his lower lip, where it hangs precariously in the balance, until suddenly he sucks it in.

"Done," he grunts, aiming the word at the giant tree rather than us.

And that's how we landed at Cielo Azul and I became Henry's Scrabble opponent.

A defining moment—unseen, like a bullet.

Two

In my dreams I'm always falling.

Maybe that's why I cling like hell to routine, even on vacation, for fear of falling into galloping chaos. So I'm trying to settle in here. I really am. I'm trying to be disciplined about not going to the dogs or anything. I've got a little schedule all established, and I stick to my rounds, trying to fit in the best I can.

That's not easy, trying to fit in, because I am definitely a sore thumb down here. I certainly look the consummate WASP. I mean, I envy one of my girlfriends back home with her dark hair and olive skin. She can pass for native just about everywhere. Great! But me, no one would ever mistake me for anything but what I am. I'm blond and tall, with long limbs, all joints and points. Even my collarbone is oversized, stretched between my shoulders like a wooden clothes hanger. I can't help but stick out here the way I do.

No matter, I'm making friends, though. I met Leo's wife, Blanca, one day at the Colon, helping in the kitchen with her two-year-old daughter, Rosaria, propped on her hip. I don't see Blanca working there very often, in spite of the fact that it certainly seems like your typical Mexican family business, crawling with cousins and in-laws. It surprised me to find out that Leo's married because he looks so young, was more surprising to find out he's got a child, and most surprising to

29

learn he owns the Colon. Some day, if I can ever figure out how to ask him tactfully, I'll have to find out how he managed to buy it (maybe he inherited it). However it happened, he can't have any extra funds, judging from the state of the rooms. And conversely, judging from the state of the rooms, he'll never have extra funds. Even the most thorough budget guidebooks don't list the Colon, and one of them even goes so far as to warn travelers against cheap rooms in San Vaciò as "too awful to recommend."

How brave we were to spend our one night at the Colon!

Blanca looks like a preteen babysitter. Thin and tiny and shy, she speaks virtually no English, but she blossoms when I praise her daughter in my *malo* Spanish.

"Muy linda," I tell her, feeling like an idiot, *"dulce, que delicado!"* hoping the words wouldn't describe corn or steak better than a little girl.

Rosaria stares and stares at me from a safe distance with those solemn, unblinking dark-pudding eyes of hers; then when I come near, she dives away with a whimper, ducking her head against her mother's sparrow chest.

This family of children—they make me feel the clock ticking, ticking away like a time bomb, while they, with their rundown one-star hotel and their priceless daughter, seem to know exactly where they're going and why. It would probably shock them to know I'm envious, or maybe it's just gringo arrogance to think that. As a matter of fact, maybe they pity me, for all my financial advantages, because I'm a twenty-something woman who's still single and childless.

No matter. *No importa.*

What exactly am I doing here, anyway? What is this supposed to accomplish? You might well ask that. I mean, that's a very good question, but kind of impossible to an-

swer. I think I may just be sort of regrouping. You certainly ought to understand why I might need to do that. Actually, I think maybe it's starting to do me some good being here. I don't know.

As to why I'm here with Blair, it's just a vacation, isn't it? He and Cal. They say they're here to surf. That's what Blair says, anyway. That's his big explanation. I'm just tagging along, right? I mean, why not? What else should I be doing?

One thing for sure, things weren't getting any better for me where I was. At least it's a change of scenery.

You never know. That could be good. Maybe it'll help. Shit.

Sometimes I wish I'd quit hearing myself talk to you. But I'm sure not going to be saying this stuff to you in person, am I?

So, what am I doing here, literally?

Nothing. Absolutely nothing. I can just see your reaction to that, standing there looking at me with shipwrecked eyes. Killing time—that's all I'm really doing here. Hey, come to think of it, you're the big expert on that. You would certainly be the ultimate expert on killing time, wouldn't you?

Other than El Colon, the rest of my routine has gravitated to the small gringo colony of San Vaciò.

Representing the expatriates is the Cafe Internet. "Technology under the coconut palms," their sign says. You have to love something like that.

It's my home away from home, so to speak. My mother would have a conniption if I severed e-mail contact, especially since we can't actually write. We can't write, because letters from the U.S. have a way of disappearing into mañana infinity here. That's supposedly because they might contain money, though there can't be a single soul in the U.S. stupid enough to mail cash into Mexico. I mean, who writes any-more, anyway? So the Cafe Internet is part of my regular schedule, a place to park myself mid-morning and communi-cate with Mama during hers. Because we're synchronized in time, Mama and I, if nothing else, since my hometown in Colorado and San Vació share time zones. In fact, they're perfectly aligned along the same longitude.

I like to picture her in our big kitchen at her sloppy desk, checking her computer screen for the circled one that tells her I'm still here, alive and well, still ticking, still attached to her by this cyber umbilical cord.

God, I miss her!

Rita, the Cafe Internet's *propietaria,* wanders over. She fills in as surrogate mom, a big, boisterous, protective hen of a woman, solicitous and worrying, wrapping me in her wings and clucking advice. Sometimes I almost expect her to reach out and automatically put her hand on my forehead to check my temperature the way Mama did when we were little. For-ever in motion, she spills constantly, not her coffee but her feelings and opinions, in flocks of words that fly out like they've just been released from captivity.

"Hi, hon," she says, my straggling-in unleashing a gush of chat. "Got a little sunburned yesterday, didn't you? Got a good sunscreen? Well, slather that stuff on, sweetie—you can't be too careful." Her own skin, if not exactly as soft as a baby's bottom, is smooth and the color of almonds, so I'm tempted to listen to her.

"How's things down at the beach, hmm?" She's like the white rabbit, though—no time for an answer. "Someone said the surf's coming up." Now she finally actually looks me in the face. "I don't know how you can sleep with it practically pounding on your doorstep."

As if the surf is something to complain about . . .

"I love the waves," I tell her. "They put me to sleep. It's the bugs on the screens that keep me awake at night."

Rita laughs, then wanders off, talking to herself. Spilling. Jeez, I almost wish she *had* put her hand on my forehead today. I'm not having such a good day. Not really. I'm feeling stuffy, bloated, lethargic, lonely. *Blah!* I'm late with my period, which never happens to me and explains eighty percent of my blahs; the rest can be accounted for by the weather, which has my exact same symptoms. I'd call the nature of the weather today "pregnant," but that would be flirting with disaster. Leo says the rainy season is closing in.

My original nonchalance over the whole late period thing has morphed gradually over the course of a few days and is now verging on abject terror. Will I never be friends with my corpus? What aggravation! Especially my goddamned latent fertility. But, hey, even my body's strengths are a thorn in my side. My well-meaning friends back home are always telling me how I'm *almost* beautiful—I would look egg-zactly like Daryl Hannah, they tell me (wondering, meanwhile, what she's up to these days)—if only my eyes were a little wider, my lips maybe fuller, my hair blonder. Otherwise, egg-zactly, though. Great! So, there are *almost* three Daryl Hannahs. There *were* almost four.

I'm sick of considering my body. An equitable truce would be acceptable. Who's in charge here, anyway?

My poor mind! As enslaved to hormonal tyranny as my ovaries, forcing me to ask questions I'd rather avoid, such as, would I want to call Blair "honey" and "dear" for the rest of my life? Is he suitable material for "wait until your daddy comes home"? As if I'd ever allow myself to become a sitcom character . . . My friends back home always swear on their lives they will never, not if hell freezes over, turn into their parents. Me, I should be so lucky—to become my parents, I mean.

Besides, what makes me think Blair would marry me, if it came down to that? Moot point. If I had his child, I'd be biologically and emotionally tied to him for life.

If I had his child. *If* I went through with a pregnancy. *If* I'm pregnant.

Help! I don't want to be asking myself these questions!

Mama!

My father, phobic as he is about self-destructive people, always tried hard to avoid sermonizing to Lily and me. Still, he couldn't resist making the suggestion at a certain point in my puberty that, "A woman would be smart to limit her lovers to those she'd be willing to marry." I think those were his exact words, as a matter of fact. He's very straight that way. He can't help it. It's like his job description, maybe even genetically engineered in his case. "That would be safe as well as ethical," he advised, just as a philosophical exercise in logic and nothing more, of course. I considered his outlook, weighed it in spite of myself without letting on to him, and eventually added it to a list I consider my iron-clad credos.

And now here I am, wondering if I've blown it.

I go ahead and buy a mug of Rita's coffee (should I even be drinking coffee, in my condition?) and I sit down at a computer. I type in the address, which already makes me feel lonely as hell.

Hi, Maminski! Your latest political commentary is scandalous (you'll be happy to know). It's pure heaven, here, really. And as a bonus, it's raining every night too (I know I shouldn't rub this in). It would be awfully good for Lily down here. I'm eating camarones every day, feeling very fat, in a beanpole kind of way. Blair's gone totally native.

He's brown as dirt from the sun, labors mulishly all day long, and piously attends Mass every Sunday. Last Sunday he crawled to the altar on bloody knees, praying for my soul all the way (please don't show this to the political correctness police, okay?). Seriously, how's my horse? Give him a peppermint for me. Is Daddy behaving himself? I suppose he swore at the sprinkler pump again this year. Did they actually accomplish a single thing this term? Ask Lily to send me an e-mail, too, okay? Tell her I'll buy her a wooden flute if she does. Love and kisses, Flor de Lis.

Of *course* I don't mention my late period to Mama, any more than I would to Blair! These are things a female has to weather alone. No wonder I'm feeling so lonely today. I have another coffee with a pastry (am I eating for two now?) while I wait for Mama's reply. I picture her checking the screen over and over again while she's fluttering around in there, watching for my message. I know she'll laugh when she reads it, then she'll try very hard to sound cheerful in her reply, like I did—the two of us leaving so much unsaid.

Our lives are in the mail now.

You can get anything you want in Mexico. The flip side of this in a "developing" country is desperation too terrible for words. But in our case, all it amounts to is a couple of new toys, neither of them decadent, and not even actually new. One is a little used Vespa we named Juanita, after Barney Fife's girlfriend. *Neeta, Wah-ah-ah-neeta.*

La dolce vita, putt-putt.

The other is an old Crown Speedgraphic camera for Blair.

So now, after mail check, Blair and I take Nita to the beach most days, stopping for supplies at the store in the alley behind us.

I love this store—seriously—I can't explain it exactly. It's just this little hole in the wall with the family living in the back. The dust from the alley works its way indoors all day long, no matter how many times they sweep it back out where it belongs. Passing by, the open door is what you notice, a dark escape hole from the heat and light and dust of the street, like the entrance to an animal den. Maybe the white rabbit's. A small army of dogs lies curled in piles of commas along the shade across the store's front, their backs against the wall. The mother runs things, keeping a hawk-eye on everything. Raising her kids and running the store. In her case the two can't be separated, because the kids are everywhere—pulling a bottle of soda from the ice water in the cooler so you don't have to get your hands wet, picking out the best orange for you, bagging your stuff, *muy rapido*. They won't let you do anything for yourself in their store. The little ones stare at you all big-eyed, but not the older kids. The older ones, they're savvy and aloof. They're very cool.

All the familiar stuff from back home is tucked away somewhere in there, but it's the local goods that fascinate me. Who decided votive candles ought to be flanked by jars of pork feet on one side and tender *nopalitos* cactus on the other? What were they thinking? The soft drinks come in old-fashioned glass bottles with crimped metal caps, the flavors inside pure tropical poetry: mandarin, lemon-lime, pineapple. "Jumex Nectars," "Guava, Mango, Tamarind."

Every time we stop, I admire the candy umbrellas made out of some mysterious material like blown glass, but I buy one of the brown sugar candies shaped like little volcanoes instead. The oldest girl, very serious and all business, takes my money without a smile. When we're ready to leave, I wave at my favorite, the youngest, with his hair cut straight as the equator across his forehead. *"Hasta pronto, Alfonso,"* I say.

"That one is Hilario," the girl behind the counter says, barely hiding her disdain.

That's okay. What I think is, if she were totally cool, she shouldn't have said anything at all. I mean, I wouldn't have.

Blair and I part ways at the beach, where a small matter of a hundred yards of riptide separate us. I flap out my beach towel and watch it settle softly onto the hot sand. Meanwhile, Blair and Cal rub sand between their hands, jerk up their boards, and march straight down to the water. They launch themselves onto the top of the surge, paddle out past the shore break, then wait out there, crouched on their boards like lions *couchant* on pedestals.

I try to stay vigilant, I really do, but eventually my attention starts wandering. You can only watch so long, after all—there's nothing you can watch forever. I've always thought we can probably stare at horror longer than beauty, but I'm probably just being morbid. As I recall, Lily accused me of that once or twice.

So, a dog distracts me, a vendor hones in, then a toddler escapes his mother and makes a dash for the water. I mean, life interferes, doesn't it?

After long lapses, I feel guilty enough to look back out there at Blair again, watching dutifully while he takes a few waves. After each ride, he flips backward, shakes the water out of his hair, and turns instantly to catch the next wave, and the next, over and over, ad infinitum.

Huh. A decidedly compulsive sport, I think, *and definitely hard on one's hairdo.* I pull my hat over my eyes and scrape a nest into the sand and lie back. Hours will pass before Blair and Cal become land dwellers again. I have no way of imagining what they're feeling, so why should I try? *Ho-hum.*

Gradually, though, almost in spite of myself, I become aware of a little clutch of Californians. I've heard about them, living only for the beach, their needs as minimal as their bathing suits. They've come up with a creative means of survival. As "Team Banana," they rent surfboards at their cafe, where their girlfriends sell their specialty, banana bread— capitalists, covering all the bases so they can afford to live down here in Mexico.

It's not like I've got anything better to do, so I end up studying these girls like they're some kind of separate species. Cocooned in a pod of American girlism, they slather up around their thong bikinis, then casually pick up their current potboilers full of sex and sadism, which they lay face down in the sand after a few minutes. They lie back, adjust their wrap-around shades, eventually drawing an arm up lazily to shade their faces. Occasionally they make the big effort to turn their heads in one direction to glance at the surf, then the other to laugh at each other (like tortoises, their heads swiveling on stationary bodies). Lounging in their private little club, while "out there" their men risk everything, offering up their lives on the sea's altar, glancing at the shore repeatedly in hopes of impressing the beach goddesses.

I catch a few words on the breeze. "What's the scariest thing you do everyday?" But I don't hear their answers, just cackling laughter, for all the world exactly like the noise of the black birds that sit in my ficus tree every evening shitting on the leaves below. Anyway I know damned well their answers have no comparison to the deeds of the men they're ignoring in the waves.

Blair finally crashes in the afternoon. By two or three o'clock I want the shade of my ficus tree and besides, the sand flies have started biting on the beach, so we make for home.

We gulp down handfuls of fruit and then we make love, because he's never too tired and I am never too sun-baked for that particular need. (How much does this have to do with my sticking with Blair, the fact that he always turns me on? He's a good swordsman and is never ever tepid when it comes to sex.) Afterward, he sleeps it off while I swing in my hammock, staring up into the dark, glossy leaves of the giant tree, which also snoozes in afternoons, drooping in the still heat, waiting for the evening breeze to resuscitate it.

If we're feeling social in the evenings, we hit the bars and bump and grind our way through salsa, merengue, and reggae with other tourists, or we might go local at the Bucañero, drinking too much *cerveza* and shouting ourselves hoarse over *ranchera* music with the Mexicans.

Mostly, though, we end up strolling the *zócalo* with the rest of the town's entire population. The two cathedrals facing each other across the plaza let loose with their bells every evening as we weave our way through the palms and pollarded trees and around the bandstand, then spiral back out. Lovers waltz past us, arm in arm, dropping out of the parade when their feelings become too intense, collapsing onto the benches in the shade of the palm trees to neck. This seems to be the national pastime. It goes on so long! Can there be any real passion in it? Meanwhile, packs of urchins hawk Chiclets and ice cream, screaming at the top of their lungs, *"Helados! Helados! Helados!"* singing the words, always in refrains of threes. Blair and I make our own pass, stepping each night on the words scrawled across one square, "Death to Yankees!" until they're almost rubbed out.

They know our routine by now at the Colon and save our favorite table for us. We take our time over dinner, sitting and staring out at the ocean like we're afraid it might disappear any moment. There's no need to worry, though, not really.

Night after night at the Colon, without fail, the breeze comes up, the little combers pile up on the beach, and someone dances across the floor with a mop. *Siempre.* Always.

Leo always takes a moment to come sit with us.

"Have you eaten yet?" we finally thought to ask him one evening. "Bring your dinner over and come eat with us." But he wouldn't do it. That would be too informal for Leo. He doesn't smoke or drink, either, so I don't really know why he takes the time. Just because, I guess. Just because he wants to practice his English, or maybe just because he finds our conversations so entertaining. Like tonight.

"So, what do you think, Leo?" Blair says, between wolfing down bites. "Is Mexico making any progress? Is anything changing for the better?"

"Jes," Leo says, his face so young and innocent you can barely stand it. "I think so. I think *el presidente,* he might make things better. But, you know, corruption in Mexico is bigger than any man, no matter how tall."

"Ah, yes," Blair says, waving his fork around like he always does whenever he has an audience. "Your corruption. Right. I've been thinking about that, you know," (swallowing another big gulp of food) "and the weird part is that it actually works— sure, I mean, maybe like a crooked walk or something, but it functions. And surprisingly well. Like maybe the purist form of capitalism, on a grassroots level, or something."

Leo sits there listening ever so patiently while Blair steamrolls on.

"You know, there's this bizarre freedom in your system. It feels freer here, without all the goddamned regulations the U.S. takes so seriously—you know—little nuisances like traffic laws, zoning ordinances, consumer protection. All that shit. But here, nothing's enforced. Yeah, it's weird, but I feel freer here."

"Maybe you're a *bandito* at heart, eh *Blaire?*"

Blair grins, liking that role immensely.

"Hey, can't you just picture it? Back in the U.S., if we had bullfights, all the matadors would be wearing helmets."

You can't help but laugh. I mean.

"Blame it on all the lawsuits," I pipe up. "It's all the fault of our tort system."

Blair gives me a look. "That's what I love about you, Iris. Miss Utterly Literal."

He turns back to Leo. "Hey," he says, actually punching the air with his fist, "I like that you don't barricade manholes. Let us all hurt ourselves, if we're that damned stupid.

"Did you know, Leo, back home in my plu-perfect town there's actually an ordinance against upholstered furniture on porches?"

I have the distinct impression Leo is utterly confused by this point.

"That's right. A thousand-dollar fine for putting a couch outdoors!"

"Yeah, but tell him the whole story," I say, always policing Blair's complete honesty, for some inexplicable reason. "Fill in the blanks. It's a university town. It's because students built bonfires with them during riots."

Blair pointedly ignores me. "Well, here, it's, like, screw all that! You can build a hovel next to a palace. You can put any color of damned Christmas lights you want all the way around your stinking, polluting transportation."

I can't believe what's coming from the mouth of this environmental activist.

Leo's eyes rove over to the kitchen and back.

"It's quick, too, your corruption. And the cost is relatively painless."

Leo finally cuts in. "I know what you're saying, *Blaire,* but you are wrong about the cost to Mexico. You only see the tip of it here. You think it is only a little *'mordita,'* the bite, the golden handshake, but it is much more terrible than that, much bigger, jes, because . . ." (he taps his index finger on the tabletop with each word) "every offense becomes open to negotiation. And Mexico's legal system becomes a *laberinto,* the bureaucracy a blockade. You don't see underneath, at Mexico's belly, where it is rotting."

Then, making us all deadly conspirators with a smoldering look, he leans forward and lowers his voice.

"You want to know how they hire police in Mexico, eh?

"They take the most violent criminals from the prisons and make them the police—the worst killers. If you don't believe this, I have a friend who goes to another town to buy a new truck. When he's driving home, they kill him for his truck. And nothing happens, because he is nobody to them. And, until now, the whole government is in on it, the president, all of them, everybody. The presidents, in the past, they torture and murder their opposition and make themselves filthy rich through corruption, then they live the rest of their lives like royalty, untouchable. No one even looks at them. But now we're looking, because now we are no longer under the rule of one party. The vultures . . . all those people who they made disappear . . . they had better watch out, because we are watching now. Mexico is facing the truth of the past . . ."

"So you have your 'disappeared ones' in Mexico," Blair says, pointing at Leo. Then he jabs at his own chest, "We've got our 'spy files' on citizens, for chrissake."

I'm not the least bit sure they're equivalent. But Blair knows all about spy files firsthand, so he's hardly objective.

Someone signals at Leo from the kitchen. He stands and heaves a big sigh and says, "I always wondered why *Los*

Unidos don just take over Mexico, anyway."

I toss down the dregs of my drink. "Like we don't have enough problems of our own," I say.

But, more and more, we stay home at Cielo Azul, reading or talking, until Cal drops by to conspire with Blair. At that point I drift over to Henry's place for our game of Scrabble. I know when I'm not particularly wanted. Besides, my duels with Henry, they're my . . . what did they call it, back in medieval times, when the landlord was entitled to his serf's bride on their wedding night? For the sake of the game, I should know this word, but I can't even look it up when I haven't got a clue (there's that catch twenty-two with dictionaries, when you think about it). "Right of rank, right of lord," something like that. It's not just one word anyway.

Anyhow, that's my obligation. I owe it, don't I?

Sure, sure, I know I'm exaggerating because I love drama, but it's true, Scrabble is the price fallen on my head for the clean bed, the ocean breeze, the giant tree, and the peace of Cielo Azul . . . And the hot water.

And it's worth every pound of flesh.

It's an easy trick to turn, anyhow. I like Scrabble, and, besides, Henry's a benevolent taskmaster. Henry's addicted, and because he cares so much, he never wins. Victory after victory falls effortlessly right into my lap. Candy from a baby and all that. Here's how it goes: He sits there an eternity, frozen, staring, sighing. So ridiculous. Finally he throws that rug of his out of his eyes. Cautiously, like he might take it back any moment, he forms "drums" by adding his "d" and "s" (and what a waste of an "s"!) to my "rum." Without even blinking, I turn it instantly into "doldrums," extending the word into a triple-word score before Henry has even replaced his two tiles. He's got a great vocabulary and a quick mind, but Henry has zilch luck because he cares too much. He never seems to draw the high-scoring letters, the "q" or the "z," or he draws the "q" near the end of the game, when the "u" and blank tiles are all gone. Henry has luck to curdle holy water.

My head is aching tonight, and I'm worried about my period. Swollen clouds have lowered in. The air is so full of electricity it feels almost impossible to breathe. I'd rather stay home and veg out, but then I think of Henry, sitting there in his cow-tongue chair, the lamplight casting a golden butterfly against the wall behind him; Henry shuffling the letters in the lid of the box, making sure they're all face-down, glancing at his watch. So I peel myself off the couch.

"Hullo, Henry," I go when he waves me in. "Are you finally going to kick my ass tonight?"

But he doesn't.

The thing is, I'm rooting for Henry by now, really I am. I don't let him win like I don't cheat at solitaire, because it would defeat the purpose (like Leo's mustache, like my awful Spanish). But, still, I'd like him to win. He's such a fine loser, too, fiddling around at reshuffling the tiles, smiling with those wolf teeth of his, his nose turning down when his lips pull back, grinning genuinely, but his eyes perplexed like maybe I'm resorting to magic to beat him so often. And it does sort of feel that way, it's so easy. He thinks I'm a fucking genius now, after so many defeats, each game increasing his awe. I'm on a Scrabble pedestal with Henry. He laughs good-naturedly when I win, then coughs and covers his mouth with that finger of his with the nail like yellow quartz.

There he sits in his logjam of cherished stuff I know by heart now—a pile of defunct golf scorecards, an old slot-car, a scuffed A&W mug, a steel letter-opener like a thin blue fish, a Bakelite ashtray marked "No Exit Cafe, Capistrano Beach." No photos, nothing sentimental, or maybe it all is. I watch his face secretly while he's studying his rack of letters. Tight-skinned over the bones like one of those mummified ice men freed from a glacier, with jagged blond brows hanging over his eyes. Fine eyes, actually, if you can ever get a look at them—except when they go all moody. Changeable, really. Sometimes they can look at you slow and deep; then they can be all quick and nervous. Smooth-skinned as a baby across the temples, tapering down to a narrow, square muzzle fuzzed over with gold stubble. Shallow grooves around his mouth—the kind that make women look old but men look rugged. He's handsome, really, in a rough, long-in-the-tooth sort of way, like a grizzled-blond Montgomery Clift if he'd lived longer. The Thinker, humped over with that finger pressed against his lips. The Skinny Thinker, because Henry is as lean as the pariah dogs slinking around San Vaciò.

"My wife used to tell her girlfriends I was all hands and feet and cock," he tells me one night between games. "She was bragging, you know, one-upsmanship. She had to be the best or have the best or biggest of everything. Of course, it's worthless now. My dick. It bends in the middle whenever there's something important for it to do."

Because Henry has begun to talk about anything and everything, whether or not I want to hear it.

Anyhow, tonight I decide to call it an early night after one game because I'm too restless to concentrate. I'm fidgeting right out of my skin.

Henry follows me to the door and steps outside with me. His palm is cold as metal when he takes my hand and leads me down the stairs towards the beach, out from under the umbrella of the ficus tree.

"Look!" he says, staring straight up. It's like San Vaciò's remoteness makes it closer to the stars. When I look, my mouth falls open and I can't seem to close it. It's like the earth is hanging onto my jaw while the sky is pulling on my eyes. I scan the whole dome, looking for the familiar constellations, which have all shifted position because, like Dorothy was no longer in Kansas, I'm no longer in Colorado.

"Where's Gemini?" I ask Henry. "The twins."

Henry hasn't let go of my hand, but either his hand is warmer or mine's colder. I can feel his pulse ticking as he takes a stronger, closer grip, turning me to the west, slightly north, and points with his free hand until I recognize it—like a pair of skinny trousers, toeing out.

"Gemini," he says, very nonchalant. "Identical twins, but one was mortal and the other immortal. Zeus disguised himself as a swan to seduce the queen of Sparta, so the myth is that they hatched from an egg. Castor, the mortal one, was a famous horseman, you know."

Henry's a walking encyclopedia, I swear. He really ought to be beating me at Scrabble.

"Inseparable. They both sailed with the Argonauts in search of the Golden Fleece. Very fateful, their being twins. Funny, they owe both their downfall and their immortality to twins. They quarreled with another set of twins and Castor was killed. Polydeuces missed Castor so much, he prayed to Zeus to share his immortality with his brother. So Zeus took pity and put them together up there among the stars for all eternity."

Henry turns his eyes from the stars and looks at me, his gaze hanging there. "Lovely, *si?*"

I don't know if he means the story or the stars or something else altogether, but it doesn't matter, either way.

"*Si.*"

The little ocean waves gleam like silver spawn. We stand there a minute, then he drops my hand when he feels me shift away.

"G'night, Henry," I call as I walk away.

"Mañana?" he asks hopefully.

"Claro." Of course.

I'm sure my belly holds trouble. There's a squirrel on a treadmill in there, lottery balls spinning. It's singing a regular whalesong.

I lie on my bed, wondering what Blair and Cal find to talk about in these ridiculous private powwows of theirs. I've asked, even though I absolutely hate women who get jealous of their lover's friends. I asked anyway, because our own conversations are shrinking in direct proportion to Blair's increased time with Cal. But all he'll say is it's only the same old shit, which means they're cramming their brains with a crazy mush of plans and hopes, inciting each other over a million perceived governmental-slash-corporate environmental abuses. He doesn't elaborate, though, so I drop it. But, still, I wonder. I used to be included in those confabs, and so did plenty of others, but now I see the two of them there in the back of the hut, their silhouettes huddled against the lamplight, heads together like coconspirators, and I don't know what I feel anymore.

I lie there thinking about my routine, what it includes, what it avoids. About Cal and Rita and the beach girls and Henry. About all the painful things in town: the creeping poi dogs and the mud houses right out of the dark ages with kids staring from the doorways. How I avoid the polluted mouth of the river, the stinking alleyways, even the jungle's darkness beyond the compound's light at night. *What do I think I'm doing down here, anyway?* I think about everything I'm avoiding in the entire rest of the world, especially back home. I knew I'd never be able to do nothing guilt-free. So I lie there assessing my capacity for cowardice, hunkering, bunkering, in my little ex-pat oasis.

And, as I'm lying there reflecting on everything I can and can't face here, a sound of sizzling begins. A frying pan is sizzling somewhere. Feeling light-headed, I get up and wander out to the porch, massaging my belly (it's going, oh man, like a washing machine) and I squint out through the screen. It's mid-June and the rain has started, slipping in behind my back. I swear, if you close your eyes, there's no difference between the sounds of sizzling heat and the fall of cool rain.

While I stand there watching through the circle of light thrown by the compound's yard lamp, the rain lays a gauze over the ocean and melts the jungle until I can't see anything but a curtain of water drawn around the porch. And I feel my period start. And I know that something else I couldn't face, the questions my body forced me to ask about Blair, have been answered, and the answer is "no."

I could swear I feel my pupils contract when I step from the black night into the store's glare. The savvy girl is at the cash register. I shake the rain off like a wet dog; then I buy some tampons and a bottle of mango nectar. I think I see a hint of a raised eyebrow at the tampons, but maybe I just imagined it. The little kids are still in there. I wrack my brain for the words, and when I'm ready to leave I say in Spanish to my favorite, "It's late. Why aren't you in bed, Hilario?" And the wise girl, barely hiding her disdain, goes, "That's Alfonso."

Three

I should know better, because Lily and I, we're twins. And that has been wonderful and awful.

We didn't include the rest of the world when we began speaking, Lily and I. We spoke to each other in our own private language, ignoring English, closing others out, because our language was a gift from the gods, feral and effortless. It involved no learning; it allowed us to delay facing life beyond the womb. We had known our language from inside the sheer walls of our amniotic sac. It's strange when you think about it, that our gestation period wasn't the solitary experience, however unconscious, of others. We had to accommodate each other from before what most people consider the beginning. We knew nothing but the shared experience, having never been alone.

Absolutely no one could tell us apart, which could be exasperating or very useful, and, since we were also two individuals, was often both. We never, ever, from our first sense of self-awareness dressed alike, but we were still mistaken for each other, until my father finally insisted our hair be cut different lengths so we could be told apart. Still, they could never be certain we hadn't lied about our identities the day it was done, so eventually, they gave up and solemnly swore us to an identity honor system we never obeyed.

One does so want to believe one's unique, after all. We were awfully fierce with each other in our rivalries, and I'm sure that's why. Oh, the fury and the petty meanness we unleashed on each other! You block that all out, if you're mercifully inclined, but since I'm least merciful to myself, I watch the mental reruns of our childhood bickering and downright cruelty without covering my eyes. We were holy terrors with each other, an unholy trinity, less one (it's an apt image, though, because we began as three, but Rose didn't survive). Our rivalry was no one's fault; Mama gave each of us plenty enough love to go around, which should have defused it, but didn't.

We loved each other, just the same. If anyone came between us, we could be a unified force, two hysterical little girls, a force worth reckoning. And we were close, mystically close, as multiples can be. We couldn't play the paper, scissors, rock game, because we always came up with the same symbol. If I thought, "Okay, I want to be scissors this time, so I'll be a rock instead," Lily would use the same thought process and we'd both smash round fists into our palms, then laugh or scream in anger, or both. We had premonitions about each other, too. We went to bed together with tandem childhood diseases (poor Mama!), we dreamt the same dreams, felt the same feelings. That's why we were so sick and tired of each other. Who can stand enduring yourself in duplicate?

To say nothing of enduring the reactions of others: "Oh, aren't they precious! Like peas in a pod!" *Blah, blah, blah.* And, really, Mama might have been foresighted enough to name us something like Sally, Barbara, and Denice. But, no, she indulged herself at our expense (and this is the only blame I can lay on my mother), she, with her romantic nature, named us Iris, Rose, and Lily. Iris, Rose, and Lily Bloom. Iris

Bloom, Rose Bloom, and Lily Bloom! Rose Bloom, a fanciful name on a headstone. But for Lily and me, it was sheer living hell. I know they're beautiful names, isolated from each other and from our family name, but the impact en masse seemed a terrible cross to bear.

Still, other than our names, I can't fault my parents, unlike most of my generation. They were wonderful people, if you want to know, decent and loving.

My father was a congressman from Colorado, a Democrat, which was a fairly rare bird in that state. His public office made for a life that was less settled than the lives of our friends "back home," though, because winning elections meant we'd spend school terms on the East Coast.

For whatever reason, he located us outside the Washington Beltway. We lived in a small coastal town south of Boston named Duxbury (home of John and Priscilla Alden and Miles Standish, if you remember your Longfellow), one of those towns anybody would like to have grown up in, but with a dark side that must've appealed to those Puritans. The landscape, especially the land bleeding down into the beach, was bleak as hell, especially in winter. Plus, Duxbury was far enough from D.C. that we mostly only saw my father weekends and summers, which meant Mama was burdened with too much responsibility, considering her nature, because she was no disciplinarian.

She was like one of us, not one of them. She couldn't hurt a fly. She was an out-and-out Socialist and believed no one, regardless of social stature, should have to suffer the boredom and futility of housework, so we lived below Puritan standards of cleanliness and survived mainly on peanut butter and jelly sandwiches when my father wasn't home. But we all shaped up for my father, not out of fear, but because he brought out the best in us. We rose to the occasion to please

51

him, all of us, including Mama, because home was so much livelier when he was there. Just to hear a masculine voice, to smell his shaving lotion in the morning, to have him laugh at our silliness, to be swung onto his shoulders—these were things you'd never jeopardize. He wasn't around enough to take for granted, especially in our female household. He was smart and could fix things that absolutely stymied the rest of us. He broadened our world by actually reading the sports and business sections, he teased us and made corny jokes, he had important telephone conversations, his hand covered my entire head. Anything that broke, he could fix it. How could I not be in awe?

Maybe it was my parents' accessibility/inaccessibility that addicted me. "Me, Iris. Look at me, Daddy! Did you see that, Mama?" Stuffing myself sick with their love, hooking my elbow into my sister's belly to be first in line for it, struggling to be The One of Two, one ovum, indivisible, with anonymity and ignominy for all. I did desperate things for attention, streaking buck naked through the campfire's light at a clambake one night; don't ask me why. Idiot that I was, I thought if I streaked fast enough, my body would blur, like in the comics, and they wouldn't know it was me, but I'd make a sensation. I can still hear the shrieks of laughter, my parents' the loudest.

I was born first and outweighed the others, which you might not think was a big deal, but it meant life or death in our case, because Rose died and Lily struggled for months. Anyway, I naturally assumed the role of "big sister," though a few minutes' and a pound's advantage were all that gave me that claim to fame. But for whatever reason, it was accepted without question by both of us, so I spent my childhood alternately protecting, bullying, and leading Lily. I knocked a boy down for pushing Lily in the bus line one morning, then pushed her myself. I was always scheming to ditch her. I'd tell her to hide, then run away and leave the game. When we rode our ponies, I galloped off, stranding her, over and over, ad infinitum.

Still, we preferred our own company to the company of other neighborhood or school kids, relishing our private intrigues and out-and-out warfare. I can see us on the beach, wearing rubber flip-flops, because they were indestructible and *de rigeur* for the beach. And sunglasses with little plastic frames in bright colors—different hues, I'm sure, because we'd have wanted it that way—two sun-browned, sun-bleached, blowzy little girls, two ducklings in a row, stuck together as if imprinted, squabbling the whole way. Fighting over the sand dabs in our red tin buckets. "Chop, chop!" Mama would call. The two little flower Blooms, spiteful as hornets, as bound to each other as to the will to live.

My father tried to spend as much time as possible at home, leaving work early to take commuter flights during the week whenever he could, which took a huge toll in time and money. We were his bookends during the evening news, his shadow on the beach. He missed some roll calls, but his constituents seemed understanding. No one ran against him the year Reagan was elected.

Lily and I were proud of our father. He was the real thing, as far as we were concerned, fighting the good fight, you know, for typical liberal stuff, all the knee-jerk liberal stuff. But, I mean, he really fought, introducing kick-ass bills or filibustering some crap the other side tried to tack on or sneak through, making speeches until he couldn't talk, for godssake. He didn't win office because he was from some political dynasty, either. I mean, his father was a blue-collar worker, but my dad didn't go around waving a log cabin about it.

We trusted him one hundred percent. We knew in our hearts he was squeaky clean when all the sexual hanky-panky of other politicians made headlines, all the pathetic, sordid stuff that makes you absolutely hate politicians. People who should know better driving off bridges, for cripessake. For one thing, our dad was no boozer. My parents were practically teetotalers. And another thing, he was a square shooter when it came to sex. Strange but true. My dad "kept his dick in his pants," as the adults said when they thought we weren't around. Chalk it up to the fact that he loved my mother a lot, or to good genetics (his father and his father's father were also good family men). Maybe all it means is he inherited a low libido. I mean, kids don't really want to think about these things when it comes to their fathers.

Of course, we already knew all about at least the mechanics of sex, Lily and I—I mean, come on, you'd have to be a moron not to know about it by age eight, or something. All you have to do is check out the mechanical parts involved to put two and two together. I mean, there's not one tribe on earth, no matter how primitive, that doesn't understand all about it, and who explained it to them?

Anyway, my father was the real thing. He practiced what he preached. He even managed to make fundraising seem halfway honorable. We knew we were leading a privileged life, but my father tried to keep things as normal as possible. Our house was modest, but then, considering the prices in Duxbury, everyone had a modest house, because the most everyday, ordinary Cape box of a house built in the 1930s with one bath started at a quarter million. I don't know what our house cost my dad back when he bought it, because parents don't tell you stuff like that when you're kids. They don't really want you to know whether or not they're loaded, because they think it'll spoil you if they are and shame you if they're not. Anyway, my father didn't make all that much money, that much we knew, and he wouldn't have lived any differently if he had; he told us that in person. Plus, he sent us to public school for all the same reasons he owned a modest house, but also including the fact that he said he'd be the one to turn the lights out, as far as public schools were concerned. That's how he was about nearly everything, though.

When we returned to our friends "back home" on the edge of the Rockies each summer, it took weeks for Lily and me to shed our uppity-ness. This elitism wasn't completely our fault, though. It was a burden we felt obligated to maintain, really, foisted onto us by our friends, by their reserve bordering on awe for my father's position and for our "sophisticated" lives "back east." It's only now, with the clarity of hindsight, that I recognize the limits of my father's stature and power.

The greatest thing my parents gave us was safe haven. We felt safe those summers, falling to sleep every night to the quiet pulsing of our automatic sprinkler system and the honking of Canada geese on the lake. We had benign, boring family barbecues where we played croquet with all the cousins. Our big lawn was kept perfectly green by the sprinkler, and trim and tidy by the yard man on his riding mower. The kids in our neighborhood played softball spring afternoons in the horse pasture and kick-the-can summer evenings, and we were invited to swim in a neighbor's backyard pool. If there was trouble in our neighborhood, we never knew it. Somehow our parents managed to keep the world at bay.

Our family's tone, if not fortune, ebbed and flowed with the nation's votes. We bore the cheesy national soap opera stoically during the political mayhem of certain terms. I think Mama's the only person in America who still likes Clinton, no matter whose dress he spoiled. ("Think anyone'll be naming their daughter Monica anytime soon?" she asked.) And when political fortune flip-flopped, I knew right away that gears would shift. Poor Mama threatened to leave the country at least once a week. She swore she didn't know how she would survive, railed against the Moral Purgatory, and made horrible faces during the news. She has to do all of this, of course, but throws her heart and soul into it with such relish that it makes us laugh.

Father was certainly more rational and dignified about events than Mama, but then, he could hardly afford to have us overhear and possibly repeat any rash reactions on his part. He egged Mama on, though, because he enjoys a good fight.

My father was defeated for two two-year terms during our high school years, so we were able to settle into a "normal" life in Colorado for the duration. Coincidental with that period of stability, Lily and I stopped competing. We'd competed in the womb, we'd had to compete for the very milk of life, but after puberty, we competed no more. Like warring married couples, we went to extremes to avoid competition, disallowing anything and anyone that might pit us against each other. We went our separate, eccentric, intense ways. Lily bought a canary that only sang when she vacuumed. She named it "Tehani," after a character in Michener's *Hawaii*. I declared Boone Caudill my ideal man and made drawings of him over and over, always with dark, solemn eyes and long braids like a Blackfoot Indian. "I got me a woman," I quoted ad nauseum in my most macho voice until I drove everyone crazy.

We drew lines around what was ours, talking volumes about everything but sharing almost nothing and then only grudgingly, and we never trespassed. If Lily's hair was long, mine was short. She was popular in school, so I hung with outsiders. I became a tomboy and rode horses, because Lily didn't. She staked a claim to classical music, our father's passion, so I turned to rock. Lily took up the flute, while I bashed away on drums. Because Lily rose to the top of her class, I gravitated to the middle, to mediocrity. She became the perfect daughter, so I was forced to rebel.

If you think about it, though, becoming opposites only reinforced our oneness. We became alter egos instead of redundancies and therefore incomplete without each other. If there'd been three of us, it wouldn't have worked out the way it did. We still shared thoughts and dreams. Whenever I found myself talking in a voice that wasn't mine or changing my gait slightly, I knew it was Lily inside me. There was an echo to my heartbeat, and that was Lily, too. Lily was a blur in my vision, and beyond her, faintly, was Rose.

Regardless of our efforts at forced opposition, it was impossible to know where Lily ended and I began. "Leave me alone!" I'd hiss and she would answer, frustrated, "What?" but understanding me perfectly.

I don't know. Maybe we flooded into each other to fill the space Rose had left.

There was trouble, naturally, when we became interested in boys, since our attraction was identical, both outgoing and incoming. I demanded absolute loyalty from my boyfriends— they had to renounce Lily one hundred percent to be with me. On the other hand, we weren't above trying a switch when it involved a boy neither of us cared for very much. We tried it only once, and, to his credit, he knew instantly, the way my horse instinctively knew us apart, and I gained faith in the depth of human perception.

And it's funny that, as Lily and I fought and scratched to be different, Mama confused us more and more. It reached the point that, when Lily's long hair fell forward, threatening to drop into her soup, Mama would reach over and tuck a strand of my short crop behind my ear.

Neither of them knew quite what to think of the separate paths taken by Lily and me, and their reactions were so opposite as to cause schizophrenia. Father was reassured by Lily's direction and mystified by mine. "I would be more than happy, My Darling Iris with the Ambrosial Eyes, to buy you a new sweater," he'd say when I appeared in a mothball-flavored long, batik skirt and baggy sweater from Goodwill. "We really can afford to dress you, you know." Meanwhile, Mama would have a heart-to-heart with Lily: "Sweetheart, don't you think your room is maybe a little too tidy? We don't want you so perfect that you're not having any fun, do we? Can't you let yourself go a little, my Frilly Lily, like Iris does?"

Father was smart enough to avoid such comparisons. When I became a Deadhead in high school, it put a scare into him, but he was cool.

"Iris," he said.

I missed that he'd stopped calling me "Iris with the Ambrosial Eyes." The whole time he'd done that, of course I thought I hated it, but when he quit, I really missed it. When they quit calling you "Pumpkin" and all the other ridiculous things they called you, you realize it's because you're not cute to them anymore. I mean, they still love you and all, but in a different way, and you know damned well they don't think you're cute anymore, and you're not. You're a long way from cute by this point.

"Iris," he said, "I worry about where you're headed. Are you really thinking for yourself? I just want you to keep questioning things, okay?"

I was pretty mortified by the whole discussion, but was actually sympathetic with him. I just didn't want him to know it.

"Are you seeing the whole picture of what you're getting into?"

I tried to make him rest easier about me. "Sure I do. We're into peace and protecting the environment and exposing government abuse, we're for Native American rights, against globalization and nuclear contamination. We're pro-animal rights, anti-industrialization, anti-consumerism . . ." I gave him the whole spiel.

"And a lot of it's noble, I'll give you that," he said, completely straight-faced. "But, what about your own personal direction, like your education? Hmm? Where are you headed with that? Are you so sure you want to move so far from the mainstream of things? Maybe the mainstream could use people like you, Iris. If you wrap yourself in a separate lifestyle and start speaking its babble, dressing in its uniform, following its priests without protest, then I worry about you . . . I worry you're losing you."

He could be convincing, my dad, but what he didn't understand was that I'd found a safe place for myself. Because you can't make it through high school alone.

If he'd said, "Why can't you be more like Lily?" I'd have taken off running in the opposite direction as fast as I could without looking back, but he didn't. I know that's what he meant, but to his credit he didn't say it.

"I'm okay, Dad. I can hang out and still be me."

"I wonder. I hope so."

I felt sorry for my dad even having to have this talk with me.

"Listen," he said. I could tell he wasn't enjoying it either, rubbing his hand over his forehead and then dragging it back through his hair, but my dad was never one to shirk his duty.

He looked pretty miserable, though.

"I know everyone hates advice," he told me. "But I only want you to remember a couple of things, Iris. Remember this . . ." (big pause for maximum effect), "you have choices. Just don't do anything that'll irrevocably hurt you, that you won't be able to pull out of if you want to. And pick your battles, okay? Don't be a loose cannon, wasting yourself on causes that don't matter. There's only so much of you to go around."

He gave me The Look. He saves this for The Big Point. "And here's my kicker," he said, " 'everything in moderation.' Think about that, Iris. I know that sounds like tepid, boring advice, but just think about it. It has to do with tolerance and maturity and reason, words that the young hate because they're not passionate. But just picture a world with no greed, Iris, with no hatred, no addictions. That would be a world of moderation. Too much of anything sucks."

My dad knew how to give speeches. He knew that last word would get my attention.

"Including moderation?" I asked, after giving it a moment's thought. I had to say something, didn't I, just to prove I'd been listening?

He laughed. "That too," he said, proving he practices what he preaches. Tolerance.

And, of course it wasn't just about me losing who I was, this concern of his. It was really about drugs. He was afraid of the drugs, but he couldn't just come out and say it, anymore than he could ask me to be more like Lily. And I don't even think he knew just how big a deal the drugs were with my friends. You have to almost wonder how parents could not know, since it was the alpha and omega of the Deadhead trip, the oracle, the magic bus; I mean, all they'd have to do was read one thing the Dead wrote, hear one song, look at one psychedelic drawing, or just remember their own scene from the sixties and seventies. You can't help but wonder what's happened to their eyesight and memories. I mean, you figure they're not that old yet.

I wish I could've reassured my dad about things, I really do, because I liked the world well enough. I wasn't as "disaffected" as my friends were. I mean, I didn't intend to completely waste myself. I just needed a group to hang with, even peripherally, to at least make it through high school. And they cared about a lot of what he cared about, they really did. And so did I, so I considered it a decent choice on my part. I couldn't explain that to him, though. Because you don't just throw the towel in and go over to the other side at that age. You're doing your job, rebelling like hell, and listening to reason would be fucking treasonous. You'd have to be crazy.

He was right about one thing, though. I did think it was boring advice at the time; I remember I did.

I still loved him, though. I hope he knew that.

Four

To tell the truth, the story of my life is that I've underestimated . . . well . . . everything.

I really have.

Blair's photos taken with the Speedgraphic are beautiful:
dark and serious, haunting. I don't know the person who took
these, but I should. I definitely should.

He woke me up last night. He sort of kicked me with his
leg in the middle of the night and said, "Wake up, Iris. You're
having a nightmare." I guess I was jerking around and making
a lot of noise or something, so he told me. I sort of knew it
anyway. I was dreaming someone pushed me from behind. It
was winter and it was night and they pushed me and I fell into
this ice-cold reservoir. So I was trying to get out of this heavy
winter coat I was wearing, underwater, so I wouldn't drown.
It was pulling me down and I couldn't get it off. I couldn't get
my arms out of it, like a straightjacket or something. I was
glad he woke me up.

There I was wearing practically nothing, sweating in the
tropical night.

There's something else I avoid in my San Vació routine
these days, something I hadn't noticed before. En route to
the Cafe Internet is an abandoned pink stucco house washed
out in the last tropical storm. A skeletal dog lies curled in fetal

position in a gully in front of the house, fragile, ears folded, never moving, barely holding on until the next wind carries it away. A crepe paper dog. I'm guessing he was left behind when the house was abandoned and no one will take him in or feed him scraps in this village where things like extra food, health care for animals, and empathy for all of God's creatures are unaffordable luxuries and maybe even cultural anomalies. I can't let myself see this. If I see it, I'll hate this place. I'll hate the world. I'll start crying and won't ever stop.

Rita teeters over on wooden legs to pour my coffee.

"Have you seen that dog down by the pink house that was washed out?" I ask her. She nods noncommittally. "Can't you take him in or feed him, or something?" I know Rita has a huge red cur with a tail that curls over his back who was also a stray, a dog she took in and named "Pizza," for some reason, who lives the good life now, lying egotistically beneath a tree out front guarding the place.

Her eyes soften, but she shakes her head firmly. "Nope. That dog is too far gone. If you fed him now, he'd die." She tries to look tough. "That dog is toast, Iris."

Like I shouldn't think about it anymore. Like I don't know that you can't save everything on earth. But all I can think is that maybe Rita's been here too long. So I take my coffee to my computer of choice and talk to my mother, but I don't mention the dog at the pink house. My mother has her own worries.

"Chicken Little" fits you to a T, don't you think, Iris? she writes. *Remember when your pet squirrel died, you asked me if he would go to heaven? You, the one who worries about stepping on ants, I shouldn't tell you about how things are around here, but you asked, so I will.*

I can't remember such a spring! This can't be our beau-

tiful Colorado, although, with all the fires, "Color Red" certainly has taken on new meaning. "Color Black" might be even more apt, I think. Well, maybe not, after all. Lily and I walked Sherlock around the pond yesterday evening—the one to the west that you like so well, not the one toward town. The sun was going down, a fiery red ball floating in an orange haze, terrible and terribly beautiful. A red-winged blackbird flew up in front of us, and when that eerie light caught the red patches on the front of his wings as he landed in a tree, they lit up like neon. The leaves he landed in were dripping red light reflected from that weird sun, and I thought, My God, Colorado's bleeding!

I've never seen a spring without a trace of moisture. They're saying it's the worst drought in four hundred years, Sweetheart, and I believe it. It feels like the whole state is on fire. There are forest fires across all the mountain ranges, two of them out of control, the largest burns in history. So there's none of our blue sky and white thunderheads this year. The sunlight shines through a smoke filter all day, every day, except when the sun drops near the horizon, when the whole edge of the earth looks on fire. The mountains are completely invisible from the smoke—we might be in Los Angeles under the worst smog, for all you can tell. And the earth seems dead. There's no smell—you know, that wonderful, wet smell you and I used to inhale with all our might whenever we drove past the alfalfa fields right after mowing. We sang out, 'Aaahhh, smell that? Earth's perfume, right?' Well, m'dear, there's only the non-smell of dry dust now.

I don't know why it's getting under my skin the way it has, but I just don't seem to have the backbone to resist it. Did I seem so spineless to you girls, growing up? I hope not. Little girls need someone with gumption to protect them until they can face the world themselves.

Oh, don't listen to me. It's just I'm feeling ganged up on—the combination of current politics and the drought is more than I can bear. It's just too much for my sensitive soul—strangling drought and soaring heat and smirking conservatives, just when my hormone levels are plunging. Don't laugh! Or do. You have no idea how much I miss your laugh around here, Sweetheart.

It's even harder on Lily. I try to get her to go out, to take Roman out for a trail ride early before the sun starts baking, but she doesn't have the heart for it. Don't be angry with me for this, okay, my child? I know how you like to keep what's yours separate from what's Lily's, but both Lily and Roman need companionship right now, so I thought it wouldn't hurt. I was sure you'd agree if you were here.

The strangest thing, Puss: you know how the whole area is full of Canada geese goslings by this time of year? I haven't seen any goslings at all. The adults are here, but they swim around idly, with no purpose.

I've forgotten what rain smells like.

Every night sheets of rain inundate San Vaciò. Henry looks up from the Scrabble board when it starts. "Here it comes," he says, eyes gleaming. He loves the rainy season.

I lie in bed later, listening to its long, slow whispering. You can almost hear the jungle sigh as it soaks up the rain. When Blair and I make love, our bodies slide apart from the humidity. We can hardly stay together, no matter how desperately we push and pull at each other, like mud wrestling. It's like the rain is a jealous lover, trying to keep us apart, nothing escaping its fury. Earth survives rain, though, and I'm like the earth, opening up for the plow—spreading, opening, yielding, embracing, quickening. At the end, I lift and arch and rise like the gulls that follow the plow, flashing white in the sun, exploding vertically into the sky.

I blow between our chests when it's over, panting, my hair completely soaked, one of us still on top of the other because we don't want to let go. But we can't bear touching, can't stand the hot stickiness of it, unless I blow.

Finally, hot and winded, we slide apart, laughing, sprawling onto our backs, rolling off each other like slippery fish. Blair gets up and walks into the bathroom without flipping on the light. Lying there in fetal position, I hear a swirl of water in the basin and I know he's in there washing his smoking gun. I wait to use the toilet until he comes back to bed. When I flip on the light, a huge centipede, at least the length of what Blair has just dangled above the basin's overflow drain, disappears quickly back down that orifice.

Everything is more extravagant in the tropics. San Vació is in the Tropic of Cancer, where the ocean is bluer, the clouds heavier, trees glossier, dirt darker, birds brighter, insects larger, and time slower. Man seems smaller in the tropics, more ridiculous, more desperate, his efforts more futile, swallowed up by the jungle, bleached by the sun, washed away by the rain. Fire and ice? Maybe in Colorado. Nothing so dramatic is necessary in the tropics. Here, rain and heat and the luxuriant excesses of growing things are plenty enough.

Henry's becoming downright invasive with his questions, but I can't find the energy to mind anymore. He smokes marijuana between games, making a mess all over his side of the board.

"Would you object . . . ?" he'd asked the first night he brought out his bowl, which made me laugh.

"It's legal for me, you know—for medicinal purposes. I

have a prescription," which made me laugh again.

"Right, Henry."

"Would you like a hit?" he asked, in that weird voice that comes out when you're holding your breath, like heels scraping a floor. "It's prime stuff."

"Some other night," I told him. It's not "legal" for me, and I've heard the horror stories about Mexican jails.

"You worry too much," he tells me, which may or may not be true. Anyway, I'm not into drugs these days. I have my reasons.

It certainly doesn't help his game. The delays while he tries to come up with a word are getting longer and longer. It doesn't matter in the Tropic of Cancer, though. *No importa.*

"How did you and Blair meet, Iris?"

This comes straight out of the blue, which he realizes, so he adds, as an afterthought, "You're looking particularly stunning tonight, by the way, but I'm feeling sharp as hell myself and think I might actually beat you tonight. Stunning or not."

"Are you going to draw your letters, Henry, or are you going to fart around trying to push your frigging finger through the bottom of that pipe?"

"Don't nag. Don't niggle. Oh! Now, there's a word I could've used in the last game! Why can't I ever think of them when I need them?"

"I have to niggle, Henry. It's my job description."

He finally draws his seven letters and shifts them around on his rack, once, twice, again, again, looking pleased with himself.

"Speaking of which, just what is your actual job description, back in the real world, Bleu?"

He came up with "Bleu" from "Bleu Iris," or "Eyes of Bleu" (even though I told him, "They're green, Henry"),

"Miss Bleu-Eyes" (regardless), or something or other. I can't even remember anymore. "Not that your given name isn't apt," he said when he first came up with "Bleu." "You have a flower-like face; I'm sure somebody's told you that." But "Bleu" it is, anyway, and he insists on the French pronunciation.

"I can't imagine who would hire you with that thing in your eyebrow."

"Lay off the eyebrow, Henry." I reassure myself by gingerly touching the bead dangling there. "I'm a student, of course."

"Like that's a full explanation."

I make the first word. "T-o-u-c-h-y." I figure I have fifteen minutes' grace now before Henry will make his play.

"What more do you want? Go ahead, spit it out, Henry."

"What career are you planning, eh, Bleu? Professional student, is that it? Nice, safe place to be for the rest of your life, etcetera, etcetera."

Henry can be very irritating. My voice develops an edge.

"Pot calling the kettle, don't you think? I mean, talk about your cloistered life, teaching history in some third-rate California school, then taking early retirement and moving to some sleepy no-name Mexican fishing village no one's ever heard of. I don't think you're in a position to lecture me about getting out in the 'real world,' Henry. I mean, here you are, lounging in your private *paradiso*, evidently set for life financially, with nothing more challenging than a Scrabble game now and then, speaking of which, you wanna set a time limit tonight, huh?"

"What's your rush, Bleu? We've got the rest of our lives."

"Maybe you do, Henry, but I actually plan to eventually find something useful to do with myself."

"And what will that be?" Henry is picking up his letters

with both hands, and lays out the word "r-e-j-e-c-t," using my "c," craftily landing his "j," worth eight points, on a triple-letter score. I'm still ahead five points, though.

I'm the one keeping score, so I finish jotting his down before answering.

"I'll let you know when I figure it out."

"Ha!" he barks. "That's the point. I thought so. You haven't the foggiest, have you?"

"What? Give me a break, Henry. Why should that delight you, mmm? Okay, have it your way. So, I'm still searching."

"You're a blank tile, that's what you are, Iris Bleu. A clean slate. *Tabula rasa*. Be careful what you let someone use you for. Be careful what's written on you."

"Oh man! You're too deep for me, Henry, you know that? Altogether too deep. I think that must be very high quality stuff you're smoking tonight."

I kick ass in that game.

I never answer Henry's questions, which I figure is only fair because I don't ask any either. Let sleeping dogs lie. Best to leave our conversations as they are, an endless exchange of adumbrations (look that one up). Henry's too nosy for my taste, anyway. I have the feeling he thinks I'm a lost soul or something, like I need his protection and guidance, but, vegetating away here as he is, he's not exactly my idea of a credible "wise man." This stay in San Vaciò is a strictly temporary situation for me, and certainly not an end-all. The same goes for Blair.

We met in Arcata. I went out there because of Luna, because Luna fired my imagination.

A sacred act, he said. Unconditional love.

My friends in Colorado were all very environmentally conscious, but passive. Okay, that's putting it mildly. Krystal, my best friend in high school, the Deadhead, she was the one who raised my consciousness, though.

She was adopted, and that screwed everything up for her whole life. She hated her adopted parents, especially her mother, I guess from the first moment, like she'd never bonded with them. She was always imagining her real mother as someone wonderful and utterly different from her adopted mother.

"I was a cutter for awhile, you know," she told me one day.

Me, from my happy, sheltered, normal life, I had no idea what she meant.

"I cut myself, see?" There were faint scars on her arms.

She was always working on her issues and mine, too. Behavior that I attributed to logic, or to normal human reactions, or to biology, or normal bumps in the road of relationships, or whatever, she interpreted as issues that needed working through. She saw issues everywhere, even in my favorite movies and novels, and that sort of ruined them for me, looking at them that way. I had commitment issues, and she would never let me off the hook. You couldn't be mad at her about it, though, because she was hardest on herself. Her major issue was abandonment, naturally, and she'd been through a couple of rebirthings to help her work through it.

She was bonkers over landfills, deadly serious about recycling. I have to admit, my family couldn't have cared less about separating out plastic, newspapers, and aluminum from our trash, but I changed all that after I met Krystal. She would practically kill me if I used Styrofoam.

"Oh my God, can you believe what my mother talks about to her friends?" she'd ask out of nowhere. "They talk about what a bitch it is to fold fitted sheets and how they hate it when the water spills over out of ice cube trays while you carry them to the freezer.

"Let's never end up like that, okay, Iris? Kill me if I ever care about crap like that, okay?"

I knew she didn't have to worry. Krystal had plenty she cared about, all of it dramatic and crucially important. She cared about the poverty at Pine Ridge Reservation, about the quality of tofu, about wearing recycled clothes, about keeping her heat turned down and a brick in her toilet to save water. About closing nuclear power plants and cleaning up toxic waste sites and oil spills, about saving the whales and the old-growth forest, about the dumping of sludge off the New Jersey coast, about acid rain, the homeless, depletion of the Brazilian rainforest, and about using animals for testing products.

She didn't care much about national unemployment, the price of oil, trade deficits, the prime rate, the Cuban embargo, divorce rates, hunger strikes in North Ireland, the JFK files, mortgage rates, the price of gold, inflation, the closing of steel plants, airline deregulation, veterans' lawsuits against Agent Orange, any sports whatsoever, Wall Street fraud, tax reform, or even affirmative action.

But in her own way, Krystal tried to improve herself and the world. She consulted spiritual guides, did daily divinations, read Tarot cards, and threw bones. She cast Rune stones, practiced pyramid and crystal power, joined drum circles. She was totally diligent with her affirmations. She had a whole book of them. If you had a zit, you read an affirmation applicable to appearance issues and how you treated yourself:

I am one with the infinite riches of my subconscious mind. It is my right to be beautiful. I am forever conscious of my true worth. I will be kind and loving to myself because I believe in my beauty. I am wonderfully beautiful. It is wonderful. I nurture my spirit by believing in my beauty. I eliminate any activity that harms myself or denies my beauty. I affirm my beauty. I believe I can recover from habits that injure myself. I am gentle and patient with my efforts to change. I do not yield to temptations. My worth is not diminished in any way by my appearance. I will judge myself not by my appearance but by my accomplishments and by the love I have given. I will not diminish the gift of life by guilt. I imagine life with healthy skin. I believe I will have perfect skin. I live each moment with serenity, joy, and gratitude.

And then your zits would disappear.

Krystal had the power to wrap people around her little finger. She was really beautiful, if you want to know—I mean, especially her hair. She was the one with ambrosial eyes, not me, because they were the color of nectar or something, and she had this perfect, glowing skin, which I could never understand, considering her vegan diet. But it was her hair that knocked you out—she twisted it into a thick rope down her back—it was reddish, but not that ugly red, nothing even close to carroty, but honey gold with a trace of papaya, impossible to describe. When she wrapped a long, batik cloth around her hips, she looked like a tropical Celtic goddess, which I know is an oxymoron, but, what can I say, that's how she looked, period.

I don't know, Krystal had power over people. Older women seemed to want to take care of Krystal. She did have a quiet, calm sort of purity about her, and her utter poverty and simple life brought out their mothering instincts, I suppose, especially if they happened to have no children of their

own. Krystal gravitated to these childless women in particular. She didn't exactly invade their lives, at least I didn't
think so at the time, but she definitely managed to insinuate
herself, until, amazingly, they opened not only their homes
and hearts to her, but their pocketbooks. She baby-sat,
house-sat, and animal-sat for them. She gave their little girls
(if they had any) riding lessons. But what she really gave
them of great value was what she gave me—her presence.
They paid for it willingly, and she took what they paid
shamelessly.

I didn't get it. One such lady had given Krystal a car, a
piece of crap hand-me-down, naturally, but still . . . Another
woman paid her board bills for her horse, Newly, and bought
her a pair of custom riding boots when Krystal's wore out. (I
mean, those boots cost a fortune!) They invited her for meals
and sent her home with extra food, all that ordinary motherly
stuff, but also bought her expensive jewelry and crystals, or
whatever she wanted. And Krystal expected these things as if
she'd earned them. She complained about her old piece of
crap car and dropped hints to her various benefactors about
buying her a better one, specifying her preference for a Volvo.
Then she read affirmations to remind herself that she was
worth it and that the universe kindly and generously provides, and, sure enough, one of her wealthy middle-aged
friends actually gave her a Volvo.

I could never tell if Krystal knew she was operating or not.
I couldn't even quite tell if she actually *was* operating. It
didn't really matter, because money issues didn't fit into our
realm anyway. Money had no part in our human be-in.

It was a terrible pain in the butt to go out to lunch with her,
if we went anywhere but a vegetarian restaurant.

"What kind of broth is this cooked in?"

There was almost nothing she could eat. She had an

73

amazing amount of food issues, let me tell you.

What else?

Krystal went to the chiropractor nearly every day until she taught me to crack her bones into place, even in her neck, which she told me few people were willing to do. It did make a horrible sound, but I was so ignorant of what might happen and I trusted her directions and her faith in me so completely that I had no fear. She thought her bones refused to stay aligned because she hadn't worked through all of her (I never would've guessed) issues. I think she'd considered multiple body piercings, but she had some kind of issues with that too and had stopped wearing her nose stud.

She was constantly on the lookout for old souls, in complete awe when she believed she'd found one. She made me envy them. I was sure I was a very, very young soul, myself.

Finally, Krystal started drifting away from me right about when Lily went away to school. Well, maybe sucked away would be more accurate, because this woman named Chandra lured Krystal into her group of followers, convincing them that they were all a reincarnation of Jesus and his disciples. She swallowed Krystal in one bite mentally. Physically too, because, the thing is, Krystal eventually moved into Chandra's big house with the rest of the tribe.

I don't know, I guess Krystal's view of the world opened up a whole parallel existence to me. I really loved Krystal. It wasn't that I bought into all of this, but it was so heartbreaking that she did, I played along with it for her sake.

But basically, it finally came to me over time, Krystal was accomplishing exactly nothing.

Unconditional love, he tells me. The ultimate cathedral.

On the other hand, here was this girl, this Julia Butterfly Hill, out in Arcata, who climbed 180 feet up into a giant redwood named Luna and didn't come down. She lived up there for two years, so Pacific Lumber Company couldn't cut down the tree. I had to go out there to see for myself.

So after a couple of years at CU in Boulder floundering around in liberal arts, I transferred to Humboldt State University, figuring I could flounder just about anywhere (admittedly there were other reasons I wanted a location change, too). By the time I reached Arcata, though, Butterfly had come down, having reached an agreement with Pacific Lumber to protect Luna, a costly settlement bought with funds Butterfly and her legion of supporters had raised during her protest. So, back on earth, with Luna's safety bought and paid for (and her own freedom, if you think about it), she went home to Arkansas or Alabama or somewhere.

By the time I left Arcata, vandals had girdled Luna with a chainsaw and no one could tell whether or not the giant thousand-year-old redwood would survive. I met Luna, but I never did meet Butterfly. I was really impressed by Luna. I hate to imagine how Butterfly felt about what had happened to her tree.

What then?

Luna and Butterfly led to Blair. So easy, drifting along the green fringe from Krystal to Luna to eco-radicals. What happened is, I met Blair in the dark. We both happened to attend a slide show at HSU about Hale-Bopp. We were both Hale-Bopp freaks. Blair was sitting with a friend in front of me, where I could study the back of his neck and the right side of his face by the light of the comet. Cosmic attraction from the start. I could also hear their conversation and I admit to eavesdropping shamelessly. He said something that stuck with me, something to the effect that the comet was so beautiful and impressive that he could understand why that group of people killed themselves to try to catch a ride on it—he said he could totally understand their rapture. That resonated with me, because I used to say stuff like that all the time before Lily did what she did.

After that, I started running into Blair around campus and in a lot of the places I hung out, at the Fogbound Coffee House, the food co-op, the Rainbow Cafe. You end up looking at someone closely, whether you want to or not, when that happens, when you keep bumping into each other that way. I mean, synchronicity certainly eventually grabs your attention, especially if you're the least bit fatalistic or even superstitious, and who isn't? The whole thing starts feeling spooky, but the fact is, there's usually a logical explanation, and in our case, we bumped into each other so often because he was an environmentalist and I was a wannabe. Simple as that. It couldn't help but happen. I mean, I wasn't stalking him, or anything (I absolutely hate that kind of thing with a purple passion). It's just that I'd set my sights on assimilating into this delectable subculture I'd found, and he was like the bull's-eye in the target.

Let me tell you, it's not easy being the Lone Ranger, sans Tonto, trying to ingratiate yourself that way. I had to work at it, use my head, make a Herculean effort, and all that. It took planning, patience, perseverance, all those "p" things. I began tagging along at various demonstrations and forest occupations. Running into Blair constantly at these events was just a fringe benefit, frosting on the cake, gravy on the potatoes, etcetera, etcetera.

Considering how I believed myself Lily's complete opposite by this time, and considering the nature of Mac, the love of Lily's life, and what had happened to them, I ought to have steered a wide path around Blair's wildness. I should have run like hell, without looking back. Me and my, "There but for fortune . . ." But I didn't.

I made it my goal to weasel in with the residents of a certain house in Arcata's outskirts called Treetops, a center for tree-sitters. I chatted them up when they shopped at the co-op, sympathized lavishly with their problems, indulged their whims, offered myself slavishly to help out with their needs. I studied them and copied their style, buying the newest Birkenstocks, reducing my possessions to what would fit in a backpack, riding my bike to work and school, drinking gallons of soy milk and eating tons of tofu. I wore a wool cap pulled down far enough to cover my eyes and baggy denim coveralls to cover everything else. I studied Zen, tied myself in yoga knots, and rooted for the total collapse of the industrial society. In other words, I renounced just about everything in the whole wide world and completely depersonalized myself. I even had my eyebrow pierced, trying to fit in. Tree-sitters were my heroes, Blair up there at the apex.

Activists are a paranoiac lot, though, and worming my way in took time and patience. None of them ever gave or asked a last name, because virtually everyone entertained the possibility they might be under police surveillance. So I was put through a sort of sifting process that winnowed out drifters, addicts, fruitcakes, and spies. Still, eventually I was allowed in.

Treetops really blew my mind. It was a rambling old crate of a house with a roof as steep and dark as a witch's hat, clanking steam radiators, and small, grimy windows that filtered out what little anemic heat and light managed to reach their surfaces through the omnipresent clouds and dense surrounding forest. Though maybe passably comely once upon a time, the place had definitely seen better days—had become derelict, a bag lady of a rat trap, if you want to know, and to boot was nowadays fraternizing with a very low class of social outcasts. The inside was a la-la-land clutter straight out of Arabian Nights: hand-painted posters, beaded string doors, tie-dyed pillows, leggy plants strangled in macramé, burnt stubs of incense turning hand-thrown clay dishes black. Everything reeking of patchouli oil. Oh, and a very fancy espresso machine.

Incoming information at Treetops was as filtered as the light, as sifted through as its inmates. Radio Free Cascadia and *The Clandestine Messenger* spouted doom and hate as non-stop as the rain. A stew of causes flowed in—a regular ideological succotash. It was impossible not to suffer seratonin and endorphin depletion at Treetops. We needed that therapeutic light simulating sunlight. We all needed to be on massive doses of Prozac or Hypericum or something, our extremism, paranoia, and morbidity a simple matter of chemical imbalance and UV deprivation. I mean, there had to be some such explanation.

And, under these circumstances, Blair shone. He was a manic amid depressives, a relatively rational voice amidst raving, nihilistic iconoclasts. It was a function of comparison. I'd landed in a lion's den and attached myself to the most amiable cat.

And he did seem amiable. There was a kind of upward mobility of the pride's most aggressive males. They relocated from Treetops into various underground houses when they crossed an invisible boundary into anarchy frontier, lured into that alternate universe by marketing forces every bit as pervasive as the capitalist consumer ads we despised. Also by too much unstructured time, by the unblemished certainty of youth that everything matters, and by the utter conviction that the apocalypse was just around the bend. Also by the need to belong and by whatever attracts us all to big fireworks displays. But Blair stayed put among the tree huggers, moderate activists whose purpose seemed noble and righteous and benign to me.

Blair and I lived together in that big house as platonic family, although Blair had a reputation more *enfant terrible* than Aristotelian. I must've caught him between women, he who was rumored to have an allergy to maidenheads. I was aware he was someone with whom, unless totally self-destructive, you wouldn't want to indulge in Erica Jong's zipless fuck. You'd want time to verify the purity of Blair's blood sample. A protective membrane between oneself and Blair would be prerequisite.

Hey, don't I know, I was on autopilot in Arcata, seduced by all that brooding Pacific Northwest beauty, by isolation and disconnection, by imagery of souls hovering above it all on platforms in swaying redwoods. And by Blair's sweet nothingness.

We met in the dark, but came together up a tree. I'd never left terra firma, though I'd schlepped food and water and clothing and reading material to a lot of those who did. I'd even emptied slop jars lowered by rope from two hundred feet up. Blair had done several stints aloft, and it became an issue between us.

"It's the greatest high you'll ever have, Iris—we're talking sacred act. Up there, you're completely engulfed in total, unconditional love in the arms of this totally ancient, living creature. It's, like, the ultimate cathedral.

"Shit, Iris! An eleven-year-old girl tree-sat up at Fall Creek!"

He kept after me and after me.

"Let's flip for it," I finally told him, and he gave me the absolute stink-eye.

So I let him drag me out to this recently abandoned platform site. I stood there at the base of this great old giant, looking where it pointed, straight up away from all the troubles of the earth, and I went up with him. And when we reached the top, it was like we'd climbed the magic beanstalk. We had that zipless fuck, swaying in the breeze like twin babes rocked in their mother's arms.

So much for my resolve, for my ironclad credos.

The thing is, I'd always considered myself brave. I love speed and had actually toyed with the idea of racing cars for a living. I was always ready for anything, no matter how insane, on my horse. I was absolutely positive that if I'd been one of the ayatollah's American hostages in Iran I'd have refused to leave when they set the women free before releasing the men—I'd have stayed with the men. I'd have shown them what Infidel women are made of! I'd always believed I understood the concept of women warriors. But now I know that was all a bunch of crap, life through the Looking Glass, because when Lily scared me, all that vanished in a flash and I ran like the white rabbit.

It took everything I had to climb that damned tree. It really did.

Five

Rita's toenails were painted red today. I never did like red toenails.

Lily and I were living in two separate worlds by our senior year in high school.

Her school friends and mine couldn't even be in the same room together, because it was like we came from two different planets. That was okay, though, because we thought their makeup was gross, their conversations incredibly stupid, and their attitude snobby, elitist, shallow, patronizing, oblivious, slavishly conformist, and completely phony. To be perfectly honest, we hoped they rotted in hell.

None of us dated the kind of guys they did (my friends wouldn't be caught dead dating anyone without long hair), as if their type would ever ask us. We didn't cross that DMZ line.

I know, I know, I'm exaggerating here. Lily really wasn't all that straight or uptight. I want it that black and white, that's all, because it's easier seeing things that way. It's a cop-out, though, because Lily was still all right. She would play classical pieces on her flute for me that were so beautiful they made me cry. "Here, listen to this," she'd say, and I'd end up crying. She even ditched Mac sometimes to go out for pizza just with me. We'd sit forever at our special booth until the owner wanted to throw us out, talking about our futures and the things we hated or loved and things that cracked us up or made us sad. Because, the thing is, we really missed each other.

I mean, Lily gives everyone the benefit of a doubt. Like for example, channel surfing. She stops for a Lawrence Welk rerun. And there's Bobby and Cindy sweating in cowboy outfits, grinning like crocodiles into the camera while they danced appallingly to horrible champagne music.

"Look," she said. "They were Mousketeers when Mama was little."

I mean, not one mean word.

She could let go and be a little crazy sometimes.

She could dance, too—I could never even come close.

We sat for hours in the U-shaped straps of the old swing set we'd long-since outgrown, discussing the twists and turns of life, rotating round and round in place, finally lifting our legs to let the swings uncoil.

We lay for hours out on the lawn watching clouds, making up stories to match their shapes.

So, I guess what I'm saying is, Lily was all right.

But then I'd have to go and ruin it. Like when Lily came in late from a date with Mac. (I mean, what kind of name is "Mac" anyway?) Mama and I were talking quietly, sitting in the kitchen with the lights dimmed, when Lily came in. It was nice, very nice, and I should've just left it at that, but from where I was sitting, I could see the back of Lily's shirt, and noticed the label was on the outside. I should've been her friend, and I actually thought about it, rationally and all, for a minute or so, but I made my choice. I busted her.

"So, Lily," I go, way louder than necessary, "so, how come your shirt's on inside-out?"

Anybody over five years old is going to know that means

she and old Mac had that shirt off and back on again in the dark in the back seat of his makeoutmobile Trans Am, or whatever the heck it was, necking away like mad practically all night. Even my mom, who is a very free thinker and pretty forgiving, would not appreciate hearing this little piece of information I'm advertising. But Lily, she gives me this desperate look, but only for, like, a nanosecond, then, cool as ice, comes back so quick she couldn't have had time enough to make it up. "Oh gosh," she goes, "I pulled it out of my closet and put it on in the dark, so I guess it must've been inside-out on the hanger." And Mama, bless her heart, never blinked an eye. And Lily just gives her this little kiss on the cheek, "Good night, Mama," and throws me this sweet smile-glare, then sashays off to bed, with me sitting there feeling like Judas. And afterward Lily doesn't even mention it to me. I mean, never.

I hated Mac right from the beginning. I hated how he treated Lily. And because I couldn't get at him, I made Lily's life miserable, rubbing salt into the wounds he made. I deviled, cajoled, browbeat, and ridiculed her. I mean, I considered anything fair game because I was trying to "save her."

He had caught Lily at a weak moment, on the rebound from her very first boyfriend, a problematical kid whose attractions were totally invisible to everyone but Lily. She had bucked a mighty tide dating him; maybe that's how Lily came to equate love with isolation, with desperation.

Then Mac appeared. When he showed up on our doorstep for that first date, she had to know he'd be accepted—embraced, even—allowing her to finally love openly, out of the closet, to finally revel in love. And she did. I mean, he was dazzling.

I have to admit he must have felt something for Lily from the first, too, something big, because he knocked himself out for that first date. He brought her something she'd been wanting forever, a photo of Abbie De Quant playing her flute, and where he'd found it, God only knows. Plus an orchid—like they were going to the prom or something—corny but effective. He'd washed his car, had it detailed, buffed, and polished. I forget what he was wearing, only that it was impressive, but it wouldn't have really mattered because Mac had something that transcended such stuff.

She'd told me he'd been noticing her in their writing class, making nice comments about her stories. She came home half agog because he'd teased her about her unshaven legs, pulling up the legs of her blue jeans and acting like he'd scratched his hand running it up her calf. I tried to imagine it happening to myself, and I could almost get it. Then again . . .

But to me, really, he was just a football thug, the coach's darling, able to charm his way out of failing grades, fistfights, and all minor scrapes. To Lily he was an icon of masculinity, a prototype of confidence. And, truthfully, I guess he was all of these.

He began driving her to and from school, then eventually took her home to meet his family, where, Lily said, it was total chaos. I know for a fact he hung out at our house a lot, ate incredible servings at dinner with us, and lapped up our family like he was starving for that, too.

He took Lily into the mountains on his motorcycle and introduced her to rock climbing. Well, he climbed while she watched. He seduced her, along with nearly everyone else, with his zest for everything and his complete lack of fear. Yeah. The whole world, and that included Lily, was there for no reason but to challenge Mac.

They became an item, as only happens in high schools and Hollywood. At the beginning, she was attracted to his pride and he was attracted to her resistance. He broke that down quickly, though, with his smooth lines. He fed Lily an entire diet of smooth lines. She began writing love notes in every class to give him when he'd show up to walk her to her next class. I never could figure out how Lily managed to get the grades she did after falling for him.

Sure, I thought, Mac could afford to be sweet when he wanted, because he thought he was so fucking superior. Okay, so he was sort of superior. But he could be cruel, too. He let her know he didn't like her to gain weight—even monitoring what she ate. I mean, he was that controlling. All he had to do was look at her and she pushed the plate away. He made her feel like she disgusted him sometimes. He told her she was wrong when she was right, and she believed him. And he flirted outrageously with other girls, but was incredibly jealous at the same. And, something she refused to believe, even though I tried to tell her after hearing it from one of my Deadhead friends, Mac bullied other kids scraping along the outermost edges of high school society. He picked on "lesser" beings, ridiculing certain girls as pariahs, physically tormenting weaker males, stabbing one that I knew of with a pen, leaving visible and invisible wounds. Yeah, leaving marks.

Never mind, though, he was her hero, regardless. She made a point of telling me how he'd smashed a guy's face for making some crack about her within Mac's hearing. That appealed to her—a display of his physical strength and his caring for her all in one.

But, if he was generous to Lily, he was anything but to just about everyone else, because Mac was no team player. He was out for individual glory and didn't care how many bodies he left in his wake. That cocky confidence in his superiority cost him any real friendships, except for Lily's. Because the truth was, except for her, Mac was actually a loner. And that's where you might judge him to be downright stupid, because he made some enemies while he outran, out-jumped, out-wrestled, and out-maneuvered the football better than everyone else.

Bad planning, because he drifted into real trouble in his senior year, when somebody—somebody he'd screwed over, no doubt—decided to make an example out of him when he was busted by another somebody for drinking. When they banished him from all sports for the duration, they destroyed Mac the Creep. The trouble is, Lily was caught in the crossfire. Because Mac pretty much fell apart after that. He hated the school and tried to force Lily to choose between her loyalty to him and her dedication to school. It killed me, seeing her in trouble with everyone and everything she cared about—her teachers and the orchestra, and especially our parents—all for his sake. Especially since it was my Lily, Lily the Perfect, everyone's darling. She was eliminated from some prized school activities because of him.

For awhile there, she was very upset, morbid even, about maybe not being valedictorian because of everything. And, the weird part is, it became a regular modern Romeo and Juliet scene. The more Mac and Lily were punished by the school, the more they became a symbol of something to the students. The whole bloody student body rallied around them in this kind of weird, muttering mutiny.

When Mac was busted for breaking into homes and stealing TV sets, no one could believe it. His parents were too preoccupied with their anger and with covering up their own failures to take any reasonable action, so they sent Mac away to a private prep school for a year. Lily was voted prom queen by the largest margin in the history of the school in her senior year, but with Mac gone, she didn't even have a date for the bloody prom. It was like she was his honored widow or something. High schools, especially in small towns, can be very strange places. Stranger than fiction.

So Lily waited, and I had to sit there and watch her waiting. And, eventually, foregone conclusion, news came back to her of a fling Mac had with another girl while he was at prep school, while she waited for him so damned chastely. She broke it off with him, but he liked the challenge of that. He called, wooing her long distance, but she held out. She was in agony the whole time though, writing pathetic love letters which ended up confetti in her wastebasket; scrunching down in the passenger seat while she had me drive past his house day after day, even though he wasn't there, just to feel closer to him. She started sleeping all the time, going to bed at seven in the evening and sleeping through half the next day. I tell you, Lily was bruised by love. She was held hostage. For Lily, love was not a many-splendored thing. Love was a wicked spell.

When he came home for the summer, she took me along while she followed his car around town, tailing him obsessively. She was suffering so much from being apart from him that I was almost happy for her when they came together again. Then again . . .

"I don't get it, Lily. What do you see in him? I mean, he's vain, he's shallow, he's got a mean streak; sure, he can be nice, but then he treats you like dirt; he's arrogant, and I don't even think he's bright. You're way too good for him."

She made me feel like a rat, though, just sitting there listening meekly to me, staring at the carpet between her bare feet. I looked down at her feet, too. She'd painted her toenails blood red, something I never do. I hate red nail polish. It looks like scabs, as far as I'm concerned. But, omitting color, each of her toenails matched mine perfectly, from the long ovals of her big toes to the weird little half-moons, barely visible, of her little toes—each a little crescent, like a wink. Or a very tiny scab. Exactly like mine.

She was wearing something soft, neutral, pale, like always. Her arms are just thin sticks, covered with down, soft and fluffy as under a dove's wing, and when she moved them around, especially when she lifted them to play her flute, they reminded me of a bird preening its feathers. The thing is, it was impossible for Lily to look awkward. When she swam she might have been made of balsa wood. Her skates left perfect traces in the ice. Picking on someone like Lily was impossible. I don't know how I did it. She hated arguing, so she let me have my way in nearly everything—everything but Mac.

"Love's not a laundry list," she fought back. "The reasons don't have to add up. They don't really matter at all. You can't understand, Iris, because you've never felt this way about anyone. I know you're right about him, but I can't help it. I love him anyway. I don't expect you to understand."

And she was right. For the first time ever, I didn't know what Lily was feeling.

"All the other girls are dying to have him for all the wrong reasons. You know how awful his parents are. I'm the only one who knows how terrible it really is for him."

Great! I thought. Could anyone but Mac manage to have it both ways? Adulation and pity.

With him back from prep school for the summer, they had three months together before Lily left for college. She'd been accepted back east by a topnotch music academy, because, if I've failed to mention it, Lily plays the flute terrifically. Lily is an absolute genius on the flute. And if you think that means there was something else Lily felt that I didn't, you'd be wrong, because, even though I can barely whistle and would way rather ride a horse than play an instrument, I'm totally swept away when Lily plays. I feel her breath blowing through that mouthpiece exactly like it's me she's playing. I feel every note just like she does. I know that for a fact.

He was late, an hour late, as usual, picking her up for a date, so I just had to butt in. I stepped into her room. I mean, I can be a real asshole sometimes that way.

In the matter of our bedrooms, there was this other great schism between Lily and me. Her room was niftily decorated, all in ivory frilly crypt or something, and very tidy, so anybody could see this was the room of someone who had her shit together. While my room, I have to admit, looked like a starship to the psychedelic hypnocratic astral mythos, so that anybody could see this was the room of someone totally derailed. Lily never set foot in my room.

So I stepped into her room, stopping just inside the doorway with my arms crossed defensively over my chest. I had dyed my hair purple with pink sprinkles on that particular day, moussing it into sharp points all over my head, more punk than Deadhead, but I allowed myself such deviations occasionally. I was wearing one of the tackiest blouses I'd ever found at Goodwill, emblazoned with a tableau of Jesus blessing a group of fishermen as a pile of fish spills from their nets. In very bright colors, I might add, especially the fish. I'm sure I looked the perfect part for someone to be giving Lily advice.

"Why do you put up with this crap from him?"

I hadn't, but I might have planned that hairdo just for this conversation.

"Why don't you tell him you have better things to do with your time? I mean, how many times has he stood you up since he's been back? The guy's a moron. I'm gonna tell him myself when he shows up tonight, I swear, Lily."

"Don't you dare, Iris. I only have a few months with Mac before I have to go back and I don't want to waste it fighting."

She looked so miserable sitting there, bothered by a pestering fly. One lousy, fat, lazy, black dive-bombing blowfly. How is it things like that dare invade our space? I swatted it away and it flew off, landing on the windowsill, where it sat rubbing its hind legs together.

I stood there with my arms crossed over my chest. Lily patted the bed beside her for me to sit down. Something about Lily is so sincere, so vulnerable, she's impossible to resist, even when you know damned well she's wrong. The only way I can explain Lily is to say that she has always, from the very beginning, had a pure heart. That's a terrible description, I know, because it sounds sentimental and phony, but still, it's the only way I can explain her. She hasn't got a mean bone in her body. She's incredibly bright and, at the same time, completely gullible. Here we are, identical twins, and it's like she grew up in a different universe than mine. I've had to wonder if that's my fault somehow.

She reached over and ran her fingers through my purple hair, ruffling the ridge of hair standing up, almost a Mohawk.

"You're so crazy, Iris. This is great! I'd never have the guts . . ." blah, blah. Softening me up.

"You know Mac isn't all bad, Iris. Why can't you ever be fair about him?" her voice soft but urgent, almost pleading.

"You always paint everything so black and white," (her, with her red toenails) "but, if he's so bad, how come your horse likes him so much? Huh? Tell me that?"

She had me there. Roman, with his infallible instincts about people, genuinely liked Mac. And Mac enjoyed spending time with horses, unlike most guys. He was patient with them, almost sensitive.

"And look how he stands up for Summer."

His sister, Summer, was hard to take: loud, rough, unattractive, and a little weird, which left her open to a lot of harassment from kids her own age of both sexes. It was true that Mac went out of his way to defend Summer. To her, he was extra kind.

To her credit, Lily didn't mention his looks in her defense. You couldn't be any better looking than Mac Culhane. I mean, he really was the perfect physical specimen. She also didn't mention courage, although he'd become a hero, not only on the football field, where he was definitely considered a fucking hero (to those who worship such things), but because he'd dived into the St. Vrain River during spring runoff to rescue a kid. Yes, he'd actually done that. Mac wasn't all that great a swimmer either (he had an Achilles heel or two), but while everyone else ran along the bank panicking, Mac dove in without stopping to think about it, bluffed the swimming, managing through sheer power and will to pull this kid from the clutches of a big hydraulic, and he hadn't even had to think about it.

Oh, he had courage. He was a third-generation football star. And his father had a Purple Heart, so he came by it honestly. Unfortunately, his father also had a drinking problem. His mother too. So Mac came by that honestly, too, and I was sure that's what was behind his escalating troubles with the law.

I was just softening up a bit when that fly came back just as Mac strolled in. He always sort of strolled, anyway, trying to look casual, but it was a swagger, no matter what. He was wearing some kind of slippery-looking print shirt, just short of being an aloha shirt, and loose cotton shorts and loafers without socks. Very casual, but he made all clothes look great. Sure, everything about Mac read "casual," except his expression. When he saw Lily, the casual was wrung right out of his face.

"Hey, baby," he said. His voice wasn't casual either, but

low and sweet. He sat down between us on the bed.

"Nice shirt, Iris. Move over," his voice instantly transformed to something completely different once he's talking to me. He pushed me over roughly, laughing that nasal, whinnying laugh of his.

"Ditto, Mac." I meant the shirt.

He didn't even think about apologizing to Lily for being late any more than he had thought about diving into that river. Consistent, if nothing else.

Then he brushes that fly away and pulls Lily's face up to kiss her, wrapping his hand behind her head, his hand so large and her neck so small that his thumb and forefinger practically touch across her throat.

I hate it when people do private things in front of me, so I look the other way. Finally, kiss over, he takes Lily's hand, and her wrist goes all limp. Lily turns to putty, her resolve, her individuality, her very "Lily-ness" melting away, vaporizing, maybe through the pulse in her wrist into the blue veins of his strong brown hand, for all I know. And Mac, this guy, this jock, this cock of the rock, this lover, wraps her into his ridiculous patterned shirt.

All very touching, but I had to have my say.

"What kept you, Mac? Busy pulling wings off butterflies?"

Lily gave me a warning look, but Mac ignored me because I was right, actually, about him not being the brightest bulb in the pack. He could never think of a decent comeback. Or maybe it was just his way of shrugging things off, you know, following his family script.

My folks were old-fashioned about such things as boys sitting on our beds with us, so I came very close to yelling "Dad!" at the top of my lungs. But I didn't. Too immature.

I flounced out of the room instead, and left them to it, whatever "it" might be. I knew they were making love by that point, the same way I knew what Lily felt when she played her flute. I just knew.

And, if you think making love was something else Lily had felt that I hadn't, you would be right about that.

Six

The little waves slap at the boat as it bucks the swells. The bow takes a big dive and the engine's tune alters ominously, but the boat recovers and plunges onward. Blair sits next to me, his knees together almost primly, a smile set in his face, hair straight up in the wind, his eyes focused nowhere, maybe on something on the inside. His skin is goose-pimpled all over like a plucked chicken, in spite of the midmorning heat. Maybe he has a case of cold feet, but I doubt it. Me, maybe, but Blair never.

All because I decided to go snorkeling.

Not alone, though—I have no intention of throwing caution to the wind, warrior or not. So I find out from the surfers' girlfriends where the snorkeling is best and safest, out around the nearest of the little islands, Isla Divino. But none of them will go with me. Leo looks utterly dismayed when I ask him if Blanca might like to go. "She don know how to swim," he says, and might as well have added, "and would never think of doing anything so loco, anyway." I hadn't asked Blair because I supposed he'd have a hard time substituting something as tame as snorkeling for the adrenal rush of surfing, but that just goes to show what I know. As it turned out, that was unfair of me. Maybe I judge Blair too harshly, always expecting the worst the way I do. Then again . . .

An old fisherman hires himself out to take people out to

the island. His boat is a ragged Joseph's coat of many peeling colors, but he sits there at the tiller, hatless, staring out to sea like a zealot, his cloudy eyes nearly disappearing into the deep wrinkles of his face. The wind is reassuringly onshore—good to know that if his sputtering motor died, we wouldn't drift to Hawaii. Sitting at the front of the boat, riding out the swells, I look at Blair and smile, realizing I feel as happy as I can ever remember. I can see to the bottom through the clear water and I wonder what happens to the blue when you look straight down.

"Look!" I tap Blair on the shoulder, hollering over the wind and the motor's whine.

Looking back to the mainland, layered against the blue Sierra Madres, is the diorama of palms, gleaming white buildings, beach palapas, and fishing boats of San Vaciò. Running with heat shimmies, the mirage melts slowly in the haze as we cross over. The thirty-minute trip feels like five.

When we land, the boatman tells us he'll wait for as long as we want, which strikes me as terribly sad—to think he would wait through eternity for such a low price. I make up my mind to be quick about my snorkeling and tip well.

The beach stretches blank and trackless, like a white ribbon wrapping the tiny rock island. There's not one green thing in view.

We wade out chest-deep, where schools of little fish are flipping out onto the water's surface, then we sink without a ripple into the water, leaving the old man sitting in the harsh sun like a statue. The world separates into above and below as if parted by a sheet of glass. Mesmerized instantly by raptures of the shallow, I've already forgotten the boatman on the other side of the glass.

Floating. Escaping the gravity of everything earthbound, I let go. The weight of the world lifts away and I feel utterly light. Separate yet part of something huge, isolated in the amniotic sac of earth's womb, floating through inner space, attached by a slender straw to my life source. Everything else is shut out, blotto.

When I lower my face into the water, the calm of the world beneath the surface feels wonderful after the roughness of the surface. Beneath me, my shadow mimics my every move with a liquid grace I know isn't really mine.

Slightly shocked by the cold water, I can hear through the ocean chamber my breath quickening in the snorkel, a nervous, metallic sound like a robot breathing. I *am* slightly nervous. This isn't my dimension, after all.

Suddenly Blair grabs my legs from behind, simulating a shark attack, and I gasp in a mouthful of sea. Choking and sputtering, I spit out my snorkel, frog-kicking frantically to keep my head above the water, because I've lost all flotation in my spasms. Blair breaks the surface next to me, grinning around his mouthpiece. We're at the compass point of the wide circular bay, the circumference awfully distant. A little panic flutters somewhere inside as the chop of the waves slaps at my face and I feel my support hollowing out from under me between waves.

If only I were a water lily . . . *help, Lily!*

Seeing the error of his ways, Blair swoops in, his expression and voice both suddenly serious. "I'm sorry, Iris. I didn't . . ."

"You didn't think! Very funny, Blair!" *Cough, cough!* "See what you've done! I could've drowned."

The hacking won't stop.

"Forgive me?"

"Don't ever do that again!"

I'm such a bitch! But, after all, it's his fault I'm nearly choking to death in water way over my head.

I reinsert my mouthpiece, blow out as hard as I can, and dive, reentering the land under the sheet of glass, forgetting instantly the other. Everything but what's before me melts away, my temper and worries wiped out.

I suppose there *are* sharks here—hammerheads anyway—and barracuda, no doubt, but the view is so dazzling, I don't care. It's worth the risk, anyway, like flying.

It *is* a kind of flying. I watch from above while a life plays out that I have no part in, keeping my distance from things with exquisite detachment. Foreign though I am, the other creatures seem unconcerned. When a school of slippery fish parts and flows around me like quicksilver, I leave no imprint in their mass. *Am I solid?* My shadow twins every movement sinuously. Silvery silica slants through rock chambers like drifting motes of anti-matter. Without the magic of water, all of this would look ordinary and disappointing.

Floating.

Oh, magic carpet, may you never land!

Blair swims beneath me and gestures a thumbs-ups toward the surface.

"Isn't this great?" He swims a circle around me, opening his arms out from his body like calipers, and it strikes me that if I swam between them they would ward off danger and entrap me.

"Let's go deeper, out beyond the surf break," he says. It's not really a request.

"I don't know, Blair . . ." I hate being so timid, but I'm not the ocean creature he is. I come from the high center of a broad continent. Heights I'm used to, but depths . . .

"C'mon, Iris!" he calls, then heads away from land without looking back, and I can't resist. I follow because I too want to go deeper. Who was it that said, "Deep, deep down we're all shallow?" Maybe the reverse is true, too. Does that make any sense?

Blair takes a breath and dives. He skims along the sandy bottom, dancing in tandem with my shadow, twisting and larking like a sea lion, as we cross into a whole rugged landscape of volcanic rock, full of sea life. Starfish like bright-gloved hands form fists around rocks, sea slugs and cucumbers roll loosely in the current between, puffer fish and purple-shelled lobsters wind their way through coral shelves the color of cotton candy.

I follow Blair farther out, concentrating on his ass in front of me rather than the bottom falling away. The water becomes colder and thicker, the current stronger, the fish larger, as Blair swims easily through the strong current without fins, hips swiveling, feet beating a regular rhythm in synch with my own pulse.

I sprint to catch him, and we surface.

"Let's go back," I gasp around my mouthpiece.

"Okay." For once, miraculously, there's no argument.

Now we flow easily with the incoming waves, heading for the steep cliff along the windward side where the floor drops off into vertical jade. Slowly it dawns on me there are no fish here. Then Blair points in both directions around us. Two sea tortoises are circling us like orbiting moons. When Blair swims toward them, they don't move away, but tighten their circle around him as if magnetized by gravitational pull, flapping and pulling themselves in spurts like seabirds bucking strong winds. Dappled voyagers, they watch us fearlessly as we swim through their world on our own odyssey.

I'm a pilot. Longing to stay suspended in this moment forever, focused on nothing, midway between ecstasy and fear, drifting willingly wherever the ocean takes me, I surrender.

There's a sensation of something sneaking up behind me, but, thinking it's only Blair again, I'm not bothered. With all the control of a note in a bottle, a wave surges up under me, lifting and heaving me into a submerged piece of the cliff. There's no sensation of pain, only a rough *bang* against the rocks, then limpness through my body as I'm sloshed away again. I tilt my mask to look down at myself and watch in fascination as a white slice opens in slow motion across my knee, the clarity magnified by the water, the whole thing like watching a movie of it happening to someone else. Then blood starts pluming out through the opening like rust-colored smoke.

You're all right, I tell myself, still calm in that moment before pain and panic set in. I swim to Blair, leaking that telltale wisp of a color that's all wrong out here in the tropical ocean: not brilliant, but dung-colored like earth, running out like sand through an hourglass. When I finally reach him, I tug on his trunks and hang on like I'll never let go.

The journey back seems a lot longer. My knee slowly soaks our white towels red, in spite of a tourniquet Blair improvises from his rubber snorkel strap and monitors carefully, releasing and reapplying according to some schedule I leave to him. I refuse to look at the wound because I already know my knee is laid wide open. *And what the hell is that thrashing around limp and helpless, drowning in our wake? Well, lookee there. If it's not a woman warrior!* The old man, poor bastard, is trying to hurry, his face all knotted up with intensity, running the motor full bore, willing us to the other shore with all his might. I didn't know old men had that kind of strength of will. I find myself focusing on this power of his, letting everything else slide about the voyage back to San Vació.

Really, I don't remember anything else until a very calm face comes into focus, a face with the concentration of a concert pianist, but studying my knee instead of the infinitesimal possibilities of eighty-eight keys. Propping myself up, looking down the length of his lowered head, all I can see are two deep furrows between a pair of sympathetically slanting brows. A straight nose hides his mouth and chin, but I can see those facial parts moving, so I try to focus harder so I can hear what he's saying, but the words sound fuzzy, like I'm still underwater.

"Ideally, we really should get her to a big hospital, you understand," he's saying, "but the logistics from here are nearly impossible. Still, I feel fairly certain I can manage here, if that's what you choose."

I realize he's talking to Blair, but I finally open my mouth and I hear my voice croak, "That's what I choose."

Oh God! Something has buckled in my heart.

I've been dreaming of Dr. Allende ever since. Blair has been sweet about the whole thing, even missing some very big surf in my behalf, but, oh God, Dr. Allende is in my bones, and I'm lost, I'm lost! Right over the edge of the abyss, headfirst into ridiculous, sometimes obscene, always painful, day-into-night-dreams. I'm a goner! How could this happen to me? After all my lectures to Lily, after listening so sensibly to my father's advice on the subject—this happened to *me*, who despises air-headed women who believe in love at first sight, who fall hopelessly for the wrong men, for men they can never have. I hate them and now I am one of them.

It's a serious wound. Not just a simple laceration, but complicated, involving inner tissue, torn ligaments, a tiny fracture, in this intricate, crucial part of me. So, I have to see Dr. Allende a lot.

So, there I am. He must wonder if I have a speech problem, running on in his fluent, cheerful English while I don't say a word. I'm afraid if I open my mouth I'll fall apart and crash into a million pieces. It embarrasses me, being so stupid. I feel myself going beet red all over, so he must wonder if I have mental problems too, or maybe a skin problem—rosacea or something. God knows what he must think of me. I want to kick myself when I limp away for what I've felt and what I haven't said and the few ridiculous things I do somehow manage to say, but I can't, of course—my knee.

And it's not like he's encouraging me. Absolutely the contrary. I know he has never once looked at me as anything but a damaged knee, a difficult case, like a concerto almost beyond his ability. Then, too, I know he's a happily married man. There are family photos in his examining room and a gold band on his ring finger as evidence. Of course he's married! If I hadn't seen the physical proof, I'd know it anyway just because he has that sense about him. Besides, it's Murphy's Law.

No one could've prepared me for this. Why him? And after a long list of contrived answers, the truth is I don't know him at all, but that doesn't seem to make any difference. Something about him makes me feel safe and wonderful, like he's someone who could protect me from myself. And that's enough.

For that matter, why me? And more significantly, why now? Some Freudian could doubtless have a field day with this question.

The whole world feels as stirred up as a bottle of shaken champagne.

And it's so ridiculous! Like the love girls in training bras feel for rock stars on stages and movie actors on screens. There may be no basis in reality, but the malady's real. Every time I go to the clinic my chest gets painful, my palms sweat, I choke up—whenever he touches my knee with those pianist's hands. Yet, perversely (and I'd be the first to admit I'm perverse), I look sickeningly forward to each visit because I'm dying for any kind of attention from him, any personal word of kindness, no matter how or what. It's terrible, this need, never satisfied. I'm terrified he might realize, certain he'd despise me if he knew what was going on inside.

Like grabbing onto a steel pipe barehanded when it's twenty below.

It's awful, love—who would want it?

I go through the motions, anyway, no matter what. What else can I do? Blair can be awfully nice sometimes, although that's mainly out of gratitude for my tolerance when he's not so damned nice. He takes me to the beach on Juanita (me hugging both machine and man, leg held carefully to one side), so I can at least soak up the sun and watch him surf in the company of others. One bonus (or not): the surfers' girlfriends take me in because I'm goddamned wounded, crippled, broken-winged. So it seems they have soft hearts after all.

"Iris! Look at you!" Andrea, their leader, yells to me my first day back on the beach. "Come on over here and tell us what happened." I have my reservations, but there's no escape when you can barely walk. Besides, Blair's right, like always—I need the company.

Andrea seems to feel responsible somehow just for having recommended Isla Divino. Through osmosis, the whole team begins to feel they had a part in my bad luck, so I'm taken under wing, my injury becoming my password, like it or not.

"Here, sit down with us. Want some fruit? How about a Coke?"

Andrea is a brunette with beautiful skin she's ruining with sun baking. She has a curvy, jiggly body, the type that will be impossible to keep thin after her twenties. And she's got a voice like a megaphone. She claims to have been a steamroller operator for a road crew in Wyoming one summer, which I don't doubt for one minute. Her personality, body, and voice all heft considerable bulk. And considering the nature of most of their conversations, this volume of hers can be a problem.

There we are, gathered at the edge of the sea like some pagan cult, prone sun worshippers cluttered on bright towels, when suddenly Andrea yells at the top of her lungs, "So, tell us Iris, how'd you lose your virginity?"

"What?" *What!*

"We've all told each other our versions, so now you've got to tell us yours."

Initiation. Trial by fire.

The rest of the group, Taz, Natty, and Dylan, snicker disagreeably. Even Henry isn't this invasive, but I know if I renege, that's the end of bonding with the surfer babes forever. Of course, I can just make up something, but I'm a terrible liar.

Andrea kick-starts me by volunteering, "Get a load of this. Natty said she was so young her first time, when the boy asked her, 'You want to get in under the covers?' she didn't get it. 'I can't,' she says, 'I've got my shoes on.'"

"Is that a riot or what?" Andrea guffaws.

"'S' pathetic," mumbles Dylan.

I lay back, adjust my shades so no one can see my eyes, and wrap my hands behind my neck, a position conducive to invention, I hope.

Do I really want to do this?

"All right. Well, there was this Dutch ice skater . . ." cadging odds that these California girls don't know much about snow and ice.

Then I sort of begin to rise to the occasion, warming up to the subject. I mean, I'm sorry, I lay it on thick.

". . . when I was fourteen," (figuring the younger, the more impressive) "this foreign student at the university . . ."

"Was he cute?" asks Natty, a willowy earth mama in ratty blond dreadlocks.

"He was a babe."

This distracts them for nearly a half-hour as they compare notes on the hottest movie star babes out there.

"Hand me the squirt gun, would ya, Taz?" Dylan asks. Dylan seems the most ambitious of the lot, videoing their boyfriends out in the surf and snapping photos with a long-range camera on a tripod, which impresses me because I can barely work a flashlight. Dylan is petite, lean, and feisty, a Schnauzer, to Andrea's rottweiler.

Taz passes Dylan a phallus-shaped orange squirt gun filled with some liquid that Dylan drinks by sucking the muzzle while squeezing the trigger. Tequila, no doubt, but I haven't got the nerve to ask.

"Anyway-y-y-y," drawls Andrea, "back to your Dutch ice skater, Iris . . ."

I start embellishing my story like I think I'm Tolstoy, until Andrea finally breaks in. "God, are you ever going to get down to it, or what?" from which point I try to hurry things along.

"When summer rolled around the neighbor asks my mom if I'd take . . ."

Omigod, a name! Rube? Claus? Melchior, Hieronymus?

". . . Nicole horseback riding."

"Nicole . . ." Andrea says, testing it out.

"We took long rides out into the country—bareback, double." I give them a meaningful look.

"Woo woo!" caws earth mama.

"Don't interrupt!" Andrea barks, like a queen on her throne.

"Okay, okay, jeez-Louise, don't have a conniption fit. Have it your way."

There is a definite pecking order among these beach girls.

"Go on," Andrea commands, but less bossy, so I assume I'm already higher in the order than Natty.

I'm beginning to want to get through this whole thing with my skin intact. I'm beginning to wish I'd just kept my mouth shut.

"One day we rode way out into the boonies. One of those hot, lazy kind of days, you know. Know what I'm talking about? Anything can happen on a day like that. A big zero kind of day, like all the dogs sleeping in the shade somewhere, and all the people sticky and antsy and half pissed-off without any reason for it. You know what I'm talking about."

Andrea heaves a big sigh and lays back, covering her face with one of her arms. "Jaysus, I'm beginning to be sorry I ever asked," she says into her armpit.

"Look, I'm getting there. Just give me a chance," I tell her.

"Yeah, give her a chance," Dylan pipes up. "Who's telling this story, anyway?"

"Yeah," the others chime. "That's right."

Andrea rotates her head, eyeballing the others with a squint. "Hey, what is this?" she says. "Some kind of conspiracy? What? A mutiny or something? Who's stopping her? Am I stopping her? God forbid! So go for it, for chrissake!"

I wait for her to calm down, which takes awhile.

"We let the horses graze and we lay down in the grass under this big old cottonwood tree. And then he kissed me, and that's all she wrote. I was gone. I wanted it. I was ready."

There. Done! Finis. Gee, maybe lying is just a matter of practice or something.

Because there's some truth in this. Because, at fourteen, my virginity was not something I wanted to hang onto indefinitely or anywhere close to indefinitely. But I was also scared, scared of pregnancy and STDs, of course, but also scared of the unknown, scared of my own inadequacies, scared of taking that irrevocable step, scared sex might not measure up. I wanted sex to be fabulous, so I waited. I waited way past age fourteen; I probably waited too damned long. Maybe not. The reason I say that is, I believe being initiated into sex is fine, as long as you're ready for it and it's your idea. A girl has to do it when the time is right for her. And other people shouldn't hold her back when she's ready. Because, actually, it's a major empowerment for women, I think, to know about sex firsthand. The thing is, you go from being this scared little rabbit, scared of men, with no understanding of what makes them tick, and scared of life because you're totally clueless about what's at the center of it, to understanding a huge chunk of what it's all about. And then you're not scared anymore. Because you learn something about your own power once you've had sex. It's not like "girl crosses threshold into womanhood," or anything. But there's no way you're a child anymore, because you know one thing afterwards you didn't know before—that a man is nothing to be afraid of, and that he can hurt you more than anything. A powerful thing to know. That's what I think about losing your virginity, this flavor-of-the-month topic with them. I don't know what the rest think, but that's what I think.

I really do.

I do know what Lily thinks, and she disagrees with me. *Right, Lily?*

She told me she thought she had a lot more control over things with Mac before "going all the way" because afterwards she was in his power and he knew it. This spells a fairly major difference between us, when I think about it, considering we're supposed to be duplicates. So maybe the truth is different for every woman.

Anyway, I'm figuring that later in their lives, long after they're no longer babes, it'll be birth experiences the beach babes talk about *ad nauseum,* and virginity will rest in peace. RIP, hymens.

"Cradle robber!" snorts Dylan.

"What? That's it? So tell us, how was it?" Andrea wants to know.

Oh God! Just when I thought I was out of the woods.

"Well, you know how it is the first time. I was nervous, naturally—you know, shy, self-conscious, and all that. And it was kind of shocking seeing myself naked outdoors like that, all that white, un-tanned skin exposed to the full light of day for the first time ever."

"Fish bellies."

"Exactly."

I can never leave well enough alone, though. "And, then I'd never seen a guy naked before."

"No way!" Andrea booms. "No fuckin' way!"

"Cross my heart."

"Hah! Look who hadn't been paying attention in Sex-Ed!"

"Oh brother, give me a break!" Taz snorts. "Like, those gory little diagrams in class where they show a cross-section of it drooping down the page like a stuffed cannelloni . . ."

"Conchiglie," says Dylan.

"Whatever . . . with a bent drinking straw shoved through it, while all the boys snicker and hide their heads in their arms on their desks, like that means you're supposed to know what to expect!"

"Right!" We cackle like little hens. *Pollitos.*

"Anyway," I finally tell them, "you know how it is the first time. Terrifying. One of life's great mysteries and you don't have a clue. And, you know, there's shame, no matter what, period.

"And it hurt."

Sympathy flows like syrup all around.

I'm onto these girls, anyway. I know, living down here, they have to know all about misery and death. But they're like the apprentice toreadors, seeing only the glory and none of the danger. They know they can be gored, but not now, not yet—not with the sun beating down so warmly and the sea singing and their young men around them. So they toy with the beast, feinting as it roars by, facing it down with their cape of oblivion—then they steamroll it.

"Anyway, you know how it is. It got better and better after the first time," I tell them, summing things up, suddenly tired of the game. "And, yeah, then it was great."

Andrea lays back. "You're all right, Iris," she says, like she's making a pronouncement.

She goes all quiet for awhile, then heaves a big sigh and tilts her head back, kind up arching up luxuriously toward the sun.

"Life's good, huh, Iris?" she says to me.

"I don't know," I tell her. "It's like mine's always on hold."

"Huh? What is it? Did I miss something?" Earth mama pops up. She'd fallen asleep.

But I'm thinking of Hub, now. I'm thinking of Hub for the whole story. And that means, at least I'm not thinking of Dr. Allende.

Bugs buzz and ping against Henry's screen, willing to die to escape the dark. The Scrabble board, lit by a pool of light, is half covered with a geometry of tiles resembling a floor plan, and Henry and I are hunched over it like a pair of colossi guarding the relic of a Roman city from a high perch. My side of the board is pristinely uncluttered, one lone water bottle sprouting from the table, but Henry's surrounds are a battle-ground of carnage and detritus: spilled hemp, assorted munchies, a half-empty beer bottle, his spectacles, the dictionary. The larger the pile, the worse his concentration.

"Didn't you mention you're a twin?" Henry asks disinterestedly after taking a millennium to make a word.

Who knows why these things pop into his head when they do? I ignore him.

"You don't like to divulge much, do you, Bleu?

"Well, listen to this."

Henry gets a newspaper regularly from the states. He's carefully folded an issue to expose the article he wants. He puts on his specs and reads from it:

London—A white couple have become the parents of black twins after a mistake by a fertility clinic during in-vitro fertilization in Britain. The mix-up was first reported Monday by The Sun.

"Ha! Talk about your identity crisis!" he laughs.

Sourly, I reach for the article to read it myself. Henry waits impatiently, like a dog waiting for his master to throw the ball. I torture him by taking my time, reading through the thing several times before looking up. I can hear Henry cracking his knuckles.

"So," he says impatiently once I've finished, "I wonder how many times it's happened before. I mean, if it hadn't involved different races, who'd have ever known, eh?"

When I hand the paper back to him, he flips through the pages and laughs triumphantly.

"Or, look! Here's another one about an eighteen-year-old woman in San Jose, California, wanting to meet the sperm donor who is her father."

This could go on forever. Returning to the game, I add the word "d-e-c-l-a-r-e" onto the "e" in "u-n-w-i-s-e." Not much count, but it's all I've got. My play is less than brilliant tonight, but I've learned to enjoy our conversations, Henry's and mine, so I let our competition slide without regrets. *No importa*.

"You've never told me a single thing about your sister, Bleu," Henry pipes up.

There's something pouting in this remark. Sometimes Henry has this nasty little attitude, like he feels aggrieved against someone and I happen to have stepped between him and his target. It's like somebody amongst us and some non-present party ought to be a sacrificial lamb, but that's not exactly it, either.

I'm trying to concentrate on my new letters, but I answer him absently, "Not true, Henry. I told you her name."

"What's she like, Bleu? Is she exactly like you? Is she a blank tile, too?"

"Nah. Yeah. Maybe . . . Look, I'm trying to concentrate here, Henry. Sort of, I guess. But not really. She plays the flute. She's fabulous on the flute."

"Ah, a flautist! You're no musician, though, huh?"

"Nope."

Sometimes he can be as bratty as a spoiled princeling.

"But you are," I say, turning the table, "aren't you? Sure, that's what I heard. Cal says you're a jazz musician. Saxophone. So, how come I never hear you playing, eh, Henry?"

I finally have his number, for once. He sits there hemming. Good, good!

"Water under the bridge," he says, all irritated. "Long

time ago, blah, blah. Yeah, I was an okay jazz man." He starts fiddling like a blind man amongst the crap at his end of the table.

"Where'd you play?" I'm not letting him off the hook.

"I haven't yet. My, my! Pay attention to the game, Bleu."

"That's not what I meant."

He knew it all along, grinning like an idiot.

"Oh, all over the place. I played all up and down the California coast, mostly southern California. I was in Laguna a lot."

"Cool! Very cool, Henry. So, why don't you play anymore?"

"I quit."

"Obviously."

He shifts in his seat, grasps one tile in his left hand, two in his right, carrying them carefully if stiffly to their destination like he's operating a backhoe, and lays them gingerly, fastidiously, on the board, adding "i-t-y" to "r-e-a-l."

"Is that it, Henry?" I hoot. "After all this time—that's it?"

He ignores me.

"Hey, bub," I goad him.

"Is your sister an escapist like you, Bleu?"

"You're so full of crap, Henry. Where do you get this stuff, anyway?"

" 'Denial,' Bleu. That'd be a good word to add to the board, if you've got the letters."

He's choosing three new tiles, picking them up from all over the pile, choosing tiles that are a shade darker than the rest, I notice. Superstitious.

"And just what exactly am I supposed to be escaping from?"

"Dunno, Bleu. But every American down here is escaping something, in case you hadn't noticed."

I lay down the word "c-r-o-c-k," near the top of the board, forming "knight" from "night" with my "k," a letter worth five, which, in this case, counts triple, twice, and with a double-word score.

"Ha!" I can't be cool about this little triumph. *"Et tu, Brute?"* I challenge ole Henry. I'm referring to both our game and his little pearl of wisdom about how we're all escaping something, but he pretends he doesn't understand and he doesn't answer me.

Seven

Blanca, Leo's young wife, looks nervously around the hut, not sure if she should sit or stand, waiting for a cue from me. I invited her for lunch, sure she would bring Rosaria along, but she came alone, and now she looks like a convent schoolgirl standing there. Her girlish face without makeup, plain white blouse buttoned all the way from her throat to her waist, where it's tucked tidily into a rather proper dark green skirt long enough to hide her knees. Her hips so narrow she reminds me of a calla flower, so her name fits (Blanca means white, and callas are white). Yes, another flower, another lily, a calla lily—a slender scape. She holds the stem of her body very still, moving only the sticks of her arms and legs around her quiet trunk, and even they move as if stirred by the slightest breeze. Though she usually wears her hair long and loose, today she's criss-crossed two long braids over the top of her head in traditional style. She makes me wish I had a hibiscus flower and the courage to tuck it into her braids. Then, if I were a painter, I'd paint her with a parrot or a monkey on her shoulder, just like Frida Kahlo.

"You look nice," I tell her, "real nice."

"Thank you," she whispers back.

"Where's Rosaria?"

"Oh, she wasn't feeling too well, so I left her with Leo's sister."

I touch her arm gently, handling her as carefully as I would a little wild animal, herding her ever so stealthily to the table near the kitchen, easing out a chair for her.

"Nothing serious, *serio*, I hope?"

She slithers into her chair like an eel. We're speaking the worst kind of Spanglish, but there's no other choice. I know maybe three hundred words of Spanish by now and Blanca knows less English, but I'm determined, and also prepared— my dictionary lies next to my plate with the flatware. I don't want to stay separate from San Vaciò's Mexican community but I also don't want this invitation to be a case of tokenism, so I'm walking a slippery slope with Blanca. Spanglish is just the language for this terrain.

"No, no. She has a new tooth coming through . . ." and she points to the place on her own lower gums.

"You like *ensalada mixta con dorado?*"

I'm certainly not going to serve Blanca tacos, for godssake, so I broiled some mahi ("dorado," down here), and tossed it with some goat cheese and the best greens I could scrounge. Andrea's crowd contributed from their own gardens, bless their pointed little hearts, and I tossed it all with a light mayo-lime dressing, so I'm all set.

Damn, I mean, this is a fishing village, after all. There's a good-sized fleet that goes out after red snapper and dorado and tuna. If you go down to the docks at the north end of town, there's a menagerie of boats in all sizes and colors, all the way from fancy cabin cruisers and big commercial trawlers to puny little pangas. The boats doze during siesta just like their owners, veiled in nets, heaving and rolling in their sleep against a backdrop of diving pelicans. A cluster of one-room stick shacks perched nearby coughs up a bunch of fishermen every morning before sunrise. The men travel miles out to sea to pull in just enough fish to feed their families. Then they return in the hot afternoon to sleep in their net hammocks under the palm trees, dead to the world, including a horde of playing children and scavenging dogs and cats attracted by the trade. When they wake up, they weave their nets, try to make repairs on their crappy tackle, and drink *cervezas*. The most successful cater to marlin and sailfish game fishermen.

I've watched them unload their catches, and it's like the *Old Man and the Sea* and all that for me—I feel terrible for the fish: big, stout, shiny things with staring eyes. To think they managed to survive this long, only to end up shredded in my salad.

I have the luxury of this wonderfully varied diet of mine, even though I know there's no way on earth I could kill a big mammal like that on my own. I only eat so damned well because there are men willing and able to kill such animals for the rest of us. I don't get it. The world is too complicated. Sometimes I wish I could just traipse through blithely without noticing these things, eat my salad in peace. I really do.

Anyway, I'm just talking. Shrimp's a major industry here, too, and I could probably kill a shrimp on my own, but I'm thinking Blanca has seen enough *cammarones* at El Colon to last her a lifetime.

"You all set?" I ask her before I take a bite.

"Perdone?"

"No importa."

Blanca studies my basic kitchen setup in awe. She eats carefully, taking little bites and chewing each mouthful a long time before swallowing. I have the feeling she's tasting sawdust. Watching Blanca, I think maybe this was a cruel idea. I've had the same feeling trying to rescue orphaned baby cottontails.

"So, tell me. Is San Vació your birthplace?"

She lays down her fork out of politeness, wiping her mouth with her napkin delicately each time I say anything, so I know this is going to be a long lunch.

"No. I was born in the mountains, but my family sent me here to live with relatives."

"And why is that?" I hope I'm not treading on anything sensitive.

"It's a much better life here. Life is simpler up there, but better here. Much safer."

"How is it simpler in the mountains?"

Now what? Poor Blanca will never finish her food. She lays her fork down again and chews and gulps, her eyes bigger with every mouthful, and I can tell that, meanwhile, she's painfully translating her answer in her mind.

"Because, in the rural villages there, a woman knows exactly what to expect in her life, and that can be good, because what's expected isn't too difficult. What's difficult is putting up with the men."

We laugh together about men. Great! Humor—a bridge, a spark, but I can tell she means it literally, too.

"So, you said it's also safer here?"

"*Si*. For the girls, yes. Better schools, and safer."

"Safer?"

"There is not much law in the mountain villages, so women have problems."

I pour Blanca some more melon juice to keep her talking.

"*Gracias,*" she whispers. She reads my expression to see if I am satisfied, and, seeing I'm not, she goes on cautiously.

"The men have things their own way in the villages."

I can tell how much effort it has taken her to say even this much, but she knows I still don't get it.

"A woman is little more than *una criada* to her male relatives there."

I look up *"criada"*: "servant."

She's amused, watching me flip through my *dictionario* frantically, searching up and down with my finger until it lands on the word, then pouncing, aha! When she sees I understand *"criada,"* she nods meaningfully at the look I give her.

"*Si.* A woman is *prohibido* from going out without a man after dark. So the streets have nothing but men, and many, many are drunk after sundown. And these men feel very brave against young girls, because stealing a cow is much more serious than *estrupro* there."

"*Estrupro.*" I flip through my dictionary: "rape." But Blanca is still talking, too involved in her story to wait for me, saying, "Still, even today, there is no justice for women out in the country."

I know Mexico is still famous for machismo; I know that women only won the right to vote in 1953. But I never knew anything about what Blanca's telling me now.

"*Si, es verdad!* I can see that you can hardly believe it, but it's true!" She's speaking rapidly now, almost all in Spanish, so I strain to understand. "There are harsh penalties for rape, but no one will investigate, even when the girl is very young, maybe no older than thirteen. No one wants to step on old customs, on the customs of the *indigenas.* The elders who judge the crimes are old men, *viejos* who think rape is just courting. And it's all forgotten if the rapist marries the girl. Otherwise, he has to pay the family ten or twenty dollars; that's all, and nothing more is done. Sometimes a man kidnaps a girl in order to marry her, and it's considered a minor *comportamiento*—harmless, even romantic. If the girl complains publicly, she is in danger of

117

becoming a *paria,* an outcast in the community."

Oh God! Something else for me to avoid here; not a suitable image for vacationing at all, for having the "nice" journey everyone urges.

"*Que lastima!* How terrible! Sometimes I hate this country." This time I've said it out loud, forgetting I'd rather cut my tongue out than offend Blanca's national pride.

"Me too, but I feel the same about yours."

Wow! Take that! She pauses just long enough to decide whether to say more, then sets her jaw and goes for it.

"You *Norteños* use all our young men for your hard labor, but treat them poorly. You force them to come into your country as criminals, though they work so hard at your worst jobs. You care more about money than people, even your own children, everybody here knows that. You don't treat your old people good. We don't think you love your families in *Estates Unidos. Gringas* love their *profesiones* and their big houses and fancy cars more than *familia.* Maybe that's why there are so many *divorcios.*"

What's going on here? Blanca has socked it to me, little, shy Blanca.

"Bravo!" I say to myself.

I search her eyes, then I say to her, exhaling the word in a gust of breath, *"Claro. "*

We've broken the ice and we know it. Whoo! We laugh giddily because we've spoken the truth to each other and survived as friends. The rest of my "ladies' lunch" sails smoothly and I'm gloriously happy afterward, hoping we've broken down a cultural and social barrier we didn't make, a barricade I believe neither of us wants. I feel sure Blanca will return the invitation and invite me to see her house, but she never does. She has me as her guest at El Colon instead, and my only consolation is that she trusts me enough to explain the reason—that her house is so poor.

"It's not for someone like you to see," she confides.

The days disappear one by one, like falling into an abyss.

Blair and I stroll along the plaza in the soft evening air, enjoying and suffering the *mariachi* band blaring *ranchera* music, *rancho romantico,* romance that probably exists somewhere in this country, but only in a place of *el imaginacion.* We have our Hollywood in the U.S.—Mexico has its *mariachis.* All fiction.

Still, I'm mortally afflicted with this fiction myself. I watch the couples as they pass us in their courting parade and I put myself in their place, arm in arm with Dr. Allende (whose first name I don't even know). Every time I look in Blair's face, I can't stop myself, I change his eyes in my mind, making them dark and serious, with brows that droop like a wounded bird's wings. It's out of my control. When we make love at night I imagine it's Dr. Allende I'm with, amazing Blair with my increase in passion. So, terrible as it is, he actually benefits from my deceit. I know I should feel ashamed, and I do, I do. Then again . . . After all, Blair uses this game, too, among others, to turn himself on during our lovemaking, rehashing past flings, until I finally had to ask him once, "Hey, is it ever me you're thinking of when we make love?" but not really caring, because I'm not in love with Blair. And because I know damned well that someday, when he's making love to someone else, he'll be imagining it's us.

I stroll along the plaza, feeling like a refugee in limbo, never mind that my feet land on solid ground with every step, stirring up the white dust swept away day after day by bent old women. These old women! Watching them at their mind-numbing duty, you could almost believe their stoops would be straightened if only their brooms were longer. *If only. If only.*

Strolling along, I take a grim pleasure in torturing myself with jealousy for all the other lovers, becoming gradually aware of the couple ahead of us winding their way through the plaza's acacias and palms. There's a touch of madness in my fascination for them, some obsessive need to fan the flames of my own misery.

Sometimes, rarely, I forget Dr. Allende and wake up feeling reborn, free to breathe, freed for a moment from my craziness. But the self-torture always returns, beyond my control. *Now I know, Lily. Now I know.*

We slowly close in on the couple ahead until I can see her face and figure beyond his. Oh man, she's the most beautiful woman I've ever seen! So perfect, it's a shock to realize she really exists, beyond movie fantasy and glossy magazine covers, without touchup or airbrushing or soft focus lens—a shock she doesn't vanish in daylight. So, this is what a woman is supposed to look like! No wonder the culture here is so macho. When you're around such beauty, maybe you can be forgiven your extravagances. Maybe Blanca was onto something about *Norteamericanas.* Have we lost touch with our femininity? One thing for sure, I've never seen such womanliness "back home," such reveling in one's own female glory. The beautiful girl keeps her eyes down. She knows one look from her would crush a man's heart into dust.

We escape the plaza's centrifugal pull, washing up into one of the satellite buildings along its edge, the Tierce Mundo Café, where we're supposed to meet Cal for dinner. It's a lively, open-air place with thatched roof and murals painted on melon-colored walls. We work our way through the patio packed with noisy gringos sipping pastel drinks. Blair takes my hand and forges a path like he thinks he's parting the Red Sea or something. I know he's no Moses, though. I know that.

Mexican waiters slip through, *muy rapido*. A big, friendly pit bull the color and size of a Brahma calf wanders around looking for someone. Inside, the room is vibrating with *musica* like a twitching beast, and at its center is Cal, dancing spastically with a woman who looks way too sensible for him. Spotting us, he breaks off dancing and waves his fins above the crowd, pointing us toward their table.

Screaming like madmen over the music, we shout introductions as we pull out our chairs, the scraping adding to the din. A waiter hustles over pronto to take our drink orders, because the Tierce Mundo doesn't espouse the *mañana* philosophy.

Cal's friend of the moment is Pat Lewis, a trim conservatively-dressed woman with an open, intelligent face and a perpetual smile which never wavers, either by nature or due to the current circumstance; you never know.

"I'm supposed to be meeting someone," she says first off, "but please don't wait, he's always late."

Cal starts slapping his arm on the table in time with the music, obviously sorry his dancing was interrupted. He flashes me a big grin, then forgets all about me the next instant, on hyper-alert, scoping the action with rapt radar. When Pat's date finally arrives, Cal excuses himself *tout de suite* and crosses the room, where I see him head-to-head with a lone, leggy girl.

Pat's date is a mousy fellow named Bertrand with staring eyes and drooping sideburns to match his mustache. He offers a limp-wristed shake to Blair when Pat introduces him, then tries to place a drink order, giving up without a struggle when he can't get the waiter's attention. So he turns his attention to food instead, spilling salsa on his shirt with his first bite, causing a fuss over it with napkin and tequila in place of water, though I don't think he really

121

gives a damn about the shirt.

The next thing you know, we're pitched headlong into one of those touch-and-go conversations akin to airplane practice landings—those fleeting meetings which fill empty hours in bars and airplane flights and waiting rooms of all types, where you barely glance off each other. People telling their whole life stories, spilling their guts, all in the highly condensed version. Travel is chocked full of them. You meet, you amaze, you part, like the raven said, evermore.

Where are you from? Where have you been? Where are you going? What do you do? As if there are easy answers . . . As if anyone really knows . . .

As it turns out, Pat is a marriage counselor from Reno, Nevada, divorced, naturally, like all marriage counselors. She seems great though, just wonderful, ready and willing, open to the universe but sensible and sage. A woman traveling on her own, she and Bertrand (who doesn't shorten it to Bert) are together by mutual consent for part of a gutsy journey she's making alone all the way through Central and South America.

This lady, with her wise eyes and permanent smile, what's going on underneath there, I want to know. So I sit there and watch the way I do, lousy voyeur and all, and there it is, right beneath the surface, something about a problem relationship back home with her daughter. It figures. I hate being cynical and everything, but flawed personal relationships are par for the course with counselors of all flavors. They really are.

Bertrand has an import business, with a shop in Tepic and another in Oakland, traveling up and down the Pacific coast hawking his wares to hotel gift shops. Since he and Pat were both heading south to Zihuatanejo, they decided to temporarily join forces. He certainly seems to have the better end of the deal . . . but that's just me.

I can tell Bertrand fancies himself quite the adventurer and an insider in Mexicana, and he just might be what he believes, but you never know. You never know what's real in these touch-and-go meetings anyway because they're not grounded long enough. It's like when you first go away to college, freed from the annoying baggage of living truthfully— you can reinvent yourself any way you please, because who will know the difference? There's no one to expose you. You can invent as many selves as people you meet when you're on your own and only "traveling through." So the ordinary garden-variety impossibility of truly knowing one another increases exponentially under these circumstances. We're all putting on the dog, anyway, as far as I'm concerned. We're all a bunch of fakers.

Well, one thing and another, and the conversation turns to what we've seen of the area, Bertrand quickly honing in on our impressions during a visit we made up into the mountains to visit a center for the Huichol Indians, whose artwork he trades.

"Sure, sure," he says, "I know the center up there *appears* to be doing wonders for the *'poor'* Huichols, without compromising their *'unique culture,'* but . . ."

By using his fingers as quotation marks, Bertrand manages to be very flamboyant and sarcastic.

"Well," I butt in, "somebody's got to protect their culture, don't they? I mean, the Indians haven't got a chance against the institutions." Digression is apropos in these touch-landing conversations, anyway. It's part of the adventure, like hopping a bus with no planned destination.

"What? What is it? Have I got something on my nose?"

Bertrand is staring.

"My point is," he goes on, "how much of this image of the Huichols as unspoiled by civilization is perpetrated for *profit?*" He zeroes in with his bulging eyes, lifting his brows almost up into his hairline.

It's no wonder I can never get anything clear in my mind! Has there ever, ever, no matter how seemingly obvious or benign the case at hand, been a consensus of opinion on anything in the whole wide world? And each side makes such a convincing argument, more or less, I end up sitting there watching opinions fly back and forth like a badminton birdie.

"C'mon!" I pipe. "The American lady who runs the center up there is married to a Huichol man!"

For once, Blair backs me up. "As far as I know, all the center's trying to do is protect the Indians and improve their living conditions. Jesus, Bertrand, it's pretty hard to believe there's a downside to it."

"I'm just saying, these people who think they're *'saviors of a dying culture'* . . ." (there go those fingers again) "who really knows why they do it? Is she some kind of monumental do-gooder, a Moonie, a Stone-Age wannabee? These types of people are always fulfilling some grandiose role, some convoluted self-image—savior, Joan of Arc, Mother Teresa. You can bet your sweet ass it's all about playing out the *'great role'* of her life," he sneers.

He's just jealous, that's all. He wishes it were himself, that's what.

Then he tones it down. "Besides, maybe change wouldn't be all that harmful to the people up there. I mean, what's wrong with them assimilating some of the *'plusses'* of modern life? You do admit there are some benefits to modern life?"

"Right," I say. "Except the people concerned about the *indigenas* don't call it 'assimilation.' They call it 'penetration.' "

"You *could* call it 'learning,' 'advancing,' 'surviving,' " he shoots back.

Would you please stop that thing with the fingers? I'm dying to tell him.

"You could," says Blair, "but, get serious, when you look at how we've fucked up our own culture . . ." This is Blair's standard spiel, very general, nothing specific, anti-nearly everything.

Anyway, that word "culture" has always seemed pretty nebulous to me.

"Isn't she trying to protect them from loggers and missionaries?" I argue weakly.

"Who's exploiting whom, here, huh?" Bertrand says, and nothing weak about it. "The people in control are vastly over-pricing Huichol art. And who was it who introduced them to yarn painting and beads, anyway, by the way?"

A-hah! I'm onto him now. Bertrand trades with the Huichols and doesn't like the prices he has to pay now that they've been enlightened.

"Okay. All right," says Blair. "But have you ever actually lived up in the Sierra with them, like the lady running the center? Answer me that."

"I'm all ears," I say.

"Not yet, but I have plans . . ."

"Hey, don't forget we have our own problems back in the States, too," Pat says finally, her mellow tone like the eye of a hurricane, "walking a tightrope between the whole melting pot thing versus ethnic identity. Just take a look at our own bilingual education mess . . ."

I knew she was bright.

"And there are things going on here we can't even imagine," Blair says, revving his activist engine, like I knew he would eventually. "I dig it, actually. Things are so raw, so 'in your face' here. I mean, a country where they take hostages for land rights!"

Blair doesn't wait to see if anyone knows what he's talking about. Nobody ever verifies facts in these touch-and-go conversations anyway.

"Hey!" he bugles, "there's a healthy respect for revolution here."

"Interesting." Bertrand stares at Blair without blinking. "So, what you're saying is you enjoy the relative lawlessness down here."

How did he know? He and Leo. I can't tell if somebody like Bertrand makes Blair more or less likely to splatter on the pavement.

"There's another take on what went on up there in Mexico City, though," Bertrand says single-mindedly.

"There's a rumor that some of the protests are nothing more than a squeeze play to get more government money for their land. You have to take these things with a grain of salt, you know."

Bertrand's smile is saturated with superiority.

"It's like this Huichol artist who brought me a Prayer Bowl covered with sacred imagery. I asked him to explain his vision, you know, his vision while he was making the bowl. He told me, and I quote, " 'Tando, I was seeing a vision of a big pot of beans cooking on the stove to feed my family.' "

"Pah! Oh man! That's just too cynical!" (I've had too much to drink by now.) "I wouldn't survive with an attitude like yours." I mean it, too.

Bertrand is unmoved. Ignoring my outburst as emotional fluff, he turns to Blair.

"If it's revolutionaries that ring your chime, you ought to head south. Go to Chiapas, or down into Guatemala, or Peru. Sure! Go to Peru! Join the Tupameros; be another Lori Berenson."

"Right. So, tell me, you ever been to any of these places?" Blair asks.

"I'm all ears," I say again. My drink seems to be really strong.

"Where you really ought to go is Costa Rica," Pat interrupts, that Mona Lisa smile never leaving her face. She has an angelic glow of sorts. I'd like to be as centered as Pat seems.

"I've heard Costa Rica's great," I say, glad for a change of direction.

"Costa Rica is heaven!" she gushes.

We haven't even ordered our food yet, so when Cal eventually drifts back to the table, he signals for a waiter.

"I'm fucking starving!" he blasts. "Oh, excuse me," he says to Pat. Not to me, though, I notice.

"Hey, Cal!" Blair hollers jovially. Yes, jovially, like he's young Hal. Sure, and Cal is Falstaff, and the Tierce Mundo is the Boar's Head, and we're all wondering what kind of king Blair will make.

"What?"

"Know where we should head next?"

"Where's that?" Cal asks less than enthusiastically, thrumming his fingers on the table because he's suddenly ravenous.

"Where the action is, down in Chiapas and Guatemala."

"There'd better be some food action right here, *muy pronto,*" he growls.

Cal asks me if he can finish my drink. I push it over and he removes the umbrella like it's a spider fallen in. He gulps it down, pulling a ridiculous face afterward.

"What the hell is that? A pink martini? What?"

"I'm not going to tell you. Don't even ask."

"Okay, I won't then. Are you even old enough to be drinking this shit, Iris?"

The huge dog wanders past just about the time the waiter finally shows up.

We manage to stumble our way through the order. Now there's time to kill until the food comes. The music whines in the background, wailing like a sick animal. I'd love to dance . . . but there's my knee. Cal drifts away, washing up against a group of attractive women, keeping an eye out for the food, though.

"Well, what do you think of the place?" Pat asks me.

Blair and Bertrand are deep in a private discussion.

"The Tierce Mundo? It's great!"

"No, I mean Mexico."

I hate being dense, but Pat is cool. She gazes at me like I'm water in the desert or something.

"Is this your first trip down here?"

"It's amazing. Completely amazing!" I yell over the noise decibel. "A different world down here—a whole different way of looking at life. I thought I was prepared from all I'd heard about it, but, really, nothing on earth could've prepared me for it." I'm losing my voice telling her.

With perfect timing, Cal skids into his seat just as the food arrives. The waiter slides the dishes into place, yelling "Hot plates!" like he'll kill us if we touch them.

Cal leans over his plate just as the dog shows up again at his elbow, panting.

"What's with this dog?" he asks, but it wanders off again.

"I guess he knows when he's not wanted," Blair says.

Trying to keep things from degenerating, I say, "So, tell us more about Costa Rica, Pat."

Pat leans forward enthusiastically. "Well, let's put it this way, if you love Colonial architecture and the whole 'wearing their hearts on their sleeves' Mexican temperament thing, if you love the Indian cultures, the peasant life of the little pueblos here—don't go to Costa Rica."

I notice Cal's foot jerking up and down jumpily.

"Costa Rica isn't like Mexico at all," Pat goes on. "There's no Colonial history, no vendors, no Indians. What it has is the best, longest-lasting democracy in Latin America, one that cares about its people. That's why there's no grinding poverty. There's a huge middle class instead, proud that no one in Costa Rica is incredibly 'rica.' " She takes a bite, carefully making it small, so she can keep talking. "Even their president lives modestly. The Ticos love that. They drive you by his simple house as part of the San Jose city tour."

Waving his fork like a scepter, Blair cuts in. "Maybe it's different from Mexico because the 'riches' never panned out down there like they did here. Money corrupts, and all that."

Pat's smile is as beatific as an altar candle, and with her there's nothing insipid about it, either.

"Whatever, it's just completely different from here. The people are reserved, not 'in your face' the way they are here. They're more sophisticated, less desperate. Maybe because there's free health care and education through university level down there for every citizen." The thought crosses my mind that Pat should be working for their PR department. "It's a wonderful place! A big part of the country's been preserved in parks, most of them so undeveloped there are no roads through them, teeming with animals and birds, insects and orchids—rare, wonderful things migrating along the isthmus." She waves her hand apologetically for running on, then can't stop herself after all. "It's got everything your heart could desire—rain and cloud forests, dry tropical forests, volcanoes, beautiful rivers. Mexico has no major river, did you know that?"

She's not really looking for an answer, though. She sighs

rather passionately. "I could have stayed forever in Costa Rica."

No one asks her why she didn't, but I'm thinking one day she might.

Could there really be anyplace on earth where people live so righteously? Is that what we're all doing down here, looking for such a place? A place existing only in the imagination.

Cal is completely preoccupied with making revolting little kissing motions with his lips at a girl sitting two tables away.

"Not me."

Bertrand and his controversy . . .

He shifts his food around in his mouth like he's playing a mouth organ, then finally sputters through his food, "I prefer the diversity here in Mexico." His Adam's apple jumps while he swallows. "I like its messiness and chaos. Mexico always seems on the verge. Doesn't really matter the verge of what. Mexico is totally surreal—an Eden full of garbage dumps."

And because I rarely have two consistent thoughts, I'm thinking I agree with Bertrand, pain in the ass that he is. I agree. I think I love this country for the same reasons I hate it.

I really do.

Drunk. Wild, shameless drunk. Blair and I can hardly wait until we reach the bed. *C'mon baby,* he pants, *I'll pet you like a kitten until you purr. We'll fuck till we float, then I'll set you loose with the stars. Kiss me, baby, I want you stuck in my teeth.*

I close my eyes, see silver flashes, then red lights like a blowtorch curling my lashes. Voltage jolts melting my eyes. *Goddamn! Goddamn!*

The little panga putts quietly upriver, and thankfully even our guide is silent, evidently not of the notion, for once, that our money's worth depends on his volume of words. The "jungle boat ride" takes us up the Decepcion River behind San Vaciò. We had avoided what we thought was nothing more than tourist bait, but were wrong because the trip is wonderful. The hum of the motor fades into the background, smothered in jungle quiet. Bathed in a green glow like the filtered light of an aquarium, leaves rain down as we float through a mirrored tunnel of green.

A snake bird, the bird that swims underwater with its head and neck aloft, perches on a mangrove root, shiny-black, its wings hanging out to dry, as still as an ornament while we drift by. A brilliant bird streaks across an oasis of openness chasing a fluorescent butterfly.

As we glide along suspended in a shimmering mirage, I trail my fingers in the green water, watching for images in the ripples like Snow White in her animated pond. And there's Lily, my own apparition, once upon a time when she was half-duckling, half-swan. Enthralled (*encantado*) by a storybook called *The Emerald Forest*, under the spell of its magic, cornering me, reading aloud whether or not I wanted to listen; scratching out a poem in gold ink about it, full of aimless adolescent angst I felt too but wouldn't admit:

A beautiful woman lived alone

In an emerald forest
Loved by all its creatures,
Who spun her a dress of silken web.

The image hangs there floating in the jade mirror, then washes away.

Oh Lily, couldn't we go back and start all over? All the way back to before the beginning, when we were floating, the three of us, all warm and contented and oblivious. Or even beyond, to the moment of conception. Was it all preordained? Couldn't we have waited a little longer to come into the world? Could we have done it separately? Couldn't we all have survived? Everything might have turned out differently then. We'd have put a dent in fate.

A cry ringing out, different from the rest, jerks me back.

"Que es?" I ask the guide. A most wonderfully silent man, he waits, listening.

There!

"Quetzal?" I ask him. I don't really know why—I know damn well there aren't any quetzals here.

Of course he sees through me and reads my wish.

"Si, claro! The bird of paradise!"

Like so many others in this country, he believes part of his job description is to make me happy.

We arrive at our destination, the turning point of our river journey, a long waterfall, thin and white as a young girl's arm. Local legend claims jaguars come to drink from the pure crystal water of the pool below the waterfall. But there's no point in trying to verify this fact with our guide, who would only lie, *"Si, claro!"* to please me.

I seek out Leo at the Colon the next morning. Except for his original lie to me about the Colon's hot water (which I excuse because we were strangers then), everything Leo has ever said has proven true. Blanca's fortunate to have a man like Leo, so diligent and good, a man who almost never lies.

I find him out behind the restaurant tinkering with the Impala, but actually, no mistake, wooing it, same as with little Blanca, who has nothing close to a 327 engine. He's pressed against its purring flanks, his head buried under the hood, and I hate to bother him, so I start to leave, just as he notices me and pulls his head out of the car's innards. It's like *coitus interruptus.* I almost hear the car moan.

"Sorry. I didn't mean to interrupt . . ."

"No, no," he waves the thought away with his hand, sweating and slightly flustered, though. *"No problema."* With his other hand he caresses the fender.

"The jungle boat guide said there are quetzals up there."

"Quetzals? No, he is only trying to please you," he frowns slightly. "These days there are only quetzal birds in the very south part of Mexico, in Chiapas, then all the way to Panama." Then when he sees my disappointment, he tries to make me happy. "But here in the jungle around San Vaciò we have macaws, you know? Si, military macaws." Egged on by my expression, he seizes the moment, "And parrots and *parakeetas* and trogons and chacalacas and flame-colored tanagers." He checks my face in the Chevy's side-view mirror, like I'm one of those birds and he's watching me through binoculars. Then he finishes up with a flourish, "And roseate spoonbills, and motmots and mangrove cuckoos and red-billed tropicbirds," pronouncing these specialized words like he needs a Rosetta stone, because he's never heard them spoken in English. I understand him, though. All these treasures out there in the jungle, one of the places I avoid. He has ticked off his list of exotic marvels like grocery items.

"So, are there really jaguars who drink at the waterfall?"

His expression softens. "Ah," he says. "Jaguars. It's possible, you know. The jungle is still so wild up there, with no people to molest them. And the jaguars come at night, when there's no one to see. So, yes, it's possible. I believe there are jaguars."

So Leo, unlike the others, doesn't lie just to please me, but like all of us may cling to false beliefs to please himself.

My love of birds comes honestly from my mother, who had a wonderful collection of books on birds. She had two huge volumes of Audubon folios I must have studied about a million times, sitting wrapped in a blanket next to the vent in my bedroom in winter with the heat turned up. God, they must've wondered about the gas bills! That's how I was, though. I was crazy about lots of things. Books, for example. My all-time favorite was a tall, thin volume of Fuertes's watercolors, *Louis Agassiz Fuertes & the singular beauty of birds*, with an elegant watercolor of a great blue heron staring out from the cover, its crest raised up like hackles, arrogant as all get-out. I think I became obsessive about that book. I gave it a kind of special power in some way. I could hardly wait to turn to certain pages to see the brightest colors imaginable leap out, the birds of Central America.

Momma planted a garden to attract birds, a wonderful, quirky space she filled with odd rocks from the mountains, plaques with wise sayings, whirligigs, teapots, birdhouses made from gourds and old boots and coffee cans, and an entire constituency of concrete frogs and mushrooms. It was a mess, a fabulous manic obsession of a folk art Gaudi, a topiary garden turned to stone by an evil spell. She saved pieces from dishes Lily and I broke accidentally while washing up after dinner (common during our ambidextrous "awkward years") and made them into mosaic birdbaths and stepping stones and coffee tables that were so wonderful Lily and I began breaking dishes intentionally as the need for materials arose. Momma must have known what was behind our clumsiness but she never scolded—our accomplice by default.

Daddy thought the neighbors might start complaining. "I don't know about your garden, Dora. It's beginning to look like Appalachia around here." He came up with a label for her garden, "The Teapot Dome Scandal." She adored his harassment but acted like it was her civic duty to put up with it.

She let Lily and me tag along out at the strip of flea markets along the highway south of town, herding us through mazes of old junk, interpreting as if the stuff were rare archeological treasures. "Oh look, girls! I used to play with one of these when I was your age!" holding up a faded spinning top or a kinked slinky. She encouraged us to find our own treasures for decorating our rooms, "things that just sweep you away," oddball objects getting the most favorable reaction from her, until eventually my room became as flamboyant as a gypsy's.

Momma drove me to and from the barn nearly every day, staying to watch my riding lessons as often as she could, and she went to every show I ever rode in. Even my dad came to shows sometimes, and I'm amazed at their sacrifice when I look back. Because there's no describing how boring it is watching kid after kid jump over eight grubby little fences on horses who'd rather be out grazing, while the sun melts your shirt onto your back and the flies settle onto you like you're made of molasses.

She read aloud to Lily and me. Oh, she made it wonderful, how she read. She made books magical. When we were little we used to push each other away trying to squeeze in next to her. "Settle down, girls, or I won't read tonight," she'd threaten—the ultimate deterrent. Once she began, we collapsed and melted together into one blob. We manipulated her shamelessly to keep her reading to us into our teens (there must have been something wrong with us, what with all of our friends avoiding their mothers like the plague). Best of all were Chekov's short stories, which she read with a fabulous fake Russian accent. "You could've been an actress!" we squealed like cats. "Don't be silly," she told us, delighted. We teased her and called her "Maminski" and "Mamuschka" and "Mamarova," and pleaded with her to explain the meanings of the stories, but she never would.

Anyway, birds. I don't know. They blow me away, they really do. They've got to be the freest thing there is, but here they are, hanging out down here with us in our backyards. Sure, their food and everything's all down here. Even so. They never go very high, do they? Maybe they don't appreciate what they've got there. Wings, I mean. Man, if I had me a set of wings . . .

Anyway, the thing is, I always thought my mother was a very happy person, satisfied and fulfilled, but I wonder when I look back now. I really do. I'm just saying. All those dreams.

Eight

Iris, I've been thinking and thinking about things.

All our good times feel like someone else's life now, don't they?

I had two daughters, silly, softhearted, joyful girls with big teeth and stuffed animals and messy rooms. Somehow, somewhere along the way while I was looking the other way, things went terribly wrong, and I just can't comprehend.

You and Lily should be happy in this time of your life when the world is still full of promise instead of regrets.

What impulses set you onto the paths you've taken?

How do I shield such moths from the flames?

How did it happen? How did my girls, of all people, fall through the cracks?

I miss you, Iris with the Ambrosial Eyes.

Love, Dad

Nine

A tropical depression is building up offshore, stirring up big waves and strong winds. Stirring up people too. Henry is all nervous and antsy. He's driving me crazy. Blair is completely zoned out, surf worshipping at the beach all day. Leo is wasting a lot of energy worrying about damage to El Colon, in case the storm comes ashore here. And me, I'm in my own private storm.

"You're awfully quiet tonight," Henry complains.

"What's gotten into you lately, sugar?" Blair wheedles.

"What's up with you?" Andrea trumpets.

Uh-oh. I can easily handle everyone but Andrea.

"What? I don't know what you're talking about."

"You're bloody boring lately, you know that, Iris?"

Being boring is a fatal flaw in Andrea's book. Coming from someone who complains constantly of boredom, this places a heavy burden squarely on my shoulders.

"What? Am I? I'm sorry. I was just thinking."

"About?"

"Oh, nothing, really."

Stupid! This pitiful excuse only spurs Andrea on.

"Come on, you can tell Aunty Andrea all about it, Iris."

I'm in the depths of despair, I want to scream, *dying a slow, tormented death. My gut is gnawing through to my heart and the pain is driving me mad.*

That would be the truth, okay, highly dramatized, if I were inclined to share it with Andrea. Because, sick as I know I am about Dr. Allende, I'm devastated that I only have maybe one more visit left with him. My knee is healing, so now he'll be sending me to the physical therapist, a sourpuss lady who smells of naphtha.

I feel ridiculous. I am ridiculous, as ridiculous as the lyrics of those insipid *ranchera* songs. My soul has become sicker and sicker, degenerating in direct proportion to my knee's healing, until I'm only able to control myself with the most heroic restraint. Even so, I can't get him out of my mind. It's so ridiculous! I can't explain. And I know it's pathetic, because it's a hopeless love. I'm not hopelessly in love with a complete shit, like Lily, but now I know how Lily felt, because, either way, it's hopeless.

I'm wretched, if anybody really wants to know, completely powerless against it. The days drag on and on like they'll never end, and the nights are even worse. I try blocking him from my mind so I can sleep, but then I suffer withdrawal like he's food and drink. So as antidote I allow myself to think about him, but I still can't sleep. Finally, exhausted, I sleep so deeply it's like I might never wake up. It's like I've come down with a tropical disease, love as dose, a bad case of love. There's no happiness in this case, just a horrible gnawing in my gut.

So then I drive myself half crazy wondering if I should tell him. Of course, I should *not*, my head tells me, and then I hate my cowardice. Maybe it would be something of value to him to know, I tell myself. Forget about whether or not he returns my feelings. Maybe it'd be something to brighten up his dutiful life, a pleasant memory for his old age, if nothing else. Then again . . .

Maybe I should have a love letter written for me by San Vació's resident poet. Leo introduced her to me—a little dried-up wisp of a woman in her nineties named Pachita, amazingly lively, still writing poems for all the local lovesick calves. Who knows? Maybe Pachita could do the trick. Then again . . .

Desesperado.

It seems a tossup whether telling him would lead to success or disaster. I mean, there's so much in the balance. I'm completely distracted from not knowing what to do, and there's this terrible hammering in my head.

It's insane.

So I'd like to scream and tear my hair in answer to Andrea's question, but instead I say calmly, "Never mind. It's just my period, Andy," and she backs off, because periods are sacrosanct.

She and the others start gossiping about the restaurant. They complain about nasty customers. They bitch about the mildew from the rains and an invasion of winged ants. They wish the local theater would show more American movies. They complain that the drinks are too weak at the Tierce Mundo. Wandering, wandering, searching for a topic of the day. Then Dylan strikes gold.

"Did you check out those Dutch tourists at the Hotel Yasmin?"

"Aha!" they yowl. They know everything that goes on at this hotel, next door to the restaurant. "This should perk you up, Iris. I mean, they were Dutch, like your wonderful Nicole."

I'm afraid to ask.

"Did you see the size of them?" Andrea shouts, brushing sand off her ample bosom.

"What I'd like to know," says Dylan, "is where are the thin, quiet, prim types of Vermeer's paintings, eh? Those lovely lasses at their needlework in dusky rooms with checkered floors."

"I have never seen so much curdled pink flesh in my life," Natty swears, hand over her heart.

"Pink?" bawls Andrea. "Don't you mean red? Beet red. Did you see the sunburn on that one chick? Ouch!"

"I don't know how she could stand that massage she won in the water aerobics contest."

"Oh sure. They were very big on exercising in the pool with Ramon. Too bad they were bigger on eating those huge buffets three times a day."

"She only went through with the massage because that cute Pedro was the masseuse."

"Ohmygod! Did you see the party that night? They had Pedro up on top of the bar, stripping down to his boxer shorts."

"They were like a bunch of piranhas, but he wouldn't go any further."

"What a bunch of lushes!" Taz says, taking a swig of whatever is in the penis-shaped squirt gun. "Bunch of sex maniacs."

Natty, gentle earth mama that she is, her dreadlocks tied up today in a two-peaked bandanna like a white yuppie Mammy, manages to stay completely out of it.

Their ridicule and racket die down slowly. It's too hot and humid with this coming storm to maintain any real heat.

I wait, biding my time.

Finally, I ask them, "You guys ever talk about anything that matters? You know, the meaning of life? Why we're here? Stuff like that?"

There's a lull while they wait for Andrea's lead.

"Hell no!" she bellows.

"Naw!" they chime.

I drag myself back to Cielo Azul for my mid-afternoon ap-

141

pointment. I shower and dress, then check myself in the mirror. See, the sickness doesn't show. Well, except maybe in my eyes. I pull down a lower lid, where things are crawling with corruption there.

Get centered! Why didn't I learn yoga, like Lily? It crosses my mind that's the first time I've envied Lily since her—her what? I mean, "mishap" certainly doesn't quite cover it. Old-fashioned euphemisms beat today's "denial," though. The point is, there were plenty of times I envied Lily—before. Let's just leave it at that. Fuck!

I drape myself across the couch and close my eyes and try to imagine the most peaceful place on earth to stop my head's pounding. *But this is it!* This *was* it, until I met the doctor.

Distract yourself!

Bent over the bowl, holding my breath while I swipe a cloth along the cool curves of porcelain, a blip of consciousness flashes onto the unexposed film of my knowing.

Ah, yes, this is definitely one legitimate difference between you and me, Lily. I do everything in reverse order of preference, but you do what you like best first.

Measuring. Always measuring.

It's hopeless. I'm seized with an uprush of emotion, my heart lurching into frantic thudding again as soon as I hear Blair pull up in Cal's pickup.

He's sacrificed an afternoon's surfing to drive me to my appointment.

"Don't do me any favors," I'd told him.

"Yum. You look great, sugar," he says now.

God, I'm such a bitch!

I tell him not to wait when we pull into the clinic, that I plan to go shopping afterwards. "I'll take a cab home." I'm too cruel to Blair. I should have just let him surf. A cab can go both ways, after all.

"Bye, baby." Blair gives me a kiss. "Try to cheer up."

I hate that kind of double-edged advice. Does that mean I've been a moping idiot? But I'm just looking for an excuse, because Blair has been on his best behavior and I've been my deceitful worst—me, with my love malaise and my surrogate fucks and my infidelity of the heart.

I have to quit thinking about my heart! All those sob songs in Spanish. *Mi corazon* this! *Mi corazon* that! Disgusting organ. But, why single it out? All my organs are worthless shit now.

I wait there in the over-decorated reception room, flipping through magazines I can't even read until the nurse finally ushers me into the examining room. She seats me on the examining table, where my butt impresses a big leaf shape in the white tissue paper covering. When she creeps away stealthily on her crepe soles, I look around the room for the zillionth time. The walls are covered with illustrations of various organs. The largest is a heart.

I hop down, defensively one-legged, off the examining table's vinyl pad, hoping no one will come in and catch me, to look again at a photo of Dr. Allende's children and wife. A formal portrait, the two children little heartbreakers, his wife pretty, staring blandly into the camera. There's no passion in that face. What is it he loves about her? I picture myself (wearing a wildly passionate expression) in her place. Hearing the tread of feet I hop back up onto the table, noisily crushing the tissue paper. When the door opens, I notice for the first time the diploma on the wall with Dr. Allende's full name: "Miguel Allende." And I feel a pang for such a lovely name. A pang in my heart.

"Good afternoon, Iris."

His smile, indifferent, professional, is completely sane in every way. His is a clean, sane, sober face, which only makes it worse.

"And how is the knee today?"

Ah, doctor! He never asks me how I am, just my knee. "The knee." Nothing about my heart in particular. He has never once even listened to my heart. I imagine him now pulling my blouse back to listen, not with a stethoscope but with his ear against my chest. I'm as insane as he is sane, but I can't stop myself. If only he *would* lay his head against my breast, maybe then I could breathe again. There's something so tight in my chest! It's like something stalking me. I really feel like I might stop breathing from the tightness.

He chats away about how well the knee has healed, running his warm hand over it.

God, oh God! Here I go again, picturing him as a pianist caressing the lid over the piano keys before lifting it to reveal what he loves. Fantasizing, I let myself go, imagining him studying the keys with controlled passion, hands poised, pausing for an instant to gather himself; then sensitively touching the pads of his fingers onto the cool, smooth ivory, allowing the piano to absorb him.

Oh I'm completely insane!

His every touch, though ordinary medical care, trips an electric surge inside me. I see myself in the mirror staring back with haggard eyes, shivering here in this tropical sauna. Sick!

Although I'd promised myself I wouldn't do anything foolish . . . I can't stop myself. I try, but it's impossible. I feel like I'll die from aching, that I won't be able to take another single breath, unless he notices.

Now what? Here I go. What the hell am I doing?

While he's busy examining my knee, my heart booming like a cannon, I begin unbuttoning my blouse as if I'm under hypnosis. I slip it off my shoulders, exposing my breasts, then, shaking like a leaf, I lean forward and slightly sideways to kiss his cheek, so gently I may have dreamt that part. Did I dream that?

Oh God! He jumps like the piano keys have sent an electric shock through him while playing. So now I'm the stalker. Too embarrassed to look up, I sit there while time grinds to a halt. Nothing happens, and I don't know for how long because the world has stopped. Burning up with embarrassment, I finally get hold of myself enough to raise my head. Then, taking courage, I raise it higher, bravely, like offering myself for sacrifice. I feel like a bud opening into a flower for him. When I finally dare to look into his face, it's completely expressionless, and I see his hand moving toward my breasts, also in slow motion.

Oh God! This is all wrong! My breasts! All wrong! Too white in this clinical light, stunning-white-white, the story I fabricated for the beach girls coming true. There's something so shocking about their whiteness! Horrifying! What was I thinking?

But it's too late. All I can do is force myself to keep staring into his eyes, which aren't looking at me anyway, but at where his hand's moving. I feel his fingers brush against my breastbone, softly as butterflies, then he pulls my blouse back together, bunching it cruelly between his fingers, and his fist thumps my chest, hard, as if to make sure the blouse will stay closed.

He turns away and says calmly, without emotion, as he's leaving, "You won't be needing to come again, Iris." And the door closes behind him with a quiet whoosh.

Ten

Cal's gone. He left San Vaciò, muttering something about "going home and facing the music." Everyone knows why he left, but no one's saying.

The tropical storm never came ashore. It veered out to sea to the north instead, but still managed to bully San Vaciò with an aftermath of giant surf.

Well, actually, regarding surf, I happen to know from Blair that "giant" is relative. What's big in San Vaciò would be considered piddling at Mavericks in northern California or at Jaws in Hawaii. When those breaks come up, forty-foot waves break miles out to sea, shaking the shore like a quake when they break, buckling the knees of those watching, even from that distance. Only the most insane surfers go out in them. There are only a handful of surfers in the world willing to risk it, men who walk a head taller than the rest of mortal mankind afterward. And everyone believes they have a death wish, though they deny it.

Cal is not among this kamikaze group, and he damned well knows it. So, when the surf comes up on the point, peaking at twenty feet, he has no intention of being heroic. Blair, on the other hand, stands on the beach leaning toward the water as if it were a magnet, glory glinting in his eyes, shaking the knots out of his muscles like a sprinter in starting blocks.

"C'mon, Carp! Let's go!"

"No way. Fuck! It's closing out."

"He's right, dude. It's not rideable," volunteers Andrea's boyfriend, Mickey, trying to sound firm, but with a sheepish look creeping over his face.

Blair sears them both with a glare.

"Clones!"

They've all removed their ankle leashes, just in case, and have left their short boards at home.

Ready or not, no one's going out, although there are plenty of surfers standing around watching. All of the spectators, even Andrea's crowd, know these men, milling around staring at the surf, are scared shitless, but there's not a shred of scorn among us, because we all love life too well. You wouldn't catch any of us out there for anything.

My expression and Cal's are no doubt identical. Eyes and mouth drawn down to slits, I watch the huge waves crest and hurl, spraying geysers when they crash, blasting gusts of mist through their wind tunnels with force enough to knock a man off his board, foaming and churning their way to shore roaring like lions.

I'm sure Blair is only posing.

Sure, sure. He'll come to his senses.

Andrea and Dylan, Natty and Taz are all oblivious.

They've seen this before, I tell myself, making excuses for them. They rattle on as usual, like the gulls nearby bickering over a dead crab.

"You know what I'd really like to learn?" Taz says to the rest, who listen idly without acknowledging.

"Aroma massage therapy."

"Yeah, great! Cool!"

"There's a problem, though."

"Huh."

"What do you do with erections?" She pronounces this last word the way she might handle the gulls' dead crab.

"No, really. See, I had a friend who was into massage, and she says it happens, you know, quite a lot, actually. So, I don't know."

They give it some serious thought, but this is a tough one. Finally, Andrea tells her, "You could just flick it with your finger," and she demonstrates rather maliciously, but she's only kidding. No one can come up with a thing.

Most of their big ideas end this way, with some impasse.

I can see Blair out there, bullying Cal, while everything in Cal's body language answers "no."

"Listen, man," he tells him, "are you going to let me go out there alone?"

Cal shakes his head, hovering firmly in place, but feeling like a trapped insect.

Blair doesn't plan on missing what he sees as the opportunity of a lifetime, though, so he plays his trump card. "All right, pussy. Have it your way, then. But just remember, did I come through for you in Arcata, or what?"

Cal wavers, kicking sand in disgust, then starts toward his board, moving toward it like he's dragging a chain. Wearing a sick expression, he jerks the board up under his arm and follows Blair like a condemned man down to the water's edge.

Blair doesn't hesitate. He sprints with telescoping strides into the surf, pumping his knees to clear the shallows. His hair flies off the back of his head like feathers when he springs forward, board death-gripped in front of him, landing with it clamped to his belly. Timing his leap with the water's rebound, he's swept out on the rip. Cal stands frozen for an instant. Then I see his head dip violently and I know he's yelled, "Shit!" into the white roar. Futile, but the word acts as his propellant, thrusting him into his own mad dash into the ocean between waves, and he's washed out on Blair's wake.

They're barely visible out there, riding the glare, absorbed by it. Only when lifted by an incoming wave are their squirming torsos visible, heaved up again and again, until finally out beyond the break, they stop paddling and sit bobbing in the water like two little humped snails.

The waves begin cresting farther and farther out into the ocean, building until they become too big to plow through, forcing Blair and Cal to paddle frantically farther out. Towed up and up, they barely breach each ridge, lifting their chests to clear the exploding spray. I know their worst nightmare is to be sucked backwards by sledge-hammering fountains, as they say, "over the falls."

The surf is threatening to "close out," to become so huge the waves implode from their own mass, falling in one great foaming piece, *whump!* across the whole bay. Closing out would mean no vertical wall to ride, no way around, no way out, no way in. They need to paddle out now, before that happens, beyond the waves to where the sea's floor is too deep to form waves, and wait there trapped outside for as long as it might take, until the ocean dies down, or until they're rescued. Or, if they're going to catch a wave, it had better be soon. They need to make their move.

The gull-girls, as usual, are clueless.

"How about electrolysis?" Natty suggests. Listlessly, though.

"Oh, right," Andrea caws. "Great idea, Nat! Then she'd be dealing with women's mustaches, armpits, and pubic hair. That'd be just peachy, wouldn't it?"

"Besides, wax jobs are going to replace electrolysis one of these days anyway," says Taz, like she's an expert on the subject. "Wax jobs are lots faster and less painful."

"La-de-da! Oh, I don't know about that, Miss Know-it-all." Natty makes a face. "Wax jobs are plenty painful. I had a Brazilian and it made me yell like a banshee. Now there's hardly anything left down there."

Dylan, shifting around in the sand, says lazily, "Too bad guys couldn't just like bushy women."

Andrea snorts. "Who says they don't? Like, has anybody ever asked them or anything?"

"Yeah, like, whatever," Taz agrees slavishly, her voice a gnat's white scratch.

The sea lulls while on the horizon a set of giant waves comes creeping in like assassins, each larger than the last.

"Oh my God," I say, scared as hell, but the gulls, shrieking and tearing at the crab, are too noisy and preoccupied to notice.

Blair and Cal start paddling out toward the point of the break with all their might to meet them, barely clearing the first wave in time. Frantically, they turn their boards toward shore, proning out to try to catch the next wave, but something backs them off, and they let the wave slide beneath them. It shivers past and crashes in one massive arm, breaking like an avalanche across the whole bay, a wave that would have eaten them alive.

Even so low in the water, sharing its perspective, they would be able to see the top of the last wave of the set looming, a rogue, already feathering, threatening to break early across its whole length.

Cal decides to make a grand play. From shore we see him give a clear signal to Blair, then he paddles like a madman. Cal is out of shape, but he's built like an ox, and, adrenaline pumping, he gores his way through, racing against the Armageddon looming behind him, licking at his heels. To catch the wave he has to match its speed, so he shoots down the face, paddling for dear life, then rises to his knees and finally to his full height. Standing with arms winged back in plunging hydrofoil, he hurtles headlong, almost daring to hope he's home free, rushed with life as he slides toward the light through a turquoise chamber.

Just as Cal begins to believe he might survive after all, Blair drops in on him. Positioned on the outside, Blair should have forfeited the wave to Cal and taken his own chances. But maybe, who knows, maybe out there alone now against all that immensity, Blair's renowned nerve failed. Maybe he didn't think he could make the next, bigger wave, and, if not, couldn't face that reckoning beyond. For whatever reason, Blair launches himself and streams down outside Cal in a near free-fall, losing control and nearly landing on top of him, forcing Cal to bail.

Cal wavers wildly then surrenders, diving into the wall of water reared up behind him, pushing off with all his might to kick his board as far as possible in the opposite direction. Man and board disappear, sucked into that exquisite aquamarine otherworld. Then, nothing—only Blair racing alone ahead of torrents of white water, making the wave.

The abandoned board is pinned down, pounded against the sand and rocks on the seafloor below. Twisted and chewed and spewed out, it reappears. Shooting like a gleaming rocket at least fifteen feet above two stories of white water, it caroms like a top, then disappears again.

But no one sees Cal.

Blair is carried past the break, where the wave melts miraculously back into the sea. We see him wheel and look back. The ocean's hackles are glaring in the sun, obliterating everything from our perspective, but Blair, looking across the sheet of glaze, spots Cal's head riding above the chop—a speck, a mote in the ocean's eye—where no one should be.

And there's nothing he can do. The next wave has already

broken and is bearing down. A man on a board in its course would be worse off than Cal. So, although he sees the tableau unfolding, all Blair can do is watch helplessly.

The spectators begin rising from their seats in the sand, slowly, awkwardly, and not all at once, but in a slow-motion chain reaction, like a flock of flamingos awakening from sleep. They stand in place, restlessly still, like prey fearful of a movement in tall grass, straining to see, until someone finally spots Cal and points.

"Okay then, how about tattoos?" Natty says to Taz. "You could become a tattoo artist." They're all facing directly into the sun to enhance their tans, away from the surf.

The wave blasts through, erasing Cal. Of course he has dived to the bottom, where he's hanging onto a rock with all his strength, talking to God about the state of his immortal soul. But no one sees him surface when the wave passes, and now that last, most monstrous wave of the set, scooping like a great hand, sucks the sea floor into itself, closes into a fist, and crashes across the bay. Hurling and pitching earthward, the thunder of it fractures the air and rattles the earth.

How long can a man hold his breath?

Even Blair, well out of its way, has to flip under his board to save himself. Shoved shoreward like a toy in a bathtub, he comes up paddling. In the short lull before the next set, he pulls towards Cal with all his might.

Glare blots out both men, even their silhouettes erased by the colorless dazzle.

"Nah," whines Taz. "I can't stand needles."

"How'd you get your tattoo, then, wimp?" Andrea asks, turning her head to check out the blue hummingbird below the dimple in Taz's butt cheek. She vaguely notices that everyone has pooled on high ground, watching something in the surf.

"I got totally smashed first. It was the worst puking hangover I ever had."

I start hobbling as best I can, following the crowd of people flushing like quail down to the south end of the beach, where Blair is paddling in with Cal, gray-faced, collapsed across the front of his board. Meanwhile, Cal's board washes up directly in front of the break—broken as cleanly in two as if cut by a laser.

The spectators crowd around, watching in a kind of worried stupor as they pump a lot of water out of Cal.

Wallowing around, waving his arms wildly, he finally comes to.

"*Depechez vous avec la civière!*" he manages to choke.

Leave it to Cal. Stuck somewhere between choking with sobs or lashing out in rage, he turns the whole thing into a magnificent joke.

As they half-carry him away, several strong men grappling him like a greased pig, he looks up at Blair.

"Fuck!" he gasps. "One more victory like that and we're done for."

"So, Blair, just when were you going to tell me?"

"What are you talking about, Iris?"

Cal's gone. I can't believe it, but I actually miss him. Things aren't the same—his departure left a big void. He moped around for a few days after the incident, uncharacteristically quiet. Then he left, but not before saying goodbye to me.

"God, I hate it when you play dumb." Blair and his fucking games. "You know what," I tell him.

For once, he sits there mute.

"You were planning all along to head south with Cal, weren't you?"

Blair, momentarily caught in a narrow space, blinks stupidly, words hovering in his throat. Then, deftly, he falls back onto the military tactic of strong offense as best defense.

"I don't get it. Tell me, Iris, why you'd believe anything that fuckhead had to say."

"A better question is why I'd believe anything you say."

We're sitting in the hut's screened porch, the dark closing in, night sounds beginning their tune up. I've fortified-weakened myself with several glasses of wine, but Blair has only had one Dos XX's, so he has the advantage.

"And tell me, if you don't mind, just what exactly Cal meant about going back 'to face the music.' Also explain, if you would, why he said you claim you're never going back."

Ugly, ugly. I'm feeling unbearably mean. I have brain fever from spending days and nights imagining how I should off myself. Should I take pills? I don't have any. Should I start the car in my closed garage? What garage? And all I've got is the Vespa. I could cut myself, but I'm afraid I'll chicken out at the last minute and screw it up. *And why would I want to live?*

Abusing myself, drowning myself day and night with hatred for my own stupidity. *Enough!* But I can't stop. I'm a prisoner—still. *It's crazy! I know, I know.*

I'll never be the focus of the doctor's passion. He'll never look at me like he could make the most beautiful music the world has ever heard. *Of course not! What was I thinking? How could I ever have imagined such a thing?* There was a passion about him, of course, but it was only a passion for his work. *Only.*

And the question isn't what he must think of me. The question is, how do I stand myself? Would I, if I could, really ruin a man's life so casually? The lives of his wife and children?

Is this what love does? *Eh, Lily?*

God! I'm a fool without a compass. It should have been me out in the ocean, not Cal. Cal came back, though. Even that bozo Cal is stronger than I am. My credos are crap. I have no gyroscope. Just how steep a slide is it to perdition? I let the weakest forces have their way with me, and Blair is just one of them.

"What did you two do in Arcata?" I ask him.

Blair knows my suspicions are unconfirmed, so he splutters, "Oh, for chrissake, Iris. If Cal is talking about facing the music, maybe he got some chick pregnant or something in Arcata. Did you ever think of that?" There's a watery vagueness to his words, though. He won't even look at me, staring out into the blank darkness instead.

"Are you listening?" he asks me.

"I heard you."

"Okay, all right, then."

I sigh. What's the point of this, anyway? Blair is who he is, and he'll do what he wants.

Suddenly I feel mortally tired. My voice quiets down. "Are you really not going back?"

He sees I've let go of my hysteria. The meanness has evaporated and I've reached the point of reason. My hair shirt has nothing to do with him anyway.

Rain begins to fall softly. The torrential downpours of the last weeks won't return for a long time. The sound of this soft rain embraces us, muffling all other sound. It insulates us, privatizes our existence, drawing a curtain around us.

The rain makes the world dreamlike and strange. It makes me feel like I'm floating a foot above reality. Why do love and rain make me feel the same? Sizzling heat and cooling rain sound exactly the same.

"I don't know," Blair says, so quietly it's barely audible above the rain. "I don't know if I'll ever go back." He straightens up, preparing a defense.

"Okay, so, yes, all right, we were going to go farther south, south to Chiapas, or Guatemala, or maybe on to Peru. Somewhere there's something worth doing, something worth caring about other than your fucking cholesterol level or your fucking cell phone model or how green you can make your fucking lawn. You and I have talked about this before, Iris, about how unexamined lives aren't worth living."

It never ceases to amaze me how everyone remembers everything differently. Whenever I try to compare memories with people, it's like we watched two different movies. No two people ever seem to draw the same conclusions.

"I can't go back to that, Iris," Blair is saying. "That's what Cal was talking about when he told you I said I 'can't' go back."

"He didn't say 'can't.' You just said it."

Blair doesn't answer. Both of us sulk in silence until I'm finally forced to say something because it feels like the darkness, the rain, the long night, need opposing.

"Would you tell me if there was some other reason?"

I'm talking to a vague shadow, because we haven't turned on any lights and there's not even a glow from the ocean because of the rain.

"You're being hypothetical, Iris. If you want to be hypothetical, then let's say no. No, I wouldn't tell you. Know why? Because what you don't know can't hurt you. You can't be asked to testify against what you don't know. You can't be an accomplice to what you don't know, Iris."

So, there's my answer.

"Weren't you even going to ask me whether or not I wanted to go south with you?"

Blair leans toward me and takes my hand. He knows infallibly where it is, in spite of the dark. I've never heard the voice he uses now, just like I'd never imagined the photographs he could take.

"You should go home, Iris," he says gently, wiping out all the distance between us.

Tears come against my will. I hate how easily they come these days.

"And what makes you so different from me?" My voice is a mess.

"You know what."

And I do. I know my own history gives me no excuse—me, with my perfect background. My utterly palatable life, softened for me by the goodness of my parents, chewed into a digestible state by them, like the food birds regurgitate down the crops of their young. Lily and I were raised on the milk of loving human kindness, which means we were completely unprepared for what lay waiting beyond the nest. There's no avoiding that life, of course, so, though there was nothing during my growing years to struggle against, there was no need to fabricate a struggle. As they say, the world provides.

Blair was born privileged, too, to a father's genius and a mother's love, so Blair should've had an inner map similar to mine, by all rights. But Blair's life had a glitch ours didn't, a problem in his program. Blair could never measure up. Blair's father expected his own mathematical genius to bloom in his only son and when it didn't, he let that destroy them all. He tormented Blair as a boy, insisting it was a matter of laziness, forcing him to grind endlessly through extra study, tutors, and summer "learning camps." When that failed, he savaged Blair and the only other target he considered responsible, his wife, cowing Blair into submission through verbal abuse of his mother, ultimately squashing both of them under his thumb. He even went so far as to tell Blair, pinning him to the wall during one of his uncontrollable outbursts, "You're not my son!"

Blair's mother had long since transferred all her love to what she called "God's creation," which understandably didn't include man. She took Blair camping and taught him fly fishing along the Rogue River in northern California, and they hiked the Sierras together. They traveled the whole coast from Santa Barbara to Longbeach, Washington, one summer, camping all the way, never beyond the sound of the surf.

It's his father Blair can't go back to.

When Blair's good, in those gold moments when he's loving, that's his mother in him.

I know all this because the only real conversations Blair and I have ever had amounted to nothing more than telling each other our life stories, trying to understand each other rather than the wide world.

Dumb as dirt. By telling our histories, we thought we'd know each other.

"Why don't women ever fall in love with nice guys?" Henry sighs loudly, his eyes riveted to the Scrabble board. It's not really a question.

He never liked Blair, and now that he's heard of Cal's near drowning, he feels he can speak out.

"Go ahead, spit it out, Henry," I encourage him, even though he's making me mad. "What exactly is it you've never liked about Blair?"

"That you're with him?" He makes this into a question.

I ignore him, which is the best way to deal with Henry sometimes. Just let him dig his own pit to fall into.

"He's a loose cannon, Bleu, and you're on deck."

"Okay, so he can be reckless. But you notice he did pull Cal out alive."

Henry pretends to study his tiles, although he's been looking at them with veritable X-ray vision for twenty minutes without coming up with a thing.

"Just barely," he mutters.

"I swear, I'm going to pick this board up and throw it across the room, if you don't make a word, Henry." I mean it, too.

"Bleu, Bleu! What's gotten into you, eh? So sad for days and days. I've been worried about you, worried you were going to do something foolish. Maybe pierce the other eyebrow." He looks at me with complete insincerity, smiling his dry wolf grin. I expect him to lick his chops any minute.

"And now, such anger! *Tch*. This is unlike you, Iris Bleu."

"Just call me Iris, Henry," I growl, hurting myself (yet again), because I like his "Bleu." I've always liked it.

"Make a word, Henry, or I'm going home." The ultimate threat.

"Doesn't that thing in your eyebrow bother you dangling there? Isn't it rather distracting during sex? I should imagine it would be in the way."

"My sex life is none of your business," I tell him, then mutter, "dirty old man."

He pretends not to have heard, casually laying out the word "b-l-i-n-d," connecting it to "f-o-l-d," for a very low count.

As he picks up new tiles he asks, all chipper as hell, "How's your knee, by the way?"

Everyone's asking me that today.

"It's fine."

"What does Miguel say about it?"

For some reason, I'd never imagined any kind of connection whatsoever existed between Henry and Dr. Allende, so his question surprises me.

"You know Dr. Allende?"

"Certainly, sure. Who do you think prescribes my ganja for me? We've known each other, quite well I'd say, since I first came to San Vaciò."

The board is nearly solid with tiles and we're down to the last few words, each of us trying to use as many tiles as possible, no matter how, so there'll be nothing left on our racks to subtract from our scores when one of us plays out.

"Aha!" I lay down my last three tiles, catching Henry with a snootful. From "venture" I make "adventurer." Quite the coup for a last play.

Henry sighs theatrically but good-naturedly as I lean back in Henry's cushy chair and stretch my arms over my head. He picks up the board and dumps the tiles, which land mostly facedown, into the lid of the game box. Then he shuffles them pretentiously, because Henry loves this part of our ritual.

They have definitely become a ritual, our little word battles.

As he loads his bowl for the next match, I watch him more closely than usual. He amuses me so much. It can't possibly be intentional on his part, can it? That innocent wolf's face of his . . .

"So, Henry . . ."

"Mmmm?" he answers, drawing on his pipe, the smoke rising over his head like a thin, coiling viper.

"Exactly what kind of history did you teach?"

" 'Merikin," he grimaces through his clenched teeth.

"Just 'American'? Like, from the Continental Congress until whenever it was you retired?"

He's holding his breath. When he exhales, he says, "America at war, through the forties. The Revolutionary, Civil, First, and Second World Wars."

"Which was your favorite?"

"You're very macabre, Iris Bleu. Wars are not like flavors of ice cream, you know. Certainly nothing delicious about war."

"You know what I mean, Henry. Which was your favorite to teach?"

He's taken another hit, so I have to wait for his answer.

"Oh, I don't know. They're all quite fascinating. But the students relate more to the most recent, so perhaps the Second World War."

"Besides, you have the ultimate evil in that war, don't you? Hitler and his henchmen. Mengele, with his experiments on twins in the death camps."

"Have the birth of our nation in that first war—that's rather exciting. Then, in the Civil War, slavery is right up there with Hitler, as far as evils are concerned, don't you think, Bleu?"

"I thought they always claimed the Civil War was over states' rights and secession, not slavery."

"What a fucking crock."

"Tut! Such language! Is that how you talked to your students, Henry?"

"You're not my student, Bleu. Don't give me any shit or I'll flunk you."

He's such a gonzo idiot. We're in no hurry to start another game. I heave a tragic sigh, watching his face in the lamplight. His lean cheeks in shadow, sandy hair falling into his face, ever-present nap of grizzled day-old stubble glistening gold in the light shining across his chin—he could be the Big Bad Wolf, I swear. Hair like autumn ruins of summer weeds. Skin like foxed newsprint. His overhanging brows so extreme, like thatch spilling over eaves, threatening to slide off onto the ground. And his eyes, hidden beneath all that straw, always smiling half-moons (I can never tell whether that gleam is sardonic or benign), glittering feverishly, but it's just their pale color in the light, the color of sapphires, but paler, almost yellow.

"So, play me something on your sax, Henry." I'm always at him about something.

"Don't have it anymore," his voice like seething sand, while outside a faint chop of waves sounds in the darkness.

"What'd you do with it?"

"I pawned it."

"What a fucking idiot you are, Henry."

He never rises to the bait, though.

"At least I answer your questions, occasionally."

"Yeah, tonight, maybe sorta."

He has fucking never answered me until tonight, so he has a lot of nerve.

"So, what'd ya want to know, Henry? Ask away."

Henry has been just lying in wait, licking his chops, like I always knew he would.

"I reiterate," he says smugly. "Why don't women ever fall in love with nice guys?"

And, of course, I have no answer for that. But I say, "I'm not in love with him, Henry."

Eleven

I can't answer for women who never fall in love with nice guys because of Hubble.

I should never have taken up with an archeologist. He seemed safe, though, stable and plodding, I mean, in an intelligent way; oblivious and self-absorbed, but in a nice way; and the sex was good, in an outstanding way, so I couldn't help myself. But I should've known that a man who spends his life scratching around in dirt was bound to unearth things in me, sooner or later. The fact that we gravitated together way out in the middle of nowhere should've been warning enough. Though life is plenty surreal, the odds were downright paranormal, and I should have realized that I would end up right at the edge of the abyss, forced to fall or fly.

I thought Hubble, the archeologist, might dig up some comforting words when I told him about what Lily did, but Hub is never what I expect. We were watching the sun go down over some buttes, remote as distant memories, before spending the night in sleeping bags way out on the prairie of the eastern plains, the night of the Perseid meteor shower. You can't help but talk about serious things on such a night. I never planned on telling Hub, but it was pulled out of me by the universe. No one can resist the universe ganging up on you like that. I think it was the same for Hubble, because he just wrapped his blanket around me when I told him, and we

163

laid back and stared and stared up into the Milky Way, like it held all the answers or something.

I left not long after.

Hub and I met in the CU library where I was cramming for finals my freshman year. We happened to choose the same study desk. There's synchronism for you. Considering the way I was frantically skimming through a year's worth of unread texts and a snarl of chaotic class notes, it's a miracle he stayed at that desk. Because Hub was a together, on-track, serious grad student, and I, well, I was a wanderer on the plains of uncertainty and inadequacy. I was a royal fuck-up.

He took me under his wing, did Hub. I became his Sancho Panza.

I'm trying not to step on ants as I walk the trail (the symbolism of that would be a helpful moral compass), like a good Hindu or humanitarian, or a squeamish hiker. Still treading lightly on the earth, because some of the philosophy from my more radical high school days with Krystal I consider definitely worth saving. So while Hub strides purposefully and obliviously ahead, me, I hopscotch behind all over the place.

It's late May and I'm tagging along on a field trip into the Pawnee Grasslands to hunt for slivers of chipped rocks, tiny curled shells, bone needles in haystacks, pieces of worked bone, or entire Tyrannosaurus Rexes, take your pick. Well, okay, the dinosaur is just fanciful thinking on my part. One was found farther north, though, up in an even more desolate part of Wyoming, where a scramble over rights to it ended in mayhem and murder, because an entire fossilized carcass is worth a million dollars. That's why I keep telling Hubble we're looking for the wrong stuff, but he knows I'm teasing, since I'm not really the mercenary type.

I watch his ass and legs moving as regularly as pistons in front of me. Hub looks very tantalizing from the back (from the front, too). I'd like to ask him to take off his shirt, but we'll never keep our minds on work if I get started. Hub is wiry, most people would say "geeky," especially with those thick glasses. But beneath those lenses is a great pair of bedroom eyes, intelligent to boot. You just have to see past the glasses. Besides, I like geeks more than anybody. I suppose there's something Freudian about that (too bad Freud gets the credit). I mean, I remember reading a literary critique of *Jane Eyre*, postulating that Charlotte Brontë's blinding of Edward Rochester was actually an emasculation calculated to make him sexually safe for her female protagonist. Wow! I don't think I'm as prudish as Charlotte. I mean, just because Hub is cerebral and scrawny and nearly blind doesn't mean he's effeminate, as far as I'm concerned, and I know for a fact I like him with all parts, mental and physical, attached.

I mean, how come the super brainy guys are *so* geeky, anyway? Is there a law or something that says testosterone makes you dumb? Does intelligence leech out hormones, or what? Teenaged girls can't help but sniff out testosterone instead of brains, though. That's an inescapable force of nature, believe me. It's too bad, too, because the geeks are the ones who end up signing everybody else's paychecks in the long run. I'm for them. I always root for underdogs, anyway. I think it's just a matter of, "to each his, her, or its own turn-on," though. Different strokes for different folks, and all that.

While my thoughts wander thus, wider than the prairie, we plod onward, bound for an exposed arroyo downstream and downwind from the Lindenmeier site (the wind being a force beyond reckoning out here). Today, though, is a rare, still day, warmly benign, and I'm filled with well-being following Hub, skirting scattered clumps of rabbitbrush following the same wash we are. All around us, as far as the eye can see, spreads the short grass and nothing else. From just about any perspective, we must look like two survivors on an empty sea, or like ants do to me, on their indeterminate journeys.

"This sure would be a beautiful place, huh, if only it weren't so damned crowded."

There's no immediate response from Hub. Then, just as I start to repeat my little quip, thinking he didn't hear me, *"He pours contempt upon princes and makes them wander in trackless wastes,"* rolls off Hub's tongue, with a crescendo on the last two words.

Knock me over with a feather. Hub and I, we've covered a lot of ground, but I have never thought of him as the slightest bit evangelistically inclined until this very moment.

"Say what?"

"Some wandered in desert wastes, finding no way to a city to dwell in."

I make a loud hoot of surprise.

"You must have a photographic memory to do that."

"Shoot, I don't know if it's 'photographic.' It's good, I guess, but repetition has a lot to do with it."

Hub really does say things like, "Shoot." He believes in "low profiles," walking softly and carrying a big stick and all that. He's explained this philosophy very carefully to me. He likes the anti-hero type. I have actually heard him say, "Aw shucks," to some very learned types.

"So what are you trying to tell me? After all this time, I'm just now finding out you're some kind of Bible freak?" This is not the kind of thing to spring on someone late in the game.

I generally avoid personal questions because they tend to be reciprocal, but these scripture sound-bites beg explanation. One doesn't figure a scientist for a lay preacher.

"Not me. My dad. A regular Bible thumper, my dad. Especially crazy about Psalms and Proverbs. Believe me, I wish he'd been into Darwin or Burton or Shakespeare instead."

"Oh, I don't know. Beauty is beauty, either way. Or humor, whatever."

His silence on the subject as we hike along for another quarter mile is like the blank space in an ellipsis.

"I'm sure he meant well," he finally says. Like it has taken this long for the words to pupate and emerge.

The dirt trail is narrow, just the width of human hips. We're walking single file, so Hub speaks up so he doesn't have to turn his head.

"You have to figure most of his generation (Hub's father was pretty old by the time Hub came along) were way more influenced by the church than by Freud, when it came to raising kids 'right.' " He puts quotation marks around the last word with his voice.

"How about Spock?"

"Too liberal for Dad."

"It's probably just as well. About Freud, I mean. I think Freud was about as wrong as all those guys before Copernicus who thought the sun orbited around the earth. I mean, women suffering from penis envy!"

Sometimes I think I'm so smart, but I can never leave well enough alone. "Just remember you heard it here first."

"Sorry, you'll have to get in line on that one."

"Shit!"

So it goes with us. I know it's not exactly Romeo and Juliet. I'm tagging along because I like Hub a lot, also digging for things that seem mystical just because they're pre-automobile and haven't been franchised. Also because I like this wide-open place with no trees to hide behind, this trackless waste. Oh, and because Hub offered to pay me to help him through the summer, and because I have nothing better to do.

Which brings up money, though I'm not mercenary. I'm just saying. What are Hub's prospects? Any woman who is less than self-destructive has to ask herself this when she begins to take someone seriously. Hub's prospects are probably okay. Right now he's living on funds from a grant (so, believe me, I'm cheap labor), but you know eventually he'll end up teaching or being a curator or something. I mean, he won't end up cleaning public toilets, not with his educational background. This reasoning, by the way, is completely insane for a person like me, who knows, above all, that A doesn't necessarily lead to B—that the twists and turns of life are way beyond our imagining.

After another time/thought gap in the ellipsis, Hub's thoughts surface from the deep fathoms of his mind. "Spock was convicted for trying to talk guys into disobeying the draft during Vietnam, you know."

"Huh. My kind of pediatrician. A regular Catcher in the Rye."

"He appealed, and it was overturned."

Hub, who denies having a photographic memory . . .

"So, Hub?"

"Yeah?"

I'm panting along, because I'm not as fit as Hub and because I don't take the heat well and it's starting to get hot, so I'm looking down at each foot stepping in front of the other, not really thinking of anything very serious. " 'Hubble.' That's for the Hubble telescope guy, right?" I know the Hubble telescope came long after Hub came, but I don't mind leaving myself open.

"Nope. It's for my mom's brother, the cowboy."

I'm pretty sure he's kidding.

It's a long way from the road to our destination; plenty of time to think, so Hub does.

"Hubble was the one to figure out some nebulae were actually other galaxies, all speeding apart at about a gazillion miles per second."

"The Big Bang theory, huh?"

Some women like their man to talk dirty to them; I like mine to talk science.

"When did he live?" *Huff, puff.* We're climbing the side of a ravine.

"I know he died in the early fifties, but I don't know exactly when he was born."

Puff. So that means he was around plenty long enough to have been Hub's namesake, telescope or no.

A couple of squeaks tell us we're near the prairie dog town. People call them barks, but it's definitely more squeak than bark, if you ask me.

"Dive, boys, dive!" Hub yells all of a sudden, like a madman or something. "You can run, but you can't hide!" Then, once they all scurry out of sight, he hollers, "It's a shame to go underground on such a nice day, PLBs." Like he thinks he's got this whole dialogue going with every species on earth or something.

We call them "poor little bastards" (or "poor little buggers" in front of people with delicate manners), because of prairie dog shoots and genocide by developers and bubonic plague and ferret reintroduction and snakes and owls and foxes and hawks, you name it. I mean, I wouldn't want to be in their shoes. They just poisoned another hundred or so with gas pellets for T-Rex, Denver's I-25 expansion. And just watch, the irony will be that as the very last prairie dog rots in his hole, they'll discover the PLBs held the genetic secret to cure AIDS and cancer and Alzheimer's. I know it'll happen that way.

Of course, a lot of farmers and ranchers think they're PLBs too, driven into the ground and to near extinction by the government, prices, weather, and agra-conglomerates. And I guess it's true. Still, you can bet they'll at least live through it. Anyway, seeing themselves as victims sure hasn't made them lay off the prairie dogs.

It's a great day to be alive! A pair of hawks are circling overhead, mountain bluebirds swoop along in front of us across the flats, and the meadowlarks are singing their heads off. Me, I love the meadowlark song. For me, it's like they're singing about the fact that winter ends and spring always comes. A lark erupts from the grass right under our feet. We've flushed his body and his voice and watch and hear him peal and peel vertically through the musical scale and the sky. A great day to be alive.

"Let the field exult, and everything in it," Hub says in his most evangelical voice.

"Amen."

When we reach the site, Hub tells me for the umpteenth time what to look for and how to do it, and we fan out, methodically scanning our separate areas. I can see him from the corner of my eye, stooping and picking at the ground. Like I said, we're downstream and downwind from the Lindenmeier site, hoping that winter's wind and snowmelt and the year's first drenching rain may have exposed something new. Hub has hopes for this area because it resembles the Big Pit of the Lindenmeier site, with eons of strata exposed by flash flooding. There, artifacts laid waiting on the surface for the Coffin brothers, amateur archeologists who were smart enough to call in professionals. That was in 1924, but it took Frank Roberts of the Smithsonian ten years to respond. I mean, better late than never . . .

"How important will it be, even if we do find more bison bones, more points, and stuff?" I holler after five minutes.

"That's your problem, Iris. You think too small. Think big! They never found any evidence of housing structures at the Lindenmeier site. They never uncovered any Folsom skeletons. We're going to make history, Iris. Our very own big bang."

I admit I'm a skeptic. When he showed me the tiny swirled shell with a hole at one end that was such a humongous big deal among archeologists because they decided it was a bead carried 600 miles to the site, I asked Hub, "What makes you think it isn't just a puka shell that was left here naturally from when this was an ocean?" But questions like that end in lengthy lectures on stratigraphy, debitage, curation, trade routes, flint knapping, fluting, cross-cultural analysis, context, drills, awls, gravers, scrapers, sourcing with UV, radiocarbon dating, population density, migration patterns, Beringia, the Llano and Plano, to say nothing of Fremont and Clovis cultures, and bead assemblages . . . until I can't remember if he ever answered me, and sure as hell wasn't going to ask again.

I stop procrastinating and start looking, but I don't see a damned thing. Right away I know there's not a damned thing there. Meanwhile I notice Hub making copious notes about chips of this and splinters of that he's gleaning from his area. He's very meticulous with his records and makes nice sketches of artifacts, settings, and even occasionally living plants and animals. I really love his sketches; I've told him I think he should make them into a book someday.

By late afternoon, hungry and thirsty (in spite of our supplies), sunburned (in spite of sunblock), and discouraged (in spite of pep talks), I brush the ants off a spot to sit down. As I do, I swear upon all that is holy, something leaps into my hand. I did not pick it up; it chose me, as God is my witness. So I stand there, staring in utter disbelief at the most perfect, beautiful Folsom point I've ever seen, made from a transparent agate with black moss floating in it. I'd recognize that rowboat shape anywhere.

"Huh-ub!" Two shaky syllables.

I give Hub credit. I know from seeing later what he'd found, pitiful little pieces that wouldn't show up under a microscope for godssake, that he had to be envious of that perfect, exquisite point lying in my palm.

"Beginner's luck," I say. I'm trying to be humble about it.

"Wow! All right, Iris! Eureka!" He's as excited and happy as a little kid, but then he gives me an X-rated kiss. I mean, he shares the moment with nothing but pure joy. And that's when the thought first creeps into my consciousness. *This is someone I could really trust.*

We add a couple of fragments of animal bones to our find through the next hours, to Hub's great delight, and with it all mapped and catalogued, start back well before dusk, seeking out, like always, a high point to watch the setting sun. Small bunches of native iris drift along a low area, with pale purple flags, bolder and fancier than most prairie flowers, standing aloof above the grass.

"The flowers appear on the earth, the time of singing has come," Hub quotes, then warbles a raspy, atonal few bars of "Buckets of Beer," just to satisfy the prophecy and because he's a little bit crazy.

Iris, though. Of course they're my favorites. I salute them as we pass.

When we reach the top of a hill, we sit there waiting for the sunset. I hug my knees up to my chest with Hub's arm around me. I'm feeling good. I'm feeling about as good as I've ever felt, and I know it. That last part really counts, as far as I'm concerned. Because it's one thing to be happy; what's huge is recognizing it.

"I saw a green flash once at night, right as the moon disappeared behind a cloud," I tell him, because I want to share something special with him, something I haven't shared with anyone else.

He looks at me, very skeptical.

"I'm sure I did," I say defensively.

"Maybe you just wished it really happened."

"I don't think that was it," but now I'm doubting myself.

Then I hear this strange humming and I'm annoyed as hell that the sound of some kid's radio-controlled airplane has invaded our special moment. But there isn't another soul in all our vast view.

"What is that noise?" I'm pretty irritated because it definitely sounds manmade.

We both search the sky until we spot the source. A bird is whipping itself through the sky, climbing straight up into a stall. Then it falls—no, hurtles—straight to earth like a rock, veering at the last instant like a kite on a string, pulling mightily against centrifugal force away from the ground, shooting itself straight up into the sky again. I've seen hummingbirds do this bizarre breeding ground display before, but they're like little insects falling, *brrrrrrrr*, with a little, trilling buzz. But this, this is a large bird, a nighthawk, a brown dive-bomber with white wing decals, and the difference in sound is exponential, a real quantum leap. This is a high-voltage hum.

"Wow, that makes the hair stand up on the back of my neck," I say.

Hub just sits there quiet for a minute.

"Eisely . . . you know the Eisely that found the 'smoking gun' at Lindenmeier?" he finally asks me.

"Sure, the one who found the vertebrae of *Bison antiquus*

with the Folsom point embedded in it that proved humans were in America ten thousand years ago?"

I'm just showing off.

"Verrry good, Ire! Impressive!" I should have known better. "Yeah, that Eisely."

"Yeah?"

"Well, he wrote a book much later. Not exactly what you'd expect from a scientist, though."

"Uh-uh?"

"Nope. It was about anthropology, all right, but it was almost mystical, very spiritual. There's a chapter about birds in it, and I've never forgotten his story about a sparrow hawk."

I bump up against him. "Well?"

"He caught it alive, to ship off to some zoo, separating it from its mate."

"Oh no! I love sparrow hawks! Those beautiful markings, like little masked bandits. They're so small, but fierce, like they think they're eagles or something." I'm almost wishing he hadn't told me.

"The mate kept flying overhead, calling and calling."

"Don't they mate for life? That's so cruel! You shouldn't have told me."

"Hey, you told me to tell you," he says defensively, laughing at me.

"I wish you hadn't, though."

"Yeah, well, he couldn't do it. Eisely. He set it free the next morning."

Hub turns his head toward me. "Some scientist, huh?"

"The quality of mercy . . ."

"Yeah."

"Wow. A scientist with a soul."

There are so many things I'd like to tell Hub, but I don't.

A mile from our room at the Pawnee Ranch B&B in

Grover, he starts up again in earnest.

"But they had a wanton craving in the wilderness." I have to laugh because he's so damned crazy.

"I hate to tell you, but I really don't think this was what your father had in mind way back when he was reading that Bible to you."

"See. That's why you have to be careful about mind control with your kids."

Later, fooling around in our room, he steps into the shower with me. *"Do not gaze at me because I am swarthy, because the sun has scorched me,"* he goes.

"You've got to be kidding!"

I could howl, it's so ridiculous. "I don't believe it. That's not from the Bible!"

"Look it up," he laughs, sliding up against me.

"Turn away your eyes from me, for they disturb me," he moans, wrapping his slippery self around me. The water makes our lips rubbery against each other. We drink it in with our kisses. *"O that you would kiss me with the kisses of your mouth! For your love is better than wine."*

Waiting in bed, he props himself on one elbow, watching me. Then he opens the covers like some kind of magic portal or something.

"Make haste, my beloved, and be like a gazelle upon the mountains of spices."

I slide between the sheets and whisper into his neck, *"His speech is most sweet, and he is altogether desirable."*

Because I know a thing or two myself.

Twelve

Hub came for a visit, Mama e-mails me, *and asked about you, as always.*

Rita is slathering some kind of lotion all over her ankles, standing with one foot propped on the seat of a chair, groaning as she stretches to reach it.

"Sunburned?" I ask her.

"Nah. I never go out in the sun around here if I can help it. Too fair, ya know? I mean, by rights I should be living in Sweden or Finland or somewhere in north Europe, not in this tropical sauna. Iceland, fer chrissake. I mean, I'm north European, right? Entirely wrong genetics for this place. Too thin-skinned for the sun around here." She scratches one ankle, then pours on more cream. "For the bugs, too."

"Oh, so the *jejenes* got to you, did they?"

"You'd think I'd know better by now than to go for an evening stroll along the beach. Even covered head to toe with the best repellant there is, spiked with pennyroyal oil."

"That works, huh?"

"Obviously not."

"Too bad about the sand flies here. San Vació would be a beach paradise otherwise, don't you think?"

"Hey, girl. I thank my stars every day for the little buggers. If it weren't for them, FONATUR would've moved in on this place long ago and turned it into another Cancun or Cabo,

God forbid!" She takes one last look at her ankle before pulling it sideways off the chair seat with her hands. It falls to the floor like a piece of firewood. *Clunk!* "Ow!" she winces.

He comes to see us fairly regularly, your X-boyfriend-rockhound, and I'm glad, because, at the risk of scaring you away from him forever, my darling, we all really like Hub, and he's good for Lily.

He says he's part of the team that's unearthing the Mammoth tusks that were found down on the Palmer Divide. Have you heard about it? An equipment operator working on a construction project near E-470 bumped into what he thought was a big rock. Then he saw the shape. Can't you just imagine, Chicken Little? Talk about life being a treasure hunt! Remember the stories I used to pass on to you and Lily about people stumbling across treasures— the jogger who picked up a rock along the road that turned out to be the largest diamond ever found in Montana? And the guy who bought a picture frame at a garage sale for one dollar with some horrible print in it? Remember, behind the print he found a priceless original map drawn by Vasco da Gama (or was it Cabeza de Vaca? No, Vasco da Gama, I think).

Excuse the detour.

Anyway, they covered the front page of the paper with a big photo of these two fabulous banana-shaped tusks curled up in the brown dust. (See, and you girls think there's no silver lining behind all the growth around here.) Oh, I wish I'd been there! It makes me want to go out and dig up the backyard, just in case, ha! Of course, Hub is "jazzed," as he puts it. Maybe he could manage to get Lily and me into the site?? How I'd love to see those tusks right where they've lain for, what'd they say? Something like 1.6 million years.

I'd like to run my hand along those incredible curves. I'll save the clipping for you. I know how much you used to love going out to Pawnee Grasslands hunting artifacts with Hub.

Speaking of photos . . . the photos arrived safe and sound, and we all love them. Even your father says Blair has talent. They're wonderful, really, just positively beautiful. My favorites are his portraits of the local people. The faces are so moving! I always did love black-and-white photography, anyway. Lily's favorite is the one of you in the hammock in front of those wild-looking roots attached to that huge tree (or vice-versa, tree attached to roots). You have such an interesting expression on your face in that photo, Iris, an expression I don't recognize, but then, it's been awhile since I've seen any expression on your face (not scolding, or anything, of course, darling). You look like you belong to that tree. And, then again, you look like you're dreaming of somewhere else. Lily claimed the photo for her own and hung it over her bed.

There's still no rain here, this brown, blistering summer. Not a drop of green is left. The monsoon flow that should've arrived weeks ago never showed, blocked by a huge high pressure that's kept us in this geede drought. I told your father I think the gods are angry with us and that we need a human sacrifice to placate them. Any volunteers? Hee, hee. But, really, you can see how ancient man would've come to believe such a thing. At least, I can (don't tell any of my PEO lady friends I said that).

I gave Roman extra carrots & a kiss on his nose today for you.

Come home, my Iris flower, and make the gods happy.

Love and a million XX's

"You're going to come watch the parade this afternoon, aren't you?" Rita asks when I stand up to leave. She's still scratching her ankles.

"Sure! I wouldn't miss it for anything in the world."

"Well, maybe I'll see you there, but you won't know it." Rita looks pleased with herself.

"Just what's that supposed to mean?"

"I'll be in costume." She's positively smirking now.

"Is that right?"

"Better believe it. It's even more of a gas that way, when no one knows who you are. You get to be anyone you want for one day."

"A blank tile."

I think I've said it to myself but must have said it out loud, judging from the confusion on Rita's face as I walk out the door.

Let's see, which festival is this one? There was the Feast of San Isidro Labrador, when seeds and animals were blessed. Then there was Navy Day, commemorated in all the seaports, even including San Vació, which held a fishing tournament, regardless that it's called *puerto olvidado*, "forgotten port." (Poor little San Vació! Of course it has a right to celebrate! Junipero Serra set sail for California from here! It was once an important boat building yard and trading center. It certainly wasn't always so *olvidado*.) Next came the Feast of Corpus Christi, my favorite so far, when people dressed their children in *indigena* costumes and converged in the plaza, decorated with flowers just for the occasion, to have the children blessed in both cathedrals. A few weeks later was Saint John the Baptist Day, an excuse for everyone to douse each other with a "blessing" of water. Clever distractions, all these religious fiestas. Opiate of the people, and all that.

Now comes the Feast of the Virgen del Carmen. All I

know is there's supposed to be a parade leading to a crappy little corral outside of town where numerous animals will be harassed for the sake of a *charreada,* a rodeo. I think I'll skip that part.

Maybe I will wear a costume. Sure, why not? Blair has begged off today with some excuse about spending the afternoon with Mickey, board-shaping or something or other. So I'm all alone. Which means, as Rita says, I could be anyone today. A blank tile. Anyone.

I gimp home to our hut. Home. I have made it home, in spite of myself. I really have. It's not mine, after all, but, unexpectedly, it turns out I'm something of a snail, carrying home around on my back, unable to rid myself of nesting instincts, for all my image of gypsy life. Even gypsies have their fringed wagons, after all. I mean, even Julia Butterfly took drawing and writing supplies with her when she climbed Luna. And a solar-powered cell phone, and her propane cook stove. Roughing it in the redwoods. She made Luna home.

So I've transformed our little piece of Cielo Azul. I bought from a vendor strands of glass beads in shades of jungle green and hung them all around our bed so they could sway in the ocean breezes and glitter in the moonlight and chime when we pass through. And block Henry's view. A painted wooden table with legs sculpted like a deer's with little cloven hooves couldn't be left behind during a trip to Tepic. A mirror ringed with shells needed a home. Henry's paltry supply of pots and pans had to be reinforced. Our bed needed new clothes. The banyan tree was lonely, so I planted flowers. The ocean roared at night, so I hung a bamboo wind chime to sing it to sleep.

Anyway, I'm familiar with metamorphosis. A costume will be easy.

I have a mask, a wonderful, ugly thing with a huge, cruel

nose. I bought it from a woman sitting on the ground wearily hawking her wares in the plaza dust one evening, selling nothing. The rest I can find in our closets and the compound's tool shed.

Henry was nowhere in sight as I scavenged through the shed—odd, because Henry never strays off the grounds of Cielo Azul. He pays a young neighbor boy to fetch his groceries and pharmaceuticals and he seems immune to recreational needs other than our nightly Scrabble game. He never has visitors, never drives his old station wagon, and rarely ever leaves the porch of his hut, though I've seen him out and about a few mornings ambling back from the beach. I was going to ask Henry to come with me, but I can't roust him. Oh well.

The streets downtown are decorated with lanterns and colored Christmas lights burning to no effect in the afternoon sun. *Watch it!* A crowd forms along all four sides of the plaza, pushing toward the streets, and I'm bumped and jostled without notice. The vendors are out in full force to take advantage of the crowds, and so are the pickpockets. I study the vendors. Some are like birds of prey and some break your hearts, like the sad, defeated faces of the young mothers who tag along behind the smallest boys, urchins whose irresistible eyes allow them to sell Chiclets to tourists for several times the going price. If you notice their shepherding mothers, you see their sadness that comes from a childhood cut too short, from being forced to learn too early about the end of romance.

"*Helados! Helados! Helados!*" a small boy sings, echoing the song sung in every plaza across Mexico. A man in a sweat-stained cowboy hat hovers over a table with a large platter of pink ice cream formed into a mound, radiating cones stuck upside-down into it, like pink punk ice cream, or a melting pink flying saucer. Another peddles a stack of identical portraits of Benito Juarez painted in unworldly, saccharin colors more sickening-sweet than the ice cream. "Chiclets?" calls one of the swarm of street urchins, because Mexico has Chiclets to spare. Because it has street urchins to spare. Because a tree that produces chicle flourishes in Mexico. Too bad it wasn't a money tree instead; then Mexico could dispense with its vendors. No, no! What am I saying? Mexican vendors are the best capitalists in the world, Mexico's puppet show, a perfect slice of Mexican life, variety show, social barometer, vending machine, all rolled into one.

I hear the music approaching, tinny and out of tune, playing several different tunes at once, blaring bravely in the heat. Over the heads of the crowd, a brightly-painted Santo wavers around in the distance, carried on the shoulders of sweating men. The town's patron saint, maybe? Or is this the *virgen?* Bright flags bearing images of saints flutter on all four corners of the Santo's throne, so I can't really see it. People reach at the figure, crying out as it passes: a reverent, respectful, ecstatic mosh pit. Children ride on their fathers' shoulders, dangling their legs down their fathers' chests like prayer shawls, their small hands gripping their fathers' hair or wrapped under their chins. Children hats, sweet- and damp-smelling.

Someone steps hard on my foot and mutters, *"Perdone, señor."* Costumed, with my height and shoulders, he thinks I'm a man. *Bueno!* A Mexican man. *Mejor!*

Costumed bands wearing huge *mariachi* hats surround the throne. Waving politicians in expensive, dark suits riding in convertibles follow the last of the *mariachis*. Then, behind them, nervous horses covered in silver mince by, tossing their riders in rhythm with the fretting *musica*. A small contingent of *policia,* perspiring profusely and wearing their holstered *pistolas* in full view, signals the end of the *posada.* But the crowd doesn't close in just yet because, following the police at a distance of one side of the plaza's square, dancing and jigging more wildly than the horses, comes a small army of buffoons and costumed revelers. Mimicking the politicians and the police, slipping in and sidestepping the muck from the horses, it's these men the crowd finally follows.

I'm like a fish in a school, swimming with the flow, riding on a current of momentum. Under my mask, my face is running with salty sweat, scalding my eyes. The crowd starts rushing, thronging toward *Calle Insurgentes.* Rash young men take the lead, passing more staid men with girlfriends or families in tow. Their faces are flushed as they rush to be the first to reach the walled street. And there I am, one of them, struggling to keep up, trying to match their energy. Reaching the *calle,* they leap to the top of the wall and turn to watch up the street, catching their breath, laughing and shoving, flashing silver teeth.

Most of those in costume lift their masks, gasping for air and trying to see better, but I leave mine on because I want to stay anonymous. I want to be accepted. The masks of the others dangle crazily from their necks like conjoined twins, empty alter-egos to the solid flesh of their human counterparts, grinning toothless smiles, watching through blank eyes. Those of us in costume are carrying wands and canes, pitchforks made of foil, noisemakers, or sparklers, so, to see us, we could almost be the armed insurrection the street is named for, a riffraff of *campesinos, paisanos,* and *indigenas* brandishing our crude weapons. There are costumes of animals, too, both real and imagined, and strange gods and goddesses, and witches. *Brujas, La Llorona,* the wailing woman, and devils and demons of all kinds, skeletons, zombies, spirits, until the fiesta starts to feel more pagan than Christian, and I could almost imagine the crowd carrying the head of a cow on a platter, or maybe the heart of a man.

A shout is heard and seconded by the spectators on the wall, a cheer for *los toros*.

San Vaciò is known for its beaches, its birds, its shrimp, its fishing, for its river—but not for its bulls. San Vaciò is at least an hour from the nearest bullfights, so the bulls running now down *Calle Insurgentes* are the runts, cowards, and rejects of the *corrida,* bound eventually for the slaughterhouse. Still, they're bulls, and every bull has its finest hour. Here they come, bellowing and snorting, bawling and farting their way down the dusty, walled street toward the arena three or four blocks away, tossing their horns in aggravation, slinging slobbers through the air in all directions. Four of these worthy opponents trot toward us, tongues lolling, tails wringing, butts smeared with shit. As they come near, suddenly they plant their front legs and balk. A handful of young men have dropped from the wall, terrifying the *toros,* who would flee posthaste but for the horsemen behind, armed with electric cattle prods. So they try to trot around these impediments, but are taunted with waving handkerchiefs and obscene gestures until they finally bolt down the street's center, plowing through the *insurgentes* who scatter before them.

And who should I see sprinting before the most irritated of the little *toros,* running for all he's worth without looking back, because he knows better than to look back at something big and powerful licking at his heels? Blair, of course, out there with Mickey, among the other fools.

And when they're nearly abreast of me, I'm seized with the urge to jump down and run for all I'm worth beside Blair, to feel that hot, sticky breath on the back of my neck, to be a woman warrior, the hostage who accepts no privileges!

. . . But there's my knee, of course.

The bull gives Blair a push, sending him up and over the wall, whether from his own propulsion or the bull's I can't tell. He lands not ten feet from me. I nod through my mask and shake my sickle at him, because, the thing is, I'm supposed to be the grim reaper, but I look like father time instead. I could also be any of a number of saints blessing him, for all he knows.

The bulls wander into the arena, where gangs of men will try to wrestle them to the ground, but I hate watching defeat, so I leave. After all, I'm only an ordinary female in an ambivalent costume. Then again . . .

I head home. By now, the plaza is full of blurred dancers and animals decked out in flowers and ribbons. The glow of the colored lights and lanterns is just beginning to be visible in the dusk. Faces in the crowd look mask-like in the low light. I pass a woman sipping a drink at a sidewalk table, dressed as an odalisque in harem pants with a mask and veil covering her face. I recognize Rita by her ankles and those goddamned red toenails, naturally.

I have a dread of running into Dr. Allende, but he's nowhere in sight. Really, I have nothing to fear, since no one, not even Blair, has recognized me in my costume anyway. Then, just as bursts of fireworks pop and flash above the palms lining the beach below, I spot Henry. He's standing there alone under a string of red lights, his sandy color burnt orange by their glow, a slim, solitary figure with a slight stoop. He looks smaller and frailer among all these other people, foreign and a bit lost. Ordinarily, I'd know how he feels, but not tonight, anonymous in my costume. After all, who out there knows whether I'm a bullfighter or a woman warrior, a fisherman or a fool? Henry is staring at me. When I look in his direction, he nods.

Thirteen

"Look at this," Blair says, shoving a recycled issue of Henry's newspaper across the table toward me. He taps his index finger on a short article:

> *Quito—U.S. environmental activist Julia "Butterfly" Hill was deported from Ecuador Thursday after her arrest for protesting an oil pipeline being built through a nature preserve, an environmental group said.*
>
> *Hill gained recognition while spending two years camped atop a redwood tree in California to save it from being cut down for lumber. She came down in 1999.*

I read it, then look up at Blair and raise my eyebrows. "So?"

"So," he says triumphantly, "look who went to Ecuador!"

"So, look who got deported."

But Blair's not listening. "You know that guy we met at the Tierce Mundo?"

"You mean, Bertrand?"

"Yeah, Nando, or whatever," he flubs the name casually. "He was telling me if you want to see really exotic Indians, like, practically Stone Age, you should go to Ecuador."

"Yeah, but was he actually there?" I say, recalling that there were a lot of places Bertrand talked about that he hadn't been to.

"He was there," Blair insists. "He told me he went to a town called Santo Domingo on their market day, just for a glimpse of *'Los Colorados'* Indians. You can drive there from Quito in a few hours. He said it was a great drive, through green valleys at the foot of Cotopaxi Volcano, then through lush mountains. You cross a wooden suspension bridge into this totally squalid little village where they mill wood. He said this mill was shooting sawdust past three scrounging pigs directly into the Toachi River, polluting the hell out of it and making a helluva racket."

"That's what can happen without the EPA." I'm not a morning person. "Santo Domingo sounds like your kind of place."

"No, no. That's not Santo Domingo. You go past that village into Santo Domingo, which is actually a busy, fairly large town, according to ole Blando, with a nice plaza full of flowers. He said the market there was a real happening, crammed with local people buying everything under the sun, everyday goods, not tourist stuff. There was this lady. He thought she was making a political speech up on a pedestal, screeching her lungs out, but she was just trying to get the crowd to buy underwear. Ha! How do you like that!" Warming to his topic. When he gets like this, his eyes positively gleam and he looks ready to pounce, and I think he's not named Jaeger for nothing. He makes it sound like Santo Domingo could be his Holy Grail and himself Don Quixote. It's something I thought I loved him for, Blair and his do-or-die causes.

"He said you had to wade through mud and garbage, starving mutts, and stray chickens. There was this stand selling plantains in bunches about two feet long, strings of at least a hundred plantains, for, like, eighty cents. People carrying chickens, dead and alive, tucked under their arms or dangling by the neck—not exactly your cellophane-wrapped

Pick-O-the-Chick. And fresh fish cooking on a rotisserie. There was all kinds of everyday stuff for sale—jewelry, rubber boots, clothes, and so on, through all the streets, but also, get this—he also saw a pile of about ten jaguar skins for sale! Imagine, Iris, jaguars!"

We haven't even had our breakfast yet. My mouth tastes like cardboard, my tongue feels fuzzy, and I need to scrape out the corners of my eyes. And Blair is in no better shape than I am. I'm thinking his timing could be better.

"You want some breakfast?" I ask, but he ignores me.

"But what was really wild, on top of all the stuff for sale, was the human circus going on. He said there was a blind black guy playing a flute for coins, and women with babies begging, and a dwarf walking through the crowd. And he saw this crippled, twisted Indian man crawling along the ground between tables in a cafe, crawling on the floor like a contortionist, begging for coins. Polio, maybe, Bertrand thought. You know, never treated.

"This was no tourist market, Iris."

I should have Blair's memory. This, from a guy who couldn't remember Bertrand's name . . .

"What about the Indians?"

"Yeah, he saw a few Colorado Indians, all right. He said their hair was plastered with so much red mud, it looked like red bark hats. They were practically naked, with nothing on but the red mud hats and breechclouts. He said they were the wildest-looking people he'd ever seen in his whole life. But then, he said the whole population looked Indian to him. He said he could see a lot of Incan influence in most of the people there. Bertrand described it as the muddiest, wildest fucking mess he'd ever seen."

Why should Blair be so mesmerized by a person like Bertrand?

And what's your point? I'm thinking, so naturally he reads my mind.

"Hey! If it's good enough for Butterfly . . ."

"It's good enough for you, huh?"

"For us, if you want to come along."

Blair certainly knows how to drive a person crazy. What I need is more complications in my life!

"So, you're really not going back, are you?"

"What's to go back, for, huh, baby? You know how I feel— like the lunatics are running the asylum." Blair's generic villains . . .

I kick him under the table. He closes the paper and tosses it, aiming for a stack near the couch but missing.

"It's too mortally, morally tiresome living in the *numero uno* country in the world." He sighs like just thinking about it may do him in. "I prefer it here. After all, who would ever bother with Mexico, too busy hurting itself to hurt anyone else?"

I've heard his arguments before, over and over. So, why don't I buy them now?

"You know what it really comes down to, Blair? You're just looking for bigger fish to fry, aren't you? Saving redwoods and protesting the WTO aren't enough for you anymore, are they?"

"Yeah, okay, so maybe that's part of it," he admits, because Blair tries to make a practice of flirting with the truth occasionally. "It definitely doesn't seem like enough anymore. Christ! I don't want to end up just another money-grubber, while people down here are just trying to get a grip.

"It's like teeth, Iris." I see one of Blair's aberrant analogies coming. "Check out how bizarre people's teeth are down here. In the U.S., even our teeth have to be perfectly fucking uniform; you know, every parent in the U.S. forking out ten grand for braces for their teenager so they can have fucking Hollywood teeth, know what I mean?"

I hate to admit it, but I do know what he means. He could be saying it better, but I understand and I agree. Mexico doesn't try to fix everything. She knows better and accepts much. There's a fatalism here that softens the suffering. Small Pacific coast villages, places like San Vaciò in particular, seem to absorb differences. There's a live and let live attitude because the only agenda is to simply live.

"I want to live where there are crooked teeth, Iris."

"What, so you can straighten them?"

"Who knows? I have to find something in this world that needs doing." He looks at me so frankly with those clear agate eyes. "I don't want to live a pale life, Iris." And, having reached that rock-solid-bottom honesty, he is utterly convincing.

Then he sits there, waiting for my response. And what am I supposed to say? I just look back at him, my insides churning, feeling a sudden impulse to reach out and tuck that feathery cockscomb of his into place.

We're both past the point of no return. Here and now is our moment of honesty. God, how I hate to blow it! But I have pressing needs closer to home than Blair does. I can't make a snap decision so lightly, even if there weren't mitigating circumstances.

I look away. We're on the porch in the steamy morning air. Small combers are piling onto the beach. A leaf from the banyan flutters earthward. A pair of doves race toward it, probably thinking it's a butterfly. Ever hopeful.

He wants to live his life so big. Me, I think I want mine small and safe.

"I don't know if I want to live in such disarray, Blair," I sigh. His body refutes my remark involuntarily, but he doesn't say anything. A true democrat, he allows me my explanation.

"I don't think I'm cut out to be extraordinary. I know I may not have a blueprint for my life yet, but I know I don't want to make other people's lives my adventures."

"So you don't think I'm sincere, then?"

"I think you may have to run along without me."

There we sit. A circle lights the Scrabble board like a stage, and Henry and I are stagehands, or maybe understudies, waiting in the dimly lit wings.

We're both hunched over the board, chins propped in our hands, like a pair of matched bookends. The game has been ridiculously slow, and we're nearly asleep in our vulturine poses. I feel like a vulture, in fact, waiting for the game to die. Here in the sleepy-eyed night of the Tropic of Cancer, we're becalmed.

"He's thinking of going south," I say without lifting my chin from my hand, so it comes out through my clinched teeth, sounding inside my head like in a tunnel.

Henry doesn't seem surprised. In fact, he doesn't budge in any way.

"And what are you going to do?" he asks, but without energy.

"I don't know yet," I answer, zombie-like.

"But, you're not thinking of going with him?" An edge has crept into his voice.

"I don't think so."

Henry flares up. "He's an adventurer, Bleu! He'd do a lot less harm if he'd take up some extreme sport. Get him a kayak, or something. But don't go with him!"

Henry has obviously never seen Blair surf.

"You think he's going to cause harm? He claims he wants to do some good."

"I think he could end up hurting a lot of people. Don't you be one of them."

This is the most aggressive I've ever seen Henry. I'm surprised by so much emotion.

"He could end up another Lori Berenson," he nearly shouts.

I don't answer because I think that's a real possibility myself.

Henry straightens himself in his chair, then heaves a big sigh. Sometimes I think of him as a kind of Sad Sack, with his scrawny body and sandy hair and his brows that hang down like a basset hound's ears, his shirt rumpled like pudding across his caving chest.

Finally he says, wearily, "I wonder how many ways a man can throw away his life . . . young men, like John Walker Lindh."

"Or he could end up the next Schweitzer."

I believe I have to allow for that possibility and that Henry should too.

"Pah!" He spits. "Kee-rist!"

This brings on a fit of coughing. I make a move to help him, but he frowns and waves scornfully for me to stay put, and it dies down.

"What you need is to toke up a little more often," I preach. I was a tattletale, too.

Our energy flags again, like we're both stuck in slow quicksand.

"He's no cannibal, Henry."

He waits, clearing his throat, then begins again, tentatively, his voice all clotted. "Ever hear of another Walker, name of William Walker?"

I shake my head.

"I didn't think so," he says, rather nastily, his voice suddenly cleared, quite loud and clear, actually, crystal clear.

Henry settles into his chair, enjoying this little opportunity to play teacher again—teacher with an attitude. "Little Grasshopper," and all that.

"Now, there was an American who thought Central America was the place to fulfill his dreams! We're talking grandiose dreams, here, Bleu. Nothing paltry about William Walker's vision of himself. Rather like Blair, I think. Napoleonic."

"Oh, come on, Henry!"

He shoos my defense away with one hand, as if it's a gnat.

"All right. If you don't want to believe me . . . But just listen up, Bleu.

"See, Walker, or should we call him 'Willie,' was born in Tennessee, just in time to be in the prime of his life when two major events collided. Lucky for him. Oh, way beyond luck, really. Because, just then, falling right into his lap, gold was discovered in California at the same time the South was preparing for secession. And here's Walker, just looking for a great cause to serve. So, he came up with the brilliant idea of forming a colony in Baja California to transport that California gold to the South. Brilliant. Logical. He wanted to finance the South's great cause, see. You remember, Iris, you and I already touched on that subject, the South's great cause?"

I've drawn my legs up into my chair, curled up like a cat, and don't really like being bothered with Henry's digression, but I nod dutifully.

"He landed at La Paz—ever been to La Paz, Bleu?" he interrupts himself, bursting his own bubble. "Well, you should go, you and that *wunderkind* boyfriend of yours. Something magical about it . . . alluring, self-contained. A must-see, believe me. I don't know what it *is* exactly I love about La Paz . . ."

"Henry!"

"Hold your horses. I'm getting there," he coughs. "Always in such a tearing hurry, Bleu. My, my, where's your attention span?"

When I move like I might stand up and go, he raises his hand in surrender. "All right. All right, then. Calm yourself, for heaven's sake. You'll give yourself a heart attack one of these days, if you're not careful, cut your life inordinately short. Really."

He's enjoying himself way too much, but finally settles back into his tale. "Yes, where was I? Walker. Willie. So . . . he landed there, in lovely La Paz—Lord, it must've been lovely back then . . . okay, okay—he and his small 'force.' It was 1853, which was, as I'm sure you know, five years after the Treaty of Guadalupe Hidalgo had been signed, which means our war with Mexico was long since over, and the new boundaries for the Gadsden Purchase were firmly in place. But, disregarding all that (and can you imagine the hubris of such a man?)—get this—the asshole declares Lower California and Sonora an independent republic. He was ready to start his own private war with Mexico. My God! I'd have given anything to have seen the expression on Santa Anna's face when he heard!" Henry laughs almost manically. "Santa Anna, who'd returned from exile to declare himself dictator for life. Can't you imagine? Can't you just see it, Bleu?"

I can see that Henry would've been a good teacher. His story is firing him up; he's making it come alive.

"The Mexicans kicked Willie's ass back to the U.S. within seven months, but Willie was not a man to be easily discouraged. Besides, other forces had been brewing which set up a great opportunity for his day in the sun."

Henry's enjoying himself immensely, the idiot, even waving his arms around in grandiose gestures.

"The plot thickens here, Bleu, because Cornelius

Vanderbilt's transit company had also seen possibilities in Central America for transporting gold and passengers across Nicaragua between the two oceans. Meanwhile, Walker had been invited by Southern liberals to lead them in the up-and-coming war they'd been stirring up with a stick, and they came up with a plan involving Vanderbilt's transit company. Yes, all these strange factions coming together, stirring things up with a big stick—such things happen in times of war—how they ever concocted the plan they came up with, it's almost beyond reckoning!"

Henry stops to sip from his beer. It's so warm and stale, he grimaces and grits his teeth at the taste.

"So Walker set sail again, this time to the Mosquito coast, landing in Nicaragua to hatch his revolutionary plan. And when he made contact with Vanderbilt's transit company, incredibly, two of its officers fell in with him, conspiring with him to gain control of the company."

Henry fixes me with a wild look.

"These two! Can't you picture them, Iris? Doubly traitorous: traitors to their federal union and to their boss and his company. Great scoundrels, don't you think?"

"If you say so, Henry."

Henry pulls his shoulders back as if I shoved him.

"That's a helluva tepid response, Bleu. Christ! Show a little spunk."

He's not going to go on if I don't, either.

"I do, Henry! I think they were lowdown skunks!"

"Okay then," he says, but it takes him a minute to get on with it, while I try to look interested as all hell. Which I am, anyway. I really am.

He finally clears his throat, once he figures I've been properly chastised.

"From what position of authority Walker seized the company's property, on the pretext of some trumped-up charter violation, is anybody's guess, but he did, and turned the company over to his two cohorts. Then, incredibly (and this whole story is certainly incredible, you have to admit), he and his 'forces' fought their way successfully into complete military mastery of Nicaragua. Yes. Just incredible!" It's like Henry's still finding it unbelievable, even as he's telling me.

"Walker became 'president' within a year's time and managed to hold onto his presidency for almost a year, somehow managing to defend it successfully against an entire coalition of Central American states trying their damnedest to oust him, before he was finally forced to surrender to the U.S. Navy to avoid capture. The Navy shipped him out, back to the U.S."

Henry's eyes are gleaming like murder.

"So, what do you do with such an adventurer, eh, Iris? Well, evidently, they didn't do enough. They merely put him on parole. And Walker, not a man to be easily dissuaded, led another foray to Nicaragua before seven months were up, if you can believe it."

I hum a bar of "Back in the Saddle Again," and Henry laughs, but chops it short because he's dying to get on with his story. He's got a point to make.

"How he must've loved the power he'd felt there, don't you see? Can't you feel it? It was something he couldn't bear giving up, this 'noble' knight with a cause. He must've become positively addicted to the idea of power, that's my guess."

Then he stops and interrupts himself, picking up his beer again.

"There's a bit of that in Blair, don't you think?"

"What? What are you talking about, Henry? Addiction to power? What a load of bull!"

Henry and his ridiculous . . .

"As in, what power?" I scoff. "As if Blair has ever had any power over anything."

"Well, the potential, then." Henry tips his bottle up, and his Adam's apple jerks a couple of times.

He lets the matter drop, wedging the bottle back into its spot on the table. "Anyway," he says, "in the case of William—and you have to wonder about this, Bleu; it's almost too incredible to believe—all the various authorities concerned seemed to have so much patience for this asshole! They returned him again to the U.S. as a prisoner on parole, but he managed to bounce back into Nicaragua in less than a year for a third try. Mind-boggling, eh?"

I nod, plenty enthusiastic, too, this time. "You'd think they'd have taken all this more seriously."

"Ah, but just wait! Because, this time he made the mistake of landing in Honduras. And in Honduras he was taken prisoner by the British Navy."

I'm hooked, and Henry knows it. He's playing me like a marlin.

"Now, one would expect the British Navy to turn Willie over to U.S. authorities yet again, wouldn't one? But maybe they'd all become tired of Willie's games. Perhaps everyone involved decided to take him seriously, as you say. Maybe Willie's hubris was no longer so amusing. Maybe he was beginning to seem a royal pain in the butt, maybe even downright dangerous. Because, imagine this, Bleu, the Brits, who must have felt no great love for Americans and their troublesome ways, turned Walker over to the Honduran authorities instead."

Henry rivets his gaze on my face.

"And the Hondurans executed him."

He turns away from me, something wild in the gesture,

lifts the bottle to his lips, and tilts his head back to swallow the rest of his beer in one gulp. Then he belches like a hippo, setting the bottle down with a loud bang, rubbing the side of his nose like it itches.

"I've been there," he says, looking down and idly straightening a few tiles on the board.

I just arch my eyebrows when he looks up again.

"To the hacienda out in the dry tropical forest where they executed him."

I wait. I know there's a little more.

"Such a beautiful old hacienda, stranded in the hot, burning forest. Sitting alone like a beautiful wedding cake. Like a bride whose bridegroom didn't show. There was no life there at all. The trees were all brown and dry. No sound of birds. Only the iguanas running along the crumbling walls, chasing each other in those vicious territorial disputes of theirs."

He lifts the bottle, eyes it against the light, and sets it back down when he remembers it's empty.

"I saw the bullet holes in the wall. It would've been such a sad place to die, Bleu. So isolated, so lonely . . . so beautiful."

His eyes light with a flash that arcs and dies, then gradually turn to watery murk. And there we both sit, savoring the sadness, forgetting the man who's the rat, remembering only that we're all equal in death, all entitled to a decent death.

I have to clear my throat. "You should write a book about it, Henry."

He doesn't answer right away, though, just sits there with his head tilted like he's listening for something, but all I can hear is the thrumming surf and, very faintly, bells tolling—a buoy or maybe the cathedral, I can't tell.

He's hypnotized himself, Henry has, listening like that, so

his answer is slow in coming and, when it finally comes, sounds fuzzy.

"No time," he says.

"But don't listen to me, Bleu." He snaps back into the real world, the ole here and now, looking abashed and apologetic for some reason.

"About Blair, you know. Don't believe anything I or anyone else predicts, anyway. We're all so full of shit, thinking we can interpret the past, let alone read the future.

"When I was in Africa," (Henry's on a roll tonight) "— that was in 1985—I traveled in Zimbabwe for awhile with a fellow from Yugoslavia, an architect building a big hotel in Herare. He told me what a free, happy, Elysian country his was. A week later, same trip but a different country, a middle-aged black South African taxi driver taking me on a tour of Soweto told me outright his dire prediction, 'Boers are tough nuts to crack, and the only thing that will change them is blood.' " Henry pauses for effect. "Both wrong. As wrong as you can get."

My throat scrapes like there's something rusted in there. "He could end up like those American activists in Bolivia." Henry knows I mean Blair. "They did some actual good down there, fighting a water grab for profit by some big American corporation. They'd doubled the price of water, gouging the poor and all." I fizzle out, then reflare weakly. "They did it peacefully. Waged a campaign over the Internet . . ." trailing off again, petering out.

"There's always that chance, Henry." I'm worried because Henry seems so depressed by his own story.

He doesn't respond to my Bolivian example, but sits there like a statue; then, when he finally moves, it's only his lips; like he's a catatonic who can only move his lips.

"Why did you come to San Vaciò, anyway, Bleu?" The

voice as catatonic as the face.

I shift in my seat because my legs have gone to sleep, squished beneath my butt from sitting lotus-like. I unfold myself and stretch them in front of me, wiggling my toes. There's nothing I can do but sigh, so I do it, and I make it plenty tragic. I'm feeling unguarded tonight, bare to the bone, really, so I tell him the exact facts.

"Shit, Henry, I came because Cal and Blair wanted to come, and I didn't want to be alone." That doesn't seem a large enough piece of the truth, though, so I add another morsel. "I came because there was nowhere else for me to go."

"How about home?" So many people telling me to go home!

"No, not there, either."

Trying to lighten things up, I tell him, "I just hope my journey here isn't some kind of 'coming of age' experience I have to go through, Henry. God forbid! Anything but that! I hope San Vaciò's not some kind of lousy fucking crossroads in my life, pull-ease." I laugh, this kind of nasty little laugh, but my joke falls flat. His smile is just a pantomime.

"Either way, north or south, I guess you'll be leaving soon, though, won't you Bleu?"

God! His face looks parched—his eyes shot with little spalls of ruin.

"I can't stay forever, Henry," I say as gently as I can.

We've completely forgotten the game. Neither of us has the heart for it now.

I stand up, gingerly, because the soles of my feet are still stinging. "Maybe I'll just hit the hay, Henry; call it an early night."

He looks up, eyes flaring.

"Don't go, yet, Bleu." I've never heard Henry plead before, so I sit back down, but not on my feet.

Then he doesn't seem to know what the hell to say. Finally he mumbles, looking away, "I just wanted to tell you not to come by for the next two nights, Bleu."

"What?"

This definitely surprises me.

"I won't be here." His voice withers. "I'm going to be in Tepic for a couple of days."

This will be the first time Henry's left San Vaciò since I've been here. He doesn't explain why, and I don't ask.

"Do you want me to watch the place for you while you're gone?"

"No, no. Don't bother, Bleu. I'll lock up and everything will be fine. There's nothing here of any real value, anyway." He looks around dolorously, his eyes tunnels of despair. "No, don't bother about it."

"Okay, Henry." I wait, but Henry has nothing else to say, so I stand up again, wait a sec, and this time I leave.

Outside, the tolling waves wash up against the sand like shoals of souls.

I'm gone from Cielo Azul the next day, anyway.

Trudging through the loose sand, I test my knee, which feels almost normal. Great! So my knee is healing but my heart is forever broken. *Always the melodramatic diva, but you know that, don't you?* I drag knee and heart across the long stretch of white sand to where Andrea and the team huddle at the line of scrimmage. Once there, I plop down in the tight end position.

"Hey, Iris!"

And, what topic have they chosen for today's skirmish? There was never a doubt in my mind, of course. Men. The topic always was, is now, and forever shall be, men. Sweet consistency. Like the lack of hot water at El Colon. Ah, the security of knowing there are some things that can always be counted on.

"You ever see yourself ever getting married, Andrea?" asks Dylan.

"Sure! Come on!" Andrea booms. She has a tuba of a voice. "We'll all get married one of these days. Hey! Babes like us aren't going to become old maids, you know. Not a chance!"

Everyone always agrees with whatever Andrea says, and so they follow suit today. Like I say, consistency.

Eventually, though, I notice Taz changing her nod from vertical to lateral (Darwin would love this), until finally she pipes up in her high-pitched, little-girl, helium-gas voice. *She and Andrea could sing a great duet.*

"I dunno, though, you guys, marriage is such a bust. I mean, have you ever seen a married couple who seemed in love for more than, like, at most, maybe a year, tops?"

All but Dylan shake their heads. "Not really." "Nah." "Nope."

"Sure," Dylan says defiantly. "Look at Paul McCartney. Look at Paul Newman."

"Both Pauls," I say. "Wonder if that means anything?"

"C'mon, you guys," Dylan urges. "Look at Mel Gibson. Look at the Reagans."

"Eeeuuw."

"Okay, then, Bob Hope."

"Double eeeuuw! Wasn't she his gazillionth wife, anyway?"

"I don't think so."

"You know who I hated to see split up?" This from Natty.

"Kenneth Branagh and Emma Thompson. Such a cool couple!"

"Yeahs" all around.

"Soooo talented!"

"It doesn't count, though, just looking at famous people anyway," Taz says, sensibly. "Just look at our parents. Does anyone want to end up with marriages like our parents?"

"Fuck, no!"

I finally put in a word. "It's all because of that rotten curse on Eve."

"There you go!" Andrea blasts. "You and your bizarre ideas, Iris. Always off on some royal screwed-up dead-end."

"No, no. I want to hear what she has to say," says Dylan. Dylan is the only one who can trump Andrea.

"Yeah, go on. Tell us, Iris," Natty seconds. "So, tell us, what?" She's only brave because Dylan went first.

"Oh! Oh!" Taz suddenly squeaks excitedly. "Wait a minute! I got it! Eve's curse! You're talking about being on the rag. That's it, isn't it?"

"Oh, for chrissake, Taz, get serious," Andrea bawls.

"Look, you guys all know this—after they were kicked out of Eden, which naturally was all the woman's fault . . ."

Jeers.

"God put a curse on Eve, don't you remember?" But no one does.

"Yeah, well, he did. You all should remember this: he cursed the serpent first, telling him he'd crawl on his belly and eat dust his whole life. He also cursed Adam; said his life would be full of sweat and toil, his garden full of weeds."

Natty murmurs, "Oh, okay, I think I remember this now." Andrea shoots her a dirty look for interrupting.

"As for Eve . . . he told Eve she would have to suffer pain in childbirth, which is pretty interesting, when you think about it."

Okay, I digress at this point. I just can't help myself, because this is the type of thing Hub loved thinking about. He's where I got all of this, anyway.

"Because that means greater human intelligence was part of Eve's curse. Women were going to pay for our evolution. Don't you think that's interesting?"

"Huh?"

"Great! I don't get it."

I've lost them.

"Sure, guys, just think about it. It's our enlarged cranium that makes childbirth so painful."

"Oh, yeah."

"Okay."

"Wow."

"Weird."

"Anyway, I just threw that in for the hell of it. What I'm getting at is the rest of God's curse on Eve, and we're all Eve, after all, right?"

"Yes, yes, sure," they all agree.

"Anyway, the curse was . . . and here's the kicker, guys . . . are you listening?" Building up the suspense a little.

I have all their attention, even Andrea's.

"I quote: *'You shall cleave to your husband, and he shall rule over you.'* " I say it kind of triumphantly, but they still don't exactly get it, so I have to backtrack and explain. I hate it when the punch line falls flat like that, so I'm pretty aggravated.

"Listen up. He cursed women by making them need men, don't you get it? And we do. And it's definitely a curse. You guys are the perfect example" (I'm punishing them for not getting the point on their own); "men are all you talk and think about." Then I back off and include myself. "Let's face it, we don't feel complete without a man. Whoever the long-bearded, eight-hundred-year-old patriarch was who wrote that two thousand years ago already understood that about women, see. And he knew it was a curse, too."

204

"Huh. Very interesting," says Andrea, like she could care less.

Dylan's thinking it over. "Maybe so, maybe we do cleave and all that, but men sure as hell don't rule over us."

"Yeah, no way. You go girl!"

"They don't have to," I say smugly. "They have our curse to help them."

"They can be fuckers," Andrea contributes. "For example, y'know that guy from nowheresville up in Wyoming who just got four million dollars for his first novel?"

But no one but Andrea has heard of this.

"He said he was only able to write it because his wife agreed to support him while he quit his job to write full time."

"So? That's nice. He's giving her credit."

"Yeah, well, just watch! First thing he'll do now that he's filthy rich is dump her for some young arm-candy trophy."

"Ain't it the truth?" somebody agrees.

"Yeah, okay. All right, but it goes both ways," Dylan argues. "You know, some bitch divorces her husband as soon as he hits pay dirt. She waits until he's loaded to cash out."

"Yeah, everything in the whole bloody U.S. is about money. So fucking bogus!" Andrea says disgustedly, blowing sand off her designer shades.

"Yeah, let's face it, marriage sucks."

"So, Andrea, you see yourself getting married?" Back where they started.

This has tired our intellects, so we burrow down into the sand, concentrating on nothing but the sun in silence.

Five minutes pass, then Dylan asks, "Pass me the squirt gun, wouldya Natty?"

Natty searches through her pile of beach necessities, through her pack and under her towel, but she can't find it. Her voice climbs the scale as she starts whining about what in the world could have happened to it, when she sees the butt-end of it sticking out from under Andrea's towel.

"Well, shit, Andrea, you're sitting on it!" she accuses, her voice dropping an octave, and she jerks it free.

"Crap! You've broken the tip off! I can't believe it! Look! It's ruint," she squawks, and displays it to all of us like Moses holding up the tablets.

"You and your fat ass, Andrea." She can't get over it, fussing and grumbling until Andrea finally mumbles, "Look, I'm sorry, okay?"

"Wha'd'you say?" Natty asks loudly, cupping her ear.

"I'm sorry!" Andrea bellows.

"Keerist!" Natty scoffs. "That's the first time I've ever had to ask her to speak up."

When the guffaws finally die down, the pack settles and things grow quiet again.

Another five minutes of peace pass before the pressure becomes more than we can stand.

"You must be real religious, huh, Iris?" Dylan asks.

I'd nearly dozed off.

"Nah," I say sleepily.

"You should stick around, Iris," Andrea says from under the towel covering her face. "Stick with us, girl. Don't go back. You keep things interesting around here. You've got good mojo."

"Yeah," they chorus.

This is nice, this agreeable consensus from Team Banana.

"You could help us at the restaurant. We could use more desserts."

"Better salads, too," Taz adds.

"Gee, guys. Thanks for the offer. I don't know, though . . ."

"Just think about it," commands Andrea.

It's not a request.

I stop by to see Leo at El Colon and offer to buy him a drink. But Leo, he doesn't drink. He's apparently the most wholesome man I've ever met—innocent, almost. But it's hard to tell about someone who speaks a different language— who's a scoundrel, who's a saint. You can't really read a man when you don't speak his language. You can't get at his true identity because you don't feel the nuances.

It's the same with a foreign place. Here, I don't always see what's beneath the surface. Because I'm a foreigner, I have no protective superstructure of instincts, no automatic cultural understanding, no long-term trusting relationships. No reason to believe anyone here would help me.

Still, what Leo says always proves true—okay, except for the little lie about the hot water. Plus he has lived all alone in my country, so he knows about being a foreigner.

He sits down at my table while I sip my drink.

"Why didn't you tell me your father is a congressman?" he scolds. "It was Blanca who finally told me. Why do I have to learn these things from Blanca?"

"What difference does it make, Leo?"

"The difference is, he must be a very wealthy man, no?"

"No. You're wrong about that. He's not all that wealthy, Leo. And why should that matter to you, anyway, huh?"

He sighs and explains carefully, diagramming things for me like I'm his preschool daughter.

"Because, Eerrrees, maybe he would like to invest in a hotel in Mexico! Maybe he has money to invest, for a tax write-off, you know, if he could just find an honest partner, someone like me, *por ejemplo.*"

I'm relieved, actually. I thought maybe Leo had some

relative with an immigration problem, or an outstanding debt, or some friends in trouble in the U.S., in jail, maybe, or something else impossible to resolve. And I'm amused. I don't know tax laws, but I seriously doubt foreign investments in losing propositions can be written off your income taxes.

"I think renovating El Colon would take more money than my father has."

"No, no, Eerrrees! That's where you're wrong! For jes two thousand American dollars I can fix El Colon up into a much better hotel. It don take so much here, you know? Because the money goes a long, long way. For two thousand *dolares* I could paint the rooms and fix the air conditioning and repair the boiler. You sure your congressman father wouldn't be interested in investing with an honest man like myself, so we could make El Colon like new?"

Nothing on earth could make El Colon like new, but because it's conceivable that Leo's dreams, if actuated, might possibly at least elevate it to budget status in the guidebooks, I'm sympathetic.

"I don't think so, Leo. No. Sorry, but I seriously doubt my father would be interested."

He looks so crestfallen, that I add, "I could ask him, though."

Leo reacts as if this evasive half-hearted encouragement is a done deal, breaking into an enormous smile that lifts the wispy mustache off his upper lip into his nose.

Oh God! I've unleashed a monster!

"I doubt he'll be interested, though," I hedge desperately, trying to temper the damage done.

Language is not the only thing in our way, Leo's and mine. In fact, sometimes it seems our lives are two separate universes, bridged only by our common humanity, which is hardly enough. Other times, we understand each other perfectly.

"I wanted to ask you something. Has Blair told you he's going to Chiapas and maybe on to Guatemala?"

Leo nods. "Well, he didn't tell me," he says, "but I heard."

"What do you think about it?"

I can see Leo would like to avoid this question, but, for some reason, he always feels obligated to answer me.

"It depends on what he's going there for, Eerrrees. Is he going there to make political trouble? Because that's what I hear."

"Where did you hear this?"

"I hear it from Cal, before he left. He had some drinks here the night before he left."

"And what if he gets involved politically down there? I know it's dangerous, Leo. I'm not asking about the danger. I'm asking what you personally think of him doing something like that."

This is why I trust Leo. He's always brave enough to be honest, except about the hot water.

"I think . . ." and he takes a minute to do just that, ". . . I think fighting for your own liberty is a brave thing. Fighting for someone else's liberty is a luxury of the wealthy."

And I think one of these days those steel balls of Blair's may just sink him.

I slurp the last of my drink, fish money from my pocket, slap it onto the table, and stand up to leave.

"I'll ask my father for you about investing in El Colon."

What can it hurt, after all?

Back home, I lie in the hammock under the banyan tree waiting for Blair. The air breathes hot and sticky on the back

209

of my neck while the sun dives over the edge of the world into the sea.

A blue lid swoops in on the night. Listening deeply, as if trying to hear other dimensions, I barely hear a humming in a lower register than ordinary sounds, some kind of subterranean hum of the universe, like a bell's vibration. I hold my breath and put my hand over my heart, and the two are in unison. So it's my heart humming in my ears, like when snorkeling.

I drift off into sleep, but wake back up when I feel something brush my face with the softest kiss. I open my eyes and see a small, dark bat has just brushed me with its wings. I watch, fascinated, while it dives again and shies off, chittering.

Another of San Vacio's spirits.

I try falling back asleep, but my thoughts get in the way.

Is there really such a thing as "the great love of one's life"? If there is, does it happen only once? Should I search the whole wide world for the same feeling I have for Dr. Allende, or would that be insanely hopeless?

Maybe "the love of one's life" isn't all it's cracked up to be, anyway. I'm definitely feeling more hopeless now than desperate. Put it this way—I feel incurable, but that feels endurable. Not at first, though. At first I was sure I couldn't stand it, the shame of what I'd done and his cold response. What I thought at first was of going home by swimming across the sea. There's no place farther from home than where I was thinking of going.

But then I thought of Lily, how she holds her flute when she plays, her elbows up and her wrists so delicate, how each note is another breath from Lily.

And I realized something good has come from all my stupidity with Dr. Allende. Being a twin, you never feel the same entitlement everybody else feels. Everything is shared, so you're always measuring your portion in your mind, always looking for your half share instead of your full share. But because I'm surviving this disease called love, I know one thing for sure. I'm not exactly like Lily—I am not Lily.

I will survive and have the full share I'm entitled to.

The strangeness of Cielo Azul feels delicious tonight. I meld into Cielo Azul, my anti-home, with its huge, tentacled octopus of a tree, and the winged ants and the bizarre night creatures—giant psychedelic insects drawn to the glow of the hut's white walls. Over the feathery ocean, the stars form a milky scrim. Here I go again, melting, disappearing into the grandiose scale of things.

I feel way too wonderful to sleep. There's something going on inside me like the bat's sonar. It's as if I'm an empath, part of the throb of the whole world, breathing the same breath together, one great huffing organism, sounding out through the cosmos.

I breathe deep, inhaling the salt sting of ocean blow. Sometimes, rarely, a wind comes down the volcanoes from inland, smelling something like my mother's compost pile—like earth and overripe vegetation and wet wood tinged with mold. Sometimes I try to believe I can even smell the Caribbean all the way from the other coast—bananas and pineapple, tropical flowers, and the musk of Mayan ruins. Anyway, that's what I try to believe. When it's dead calm, I smell the town, a blend of wood smoke and steam and cooking food, truck fumes, fish guts, liquor, piss, and disinfectant. But mostly, like now, I smell the ocean.

The ocean goose pimples when the breeze sweeps across. In it I see San Vaciò, a string of little rosettes of lights, shivering like paper shadows.

"Are you talking to me, God?"

I say it again, out loud, in my best Robert De Niro imitation, like in *Taxi Driver*. "You talkin' to *me?*" Smiling like I'm crazy or something.

Then I fall asleep again in spite of myself and dream of Lily's beautiful woman in the emerald forest. Beside her is a resplendent bird with all the colors of the rainbow in its long tail. The woman wears a shimmering dress, and orchid flowers are woven into her hair. She strokes a jaguar crouched at her feet, lapping water from a crystal pool. Alone with her animals, she's the only human in the forest, the only creature of her kind. There's no other like her, and the world around her is filled with peace and harmony. In this dream I'm not falling, and nothing is disappearing just beyond my grasp. *Don't wake up! Don't wake up!*

This time when I wake, it's because something's not right. It feels like something near me is definitely in trouble. So I sit up and take a good look around the compound, but I don't see anything out of the ordinary. The night crackles. *Didn't something just move inside Henry's hut?* I slip out of the hammock and tiptoe up behind his hut as quietly as the banyan leaves allow, creeping up like a poacher, thinking, *Ugh! We ought to rake these up—get rid of the cockroaches.*

Thinking stuff like that when I'm scared helps in some goofy way.

When I reach the hut and peek through the screen, I can't see a thing, so I go around to the front and climb the porch stairs, careful to avoid the planks that creak.

Nothing. Huh.

I turn to go. Still, something's wrong, I just know it in my gut, so I pull on the door and it opens.

Henry said he was going to lock this.

At this point I know I should go for help and leave the

whole damned thing up to someone braver, but something stronger than fear draws me inside. *Curiosity killed the kitty cat.* Too chicken to call out, I slink molten-like into the room. It's as still as a tomb in there, so I flip on the light.

What's this? What the hell is going on? Oh man!

There's Henry, lying in fetal position on the couch curled around his saxophone, the two of them wrapped together like twin embryos, ringed by a circle of irregular-sized empties gleaming like church organ pipes.

Hah! So, Henry's a binge drinker. Talk about your—I never would've guessed. No wonder he wanted a little privacy! Oh man!

I figure I really should just sneak away before he sees me, to save him face and all (I really just want to get the hell out of there so bad)—only, I don't know, he just doesn't look right, not even for someone on a bender. I can't just up and leave. So I walk over to him—not really wanting to see him like this—looking anywhere but at Henry, and then I shake him by the shoulder from as far away as possible. But all that happens is his corpus rolls away from the sax, belly-up like a dead fish, which makes me jump a bloody mile.

That's it! Get serious. You have to look, idiot!

So, I squat down on my haunches, eye to eye, and check out his breathing closely and carefully. Yes, okay, so he's breathing, all right, but oh God! Each breath is just terrible. *Cripes!* I shake him harder, *shaken not stirred,* but he won't come to. *Come on, Henry! Come on, come on! Wake up, you asshole, you!*

Finally, he barely comes around, Zombie-like, a look rising, then sinking again in his eyes like faces in a window. I panic. I mean, I feel it flood my whole body—heart, head, everything—rattling, like rat-a-tat-tat. *Okay, okay, stay calm!* But it's no use. My heart is a train pounding. I can't control my heart; never could. Then I notice a small collection of prescription meds on the table next to the couch and my pulse leaps madly.

What's this? This can't be happening again!

The weak coughs of the Vespa sputtering into the compound make me cry out loud. I spring up and run out to Blair for help. Henry's old banger of a car is nowhere in sight, so I race back in as fast as I can and call a cab while Blair tries to wake Henry. And then I dial the clinic, my hands shaking like I'm freezing to death.

Fourteen

Dear Iris,

You asked me to talk to you about it, to tell you my feelings. In a way, it breaks my heart, just the fact that you asked. I suppose the only reason you have asked at all is because there are so many miles between us, which means maybe everything actually has a silver lining, after all. Unfortunately, I don't believe I can possibly explain. I would if I could, my darling. God knows, you certainly deserve to know. I think the best I can do is describe what happened that day from my viewpoint, a day I've played over and over in my mind until I'm half crazy from it. Maybe that will help. Maybe it's what you need and maybe it will help me, too. Anyway, I think it's the best I can do.

When Lily left for her music academy, I went from having the two of you around all the time to no one.

Both of you suddenly gone.

Lily. The quiet one, the perfectionist. Never able to do anything well enough to suit herself. Always kicking herself up one side and down the other. Thinking she's "ugly." Amazing!

And you. Bound to save the world. Rescuing, rescuing every stray out there. All rough edges about it, though. Never letting your guard down in front of anybody.

My two girls.

Oh, I know there's more to you than that. It's not that black and white. You're all intermingled, you two, no matter what.

215

Really, when you think about it, I hadn't seen much of Lily that summer anyway, because Mac was in town and didn't seem to like coming around our house much, so Lily was nearly always out with him. (It was strange, him not wanting to be around us anymore, wasn't it? It seemed to me he used to find solace here. Didn't it seem that way to you, too?) I almost saw more of you, even though you had moved out, because you and Hub stopped by on your way to and from the plains so often.

How could two girls who looked so identical be so different? How could you be attracted to such opposite types of men?

It was hard to be fair, when I liked Hub so well and thought Mac so bad for Lily. A parent doesn't dare interfere too much for fear of causing a backlash, but you remember, I did try talking to Lily. I believe you did too, didn't you? There was just no reaching her.

I can't help but blame myself, though. By the time she left for the East Coast, she seemed so miserable. I hated sending her off so far away where she didn't know a soul, but she kept insisting she'd be all right, and I thought her flute would be her magic ticket. Mac had promised to call her regularly from San Francisco. And Lily did seem to settle in. She called and e-mailed, rambling on about her roommate and the music studios and how she missed Sherlock, all seemingly normal adjustments.

I didn't really see it coming at all. Like a bullet. I blame myself for that, because a mother should know, I think, when there's serious trouble. How could I not know?

When you came by with Hub on a trip out to the grasslands that morning, the two of you were laughing and hanging onto each other like puppies. It made me happy just watching you, remembering what it was like, how wonderful it can be.

You visited awhile then drove off together, planning to stay a couple of nights out in Grover at that bed and breakfast you liked out there. Your father was on the phone in his office most of the day, but later that afternoon we took our regular walk around the lake with Sherlock. I remember it was such a beautiful day! There were big thunderheads building up over the mountains and flocks of blackbirds trying to fly upwind. The last cutting of hay had been mown and the farmers were trying to get it in before it rained. A pair of white-tailed deer ran away from us. We had a lovely walk. Still, there was the smell of something dead—that sickening-sweet smell, something hidden in the tall grass. But we just called Sherlock over and walked past. Because that's what you do.

Your dad was in great spirits about the upcoming term. He's always happiest at the prospect of locking political horns, anyway, don't you agree? I was feeling low, though, thinking how lonely I'd be once he left, alone in my house for the first time ever, my family all scattered. Remember? I was worried about how dividing my time between Colorado and Washington was going to be hard on Sherlock, so you were looking into finding a way to take him. It's funny. I never feel right trusting anyone else with my animals, though. I worry, no matter what. I don't believe anyone else will take care of them the way I do. (I'm sorry, Sweetheart, not even you.) I know that's ridiculous.

Not long after our walk we got the call about Lily, and your father left to catch a flight out there to bring her home. Then I called you. It all happened so fast, I hardly had time to feel anything. But calling you made it real. Calling you that evening was the hardest thing I've ever had to do, Iris.

And now look, you've run off, first to the top of a redwood tree, and now to some Mexican backwater.

I just don't understand at all.

Why do you think women today still seem as destined for self-destruction as ever? I read that girls in China are as willing to have their legs broken to become taller in this day and age as their great-grandmothers were to bind their feet. Such terrible things ought to have changed, don't you think?

Tell me, Iris, what is there in the nature of women . . . ?

My girls, my girls!

Forgive me, my Iris flower. It's just that I love you both so much it's scary.

Fifteen

The thing is, Lily had to know when she did that to herself she was scarring me. But then, vice-versa too, and I've never let that stop me from hurting her.

It's a horrific phone call to get from your mother. We all should've been able to stop it from happening somehow. We should have run Mac off long before, but of course, that wouldn't have made any difference. There was no keeping them apart, and, besides, it wouldn't have repaired the hole in Lily.

Lily was already home by the time I got there. Mama came out to meet us, to head us off, really, when Hub's car pulled in. She looked terrible, like maybe she spent the night in a chair, blinking now against the bright sun like it was heavy snow falling on her. Her face—with features too large and pointy for anyone to think conventionally pretty, but, really, a wonderful face, perfectly aligned, symmetrical, with big, striking eyes—all twisted out of shape as she leans over and looks into the car. She's got her fists jammed into her pockets, like she wants to pile-drive herself into the earth, but really, it's because she doesn't know what else to do with her hands. When finally she pulls one out, it's to drag her fingers shakily through her ragged hair, her head tilted absently. She hardly looks at me. She cannot meet my eyes. I wonder if she's blaming herself, like I am. We'd have had to undo what had been done to be any comfort to each other, so we were no comfort at all. Dad's the one who's always been solid, anyway, not Maminski. Mama, she's like the breeze that twirls the leaves on your patio. She always relies on Dad for strength, but this—this had shaken him, she tells me now, this chink in his armor another fearful revelation for her. She wiped her sleeve across her eyes.

"He and Lily are both still asleep after a long, long night," she tells me.

"Let him sleep," she said, almost pleading. "He's so exhausted." Like she wasn't.

I needed to see Lily, though, and absolutely could not wait. So I crept into her room, that girlishly prim room of hers, and eased down into her chair to watch her sleep.

Mama tiptoed past, whispering to Sherlock to go lie down. Sherlock has a habit of tailing people when he thinks something's wrong. Mama couldn't sit still, so she kept doubling back on herself, nearly stepping on the woeful dog. *"Go lie down!"* she whispered harshly, completely exasperated with him, creeping around and whispering like someone guilty of a crime; like Lily, having done something so extraordinary, might overhear her doing ordinary things.

Watching Lily always makes me feel like some kind of skewed replica or something. *That's how I look sleeping. That's how people see me.* That's how it makes me feel. But not that morning, because I was shocked into seeing Lily as herself for the first time in my life. She looked scary, with her mouth thrown open, arms all akimbo, tangled and mangled and corkscrewed into the bedclothes, lifeless. It scared the hell out of me.

I sat there a long time, trying to get used to the whole idea. I couldn't've moved, anyway, not if my life had depended on it, because she looked wonderful, too, once I calmed down.

Wonderfully alive. As unguarded and unknowing as a princess in a deep, dark winter sleep under an evil spell. But that was strange too, seeing that.

Finally, after I calmed down a little, I went back to the kitchen and found Mama adrift. She had run out of nothing to do and was standing there staring out the window, her arms wrapped around her chest like a straightjacket; like she was trying to hold everything together with the pressure of her own arms. Thinking of something to anchor her, I came up with, "Let's fix some eggs!" which we did, comforted by the routine. Anything to keep us from thinking. Just watching her crack the eggs on the side of the frying pan was soothing somehow. She always makes a game of trying to crack them one-handed, banging them just hard enough on the side of the pan to split the shells without breaking the yolks. Then spreading the two pieces apart with a lift of her thumb and little finger in opposite directions until the yolks drop, *plop!* palming the halved shells into each other with a twist of her hand, then tossing them loftily, airily, into the sink. *Airy fairy*. She pretends she's great at this, but ordinarily she's only successful about half the time, because her touch isn't in synch; she gets silly about it and the yolks shatter and bleed into the whites, polluting the whole mess, cooking into one solid, compromised off-orange disk. (Poor Mama! Never could keep her eggs properly separated!) But that morning she performed her little feat flawlessly. Go figure. Just because her heart wasn't in it at all, that's why; her heart was a million miles away.

Then, of course, we couldn't eat a bite. We just thought we ought to eat, but couldn't. We couldn't eat a thing. We couldn't even give the eggs to Sherlock because he's too fat and they're bad for him. Swell. Mama saved them for when Lily woke up, though, just in case. As if. She wrapped them up ever so carefully and settled them softly onto the refrigerator shelf like they might still shatter. It was almost as if she didn't have the strength to push the plate onto the shelf.

I wandered back into Lily's room because there was nowhere else in the world to go, and watched from the chair again, throwing my legs over the arm. I couldn't have told you what I was thinking, sitting there like that. All kinds of shit went racing through my head. Anyway, I just sat there, all fucked-up that way, until she finally woke up.

She saw me and smiled before she remembered, a rare smile because it happened in that innocent, rarified, pre-knowing gap of time. Then I saw the memory hit her and that wonderful smile disappeared . . . an awful thing to watch, like watching the fall from grace when those first two screw-ups went from total innocence directly to a sneak preview of every horrible thing in the world they'd just unleashed. You could see it all in her eyes, the look of a spilled future.

"Hey," she said.

And what was I supposed to do now? How could we possibly broach the unthinkable?

Lily saved me, though, always bailing me out. She smiled again sleepily and patted the bed beside her and that was all I needed. I can't remember my feet touching the floor as I dove in. Wrapped together, both of us held onto each other for dear life, like castaways drifting away from Eden, trying to find our way back into paradise.

"Why'd you do it, Lily?"

I should've let it pass, though. Her face shattered. She couldn't answer right away.

We settled into the bed and into each other, gradually, like butter melting slowly in hot sun.

"I'll tell you everything, Iris. You're the one I want to tell."

She seemed smaller, like she'd shrunk somehow, and I could barely hear her, she was speaking so softly, but I couldn't get any closer.

Then she tells me.

"I thought it would send him a message."

Her hair smelled like cinnamon. Nested like fledglings, I was careful to avoid the bandage on her neck. No way. I didn't want to know.

"He came to see me right after I moved in."

She and her voice both raised up a little in alarm.

"God! He was so screwed up, Iris!"

She faltered then and sank back down, weightless as a shadow.

"It was something too scary to imagine, what he did to himself. I mean, syringes, Iris!" The way she said it, it might have been guillotines.

"Heroin! I think it was heroin he was using!"

She stared at me with stricken eyes, as if daring me to believe her. I couldn't look back, though. It was like looking at stigmata.

"What could he have been thinking? Did he think the rules didn't apply to him? Did he think he had some kind of lousy *impunity* or something, for godssake?"

Small town ex-hero goes big-time, one way or another . . . Mac and his visions of grandeur!

"Maybe by then he wasn't thinking," I told her weakly, grasping for something to soothe her. "Or maybe he'd passed the point of caring," like there was actually a logical explanation for any of this.

There was no way I could fix it, though, no matter what. I knew that.

"How could I really know what was going on, though? Answer me that! It was just completely beyond my wildest imagination.

"He was cannibalizing himself, you know? Like when an animal chews its own leg off to escape a trap. But he'd set the trap. How could I watch and do nothing? You tell me!" Her voice flailing like a harried bird's.

She raised herself onto her elbow to look at me, but I wouldn't look back.

"It's so slow, Iris!" she said, practically shouting. "You start thinking, if only he'd hurry it up! Get it over with! 'Torturous' implies slow, right? It was like watching him die through slow, miserable, self-inflicted torture, that's what."

I knew I couldn't calm her. Not me, not anything on earth.

Her elbow gave out, and she dropped back down into the covers, swaddled by the warm tangle of sheets and pillow and me.

"And he was poisoning me, too—like I was drugged too.

"So eventually it came to me. The only thing to do was to end it quickly for him."

I shifted involuntarily.

"Oh man!"

"I know, I know—you can hardly believe that, because you're in a rational position. But don't tell me you don't understand, Iris. I know you could never, ever watch any creature on earth suffer like that and sit there and do nothing about it. Besides, you've got to realize, it was twisting my mind, watching everything I loved about him being erased bit by bit like that. I mean, he was murdering our futures!

"I couldn't stand it, that's what it finally came down to. I wanted to either see him well or never see him again."

She took a deep breath like a tired swimmer, holding it a long time before exhaling.

"But, then, just walking away from it wasn't really an option, was it?"

Arguing both sides rationally.

"No, that wouldn't have worked at all . . . because I'd still be imagining what was happening to him. It would still be happening, and I'd know it. So I was trapped too. Me too. No way out without cannibalizing myself, too."

Sherlock wandered into the room and dumped himself on the floor, looking up at us sheepishly and pelting it with his tail a few times.

"And then, I knew I couldn't do the other—you know, end it for him—no matter what. Whether they shoot horses or not. Never. I thought about it, though, I really did. And I know that's terrible. Somehow I have to find a way to live with that."

God, Lily!

"But there was no way. The only suffering I could stop was my own."

"But . . ." I was barely whispering, "I mean, did something . . . What precisely happened?"

A torrent came pouring out of her.

"When he showed up he was flying, just absolutely flying. It was terrifying! I tried to talk to him about what was going on, but he wouldn't listen. He just exploded." She squeezed my arm. "You remember how explosive he could be. But this was beyond anything I'd ever seen, Iris." I nodded against her chest. "So then I backed off. And . . .

". . . we slept. We slept a long time, I hardly remember. And then we woke up . . . and . . . I don't know . . . we made love. We made love the whole rest of the night. And it was as sweet as it had ever been with him.

"Oh, Iris!"

225

God! I couldn't stand looking back at her.

"I shouldn't have, I know, but I couldn't help myself."

"Hey. Hey!" *Shush.* "You don't have to explain, Lily."

She shook her head. I was absolutely wrong.

I plucked a piece of lint out of her hair. Lily's beautiful sleavesilky hair all stubbed into tats. Trying to make her perfect again.

"I'd been so lonely, Iris. My roommate was horrible, and I hadn't made any friends yet. I felt so alone!"

Shush, shush!

I hated picturing it. Lily's no good alone.

"If only I were stronger, like you."

How could Lily be so wrong? I shook my head, like trying to rid it of moths.

"Yes," she said. "Oh, yes."

I still didn't want to look at her—backing off, sculling my oars in her turbulence. I couldn't bear having her see me seeing her like that, like a mirror reflecting a mirror.

"The next day he disappeared without a word. And then he just didn't come back—nothing—after *that* night.

"So I started calling and calling California—I must've called a million times—until he finally answered.

"I tried to talk to him again about what he was doing to himself. But he wouldn't listen! He didn't want to hear it, not one word.

"Oh, Iris," she whispered, fading out, "he'd never been so cruel. He said horrible, unspeakable things to me.

"He couldn't have remembered that night we'd had—he couldn't've."

She gripped my arm until it hurt.

"God, oh, God! You can't imagine how it feels to see someone you love disappearing before your very eyes."

But I looked straight at Lily and thought, *"Oh yes I can."*

Sherlock panted loudly a couple of times, moaned, then stretched out full length onto his side.

Lily went on. "He hung up . . . *'Click!'* then wouldn't answer. It rang and rang . . . but he never answered again."

Her tone free fell into despair.

"I heard that phone ringing forever and ever.

"I tried to forget it. Tried to stop the ringing. Tried to erase the whole thing from my mind. Just forget about him—that's what I'd do. What's he to me, anyway? He's just a guy I happened to run into, right?"

A train wreck, that's what I thought. *A hit-and-run by a run-amok Mack truck.*

"But I couldn't."

Her hand began stroking my arm gently, slowly up and down along the blue vein on the inside.

I needed to pee. I needed to blow my nose—bad.

"Don't you see? I thought there'd never be anything in my life to replace his love. Nothing that had happened since our good times seemed as good to me. Not even close. And I just didn't think I could live with that kind of future, so alone, knowing it was over, knowing what he was doing to himself. I couldn't stand my own imagination. You get it, Ire, don't you? Of course you do. You've always understood every single thing, haven't you?"

I nodded.

"It was an impasse, see? Despair and dreams stalemated."

The thing is, I knew. I knew exactly. *The abyss.*

"I thought killing myself with pills would send him a clear message, see?"

Explaining and explaining, until I'd understand absolutely everything. Unraveling her mess.

"But then, I tried to save myself afterward, you know—they told you that, didn't they? I was hoping I could undo things without anyone else finding out. God! I really didn't want anyone else to have to know. But when I realized I wasn't going to stay conscious, I dialed 911."

I lay there, terrified for her, terrified for us both. *Just how alike are we?*

"I was thinking about us," she said, like she'd heard my thought, "before I called for help—about all the great things we used to do together when we were little."

And all I can ever remember are our fights and frustrations.

"That's what made me realize I didn't want to die, Iris. I was thinking about you."

Lily should never have said that. It was a burden I couldn't bear.

Sometimes I wonder if, because I'm a twin, I'm less than whole. But maybe everyone feels that way. I have no way of knowing.

"What about this . . . ?" I finally asked, not quite touching the gauze on her neck. Something of the singed wing of a moth about it.

"The paramedics had to do an emergency tracheotomy because I quit breathing."

Spoken so matter-of-factly.

"Want to see?"

I shook my head, *no!*

"It's not so horrible, Ire. Just a little incision. They just made a small hole to breathe through. It wasn't so different from blowing into my flute. They already closed it surgically. They say I'll be back to myself before I know it."

Still . . . I shook my head.

"No, Lily."

I didn't want to see it. Flute or no flute . . . it was horrible.

Where she'd touched her neck, pointing to it, pain shot through me.

I hung around for the next few weeks, waiting for our family to feel normal again, trying to adjust to the whole idea and wanting to be supportive, but scared shitless the whole time. Scared she'd do it again. Scared of the medications in the cupboard, of the razor in the shower. Scared of what the therapist was telling her. Scared of being so much like her. No matter what they'd told her, none of us would return back to ourselves, not for a long, long time, and I knew it.

Hub had told me about suns imploding when their fuels run out, exploding into supernovas or collapsing into black hole vacuums, immense vortexes swallowing everything in their paths into some unknown, drifting through the universe, even through our own Milky Way, heading toward earth. And that worried me. Huge, solid things that are supposed to stay intact and in place forever, melting and blowing up and drifting around like flotsam . . .

I never did cry about it, though, because it's always, like, the more I cry, the less I do about things.

She'd left a note, "What could be more beautiful than love and death," with the word "love" crossed out. God! I understood it all too well when she told me. Not about the love part, but about death. I understood perfectly every single thing about what Lily had done, because I believe what she did is the ultimate inalienable human right. The ace up our sleeves, that's what, a way out, just in case. And that scared hell out of me, too.

So I stayed a couple of weeks, and then I went out to Arcata, where all these people were sitting in trees, way up there above the earth. I tried to explain to Hub when I left, but there was no explaining it.

When I was up in that tree with Blair, I thought about how I'd never asked Lily how she felt about being a twin. And I thought about how the mark on her neck, right there where her throat curves backward like a swan's, meant that now we could always and forever be told apart from each other.

Sixteen

Now here I am, sitting in a chair next to Henry in the clinic having the worst kind of *déjà vu.*

Mexican taxi drivers have seen it all. But the self-important little man who watched Blair carry Henry to the car like a child fallen asleep at a friend's house while his parents played cards, then opened his trunk so I could stash Henry's sax and Scrabble board, then watched in his rearview mirror as I blubbered over Henry's head in my lap while Blair trailed us, wavering radically, in the putting Vespa—that poor taxi driver must have gained a new perspective on humanity's capacity for farce.

I'm back in the *clinica,* where I thought I'd never step foot again, sitting in a chair, watching Henry sleep. *Déjà vu,* all over again. Like the song—I'm sure I read it somewhere, too.

Blair went home once everything was under control, but I told him I wanted to stay with Henry until his eyes opened.

No argument. Funny, we seem to be arguing less these days.

I pull up my chair, screeching its objections, close enough to the bed to take Henry's hand. I study the skin, grainy and sand-colored, a map of blue veins spreading across the back of his hand, bony knuckles like tree-branch joints, and I follow one long, strong finger down to the golden nail. I lift his hand to look closer. Yes, it's shiny gold. Something gold

231

in Henry comes out through his nails, flowing clear to his fingertips.

Dr. Allende slips into the room before I can replace Henry's hand and scoot my chair back.

"He's going to be all right, Miss Bloom. He was very dehydrated and had a bad reaction from the combination of the drugs and alcohol. He knows he's not supposed to drink with these drugs. I don't understand why he did this."

He checks Henry's IV.

I clear my throat. I have to do it twice.

"Do you think he did it deliberately?" I go. "Was this . . . you know . . . ?" I just can't say it out loud.

"A suicide attempt?" he finishes for me. "No. No, I don't think so. It was good you brought his medications in. We checked the dates of the prescriptions against the amounts in the vials, and it doesn't appear that he took more than his normal doses."

Watching him examine Henry's breathing like he had my knee, with a concentration like the love of a musician for his instrument, my misery floods back into the space I'd worked so hard to empty.

"It's not like Henry has no reason to be depressed, but he has always welcomed each day so greedily . . . it would be hard for me to believe."

I can feel the doctor studying me now, following with his eyes from where I hold Henry's hand to the side of my face, and everywhere his eyes travel, I can't stop a flush from following.

"Has he told you how sick he is?"

I barely shake my head.

"Maybe I shouldn't tell you—but he's a very sick man, Iris. Late stage cancer."

I start to sniffle, then laugh a little burst through it.

"And I always thought he was . . . ." ("bullshitting," I want to say) "lying . . ." (I actually say, though, because it's Dr. Allende) "about the marijuana."

The buzz of the electric clock on the wall seems awfully loud.

"How long does he have?"

"Not long. Less than a year. A matter of months, certainly." He starts toward the door, but changes his mind. "Henry is a good man, you know."

"I know."

"I mean, he's been good to many people here. Henry has done some very good things for the people of San Vaciò, for the whole community."

I didn't know.

"He hasn't really told me anything, not really. We play Scrabble and spend hours together, but we don't tell each other anything about anything. Isn't that crazy?"

"It's how people are," shrugs the doctor, like he really knows.

Here I've been thinking Henry's Timon of Athens or somebody and all the time he's Lord Jim. I laugh, small and silly.

I can feel Dr. Allende's gaze on my face the whole time.

"I think maybe you're a good person, too, Iris."

I shake my head firmly, left and right, mad because I can't stop a tear rolling down my cheek.

"Yes, I think I misjudged you."

I shake my head stronger, grimly, left, right.

"I'm sorry, Iris," he says softly. "I was angry. I thought you were maybe just another adventurous *gringa*, believing all Mexican men are faithless womanizers. But now, I don't believe you did this lightly."

He places his hand on my shoulder, and it's like a benediction.

"I'm sorry."

Then he adds, even more softly, "I could have been kinder."

The thing is, I should feel better, but I don't. I feel like a jellyfish spreading through the water, an aqueous, floating blob seeping through my own skin.

"Hasn't Henry got any chance at all?" I sniff hoarsely.

Dr. Allende pats my shoulder before taking his hand away.

"There's always a chance. People sometimes defy science, defy all the odds. But we don't count on that."

Then he lays his hand on my head, and I feel a current flowing into me.

And then he leaves the room.

It's a long wait until Henry wakes up, but I'm still there holding his hand when he does.

"Bleu?" he asks fuzzily.

"Hey, Henry. How you feeling?" I ask him.

"What the hell am I doing here? I just meant to have a good wallow in peace."

"We were worried. We couldn't wake you up."

"God, I feel like such shit."

"You deserve it."

He looks at me sitting there, then looks up at the ceiling.

He pushes back deep into the pillow. Then he rolls his head toward me, searching my face for a minute. He lifts up, straining the cords in his neck.

"Miguel told you, didn't he?"

I nod, and he throws his head back into the pillow in frustration—hard, like pitching something disgusting into the garbage.

He lies there smoldering for a minute, then, because he's Henry, he calms down and asks reasonably, "Do you think we could really talk, now, Bleu, you know, once I get out of here? Back at Cielo Azul?"

I nod again. "Sure, Henry. I think it's about time."

We look at each other.

"You first, though," I tell him.

Seventeen

"Iris," he goes.

"I'm leaving tomorrow, taking the morning bus south, Iris."

We're at El Colon. There are new hand-written menus tonight, a feature Leo decided to introduce. I notice a new entree, "Tibon Steka," and some dishes that sound distinctively Carribe, like fried bananas stuffed with cheese. Leo tells us a relative moved here from way south on the Caribbean coast to join the kitchen staff. Sometimes I think El Colon will make it just fine without any outside investment.

When he brought our menus, Leo gave me a questioning look, which Blair spotted. I signaled Leo over and whispered that I hadn't talked to my father yet. "I will, though, soon," I promised.

"What's that all about?" Blair asked.

"Nothing. Trust me, nothing."

Now he's dropped this bomb, now that we've finished eating and we're sitting here enjoying the breeze that does its part to sweep the pink-checkered marble floor clean every evening. I'm not surprised, though. I saw it coming.

"Well, *vaya con Dios*," I say, smiling as if I could care less, but I actually mean it; I just can't say it that way. "Thanks for all your help with everything—you know, my knee and Henry—everything."

We're both trying like hell to be decent about this, unemotional, to make it easier on each other.

So he says, "Take good care of Henry, huh?" Unnecessary parting advice. *De rigueur* in cases like these.

"Yeah, sure. You know I will. I'll be the daughter he never had."

"He has a daughter, you know."

"I can't believe he's told you things he hasn't told me!"

"Not all that much younger than us. That's who the empty hut's saved for."

"The one that's never occupied."

"That's right. Don't ask; I don't know all that much."

He looks like he'd already like to be halfway to Chiapas, which saddens me.

"Anyway, Iris, I don't think Henry looks at you like a daughter."

"That's exactly how he looks at me, Blair. You're fucking crazy."

Blair laughs, triggering a little warning signal in the hairs on the back of my neck, because this laugh reminds me of Mac's that day in Lily's bedroom.

"Come on, Iris! Anybody in their right mind can see Henry's in love with you!"

I'm beginning to wonder if love is just a game of musical chairs.

He laughs that arrogant laugh again, then he looks at me with a ridiculously amused expression on his mug and says, "Hey, he's not *that* old, you know.

"Why do you think he got so plastered, huh? He knows you'll be leaving soon, right? Figure it out."

"It just could be, Blair, the fact that he's terminally ill is more devastating to him than my leaving."

"Open your eyes. Just look at the timing, Iris."

"You've made your point," I growl. "Let's drop it, okay? Let's not get into it. Let's talk about something else, okay?"

No one ever takes that kind of suggestion gracefully, though, so we both sulk awhile.

Finally he says, "Look, I'm taking the camera with me, but I'll leave you the papers to the Vespa. When you leave, give them to Leo, like I promised, all right?"

I nod, starting to feel miserable.

"Okay?" he asks me, ducking down to get my attention. "I'm sure Henry'll let you drive that heap of his."

"Okay?" he says again when I don't move. So I nod my head and finally I look up at him. Really look.

"Hey you," I go. "I care about you. Be careful, Blair, okay? Go easy, for once."

I search his face, looking closely for once, committing it to memory, because I know it won't be there tomorrow. I'm going to miss the freckles along the bridge of his nose, the mole that causes him so much trouble when he shaves, all that smug confidence of his. What kind of king will he make?

"And please," I say, begging shamelessly for once, because there's no reason not to anymore, "please, stay in touch with me."

He takes my hand. "I will, baby."

He turns it over and kisses my palm. "I love you, you know, Iris."

And, for once, I believe him.

I really do.

That night I dream I'm way up in the air standing alone on the wings of a plane, holding my saddle in front of me, with nothing to support me. All around me are other circling planes with people doing the same thing. As the plane descends, I struggle to keep my balance, while others begin top-

pling off, falling from high up, shrinking to specks, smacking into the ground on their backs. I feel angry that the people in charge haven't thought of some way to support and protect us out there on our wings. Fighting to stay on, I feel seasick from the plane's swaying. Finally, with only forty feet left to descend, I realize I'm going to fall. My knees buckle, and, like the others, I fall backward, the ground flying up at me. I land safely on my feet, still holding my saddle in front of me, the seasickness disappearing the instant my feet touch the ground.

Blair's gone, and now I don't feel I can stay at Cielo Azul much longer.

"Does Cielo Azul mean 'Blue Heaven' or 'Blue Sky?' " I ask Henry. "It makes a big difference, you know."

We're at our Scrabble again, because it's our forum. If we're going to talk, this is our agora.

"Dunno. You decide. Take your pick."

"You said you'd talk to me, Henry." *J'accuse.*

"And I meant it. Ask away, Bleu, anything but the meaning of Cielo Azul."

"All right then—level with me—the booze and pills. Were you trying to . . . ?" I still can't say it.

"Do myself in? Is that what you believe? God, no! I told you, I just gave in to a bit of self-pity, that's all, a little harmless baptism of my sorrow."

"Cross your heart?"

"Oh, so you believe I have one, do you?

"If you're not going to take my word, Bleu, believe what you want."

"So then, it's death you're escaping down here, isn't it?"

Henry looks up over his sharp nose. "My, my, Bleu. Go right for the jugular, huh?"

Looking back down at the board, he sighs. "No. You've got it all wrong, as usual." He doesn't say this meanly, though.

"There's no escaping death, of course; I'd never be so foolish as to try something like that." He looks up again and raises his brows. "That's not to say that I don't prefer the kind of death I'll have here to the dry, sanitized, institutional methods of dying in the good ole U.S. of A. At least here, I'll have some control over how I go.

"Don't you think it appropriate that I wanted to be in the Tropic of Cancer, Bleu?" he smiles snidely.

"Not funny, Henry. Rotten graveyard humor."

"Bet that expression comes from Shakespeare's grave diggers."

"So, what then?"

"What 'what'?"

"What the hell are you escaping down here, Henry?" Shit! Now I've gone and raised my voice at him, something I told myself I wouldn't do anymore.

"Oh, yes. That."

"You did agree to go first."

"Need a refresher there, Iris?" He peers over at my glass.

"I'm fine."

"Okay. Well. If you really must have some kind of horrible confession, then . . . I see you've braced yourself."

I've done nothing of the sort.

"I suppose I did promise, didn't I? Nothing like taking advantage of a man when he's down."

"Henry . . . !"

"Okay. What I'm escaping from. Ahem. Here it is, then. Very awkward, though. Hmm. Let's see. Mmmm . . ." Delaying, as only Henry can.

"Let's put it this way. Yes, that'll work. Y'see, Iris of the

Bleu Persuasion . . ." finally he spills it, ". . . my early retirement wasn't completely voluntary, to tell the precise truth."

Now we're at the crux of things, so I'm careful not to interrupt in any way. The crux is such a delicate place to be. *Poof!*
And it's gone.

"Actually, Bleu," he exhales another long sigh, "actually,
they requested that I leave permanently because I'd cost
them too much money." He sips his water. Dr. Allende made
him promise no alcohol.

"I'd become too costly, you see. There was this little
matter of a sexual harassment suit. Actually, to be exact,
there were two harassment suits." He looks at me to see how
shocked I am, but I've made my face a blank.

"You'd have made an excellent poker player, Bleu."

Another sigh, big, tragic, almost whistling. "Anyway, the
first I had coming. I was quite smitten with a grad student,
and I made several passes at her. Then, when she didn't respond, I made her life rather miserable, I admit. I blackmailed her, held her master's degree hostage, until she filed a
complaint. I acted horribly."

I can tell he'd like me to forgive him for the whole thing.
Like it's up to me.

"I couldn't stop myself, you see.

"The second complaint, I didn't deserve, I swear. It was
that era, you know, when there was an epidemic of sexual harassment suits in campuses all across the country. A student
blackmailed me; call it a case of classic karmic payback. I had
it coming; that's why I didn't fight it. She didn't like the grade
I gave her, so made an accusation. Strike two!

"Truth is, I was sick of teaching anyway. It was the era of
political correctness, and that ruined teaching for me. P.C.
was the death of free discussion." Henry makes a slight detour. "My God! In the early seventies professors had to be

dead honest, had to answer for everything they did. We called them on every word, every thought in their heads, all their cherished views. We overturned all their fossilized methods. It must've been a great time to be teaching, the seventies! But when political correctness became standard issue, we all became bored to death with each other again. No one would volunteer a word from that day forth. There was nothing but total apathy in the classroom again. Looking out, you saw apathy sitting in every seat.

"All the great upheaval of the seventies—Vietnam, civil rights, women's lib—it all subsided and campus life began a long, slow slide to where it is today, a twenty-some-percent voter turnout and eighty-percent approval rating for this ghastly current administration.

"Anyway, I was ready to go, so when the school made me a nice severance offer to get rid of me quickly, I went quietly. I can't complain, you know. I never have complained, actually. But it did ruin my family."

His face drops. "My wife and I had already split up years before all of this and were sharing custody of my daughter. But after the incident, Noelle refused to see me anymore. She was a preteen, you know. Pretending she didn't know her parents anyway. Now she didn't have to pretend with me anymore.

"I hung around, trying to redeem myself somehow, drifting up and down the coast playing jazz clubs, but when I was diagnosed, I eventually decided to leave. Cheaper medicine down here. Other reasons, too. So, I left. End of story."

He heaves a sigh. "It's all a moot point now, anyway." He looks down at the board with a blank stare, then glances up. "Your turn, Bleu."

I'm thinking he wants me to tell him what I'm escaping, but then he tilts his head at the board.

I look at the same tiles that have been there for half an hour and try to come up with a stellar word. Stellar is tough, though, when your heart just isn't in it.

Besides, Henry pipes up with an addendum. "I'll tell you something else you ought to know, now that Blair's gone. If you're interested, that is. A little lagniappe for you. Two for the price of one. Buy one, get one free."

I go ahead and lay down the word "elude."

"Shoot!" I say, but Henry thinks I'm commenting on my play, so I have to rephrase. "I'm interested. Whatever you have to say, I'm interested, Henry."

"There's a reason Blair wouldn't go back, you know."

Oh yeah, I'm definitely interested in this.

"I figured, but I didn't push it because he didn't want to tell me."

"You're too easy, Bleu."

"Too cowardly, you mean."

"Yup. Fatally flawed."

"I know. What'd he do, Henry?"

"Cal spilled it one night. He was terrible at keeping his mouth shut if you poured him a couple of Scotches, you know."

"I'm figuring that out."

"He told me he and Blair were in on a couple of 'actions,' as he called them, while they were in California. They did sound awfully nefarious, too, these 'actions.' "

"Come on, Henry!"

God! You'd think he'd be in more of a hurry, considering.

"There was something about torching a large quantity of SUVs in Eugene, and a failed attempt at blowing up an oil tank or setting fire to an oil company, or some such thing that would've made an awful bang."

"Oh my God!" Not Hal. Hotspur!

243

I feel as if Henry has just yanked me right out of my skin. *Sure!* My ignorance crashes like a line of dominos. No wonder the sudden exodus to Mexico!

Two of the more radical "anarchists" living with Cal had been busted. And Henry's right about the details. They had set fire to an entire fleet of new SUVs in the early morning hours. The authorities claimed a million dollars' worth of damage was done. They were also charged with attempted arson at a Eugene oil company . . . charges they denied. When the sentencing was made public, Cal and Blair freaked. "Dirt" was sentenced to twenty-three years in prison, and "Wolf" to eight. It was an astonishingly harsh sentence that blew all our minds, so I didn't wonder at Cal's and Blair's reactions. It wasn't long after that Cal split, with the understanding that Blair would wait a few weeks, then follow. And me, little Miss Muffet, I thought they were just taking off on a legit surfing vacation!

"So, you see why I wasn't too optimistic about Blair's prognosis for 'doing good,' Iris. I'm sorry I didn't feel I could tell you at that point. Maybe I shouldn't be telling you now. But, there's a nasty little twist to the tale that Cal told me that I think you should know about.

"He said a firefighter was injured trying to douse the SUVs. Cal was quite upset about it, because they'd never planned to hurt anybody. What disturbed him, especially in view of the experience he'd just had nearly drowning in the surf, was that Blair never expressed any regrets whatsoever about the poor bastard who got in the way of their pyrotechnics."

For godssake, when Henry comes clean, he rocks! And I know, without ever having to ask Blair, it's all true. No need to ask.

"I take it you had no idea." All he has to do is look at my

face. "I didn't think you did."

"How could I be so stupid?" Asking myself, really, but I say it out loud.

"You didn't see it in him?"

I'm trying to explain it to myself as much as Henry, I realize.

"No. I mean, I knew he had a wild streak and liked a little vicarious danger, but he didn't seem any different from the rest of us living at Treetops. We were all doing what we did out of respect for life. We were all non-violent pacifists."

"Nothing at all? No signs? No indicators?"

"Well, I knew he'd become discouraged with using official means. He had tried the whole official route, you know, but got more and more discouraged. He'd originally worked with a bona fide consumer advocate group, some Nader thing, but he was half done-in from it, from spending a year of his life trying to expand Oregon's bottle bill. Maybe you remember it? 'The Snapple bill'? You know. The beverage industry slammed the group with misleading ads, and broke the bill's back. I know Blair felt totally compromised by the whole experience."

My head feels like a war zone.

"Still, that doesn't really seem enough."

"Wait!" I hold up a finger like I'm trying to shush time and space. "Just a minute!"

I jump up and bang through the screen door both ways, running to and from my hut, returning waving a clipping wildly like I'm flagging a train.

"Here, you want me to read it, or you want to read it yourself?"

"Crap! What happened to my reading glasses?" he says, dithering and fussing through his pile of clutter, the light blooming a roan halo on his hair.

Still panting for breath, I can't be bothered waiting for Henry to hunt down his specs.

"Here. Never mind, Henry."

I read:

Blair Jaeger, a 25-year-old protester who stormed into a Portland department store and spray-painted clothing, pleaded guilty Monday to one felony count and one misdemeanor count of criminal mischief.

District Judge, blah, blah, sentenced Jaeger to a two-year deferred judgment on the felony and probation for the misdemeanor.

If Jaeger stays out of trouble, the felony conviction will be dismissed in two years.

Jaeger was one of four protesters to enter the store as part of a nationwide protest against the department chain. The protesters said the retail chain was buying clothing made in Nicaraguan sweatshops.

As part of their investigation, police searched the offices of the Arcata Justice and Peace Committee, seizing membership lists and other materials. That led the American Civil Liberties Union to sue Arcata for allegedly keeping "spy files" on citizens in violation of policy. The lawsuit is pending.

Jaeger spent six months in jail for contempt after refusing to name the other protesters. They later came forward and their cases are pending.

I look up and wait expectantly.

"I see," he goes, rubbing his jaw.

"See? Not so black and white, after all, is it, Henry?"

"I never said he was all bad. He is very rash, though, you have to admit, Bleu."

"Yeah, well. Like, we don't all have the advantage of your age, your admirable restraint, your impeccable judgment, Henry."

"Ouch! You can sting, can't you, Bleu? But I deserve that."

"Fuck, Henry, we've all got something coming to us. Forget it. Forget I said that. I'm a fine one to talk."

The night feels as damp as a snail's bed, and me, I still have miles to go. So I haul out my stagnant archives and tell him all about how I ran out on Lily, baring my shame-wounded soul while the moon drags the tide. And the telling is a milestone—he's the first outside of Hub to hear it from me.

This is the second game we won't finish. We both sit there, mute, like lumps of laundry, listening to the waves lapping, watching the coils of orbiting moths while the palm trees shiver outside the window. I put my head down on my arms, like I could be bowing to the Scrabble gods.

I'd like to hang onto this silence. It's a lovely, weighty silence; one that feels like breaking it would be something cataclysmic. But there are things to say.

"I know my poor father thinks Lily and I have fallen through the cracks."

I look into Henry's eyes, pale as ice, dark chinks in them like shadows in woods.

"Don't you think it's too early to tell, though, Henry?"

"I don't know, Bleu."

That's not the answer I wanted.

"Anyone and everyone can fall through the cracks," he says, "just because there are so many. Like Everest, just because they're there."

"You think Hillary ever actually said that?"

"Why on earth not?"

When I stir to go, Henry cracks his knuckles.

"You could stay here, Iris."

Not "Bleu," but "Iris." I don't answer because I don't get his drift.

"Why do you have to go anywhere? Couldn't you just stay here in San Vaciò?" His eyes like a rabbit's.

But, I don't know, I don't think he actually expected an answer. I really don't.

Eighteen

Dear Iris with the Ambrosial Eyes. Remember when your father used to call you that? You always pretended to hate it. But you are ambrosial, my love, for sending Lily the wooden flute. You know she hadn't touched her flute since coming home. But she laid that flute you sent her on the nightstand next to her bed. Then she began holding it and holding it, even while she slept. Do you know how wonderful it is to hear her play again? Of course you know! You always see everything, don't you? You feel everything Lily does—I think you feel everything that happens in the whole wide world. I know that's why you're hiding out down there in the jungle. And don't think for a second I'm scolding you! I understand, Chicken Little, believe me. I would hide too, if I could, if I were your age, if she were my twin instead of my daughter. Besides, I could never scold you when I can hear Lily playing in the next room. A wooden flute sounds like something straight out of heaven, don't you think?

But listen, there's something I need to tell you in person, so could you please telephone this evening? Don't worry! Everyone in the family is all right, I promise. Lily is fine. But there's something you should hear direct from us, so please call, okay?

Mama never refers to the suicide attempt directly.

They all think I see everything.

I wonder if they really know just how much I see.

I see Lily sitting in a booth across from me, telling me about all her dreams for the future. She's eating pizza, a long string of cheese dangling from her chin like a goatee. She laughs and catches the end of it with her finger and loops it back up onto her tongue, sucking in air, *ooh! ooh!* because it's burning hot.

I see Mama bottle-feeding four abandoned kittens, holding them in a towel on her lap while she watches evening TV. Crying inconsolably when one of them didn't survive. How the last one living, a gray tabby, still begs to be in her lap now, too old to jump up uninvited anymore. I see her interest in jars of butterfly cocoons and ant farms outlasting ours. How her eyes melted in disappointment when we argued.

Daddy, rigging our fishing poles and baiting our hooks for us when we were little. Un-snagging our lines, over and over; not getting to fish himself at all. Carrying us back to the car by lantern light. Grease-painting hobo faces on us at Halloween. Reaching over the arm of his recliner to put his reading glasses on the sleeping dog's nose.

I wonder if they know how much I see.

I keep the record straight.

The sound of Mama's voice completely shatters me when I call home that evening, but I wouldn't let her know for anything.

We go through all the typical ceremonial chit-chat to get to the crucial message, everything carefully coded, meted out in a certain order, delivered with feigned lightheartedness, me, sitting there twirling a strand of my hair around my finger. Killing time. When we've gone through the whole ritual, she shifts into the necessary voice and drops the bomb.

"Mac is dead, Iris."

"Oh my God!" I know I should feel for Mac, but, without even thinking, I nearly shout it out, "Is Lily all right?"

"She's all right, Iris." Mama musters every iota of firmness she's capable of, "I swear."

But all the terror has flooded back. "You don't think she'd do anything . . . ?"

I can't speak directly about it either.

"No, I don't, Iris. I think she's coping well, I really do. She wants to talk to you."

She sounds so calm, my Mamarova. That's reassuring. Mama never could hide anything, after all.

"God. Mac, dead. What . . ."

"He fell out of a window in some awful neighborhood in San Francisco."

I have an image—a body falling, splintered glass.

I saw a wild goose shot out of the sky one December afternoon, back home in Colorado. Flying along so innocently, all of a sudden its flight interrupted from out of nowhere, the big body flopping down in a spiral, helixing down, its great wings useless, smacking into the dirt. A sudden, thudding, final ending to its own grand design. I hated having to see that. I remember wishing I could erase it from my mind at the time. And now, I don't want to watch this movie ever again, *never* again, so I just block it out, forever and ever, amen.

The thing is, too, at the same time I'm wondering if San Francisco has any "awful" neighborhoods.

I don't know what's wrong with me, even thinking something like that, something too frivolous to utter. The perfect emotional escape hatch, I guess. The crummy human condition. Anyway, beyond my control. Someday maybe I'll be able to pretend thoughts like these don't exist.

"He fell?" I'm remembering exactly how athletic he was.

There's a pause at the other end. "They don't know, actually, whether he fell or was pushed."

"Drugs?"

"They're nearly certain it was. It had to be, didn't it?"

A horrible end, no matter how I felt about him.

"Let me talk to Lily now, okay?"

Lily and I don't really sound alike, I don't care what anyone says. Her voice is softer than mine, almost velvety, and vulnerable, which, believe me, is painful to hear right now.

"Is that you, Iris?"

She sounds breathless, but it could just be from running to the phone.

I hear the delayed click of Mama hanging up, a reluctant echoing non-sound. It strikes me that Lily is probably talking from her own bedroom.

"Lily!" I can't stop myself from wailing. "Are you all right?" I'm scared for her, but I don't want her to know, not for anything in the world, so I try to make myself sound calmer.

"No. But I'm going to be all right." There's something so solid in the way she says it, the terror inside me damps down to nothing, and I believe her, completely.

We two are speaking in codes, dualing-dueling, but even so, we always understand each other perfectly, no matter that our conversations are so often inversions of each other's—so she knows I'm scared for her, and I know she's telling me the truth.

"You know I couldn't stand him, Lil, but, even so, I'm so sorry, that's all I'm saying. I'm sorry."

Somehow, I don't know what happened exactly, but I don't catch most of what she says next, about how she feels about Mac's death. I hadn't the faintest idea, but I swear I'd die before I'd ask her to repeat it.

Oh God, what's wrong with me? How and why did I miss this, of all things?

All I hear is the ending, ". . . no more pain."

It's like we're at cross-purposes, my consolation and her reassurances.

Then she says, "Things are no good around here, Iris. Mama creeps around, sneaking up to peek in on me sixty times a day, and Dad sits around in his knickers half the morning watching the golf channel."

"But he doesn't even play golf."

"That's what I'm telling you. It's terrible around here. Something's got to give."

She's just trying to make me laugh, and it works. But then when it ends, an embarrassing silence hangs between us.

"There's something I didn't tell you about that night, Iris."

She doesn't sound quite ready to tell me even now (I can almost hear her brows furrowing), but then she does it anyway.

"The trouble is, I don't know how you'll take this. I don't want you to think I'm crazy."

"Oh, Lily . . ."

"No, really. It's just that . . .

"I swear I saw something that night, right before I passed out." She exhales shakily. But I hear it loud and clear through all the longitude between us.

"I saw this light and heard a voice. Don't think I'm crazy. I know, I know, people will just think I was hallucinating, but it was clearer than your voice is now, Iris."

I stay mum because anything I could say would be all wrong.

"The voice asked me what I'd done—not scolding or anything, though—kind and gentle, like, 'What have you done?' And then it told me I was loved." Her own voice is cautious and quiet now.

Great! Something else that'll remain unique to Lily, something else invisible that we won't have in common!

I mean, for me it's like, "God: Address Unknown."

But maybe . . . maybe like Polydeuces, Lily will share her immortality with me.

"Oh, Lily," I tell her, "you *are* loved."

She ignores that as a non-sequitur.

"No, no, don't stop me, Iris. I have to finish telling you.

"There was this rush of reassurance! I felt so secure . . ." Her voice drops an octave. "I'll never hurt myself again, Iris, not for anything. Not for anyone."

So Lily will have her full share, too, and we can stop measuring, always measuring.

Then she says, in the voice I've known since that private feral language of the womb, "You don't have to be scared of me anymore, Ire. Please come home."

I cough away from the receiver, but it's no use. I know I can't hide from Lily anymore. So she hears my voice as it really is, scalding and curdling, struggling to answer. Because there's something I want to tell her through my crying—something I've been thinking and thinking about for weeks, an idea that's been blooming in my head, spreading like waves crossing the ocean.

Nineteen

A blank tile supercedes all tiles.

There's just enough red to it, the way Henry's hair flames up in the light, it could go either way, halo or horns. So, which is he, angel or devil? We've finished our meal and his smokes are coiling up around him like a viper, but it could be like a magic act, too, like smoke and mirrors. Then too, it's like maybe a divine revelation is about to happen, and Henry's the apparition. Henry—elusive as always. Or is it my own mind that's so vaporous? Maybe it's only the trickery of night, or of San Vaciò, or maybe it's reality as a whole.

No importa.

Anything could happen. Tonight is my birthday. That is, today is our birthday, Lily's and mine. And Henry's! Strangely enough, unless he's fibbing, Henry claims to be our triplet; what with Rose, our quadruplet (so, I guess with Daryl Hannah, that makes five of us). Synchronism. I'm just saying.

It doesn't really matter about birth dates, anyway, except when you're twins.

Henry made a big deal out of it, though, beyond all my expectations.

"Come to dinner," he said.

"What? You cook? And what about cockroaches?"

255

Then it was so fine, I'm ashamed I gave him such a hard time.

There's something so touching in all the extra touches. Very nice, cool jazz curling up like incense from some hidden corner—a first, because I didn't even know Henry owned a sound system. I had begun to think Henry was some sort of music anchorite. He'd cleaned the place up and put a checkered tablecloth on the table and even garnished it with one of those Chianti bottles with the globby wax half picked off. The plates matched and the silverware was done properly, right down to napkins under the knives and spoons. Paper, okay, but who cares anyway?

I felt like a cat being stroked. Most birthdays are doomed to disappointment, especially mine, always shared with somebody else.

"I shouldn't have doubted you," I tell him.

"You shouldn't have."

"How come you only agree with me when I'm wrong?"

"Still."

"All right, so I already admitted it. You never cease to amaze me. No kidding."

"Ah, well. Now you're blowing smoke up my ass."

"Hah! Why on earth would I do such a thing?"

"Ease the pain of defeat."

That's because he's challenged me to a birthday match.

"What do you say, Bleu? Winner takes all tonight. Scrabble Championship of the World. What do you say?"

Henry looks quite dashing, auspicious, even. He seems to have had his hair cut especially for the occasion, and by a proper barber, too. This is definitely an improvement over his usual (I've suspected him of cutting his own using a very dull pair of scissors). He had a shave, too, so I scrubbed my hand on his cheek when I stepped into the porch, just to take advantage of something I may never see or feel again.

He's put on a white long-sleeved dress shirt with the collar open, without rolling up the sleeves for once. It looks suspiciously new. No knobby knees tonight, either, because he's wearing a pair of dark slacks. Also a pair of sandals, which suit him fine because his feet, like his hands, have character—thin and bony, classy, with narrow greyhound ankles and highbrow arches.

"I like your sandals," I tell him. "Matter of fact, everything is nice. You look nice."

There even seems less slump to him. I give him a little peck on his cheek, just a little sequin of a kiss as distraction, so he needn't feel he has to reciprocate my compliment, since I haven't dressed for the occasion. I'm my normal, sloppy self.

I did bake a coconut cake, though, as close as I could get to a Hawaiian Haupia cake, which I consider the pinnacle of all cakedom.

"So you want some dessert?" he asks me now.

"I couldn't. I'm stuffed. Besides, that's for you."

"You don't expect me to eat the whole thing myself?"

"I do."

"I know!" he says after a moment's thought, "I'll divvy it up and freeze it."

"There you go."

"You'll break down, anyway. You can't resist. I know you."

"You don't know squat."

With unctuous ceremony, he puts it away for later, leering like The Big Bad Wolf.

He won't let me help clear the dishes, either.

"They can wait for tomorrow when it's not our birthdays," he tells me, then stashes them all out of sight down in the sink when I can't stop eyeing the stack.

"You're so compulsive, Bleu," he says. But that's not true.

"There!" he says, dusting off his hands. "That takes care of that."

The night engulfs us as we settle down to our game.

Then, for some reason, maybe some bizarre confluence of the stars, it actually happens. The championship of the world. I knew anything could happen; I felt it in my bones.

The battle is ferocious, Henry and I taking no prisoners, alone in our pool of light, cheered on by frantic insects pressing in on us against the screens like they're boxing-ring ropes. We've told each other everything there is to tell by now, so there are no more conversational interruptions, no emotional distractions, no game-playing beyond the match at hand. Nothing in the world but a blank, fallow space waiting for us to play God—to create language and declare it good, Henry and I the first explorers of a whole new world, assigning names to everything.

And then, I don't know how it happens, tonight Henry is absolutely undisputed captain of the expedition, leading from the push-off, even winning the draw to see who goes first with a blank tile, because a blank tile supercedes all other tiles in this case.

"What a lucky dog you are."

I despise whining, but there I go.

"This has got to stop!" I say, definitely whimpering.

But . . . I mean . . . his words! In Scrabble, strategy forces you to go for score rather than originality, which means smart play isn't always the glitziest, so in Scrabble, like life, artistry is quashed by rules.

But Henry is dazzling tonight, soaring. His words shining. "Abjure," "elegy," "Pelagic!" "Divine," "rapier," "ecstasy," "defy."

"Where are you getting these?" I ask cravenly.

Plus, he's winning.

I can't remember—did the Romans assimilate their conquered?

"I don't like this one bit. This is a scorched-earth policy, Henry. You're leaving me with nothing, absolutely nothing."

No openings, no possibilities, no comparables. Henry, intimidating, humiliating, pillaging, all but raping. It's a Scrabble Blitzkrieg.

I rub my aching temples.

"Need a break?" he asks, all sympathy.

No response.

"Seriously," he says.

"I'm fine," I go.

"Okay, then. Have it your way."

By the time we're down to the last draw of tiles, I'm studying Henry with new eyes. The score is close, not accurately reflecting his play's superiority. For my big finale I try making the most of my last tiles by playing one letter very cagily for a high count, which squeaks me out into the lead.

"Hah! Take that you villain! Go ahead, do your worst."

I had to go and say that.

Now, the thing is, truthfully, I've never considered Henry to have a poker face. I have always and forever been able to tell when he has something up his sleeve. But, coolly, blank-faced and without his usual delay, he picks up tile after tile out of his rack and places them in the upper right corner of the board. Building backwards, just to keep me guessing I suppose, he starts from the first letter of an existing word, an "s."

"No one builds a word backwards!" I gripe. "That's downright dyslexic, Henry."

His rack is sitting there as empty as the Gobi desert: "l-a-z-t-e-blank-q."

With something of a satiated crocodile in his expression, he begins counting: "Let's see, now . . . the 'z,' that's worth ten, then landing on a double letter score equals twenty, plus seven, eight, blah-blah; tripled because of the triple word score; plus the score of the word I added onto. Oh, and plus another fifty points for using all my tiles."

Then, sitting there looking at his bloody masterpiece, he finally crows triumphantly, "Quetzals!"

And then, just because he's Henry, he looks up at me sheepishly and adds a little explanatory footnote to save me face.

"See, I needed a 'u,' but they'd all been played, so my only hope was to draw that last blank, and what do you think I got for my final draw? Pure, unadulterated luck, Bleu."

So Henry's first and last draws of the game were both blanks.

I'm speechless. It needs no answer, anyway. It was inevitable, wasn't it? You can't fight something like divine intervention. I'm wiped out.

Henry went out big!

His face is a mask of complete innocence, but something has to be said.

I lean back, staring at the board like I still can't believe it, then I look up as Henry makes a move to scoop up the tiles.

"Leave 'em be, Henry. I want to look a minute."

He withdraws his hands obediently, and I sit there re-reading all of his glorious plays.

"That was an amazing game," I say.

Then, sitting there, staring straight at me in all seriousness, he blindsides me.

"You let me win, didn't you, Bleu? For my birthday . . . you let me beat you."

"Oh for . . . don't be fucking ridiculous, Henry! Where do

you get that? Besides, it's both our birthdays. Don't be an idiot. You just played the most fantastic game of Scrabble I've ever seen."

I'm feeling a little giddy. I can't seem to think straight. Henry also seems very mellow tonight, though that could be accounted for by what he's smoking. It could just be I'm affected by my own serendipity, though. Maybe Henry's apparent bliss is only my own interpolation, a misconception, or maybe a case of osmosis. Maybe it's just because it's our birthdays.

"You sure you didn't let me win, Bleu?"

He's beginning to irritate me.

"Let up, Henry."

But he doesn't.

"—Like a mercy fuck?"

A squawk escapes, like from a startled parrot, as I'm seized with laughing mania, which Henry also catches by osmosis, until we're howling a hooting duet.

"You're crazy. You've got to be kidding! What swill!" I gasp, and we explode again, bound hand and foot by our mad dog hysteria, shrieking at the joke of our existence until there's nothing left.

It takes a long time for all the silliness to trickle out. When it does, it leaves an awful silence.

Finally, Henry starts picking at the damned lint on the cushion. Without looking up, talking into the stupid cushion, he says, "I've got a coupla presents for you, Bleu."

Ah, Henry.

"Me too," I go.

"You first, though," I say, because, I don't know, I just always have to make Henry go first.

So he disappears into his tiny hole of an office, like a wading bird the way he dabs each foot in front of the other. I don't even hear him come back, but there he stands, poking an envelope at me, silhouetted in the light. He thinks his face is blank, but he's obviously bursting with suspense.

"What's this?" The old ritual.

"Go on, open it!"

Open, open.

"But, what is it?"

"It's the deed to Cielo Azul."

"I can see that."

I mean, I'm looking right at the bloody thing.

"It's yours, Bleu. Happy birthday." He smiles this sickly little smile, childishly shy because he knows how large this is, his eyes so filled with little truant fantasies, I can't look.

"Oh, don't be ridiculous, Henry. You know I can't take this."

"I'm completely serious, Bleu. I want to give it to you. I've got no one else to leave it to. My daughter obviously doesn't intend to reconcile with me, no matter what. And you love it so."

Me and my transparency. It's true, I love Cielo Azul. I love San Vaciò. I didn't mean to, but it grew on me in spite of itself, in spite of myself, and I couldn't stop falling in love with it any more than with Dr. Allende.

I love it. Mexico, all of it, awful and irresistible. Wearing its heart on its sleeve, living publicly in every alley and street, baring its wounds shamelessly, pissing itself in its streets. Piety and cruelty its twin personalities throughout its history. Mexico, like a delicate, shimmering hummingbird feeding on carrion, and I can't help but love it anyway.

The thing is, you don't get to choose who you love or where you belong.

But still, I can't accept this gift from Henry, and he knows it.

"I've had it signed over to you in the event of my death, Bleu. All you have to do is see my lawyer."

I shake my head, but his gaze is so strong.

The bugs slice through the dark.

"It's all in place for you. You can decide what to do with it. Donate it to the city as a park, if you don't want it. But it's yours when I go."

His rug of hair is glowing like a tiara in the stele of lamplight.

I can't budge. I feel as stuck as the limpets out on the tidepool rocks. A gecko climbs up the screen in front of me, hanging on with its spatulate fingers, then drops out of sight when it can't keep a grip.

"I know, I know," Henry says. "You don't accept, but you've got no choice. Look at it this way, Bleu, with Cielo Azul, you'll never end up homeless, even if you should fall through the cracks."

He's making me feel like shit. This gift is more work than fun for Henry, but I guess he expected that.

"Anyway," he sighs, "as a contingency plan, I have something else for you. Something you can't refuse."

Reaching behind his pile of precious junk, he produces his saxophone, glittering like the sun with its own interior light source.

"Henry!"

He wets the mouthpiece and plays a couple of bars, hokey, very corny. "Mister Sandman, send me a dream . . ."

I shoot him a look.

"I'm clairvoyant," he grins.

"Everyone sees through me."

Then, without fanfare or introduction, without missing a beat, he closes his eyes and dissolves into the blues, making love to that mouthpiece, biting it gently with his wolf's teeth, sending through it his life's breath in a long, cool sobbing that pulls like wind through a cemetery.

Stop! Please Henry, you're torturing me.

It's as if my vertebrae are the finger keys. He's in another dimension, though. I know if I touched him, he wouldn't feel it, but oh God I'm feeling it . . . *I don't want to do this.*

"Don't cry, Iris."

He lays the sax across his lap, gently, like a sleeping child.

"I didn't mean to make you cry."

God, I hate crying in front of people! "Are you happy now?"

"Now you see why I don't play anymore."

And I do. I finally get it. I wave my hand at the still-echoing tune like I'm trying to catch the trailing tail of the notes that just ran me over. Might as well try to catch the breeze of a passing train.

"What was that?"

"Billie Holiday. 'Blue Monday.' "

"It's the saddest damned thing I ever heard."

"Yeh. You and everyone else. It was illegal to air that tune during the Depression, you know. Too many people jumped off window ledges."

"So, *why* . . . ?"

"Something superlative for your birthday, Bleu. The only thing, really, no matter what."

He exposes his snaggle tusks in a smile.

"You're a strange one, Bleu. You'd think a girl with such a floriferous name would realize the sting of the bee is part of the honey."

Henry lowers the sax into its case like he's laying something sacred into a sarcophagus.

"You won't stop playing?"

He shakes his head.

"You amaze me, you know that?"

"You too." And that's as close as we've ever come.

Then he has to go and ruin it.

"Stay with me, Bleu. Don't go." His eyes cut into me like scissors. "I'll pay you to stay. Or you can do a few chores to earn your keep, if you really feel you have to."

Wrapping his arms around the case, he pulls it up against his chest, then, his face changing shape like a sand dune in wind, he shoves the case between us.

"You know I'm not making a sexual offer. I already told you all about that, how it bends in the middle."

I choke out a laugh in spite of myself, and Henry sputters a few sick clucks himself.

"Don't, Henry. You don't have to . . ."

Then he goes all deadly serious.

"I repent my sins, you know."

Like I'm his confessor.

"Stay, Bleu," he says, his voice faltering. "I don't want to be alone." The plea so destitute a lamentation it stops our laughing dead in its tracks.

Oh, the fugitive look he gives me! I could bury my face in that look.

"Sure," he says, "I could hire someone from the village, but I want someone who cares about me."

Then he leans toward me, his hands on his knees, his nails like polished agates against his dark slacks. Taking one of my hands, he presses it against his cheek. *Ah, so that's why he shaved.* Feeling my life pulse, he holds it there for a long time, too long, like when he kept us in suspense about renting Cielo Azul to us, like that time he pointed out Gemini to me in the night sky. Then, reluctantly, he finally lets it drop.

"You do, don't you, Bleu . . . ?"

His pale eyes, bottomless as the jaguar's pool, flicker in

265

the light, seeping utter loneliness.

". . . care about me."

The thing is, there aren't answers for everything, and there are exact answers for almost nothing. I used to think there were. I thought for a long time that science would solve all the world's problems with perfect, tidy little answers. It's funny, though, I never thought God would, not even when I was little.

And then, there are so many answers I'm afraid to face. Henry and I have kept such a safe distance between us—the span of a Scrabble board, to be exact. Our relationship has been through letters arranged on a board, a pen pal correspondence, for all that we've been within such close physical reach of each other the whole time.

Then too, so much can't be defined. It seems there are as many shades of love as shadows of the sun.

But, as for staying on at Cielo Azul . . . that answer has been there buried all along, fermenting, slowly percolating to the surface.

"I'm not going, Henry."

I hadn't known.

"Don't even worry about it, because I'm not planning on leaving. I'll stay as long as it takes." Something inside forces another little grating laugh.

"Who knows, I may stay forever."

Henry sits there as still as the shadows pooled in the light.

"And forget paying me." He starts to object. "Yeah, just forget it, Henry. I can make it on my own. I've had an offer from the banana girls, you know. Or maybe Rita could use my help part-time or something. God, local wages! Taking a job away from a local! Anyhow, I'll figure a way.

"Don't worry about it," I tell him. And I will. I'll figure something out. I have to.

So there's my real birthday present for Henry, something I hadn't planned, hadn't even known was mine to give. Serenity. It alters his features gradually, flooding his face like water slowly filling a cistern to the rim. And I remember from somewhere way back the words, *a peace which surpasseth all understanding,* or something like that. Something else superlative.

"I knew you would, Bleu. Someone with so much compassion for a tree . . ." he says, which makes us both smirk.

As if a few birthday presents could make everything right with the world . . .

I force myself to sound cheery. "My turn!"

"Cover your eyes," I tell him, bossy so he'll actually cooperate, then, the deed accomplished, "Okay!" I call out, presenting myself in the spotlight, twirling around, light as air in front of him. Me, Miss Tall and Bony, light as air, *"Ta-dah!"*

But Henry doesn't get it, so I have to repeat the whole routine, all wooden now.

"Henry! Don't you notice anything?"

Mr. Completely Blank.

"I took it out, just for you!"

Still nothing. *Clunk!*

Can this be the same man who turned a Scrabble match into a quetzal bird?

"My eyebrow stud!"

"Aahhh." That's all he has to say.

"Is that all you can say?"

"Uh-huh."

"Well, shit, that certainly turned out to be a big dud. You'd think, with all your bitching . . . God, Henry! Okay, well, one down and two to go." I hold up two fingers in a V, like to a preschooler. Henry looks immovable, though, like maybe I should snap my fingers to wake him up, *snap!*

"Momentito!"

I run and grab a package from under the porch step where I'd stashed it, slamming the screen door on the way out and then back in a heartbeat later. Henry is sitting there like a golden idol, like he hasn't moved a muscle.

I hold my package out to him. "Here."

"What's this?"

I've wrapped it for him in an especially fine episode of *Doonesbury*, his favorite comic strip. Henry uncovers it like I knew he would, slowly and methodically.

"Very clever, Bleu."

I knew he wasn't one to miss much or let things slide. He peels the paper away carefully and straightens it out, smoothes it all out perfectly flat with his palm, and sets it aside gingerly, then takes forever reading the comic, without even looking at the gift. *Christ!* Then, finally, he brings what was inside up close to his face, honing in. It's a shot Blair took of us playing Scrabble. Seen from below, neither of us has shifted our focus, I from the game, nor Henry from me. Maybe because of the angle, maybe because it's black and white, we look famous and important, like somebodies in the spotlight. Henry, intense, grizzled, the light shining through him like late sunlight through autumn leaves; and me, scowling and high-toned and unaware, bones casting shadows over my eyes and mouth, concealing their signals. We look fabulous, Henry just like Montgomery Clift, and me, I look classy, beautiful even, and not just almost, and nothing like Daryl Hannah either. Together, the two of us, whether we like it or not, forever. It's like one of those big, glossy magazine photos of movie stars from the fifties. It reminds me of a photo from one of my art history books of Marcel Duchamp playing chess with someone long dead whose works sell for ten million dollars today, though no one would pay a plug nickel for them while the poor slob was living. It's a great photo, really, audacious and sad and wonderful all at once. There's all kinds of stuff in there I can't even lay my finger on. I put it in a nice frame, too.

"Maybe Blair's all right after all," Henry mutters. "Maybe he's not as big a zero as he seemed." And having made such a huge concession, he fumbles around and clears a space to set the photograph among his treasures next to the Scrabble board. The only photo in his whole place.

Still. There's something about it all . . . I don't know.

"Well, look, I really better go."

I like quick clean exits, that's what I like—it makes me squeamish otherwise, whenever moments start to feel momentous. So I sort of slither upright and amble over to the door as casually as possible, leaving Henry's deed to Cielo Azul lying there neutrally on the Scrabble board, covering his great last play.

"Okay. Well, don't eat that cake all at once, now," I warn him, though it wouldn't matter—he's so skinny and the cake is so light.

" 'Night, Henry. Thanks for the great birthday."

He walks me to his door, hovering like an usher, stopping at the threshold and folding himself awkwardly into the doorway over me.

"Well?" he says.

"Well what?"

He hovers over me like that, close.

"The last gift, Bleu?"

Ah, I knew Henry was too sharp to forget.

"It's all in the timing, H."

So then I answer that question I dodged about caring. Breathing life into him if only I could, as he had into his sax, I

269

reach up and put my arms around his neck and pull his head down. Then I kiss Henry square on the lips, pressing my teeth and my whole damned body against him with such a kiss, *such a kiss*, that even his broken dick, even if it were the dick of Lazarus himself, is forced to life, forced to feel the flow of my life force, the force of all life's will and yearning.

Twenty

I guess you don't get to choose what you do with your life anymore than you get to choose who you love. I guess, like love, life chooses you.

I keep telling myself any mess can be cleaned up, you know, mopped up after. Like Prince William Sound. It's just a matter of how much effort has to go into it and how long it takes. Anything can be set right, though. Anyhow, that's what I keep telling myself these days.

I've been asking all over San Vaciò if there were quetzal birds here before the Spanish came, before Junipero Serra's time, but no one can answer me for certain. A lot of people seem to think there were, but no one's sure.

The thing is, my family will be coming soon and I want to show Lily the jungle along the river and take her on that boat ride to the jaguar's pool. I really need to know whether there were ever quetzals there. I don't know why it matters; it just does. Keeping the record straight.

They're going to stay at Cielo Azul for at least two weeks. Mama can listen to the rain and the prehistoric silence and sink into the green. I'm thinking Lily will gain a new perspective on just about everything. I mean, everything. And Hub may come down for a few days too, just to see some ruins, so he says.

Poor Hub. He was collateral damage when Lily scared me off.

Mamuschka forwarded an e-mail from Krystal—a cyber-amends, one of twelve steps in the right direction. Poor Krystal! With all her abandonment issues, apologizing for forsaking me for Chandra and the surrogate disciples at such a critical point in my life. Such a sad little tome! With no news of her current situation, just that cold, cryptic where-she's-@ address along the top. I'm fairly certain she's abandoned the reincarnated apostles, though. Her message bore no resemblance whatsoever to St. Paul's letters to the Corinthians. Anyway, I e-mailed her back right away.

There's been no news from Cal, but I did hear from Blair, who made it to Chiapas. I don't know whether to be mad or amazed at him for not spilling his guts to me about what he did back in Arcata. I can hardly believe he had enough restraint to keep me out of it. Thank God all I know is hearsay and neither of us plans to go back anytime soon, or I'd have to come up with the moral backbone to decide whether or not to do the right thing and talk to the authorities. At least for now I don't have to go there. I think about it, though. A lot. It's something I'd like to discuss with my father. Anyway, from the sound of it, he's fallen in with good company in Chiapas—reasonable radicals—but you never know. I like to think Blair will do something good like he said. I want to believe anyone he gets into trouble, he'll rescue, like he did Cal. Nobody will be hurt, that's what I want to believe. He won't be another Mac.

Even Blanca, shy little sparrow. I mean, you just never know. Whizzing around San Vació on Juanita these days, fledged.

The thing is, I've been wrong about so many things. Like I said, I've underestimated just about everything.

It finally dawned on me, for example, that Henry's been letting me win at Scrabble. This whole time, he's been letting the pitch go by. Why he blew his cover on my birthday, I have no idea, and I'm not giving him the satisfaction of asking, either.

So, maybe I'm wrong about my father, too. Maybe he's just been waiting to buy into a rundown, pink hotel in a town whose name means nothing.

Poor Mexico! Can she dare absorb one more *gringa*, trailing all her troubles behind her like the quetzal's long tail? Dragging along my glorious, lustrous, magnificent train of troubles.

I'd bet on it, but, like I said, I've been plenty wrong.

Something I know for sure, though.

Call me crazy, but I know this, absolutely. I know there's still a quetzal bird somewhere out there in the jungle around San Vació.

> *What I believe—I believe if I go deep enough,*
> *if I wait long enough,*
> *if I make myself quiet enough, it'll come to me.*
> *Unseen, like a bullet.*

I really do.

About the Author

Since the age of seven, Barbara Haynie grew up "mostly outdoors" on the eastern slope of the Rockies. She wandered through a variety of majors in her twenties, finally earning a Bachelor of Fine Arts degree at age fifty. She has been a landscape designer in a nursery business owned with her husband since 1969. Together, they have seen their share of islands and continents, having traveled nearly everywhere except the Far East.

Currently, she lives in a forest behind her nursery, where she can see her two horses from her kitchen window and ride along the Poudre River.

Her first novel, *The Terrain of Paradise*, was published in 2002 by Five Star Publishing.

AROUND PARLIAMENT
See pages 104–119.

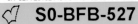

Around Városliget

Central Pest

AROUND VÁROSLIGET
See pages 140–151.

CENTRAL PEST
See pages 120–139.

Budapest Card

Your tourist pass for 48 or 72 hours

"the whole city in your pocket"

Budapest Card

Budapest Kártya

signature
aláírás

- · unlimited travel on public transport
  - · free or discounted admission to 60+ museums and selected sights
- · discounted admission to selected cultural and folklore programmes
  - · discounted city sightseeing tours
- · discounted admission or reductions to thermal baths, in restaurants, shops and numerous other services

The Budapest Card is on sale in hotels, tourist information offices, travel agencies, and main underground ticket offices.

Purchase your Budapest Card online at www.budapestinfo.hu

EYEWITNESS TRAVEL

BUDAPEST

EYEWITNESS TRAVEL

BUDAPEST

MAIN CONTRIBUTORS:
BARBARA OLSZAŃSKA, TADEUSZ OLSZAŃSKI

DK

LONDON, NEW YORK,
MELBOURNE, MUNICH AND DELHI
www.dk.com

PRODUCED BY Wydawnictwo Wiedza i Życie, Warsaw SERIES EDITOR Ewa Szwagrzyk
CONSULTANTS András Hadik, Małgorzata Omilanowska,
Katalin Szokolay
EDITORS Joanna Egert, Anna Kożurno-Królikowska,
Bożena Leszkowicz
DESIGNER Paweł Pasternak

Dorling Kindersley Ltd
PROJECT EDITOR Jane Oliver
EDITORS Felicity Crowe, Nancy Jones

TRANSLATORS
Magda Hannay, Anna Johnson, Ian Wisniewski

PHOTOGRAPHERS
Gábor Barka, Dorota and Mariusz Jarymowiczowie

ILLUSTRATORS
Paweł Mistewicz, Piotr Zubrzycki
REPRODUCED BY Colourscan, Singapore
Printed and bound by South China Printing Co. Ltd., China

First published in Great Britain in 1999
09 10 9 8 7 6 5 4 3 2 1
Reprinted with revisions 2000, 2001, 2004, 2007, 2009

Published in the United States by DK Publishing, 375 Hudson Street,
New York, New York 10014

Copyright 1999, 2009 © Dorling Kindersley Limited, London

ISSN 1542-1554
ISBN: 978-0-75666-107-6

FLOORS ARE REFERRED TO THROUGHOUT IN ACCORDANCE WITH EUROPEAN
USAGE; IE THE "FIRST FLOOR" IS THE FLOOR ABOVE GROUND LEVEL.

Front cover main image: Chain Bridge, Budapest

We're trying to be cleaner and greener:

- we recycle waste and switch things off
- we use paper from responsibly managed forests whenever possible
- we ask our printers to actively reduce water and energy consumption
- we check out our suppliers' working conditions – they never use child labour

Find out more about our values and best practices at www.dk.com

---

The information in this
Dorling Kindersley Travel Guide is checked regularly.
Every effort has been made to ensure that this book is as up-to-date
as possible at the time of going to press. Some details, however,
such as telephone numbers, opening hours, prices, gallery hanging
arrangements and travel information are liable to change. The
publishers cannot accept responsibility for any consequences arising
from the use of this book, nor for any material on third party
websites, and cannot guarantee that any website address in this
book will be a suitable source of travel information. We value the
views and suggestions of our readers very highly. Please write to:
Publisher, DK Eyewitness Travel Guides, Dorling Kindersley,
80 Strand, London, WC2R 0RL, Great Britain.

◁ **The Parliament building** *(see pp108–9)*, standing on the Danube

---

CONTENTS

Pallas Athene on the Old Town Hall

INTRODUCING
BUDAPEST

**Hungarian crest adorning a wall
close to the Tunnel** *(see p100)*

The Hungarian National Gallery *(see pp74–7)*, in the former Royal Palace

View across the Danube towards
St Stephen's Basilica *(see p116–17)*

Porcelain in the Museum of
Applied Arts *(see pp136–7)*

Barrel-organ player in the historic
Castle District *(see pp68–85)*

The landmark domes and towers of four of Budapest's most striking places of worship

HOW TO USE THIS GUIDE

This Eyewitness Travel Guide helps you get the most from your stay in Budapest with the minimum of difficulty. The opening section, *Introducing Budapest*, locates the city geographically, sets modern Budapest in its historical context and describes events through the entire year. *Budapest at a Glance* is an overview of the city's main attractions. *Budapest Area by Area* starts on page 66. This is the main sightseeing

Plotting the route

section, which covers all of the important sights, with photographs, maps and illustrations. It also includes day trips from Budapest and three walks around the city. Information about hotels, restaurants, shops and markets, entertainment and sports is found in *Travellers' Needs*. The *Survival Guide* has advice on everything from using the postal service and telephones to Budapest's public transport system and medical services.

FINDING YOUR WAY AROUND THE SIGHTSEEING SECTION

Each of six sightseeing areas in Budapest is colour-coded for easy reference. Every chapter opens with an introduction to the area of the city it covers, describing its history and character, and has one or two *Street-by-Street* maps

illustrating typical parts of that area. Finding your way around the chapter is made simple by the numbering system used throughout. The most important sights are covered in detail in two or more full pages.

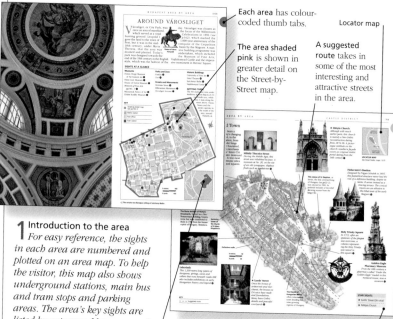

Each area has colour-coded thumb tabs.

Locator map

The area shaded pink is shown in greater detail on the Street-by-Street map.

A suggested route takes in some of the most interesting and attractive streets in the area.

1 Introduction to the area
For easy reference, the sights in each area are numbered and plotted on an area map. To help the visitor, this map also shows underground stations, main bus and tram stops and parking areas. The area's key sights are listed by category: Museums and Galleries; Churches; Historic Streets and Squares; Palaces and Historic Buildings; Hotels and Baths; and Parks and Gardens.

A locator map shows where you are in relation to the other areas in the city centre.

2 Street-by-Street map
This gives a bird's-eye view of interesting and important parts of each sightseeing area. The numbering of the sights ties up with the area map and the fuller description on the pages that follow.

The list of star sights recommends the places that no visitor should miss.

BUDAPEST AREA MAP

The coloured areas shown on this map (*see inside front cover*) are the six main sightseeing areas used in this guide. Each is covered in a full chapter in *Budapest Area by Area* (pp66–167). They are highlighted on other maps throughout the book. In *Budapest at a Glance*, for example, they help you locate the top sights. They are also used to help you find the position of the three walks (pp168–75).

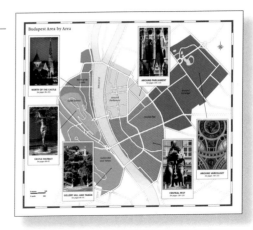

Budapest Area by Area

Numbers refer to each sight's position on the area map and its place in the chapter.

Practical information provides everything you need to know to visit each sight. Map references pinpoint the sight's location on the Street Finder map (pp242–53).

Façades of important buildings are often shown to help you recognize them quickly.

The visitors' checklist provides all the practical information needed to plan your visit.

3 Detailed information on each sight
All the important sights in Budapest are described individually. They are listed in order following the numbering on the area map at the start of the section. Practical information includes a map reference, opening hours, telephone numbers and admission charges. The key to the symbols used is on the back flap.

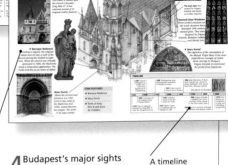

Stars indicate the features no visitor should miss.

4 Budapest's major sights
Historic buildings are dissected to reveal their interiors; museums and galleries have colour-coded floorplans to help you find important exhibits.

A timeline charts the key events in the history of the building.

INTRODUCING
BUDAPEST

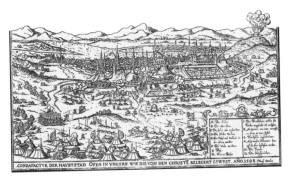

FOUR GREAT DAYS IN BUDAPEST

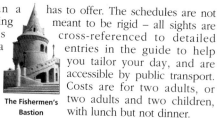

It can be difficult to plan a visit to this historic, sprawling city, particularly if time is short. These four days provide a taste of Budapest, with a variety of sights and experiences, and together include much of the best in architecture, museums, shopping and fun that the city

The Fishermen's Bastion

has to offer. The schedules are not meant to be rigid – all sights are cross-referenced to detailed entries in the guide to help you tailor your day, and are accessible by public transport. Costs are for two adults, or two adults and two children, with lunch but not dinner.

Passengers ride the antique Sikló funicular railway up Castle Hill

A DAY ON CASTLE HILL

- Art at the Royal Palace
- Lunch in a Castle courtyard
- Concert at Mátyás Church
- A subterranean Labyrinth

TWO ADULTS allow at least 10,000 HUF

Morning

Buda's **Castle District** (see pp69–85) towers over Pest. Winding paths lead up Castle Hill from Clark Adám tér, but the traditional way up is by the **Sikló** (see p69), a 100-year-old funicular railway. Start the day with a tour of the grounds of the **Royal Palace** (see pp70–1). Take time to admire the Romantic design of **Mátyás Fountain** (see p72), and to visit the wonderful collection of 19th-century Hungarian paintings at the **National Gallery** (see pp74–7). Leave the Palace area through the ornamental Habsburg Gate, then stop at **Rivalda** (see p196) for a splendid al fresco lunch.

Afternoon

A short walk along Tárnok utca into central Buda, past myriad souvenir shops, leads to **Fishermen's Bastion** (see p80). From here there are glorious views of Pest, especially **Parliament** (see pp108–9) and **Chain Bridge** (see p62), almost directly below. Do not fail to visit ancient **Mátyás Church** (see pp82–3) – where there are organ concerts some summer evenings – before walking along the wonderfully preserved streets of Buda's Old Town. Follow Fortuna utca round to Kapisztran tér and the tall, ruined tower of **St Mary Magdalene** (see p84).

Peerless **Lords' Street** (see p85), with its gothic details and peaceful courtyards, leads to the bizarre subterranean **Labyrinth** (see p85). Nearby **Alabárdos** (see p196) is the perfect place for an early dinner in a medieval setting.

THE FINER SIDE OF LIFE

- A morning at the spa baths
- The Museum of Fine Arts
- A walk to the Opera House
- Dinner at Gresham Kávéház

TWO ADULTS allow at least 17,500 HUF

Morning

Start with coffee in **Gerbeaud Cukrászda** (see p206), the city's most famous café. Then ride the beautifully preserved **Millennium Line** (see p238) to **Széchenyi Baths** (see p151), and spend at least three hours indulging in bathing, sauna and massage in glorious imperial surroundings. Stop for lunch at **Gundel Étterem** (see p204).

Afternoon

Walk off the effects of lunch in the **Museum of Fine Arts** (see pp146–9), which houses

One of three outdoor pools at Széchenyi Baths, the hottest in Budapest

◁ The coronation of Franz Joseph I by Ede Heinrich (1819-1885)

Hungary's finest collection of foreign art in a monumental building facing **Heroes' Square** (*see pp142–3*).

On leaving the museum, walk past the **Millennium Monument** (*see p145*) and down Andrássy út – a superb avenue of embassies and consulates, giving way to restaurants and shops – and stop at one of the many cafés on **Liszt Ferenc tér** (*see p206*). The highlight of Andrássy út is No. 22, the **State Opera House** (*see pp118–9*), which offers guided tours in the late afternoon. From here, walk along lower Andrássy út, over Erzsébet tér, to the **Gresham Palace** hotel (*see p114*), facing Chain Bridge. Finally, spend the evening dining at the informal **Gresham Kávéház** (*see p199*), famous for its "Three Foie Gras", a Hungarian speciality.

Children relax at Budakeszi Wildlife Park in the Buda Hills

FAMILY FUN AL FRESCO

- **A tour of the Buda Hills on the Children's Railway**
- **A walking safari round Budakeszi Wildlife Park**
- **Supper and folk music**

FAMILY OF 4 allow at least 17,500 HUF

Morning
Head for the **Buda Hills** (*see p161*) by means of the Széchenyi Hill cog railway (*5am–11pm, tel. 355 41 67*), which begins at Szilagy Erzsébet fasor, just north of Moszkva tér metro station. At the top, a short walk leads to the TV tower (closed) and the terminus of the **Children's Railway** (*open May–Aug: 10am–5pm*). The steam engine departs on the hour and meanders through the Buda hills to Hűvösvölgy, passing the **Erzsébet Look-Out Tower**. Disembark at Szép Juhászné station for lunch at the outdoor café.

Afternoon
A well-marked path runs from the café to **Budakeszi Wildlife Park** (*open Mar–Oct: 9am–6pm; Nov–Feb: 9am–3pm.*

Tel. 023 45 17, 83). The park is set across 3 sq km (1 sq mile) and contains a wide variety of animals, from wild boar (which also roam the surrounding country-side), to wolves. There is a separate reserve for plants and flora. A walking safari tours the best of both areas. The on-site restaurant is a great place for supper, and offers folk music after 6pm. At going-home time the Children's Railway will be closed, but bus No. 22 runs from the park to Moszkva tér.

HISTORY AND SHOPPING

- **The surviving monuments of the Jewish Quarter**
- **A Middle Eastern lunch**
- **Shopping on Váci utca and in Central Market**

TWO ADULTS allow at least 8,700 HUF

Morning
Start at the **Hungarian National Museum** (*see pp130-3*), where Sándor Petőfi read his *National Song* in 1848 (*see p31*). Spend an hour amongst the treasures of Hungary's turbulent past, then go to another historic location – the **Jewish Quarter** (*see p134*). The **Great Synagogue** on Dohány utca is a splendid Byzantine-style building, attached to which is the **Jewish Museum**. The **Holocaust Memorial** is found in the synagogue's courtyard. The rest of the quarter is known for its gift shops and book stores, and the less ostentatious synagogues on Rumbach S. utca and Kazinczy utca. On the same street, stop for an authentic kosher lunch at **Carmel Pince** (*see p200*).

Afternoon
Váci utca (*see p127*) offers great shopping at its northern end – for souvenirs, fashion and fine Hungarian porcelain at Goda (No. 9). Do visit the **Inner City Parish Church** (*see pp124–5*), then cross Kossuth Lajos út, and head south past the **Klotild Palaces** (*see p127*) and more shops, to Fővám tér. Rest here in a café. Across the road is the final retail challenge of the day – the huge, renovated **Central Market Hall** (*see p211*).

One of the many busy terrace cafés that line Váci utca

Putting Budapest on the Map

The capital of the Republic of Hungary, Budapest has over 1.8 million inhabitants, a fifth of the country's total population. The city is situated on the Danube and covers an area of 525 sq km (200 sq miles). One third of the city is taken up by hilly Buda and Óbuda, on the western bank of the Danube, and the remaining two thirds by flat Pest, on the eastern bank. Budapest has a pivotal location at the heart of central Europe. From here one can easily reach other major cities such as Vienna, Zagreb, Bratislava, Belgrade, Bucharest and Prague.

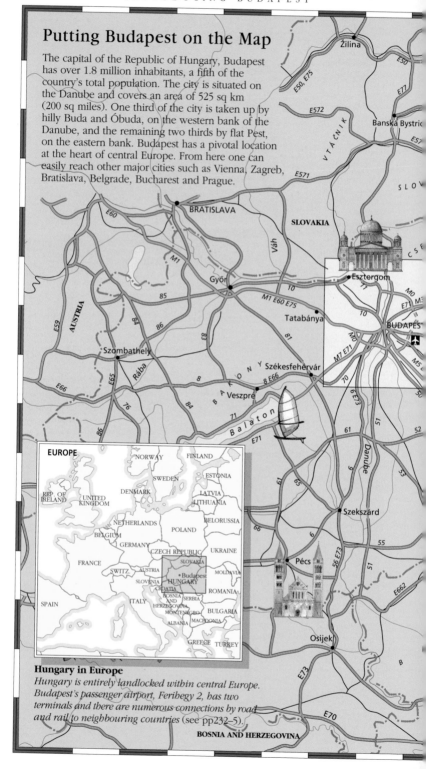

Žilina

Banská Bystric

BRATISLAVA

SLOVAKIA

Győr

Esztergom

Tatabánya

BUDAPES

Szombathely

Székesfehérvár

Veszpré

Balaton

Szekszárd

Pécs

Osijek

EUROPE

NORWAY   FINLAND

SWEDEN   ESTONIA

REP. OF
IRELAND   DENMARK   LATVIA

UNITED   LITHUANIA
KINGDOM

NETHERLANDS   BELORUSSIA

POLAND

BELGIUM
GERMANY

CZECH REPUBLIC   UKRAINE

FRANCE   SLOVAKIA

SWITZ. AUSTRIA   HUNGARY   MOLDAVIA
              Budapest

SLOVENIA
              CROATIA   ROMANIA

SPAIN   ITALY   BOSNIA
              AND   SERBIA
              HERZEGOVINA   BULGARIA
                       MONTENEGRO
                       ALBANIA   MACEDONIA

              GREECE   TURKEY

Hungary in Europe

*Hungary is entirely landlocked within central Europe.
Budapest's passenger airport, Ferihegy 2, has two
terminals and there are numerous connections by road
and rail to neighbouring countries (see pp232–5).*

BOSNIA AND HERZEGOVINA

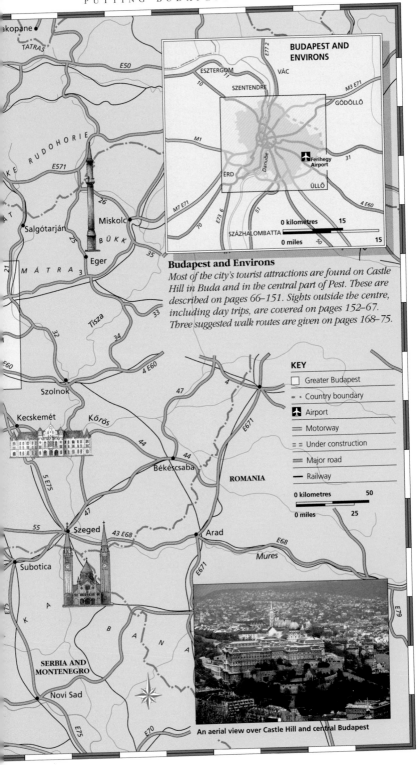

BUDAPEST AND ENVIRONS

ESZTERGOM
VÁC
SZENTENDRE
GÖDÖLLÖ
ÉRD
Ferihegy Airport
ÜLLÖ
SZÁZHALOMBATTA

0 kilometres   15

0 miles   15

Budapest and Environs

Most of the city's tourist attractions are found on Castle Hill in Buda and in the central part of Pest. These are described on pages 66–151. Sights outside the centre, including day trips, are covered on pages 152–67. Three suggested walk routes are given on pages 168–75.

Miskolc
Salgótarján
BÜKK
Eger
MÁTRA
Tisza
Szolnok
Kecskemét
Körös
Békéscsaba
ROMANIA
Szeged
Arad
Mures
Subotica
BANAT
SERBIA AND MONTENEGRO
Novi Sad

KEY

☐ Greater Budapest

– · Country boundary

✈ Airport

═ Motorway

= = Under construction

═ Major road

── Railway

0 kilometres   50

0 miles   25

An aerial view over Castle Hill and central Budapest

Central Budapest

Detail on the Stock Exchange

The centre of town includes Castle Hill (district I) on the western bank of the Danube and districts V, VI, VII, VIII and IX of Pest on the river's eastern bank, bounded by the city's original tram line. The Roman numerals denote the official administrative districts *(see p223)*. For the purposes of this guide, the centre is divided into six areas. Each area has its own chapter containing a selection of sights that convey its character and history. Sights on the outskirts of the city, and suggested day trips and walks, are covered in separate chapters.

Calvinist Church
Situated close to the Dan this church is distinguis by its eye-catching, poly chromatic roof (see p1

Royal Palace
The Royal Palace has been destroyed and painstakingly rebuilt many times. It was last meticulously reconstructed after World War II, to the form that the Habsburgs had given it (see pp70–71).

Liberation Monument
This statue of a woman holding aloft the palm of victory was created by the Hungarian sculptor Zsigmond Kisfaludi Stróbl. Situated in a park on Gellért Hill, the monument is visible from all over the city. It is now one of the symbols of Budapest (see p92).

0 metres   500
0 yards   500

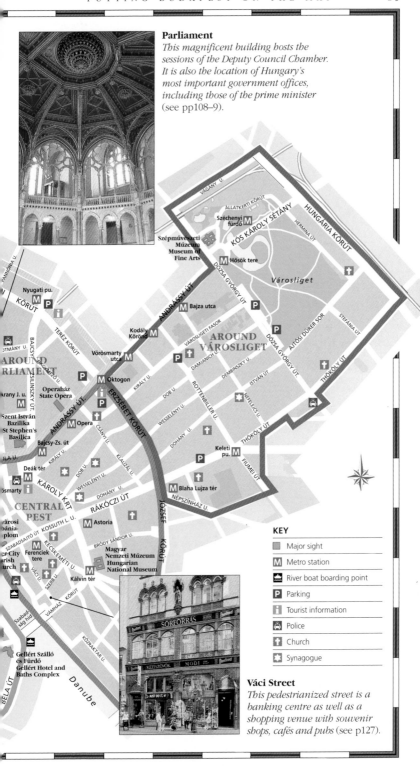

Parliament
This magnificent building hosts the sessions of the Deputy Council Chamber. It is also the location of Hungary's most important government offices, including those of the prime minister (see pp108–9).

Vágány u.

ÁLLATKERTI KÖRÚT

Széchenyi fürdő

KÓS KÁROLY SÉTÁNY

HUNGÁRIA KÖRÚT

HERMINA ÚT

Szépművészeti Múzeum Museum of Fine Arts

M Hősök tere

DÓZSA GYÖRGY ÚT

Városliget

Nyugati pu. **P**

KÖRÚT

TERÉZ KÖRÚT

ANDRÁSSY ÚT

M Bajza utca

STEFÁNIA ÚT

PANNÓNIA U.

ÓTMÁNY U.

BAJCSY-ZS. U.

ISILINSZKY U.

Kodály Körönd **M**

VÁROSLIGETI FASOR

AROUND VÁROSLIGET

AJTÓSI DÜRER SOR

THÖKÖLY ÚT

AROUND PARLIAMENT

Vörösmarty utca **M**

P

DAMJANICH U.

DÓZSA GYÖRGY ÚT

Arany J. u.

M

P Oktogon

KIRÁLY U.

DEMBINSZKY U.

ISTVÁN ÚT

Operaház State Opera

ANDRÁSSY ÚT

ERZSÉBET KÖRÚT

DOB U.

ROTTENBILLER U.

Szent István Bazilika St Stephen's Basilica

M Opera

CSÁNYI U.

WESSELÉNYI U.

NEFELEJCS U.

THÖKÖLY ÚT

Bajcsy-Zs. út

KIRÁLY U.

DOHÁNY U.

Keleti pu. **M**

P

ILA U.

Deák tér **M**

DOB U.

KLAUZÁL U.

FIUMEI ÚT

KÁROLY KRT

WESSELÉNYI U.

ösmarty

M

KÁROLY KRT

DOHÁNY U.

M Blaha Lujza tér

CENTRAL PEST

RÁKÓCZI ÚT

NÉPSZÍNHÁZ U.

árosi bánia- plom

KOSSUTH L. U.

M Astoria

JÓZSEF KÖRÚT

SZABADSAJTÓ ÚT

BRÓDY SÁNDOR U.

e City arish urch

M Ferenciek tere

KECSKEMÉTI U.

KEY

VÁCI U.

SZERB U.

Magyar Nemzeti Múzeum Hungarian National Museum

▪	Major sight
M	Metro station
⛴	River boat boarding point
P	Parking
ℹ	Tourist information
▣	Police
✝	Church
✡	Synagogue

Kálvin tér

VÁMHÁZ KÖRÚT

Szabad- ság híd

KÖZRAKPART

Gellért Szálló és Fürdő Gellért Hotel and Baths Complex

BÉLA U.

Danube

Váci Street
This pedestrianized street is a banking centre as well as a shopping venue with souvenir shops, cafés and pubs (see p127).

THE HISTORY OF BUDAPEST

As early as the Palaeolithic era, there were settlements in the area of Budapest: the narrowing of the Danube made the crossing of the river easy at this particular spot. In around AD 100, the Romans established the town of Aquincum here. Their rule lasted until the early 5th century AD, when the region fell to Attila the Hun. It was subsequently ruled by the Goths, the Longobards and, for nearly 300 years, by the Avars.

The ancestors of modern Hungarians, the Magyars, migrated from the Urals and arrived in the Budapest region in 896. They were led by Prince Árpád, whose dynasty ruled until the 13th century. At the turn of the first millennium, St István, whose heathen name was Vajk, accepted Christianity for the Hungarians. As their first crowned king, István I also laid the basis of the modern Hungarian state.

It was Béla IV who, in 1247, after the Mongol invasion, moved the capital to Buda. Much of the expansion of Buda took place under kings from the dynasty of the Angevins. Buda reached a zenith during the reign of Mátyás Corvinus in the 15th century, but further development was hindered by the advancing Turks, who took the region and ruled Buda for 150 years.

Crest of the Hunyadis

Liberation by the Christian armies resulted in the submission of the country as a whole to the Habsburgs. They suppressed all nationalist rebellions, but at the same time took care of economic development. Empress Maria Theresa and Archduke Joseph, the emperor's governor, made particular contributions to the modernization of both Buda and Pest. Yet, the slow pace of reforms led to an uprising in 1848, which was brutally crushed by Franz Joseph I. Compromise in 1867 and the creation of an Austro-Hungarian Empire stimulated economic and cultural life once more. Soon after, in 1873, Buda and Pest were united to create the city of Budapest.

Following World War I, the monarchy fell and Hungary lost two thirds of its territory. The desire to regain this contributed to its support of Germany in World War II. However, Budapest was taken by Russian troops in 1945 and large sections of it levelled. Under the subsequent Communist rule, the popular uprising of 1956 was ruthlessly suppressed by Soviet tanks but it initiated a crisis that shook the regime. Free elections took place in 1990, resulting in the victory of the democratic opposition, and the emergence of a new bourgeoisie.

Dating from 1686, when the Turks were expelled, this map shows the fortified towns of Pest and Buda

◁ Gyula Benczúr's *The Baptism of Vajk*, displayed in the Hungarian National Gallery *(see pp74–7)*

The City's Rulers

In the 13th century, Béla IV built a castle in Buda and designated the town as his new capital. Until that time, the Árpád dynasty, the first family of Hungarian kings, had ruled their domain from elsewhere. When, at the beginning of the 14th century, there were no male heirs to the Árpád throne, Hungary began a long period during which it was mainly ruled by foreign kings including the French Angevins and the Polish Jagiełłos. Under Mátyás Corvinus, a great Hungarian king, Buda became one of Europe's most impressive cities. The Habsburgs, while suppressing national insurrections, rebuilt Buda and Pest after the devastation left by the Turks, adding fine pieces of architecture.

1440–44
Władysław (Uláiszló) I of Poland

1637–
Ferdinand

1301–5
Wenceslas II of Bohemia

1541–66
Sultan Süleyman, "the Magnificient"

1385–6
Charles II of Durazzo

1608–19
Mátyás II

1386–95
Maria (crowned)

1490–1516
Władysław (Uláiszló) II

1272–90
Ladislas IV, "the Cuman"

1526–64
Ferdinand I

1437–9
Albert of Austria

1270–72
István V

1307–42
Charles I Robert of Anjou

1200	1300	1400	1500	160•
ÁRPÁDS	ANGEVINS		JAGIEŁŁOS	OTTOMANS
1200	1300	1400	1500	160•

1445–57
Ladislas V, "Posthumus"

1290–1301
András III

1382–5
Maria (uncrowned)

1235–70
Béla IV

1458–90
Mátyás I, "Corvinus"

1516–26
Louis II

1526–40
János I Szapolyai

1342–82
Louis I (Lajos), "the Great"

1564–76
Maximilian I

1576–1608
Rudolf I

1305–7
Otto Wittelsbach of Bavaria

1387–1437
Sigismund of Luxembourg (initially as Maria's consort)

1619–37
Ferdinand II

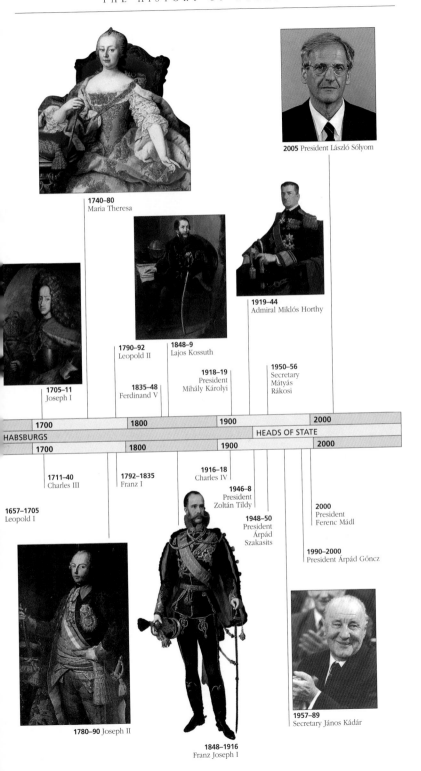

2005 President László Sólyom

1740–80
Maria Theresa

1919–44
Admiral Miklós Horthy

1790–92
Leopold II

1848–9
Lajos Kossuth

1950–56
Secretary
Mátyás
Rákosi

1918–19
President
Mihály Károlyi

1705–11
Joseph I

1835–48
Ferdinand V

1700   **1800**   **1900**   **2000**

HABSBURGS   HEADS OF STATE

1700   **1800**   **1900**   **2000**

1711–40
Charles III

1792–1835
Franz I

1916–18
Charles IV

1946–8
President
Zoltán Tildy

1657–1705
Leopold I

2000
President
Ferenc Mádl

1948–50
President
Árpád
Szakasits

1990–2000
President Árpád Göncz

1780–90 Joseph II

1848–1916
Franz Joseph I

1957–89
Secretary János Kádár

Early Settlers

Bronze Age vessel

Traces of settlements in the region by the Scythians and the Celtic Eravi date from around 400 BC onwards. In the 1st century AD, the Romans conquered the area as their province of Pannonia and soon established Aquincum (see pp162–3) within the limits of the modern city. Little evidence remains of the next rulers, the Huns, who were followed by the Goths and the Longobards. For nearly three centuries, starting in around AD 600, the Avars were pre-eminent. In 896, the Magyars swept into the region and laid claim to what would later become the Hungarian state.

EXTENT OF THE CITY

■ AD 300   □ Today

Bronze Decorations
In the 2nd century AD, Roman carts were often decorated with bronze plaques. This example depicts (from left): a satyr, Bacchus, god of wine and Pan, god of shepherds, under a palm frond. It was found in Somodor.

Workshops and shops, known as *tabernae*, were enclosed and faced onto the street.

The Sun God Mithras
The Persian god Mithras was adopted by the Eravi and his cult survived into the Roman period. This bronze image dates from 2nd–3rd centuries AD.

RECONSTRUCTION OF THE MACELLUM
This solidly built, square market hall was the focus for trade in the Roman town of Aquincum. At its centre was a courtyard with stalls, shops and workshops built around.

TIMELINE

10,000 BC Remains dating from the Palaeolithic era indicate the existence of a settlement in the Remeda Cave in Buda.

Silver Celtic coin dating from the 4th century BC

c. 50 BC Celtic Eravi settlement on Gellért Hill (see pp88–9)

c. AD 100 The town of Aquincum is established by the Romans

800 BC Tombs with Iron Age urns at Pünkösdfürdő.

400 BC Scythians in the region

10,000	5000	1000	AD 1

5000 BC Stone Age settlements in Talxina and along the Danube

Scythian ornamental gold stag

AD 89 Romans establish a permanent army camp in modern-day Óbuda

AD 106 Aquincum becomes the capital of the Roman province of Lower Pannonia

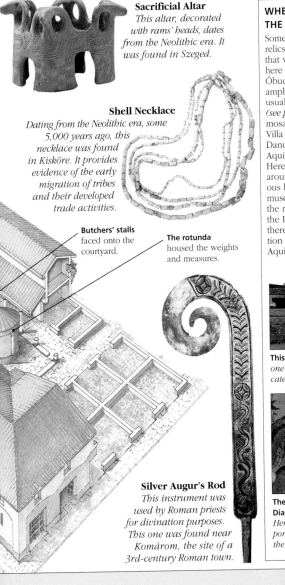

Sacrificial Altar
This altar, decorated with rams' heads, dates from the Neolithic era. It was found in Szeged.

Shell Necklace
Dating from the Neolithic era, some 5,000 years ago, this necklace was found in Kisköre. It provides evidence of the early migration of tribes and their developed trade activities.

Butchers' stalls faced onto the courtyard.

The rotunda housed the weights and measures.

Silver Augur's Rod
This instrument was used by Roman priests for divination purposes. This one was found near Komárom, the site of a 3rd-century Roman town.

WHERE TO SEE THE EARLY CITY

Some quite considerable relics of the Roman legions that were once stationed here can be seen in modern Óbuda. The remains of an amphitheatre are near an unusual underground museum *(see p170)*, while magnificent mosaics adorn the Hercules Villa *(p171)*. Further up the Danube are the ruins of Aquincum itself *(pp162–3)*. Here visitors can wander around the remains of various buildings and enter a museum. On the Pest side of the river, just to the north of the Inner City Parish Church, there is a small, open-air section of remains from Contra Aquincum *(p122)*.

This Roman amphitheatre, *one of two in Aquincum, indicates the status of the town.*

The mosaic of Hercules and Diana, *which survives at the Hercules Villa, was probably imported from Alexandria during the 2nd or 3rd century AD.*

Ornate earring from the 7th century AD

c. 140–60 Two amphitheatres are built to serve Aquincum's growing population

409 The Huns, under Attila, conquer Aquincum

c. 600–896 The Avars rule the region

200 | **400** | **600** | **800**

194 Aquincum is promoted to the status of a Roman colony

294 Contra Aquincum is founded on the eastern bank of the Danube

453 Collapse of the Huns' domination

Carving of the Sun God Mithras

896 Magyar (Hungarian) tribes take over Pannonia

The Árpád Dynasty

Hair clasp from the 9th century

After a long journey beginning in the Urals region in Russia, nomadic tribes of Magyars eventually settled in Pannonia in AD 896. Following a period of internal disputes, the tribes made a blood-bonded alliance and chose one leader, Árpád. While Géza I made contact with missionaries, it was his son, István I, who accepted Christianity for his people. Their first crowned king, István organized the state according to the European, feudal model. Initially under the Árpáds, Esztergom (see p164) was the country's capital and later Székesfehérvár. The development of Buda, Pest and Óbuda began in the second half of the 12th century, but was interrupted by the Mongol invasion of 1241.

EXTENT OF THE CITY

🟩 *1300*   ⬜ *Today*

Christ is depicted twice in the middle section of the coat; in each case He is larger than the surrounding figures.

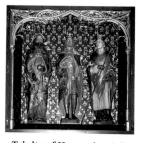

Trinity of Hungarian Saints
The figures of three saints, King István, his son Imre and Bishop Gellért, are presented on this colourful triptych in the Chapel of St Imre in Mátyás Church (see pp82–3).

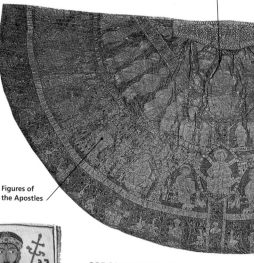

Figures of the Apostles

King Géza I
Géza I (1074–77), the father of King István, is represented on an enamel plaque decorating the Crown of the Árpáds.

CORONATION COAT
This silk coronation coat was made in 1031 for the Árpád kings. It has a pearl-beaded collar and is embroidered with the figures of Christ, Mary, the Apostles and the Prophets.

TIMELINE

Sculpture of King István I by Imre Varga

c.900 Árpád settles on Csepel Island (in modern-day Budapest) and his brother Kurszán in Óbuda

Coronation sword

850	900	950	1000	1050

973 Prince Géza invites missionaries into the region

1001 Coronation of István (Stephen) I

1046 Revolt by pagans and the martyr's death of Bishop Gellért, thrown in a barrel into the Danube

Crown of the Árpáds

This gold crown, ornamented with jewels, pearls and enamel, was created by joining two existing crowns. The lower, Byzantine one was known as the "Greek crown" and the upper one as the "Latin crown".

Bone artifacts

Bone items such as shepherds' staffs often had carved handles.

Figures of the Prophets

King István's coin

The first Hungarian coin, the denar, was produced soon after AD 1000, during King István's reign.

Tympanum

This 11th-century church tympanum, from Gyulafehérvár in modern Romania, is in the Hungarian National Gallery (see pp74–7).

WHERE TO SEE THE MEDIEVAL CITY

Only a few monuments survive from the Middle Ages. Among the notable ones that still remain are the crypts in Mátyás Church (see pp82–3), and the elevations and cellars of some historic houses in the Castle District (a few of which are now converted into wine bars). The reconstructed lower chambers of the Royal Palace (pp70–71) and parts of its fortifications also date from the medieval era.

This 19th-century copy *of the Romanesque Ják Church (see p143) reveals how the Árpáds adopted European styles.*

Gothic niches *can be seen by the entrances to many houses in the Old Town (see pp78–9).*

1188 Béla III moves his headquarters to Óbuda and sets out on Frederick Barbarossa's crusade

1222 "Golden Bull" grants nobility privileges including tax exemption

1241 Mongol invasion

1247 Béla IV builds castle in Buda, which becomes capital of Hungary

1267 Béla IV announces new "Golden Bull"

| 1100 | 1150 | 1200 | 1250 | 1300 |

Magyar belt buckle dating from the 10th century

1244 The citizens of Pest are granted civic rights

1255 The citizens of Buda get civic rights

1301 Death of King András III, last king of the Árpád dynasty

Gothic and Renaissance Eras

Tabernacle of the Inner City Parish Church

As a result of the efforts of the Angevins and Sigismund of Luxembourg, the Gothic style reached Buda in the 14th century. Buda's palace and the summer palace in Visegrád were both extensively rebuilt. Shortly after defeat by the Turks at Varna, Hungary regained control of Belgrade and, for a while at least, halted their invasion. Mátyás Corvinus, the son of hetman János Hunyadi, the victor of Belgrade, became king. Under Mátyás's rule Hungary was turned into the greatest monarchy of Middle Europe, and, as a result of his marriage to Beatrice, a Neapolitan princess, the Renaissance began to blossom in the country.

EXTENT OF THE CITY

■ c. 1480   □ Today

Castellan Ferenc Sárffy was the commander of Győr Castle.

Hungarian soldier

Illuminated letter from the Philostratus Codex
This letter depicts the son of King Mátyás I, Johannus Corvinus, after he took Vienna. It is housed in the Széchenyi National Library (see p72).

Royal Medallion
An unknown master from Lombardy commemorated King Mátyás I in this marble silhouette dating from the 1480s.

Gold Seal
This gold seal, which belonged to King Mátyás I, is indicative of the affluence enjoyed by Hungary while he was on the throne.

Ulrik Czettrich, an officer of the royal household, discovered the body of Louis II on the marshy bank of the Csele river.

TIMELINE

Ciborium dating from the 14th century

1355 Óbuda's citizens gain civic rights

1370 Louis I enters a political union and becomes king of Poland

1385 Sigismund of Luxembourg marries Maria

1395 University established in Óbuda

| 1350 | 1375 | 1400 | 142 |

1342 Louis I, "the Great", becomes king

1387–1437 Rule of Sigismund of Luxembourg. He enlarges the Royal Palace *(see pp70–71)*

1335 Treaty on co-operation and succession signed by the kings of Hungary, Poland and Bohemia in Visegrád

1382 After death of Louis I, one daughter, Maria, becomes queen of Hungary and another, Jadwiga, queen of Poland

Wine Cups
This pair of elaborate Renaissance wine cups, dating from the 16th century, is designed to fit together to form a covered receptacle.

Crest of King Mátyás Corvinus
Inscribed with the date 1470, this crest commemorates the building of significant additions to Mátyás Church (see pp82–3), which was then renamed after the king.

WHERE TO SEE THE GOTHIC AND RENAISSANCE CITY

The full bloom of the Gothic period took place in Hungary in the 14th century. Mátyás Church *(see pp82–3)* has portals that survive from this era. Renaissance art reached Hungary thanks to Italian masters brought by Mátyás's second wife, Beatrice. Both the Royal Palace *(pp70–71)* and the summer palace at Visegrád *(p164)* were outstanding pieces of Renaissance architecture. Since the storming of Buda by the Turks, only a few remnants of the former splendour have remained.

A chapel of the Royal Palace *from the period of Angevin rule can be seen in the Budapest History Museum (see p72).*

This portal of Mátyás Church *dates from the 14th century. In the 19th century, a Neo-Gothic porch was built around it.*

King Louis II

Hungarian knight

THE DISCOVERY OF LOUIS II'S BODY
At the Battle of Mohács, on 29 August 1526, King Louis II lost his life together with thousands of Hungarian and Polish knights. The tragic scene of the finding of his body was recreated by Bertalan Székely in 1859.

1440 Władysław III of Poland is Władysław I of Hungary

1456 Victory over Turks at the Battle of Belgrade

1473 *Chronica Hungarorum*, the first book to be published in Hungary, is printed by András Hess

1514 Peasant revolt under György Dózsa

Władysław II *(ruled 1490–1516)*

1450	1475	1500	1525	1550

1458–1490 Reign of Mátyás Corvinus

1444 Władysław I is killed during the Battle of Varna

1478 Law is passed threatening landlords who fail to maintain their buildings with dispossession

1526 Defeat by the Turks at the Battle of Mohács. King Louis II perishes during the fighting

Shield of soldier in the army of Mátyás Corvinus

The Turkish Occupation

Ottoman plate

After the battle of Mohács, the Turks razed Buda, but they temporarily turned their attention elsewhere and did not return to occupy it until 1541. When they then moved into the Royal Palace *(see pp70–71)*, Buda became the capital of Ottoman Hungary, while eastern Hungary and Transylvania were feudal suzerains. The Ottomans soon converted the city's churches, including Mátyás Church, into mosques and also built numerous Turkish baths *(see pp50–53)*. The Habsburgs tried relentlessly to recover Buda during this period. Their sieges destroyed the city progressively and when, in 1686, the Christian armies eventually recovered it the scene was one of devastation.

EXTENT OF THE CITY

▨ 1630	☐ Today

Turkish fortress on Gellért Hill

The Rudas and Rác Baths

The Liberation of Buda in 1686
After a bloody siege, the Christian army, led by Prince Charles of Lorraine, entered Buda and liberated it from the Turks. This painting by Gyula Benczúr, dating from 1896, depicts the event.

CITERIORIS Regni auata

Ottoman Tombstones
A few inscribed Ottoman tombstones, topped by distinctive turbans, remain to this day in Tabán (see p94).

PEST AND BUDA IN 1617
Georgius Hurnagel's copperplate print shows the heavily-fortified towns of Pest and Buda in a period when much of Hungary was firmly under Turkish rule.

TIMELINE

1526–41 Turks conquer Buda on three occasions		**1541–66** Reign of Sultan Süleyman I, "the Magnificent", who considered himself the Turkish king of Hungary		**1602–3** Austrians, led by General Herman Russworm, fail in attempts to storm Pest and Buda
	1529 János I Szapolyai, the Hungarian monarch, pays homage to Sultan Süleyman I			
1525	**1545**	**1565**	**1585**	**1605**

1530–40 János I Szapolyai rebuilds Buda

1542 The Austrians lay siege to Buda

Austrian siege of Buda

1594 Bálint Balassi, Hungary's first great lyric poet, is killed taking part in a battle against the Turks at Esztergom *(see p164)*

Campaign Tent

This Turkish leader's tent, decorated with appliqué work, was used during the siege of Vienna in 1683.

Mátyás Church *(see pp82–3)* was converted into a mosque.

Ottoman Coat

This 16th-century leather coat was supposedly taken from the battlefield of Mohács (see p25).

Ottoman Jug

Dating from the 17th century, this copper vessel was found in Buda during the reconstruction of the Royal Palace (see pp70–71).

WHERE TO SEE THE TURKISH CITY

Almost all Turkish buildings were razed by their successors, the Habsburgs, during or after the recapture of the city. Churches which the Turks had used as mosques were converted back again, although some *mihrabs*, the niches pointing towards Mecca, were left. These can be seen in the Inner City Parish Church *(see pp124–5)* and in the Capuchin Church *(p100)*. Among the few wonderful examples of classical Ottoman architecture to survive are the Rudas, Rác *(p95)* and Király Baths, and the Tomb of Gül Baba, a Turkish dervish *(p101)*.

The Király Baths, *built in the 16th century by Arshlan Pasha, remain an impressive Ottoman monument (see p101).*

The Rudas Baths *have an original Turkish dome covering their central chamber (see p93).*

Ottoman tablet with calligraphy

1634 György I Rákóczi, prince of Transylvania, joins an anti-Habsburg alliance with France and Sweden

1684 Start of ultimately successful siege of Buda by the Austrians

Viennese sword dating from the 17th century

1625	1645	1665	1685

1624 Signing of the Treaty of Vienna

1648 Death of György I Rákóczi

Gold five-ducat coin from 1603, showing the prince of Transylvania's crest

1686 Christian troops enter Buda. The end of Turkish rule in Hungary

Habsburg Rule

In order to gain control of Hungary, the Habsburgs encouraged foreign settlers, particularly Germans, to move into the country. This policy led to a national uprising in 1703–11, led by the prince of Transylvania, Ferenc II Rákóczi. Only in the second half of the 18th century, particularly under Empress Maria Theresa, did the reconstruction of Buda, Óbuda and Pest begin in earnest. This was accompanied by economic development and a further increase in the country's population. The university at Nagyszombat (now Trnava in the Slovak Republic) moved to Buda in 1777, and subsequently to Pest in 1784, and was an important factor in their expansion.

Order created by Maria Theresa

EXTENT OF THE CITY

☐ 1770   ☐ Today

Maria Theresa holds the infant Joseph, the successor to her throne.

The Return of the Crown to Buda *(1790)*
A vast ceremonial procession of commissioners marked the arrival in Hungary of royal insignias from Vienna, a sign of peace between the two countries.

Ferenc II Rákóczi
This fine portrait by Ádám Mányoki depicts Ferenc II Rákóczi, the leader of the national uprising of 1703– 11 and a figure much loved by the Hungarian people.

"VITAM ET SANGUINEM"
In 1741, the Hungarian states swore on "life and blood" their loyalty to the Habsburg Empress Maria Theresa. This copperplate print by Joseph Szentpétery depicts the scene of the oath-taking.

TIMELINE

1687 Under Austrian pressure, the Hungarian parliament gives up its right to elect a king and accedes to the inheritance of the throne by the Habsburgs

1702 The Jesuits open a college and theological seminary

1703 The Prince of Transylvania, Ferenc II Rákóczi, leads a rebellion by the Hungarians against the Habsburgs

1729 The start of the reconstruction of Pest's suburbs

1690	1705	1720	1735

1689 Bubonic plague devastates the population of Buda and Pest

Royal postal carriage

1711 Suppression of Rákóczi's rebellion; a second bubonic plague decimates the city

1724 The population of Buda and Pest reaches 12,000 people

1723 Great Fire of Buda

Triple-jug of the Andrássy family
These silver jugs are joined by a miniature of the castle belonging to the Andrássy family, at what is now Krásna Hôrka in the Slovak Republic.

Hungarian aristocrats swear on their lives to protect Maria Theresa's throne.

Dress *(c. 1750)*
This dress, typical of Hungarian style with its corset which was tightened by golden cords, was worn by a lady from the noble Majtényi family.

Ferenc II Rákóczi's Chair
Richly upholstered, this graceful 18th-century chair from Regéc Castle is typical of the style of the period.

WHERE TO SEE THE HABSBURG CITY

Having taken Buda and Pest from the Turks in the late 17th century, the Habsburgs set about rebuilding them in the 18th century, mainly in the Baroque style. Famous buildings from this era include the Municipal Council Offices, St Anne's Church *(see pp102–3)*, St Elizabeth's Church *(p101)* and the University Church *(p139)*.

St Anne's Church, *which was built between 1740–1805, astonishes visitors with its magnificent Baroque interior.*

The Municipal Council Offices *in the heart of Pest have a portico decorated with allegorical figures by Johann Christoph Mader (see p127).*

5–71 Building of the sburg Royal Palace

The magnificent Habsburg Royal Palace

1788 First Hungarian newspaper, *Magyar Merkurius*, begins printing

A hussar, or soldier

1778 Roman remains are discovered in Óbuda

1750	1765	1780	1795

1752 A regular postal service operates between Buda and Vienna

1766 A floating bridge links Buda and Pest

1792 Convocation of parliament and the coronation of Franz I

46–57 Construction of the Zichy lace in Óbuda *(see p171)*

1777 University moves from Nagyszombat to Buda; later relocates to Pest

1784 Establishment of Ferenc Goldberger's textile factory in Óbuda

National Revival and the "Springtime of Revolutions"

The dynamic economic development of Buda and Pest began at the start of the 19th century. Pest, in particular, benefited from favourable circumstances for the grain trade and became, in the Napoleonic Wars, an important centre for the Habsburg monarchy. A national revival and rekindling of cultural life took place after the Napoleonic Wars. The Hungarian National Museum and many other public and private buildings were built at this time. Yet, Hungarian reformers were hampered by the Viennese royal court and an uprising erupted in the spring of 1848. This rebellion was suppressed by the Habsburgs, with the help of the Russian army, and a period of absolutism followed.

Hungarian crest

EXTENT OF THE CITY
■ 1848   □ Today

Count György Andrássy, offered 10,000 forints towards the building of the Hungarian Academy of Sciences.

The Advance of the Hussars
In this watercolour, painted in 1850, Mór Than depicts fighting in the Battle of Tápióbicske of 1849. The Hungarian side was led by a Polish general, Henryk Dembiński.

The Great Flood
This bas-relief, made by Barnabás Holló in 1900, shows a heroic rescue by Count Miklós Wesselényi during the Great Flood of 1838.

THE FOUNDING OF THE ACADEMY
In 1825, István Széchenyi put up 60,000 forints towards the building of Hungarian Academy of Sciences *(see p114)*, a move which led to a national effort to collect funds for it. Barnabás Holló created this bas-relief depicting the major donors.

TIMELINE

1802 Count Ferenc Széchenyi donates collections which will form the basis for Széchenyi National Library *(see p72)* and Hungarian National Museum *(see pp130–33)*

1809 Royal court moves from Vienna to Buda as Napoleon advances. Despite his offer of Hungarian independence, the Hungarians back the Habsburgs

1817 First steamboat sails on Danube in the environs of Buda and Pest

| 1800 | 1805 | 1810 | 1815 | 1820 |

1808 Establishment of the Embellishment Commission, led by Governor Archduke Joseph

Boats on the Danube

Lajos Batthyány Eternal Flame

This lamp, designed by Móric Pogány, has burnt since 1926 in Liberty Square (see p110). It was there that the Austrians shot Lajos Batthyány, the first prime minister of liberated Hungary, on 6 October 1849.

National Song

The 1848 uprising was sparked on 15 March when Sándor Petőfi recited his poem, Nemzeti Dal *(National Song), outside the Hungarian National Museum.*

WHERE TO SEE THE NEO-CLASSICAL CITY

In the early 19th century, the Embellishment Commission, set up by Archduke Joseph and led by architect János Hild, prepared a plan for the development of Pest in which its centre was redesigned on a pattern of concentric streets. Monumental Neo-Classical buildings were built here and to this day they form the heart and the character of this area. Structures to look for in particular include the Hungarian National Museum, the Chain Bridge and several houses located on József Nádor Square *(see p126).*

The Hungarian National Museum, *which was built in 1837, is among Hungary's finest examples of Neo-Classical architecture (see pp130–31).*

The Chain Bridge, *the first permanent bridge over the Danube, was built by Adam Clark in 1839–49 (see p63).*

Count István Széchenyi, an energetic force for change, is regarded as the one of the greatest Hungarians.

György Károlyi

Buda and Pest in 1838

Seen here in the year before the construction of the Chain Bridge, the Danube was an important means of transport.

1825–48 Period of major projects; establishment of the Hungarian Academy of Sciences, Hungarian National Museum and National Theatre

Poet Sándor Petőfi (1823–49)

1840 Language Act: Hungarian takes over from Latin as the official language of the nation

15 March 1848 Uprising begins

1847 Death of Archduke Joseph, emperor's governor

1825	1830	1835	1840	1845

1830 István Széchenyi publishes his book, *On Credit*. It is seen as the manifesto for the fight for modern Hungary

The Great Flood

1838 Catastrophic Great Flood results in destruction of half of Pest's buildings

1846 First railway line in the city, linking Pest and Vác

1849 After stout resistance, the Russian army, under the command of General Ivan Paskievicz, suppresses uprising

Compromise and the Unification of Budapest

After suffering a defeat by Prussia in 1866, the Habsburgs realized the necessity of reaching an agreement with Hungary and the Compromise brokered in 1867 proved to be of tremendous importance for the future of Buda, Óbuda and Pest, as it created political stability and prosperity and marked the beginning of rapid industrialization in the country. The option of uniting the three cities had been considered since the opening of the Chain Bridge in 1849. It eventually came about in 1873 and Budapest soon found itself among Europe's fastest growing metropolises. In 1896, Városliget was the focal point for Hungary's Millennium Celebrations (see p142).

EXTENT OF THE CITY

☐ 1873   ☐ Today

The Citadel (see p92) on Gellért Hill

Castle District

Hungarian Wine Cup
This 19th-century wine cup is embellished with the Hungarian crest, which incorporates the Crown of the Árpáds (see p23).

Ferenc Deák
(1803–76)
A great statesman, Deák was an advocate of moderate reforms. He argued persuasively in favour of accepting the Compromise reached with the Habsburgs in 1867.

Today's Boráros tér, where goods were once traded.

Decorative Pipe *(1896)*
Made in the year of Hungary's Millennium Celebrations, this pipe of "heavenly peace" includes figures of the Árpád kings and Emperor Franz Joseph.

TIMELINE

1854 Martial law ends five years after 1848–9 uprising

1856 Tunnel (see p100) built by Adam Clark under Castle Hill

Entrance to the Tunnel

1875 Opening of the Franz Liszt Academy of Music (see p129), with the composer as its principal

1850	1860	1870	1880

1859 Synagogue on Dohány utca (see p134) completed

1864 Opening of the Great Market Hall (see p203)

1873 The unification of Buda, Óbuda and Pest as one city, with a total of 300,000 inhabitants

1867 Compromise with Austria, giving Hungary independence in its internal affairs. Creation of the Dual Monarchy; Emperor Franz Joseph accepts the Hungarian crown

Monument to Hungarian Soldiers Killed in World War I

This bas-relief, by János Istók, commemorates the dead of World War I, in which Hungary fought on the German side. It is located next to the main entrance to the Servite Church (see p128).

"Handcuff" Bracelet

Following the defeat of the national uprising of 1848–9, Hungarians sought to symbolize their oppression even in pieces of jewellery.

WHERE TO SEE THE HISTORICIST CITY

Historicism had a profound influence on the form of the rapidly developing metropolis at this time. A wonderful example of the style is the Hungarian Academy of Sciences. Among others are Parliament *(see pp108–9)*, St Stephen's Basilica *(pp116–17)*, the Museum of Fine Arts *(pp146–7)*, the New York Palace *(p129)* and many of the buildings that stand on Andrássy Street *(p144)*.

The Hungarian Academy of Sciences *is housed in this fine Neo-Renaissance palace dating from 1864 (see p114).*

St Stephen's Basilica *was built over a period of 60 years by three architects. It was finished in 1905 (see pp116–17).*

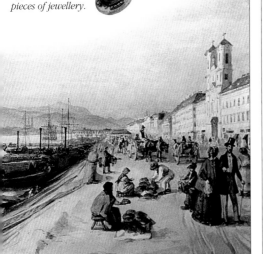

TRADING ON THE PEST EMBANKMENT

Completed in 1887, this painting by Antal Ligeti shows the Pest embankment at a time when the city was booming. Manufactured goods and grain were sent along the Danube for sale in Germany and the Balkans.

1894 Body of Lajos Kossuth *(see p106)* is returned from Turin

1904 Grand opening of Parliament *(see pp108–9)*

Old Upper House Hall in Parliament

1916 Franz Joseph dies and Charles IV becomes king of Hungary

1890	1900	1910	1920

1896 First metro line and several museums opened

1909 Airport opened in Rákos, now Kőbánya

1900 With a population of 773,000, Budapest is Europe's fastest growing city

1914 Hungary enters World War I on the German side

1918 Abdication of Charles IV marks end of the Austro-Hungarian Empire

Modern Budapest

Poster for Unicum liqueur (see p193)

Hungary paid a high price for its alliances first with Austria and later with Nazi Germany. Following defeat in both World Wars, the country had lost a large portion of its territory. As a result of the Yalta Agreement of 1945, it then found itself within the Soviet-controlled zone of Europe. Stalinism took on a particularly ruthless form here and led to the 1956 Uprising, which was brutally put down by Soviet tanks on the streets of Budapest.

Efforts towards reform, undertaken by János Kádár, brought some changes but political opposition was not tolerated. In 1989, the Communists were ousted and Hungary at last regained control of its own affairs.

1944 Efforts to withdraw from World War II end with German troops entering the country. A ghetto is established in Budapest and the extermination of Hungarian Jews begins. As the Russian army approaches the city, all bridges across the Danube are blown up

1945 After a siege lasting six weeks, the Russian army takes Budapest

1946 Proclamation of Republic of Hungary. Smallholders' Party wins elections

1919 Communists take over government and declare the Hungarian Soviet Republic

1941 Hungary enters World War II on Germany's side

1947 After falsification of election results, Communists control the whole country

1939 Hungary neutral at beginning of World War II. Accepts refugees after capitulation of Poland

1957 János Kádár is first secretary of Hungarian Socialist Workers' Party

1922 Reopening of the State Opera House (see pp118–19) after World War I

1949 Stalinist terror prevails. Cardinal Mindszenty (see p111) goes on trial. László Rajk, secret police chief, sentenced to death by Moscow loyalists

1928 Budapest is a free port on Danube

1937 Sixth and last visit of author Thomas Mann

| 1920 | 1930 | 1940 | 1950 |

| 1920 | 1930 | 1940 | 1950 |

1935 Tabán (see p94) levelled and transformed into a park

1938 Eucharistic Congress

1953 The national football team beats England 6–3 at Wembley

1925 Radio Budapest broadcasts its first programme

1948 Mátyás Rákosi leads Hungarian Socialist Workers' Party, created by Communists

1919 Admiral Miklós Horthy enters Budapest; many killed in the period of "White Terror". Horthy becomes regent

1945–1 August 1946 Monetary reform. Banknotes valued at one billion pengő are printed during rampant inflation. There is not enough room for all the zeros to be shown on the notes

1918 Democratic revolution; Hungary declared a republic. Mihály Károlyi selected as the country's first president

1956 National uprising is suppressed through Soviet intervention

1958 The leader of the 1956 Uprising, Prime Minister Imre Nagy, is executed

1960–66 Rebuilding of Castle District *(see pp68–85),* including Royal Palace, and the Danube bridges

October 1989 Republic of Hungary is proclaimed once more. The national emblem is changed

September 1989 Hungary opens its borders to allow refugees to flee from East Germany to the West

1964 The Elizabeth Bridge *(see p63)* reopens to traffic, having been totally reconstructed

1981 Director István Szabó receives an Oscar for his film *Mefisto*

February 1989 Round- table talks between opposition parties and ruling socialist government

1991 Warsaw Pact is dissolved. Russian army leaves Hungary

1994 Election won by the Hungarian Socialist Party

1998 Election won by the Citizens' Party

2002 Election won by the Hungarian Socialist Party. Imre Kertész receives the Nobel prize for Literature

2007 Hungary joins the Schengen open-borders agreement

1970	1980	1990	2000

1970	1980	1990	2000

1968 Introduction of new economic system known as "goulash-Communism"

1987 UNESCO places the historic Castle District and the Banks of the Danube on its list of world heritage sights

June 1989 Ceremonial funeral for Imre Nagy and rehabilitation for other leaders of 1956 Uprising

1990 The Democratic Hungarian Forum wins free elections. József Antall becomes the first prime minister to be elected in a democratic process; Árpád Göncz is elected president

2004 Hungary becomes a member of the EU

1993 Pope John Paul II visits Hungary

1970 Opening of a new metro line

1991 Václav Havel, József Antall and Lech Walesa sign an agreement in Visegrád *(see p164)* between Czechoslovakia, Hungary and Poland

BUDAPEST AT A GLANCE

Often described as the "Little Paris of Middle Europe", Budapest is famous not only for the monuments reflecting its own 1,000-year-old culture, but also for the relics of others who settled here. Remains from both Roman occuption, and, much later, rule by the Turks can still be seen in the city. After Turkish rule, union with Austria had a partic-ular influence on the city's form and style. Descriptions of nearly 150 places of interest can be found in the *Area by Area* section of the book. However, to help you make the most of your stay, the following 20 pages are a guide to the best Budapest has to offer. Museums and galleries, churches and synagogues, palaces and historic buildings, baths and pools are presented, together with the influence of Secession in the city. Each sight is is cross-referenced to its main entry. Below are the sights not to be missed.

BUDAPEST'S TOP TEN SIGHTS

Váci Street
See p127.

Gellért Monument
See p93.

Gellért Baths
See pp90–91.

Parliament
See pp108–9.

National Museum
See pp130–33.

State Opera House
See pp118–19.

Margaret Island
See pp172–3.

Danube and Chain Bridge
See p62.

Mátyás Church
See pp82–3.

National Gallery
See pp74–7.

◁ **The Neo-Renaissance façade of the City Council Chamber** *(see p138)* in the centre of Pest

Budapest's Best: Museums and Galleries

Unlike many other European cities – such as Paris with the Louvre and Madrid with the Prado – Budapest does not have a museum founded from a royal treasury because Hungary was for so long ruled by foreign powers. In the early 19th century, however, the modern aristocracy, backed by an increasingly affluent middle class, began to take an interest in preserving historic objects for the nation. Today, there are over 60 museums and galleries in Budapest, ranging from those with collections of international significance to others of much more local interest. For more information on museums and galleries see pages 40–41.

Museum of Military History
This museum has interesting displays illustrating the history of Hungarian weaponry.

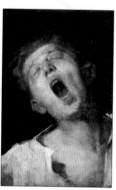

Hungarian National Gallery
The Hungarian art displayed here dates from the Middle Ages right through to the 20th century. The Yawning Apprentice (1868), by the great Mihály Munkácsy, is among the highlights of the collection.

North of the Castle

DANUBE

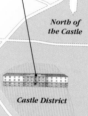

Castle District

Budapest History Museum
This Gothic work is one of the medieval treasures of the Budapest History Museum. The oldest exhibits are located in the original, lower-floor rooms of the Renaissance Royal Palace.

Gellért Hill and Tabán

| 0 metres | 500 |
| 0 yards | 500 |

Semmelweis Museum of Medical History
Doctor Ignác Semmelweis, famous for his discovery of how to prevent puerperal fever, was born in 1818 in the house where the museum is now situated.

Ethnographical Museum

Among the exhibits at this museum illustrating the material culture of the Hungarians is this jug, dating from 1864, made by György Mantl. There are also impressive displays concerning tribal societies in other parts of the world.

Museum of Fine Arts

The wonderful Portrait of a Man *(c.1565), by Paolo Veronese, is one of many Old Masters in this splendid collection of paintings and sculpture.*

Around Parliament

Around Városliget

Central Pest

Jewish Museum

Located in several rooms beside the Great Synagogue, this museum covers the Holocaust in this country and displays religious objects.

Hungarian National Museum

Beautiful frescoes by Károly Lotz and Mór Than decorate the elegant staircase of Hungary's oldest museum.

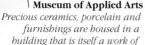

Museum of Applied Arts

Precious ceramics, porcelain and furnishings are housed in a building that is itself a work of art, surmounted by a magnificent, oriental-style dome.

Exploring the Museums and Galleries

Most of the city's museums and galleries are located in historic buildings. These include the spacious chambers of the restored Royal Palace, which in the 1970s and 1980s were designated as the premises of several museums, including the Hungarian National Gallery. The largest museums – including the Hungarian National Museum and Budapest History Museum – also stage temporary exhibitions that are popular with both locals and tourists.

Processional crucifix

Sculpture of Imre Varga at the gallery named after him *(see p171)*

HUNGARIAN PAINTINGS AND SCULPTURE

There are two important venues that should be on the itinerary of anyone interested in viewing the finest examples of Hungarian art.

At the **Hungarian National Gallery**, seven chronological sections present paintings and sculpture dating from the Middle Ages up until modern times. The sequence begins in the Lapidarium, where fragments of recovered medieval stone sculptures from the castles of the first Hungarian kings are exhibited.

As a rule, very few examples of Gothic and Renaissance art survive in Budapest because of the pillage inflicted by the Turks during their rule. However, a fine collection of altar retables from the 15th and 16th centuries are on display in the Hungarian National Gallery. In the 19th century, Hungarian painting developed and flourished, at the same time reflecting all the major international modern art movements. The Hungarian style can be seen particularly in the works of Pál Szinyei-Merse, Mihály Munkácsy and László Paál. For sculpture, meanwhile, the main names to look out for are István Ferenczy, Zsigmond Kisfaludi Stróbl and Imre Varga.

It is portraits, rather than paintings and sculpture, that are shown at the **Hungarian National Museum**. These provide a fascinating insight into the country's history.

The **Vasarely Museum** has a collection of 300 works by Hungarian-born artist Victor Vasarely. He moved to Paris in 1930 and became famous as one of the main exponents of the Op Art movement.

EUROPEAN PAINTINGS AND SCULPTURE

Masterpieces by the finest European artists, from medieval times to the modern day, are also divided between two museums in Budapest.

The **Museum of Fine Arts** has a magnificent collection of Italian paintings, dating from the 14th century up to the Baroque period, by masters such as Titian, Antonio Correggio, Paolo Veronese, Giambattista Tiepolo and Jacopo Tintoretto. However, it is the *Esterházy Madonna* (1508) by Raphael, that is the jewel of the Italian collection. Equally splendid is the exhibition of Spanish paintings, which is one of the largest in the world. Works by Goya include *The Water Carrier* (c.1810). There are seven canvases by El Greco and others by Francisco de Zurbarán and Bartolomé Esteban Murillo. Other galleries within the museum represent artists of the Netherlands and Germany, as well as British, French and Flemish masters. The museum also owns more than 100,000 drawings and engravings by the Old Masters, while its modern art collection includes some notable works.

Modern European paintings can also be viewed in the **Ludwig Museum of Contemporary Art**. All the canvases belong to the Peter Ludwig Foundation of Germany. Highly prized works here include two paintings by Pablo Picasso, *Mother and Child* and *Musketeer*.

Pablo Picasso's *Musketeer* (1967), in the Ludwig Collection

The Jewish Museum, located beside the Great Synagogue

HISTORY

The history of Budapest, and that of Hungary as a whole, is illustrated in several museums. Relics from the Roman era can be found at the **Aquincum Museum** and at a handful of museums, including the **Roman Camp Museum**, in Óbuda.

The most important national historic treasures are housed in the **Hungarian National Museum**. The Coronation Mantle, dating back to the 11th century, is included in this collection.

Medieval seals and Gothic statuary are among the exhibits at **Budapest History Museum**. At the **Museum of Military History**, displays chart various Hungarian struggles for liberty, including the 1956 Uprising (see p34).

The **Jewish Museum** has a room covering the Holocaust, as well as many ritual objects. The collection of the **Lutheran Museum**, situated next to the Lutheran Church, includes a copy of Martin Luther's will.

MUSIC

Two of the museums featured in this book, the **Franz Liszt Museum** and the **Zoltán Kodály Museum**, are dedicated to internationally renowned composers. In each case, the setting is the apartment where the composer lived and worked, and on display are the instruments they played, musical scores and photographs.

A more general view of Hungarian music is on offer at the **Museum of Musical History**, located in a Baroque palace on Mihály Táncsics Street. Displays feature the development of instruments and music in the 18th and 19th centuries; a special section is dedicated to Béla Bartók.

ETHNOGRAPHY AND ORIENTAL CRAFTS

Lavish folk costumes, as well as many other everyday items that belonged to the people of the region, can be viewed in the beautiful interiors of the **Ethnographical Museum**. The museum also has a section that focuses on the primitive tribes of Africa, America and, particularly, Asia. It is in Asia that the Hungarians seek their roots as it is from there that the Magyars are thought to have come.

This fascination with the Orient has led to the foundation of two other museums displaying Eastern artefacts. The **Ferenc Hopp Museum of Far Eastern Art** has assorted Indian objects; its Chinese and Japanese collections are displayed at the **Ráth György Museum**.

DECORATIVE ARTS

Housed in an extraordinary building designed by Ödön Lechner (see p56), the **Museum of Applied Arts** gives an impressive overview of the development of crafts from the Middle Ages onwards. Meissen porcelain is exhibited alongside oriental carpets and

Stained-glass window at the Museum of Applied Arts

Hungarian pieces. The display relating to the Secession (see pp54–7) is striking. The museum's permanent collection was founded in 1872. Major exhibitions tend to change each year, while smaller national and foreign displays change monthly.

SPECIALIST MUSEUMS

The **Semmelweis Museum of Medical History** explores the work of a doctor called Ignác Semmelweis, who discovered how to prevent puerperal fever. This affliction had previously been a serious threat for women who had recently given birth. The **Golden Eagle Pharmacy Museum** is situated in a building that first opened as a pharmacy in 1681. Many original fixtures are intact and pharmaceutical exhibits are displayed.

Railway enthusiasts of all ages will appreciate the **Transport Museum** on Hermina Street, with its enormous collection of model trains and exhibits on the evolution of air, sea, road and rail transport.

Budapest's Best: Churches and Synagogues

There are very few medieval and Renaissance churches still standing in Budapest. This is mainly due to the fact that the Turks, during their 150-year rule, turned all churches into mosques, which were later destroyed during the attacks on Buda and Pest by the Christians. The reconstruction of old churches and the building of new ones started in the late 17th century, hence the prevalence of Baroque and Neo-Classical styles.

Capuchin Church
Two Turkish windows remain from the time when this church was used as a mosque, alongside fragments of its medieval walls.

St Anne's Church
Built in the mid-18th century, this is one of the most beautiful Baroque churches in the city. The joined figures of St Anne and Mary decorate the centre of its façade.

North of the Castle

DANUBE

Castle District

Mátyás Church
Romanesque and Gothic styles are both evident in the coronation church of the Hungarian kings. The Neo-Gothic altar dates from the 19th century.

Gellért Hill and Tabán

Rock Church
In the rocky interior of St István's Cave, on the south side of Gellért Hill, the priests of the Pauline order established a church in 1926. It was designed to imitate the holy grotto at Lourdes.

| 0 metres | 500 |
| 0 yards | 500 |

St Stephen's Basilica
A bas-relief by Leó Feszler, representing the Virgin Mary surrounded by Hungarian saints, decorates the main tympanum of St Stephen's Basilica. This imposing church was built between 1851–1905.

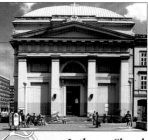

Lutheran Church
This Neo-Classical church was completed by Mihály Pollack in 1808. The impressive façade was added half a century later by József Hild.

Around Városliget

Around Parliament

Central Pest

Great Synagogue
Two Moorish-style minarets, each topped by an onion-shaped dome, dominate the exterior of the largest synagogue in Europe.

Franciscan Church
The magnificent 19th-century paintings that decorate the interior of this Baroque church are by Károly Lotz.

Inner City Parish Church
Dating from 1046, this church is Pest's oldest building. A figure of St Florian, the patron saint of fire fighters, was placed on the wall beside the altar after the church survived the great fire of 1723.

Exploring the Churches and Synagogues

Detail on St Elizabeth's Church

Most of the city's churches are found around the centres of Buda and Pest. Only a few sacred buildings of architectural interest are situated on the outskirts of the city. The greatest period of construction took place in the 18th century, after the final expulsion of the Turks. Another phase occurred in the second half of the 19th century, producing two of Budapest's grandest places of worship: St Stephen's Basilica and the Great Synagogue. Religious buildings were neglected after World War II, but thanks to restoration some have now regained their former splendour.

Reconstructed Gothic window of the Church of St Mary Magdalene

MEDIEVAL

Both **Mátyás Church** and the **Inner City Parish Church** date originally from the reign of Béla IV in the 13th century. Glimpses of their original Romanesque style can be seen, although each church was subsequently rebuilt in the Gothic style. After being sacked by the Turks in 1526,

Mátyás Church was given a Baroque interior by the Jesuits who had at that time taken it over. Finally, the church was returned to a likeness of its medieval character between 1874–96, when all Baroque elements were systematically removed and it was given a Neo-Gothic shape.

The **Church of St Mary Magdalene**, built in 1274 in the Gothic style, was almost completely destroyed in 1945. All that remains intact today is the 15th-century tower with its two chapels. A Gothic window has also been rebuilt.

St Michael's Church, founded in the 12th century on Margaret Island, was completely destroyed by the Turks. However, in 1932 it was reconstructed from its original Romanesque plans.

BAROQUE

In the 18th century, 17 churches were built in Pest, Buda and Óbuda, all of them in the Baroque style. The influence of the Italian architectural school is visible in many of them, although only

University Church was built by an Italian architect, Donato Allio. Under Habsburg rule, the leading architects working in the city, András Meyerhoffer, Mátyás Nepauer and Kristóf Hamon, often chose to follow Austrian examples.

University Church and **St Anne's Church** are generally considered to be the most beautiful buildings in the city dating from this era. The former astonishes visitors with its beautifully carved stalls and pulpit, and with the paintings by Johann Bergl adorning its vaults. St Anne's Church has a magnificent Baroque façade and reveals the influence of southern German Baroque in its oval floor plan. Inside, there is a lavish altar and pulpit designed by Károly Bebó.

The **Franciscan Church**, which is situated in the centre of Budapest and dates from 1758, has a wide Baroque nave and a main altar created by Antal Grassalkovich.

The interior of the Servite Church (1725), with its Baroque altar

SPIRES AND DOMES

The Gothic spire belonging to the Church of St Mary Magdalene and the Neo-Gothic spire of Mátyás Church are among Budapest's main landmarks. The twin Baroque towers of St Anne's Church and the soaring spire of the Calvinist Church rise above the Danube in Buda. On the Pest side, the dome of St Stephen's Basilica and the minarets of the Great Synagogue dominate.

Gothic spire of the Church of St Mary Magdalene

Baroque towers of St Anne's Church

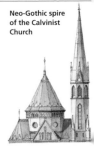

Neo-Gothic spire of the Calvinist Church

NEO-CLASSICAL AND HISTORICIST

In 1781, Joseph II passed an edict permitting the building of Protestant churches. The city already had many Catholic churches and Protestant communities now started to build their own places of worship in the prevailing style of the time, Neo-Classicism.

One of the first to go up was the **Lutheran Church**, on Deák Ferenc tér, completed in 1808 by Mihály Pollack, a gifted master of Neo-Classical architecture. The white, ascetic interior of the church, with its two-floor gallery, was ideally suited to the nature of this place of worship. The majesty and simplicity of the Neo-Classical style corresponded with the more austere nature of Protestant belief. József Hild, another master of the style, later extended the church. He added the portico with its Doric columns, linking the church with the presbytery and a school. The complex as a whole is one of the best examples of Neo-Classical architecture in Budapest.

On a more modest scale is the **Calvinist Church**, built in the Neo-Gothic style between 1893–6.

When plans for it were drawn up by József Hild in 1845, **St Stephen's Basilica** was intended to be the pinnacle of Neo-Classical architecture. However, several delays, including the collapse of its dome at one point, meant

Baptismal font at the Lutheran Church

that the realization of the original design was impossible. Following Hild's death in 1867, Miklós Ybl continued the project. He departed from Hild's plan, incorporating Renaissance-style features. The Basilica was finally completed by a third architect, József Kauser, in 1905.

LATE 19TH- AND 20TH-CENTURY

The two most stunning synagogues in Budapest were designed by Viennese architects in the second half of the 19th century.

Ludwig Förster constructed the **Great Synagogue** in Byzantine-Moorish style in 1859 and Otto Wagner, an important Secession architect *(see pp54–7),* realized one of his first projects in 1872. This was the **Orthodox Synagogue** on Rumbach utca, which also incorporated Moorish ideas.

Closely linked to the Secession style is the Hungarian National Style, based on an idiosyncratic combination of ethnic motifs and elements from folk art. This style is most visible in two churches by Hungarian architects. Ödön Lechner, the originator of the Hungarian National Style, completed **Kőbánya Parish Church**, on the outskirts of Budapest, in 1900. Meanwhile, Aladár Árkay built **Városliget Calvinist Church** in 1913. These two churches display a striking combination of

The Byzantine-Moorish interior of the Great Synagogue

colourful ceramics, Eastern-style ornamentation and also Neo-Gothic elements.

Moorish-style towers of the Great Synagogue

Dome of the eclectic St Stephen's Basilica

Budapest's Best: Palaces and Historic Buildings

Detail on the façade of Károly Palace

Budapest boasts historic buildings and palaces in a broad range of architectural styles. The majority represent the Neo-Classicism, Historicism and Secession of the 19th and early 20th centuries, when a dynamic development of the capital took place. All but a few Gothic and Renaissance details were lost in the destruction of Buda and Pest by Christian troops in 1686, but some examples of its Baroque heritage remain. This map gives some highlights, with a more detailed look on pages 48–9.

Royal Palace
This palace has a turbulent history dating back to the 13th century. Its present form, however, reflects the opulence of the 19th century. Today the palace houses some of the city's finest museums.

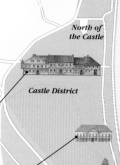

North of the Castle

Castle District

Houses on Vienna Gate Square
This charming row of four houses was built in the late 18th and early 19th centuries on the ruins of medieval dwellings. The houses are adorned with decorative motifs in the Baroque, Rococo and Neo-Classical styles.

Gellért Hill and Tabán

Sándor Palace
The original friezes that decorated this 19th-century palace were recreated by Hungarian artists as part of its restoration. The palace is now the headquarters of the President of the Republic of Hungary.

Várkert Casino
This Neo-Renaissance pavilion was built by Miklós Ybl (see p119) as a pump house for the Royal Palace. It now houses the luxurious Várkert Casino.

Hungarian Academy of Science

The façade of the academy is adorned with statues by Emil Wolff and Miklós Izsó, symbolizing major fields of knowledge: law, natural history, mathematics, philosophy, linguistics and history.

Gresham Palace

Now housing a Four Seasons Hotel, this splendid example of Secession design was built in 1905–7 by Zsigmond Quittner.

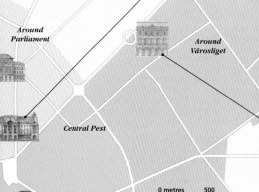

Around Parliament

Around Városliget

Central Pest

0 metres	500
0 yards	500

Pallavicini Palace

Gustáv Petschacher built this Neo-Renaissance mansion on Kodály körönd in 1882. The inner court-yard was copied from the Palazzo Marini in Milan.

Ervin Szabó Library

The grand, Neo-Baroque palace that now houses this library was originally built in 1887 for the Wenckheims, a family of rich industrialists.

Péterffy Palace

This plaque, commemorating a flood of 1838, was placed on one of the few Baroque mansions that remain in Pest. The house was built in 1756.

Exploring the Palaces and Historic Buildings

Little more than fragments remain of Budapest's Gothic and Renaissance past. However, some Baroque buildings have survived in Buda's Castle District and Víziváros. Neo-Classicism, on the other hand, has a much wider presence; there are many apartment buildings, palaces and secular monuments built in this style, especially around the old fortification walls of Pest on the eastern side of the Danube. Historicism dominated the architecture of the second half of the 19th century. It played a vital role in the enlargement of the city as it expressed and celebrated the optimism of the era.

Façade of the Gross Palace, built by Jószef Hild in 1824

BAROQUE PALACES AND BUILDINGS

Many buildings in the Castle District and neighbouring Víziváros, around Fő utca, have retained their original Baroque façades. The main entrance of the **Hilton Hotel**, formerly a 17th-century Jesuit college, is a fine example.

Other outstanding instances of this style are the four houses on **Vienna Gate Square, the Batthyány Palace** on Parade Square and the **Erdődy Palace** on Mihály Táncsics Street, now the Museum of Musical History.

The **Zichy Palace** in Óbuda is a splendid Baroque edifice, and the buildings of the former **Trinitarian Monastery**, now the Kiscelli Museum, stand as significant models of the style.

There are only two Baroque monuments remaining in Pest. The **Péterffy Palace**, a mansion that stands below the current street level, dates from 1755. Pest's other Baroque edifice was, however, the first to be built in either Buda or Pest. The huge complex of the **Municipal County Offices**, formerly a hospital for veterans of the Turkish wars, was constructed by the Italian master Anton Erhard Martinelli. It was greatly admired by Empress Maria Theresa, who declared it to be more beautiful than the Schönbrunn Palace in Vienna.

NEO-CLASSICAL PALACES AND BUILDINGS

Neo-classicism, influenced by ancient Greco-Roman design, was popular in the first half of the 19th century as it reflected the confidence of this period of national awakening and social reform. Many monumental Neo-Classical structures were produced, including the Chain Bridge, built in 1839–49. The leading Neo-Classical architect was Mihály Pollack, who built the **Hungarian National Museum**.

Two stunning Neo-Classical palaces deserve particular mention – **Sándor Palace** in Buda and **Károlyi Palace** in Pest. The first stands on Castle Hill, by the top of the funicular railway, and impresses visitors with its harmonious elegance. The second, now housing the Petőfi Literary Museum, gained its present form in 1834 after considerable reconstruction.

A group of particularly attractive Neo-Classical houses is situated on **József Nádor Square**. Some of their features, such as the pillars, projections and tympanums, merit individual attention.

In 1808, the Embellishment Commission was set up by the Austrian architect János Hild to develop Pest. He and his son, József Hild, who built the **Gross Palace** in 1824, were both involved in the general restoration of the city. Having studied architecture in Rome, they created many splendid Italianate buildings.

The outstanding Baroque façade of Erdődy Palace, Museum of Musical History

HISTORICIST PALACES AND BUILDINGS

In the second half of the 19th century, Historicism took precedence over Neo-Classicism. After the unification of Buda, Óbuda and Pest in 1873, Historicism had a significant influence on the city's architectural development. In this period Budapest gained an eclectic mix of new apartment buildings and palaces, as Historicist architects sourced different genres for inspiration. Miklós Ybl, whose work includes the **State Opera House** and the expansion of the **Royal Palace**, looked to the Renaissance, while Imre Steindl designed a Neo-Gothic **Parliament** (to which a Neo-Renaissance dome was added). Frigyes Schulek's **Fishermen's Bastion** features

Neo-Gothic and Neo-Romanesque designs.

The **Vigadó**, a concert hall built by Frigyes Feszl between 1859 and 1864, is often thought of as the most magnificent Historicist building, with its façade richly decorated with relief sculptures and busts of the great Hungarians. However, the complex of three French-style, Neo-Renaissance palaces, Festetics, Károly and Esterházy, in **Mihály Pollack Square**, is also considered by many to be a fine example.

The **Drechsler Palace** in Andrássy út is a marvellous model of Neo-Renaissance design, while the **Divatcsarnok** department store features Lotz's Hall, stunningly decorated with paintings and gold. The twin apartment buildings known as the **Klotild Palaces** incorporate Spanish-Baroque motifs and

Sculptures on the Vigadó façade

Beautiful Neo-Baroque interior of the New York Palace

can be admired near the Elizabeth Bridge. Perhaps one of the most extravagant of all the examples of Historicism in the city is the Neo-Baroque **New York Palace** by Alajos Hauszmann, which has a luxurious interior of marble columns and rich colour.

DECORATIVE FEATURES

The façades of many palaces and buildings still display the rich sculptural decoration characteristic of the various styles of architecture prevalent in the city. These features include coves, cartouches, finials, relief sculptures and ornamental window frames.

Regrettably, almost no original Gothic detail remains in Budapest, but niches or pointed arches decorating old apartment buildings can be spotted in the Old Town.

Baroque elements are still evident in fine buildings such as the Zichy Palace and the Erdődy Palace. Decorative Neo-Classical features,

such as borders and tympanums, are visible on many buildings from the first half of the 19th century.

A finial with cartouche on the Neo-Classical Károlyi Palace

Relief on the Hungarian National Bank (1905)

Cove detail on the façade of the Staffenberg House

Ornate window frame adorning the house at 21 József Nádor utca

Budapest's Best: Baths and Pools

Budapest is one of the great spa cities of Europe. Numerous natural hot springs pour out over 80 million litres (18 million gal) of richly mineralized water every day. The greatest concentrations of natural springs are situated in Óbuda, near Gellért Hill, on the Buda embankment near Margaret Bridge and on Margaret Island itself. Baths have existed here since Roman times, but it was the Turks who best exploited Budapest's natural resources. Today there is a wide choice of therapeutic and recreational baths and pools.

Palatinus Strand
With seven swimming pools, hot springs, water slides and a restful location on Margaret Island, this spa is perhaps the most beautiful in Europe.

Hajós Olympic Pool
The pool was designed by Alfréd Hajós, who won Hungary's first Olympic gold medal for swimming in 1896, and on the walls of the swimming hall hang gold-engraved marble plaques citing Hungary's numerous Olympic champions.

North of the Castle

Castle District

DANUBE

Lukács Baths
These 19th-century thermal pools are open all year round, and attract both tourists and the locals of Budapest.

Gellért Hill and Tabán

Király Baths
Dating from 1566, these baths were built by the Turks and have many authentic Ottoman features.

Rác Baths
The original Ottoman pool and cupola are hidden behind a 19th-century façade.

Dagály Strand
Half a century ago, it was discovered that the water in a pond on this site was beneficial to health. Now a huge open-air complex of swimming pools, children's pools and a hydrotherapy and fitness centre is located here.

Around Városliget

Széchenyi Baths
This spa has the hottest thermal baths in Budapest and the added attraction of magnificent Neo-Baroque architecture. The warmth of the water is such that these baths are popular even during the winter season.

Around Parliament

Central Pest

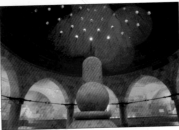

Rudas Baths
The most famous of the Turkish baths were constructed during the 16th century. They still have an original Ottoman cupola and octagonal pool.

Gellért Baths
The main indoor swimming pool of this popular Buda spa delights bathers with its beautiful Secession interior, marble columns and colourful mosaics.

0 metres	500
0 yards	500

Exploring Budapest's Baths and Pools

Heated deep inside the earth, the waters of the mineral-rich hot springs which bubble up through fractures in the rocky hills of Buda and Óbuda have given the city a Turkish-influenced bathing culture which has survived even the rigours of Communism. A total of 31 spa-water pools and thermal baths, with entrance fees kept low by generous government subsidies, make taking the waters an unmissable treat for visitors to Budapest.

THE TURKISH INFLUENCE

Although the ruins of Roman thermal baths dating from the 2nd century AD have been found in Óbuda, it was only under the Ottoman occupation of the 16th–17th centuries (see pp 26–7), that the bathing culture really took hold in Budapest.

Four stunning Turkish-built baths, some of the few remaining examples of Ottoman architecture in Budapest, are still in operation. The **Rudas**, the **Rác**, the **Király** and the **Komjády** (formerly known as Császár) were all built in the 16th century, and are constructed on a single model. A marble staircase leads into a chamber containing a dome-topped, octagonal thermal pool, which is surrounded by smaller dome-covered pools at temperatures ranging from icily cold to roastingly hot. The most beautiful are almost certainly the Rudas Baths, followed closely by the Király Baths. The Rác Baths have undergone extensive restoration work and will re-open in the spring of 2009 as a spa and hotel complex. The Császár Baths have been absorbed into the Lukács Baths complex (see below).

Many of the city's newer baths are for both men and women. The Turkish baths, however, remain resolutely single-sex, though the Rudas Baths are open to men during the week and women at weekends; and the Rác and the Király Baths open to men and women on alternate days. There is no need to wear a bathing suit, as a small apron is provided.

AFTER THE TURKS

The late 19th and early 20th century was a new golden age for Budapest (see pp32–3), and saw the building of a number of splendid baths. Many have spring-water swimming pools attached.

Opened in 1894 the Neo-Classical **Lukács Baths** offer two outdoor swimming pools as well as the 16th-century Császár thermal pool. The **Széchenyi Baths**, opened 20 years later on the Pest side of the river, make up the biggest bathing complex in Europe. In addition to the usual indoor thermal pools, they also boast outdoor thermal and swimming pools, complete with sun terraces. With the hottest spa-water in the city, the outdoor thermal pool is popular even in the depths of winter.

As well as the thermal pools, Budapest's bathing establishments also include a steam room and sauna. Professional massages are almost always available for a small fee. Some places offer medicinal mud and sulphur baths. You will be invited to take a shower, and a short nap in the rest room before you leave.

Swim in style at the Rudas Baths

SPA HOTELS

Nestling at the foot of Gellért Hill, the beautiful **Gellért Hotel and Baths Complex** is the oldest and most famous of a handful of luxury hotels in Budapest offering swimming and thermal pools, steam rooms, sauna and massage. The renowned Gellért Baths were opened to the general public in 1927, and include a fabulous, marble-columned indoor swimming pool, a labyrinth of thermal baths (one set for men and one for women), single-sex nudist sun-bathing areas and an outdoor swimming pool. A hugely popular wave machine is switched on in the latter for ten minutes in every hour.

A second wave of spa-hotels were built in the 1970s and '80s. Set on Margaret Island, the modern, squeaky-clean and extremely luxurious **Danubius Health Spa Resort Margitsziget**, is linked by an underground passage to the older **Danubius Grand Hotel Margitsziget**. In addition to the usual range of baths and pools, treatments

Outdoor pool at the Gellért Hotel and Baths Complex

include manicure, pedicure and a solarium. The late 1980s saw the arrival of two new spa hotels, the **Danubius Health Spa Resort Helia** not far from the Pest riverbank and, on the Buda side, the **Ramada Plaza Budapest**, facing north towards Óbuda. Both make use of the hot springs on Margaret Island, and offer gyms, bars and restaurants as well as swimming pools and thermal baths.

Széchenyi Baths, the biggest bathing complex in Europe

THE HEALING WATERS

The citizens of Budapest are great believers in the social, psychological and medical benefits of the thermal baths. Office workers will often visit the public baths as early as 6am, to prepare for the day. Others like to visit at the end of the day, at 6pm, to relax, recharge and work up an appetite. Most of the baths employ staff who can offer advice on the most appropriate pools and special treatments for a particular ailment. The warm, mineral-rich spa waters are extremely good for general relaxation. They can also be helpful in the relief of a number of specific complaints, including post-traumatic stress, joint and muscle damage, rheumatism and menstrual pain. Budapest's public baths are also extremely good value for money. Admission is usually no more than 500 forints, and a 15-minute massage costs the same. All baths employ expert masseurs.

An ornamental tap, typical of the architectural detail found in Budapest's historic baths

SWIMMING AS SPORT

Many Hungarians are excellent swimmers, and the country has chieved great success in competitive water sports. In addition to Budapest's many recreational pools, sports pools include the **Hajós Olympic Pool** complex on Margaret Island. The complex consists of three sports pools, two outdoor, including one at full Olympic size, and one indoor. The pools are used for professional training, but are also open to the public. Together with the Komjádi Béla Swimming Stadium on Árpád Fejedelem útja, the Hajós Olympic Pool is the place to go to see professional swimming, diving or water polo.

A DAY AT THE STRAND

Designed as a complete bathing day out, the strands of Budapest are a phenomenon not to be missed. A total of 12 strands in the city testifies to their popularity. Outdoor swimming and thermal pools are surrounded by grassy sun-bathing areas. Trampolines and ping-pong and pool tables offer a change from the water, while ice creams, beers and hot dogs add to the summer-holiday atmosphere.

The lovely **Palatinus Strand**, set in a large area of

Sculpture at the Római Strand

parkland on Margaret Island, boasts seven outdoor pools, some thermal and some for swimming, complete with water slides and wave machines. Just east of the Pest river bank is the vast, modern **Dagály Strand** complex. Built after World War II, it includes 12 pools, with space for up to 12,000 people. Other strands worth visiting include **Római Strand** in Óbuda in the north of the city. Three pools have been carefully rebuilt here, on the site of some Roman baths, together with a not-so-Roman water chute. To the north of the city at Csillaghegy on the HÉV suburban train line, **Csillaghegy Strand** consists of four pools set in picturesque grounds, and includes a popular south-facing nudist beach.

WHERE TO FIND THE BATHS AND POOLS

Budapest's Best: the Secession

Decoration on a house on Áldás utca

Visitors to Budapest are often impressed by its wonderful late 19th and early 20th century buildings. The majority of these are found in central Pest and around Városliget; Buda was already developed at this stage and so boasts few examples. The movement started among groups of avant-garde artists in Paris and Vienna, from where the term Secession comes. In Budapest, the Secession style was also the inspiration for the development of the Hungarian National Style. Further details are given on pages 56–7.

The School on Rose Hill
Károly Kós and Dezső Zrumeczky used motifs from village houses in Transylvania to give this building on Áldás utca its character.

Woman with a Birdcage (1892)
This painting by József Rippl-Rónai has an atmosphere of mystery and intimacy typical of Hungarian art of the period. It hangs in the Hungarian National Gallery (see p77) today.

North of the Castle

Castle District

DANUBE

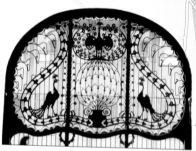

Ironwork Gates of Gresham Palace
Two peacocks, a classic Secession motif, decorate the wrought-iron gates of the Four Seasons Gresham Palace hotel. The building was built by Zsigmond Quittner and the Vágó brothers between 1905–7.

Gellért Hill and Tabán

Gellért Hotel and Baths Complex
Supported by flattened arches, a glass roof adds to the tranquil appeal of this hall in the famous spa at the Gellért Hotel. The Secession interiors created here are among the most splendid to be found in Budapest.

Post Office Savings Bank
The main staircase of this building by Ödön Lechner is embellished by fine balusters, rounded lamps and decorative windows.

Entrance to the Zoo
Kornél Neuschloss made ingenious use of elements of Hindu architecture when he created this amusing gate guarded by two elephants.

Around Városliget

Around Parliament

Central Pest

Sipeky Balázs Villa
Built between 1905–6, this fanciful villa is perhaps the most representative example of the Secession style in Budapest. It was designed by Ödön Lechner.

Philanthia Florist's
This extraordinary florist's is on Váci utca. The interior of the shop is in the Secession style, while the building itself is Neo-Classical.

| 0 metres | 500 |
| 0 yards | 500 |

Apartments on Bartók Béla utca
Ödön Lechner was the leading exponent of the Hungarian National Style. He built this apartment block, with a studio for himself on the fourth floor, in 1899. The block is at 40 Bartók Béla utca.

Exploring Secession Budapest

The Secession movement crossed artistic boundaries, influencing painting and the decorative arts as well as architecture. Colourful, sometimes fantastical designs are instantly recognizable hallmarks of the style. The Hungarian National Style drew heavily on this general trend, incorporating motifs from old Hungarian architecture, particularly that of Transylvania, folk art and even oriental features.

Secession ornament

Vase designed by István Sovának, in the Museum of Applied Arts

József Rippl-Rónai's *Woman in White-Spotted Dress* **(1899), in the Hungarian National Gallery**

PAINTINGS AND DRAWINGS

The main exponents of Secession art in Hungary were József Rippl-Rónai, János Vaszary and Lajos Gulácsy.

Rippl-Rónai spent many years in Paris, at the time when the Art Nouveau movement was beginning to flourish. *Lady in Red*, which he painted in 1899, was the first Hungarian painting in the Secession style. Many of Rippl-Rónai's works are on show in the **Hungarian National Gallery**. There is also a tapestry version of *Lady in Red* in the **Museum of Applied Arts**.

The work of János Vaszary was heavily influenced by both German and English art. His finest pictures, which include *Golden Age* and the mysterious *Adam and Eve*, can be admired in the Hungarian National Gallery. Lajos Gulácsy was influenced by the Pre-Raphaelite movement and his pictures are often symbolic. Many of his paintings, too, can now be viewed in the Hungarian National Gallery. The artists' colony based at Gödöllő was an important centre for painters working in the new Secession style. Its founder, Aladár Körösfői-Kriesch, created numerous works, including a fresco entitled *The Fount of Youth* which decorates the **Franz Liszt Academy of Music**.

DECORATIVE ARTS

New ideas in the decorative arts at this time were closely related to architectural developments. Ödön Lechner began to make use of colourful ceramic tiles, acquired from his father-in-law's brickyard in Pécs in southern Hungary, not only to cover roofs but also as a decorative element.

The owner of this brickyard, Vilmos Zsolnay, discovered an innovative method of glazing tiles and ceramics. This proved so successful that the the brickyard was turned into a factory specializing in their production. Zsolnay's factory eventually made most of the vivid and distinctive ceramic tiles covering the Secession buildings in the city.

Zsolnay also employed leading designers to create ranges of dinner services, vases and candlesticks. For these he was awarded the Gold Medal of the Legion of Honour at the World Fair in Paris. And at an exhibition organized in 1896, to mark the millennial anniversary of the Hungarian Kingdom, the

ÖDÖN LECHNER (1845–1914)

The most influential architect of the Hungarian Secession, Ödön Lechner trained in Berlin before completing his apprenticeship by working in both Italy and France. His quest was to create an identifiable Hungarian National Style, by combining Secession motifs with elements from Hungarian folk art and Hindu designs. The colourful ceramics that he often used

Portrait of Lechner

became his signature. Among the buildings that Budapest owes to him are the Museum of Applied Arts, the Post Office Savings Bank and the Institute of Geology. Behind the ingenious and fantastical exteriors, Lechner's buildings have wonderfully simple, functional and superbly lit interiors.

factory introduced its most beautiful pieces.
Gresham Palace and the **Gellért Hotel and Baths Complex** are among the many buildings in the city that are embellished by ornamental wrought-iron gates, gratings and banisters that incorporate Secession motifs.

INTERIOR DECORATION

Among the interiors of the era, those of the **New York Palace** *(see p129)* are a real jewel. Decked out in the best materials, including bronze and marble, they retain the splendour of their original, Neo-Baroque form.

Also worth visiting are the **Hungarian National Bank** and the **Post Office Savings Bank**, with their furnished secure rooms and ornate door and window frames. The interior of Philanthia, a florist's shop, is another wonderfully

Window created by Miksa Róth, at the Hungarian National Bank

preserved example of decor from the Secession.

Exhibitions of attractive Secession furniture are a feature of both the Museum of Applied Arts and also the **Nagytétény Palace**.

ARCHITECTURE

Hungarian architecture of the *fin de siècle* is characterized not only by decorative forms using glazed ceramics, but, more fundamentally, by the implementation of modern technical solutions. Reinforced concrete, steel and glass were used together, and large, light-filled interiors were often achieved. The central hall of the Museum of Applied Arts is a fine example of this. Aside from Ödön Lechner, the most important of the Hungarian Secession architects, others who contributed significant buildings in the prevailing style included Béla Lajta, Aladár Árkay, Károly Kós and István Medgyaszay.

Béla Lajta, a pupil of Lechner, designed the **Rózsavölgyi Building**, with its distinctive geometrical ornamentation, on Martinelli tér. Also among his buildings is the extraordinary former **Jewish Old People's Home**, at No. 57 Amerikai út. With sophisticated ornamental details based on folk designs, **Városliget Calvinist Church** was the creation of Aladár Árkay. Károly Kós was a highly original member of this set. Fascinated by the traditional architecture of Transylvania, he trawled the whole of that region, making drawings of the village churches and manor houses he encountered. Motifs from these buildings were later transferred to the aviary at Budapest's **Zoo** and the houses of the **Wekerle Estate**.

Frieze on the Rózsavölgyi Building

WHERE TO FIND SECESSION BUDAPEST

A Secession cabinet, displayed in the Museum of Applied Arts

DECORATIVE MOTIFS

Stylized folk motifs derived from embroidery and also oriental patterns were often employed in Budapest's decorative arts during this period. Secession motifs such as feline forms, based on Viennese and Parisian examples, also feature.

Sunflower motif adorning the Post Office Savings Bank

Secession lettering on the sign of Philanthia Florist's

Colourful mosaic at No. 3 Aulich utca

BUDAPEST THROUGH THE YEAR

Set in the middle of Hungary, Budapest enjoys a continental climate with sharply defined seasons, each of which brings its own attractions, from traditional feast days to cultural and sporting events. Historically a centre of cultural, and especially musical, activity, Budapest continues the tradition with many musical events including the

Spring Festival logo

Spring Festival, an international celebration of classical music and ballet, and the smaller Budapest Contemporary Music Weeks, devoted to contemporary classical music. Many hotels and tourist offices provide a programme of the events taking place in the city, as do the English-language weeklies.

SPRING

Spring makes a welcome return to the city in March, with sunshine and fresh, warm days. Budapest turns green and the Spring Festival sees the arrival of some of the year's first tourists.

MARCH

The Spring Uprising (*15 Mar*). A public holiday marks the day in 1848 when the youth of Buda, led by the poet Sándor Petőfi, rebelled against the Habsburg occupation of Hungary (*see pp30–31*). Thousands of people take to the streets to lay wreaths and light eternal flames, wearing the national colours of red, white and green. There are speeches and street theatre, especially in front of the Hungarian National Museum (*see pp130–33*).
Spring Festival (*the last two weeks of Mar–mid-Apr*).
www.festivalcity.hu

Parade in the Castle District during the Spring Festival

Top national and international musicians gather for several weeks of music and dance in churches and concert halls all over the city. The emphasis of the festival is on the classical tradition, but also in evidence are folk music and dance, as well as pop and jazz.

APRIL

Easter is an important religious event in Hungary and the Easter service is well worth attending in one of the city's many churches. On the

morning of Easter Monday young men spray their female friends and relatives with perfume or water, a ritual which is said to keep the recipients beautiful until the following year. Painted eggs are given in return.
Festival Celebrating the Day of Dance (*end Apr*).
www.nemzetitancszinhaz.hu
The National Dance Theatre and the Association of Hungarian Dance Artists organize this festival every year, with participation from top Hungarian dance groups and foreign guest artists.
Horse Racing (*Sun, Apr–Oct*). April sees the beginning of the flat-racing season. Place your bets at the busy and charmingly down-at-heel Kincsem Park race course on Albertirsai út.
Budapest International Book Festival.
www.bookfestival.hu
Organised in co-operation with the Frankfurt Book Fair, this festival is the most important event in Hungary's publishing year, both for the publishing industry and for the general public. It is held at a modern new venue in the Millenáris Park.

MAY

May Day (*1 May*). No longer a compulsory display of patriotism, May Day celebrations take place in public parks all over the city and involve craft markets, street performers and sausage and beer tents. A dip in the local thermal bath or swimming pool (*see pp50–53*), is another popular May Day activity.

Springtime magnolia blossom on Margaret Island

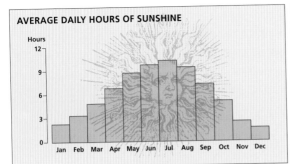

AVERAGE DAILY HOURS OF SUNSHINE

Hours
12
9
6
3
0
Jan Feb Mar Apr May Jun Jul Aug Sep Oct Nov Dec

Sunshine Chart
Budapest enjoys some of the sunniest weather in Europe, with an average of eight hours of sunshine each day from April to September. During the sticky months of high summer (June, July and August), the Buda hills provide a welcome refuge from the heat of the city.

SUMMER

The long hot days of summer are made for relaxing on Margaret Island or sun-bathing at some of the city's twelve open-air pools.

JUNE

Open-Air Theatre Festival
(Jun–Aug). **www**.szabadter.hu
Margaret and Óbuda Islands provide two of the major venues for this summer-long, open-air arts festival.
Budapesti Búcsú *(last weekend in Jun).* **www**.festivalcity.hu
A mixture of music, dance and theatre celebrates the departure from Hungary of Soviet troops in 1991.
Danube Carnival Inter-national Cultural Festival
www.dunaart.com
Various venues host music and dance events.

Formula One racing in the Hungarian Grand Prix

JULY

Hungarian Grand Prix *(end Jul).* **www**.hungaroring.hu
The biggest event in the Hungarian sporting calendar takes place east of the city, at Mogyoród race track.
Chain Bridge Festival
(weekends in Jul & Aug).
www.festivalcity.hu
A lively series of free events including concerts and dance,

traditional arts and crafts, street theatre, parades and activities for children.
Concerts in St Stephen's Basilica *(Jul–Aug).* Monday evening organ concerts in the city's largest church *(see pp116–17)* provide a perfect opportunity to study the lav-ish interior decoration of this extraordinary building.
Budafest Summer Music Festival *(Jul or Aug).*
www.viparts.hu
Look out for the series of shows at the State Opera House *(see pp118–19).*

AUGUST

St István's Day *(20 Aug).*
St István, the patron saint of Hungary, is celebrated with mass in St Stephen's Basilica followed by a huge procession. The day ends with fireworks on Gellért Hill *(see pp88–9)* and along the Danube.
Sziget Festival *(Aug).*
www.sziget.hu
Ten stages and a camp site are set up on Óbuda Island for this popular week-long festival of rock, folk and jazz, which features top bands such as REM and Iron Maiden.

Fireworks on Gellért Hill to celebrate St István's Day

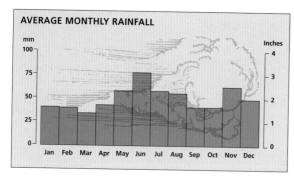

AVERAGE MONTHLY RAINFALL

Rainfall Chart

Budapest is a fairly dry city. Typically, it rains very heavily for two days or so, then is dry for several weeks. June is the wettest month, with May, July, August and November only slightly dryer. Autumn is usually the dryest season, while there is some snowfall in the winter months.

AUTUMN

One of the many treats of autumn in Budapest is a visit to one of the city's fruit and vegetable markets, where you can feast your eyes on a vast array of jewel-coloured vegetables and fruit.

SEPTEMBER

Jewish Summer Cultural Festival *(end Aug–beg Sep).* www.zsidonyarifesztival.hu This multicultural festival includes a Jewish book fair, an Israeli film festival, art exhibitions, and cuisine presentations.

Budapest Wine Festival *(2nd week of Sep).* Wine makers set up stalls for wine tastings and folk dancing on Buda's Castle Hill *(see p69)* and in squares around the city.

OCTOBER

Plus Budapest International Marathon and Running Festival *(Oct).* There is a marathon, a relay race, a mini-marathon and a family running competition for participants. Concerts and events are held for spectators. **Autumn Festival** *(mid-Oct).* Several weeks of contemporary film, dance and theatre at venues across the city.

A colourful food stall in one of Budapest's covered markets

Vienna-Budapest Super Marathon Running Competition. This competition aims, through sport, to strengthen ties between central European countries, particularly those of Austria and Hungary, and celebrates open European borders. www.szupermarathon.hu. **Remembrance Day** *(23 Oct).* This is a national day of mourning to remember the 1956 Uprising, when 30,000 people were killed by Soviet tanks and 200,000 fled the country. Wreaths are laid in Municipal Cemetery *(see pp158–9)*, on the grave of the executed leader Imre Nagy *(see p34).*

NOVEMBER

Budapest Christmas Fair *(26 Nov–24 Dec).* The Budapest Christmas Market transforms Vörösmarty Square into a festive marketplace, where Hungarian artists and craftsmen display their work and national dishes are served. www.budapestinfo.hu

Performers take part in the Open-Air Theatre Festival

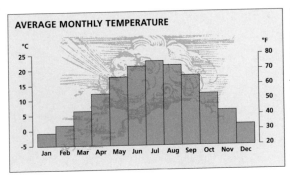

AVERAGE MONTHLY TEMPERATURE

Temperature Chart
Seasons in Budapest are sharply defined. Daytime temperatures rise rapidly from March onwards. By June, the thermometer often reaches 30°C (90°F) and more. September sees cooler weather, with temperatures falling rapidly to lows of well below freezing in January.

WINTER

Despite the cold weather, winter can be an exciting time to visit Budapest. Open-air ice-skating takes place from November, roast-chestnut sellers appear on the streets and a Christmas tree is erected in Mihály Vörösmarty Square.

DECEMBER

Budapest Christmas Fair *(26 Nov–24 Dec)* continues.
Silver and Gold Sunday *(2nd-to-last Sunday before Christmas)*. All the city's shops stay open for this Sunday of serious Christmas shopping.
Mikulás *(6 Dec)*. On *Mikulás*, or St Nicholas Day, children leave their shoes on the window sill for Santa Claus to fill.
Christmas *(25–26 Dec)*. The city shuts down for two days. Celebrations begin with a family meal of carp on 24 Dec.
Szilveszter *(31 Dec)*. Budapest celebrates in style on New Year's Eve, with music in Vörösmarty and Nyugati Squares until dawn, and fireworks. Public transport is free and runs all night.

Seeing in the New Year, a stylish affair in Budapest

Christmas tree in Mihály Vörösmarty Square

JANUARY

New Year's Gala Concert *(1 Jan)*. This cheerful occasion is an excellent way to start the new year. Outstanding Hungarian and foreign artists perform excerpts from European opera and musicals, providing a lively evening of music. **www.viparts.hu**

FEBRUARY

Hungarian Film Festival *(early Feb)*. This two-day celebration of Hungarian film has been run by the *Magyar Filmszemle* since 1969, to attract funding to a hard-pressed industry. Many films are subtitled. **www.szemle.film.hu**
Masked-Ball Season *(Feb)*. Budapest forgets the cold weather to welcome the coming of spring, and the arrival of the *farsang*, or fancy dress masked-ball season. The climax of the season is the spectacular Opera Ball and a masked procession, on the last Saturday and Sunday before Lent, respectively. **www.operabal.com**

Shopping for Christmas

PUBLIC HOLIDAYS

Public holidays mainly follow the Christian calendar. Two days mark cataclysmic events in Magyar history, while one, May Day, is a reminder of the country's socialist past.

New Year's Day (1 Jan)
Spring Uprising (15 Mar)
Easter Sunday (variable)
Easter Monday (variable)
Whit Monday (variable)
May Day (1 May)
St István's Day (20 Aug)
Remembrance Day (23 Oct)
All Saints' Day (1 Nov)
Christmas Day (25 Dec)
Boxing Day (26 Dec)

Margaret Bridge to Elizabeth Bridge

Crown on Elizabeth Bridge

A trip on a river boat along the Danube provides a unique panorama of the city. Most major cities have a river at their heart. However, the Danube historically played a different role in this case, for centuries dividing the separate towns of Buda and Pest. Several road bridges today link the two halves of the modern city. All had to be reconstructed this century after being destroyed by the retreating Nazi army towards the end of World War II.

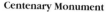

Centenary Monument
This monument was erected in 1973 to commemorate the centenary of the joining of Buda, Óbuda and Pest as Budapest. It stands on Margaret Island (see pp172–3), close to Margaret Bridge.

MARGIT

St Francis's Wounds Church
This Baroque church, built for an order of nuns, has its front facing away from the Danube. The hospital and hostel run by the sisters face the river (see p101).

BATTHYÁNY
TÉR

Mátyás Church
With medieval origins, the tower of this church has been rebuilt several times. It overlooks the Hilton Hotel and the Fishermen's Bastion (see pp82–3).

St Anne's Church
can be recognized by its twin, slender Baroque towers.

LÁNCHÍ

Chain Bridge was built between 1839–49 at the inititiative of Count István Széchenyi *(see p31)*. It was designed by Englishman William Tierney Clark and built by the unrelated Scot, Adam Clark. The bridge extends for 380 m (1,250 ft), supported by two towers – a major feat of engineering at the time.

KEY

Ⓜ Metro

⛴ River boat boarding point

Margaret Bridge was built by the French engineer Ernest Gouin, at the point where the Danube becomes a single body once more after dividing to flow around Margaret Island. The bridge is distinguished by its unusual chevron shape. It was erected in 1872–6, and between 1899–1900 access from the bridge onto the island was added. Sculptures by Adolphe Thabart decorate its columns.

Parliament
The magnificent, high dome of the Parliament building is visible from every point along the Danube in central Budapest (see pp108–9).

Much of the eastern bank of the river is characterized by fairly uniform architecture. Variation is provided here by the dome and towers of St Stephen's Basilica *(see pp116–17).*

```
0 metres        300
0 yards         300
```

Hungarian Academy of Sciences

Elizabeth Bridge, constructed in 1897–1903, was at that time the longest suspension bridge in the world. Destroyed in 1945, it was rebuilt in its current form by Pál Sávolya.

The bridgehead of Chain Bridge is guarded by two vast stone lions sculpted by János Marschalkó. According to an anecdote János was heartbroken because he forgot to give the lions any tongues, so he drowned himself in the river. In fact the lions do have tongues, but they are not easily visible.

VÖRÖSMARTY TÉR

FERENCIEK TÉRE

RZSÉBET HÍD

Piers, from which passenger cruises operate daily in summer, are spaced frequently along the Danube in central Budapest.

Elizabeth Bridge to Lágymányosi Bridge

Like Paris, Budapest has fully exploited the opportunities given by its river. The most important and beautiful buildings of Buda and Pest crowd along the banks of the Danube. These include the Royal Palace, churches, historic palaces and the Gellért Hotel and Baths Complex.

Royal Palace
The monumental Habsburg Royal Palace that once occupied this spot was destroyed during World War II, then reconstructed to reveal defensive walls and royal chambers that date from the Middle Ages (see pp70–71).

Inner City Parish Church
This church was built in the 12th century on the ruins of Roman Contra Aquincum's walls. The spot was, from early times, an important place for crossing the river (see pp124–5).

Gellért Hotel and Baths Complex
The architects of this hotel maximized its river façade to make it as imposing as possible (see pp90–91).

Technical University
The university campus occupies almost the entire space between Liberty Bridge (Szabadság híd) and Lágymányosi híd (see p157).

VÖRÖSMARTY TÉR

FERENCIEK TERE

ERZSÉBET HÍD

SZABAD

The embankment walk near Petőfi Bridge extends along the length of the Danube on the Pest side. It is a favourite place to meet or to go for a stroll, and is lined by smart hotels and restaurants.

Little Princess (1989), perched by the tram rails on the Pest side of the Danube, was so liked by Charles, Prince of Wales, on his visit here that he invited its designer, László Marton, to exhibit in London.

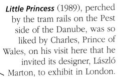

Liberty Bridge was built between 1894–9 by Hungarian engineer János Feketeházy. Opened by Emperor Franz Joseph, it initially took his name. All its original features were retained when it was rebuilt after World War II: on top of the bridge there are legendary Hungarian *turul* birds and royal crests.

Corvinus University

Formerly a customs' headquarters, this building has an elegant façade decorated with ten allegorical figures. These are the work of German sculptor August Sommer (see p138).

Lágymányosi Bridge, Budapest's most modern and southernmost bridge, is pictured here under construction. Opened in 1996, it is designed to carry traffic on a ring road bypassing the city centre.

KÁLVIN TÉR
Ⓜ

PETŐFI HÍD

LÁGYMÁNYOSI HÍD

BUDAPEST AREA BY AREA

CASTLE DISTRICT

The hill town of Buda grew up around its castle and Mátyás Church from the 13th century onwards. At 60 m (197 ft) above the Danube, the hill's good strategic position and natural resources made it a prize site for its earliest inhabitants. In the 13th century, a large settlement arose when, after a Tartar invasion, King Béla IV decided to build his own defensive castle and establish his capital here. The reign of King Mátyás Corvinus in the 15th century was an important period in the evolution of

Bas-relief on the Eugene of Savoy monument

Buda, but it suffered neglect under Turkish rule during the next century and was then destroyed by Christian troops. The town was reborn, however, and assumed an important role during the 18th and 19th centuries under the Habsburgs. By the end of World War II, the Old Town had been almost utterly destroyed and the Royal Palace burnt to the ground. Since the war the Royal Palace and Old Town have been reconstructed, restoring the original allure of this part of the city.

SIGHTS AT A GLANCE

Churches
Buda Lutheran Church ⑰
Church of St Mary Magdalene ⑱
Mátyás Church pp82–3 ⑪

Museums and Galleries
Budapest History Museum ①
Golden Eagle Pharmacy
  Museum ⑧
House of Hungarian Wines ⑩
Hungarian National Gallery
  pp74–7 ④

Labyrinth of Buda Castle ㉒
Museum of Military History ⑳
Széchenyi National Library ②

Historic Streets and Squares
András Hess Square ⑭
Holy Trinity Square ⑨
Lords' Street ㉑
Mihály Táncsics Street ⑮
Parade Square ⑤
Parliament Street ⑲
Vienna Gate Square ⑯

Palaces, Historic Buildings and Monuments
National Dance Theatre ⑦
Fishermen's Bastion ⑫
Hilton Hotel ⑬
Mátyás Fountain ③
Sándor Palace ⑥

GETTING THERE
Castle Hill and the Old Town are largely pedestrianized, but there are a couple of car parks where cars and coaches can park for a fee, allowing visitors to walk to the area. Bus 16 runs from Clark Ádám tér to Dísz tér, and a funicular railway (Sikló) connects Clark Ádám tér to Szent György tér. There is also a minibus (Várbusz) that arrives at this square from Moszkva tér to the north.

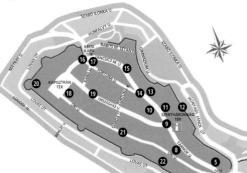

0 metres   400

0 yards   400

KEY

▮ Street-by-Street map
  See pp70–71

▮ Street-by-Street map
  See pp78–9

ℹ Tourist information

◁ **Fountain on Tárnok utca in the Old Town**

Street-by-Street: The Royal Palace

The Royal Palace has borne many incarnations during its long life. Even now it is not known exactly where King Béla IV began building his castle, though it is thought to be nearer the site of Mátyás Church (see pp82–3). The Holy Roman Emperor Sigismund of Luxembourg built a Gothic palace on the present site, from which today's castle began to evolve. In the 18th century, the Habsburgs built their monumental palace here. The current form dates from the rebuilding of the 19th-century palace after its destruction in February 1945. During this work, remains of the 15th-century Gothic palace were uncovered. Hungarian archeologists decided to reveal the recovered defensive walls and royal chambers in the reconstruction.

An ornamental gateway, dating from 1903, leads from the Habsburg Steps to the Royal Palace. Nearby, a bronze sculpture of the mythical turul bird guards the palace. This statue marks the millennium anniversary of the Magyar conquest in 896.

★ Mátyás Fountain
In the northwest courtyard of the Royal Palace stands the Mátyás Fountain. It was designed by Alajos Stróbl in 1904 and depicts King Mátyás Corvinus and his beloved Ilonka ❸

Lion Gate, leading to a rear courtyard of the Royal Palace, gets its name from the four lions that watch over it. These sculptures were designed by János Fadrusz in 1901.

TIMELINE

1255 First written document, a letter by King Béla IV, refers to building a fortified castle	**c.1400** Sigismund of Luxembourg builds an ambitious Gothic palace on this site	**1541** After capturing Buda, the Turks use the Royal Palace to stable horses and store gunpowder	**1719** The building of a small palace begins on the ruins of the old palace, to a design by Hölbling and Fortunato de Prati	**1881** Miklós Ybl (see p119) begins programme to rebuild and expand the Royal Palace

1200	1400	1600	1800

c.1356 Louis I builds a royal castle on the southern slopes of Castle Hill	**1686** The assault by Christian soldiers leaves the palace completely razed to the ground	**1849** Royal Palace is destroyed again, during an unsuccessful attack by Hungarian insurgents	Turul *bird*
1458 A Renaissance palace evolves under King Mátyás	**1749** Maria Theresa builds a vast palace comprising 203 chambers		

The dome of the Royal Palace
was rebuilt in the Neo-Classical style after the Neo-Baroque dome, designed by Alajos Hauszmann, was destroyed in the razing of the palace in World War II.

LOCATOR MAP
See Street Finder, maps 1, 3 & 9

| 0 metres | 50 |
| 0 yards | 50 |

A statue of Prince Eugene of Savoy, by József Róna, was unveiled in 1900. It commemorates the battle of Zenta in 1697, victory at which was a turning point in the Turkish war. The bas-reliefs on the base depict scenes from the battle. Two Turkish prisoners cower by the feet of the prince.

★ **Hungarian National Gallery**
Artworks depicting Hungary's turbulent history are displayed here. Periods of both foreign domination and patriotic home rule are brought to life through the gallery's extensive collection ❹

KEY

– – – Suggested route

BUILDING THE ROYAL PALACE

In the 15th century, a Gothic Royal Palace was built on the site, but it was rebuilt in the Renaissance style by King Mátyás in 1458. After the Turkish occupation it was razed and reborn on a smaller scale. Maria Theresa further developed the palace and it was rebuilt again after World War II to a design originally completed in 1905.

| ▨ 15th century | ▨ 1749 |
| ▨ 1719 | ▨ 1905 |

STAR SIGHTS

★ Hungarian
National Gallery

★ Mátyás Fountain

Renaissance majolica floor from the 15th century, uncovered during excavations on Castle Hill and displayed at the Budapest History Museum

Budapest History Museum ●

Budapesti Történeti Múzeum

Szent György tér 2. **Map** 3 C1 (9 B4). *Tel* 225 78 16. ▨ 5, 16, 78, Várbusz. ◯ Mar–Oct: 10am–6pm daily (Tue Mar–May & Sep–Oct); Nov–Feb: 10am–4pm Wed–Mon. ▨ ▨ **www**.btm.hu

Since the unification of Budapest in 1873, historic artifacts relating to Hungary's capital have been collected. Many are now on show at the Budapest History Museum (also called the Castle Museum).

During the rebuilding that followed the destruction suffered in World War II, chambers dating from the Middle Ages were uncovered in the south wing (wing E) of the Royal Palace. They provide an insight into the character of a much earlier castle within today's Habsburg reconstruction.

These chambers, including a tiny prison cell and a chapel, were recreated in the basement of the palace. They now house an exhibition, the Royal Palace in Medieval Buda, which displays authentic weapons, seals, tiles and other early artifacts.

On the ground floor, Budapest in the Middle Ages illustrates the evolution of the town from its Roman origins to a 13th-century Hungarian settlement. Also on this level are reconstructed defensive walls, gardens, a keep, and Gothic Statues from the Royal Palace dating from the 14th and 15th centuries. The statues were uncovered by chance in the major excavations of 1974. On the first floor, Budapest in Modern Times traces the history of the city from 1686 to the present.

Széchényi National Library ●

Nemzeti Széchényi Könyvtár

Szent György tér 6. **Map** 3 C1 (9 B4). *Tel* 224 37 00. ▨ 5, 16, 78, Várbusz. ◯ 10am–8pm Tue–Sat. ◯ Sun. **www**.oszk.hu

A magnificent collection of books has been housed, since 1985, in wing F of the Royal Palace, built in 1890–1902 by Alajos Hauszmann and Miklós

Corviniani illuminated manuscript in the Széchényi National Library

Ybl *(see p119)*. Previously, the library was part of the Hungarian National Museum *(see pp130–33)*.

Among the library's most precious treasures is the *Corviniani*, a collection of ancient books and manuscripts that originally belonged to King Mátyás Corvinus *(see p24–5)*. His collection was one of the largest Renaissance libraries in Europe. Also of importance are the earliest surviving records in the Hungarian language, dating from the early 13th century.

The library was established by Count Ferenc Széchényi in 1802. He endowed it with 15,000 books and 2,000 manuscripts. The collection now comprises five million items; everything that has been published in Hungary, in the Hungarian language or that refers to Hungary is here.

Crest on the Lion Gate in a courtyard at the Royal Palace

Mátyás Fountain ●

Mátyás Kút

Royal Palace. **Map** 1 C5 (9 B3). ▨ 5, 16, 78, Várbusz.

The ornate fountain in the northwest courtyard of the Royal Palace (situated between wings A and C) was designed by Alajos Stróbl in 1904. The statue is dedicated to the great Renaissance king, Mátyás, about whom there are many popular legends and fables.

The Romantic design of the bronze sculptures takes its theme from a 19th-century ballad by the poet Mihály Vörösmarty. According to the tale, King Mátyás, while on a hunting expedition, meets a beautiful peasant girl, Ilonka, who falls in love with him. This representation shows King Mátyás disguised as hunter, standing proudly with his kill. He is accompanied by his chief hunter and several hunting dogs in the central part of the fountain. Beneath the left-hand columns sits Galeotto Marzio, an Italian court poet, and the figure of the young Ilonka is beneath the columns on the right.

In keeping with the romantic reputation of King Mátyás, a new tradition has grown up concerning this statue. The belief is that anyone wishing to revisit Budapest should throw some coins into the fountain to ensure their safe return.

Hungarian National Gallery ❹

Magyar Nemzeti Galéria

See pp 74 – 7.

Batthyány Palace on Parade Square retains its original Baroque façade

Parade Square ❺

Dísz Tér

Map 1 B5 (9 A3). 🚌 *Várbusz.*

Parade Square is named after the military parades that were held here in the 19th century. At the northern end of the square is the Honvéd Monument, built in 1893 by György Zala. It honours and commemorates those who died during the recapture

The western elevation of the Neo-Classical Sándor Palace

of Buda from Austria in the 1848 revolution.

The house at No. 3 was built between 1743–8, by József Giessl. This two-floor Baroque palace was the home of the Batthyány family until 1945. Although the building has been frequently remodelled, the façade remains intact.

A few houses on Parade Square incorporate medieval remains. Such houses can be seen at Nos. 4–5 and No. 11, built by Venerio Ceresola. The former has seat niches dating from the 13th century.

Sándor Palace ❻

Sándor Palota

Szent György tér 1–3. **Map** 1 C5 (9 A3). 🚌 *5, 16, 78, Várbusz.* ⬤ *to the public.*

By the top of the cog-wheel railway stands the grand Neo-Classical mansion, Sándor Palace. It was commissioned in 1806 by Count Vincent Sándor from architects Mihály Pollack and Johann Aman.

The bas-reliefs that decorate the palace are the work of Richárd Török, Miklós Melocco and Tamás Körössényi. The decoration on the western elevation depicts Greek gods on Mount Olympus. The southern elevation shows Count Sándor being knighted and the northern elevation features a 1934 sculpture of Saint George by Zsigmond Kisfaludi Stróbl.

Sándor Palace functioned as the prime minister's official residence from 1867 to 1944,

when it was severely damaged in World War II. The building has been completely restored, and it is now the official residence of the President of Hungary.

National Dance Theatre ❼

Nemzeti Táncszínház

Színház utca 1–3. **Map** 1 C5 (9 A3). *Tel 201 44 07 or 375 86 49.* 🚌 *5, 16, 78, Várbusz.* **Box Office** 🕐 *1–6pm Mon–Sun.* **www**.nemzetitancszinhaz.hu

An unlikely assortment of institutions have stood on this site. The church of St John the Evangelist, founded by King Béla IV, stood here in the 13th century. This church was then used as a mosque under Ottoman rule, and in 1686 it was demolished by the Christian armies that retook the city. In 1725 the Carmelite order built a Baroque church in its place and this building was first converted into a theatre in 1786, during the reign of Emperor Joseph II. Farkas Kempelen, a famous Hungarian designer added a Rococo façade and seats for 1,200 spectators. The first plays were in German and it was not until 1790 that any work was staged in Hungarian. Beethoven's concert of 1800 is commemorated by a plaque.

The building was damaged in World War II and restored in 1978. The National Dance Theatre now performs here.

Hungarian National Gallery ●

Established in 1957, the Hungarian National Gallery houses a comprehensive collection of Hungarian art from medieval times to the 20th century. Gathered by various groups and institutions since 1839, these works had previously been exhibited at the Hungarian National Museum *(see pp130–33)* and the Museum of Fine Arts *(see pp146–9)*. The collection was moved to the Royal Palace (wings B, C and D) in 1975. There are now six permanent exhibitions, presenting the most valuable and critically acclaimed Hungarian art in the world.

Sisters by Erzsébet Schaár

St Anne Altarpiece
(c.1520)
Elaborately decorated, this folding altarpiece from Kisszeben is one of the Gothic highlights in the gallery.

Madonna of Toporc
(c. 1420)
This is a captivating example of medieval wood sculpture in the Gothic style. It was originally crafted for a church in Spiz (now part of Slovakia).

First floor

Madonna of Bártfa
(1465–70)
This painting of a Madonna and Child is from a church in Bártfa (now in Slovakia). It is thought to have been painted in Cracow, Poland.

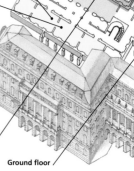

★ **The Visitation** *(1506)*
This painting by Master MS is a delightful example of late Gothic Hungarian art. It is a fragment of a folding altarpiece from a church in Selmecbánya in modern-day Slovakia.

Ground floor

Main entrance

STAR EXHIBITS

★ The Visitation

★ Picnic in May

KEY

☐ Stone sculptures and artifacts
☐ Gothic works
☐ Late Gothic altarpieces
☐ Renaissance and Baroque works
☐ 19th-century works
☐ Early 20th-century works
☐ Temporary exhibitions

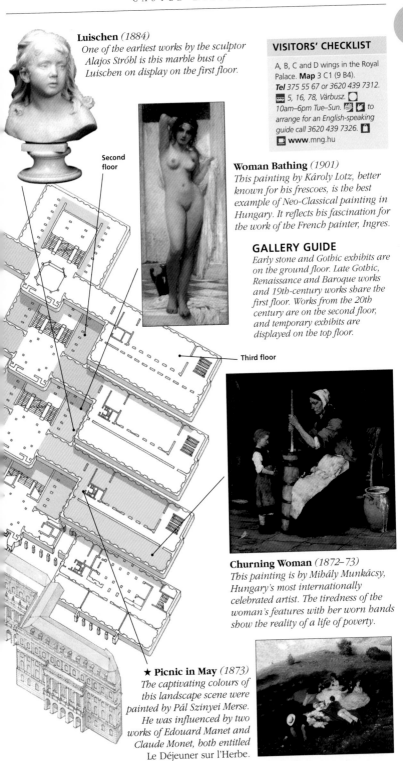

Luischen *(1884)*
One of the earliest works by the sculptor Alajos Stróbl is this marble bust of Luischen on display on the first floor.

VISITORS' CHECKLIST

A, B, C and D wings in the Royal Palace. **Map** 3 C1 (9 B4).
Tel 375 55 67 or 3620 439 7312.
5, 16, 78, Várbusz.
10am–6pm Tue–Sun. to arrange for an English-speaking guide call 3620 439 7326.
www.mng.hu

Second floor

Woman Bathing *(1901)*
This painting by Károly Lotz, better known for his frescoes, is the best example of Neo-Classical painting in Hungary. It reflects his fascination for the work of the French painter, Ingres.

GALLERY GUIDE
Early stone and Gothic exhibits are on the ground floor. Late Gothic, Renaissance and Baroque works and 19th-century works share the first floor. Works from the 20th century are on the second floor, and temporary exhibits are displayed on the top floor.

Third floor

Churning Woman *(1872–73)*
This painting is by Mihály Munkácsy, Hungary's most internationally celebrated artist. The tiredness of the woman's features with her worn hands show the reality of a life of poverty.

★ Picnic in May *(1873)*
The captivating colours of this landscape scene were painted by Pál Szinyei Merse. He was influenced by two works of Edouard Manet and Claude Monet, both entitled Le Déjeuner sur l'Herbe.

Exploring the Hungarian National Gallery

Secession poster

The works are displayed in six permanent exhibitions and give a thorough insight into Hungarian art from the early Middle Ages to the present day. Although one-and-a-half centuries of Turkish occupation and wartime destruction interrupted the development of Hungarian art, the birth of national pride in the 19th century allowed a new indigenous style to develop. Among the most interesting are the Hungarian paintings of the late 19th century, when a greater diversity of styles came to the fore.

The Habsburg Crypt, with the sarcophagus of Palatine Archduke Joseph

THE LAPIDARIUM

On the ground floor, to the left of the main entrance, is a display of stone objects discovered during the reconstruction of the Royal Palace *(see p70)*. Called the Lapidarium, it includes sculptures and fragments of architectural features, such as balustrades and windows, that decorated the royal chambers during the Angevin and Jagiełło eras *(see p18)*. The most valuable exhibit, however, is a sculpture of King Béla III's head, which dates from around 1200.

Also in this first section are two marble bas-reliefs of King Matthias and his wife Beatrice, by an unknown Renaissance master from Lombardy.

The second section exhibits late Gothic and Renaissance artifacts from other palaces in Hungary. There are pillars and balustrades from the palace at Visegrád and bas-reliefs from a chapel in Esztergom.

GOTHIC WORKS

A collection of painted panels, sculptures and fragments of altar decoration is opposite the Lapidarium. Note, however, the image of the *Madonna of Bártfa*, which is a rare complete example from the Gothic period.

The sculptures of the "Beautiful Madonnas" are executed in the Soft Style. This style

King's head sculpted from red marble

is characterized, as its name suggests, by the sentimental and gentle imagery of the Madonna playing with the Christ child.

The Visitation, a magnificent late Gothic work by Master MS, is, in fact, only the main section of an altar; the other pieces are now in Esztergom *(see p164).*

RENAISSANCE AND BAROQUE WORKS

The exhibition begins with a still life by Jakab Bogdány (1660–1724) and portraits by Ádám Mányoki (1673– 1757) *(see p28)*, who actually settled outside Hungary. As a result of the powerful influence of the Habsburgs during this period *(see pp28–9)*, Baroque art was overwhelmingly dominated by Austrian artists. Painters such as Joseph Dorfmeister and Franz Anton Maulbertsch and sculptors Georg Raphael Donner and Philipp Jakob Straub were the acknowledged masters. Jan Kupetzky's portraits are also exemplary models of this era.

The sculptures by Donner and the sacred paintings of Dorfmeister conclude this section of the gallery.

LATE GOTHIC ALTARPIECES

One of the star exhibits of this collection is the imposing late Gothic altarpiece. Arranged in the Great Throne Room, the majority of these vast altarpieces date from the 15th and early 16th centuries.

The Great Throne Room, displaying the collection of folding altarpieces

Architecturally these altarpieces are pure Gothic, while adorned with sculptures and paintings revealing a Renaissance influence. This is evident in the altars of St Anne and St John the Baptist from a church in Kisszeben (now Sabinov in Slovakia), which date from 1510–16. The most recent altarpiece dates from 1643 and is from the church of Our Lady Mary in Csíkmenaság.

Christmas (1903) by Jozsef Rippl-Ronai, a leading Hungarian artist

Bertalan Székely's *Women of Eger* (1867), depicting the Turkish wars

19TH-CENTURY WORKS

The wonderful collection of works from this period reflects the rise of fine art in Hungary in the 19th century.

Historicist art developed during this period. Among those distinguishing themselves in particular were Gyula Benczúr and Bertalan Székely, who produced the epic works *The Recapture of Buda in 1686* (1896) and *Women of Eger* (1867) respectively. The latter depicts the women of the town defending the Castle of Eger against the Turks.

Viktor Madarász's work *The Mourning of László Hunyadi* (1859) refers to the execution of László Hunyadi by the Habsburgs in 1457. It alludes, too, to the execution of many Hungarians after the crushing of the uprising against Austria in 1849 *(see pp30–31).*

European developments in fine art can also be seen in Hungarian painting from the late-19th century. The influence of Impressionism, for example, is best seen in Pál Szinyei Merse's *Picnic in May* (1873).

Hungarian Realism is expressed in the work of László Paál and Mihály Munkácsy, the latter being widely regarded as the country's greatest artist. Paintings by Munkácsy which deserve particular attention are *The Yawning Apprentice* (1869), *Dusty Road* (1874), the still life *Flowers* (1881), and – most notably – *Woman Carrying Brushwood* (1870), which was painted at the zenith of his career.

It is also worth spending a few moments seeing the paintings of the Neo-Classical artists. The work of Károly Lotz, who is perhaps better known for his frescoes that can be seen on walls and ceilings around Budapest, is exhibited here.

20TH-CENTURY WORKS

Examples of work from the Secession era through to Expressionism and Surrealism, and even contemporary art are exhibited here. They provide a comprehensive review of 20th-century Hungarian art.

József Rippl-Rónai studied in France with Gaugin and Toulouse-Lautrec. His work shows the influence of the Secession style in *The Palace in Körtyvélyes* and *Woman with a Birdcage*. But one of the most engaging artists from the early-20th century is Károly Ferenczy whose *The Paintress* (1903) exemplifies the serene qualities of his work.

Tivadar Kosztka Csontváry is an artist whose work did not follow any conventional style but was greatly admired,

even by Pablo Picasso. One of his paintings in particular, the *Ruins of the Greek Amphitheatre in Taormina* (1905), captures his abstract interpretation of the world.

The Eight, a group of artists who set up the first Hungarian avant-garde school, were active between the two world wars. Notable examples of their work are *Young Girl with a Bow* by Béla Czóbel, *Woman Playing a Doublebass* by Róbert Berény, *The Oarsmen* by Ödön Marffy, *Landscape* by Lajos Tihanyi and *Riders at the Edge* by Károly Kernstok.

The best works of Hungarian Expressionism can be seen in the paintings *Along the Tracks*, *For Bread* and *Generations*, by Gyula Derkovits.

Among the sculptures on display, the most interesting are *Raising Oneself* and *The Sower*, by Ferenc Medgyessy, and *Standing Girl*, by Béni Ferenczy. The exhibition is completed by a section featuring contemporary artists.

The Paintress by Károly Ferenczy (1903), a typically peaceful work

Street-by-Street: the Old Town

Bas-reliefs on a house on Fortuna utca

Buda's old town has been a barometer of Hungary's changing fortunes. It developed, to the north of the Royal Palace, from the 13th century. Under kings such as Sigismund, it flourished, and wealthy German merchants set up shops in Lords' Street (Úri utca) to supply the court. The area was later destroyed by the Turks and again by their evictors. It was most recently rebuilt after World War II, but genuine relics can be hunted out in its cobbled streets and squares.

Mihály Táncsics Street
During the Middle Ages, this street was inhabited by Jews. A museum at No. 26, on the site of an old synagogue, displays finds such as tombstones ⓯

The State Archive of Historic Documents, located in a Neo-Romanesque building, houses items that were transferred to Buda in 1785 from the former capital of Hungary, Bratislava.

Surviving tower of the Church of St Mary Magdalene

BÉCSI KAPU TÉR

ORSZÁGHÁZ UTCA

ÚRI UTCA

FORTU...

Defensive walls

0 metres   50
0 yards   50

Labyrinth of Buda Castle
This 1,200-metre long system of dungeons, springs, caves and cellars that runs beneath Castle Hill also includes exhibitions on early Hungarian history and legend ㉒

★ Lords' Street
Once the homes of aristocrats and merchants, the houses on Úri utca have medieval foundations. Many have Gothic details and peaceful courtyards ㉑

KEY

– – – Suggested route

★ **Mátyás Church**
Although with much earlier parts, this church is mainly a Neo-Gothic reconstruction dating from 1874–96. A picturesque vestibule on the church's southern façade covers an original Gothic portal dating from the 14th century ⑪

LOCATOR MAP
See Street Finder, maps 1 & 9

This statue of St Stephen, or István, the first crowned king of Hungary *(see pp22–3)*, was erected in 1906. Its pedestal includes a bas-relief showing scenes from the king's life.

Fishermen's Bastion
Designed by Frigyes Schulek in 1895, this fantastical structure never had the role of a defensive building, despite its name. It serves instead as a viewing terrace. The conical towers are an allusion to the tribal tents of the early Magyars ⑫

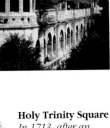

Holy Trinity Square
In 1713, after an epidemic of the plague was overcome, a column representing the Holy Trinity was raised in this square ⑨

Golden Eagle Pharmacy Museum
From the 18th century a pharmacy called "Under the Golden Eagle" traded in this medieval house, now a museum ⑧

House of ...garian Wines
...rs wine-tasting
...rs detailing the
...e-growing
...ons of Hungary.

STAR SIGHTS

★ Lords' Street (Úri utca)

★ Mátyás Church

Golden Eagle Pharmacy Museum ❽

Aranysas Patikamúzeum

Tárnok utca 18. **Map** 1 B5 (9 A2).
Tel 375 97 72. 🚌 16, *Várbusz.*
⭕ *Mid-Mar–Oct: 10:30am–6pm
Tue–Sun; Nov–mid-Mar: 10:30am–
4pm Tue–Sun.*

This pharmacy was opened
in 1688 by Ferenc Ignác
Bösinger and traded under the
name the "Golden Eagle" from
1740. It moved to this originally
Gothic building, with its Baroque interior and Neo-Classical
façade, in the 18th century.
The museum opened here in
1974. It displays pharmaceutical items from the Renaissance
and Baroque eras.

Holy Trinity Square ❾

Szentháromság Tér

Map 1 B4 (9 A3).
🚌 *Várbusz from Moszkva tér.*

This square is the central
point of the Old Town.
It takes its name from the
Baroque Holy Trinity Column,
originally sculpted by Philipp
Ungleich in 1710 – 13, and restored in 1967. The column
commemorates the dead of
two outbreaks of the plague,
which struck the inhabitants
of Buda in 1691 and 1709.
   The pedestal of the column
is decorated with bas-reliefs
by Anton Hörger. Further up
are statues of holy figures and
at the summit is a magnificent
composition of the figures of
the Holy Trinity. The
central section of the column
is decorated with angelic
figures surrounded by clouds.
   Buda's Old Town Hall, a
large Baroque building with
two courtyards, was also built
on the square at the beginning
of the 18th century. It was
designed by the imperial court
architect, Venerio Ceresola,
whose architectural scheme
incorporated the remains of
medieval houses. In 1770 –74
an east wing was built, and
bay windows and a stone
balustrade with Rococo urns,
by Mátyás Nepauer, were also
added. The corner niche,
opposite Mátyás Church,
houses a small statue by Carlo
Adami of Pallas Athene.
   At No. 6 is the House of
Hungarian Wines with an
extensive selection of wines
to sample and buy.

House of Hungarian Wines ❿

Magyar Barok Háza

1014 Szentháromság tér 6.
Map 1 B4 (9A2). *Tel* 212 10 31.
🚌 *Várbusz from Moszkva tér.*
⭕ *noon–8pm daily.* 📷
www.magyarborokhaza.hu

At No. 6 on the square,
opposite the Hilton Hotel, the
House of Hungarian Wines
represents all 22 of the
country's wine-producing
regions and stocks
approximately 700 different
wines. Some 55 of these
are made available to
visitors for tasting. The
wider aim of the
House is to stock the
complete range of
wines produced in Hungary
in a single location, to aid
appreciation and unders-
tanding. The House also aims
to raise the profile of
Hungarian wines both
nationally and internationally.

Mátyás Church ⓫

Mátyás Templom

See pp82–3.

A statue of St István stands in
front of the Fishermen's Bastion

Fishermen's Bastion ⓬

Halászbástya

Szentháromság tér. **Map** 1 B4 (9 A2).
🚌 *Várbusz from Moszkva tér.*
⭕ *9am–11pm daily.* 📷 *Mar–Oct.*

Frigyes Schulek designed this
Neo-Romanesque monument
to the Guild of Fishermen in
1895. It occupies the site of
Buda's old defensive walls and
a medieval square where fish
was once sold. The bastion is
a purely aesthetic addition to
Castle Hill and boasts beautiful
views of the Danube and Pest.
In front of it stands a statue of
St István, the king who
introduced Hungary
to Christianity.

Buda's Old Town Hall, its clock tower crowned with an onion-shaped dome, on Holy Trinity Square

Bas-relief depicting King Mátyás on the façade of the Hilton Hotel

Hilton Hotel 🄳

Hilton Szálló

Hess András tér 1–2. **Map** 1 B4 (9 A2). **Tel** 889 66 00. Várbusz. www.hilton.com

Built in 1976, the Hilton Hotel is a rare example of modern architecture in the Old Town. Controversial from the outset, the design by the Hungarian architect Béla Pintér combines the historic remains of the site with contemporary materials and methods.

From 1254 a Dominican church, to which a tower was later added, stood on this site, followed by a late-Baroque Jesuit monastery. The remains of both these buildings are incorporated into the design. For example, the remains of the medieval church, uncovered during excavations in 1902, form part of the Dominican Courtyard, where concerts and operettas are staged during the summer season.

The main façade comprises part of the façade of the Jesuit monastery. To the left of the entrance is St Nicholas's Tower. In 1930, a replica of the 15th-century German bas-relief of King Mátyás, considered to be his most authentic likeness, was added to this tower.

András Hess Square 🄴

Hess András Tér

Map 1 B4 (9 A2). Várbusz frov m Moszkva tér.

This square is named after the Italian-trained printer who printed the first Hungarian book, *Chronica Hungarorum*, in a printing works at No. 4 in 1473. The house was rebuilt at the end of the 17th century as an amalgamation of three medieval houses, with quadruple seat niches, barrel-vaulted cellars and ornamental gates.

The former inn at No. 3 was named the Red Hedgehog in 1696. This one-floor building has surviving Gothic and Baroque elements.

The square also features a statue by József Damkó of Pope Innocent XI, who was involved in organizing the armies who recaptured Buda from the Turks. It was built to mark the 250th anniversary of the liberation, in 1936.

Hedgehog on the façade of No. 3 András Hess Square

Mihály Táncsics Street 🄵

Táncsics Mihály Utca

Map 1 B4 (9 A2). Várbusz. **Museum of Musical History Tel** 214 67 70. Partly for reconstruction.

Standing at No. 7 is Erdődy Palace, built in 1750 – 69 for the Erdődy family by Mátyás

Nepauer, the leading architect of the day. It features outstanding Baroque façades. Like many houses on this street, it was erected on the ruins of medieval houses.

In 1800, Ludwig van Beethoven, who was then giving concerts in Budapest, resided here for a short period.

The palace now houses the Museum of Musical History and the Béla Bartók archives. A permanent exhibition illustrates musical life in Budapest from the 18th to 20th centuries, and includes the oldest surviving Hungarian musical instruments. The Royal Mint stood on the site of No. 9 during the Middle Ages, and, in 1810, the Joseph Barracks were built here. These were later used by the Habsburgs to imprison leaders of the 1848 – 9 uprising, including Mihály Táncsics himself.

An original mural has survived on the façade of the house at No. 16, which dates from around 1700. It depicts Christ and the Virgin Mary surrounded by saints. The bas-reliefs on the gateway are, however, from a Venetian church.

Relics of Buda's Jewish heritage can be found at Nos. 23 and 26. The remains of a 15th-century synagogue stand in the garden of the mansion at No. 23. During archeological excavations, tombs and religious items were also found in the courtyard of No. 26.

The Museum of Musical History on Mihály Táncsics Street

Mátyás Church ⓫

The Parish Church of Our Lady Mary was built on this site between the 13th and 15th centuries. Some of the existing architectural style dates from the reign of Sigismund of Luxembourg, but its name refers to King Mátyás Corvinus, who greatly enlarged and embellished the church. Much of the original detail was lost when the Turks converted the church into the Great Mosque in 1541. During the liberation of Buda the church was almost totally destroyed, but was rebuilt in the Baroque style by Franciscan Friars. The church sustained more damage in 1723, and was restored in the Neo-Gothic style by Frigyes Schulek in 1873–96. The crypt houses the Museum of Ecclesiastical Art.

Rose Window
Frigyes Schulek faithfully reproduced the medieval stained-glass window that was in this position during the early Gothic era.

Béla Tower
This tower is named after the church's founder, King Béla IV. It has retained several of its original Gothic features.

★ Baroque Madonna
According to legend, the original statue was set into a wall of the church during the Turkish occupation. When the church was virtually destroyed in 1686, the Madonna made a miraculous appearance. The Turks took this as an omen of defeat.

Main Portal
Above the arched west entrance is a 19th-century bas-relief of the Madonna and Child, seated between two angels. The work is by Lajos Lantai.

STAR FEATURES

★ Baroque Madonna

★ Mary Portal

★ Tomb of King Béla III and Anne de Châtillon

★ **Tomb of King Béla III and Anne de Châtillon**
The remains of this royal couple were transferred from Székesfehérvár Cathedral to Mátyás Church in 1860. They lie beneath an ornamental stone canopy in the Trinity Chapel.

VISITORS' CHECKLIST

Szentháromság tér 2. **Map** 1 B4
(9 A2). **Tel** 355 56 57.
Várbusz. ◯ 9am–5pm Mon–Fri,
9am–1pm Sat, 1–5pm Sun.
◻ ◻ **Museum** ◯ 9am–5pm

Pulpit
The richly decorated pulpit includes the carved stone figures of the four Fathers of the Church and the four Evangelists.

The roof is decorated with multicoloured glazed tiles.

The main altar was created by Frigyes Schulek and based on Gothic triptychs.

Stained-Glass Windows
Three arched windows on the south elevation have beautiful 19th-century stained glass. They were designed by Frigyes Schulek, Bertalan Székely and Károly Lotz.

★ **Mary Portal**
This depiction of the Assumption of the Blessed Virgin Mary is the most magnificent example of Gothic stone carving in Hungary. Frigyes Schulek reconstructed the portal from fragments.

TIMELINE

c.1387 Church redesigned as Gothic hall-church by Sigismund of Luxemburg

1458 Thanksgiving mass following the coronation of Mátyás Corvinus

1541 Turks convert church into a mosque

1686 After liberation of Buda from Turkish rule, church is almost destroyed. New church built with a Baroque interior

Holy figures on the pulpit

1250	1350	1450	1550	1650	1750	1850	1950

1309 Coronation of the Angevin king Charles Robert

1255 Church originally founded by King Béla IV after the Mongol invasion

1526 Cathedral burnt in the first attack by Turks

1470 Mátyás Tower is completed after its collapse in 1384

1896 Frigyes Schulek completes the reconstruction of the church in the Neo-Gothic style

1945 Church is severely damaged by German and Russian armies

1970 Final details are completed in post-war rebuilding programme

Vienna Gate, rebuilt in 1936, commemorating the liberation of Buda

Vienna Gate Square **16**

Bècsi Kapu Tér

Map 1 B4.
🚌 Várbusz from Moszkva tér.

The square takes its name from the gate that once led from the walled town of Buda towards Vienna. After being damaged several times, the old gate was demolished in 1896. The current gate, based on a historic design, was erected in 1936 on the 250th anniversary of the liberation of Buda from the Turks.

The square has a number of interesting houses. Those at Nos. 5, 6, 7 and 8 were built on the ruins of medieval dwellings. They are Baroque and Rococo in design and feature sculptures and bas-reliefs. The façade of No. 7 has medallions with the portraits of Classical philosophers and poets; Thomas Mann, the German novelist, lodged here between 1935–6. No. 8, meanwhile, is differentiated by its bay windows, attics and the restored medieval murals on its façade.

On the left-hand side of the square is a vast Neo-Romanesque building with a beautiful multicoloured roof, built in 1913–20 by Samu Pecz. This building houses the National Archive, which holds documents dating from before the battle of Mohács in 1526 and others connected with the Rákóczi and Kossuth uprisings (see pp 25, 31 and 38).

Behind the Vienna Gate Square is a monument built in honour of Mihály Táncsics, the leader of the Autumn Uprising. It was unveiled in 1970.

Buda Lutheran Church **17**

Budavári Evangélikus Templom

Bécsi kapu tér. **Map** 1 B4.
Tel 356 97 36. 🚌 Várbusz. ♿

Facing the Vienna Gate is the Neo-Classical Lutheran church, built in 1896 by Mór Kallina. A plaque commemorates pastor Gábor Sztéhló, who saved 2,000 children during World War II.

At one time, a painting by Bertalan Székely, called Christ Blessing the Bread, adorned the altar, but it was unfortunately destroyed during the war.

Church of St Mary Magdalene **18**

Mária Magdolna Templom Tornya

Kapisztrán tér 6. **Map** 1 A4.
🚌 Várbusz.

Now in ruins, this church was built in the mid-13th century. During the Middle Ages, Hungarian Christians worshipped here because Mátyás Church was only for use by the town's German population. The church did not become a mosque until the second half of the Turkish occupation, but it was severely damaged in 1686, during the liberation of Buda from the Turks. An

order of Franciscan monks subsequently took possession and added a Baroque church and tower.

After World War II, all but the tower and the gate were pulled down. These now stand in a garden, together with the reconstructed Gothic window.

Parliament Street **19**

Országház Utca

Map 1 A4 & 1 B4.

This street was once inhabited by the Florentine artisans and craftsmen who were working on King Mátyás' Royal Palace (see pp70–71), and it was known for a time as Italian Street. Its present name comes from the building at No. 28, where the Hungarian parliament met from 1790–1807. This building was designed in the 18th century by the architect Franz Anton Hillebrandt as a convent for the Poor Clares. However, Emperor Joseph II dissolved the order before the building was completed.

Numerous houses on Parliament Street have retained attractive Gothic and Baroque features. No. 2, now with a Neo-Classical façade, is the site of the Alabárdos Étterem (see p196), but its history dates back to the late 13th century. In the 15th century, Sigismund of Luxembourg built a Gothic mansion here and some details, such as the colonnade around the courtyard and the murals on the second floor, have survived until the present day. The entrance to No. 9 features the Gothic traceried seat niches that were popular in Buda at this time. In front of the Neo-Classical house at No. 21 is a statue of Márton Lendvay (1807–58), who was a famous Hungarian actor and member of the National Theatre.

The reconstructed Baroque tower of the Church of St Mary Magdalene

Museum of Military History 20
Hadtörténeti Múzeum

Tóth Árpád Sétany 40. **Map** 1 A4.
Tel 356 95 22. 🚌 *Várbusz.*
🕐 Apr–Sep: 10am–6pm daily;
Oct–Mar: 10am–4pm daily.
🕐 Monday. 🖥 **www**.hm-him.hu

The museum is located in a wing of the former Palatine barracks. It houses a wide range of military items relating to the skirmishes and wars that have afflicted Budapest from before the Turkish occupation to the 20th century. Uniforms, flags, weapons, maps and ammunition from as far back as the 11th century give an insight into the long, turbulent history of Budapest.

Of particular interest is the exhibit concerning the 1956 Uprising. Photographs illustrate the 13 days of demonstrations that ended in a Soviet invasion. and a huge civilian death toll.

Lords' Street 21
Úri Utca

Map 1 A4, 1 B4 and 1 B5 (9 A2).
🚌 *Várbusz.* **Telephone Museum**
Tel 201 81 88. 🕐 10am–4pm
Tue–Sun.

The buildings in Lords' Street were destroyed first in 1686 and again in 1944. Reconstruction in 1950– 60 restored much of their original medieval character. Almost all have some remnant of a Gothic gateway or hall, while the façade is Baroque or Neo-Classical.

An excellent example of a Gothic façade can be seen on Hölbling House at No. 31. Enough of its original features survived the various wars and renovations to enable architects to reconstruct the façade in considerable detail. The first-floor window is a particularly splendid Gothic feature. The houses opposite are also examples of this restoration work.

The building at No. 53 was rebuilt between 1701–22 as a Franciscan monastery, but in 1789 it was restyled for use by Emperor Joseph II. In 1795, Hungarian Jacobites, led by Ignác Martinovics, were imprisoned here; a plaque records this event. A well featuring a copy of a sculpture of Artemis, the Greek goddess of hunting, by Praxiteles, was set in front of the house in 1873.

There are two museums located on Lords' Street. The Telephone Museum, at No. 49, is a former telephone exchange and one of the most fun and interactive museums in the city. At No. 9 is the entrance to the Labyrinth (*see below*), a relatively new attraction.

Labyrinth of Buda Castle 22
Budavári Labirintus

Úri utca 9 & Lovas út 4. **Map** 1 B5.
Tel 489 32 81, 212 02 87.
🚌 *Várbusz.* 🕐 9:30am–7:30pm
daily; oil lamps lit 6–7:30pm. 🖥
English, German; personal tours from
8pm. 🖥 **www**.labirintus.com

The haunt of prehistoric man some half a million years ago, the Labyrinth of Buda Castle comprises a 1,200-metre (1,000-yard) section of the impressive complex of caves, cellars, dungeons and springs that run beneath Castle Hill to a depth of several storeys. The complex, which was created by the action of hot spring water on calcareous rock, has

One of many tufa-clad caves in the ancient, subterranean Labyrinth

been used variously as a storage area, a refuge and a secret military installation. Now it contains a series of imaginative and unusual themed exhibits. "Prehistoric Labyrinth" contains copies of the most celebrated cave paintings in Europe; "Historical Labyrinth" is populated by figures from Hungarian myth and legend; and "Gallery" is a collection of reconstructions and representations of labyrinths from various ages and cultures. From 6pm, oil lamps are lit. Personal tours, conducted in the dark, "for those who are not afraid of themselves", can be arranged.

Lords' Street, which runs the full length of the Old Town

GELLÉRT HILL AND TABÁN

Carving on the altar in the Cave Church

Rising steeply beside the Danube, Gellért Hill is one of the city's most attractive areas. From the top, at a height of 140 m (460 ft), a beautiful view of the whole of Budapest unfolds. The Celtic Eravi, who preceded the Romans, formed their settlement on the hill's northern slope (see p94). Once called simply Old Hill, many superstitions and tales are connected

with it. In 1046, heathen citizens threw a sealed barrel containing Bishop Gellért, who was trying to convert them to Christianity, from the hill to his death. Afterwards, the hill was named after this martyr. Gellért Hill bulges out slightly into the Danube, which narrows at this point. This made the base of the hill a favoured crossing place, and the settlement of Tabán evolved as a result.

SIGHTS AT A GLANCE

Museums
Semmelweis Museum of
Medical History ⑫

Churches
Rock Church ②
Tabán Parish Church ⑩

Historic Buildings
Citadel ④
Golden Stag House ⑬

Hotels and Baths
Gellért Hotel and Baths
Complex pp90–91 ①
Rác Baths ⑨
Rudas Baths ⑥

Districts, Squares and Monuments
Liberation Monument ③
Miklós Ybl Square ⑪
Queen Elizabeth
Monument ⑦
Statue of St Gellért ⑤
Tabán ⑧

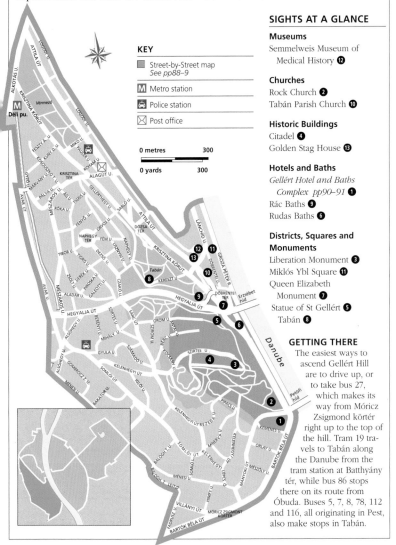

KEY

■ Street-by-Street map
See pp88–9

Ⓜ Metro station

🚓 Police station

⊠ Post office

0 metres 300
0 yards 300

GETTING THERE
The easiest ways to ascend Gellért Hill are to drive up, or to take bus 27, which makes its way from Móricz Zsigmond körtér right up to the top of the hill. Tram 19 travels to Tabán along the Danube from the tram station at Batthyány tér, while bus 86 stops there on its route from Óbuda. Buses 5, 7, 8, 78, 112 and 116, all originating in Pest, also make stops in Tabán.

◁ The Statue of St Gellért, dedicated to a murdered 11th-century bishop

Street-by-Street: Gellért Hill

The hill to the south of Castle hill was long regarded as a notorious spot. In the 11th century, Prince Vata, brother of King István, incited a heathen rebellion here that resulted in the death of Bishop Gellért. During the Middle Ages, witches were even reputed to celebrate their sabbath here. Under the Turks, a small stronghold was first built on the hill to protect Buda. In 1851, the Austrians placed their own bleak and intimidating Citadel at the summit. Not until the end of the 19th century did the popular image of Gellért Hill begin to change, when it became a venue for picnicking parties. In 1967, the area around the Citadel was made into an attractive park.

Queen Elizabeth Monument
Close to the entrance to Elizabeth Bridge stands this statue of Emperor Franz Joseph's wife, who was popular with the Hungarians **7**

★ Statue of St Gellért
Blessing the city with his uplifted cross, the martyred Bishop Gellért is regarded as the patron saint of Budapest **5**

Citadel
Once a place to inspire terror, the Citadel now hosts a hotel, restaurant and wine bar, where people can relax and enjoy the view **4**

HEGYALJA ÚT

0 metres   500

0 yards   500

KEY

━ ━ ━ Suggested route

Liberation Monument
At the foot of the Liberation Monument, towering above the city, are two sculptures, one representing the battle with evil **3**

STAR SIGHTS

★ Rock Church

★ Statue of St Gellért

Rudas Baths
These famous Turkish baths, which date from the 16th century, have a characteristic Ottoman cupola **6**

LOCATOR MAP
See Street Finder, maps 3, 4 & 9

The observation terraces on Gellért Hill provide those who climb up to them with a beautiful panorama over the southern part of Buda and the whole of Pest

THE RESERVOIR

In 1978, a reservoir for drinking water was established close to the Uránia Observatory on Gellért Hill. The surface of the reservoir is covered over and provides a point from which to observe the Royal Palace (*see pp70–71*) to the north. A sculpture by Márta Lessenyei decorates the structure.

★ **Rock Church**
This church was established in 1926 in a holy grotto. Under the Communists, the Pauline order of monks was forced to abandon the church, but it was reopened in 1989 **2**

Sculpture by Márta Lessenyei on Gellért Hill's reservoir

SZENT GELLÉRT RAKPART

Gellért Hotel and Baths Complex
One of a number of bath complexes built at the beginning of the 20th century, this magnificent spa hotel was erected here to exploit the natural hot springs **1**

Gellért Hotel and Baths Complex ❶

Stained-glass window by Bózó Stanisits

Between 1912–18, this hotel and spa was built in the modernist Secession style *(see pp54–7)* at the foot of Gellért Hill. The earliest reference to the existence of healing waters at this spot dates from the 13th century, during the reign of King András II and in the Middle Ages a hospital stood on the site. Baths built here by the Ottomans were referred to by the renowned Turkish travel writer of the day, Evliya Çelebi. The architects of the hotel were Ármin Hegedűs, Artúr Sebestyén and Izidor Sterk. Destroyed in 1945, it was rebuilt and modernized after World War II. The hotel has several restaurants and cafés. The baths include an institute of water therapy, set within Secession interiors, but with modern facilities.

Outdoor Wave Pool
An early swimming pool with a wave mechanism, built in 1927, is situated at the back of the complex, looking towards Gellért Hill behind.

★ Baths
Two separate baths, one for men and one for women, are identically arranged. In each there are three plunge pools, with water at different temperatures, a sauna and a steam bath.

Balconies
The balconies fronting the hotel's rooms have fanciful Secession balustrades that are decorated with lyre and bird motifs.

★ Entrance Hall
The interiors of the hotel, like the baths, have kept their original Secession decor, with elaborate mosaics, stained-glass windows and statues.

Sun Terraces

Situated in the sunniest spot, these terraces are a popular place for drying off in the summer.

VISITORS' CHECKLIST

Szent Gellért tér. **Map** 4 E3.
Tel 466 61 66. 🚌 7, 7A, 86.
🚋 18, 19, 47, 49. 🅿 ♿ 🔲
🍴 🏨 **Baths** Kelenhegyi út.
⏰ 6am–5/6pm daily. 🈚 🅿 ♿
www.budapestspas.hu

Hot pool with
medicinal
spa water

Eastern-Style Towers

The architects who designed the hotel gave its towers and turrets a characteristically oriental, cylindrical form.

Main Staircase

The landings of the main staircase have stained-glass windows by Bózó Stanisits, added in 1933. They illustrate an ancient Hungarian legend about a magic stag, recorded in the poetry of János Arany.

Restaurant Terrace

From this first-floor terrace, diners can appreciate a fine view of Budapest. On the ground and first floors of the hotel there are a total of four cafés and restaurants.

★ Main Façade

Behind the hotel's imposing façade are attractive recreational facilities and a health spa that is also open to non-guests. The entrance to the baths is around to the right from the main entrance, on Kelenhegyi út.

STAR FEATURES

★ Baths

★ Entrance Hall

★ Main Façade

Gellért Hotel and Baths Complex **1**

Gellért Szálló és Fürdő

See pp90–91.

Rock Church **2**

Sziklatemplom

Gellért rakpart 1a. **Map** 4 E3.
Tel 385 15 29. ⏱ *9am–8pm daily.*
🚌 7, 7A, 86. 🚋 18, 19, 47, 49.

On the southern slope of Gellért Hill, the entrance to this grotto church is a short walk from the Gellért Hotel and Baths Complex. Based on the shrine at Lourdes, the church, designed by Kálmán Lux, was established in 1926.

The church was intended for the Pauline order of monks, which was founded in the 13th century by Eusebius of Esztergom. In 1934, 150 years after Joseph II had dissolved the order in Hungary,15 friars arrived back in the city from exile in Poland. However, their residence lasted only until the late 1950s, when the Communist authorities suspended the activities of the church, accusing the monks of treasonable acts, and sealed the entrance to the grotto.

The church and adjoining monastery were reopened on 27 August 1989, when a papal blessing was conferred on its beautiful new granite altar, designed by Győző Sikot. To the left within the grotto is a copy of the *Black Madonna of Czestochowa* and a depiction of a Polish eagle. Visitors will also see a painting of St Kolbe,

a Polish monk who gave his life to protect other inmates at Auschwitz concentration camp. A memorial plaque lists the names of the camps where Polish soldiers were interned during World War II, together with the towns and schools where Polish refugees were sheltered in those years.

At the entrance to the church stands a statue of St István. The monastery can be reached through the Chapel of St István inside. Here, it is worth pausing to look at Béli Ferenc's exquisite wooden sculptures.

Liberation Monument **3**

Felszabadulási Emlékmű

Map 4 D3. 🚌 27.

Positioned high on Gellért Hill, this imposing monument towers over the rest of the city. It was designed by the outstanding Hungarian sculptor Zsigmond Kisfaludi Stróbl and set up here to commemorate the liberation of Budapest by the Russian army in 1945 *(see p34)*. The monument was originally intended to honour the memory of István, son of the Hungarian Regent Miklós Horthy, who disappeared in 1943 on the eastern front. However, after the liberation of the city by Russian troops, Marshal Klimient Woroszyłow spotted it in the sculptor's workshop and reassigned it to this purpose.

The central figure on the monument is a woman holding

The Liberation Monument, standing at the top of Gellért Hill

aloft a palm leaf. Standing on its pedestal, this reaches a height of 14 m (46 ft). At the base of the monument there are two allegorical compositions, representing progress and the battle with evil.

The arrival of the Russians in Budapest was a liberation but also the beginning of Soviet rule. After Communism's fall, a figure of a Russian soldier was removed from the monument to Statue Park *(see p160)*.

Citadel **4**

Citadella

Map 4 D3. 🚌 27. ⏱ *daily.*
🏨 **Hotel Citadella *Tel*** 466 57 94.
Citadella Restaurant *Tel* 386 48 02. ⏱ *11am–11pm daily.*
www.citadellarestaurant.com

After the suppression of the uprising of 1848–9 *(see pp30–31)*, the Habsburgs decided to build a fortification on this strategically important site. Constructed in 1850–54, the Citadel housed 60 cannons, which could, in theory, fire on the city at any time. In reality, from its very inception the Citadel did not fulfil any real military requirements, but served rather as a means of intimidating the population.

The Citadel is some 220 m (720 ft) long by 60 m (200 ft) wide, and has walls 4 m (12 ft) high. After peace was agreed with the Habsburgs, Hungarian society continually demanded the destruction of the Citadel, but it was not until 1897 that the Austrian soldiers left their barracks here. A section of its

Entrance to the Rock Church, run by the Pauline order of monks

entrance gateway was then symbolically ripped out.

After much discussion in the early 1960s, the Citadel was converted into a leisure complex. A restaurant *(see p196)*, hotel *(see p182)* and even a nightclub now attract customers up Gellért Hill. From the old defensive walls of the Citadel there is a spectacular panorama of the city.

Statue of St Gellért ❺

Szent Gellért Emlékmű

Map 4 D2. 🚌 27. *(And a long walk. Go via the steps by Elizabeth Bridge.)*

In 1904 a vast monument was established on the spot where Bishop Gellért was supposedly murdered in the 11th century. It is said the bishop was thrown into the Danube in a barrel, by a mob opposed to the adoption of Christianity. St Gellért holds a cross in his outstretched hand and a Hungarian convert to Christianity kneels at his feet.

The statue was designed by Gyula Jankovits; the semicircular collonade behind it is by Imre Francsek. A spring that bubbles up here was used to create the fountain.

Overlooking the Elizabeth Bridge, the monument can be seen from throughout the city.

The main plunge pool at the Rudas Baths, covered by a Turkish cupola

Rudas Baths ❻

Rudas Gyógyfürdő

Döbrentei tér 9. **Map** 4 D2 (9 C5). **Tel** 356 13 22. **Spa Baths** ⬜ 6am–8pm Mon–Fri, 6am–5pm Sat & Sun, 10pm–4am Fri & Sat. **Swimming pool** ⬜ 6am–6pm Mon–Fri, 6am–2pm Sat & Sun. **www**.budapestspas.hu

Dating originally from 1550, these baths were extended in 1566 by Sokoli Mustafa, an Ottoman pasha. The main part of the baths, dating from this period, have an octagonal plunge pool and four small corner pools with water of varying temperatures.

In recent years the baths have been modernized and include a mixed swimming pool. The spa pools are mixed on weekends, but Tuesdays are reserved for women and the rest of the week for men.

Queen Elizabeth Monument ❼

Erzsébet Királyné Szobra

Döbrentei tér. **Map** 4 D2 (9 C5).

This monument to Queen Elizabeth, wife of Habsburg Emperor Franz Joseph, was created by György Zala.

The statue was erected in its present location in 1986. It stands close to the Elizabeth Bridge *(see p63)*, which was also named after the empress, who showed great friendship to the Hungarians. The statue stood on the opposite side of the river from 1932 until 1947, when the Communists ordered it to be taken down.

The landmark Gellért Monument overlooking the Elizabeth Bridge

Tabán 8

Map 3 C1, C2, C3 (9B5).
18, 19. 5, 78, 112.

The Tabán now consists of a pleasant park and a few historic buildings, but was once very different. In the early 20th century this district, nestling in between Castle Hill and Gellért Hill, was a slum which was cleared as part of a programme to improve the city. Only a few buildings, including Tabán Parish Church, escaped the demolition.

Natural conditions ensured that this was one of the first places in the area where people chose to live. The Celtic Eravi were the first to make a settlement here, while the Romans later built a watchtower from which they could observe people using a nearby crossing point over the river. The first reference to bathing in thermal waters in Tabán dates from the 15th century. The Turks took advantage of this natural asset and built two magnificent baths here, the Rác Baths and the Rudas Baths (see p93), around which a blossoming town was established. Apart from the baths, virtually everything was destroyed in the recapture of Buda in 1686 (see p26).

In the late 17th century, a large number of Serbs, referred to in Hungarian as Rács, moved into the Tabán after fleeing from the Turks. They were joined by Greeks and Gypsies. Many of the inhabitants of the Tabán at this stage were tanners or made their living on the river. On the hillside above grapevines were cultivated. By the early 20th century, though picturesque, the district was still without proper sanitation. The old, decaying Tabán, with its numerous bars and gambling dens, was demolished and the present green space established in its place.

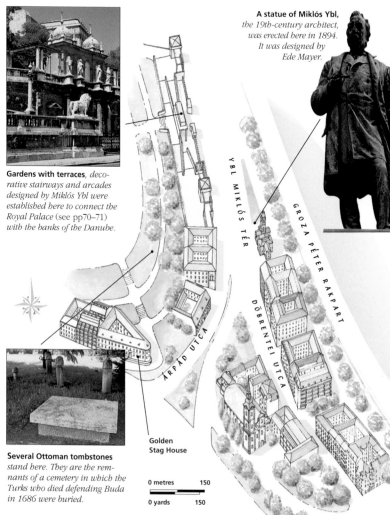

Gardens with terraces, *decorative stairways and arcades designed by Miklós Ybl were established here to connect the Royal Palace (see pp70–71) with the banks of the Danube.*

A statue of Miklós Ybl, *the 19th-century architect, was erected here in 1894. It was designed by Ede Mayer.*

YBL MIKLÓS TÉR

GROZA PÉTER RAKPART

DÖBRENTEI UTCA

ÁRPÁD UTCA

Golden Stag House

Several Ottoman tombstones *stand here. They are the remnants of a cemetery in which the Turks who died defending Buda in 1686 were buried.*

| 0 metres | 150 |
| 0 yards | 150 |

Rác Baths ❾

Rác Gyógyfürdő

Hadnagy utca 8–10. **Map** 4 D2 (9 B5). **Tel** 487 03 13. 🚊 18, 19. ⏰ Re-opening 2009, call for opening hours

Taking their name from the Serbian, or Rác, people who once lived here, the baths date back to the Turkish era *(see pp26–7)*. This is not clear from the outside, as the baths were redeveloped in 1869 to a design by Miklós Ybl. Inside, however, original Ottoman features include an octagonal pool and cupola. The baths are being redeveloped into a modern, luxurious spa and hotel complex, due to open in the spring of 2009.

The façade of the Rác Baths

Tabán Parish Church ❿

Tabáni Plébániatemplom

Attila út 11. **Map** 4 D1 (9 C5). **Tel** 375 54 91. 🚊 18, 19.

A temple is thought to have stood on this site even in the reign of Prince Árpád. In the Middle Ages a church was built here, which was converted into a mosque by the Turks and subsequently destroyed. In 1728–36, after the Habsburgs had taken control of the city, a second church was erected to a design by Keresztély Obergruber. Mátyás Nepauer added the tower in the mid-18th century. In 1881 the façade was extended and the tower crowned by a Neo-Baroque dome.

Inside the church, on the right-hand side under the choir gallery, is a copy of a

Tabán Parish Church, with its Neo-Baroque domed tower

12th-century carving entitled *Christ of Tabán*; the original is now in the collection of the Budapest History Museum *(see p72)*. The altar, pulpit and several paintings adorning the walls of the church all date from the 19th century.

Miklós Ybl Square ⓫

Ybl Miklós Tér

Map 4 D1 (9 C4). 🚊 19.

It is no coincidence that the important architect Miklós Ybl *(see p119)* is commemorated by a statue in this square, close to many of his buildings. Among Ybl's most monumental projects were the State Opera House *(see pp118–19)*, St Stephen's Basilica *(see pp116–17)* and also a large-scale rebuilding of the Royal Palace *(see pp70–71)*.

The Várkert Kiosk, on the square, was also built by Ybl. Initially it pumped water up to the Royal Palace, but in 1903 it was converted into a café. The building also contains the Casino-Valentine Restaurant.

Semmelweis Museum of Medical History ⓬

Semmelweis Orvostörténeti Múzeum

Apród utca 1–3. **Map** 4 D1 (9 B4). **Tel** 375 35 33. 🚊 18, 19. ⏰ Mar–Oct: 10:30am–6pm daily; Nov–Feb 10.30am–4pm. 🍴 📷 🚫

This museum is located in the 18th-century house where Dr Ignáz Semmelweis was born in 1818. He is renowned for his discovery of an antiseptic-based prevention for puerperal fever, a fatal condition common among women who had recently given birth.

The history of medicine from ancient Egypt onwards is portrayed in the museum, which includes a replica 19th-century pharmacy. Semmelweis's surgery can also be seen with its original furniture. In the courtyard is a monument called *Motherhood* by Miklós Borsos.

Golden Stag House ⓭

Szarvas Ház

Szarvas tér 1. **Map** 3 C1 (9 B4). **Tel** 375 64 51. 🚊 19.

Standing at the foot of Castle Hill is this distinctive early 19th-century house. It received its name from the inn that opened here called "Under the Golden Stag" – above the entrance you will see a bas-relief depicting a golden stag pursued by two hunting dogs. The building still accommodates a restaurant of that name, Aranyszarvas, which specializes in game dishes. There is also a separate wine bar located in the cellar.

Bas-relief above the entrance to Golden Stag House

NORTH OF THE CASTLE

Between Castle Hill and the western bank of the Danube, extending north from the Chain Bridge towards Margit körút, is the area known as Víziváros or Water Town. This area gained its name in the Middle Ages due to constant flooding. It was originally an area inhabited by artisans and fishermen who, consequently, remained poorer than their neighbours on Castle Hill. Today,

Decoration on the Millacher Fountain

the church towers of Víziváros create a wonderful vista along the western bank of the Danube.

In the Middle Ages and during the 150 years of Turkish occupation this area north of Castle Hill was fortified by a system of walls. A short section of these walls still exists by No. 66 Margit körút, and is commemorated by a plaque. The tomb of Gül Baba, a Turkish dervish, is in the north of the area. It is one of the few surviving Ottoman monuments.

SIGHTS AT A GLANCE

Churches
Calvinist Church ❸
Capuchin Church ❷
St Anne's Church pp102–3 ❹
St Francis's Wounds Church ❻

Historic Buildings and Monuments
Tomb of Gül Baba ❽
Tunnel ❶

Squares
Batthyány Square ❺

Baths
Király Baths ❼
Lukács Baths ❾

GETTING THERE
This area is well served by Public transport. Buses 4, 16, 86 and 105 run to Clark Ádám tér (next to the Chain Bridge). Tram 19, metro line M2 (red) and the HÉV suburban train converge at Batthyány tér. The tram and HÉV run parallel with the Danube, the tram from the south, the HÉV from the north. The M2 metro links the area with Pest to the east.

KEY

▨	Street-by-Street map *See pp98–99*
🚊	HÉV station
Ⓜ	Metro station
⊠	Post office
⛴	River boat boarding point

◁ **The Calvinist Church, viewed from the Danube, beautifully illuminated at night**

Street-by-Street: Víziváros

Fő Utca, the main street of Víziváros (Water Town), runs the length of the neighbourhood. Numerous cafés and restaurants, spectacular Baroque monuments, and a promenade along the Danube give this area a charming atmosphere. A fine array of churches, in an interesting assortment of architectural styles, reflect the history of the area as far back as the Middle Ages. From the Danube promenade the panorama of Pest opposite, with Parliament (see pp108–9) in the foreground, can best be viewed.

★ **St Francis's Wounds Church**
The Baroque pulpit in this church was carved by the Franciscans, for whom the church was built in the mid-18th century ⑥

The Hikisch House was built on top of medieval walls. The façade, dating from 1795, features bas-reliefs of cherubs carrying out different tasks. Other reliefs depict allegories of the four seasons.

The White Cross Inn, one of Budapest's earliest inns, was established in 1770. Its asymmetrical façade was created by joining two houses together. Among those reputed to have stayed here are Emperor Joseph II and also Casanova.

0 metres   100

0 yards   100

STAR SIGHTS

★ Bathyány Square

★ St Anne's Church

★ St Elizabeth's Church

★ **Batthyány Square**
A monument to Ferenc Kölcsey (1790–1838) overlooks this square. He was a literary critic and political commentator of the early 19th century, and also wrote the prayer Lord, Bless Hungary, which is used as the lyrics for the Hungarian national anthem ⑤

KEY

 Suggested route

★ **St Anne's Church**
Characteristic of the late Baroque period, the interior of this church is quite stunning. The main portal is decorated with allegorical sculptures of Faith, Hope and Charity ❹

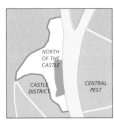

LOCATOR MAP
See Street Finder, maps 1 & 9

Calvinist Church
The roof of this church, built in 1893–6, is covered with colourful ceramic tiles from the Zsolnay factory (see p56). They are a strong focal point in the panorama of Buda ❸

B E M   R A K P A R T

A Monument to Samu Pecz
stands beside one of his most important buildings, the Calvinist Church. Pecz was a follower of the Neo-Gothic movement and constructed many other important buildings in the city.

Capuchin Church
In its original medieval form, this church underwent conversion into a mosque at the hands of the Turks. Many Gothic elements have survived, however. Its present structure dates from 1854–6 ❷

To Clark Ádám tér and the Chain Bridge

F Ő   U T C A

Kapisztory House,
at No. 20 Fő utca, was built in 1811 for the Greek merchant, Joseph Kapisztory. Its unusual turretted cylindrical window is an attractive feature of this street.

The imposing entrance to the Tunnel on Clark Ádám tér

Tunnel **1**

Alagút

Clark Ádám tér. **Map** 1 C5 (9 B3).
16, 86.

The Scottish engineer Adam Clark settled in Hungary after completing the Chain Bridge *(see p62)*. One of his later projects, in 1853–7, was building the Tunnel that runs right through Castle Hill, from Clark Ádám tér to Krisztinaváros. The Tunnel is 350 m (1,150 ft) long, 9 m (30 ft) wide and 11 m (36 ft) in height.

The entrance on Clark Ádám tér is flanked by two pairs of Doric columns. This square is the city's official centre because of the location here of the Zero Kilometre Stone, from which all distances from Budapest are calculated.

The Tunnel's western entrance was originally ornamented with Egyptian motifs. However, it was rebuilt without these details after it was damaged in World War II.

Capuchin Church **2**

Kapucinus Templom

Fő utca 32. **Map** 1 C4 (9 B2). *Tel* 201 47 25. by arrangement.
The origins of this church date from the 14th century, when the mother of Louis I, Queen Elizabeth, decided to establish a church here. Fragments of walls on the northern façade survive from this time.

During the Turkish occupation *(see pp26–7)*, the church was converted into a mosque. Features from this period, such

as the window openings and and the doorway on the southern façade, have remained despite the fighting of 1686.

Between 1703–15 the church was rebuilt, following a Baroque design created by one of the Capuchin Fathers.

In 1856 the church was again restyled, by Ferenc Reitter and Pál Zsumrák, who linked the differently styled façades harmoniously together. The statue of St Elizabeth on the mid-19th-century Romantic façade also dates from 1856.

The altar of the Capuchin Church

Calvinist Church **3**

Református Templom

Szilágyi Dezső tér 3. **Map** 1 C4 (9 B2). *Tel* 457 01 09.

One of Budapest's more unusual churches, the Calvinist Church was built by Samu Pecz between 1893–6 on the site of a former medieval market. It is one of the major examples of his work.

Despite the use of modern tiles on the roof, the church is

Neo-Gothic in style. It is also interesting to note that Pecz used this traditional design of medieval Catholic churches for a Calvinist church, which has very different liturgical and ecclesiastical needs.

St Anne's Church **4**

Szent Anna Templom

See pp102–3.

Batthyány Square **5**

Batthyány Tér

Map 1 C3 (9 B1). Batthyány tér.

Batthyány Square is one of the most interesting squares on the Danube's western bank. Beautiful views of Parliament and Pest on the opposite bank unfold from here.

In 1905, the square was renamed after Count Lajos Batthyány, the prime minister during the Hungarian uprising of 1848–9 *(see pp30–31)*, who was shot by the Austrian army.

The square features buildings in many different styles. The Hikisch House, at No. 3, dating from the late 18th century, is late Baroque. It is notable for the bas-reliefs on its façade depicting the four seasons. The White Cross Inn, at No. 4, also late Baroque, features Rococo decoration. On the western side of the square is the first covered market in Buda, dating from 1902. Though damaged in World War II, it is now fully restored.

The Hikisch House, with bas-reliefs representing the four seasons

St Francis's Wounds Church ➏

Szent Ferenc sebei-templom

Fő utca 41–43. **Map** 1 C3 (9 B1).
Tel 201 80 91. Ⓜ *Batthyány tér.*

In 1731–57 a church was built for the Franciscan order on the ruins of a former mosque, to a design by Hans Jakab. In 1785, after he had dissolved the Franciscan order, Emperor Joseph II gave the church to St Elizabeth's Convent.

The Baroque interior is adorned with late 19th-century frescoes, including one of St Florian protecting Christians from a fire in 1810. Their resonance is due to their recent restoration. The original pulpit and pews, carved by the friars, have remained intact.

In the early 19th century, a hospital and hostel were built adjacent to the church. These were run by the Elizabeth Sisters.

Király Baths ➐

Király Gyógyfürdő

Fő utca 84. **Map** 1 C2.
Tel 202 36 88. Ⓜ *Batthyány tér.*
◯ *7am–6pm Mon, Wed, Fri (women); 9am–8pm Tue, Thu, Sat (men).* ⓐ

The Ottoman Király Baths are one of the city's four remaining Turkish baths *(see p50–53)*. Built from 1566–70, with 19th-century neo-classical additions, they retain many original features, the most beautiful being the central cupola hall with its octagonal pool. From here radiate out the smaller pools of different temperatures, the steam rooms and saunas.

At the end of Fő utca, in the square that bears his name is the monument to the Polish general József Bem. The hero of the 1848–9 uprisings, he is depicted with his arm in a sling. It was in this state, in the front line of the Battle of Pisk, that he inspired the Hungarian troops to attack the bridge and achieve victory over the Habsburg armies. Memorable words, which he uttered during the battle, are engraved on the base of the monument.

Tiles on the Tomb of Gül Baba

Tomb of Gül Baba ➑

Gül Baba Türbéje

Mecset utca 14. **Map** 1 B1. 🚌 91.
◯ *May–Sep: 10am–6pm Tue–Sun; Oct–Jan: 10am–4pm Tue–Sun.* ⓐ

Gül Baba was a Muslim dervish and member of the Bektashi order, who died in 1541, just after the capture of Buda. He was one of the few Turks who was respected and revered by the people of Hungary. His remains now lie in a tomb built between 1543 and 1598.

According to legend, it was Gül Baba who introduced roses to Budapest. From this came both the name of this area, Rózsadomb, meaning Rose Hill, and Gül Baba's own name, which in English means Father of Roses. Fittingly, his tomb is surrounded by a lovely rose garden.

A 400-year-old dome covers the octagonal tomb. Inside, the sarcophagus is draped in green cloth with gold citations from the Koran. Pictures, religious items and beautiful rugs also adorn the tomb.

It is a well-known place of pilgrimage for Muslims.

Lukács Baths ➒

Lukács Gyógyfürdő

Frankel Leo út 25–9. **Map** 1 C1.
Tel 326 16 95. ◯ *6am–7pm Mon–Fri; 6am–5pm Sat & Sun.* ⓐ
🅿 17. www.budapestspas.hu

This famous spa is named after St Luke. Although the Neo-Classical complex was established in 1894, the baths are one of a number still operating in the city *(see pp50–53)* that date back to the period of Turkish rule.

Set in peaceful surroundings, the complex comprises the 16th-century Komjády (Császár) thermal baths and two outdoor swimming pools. Natural hot springs keep these pools heated all year round; bathing is comfortable even in winter.

It is also worth entering the overgrown courtyard to see a statue of St Luke, dating from 1760, and the plaques inscribed with thanks by bathers from around the world who benefited from the healing waters.

Lukács Baths, with beautiful old plane trees growing outside

St Anne's Church ➍

Budapest is home to many churches, but the twin-towered parish church of Víziváros is one of its most beautiful Baroque examples. Initially a Jesuit church, the architect who first designed it is unknown. Building was begun in 1740 by Kristóf Hámon and completed after his death by Mátyás Nepauer. In 1763 an earthquake seriously damaged the building and the dissolution of the Jesuit order ten years later further delayed the completion of the church. Thus it remained unconsecrated until 1805. The rectory now houses the Angelika café.

Crucifix on the St Cross altar

The twin towers are crowned by magnificent Baroque spires.

Façade
Buda's coat of arms appears in the centre of the tympanum. The symbol of the Trinity is above this, between two kneeling angels.

★ Pulpit
This magnificent, late Baroque pulpit was created by Károly Bebó in 1773. It features gilded details and angels that embody theological virtues. The reliefs were added at a later date.

Main entrance

Organ
The organ case from a former Carmelite church on Castle Hill was transferred to St Anne's Church in the late 18th century, after the dissolution of the order by Emperor Joseph II.

★ Painted Ceiling
The painted ceiling in the cupola of the chancel depicts the Holy Trinity. It was painted in 1771 by Gergely Vogl. There are also Neo-Baroque frescoes in the nave dating from 1938.

VISITORS' CHECKLIST

Batthyány tér 7. **Map** 1 C3 (9 B1).
Tel 201 34 04. Ⓜ Batthyány
tér. ◯ Only for services.
✝ daily. **Angelika café** ◉
Currently closed for renovations

★ High Altar
The sculptures depict Mary, as a child, being brought into the Temple of Jerusalem by St Anne, her mother. Completed in 1773, it is regarded as one of the most beautiful works of Károly Bebó.

Church Pew
The choir pews are decorated with intricately carved wooden panels which feature figurative scenes.

Baptismal Font
Concealed behind a pillar, this baptismal font has a carved pedestal and a simply, but beautifully, decorated cover.

Side Altar
This late Baroque altar of St Francis the Saviour, like the altar of St Cross on the opposite side of the church, is the work of Antal Eberhardt and dates from 1768. The picture in the centre was, however, executed by Franz Wagenschön.

STAR FEATURES

★ High Altar

★ Painted Ceiling

★ Pulpit

AROUND PARLIAMENT

Towards the end of the 18th and throughout the 19th century Pest underwent a series of huge changes. In 1838 a flood destroyed most of the rural dwellings that had occupied the area until that time. The unification of Budapest in 1873 and the 1,000-year anniversary, in 1896, of the Magyar conquest also boosted the city's development. The medieval walls that originally

An ornate lantern on the Parliament

marked Pest's limits were crossed as the area was gradually urbanized. This period produced a number of the most important buildings in Hungary, including St Stephen's Basilica, Parliament and the Hungarian Academy of Sciences, which were built in a variety of revivalist styles. Many Neo-Classical residences were also built, particularly on Nádor utca, Akadémia utca and Október 6 utca.

SIGHTS AT A GLANCE

Historic Buildings and Palaces
Central European University ⑥
Drechsler Palace ⑫
Gresham Palace ⑧
Hungarian Academy of Sciences ⑨
Ministry of Agriculture ③
Parliament pp108–9 ①
Post Office Savings Bank ⑤
Radisson Béke Hotel ⑬

Museums
Ethnographical Museum ②

Squares
Liberty Square ④
Roosevelt Square ⑦

Theatres
Budapest Operetta Theatre ⑭
State Opera House pp118–19 ⑪

Churches
St Stephen's Basilica pp116–17 ⑩

GETTING THERE
The M2 metro line (red) runs to Kossuth Lajos tér and the M3 metro line (blue) runs to Arany János utca. Tram 2 runs north along the Danube and terminates past Parliament at Margaret Bridge. Trolley buses 70 and 78 also serve this area.

KEY

▨	Street-by-Street map *See pp106–7*
▨	Street-by-Street map *See pp112–13*
Ⓜ	Metro station
⊠	Post office
ⓘ	Tourist information

0 metres 500
0 yards 500

◁ **Neo-gothic spires, flying buttresses and stained-glass windows on Hungary's Parliament**

Street-by-Street: Kossuth Square

Brigadier Woroniecki

This square expresses well the pomp and pride with which Pest was developed during the 19th and early 20th centuries. Parliament dominates the square on the Danube side, but equally imposing are the Ministry of Agriculture and the Ethnographical Museum on the opposite side. Several monuments commemorate nationalist leaders and provide a visual record of Hungary's recent political history.

★ **Ethnographical Museum**
Among 170,000 exhibits amassed in the museum's collection is a captivating collection of folk costumes representing the various nationalities and ethnic groups in Hungary ❷

★ **Parliament**
This building has become the recognized symbol of democracy in Hungary, despite the dome being crowned by a red star during the Communist period ❶

Attila József was a radical poet whose work sensitively explored the human condition. In 1937 he committed suicide, aged 32. This statue by László Marton dates from 1980.

LAJOS KOSSUTH (1802–94)

The popularity of Lajos Kossuth among the Hungarian people is immense. He led the 1848–9 uprising against Austrian rule *(see pp30–31)*, and was one of the most outstanding political figures in Hungary. He was a member of the first democratic government during the uprising, and briefly became its leader before being exiled after the revolt was quashed in 1849.

Stained-glass window depicting Lajos Kossuth

BALASSI BÁLINT U

0 metres   150
0 yards   150

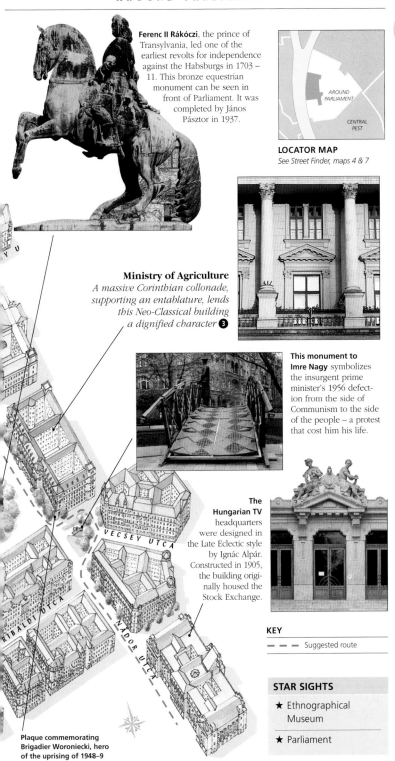

Ferenc II Rákóczi, the prince of Transylvania, led one of the earliest revolts for independence against the Habsburgs in 1703 – 11. This bronze equestrian monument can be seen in front of Parliament. It was completed by János Pásztor in 1937.

LOCATOR MAP
See Street Finder, maps 4 & 7

Ministry of Agriculture
A massive Corinthian collonade, supporting an entablature, lends this Neo-Classical building a dignified character ❸

This monument to Imre Nagy symbolizes the insurgent prime minister's 1956 defection from the side of Communism to the side of the people – a protest that cost him his life.

The Hungarian TV headquarters were designed in the Late Eclectic style by Ignác Alpár. Constructed in 1905, the building originally housed the Stock Exchange.

KEY

- - - Suggested route

STAR SIGHTS

★ Ethnographical Museum

★ Parliament

Plaque commemorating Brigadier Woroniecki, hero of the uprising of 1948–9

Parliament ❶

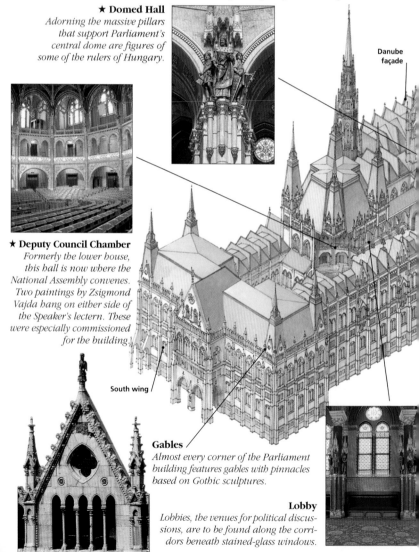

One of the pair of lions at the main entrance

Hungary's Parliament is the country's largest building and has become a symbol of Budapest. A competition was held to choose its design, the winner being Imre Steindl's rich Neo-Gothic masterpiece built between 1885–1902. Based on the Houses of Parliament in London, completed by Charles Barry in 1835–6, it is 268 m (880 ft) long and 96 m (315 ft) high, and comprises 691 rooms.

Aerial View
The magnificent dome marks the central point of the Parliament building. Although the façade is elaborately Neo-Gothic, the ground plan follows Baroque conventions.

★ Domed Hall
Adorning the massive pillars that support Parliament's central dome are figures of some of the rulers of Hungary.

Danube façade

★ Deputy Council Chamber
Formerly the lower house, this hall is now where the National Assembly convenes. Two paintings by Zsigmond Vajda hang on either side of the Speaker's lectern. These were especially commissioned for the building.

South wing

Gables
Almost every corner of the Parliament building features gables with pinnacles based on Gothic sculptures.

Lobby
Lobbies, the venues for political discussions, are to be found along the corridors beneath stained-glass windows.

Dome
The ceiling of the 96-m (315-ft) high dome is covered in an intricate design of Neo-Gothic gilding combined with heraldic decoration.

VISITORS' CHECKLIST

Kossuth Lajos tér. **Map** 2 D3 (9 C1). *Tel* 441 49 04. 🚊 *2, 2A.* Ⓜ *Kossuth tér.* 🚌 *70, 78.* 🕐 *English 10am, noon, 2pm.* 🎫 *Free adm with EU passport.* ♿ ▯

Gobelin Hall
This hall is decorated with a Gobelin tapestry illustrating Prince Árpád, with seven Magyar leaders under his command, signing a peace treaty and blood oath.

North wing

Old Upper House Hall
The Old Upper House Hall is now used for holding international conferences. It is virtually a mirror image of the National Assembly Hall.

e Royal signia, excluding the ronation Mantle *e p132),* are kept the Domed Hall.

The main entrance on Kossuth Lajos tér

STAR FEATURES

★ Deputy Council Chamber

★ Domed Hall

Main Staircase
The best contemporary artists were invited to decorate the interior. The sumptuous main staircase features ceiling frescoes by Károly Lotz and sculptures by György Kiss.

The magnificent façade of the Ethnographical Museum

Parliament ●
Országház

See pp108–9.

Ethnographical Museum ●
Néprajzi Múzeum

Kossuth Lajos tér 12. **Map** 2 D3 (9 C1). *Tel* 473 24 41. Ⓜ Kossuth Lajos tér. ◯ 10am– 6pm Tue–Sun. 📷 📹 💻 www.neprajz.hu

This building, designed by Alajos Hauszmann and constructed between 1893 – 6, was built as the Palace of Justice and, until 1945, served as the Supreme Court.

The building's design links elements of Renaissance, Baroque and Classicism. The façade is dominated by a vast portico crowned by two towers. It also features a gable crowned by the figure of the Roman goddess of justice in a chariot drawn by three horses, by Károly Senyei. The grand hall inside the main entrance features a marvellous staircase and frescoes by Károly Lotz.

The building was first used as a museum in 1957, housing the Hungarian National Gallery *(see pp74–7)*, which was later transferred to the Royal Palace. The Ethnographical Museum has been here since 1973.

The museum's collection was established in 1872 in the Department of Ethnography at the Hungarian National Museum *(see pp130–33)*. There are now around 170,000 exhibits, although most are not on display. The collection includes artifacts reflecting the rural folk culture of Hungary from the prehistoric era to the 20th century. A map from 1909 shows the settlement of the various communities who came to Hungary. Ethnic items relating to these communities, as well as primitive objects from North and South America, Africa, Asia and Australia, can also be seen.

The museum has two very informative permanent displays: Traditional Culture of the Hungarian Nation, and From Primeval Communities to Civilization.

Ministry of Agriculture ●
Földművelésügyi Minisztérium

Kossuth Lajos tér 11. **Map** 2 D3 (9 C1). Ⓜ Kossuth Lajos tér.

On the southeast side of Kossuth Square is this huge building, bordered by streets on all its four sides. It was built for the Ministry of Agriculture by Gyula Bukovics at the end of the 19th century.

The façade is designed in a manner typical of late Historicism, drawing heavily on Neo-Classical motifs. The columns of the colonnade are echoed in the fenestration above the well-proportioned pedimented windows.

On the wall to the right of the building two commemorative plaques can be seen. The first is dedicated to the commanding officer of the Polish Legion, who was also a hero of the 1848–9 uprising *(see p30–31)*. Brigadier M Woroniecki, who was renowned for his bravery, was shot down on this spot by the Austrians in October 1849.

The second plaque honours Endre Ságvári, a Hungarian hero of the resistance movement, who died in the fighting against the Fascists in 1944.

The two sculptures in front of the building are by Árpád Somogyi. The *Reaper Lad* dates from 1956 and the *Female Agronomist* from 1954.

Liberty Square ●
Szabadság Tér

Map 2 E4 (10 D1). Ⓜ Kossuth Lajos tér, Arany János utca.

After the enormous Neugebäude Barracks were demolished in 1886, Liberty Square was laid out in its place. The barracks, built for the Austrian troops, once dominated the southern part of Lipótváros (Leopold Town). It was here that Hungary's first independent prime minister, Count Lajos Batthyány was executed on 6 October 1849. Since 1926, an eternal flame *(see p31)* has been burning at the corner of Aulich utca, Hold utca and Báthory utca to honour all those executed during the uprising.

Two particularly impressive buildings by Ignác Alpár are on opposite sides of the square. The former Stock Exchange, now the Hungarian TV headquarters (Magyar Televízió székháza), dates from 1905 and shows the influence of the Secession style. The Hungarian National Bank (Magyar Nemzeti Bank) is decorated in a pastiche of Historicist styles and also dates from 1905.

Bas-reliefs on the former Stock Exchange

Beautiful Secession interior of the Post Office Savings Bank

tendrils and icons taken from nature. The bees climbing up the gable walls represent the bank's activity and the pinnacles, which look like hives, represent the accumulation of savings. These features were intended to be accessible to the people who banked here.

The building is not officially open to the public, but it is possible to see the Cashiers' Hall during office hours.

Central European University 6

Közép-Európai Egyetem

Nádor utca 9. **Map** 2 E5 (10 D2). *Tel* 327 30 00. Ⓜ *Kossuth Lajos tér.* **www**.ceu.hu

This Neo-Classical palace on Nádor utca, in the direction of Roosevelt Square, was built in 1826 by Mihály Pollack for Prince Antal Festetics. Since 1993 it has housed the Central European University.

Founded by the American millionaire George Soros, who was born in Budapest, this international educational establishment is open to students from central and eastern Europe and the former USSR.

The university offers postgraduate courses in subjects ranging from history and law to political and environmental sciences. In Budapest, the Soros Foundation finances numerous other ventures and it has branches in all the central European countries.

An obelisk by Károly Antal stands at the northern end of the square commemorating the Red Army soldiers who died during the siege of Budapest in 1944– 5. A second statue is to the US general Harry Hill Bandholtz. He led the allied forces that thwarted the Romanian troops looting the Hungarian National Museum.

Post Office Savings Bank ❺

Postatakarék Pénztár

Hold utca 4. **Map** 2 E4 (10 D1). Ⓜ *Kossuth Lajos tér.*

A masterpiece by Ödön Lechner, the former Post Office Savings Bank was built between 1900– 1901. Chiefly a Secession architect, Lechner *(see p56)* combined the curvilinear motifs of that style with motifs from Hungarian folk art to produce a unique visual style for his work.

Approaching the Post Office Savings Bank, one can see glimpses of the details that

have made this building one of Pest's most unusual sights. The construction methods, interior design and exterior detailing of the building are remarkable. Lechner commissioned the tiles used in the design, including the vibrant roof tiles, from the Zsolnay factory *(see p56)*. The façades are decorated with floral

---

THE AMERICAN EMBASSY

This beautiful house, at No. 12 Liberty Square, was designed by Aladár Kálmán and Gyula Ullmann and built between 1899– 1901. The façade is decorated with bas-reliefs featuring motifs typical of the Secession style.

By the entrance to the embassy is a plaque with an image of the Catholic Primate, Cardinal Joseph Mindszenty, who was part of the movement seeking to liberate

Plaque commemorating Joseph Mindszenty

Hungary from the Communists after World War II. He was imprisoned by the regime in 1949 and was mistreated for many years. Released during the 1956 uprising, he asked for political asylum in the embassy. He lived here for 15 years in internal exile until, in 1971, the Vatican finally convinced him to leave Hungary.

Street-by-Street: Roosevelt Square

In 1867, a cermonial mound was made of earth from
all over the country to celebrate the coronation of
Franz Joseph as king of Hungary. Today, the historic
earth has been dug into the ground where Roosevelt
Square now stands. At the head of the Chain Bridge on
the eastern bank of the Danube, it features many of
Pest's most beautiful buildings, such as the Hungarian
Academy of Sciences, to the north of the square, and
Gresham Palace, to the east. The square was named
after American president Franklin D Roosevelt in 1947.

No. 1 Akadémia utca was
built in the Neo-Classical
style by Mátyás Zitterbarth
the younger, in 1835.
A plaque shows that in
November 1848 General
József Bem *(see p101)*
stayed here when it was
the Prince Stephen Hotel.

★ **Gresham Palace**
*One of the most expressive
examples of Secession architecture in Budapest, now a
Four Seasons hotel* **8**

**House
designed by
József Hild
in 1836**

★ **Hungarian Academy
of Sciences**
*The debating hall of the Hun-
garian Academy of Sciences
is decorated with sculptures
by Miklós Izsó and ceiling
paintings by Károly Lotz* **9**

**The Chain
Bridge** *(see p62)*
was built between
1839 – 49 and was
the city's first
permanent river
crossing. It was
destroyed by the
German forces in
World War II and
was reopened in
1949, 100 years after
it was first finished.

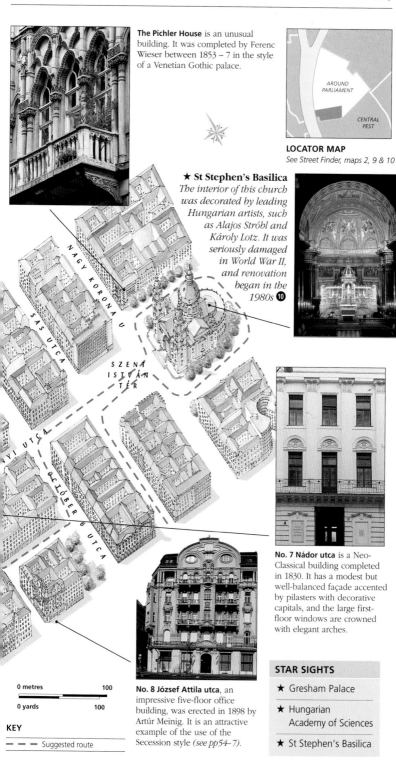

The Pichler House is an unusual building. It was completed by Ferenc Wieser between 1853 – 7 in the style of a Venetian Gothic palace.

LOCATOR MAP
See Street Finder, maps 2, 9 & 10

★ **St Stephen's Basilica**
The interior of this church was decorated by leading Hungarian artists, such as Alajos Stróbl and Károly Lotz. It was seriously damaged in World War II, and renovation began in the 1980s ❿

No. 7 Nádor utca is a Neo-Classical building completed in 1830. It has a modest but well-balanced façade accented by pilasters with decorative capitals, and the large first-floor windows are crowned with elegant arches.

No. 8 József Attila utca, an impressive five-floor office building, was erected in 1898 by Artúr Meinig. It is an attractive example of the use of the Secession style *(see pp54–7).*

0 metres   100

0 yards   100

KEY

– – – Suggested route

STAR SIGHTS

★ Gresham Palace

★ Hungarian
   Academy of Sciences

★ St Stephen's Basilica

Monument to Ferenc Deák, dating from 1887, in Roosevelt Square

Roosevelt Square ❼
Roosevelt tér

Map 2 D5 (9 C3). ▦ 16. ▦ 2.

Previously, Roosevelt Square was known by several different names – Franz Joseph Square and Unloading Square among others – but it received its current title in 1947. It is located at the head of the Pest side of the Chain Bridge, and is home to many beautiful and important buildings.

At the beginning of the 20th century the square was lined with various hotels, the Diana Baths and the Lloyd Palace designed by József Hild. The only building from the previous century still standing today is the Hungarian Academy of Sciences. The other buildings were demolished and replaced by the Gresham Palace and the Bank of Hungary, on the corner of Attila József utca. Two large modern hotels, the Sofitel Atrium Budapest (see p184) and the Inter-Continental Budapest (see p186), stand on the southern side of the square.

There is a statue to Baron József Eötvös (1813–71), a reformer of public education, in front of the Inter-Continental. Situated in the centre of the square are monuments to two politicians who espoused quite different ideologies: Count István Széchenyi (1791 – 1860), the leading social and political reformer of his age, and Ferenc Deák (1803 – 76), who was instrumental in the Compromise of 1867, which resulted in the Dual Monarchy (see p32).

Gresham Palace ❽
Gresham Palota

Roosevelt tér 5 – 7. **Map** 2 D5 (9 C3). **Tel** 268 60 00. ▦ 16. ▦ 2. **www**.fourseasons.com/budapest

This Secession palace aroused both controversy and praise from the moment it was built. One of Budapest's most distinctive pieces of architecture, it was commissioned by the London-based Gresham Life Assurance Company from Zsigmond Quittner and the brothers József and László Vágó, and completed in 1907.

This enormous edifice enjoys an imposing location directly opposite the Chain Bridge. The façade features characteristic Secession motifs (see pp54 – 7), such as curvilinear forms and organic themes. The ornately carved window surrounds appear as though they are projecting from the walls, blending seamlessly with the architecture. The bust by Ede Telcs, at the top of the façade, is of Sir Thomas Gresham. He was the founder of the Royal Exchange in London and of Gresham's Law: "bad money drives out good".

On the ground floor of the palace there is a T-shaped arcade, covered by a multi-coloured glazed roof. The entrance to the arcade is marked by a beautiful wrought-iron gate with peacock motifs. Still the original gate, it is widely regarded as one of the most

Bust of Sir Thomas Gresham on the façade of the Gresham Palace

splendid examples of design from the Secession era. Inside the building, the second floor of the Kossuth stairway has a stained-glass window by Miksa Róth, featuring a portrait of Lajos Kossuth (see p106).

In 2004 the palace opened as a Four Seasons Hotel, the second in Central Europe, and the first in Hungary. Visitors can wander in and admire its many splendours.

Miklós Izsó's sculptures inside the Hungarian Academy of Sciences

Hungarian Academy of Sciences ❾
Magyar Tudományos Akadémia

Roosevelt tér 9. **Map** 2 D4 (9 C2). **Tel** 411 61 00. ▦ 16. ◯ 11am–4pm Mon–Fri. **www**.mta.hu

Built between 1862–4, this Neo-Renaissance building was designed by the architect Friedrich August Stüler.

The statues adorning the façade represent six disciplines of knowledge – law, history, mathematics, sciences, philosophy and linguistics – and are the works of Emil Wolf and Miklós Izsó. On the Danube side are allegories of poetry, astronomy and archeology, and on the corners of the building are statues of renowned thinkers including Newton, Descartes and Révay. The interior features more statues by Miklós Izsó, and the library, on the ground floor, has a priceless collection of academic books.

The Neo-Renaissance façade of the Drechsler Palace

St Stephen's Basilica ⑩
Szent István Bazilika

See pp116–17.

State Opera House ⑪
Magyar Állami Operaház

See pp118–19.

Drechsler Palace ⑫
Drechsler Palota

Andrássy út 25. **Map** 2 F4 (10 E2). Ⓜ *Opera.*

Soon to be a 5-Star hotel, and formerly the State Ballet Institute, the Drechsler Palace was originally built as Neo-Renaissance apartments for the Hungarian Railways Pension Fund in 1883. It was designed by Gyula Pártos and Ödön Lechner to harmonize with the façade of the State Opera House *(see pp118–19)*.

Its name derives from the Drechsler Café, which occupied the ground floor of this building towards the end of the 19th and in the early 20th century.

Radisson SAS Béke Hotel ⑬
Radisson SAS Béke Hotel

Teréz körút 43. **Map** 2 F3. *Tel* 889 39 00. Ⓜ *Oktogon.* **www**.danubiushotels.wm/beke

This elegant hotel was built in 1896 as an apartment building, and in 1912 was restyled by Béla Málnai as the Hotel Brittania. A mosaic of György Szondi, a Hungarian captain who fought against the Turks in the 16th century, was added to the façade at this time.

In 1978 the hotel was taken over by the Radisson group, which restored the rich interiors. Notable features are the stained-glass windows in the Szondi Restaurant, by Jenő Haranghy, illustrating the works of Richard Wagner. The Romeo and Juliet conference room and the Shakespeare Restaurant are named after the murals that decorate them. The café serves cake and coffee on porcelain from the Pécs factory *(see p56)*.

Budapest Operetta Theatre ⑭
Budapesti Operett Színház

Nagymező utca 17. **Map** 2 F4 (10 F1). *Tel* 472 20 30. 🚋 *4, 5, 6.* **www**.operettszinhaz.hu

Budapest has a good reputation for musical entertainment, and its operetta scene *(see p216)* is over 100 years old. Operettas were first staged on this site in the Orfeum Theatre, designed in the Neo-Baroque style by the Viennese architects Fellner and Helmer, in 1898. The project was financed by the impressario Károly Singer-Somossy.

In 1922, the American entrepreneur Ben Blumenthal redeveloped the building and opened the Capital Operetta Theatre, which then specialized in the genre. After 1936, this theatre became the only venue for operetta in Budapest.

The repertoire of the theatre includes the works of both international and Hungarian composers of this genre, including Imre Kálmán, Ferenc Lehár and Pál Ábrahám, who wrote the *Csárdás Princess*.

Entrance to the Budapest Operetta Theatre on Nagymező utca

St Stephen's Basilica ❿

St István's coronation

Dedicated to St Stephen, or István, the first Hungarian Christian king *(see p22)*, this church was designed by József Hild in the Neo-Classical style, using a Greek cross floor plan. Construction began in 1851 and was taken over in 1867 by Miklós Ybl *(see p119)*, who added the Neo-Renaissance dome after the original one collapsed in 1868. József Kauser completed the church in 1905. It received the title of Basilica Minor in 1938, the 900th anniversary of St István's death.

Dome
Reaching 96 m (315 ft), the dome is visible from all over Budapest.

St Matthew
St Matthew is one of the four Evangelists represented in the niches on the exterior of the dome. They are all the work of the sculptor Leó Feszler.

Observation point

Tower
A bell, weighing 9,144 kg (9 tons) is housed in this tower. It was funded by German Catholics to compensate for the original bell, which was looted by the Nazis in 1944.

Main Portal
The massive door is decorated with carvings depicting the heads of the 12 Apostles.

Mosaics
The dome is
decorated with
mosaics designed
by Károly Lotz.

★ **Main Altar**
In the centre of the altar
there is a marble statue of
St István by Alajos Stróbl.
Scenes from the king's life
are depicted behind the altar.

★ **Holy Right Hand**
Hungary's most unusual relic is
the mummified forearm of
King István. It is kept in the
Chapel of the Holy Right Hand.

**Figures of the 12
Apostles**, by Leó
Feszler, crown the
exterior colonnade
at the back of
the church.

**St Gellért and
St Emericus**
This portrayal of
St Gellért and his
pupil, St Emeryka,
is the work of
Alajos Stróbl.

★ **Painting by
Gyula Benczúr**
This image shows King István,
eft without an heir, dedicating Hungary
to the Virgin Mary, who became
atrona Hungariae, the country's patron.

STAR FEATURES

★ Main Altar

★ Holy Right Hand

★ Painting by
   Gyula Benczúr

State Opera House ⓫

Opened in September 1884, the State Opera House in Budapest was built to rival those of Paris, Vienna and Dresden. Its beautiful architecture and interiors were the life's work of the great Hungarian architect, Miklós Ybl. The interior also features ornamentation by Hungarian artists, including Alajos Stróbl and Károly Lotz. During its lifetime, the State Opera House has seen some influential music directors, including, Ferenc Erkel, composer of the Hungarian opera *Bánk Bán*, Gustav Mahler and Otto Klemperer.

Decorative lamp with putti

Façade

The decoration of the symmetrical façade follows a musical theme. In niches on either side of the main entrance there are figures of two of Hungary's most prominent composers, Ferenc Erkel and Franz Liszt (see p144). Both were sculpted by Alajos Stróbl.

Murals

The vaulted ceiling of the foyer is covered in magnificent murals by Bertalan Székely and Mór Than. They depict the nine Muses.

★ Foyer

The foyer, with its marble columns, gilded vaulted ceiling, murals and chandeliers, gives the State Opera House a feeling of opulence and grandeur.

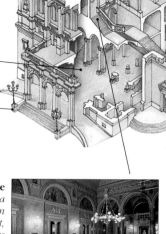

Main entrance

Wrought-iron lamps illuminate the wide stone staircase and the main entrance.

★ Main Staircase

Going to the opera was a great social occasion in the 19th century. A vast, sweeping staircase was an important element of the opera house as it allowed ladies to show off their new gowns.

Chandelier

The main hall is decorated with a bronze chandelier that weighs 3,050 kg (3 tons). It illuminates a magnificent fresco, by Károly Lotz, of the Greek gods on Olympus.

VISITORS' CHECKLIST

Andrássy út 22. **Map** 2 F4 (10 E2).
Tel *331 25 50 or 353 01 70 (box office).* M *Opera.* 🎦 🚫 ♿ 🚻
🎬 *3pm & 4pm.* www.opera.hu

Central Stage

This proscenium arch stage employed the most modern technology of the time. It featured a revolving stage and metal hydraulic machinery.

The side entrance has a loggia that reflects the design of the main entrance.

★ Royal Box

The royal box is located centrally in the three-storey circle. It is decorated with sculptures symbolizing the four operatic voices – soprano, alto, tenor and bass.

MIKLÓS YBL (1814 – 91)

The most prominent Hungarian architect of the second half of the 19th century, Miklós Ybl had an enormous influence on the development of Budapest. He was a practitioner of Historicism, and tended to use Neo-Renaissance forms. The State Opera House and the dome of St Stephen's Basilica are examples of his work. Ybl also built apartment buildings and palaces for the aristocracy in this style. A statue of the architect stands on the western bank of the Danube, in Miklós Ybl Square *(see p95).*

Bust of Miklós Ybl

STAR FEATURES

★ Foyer

★ Main Staircase

★ Royal Box

CENTRAL PEST

Bas-relief on the façade of
the City Council Chamber

At the end of the 17th century much of Pest was in ruins and few residents remained. Within the next few decades, however, new residential districts were established, which are today's mid-town suburbs. In the 19th century, redevelopment schemes introduced grand houses and apartment blocks, some with shops and cafés, as well as secular and municipal buildings. Perhaps the most prominent example of this work is the Hungarian National Museum. At this time Pest surpassed Buda as a centre for trade and industry. This was partly due to the area's Jewish community, who played an active role in its development.

SIGHTS AT A GLANCE

Churches
Calvinist Church **22**
Chapel of St Roch **18**
Franciscan Church **31**
Great Synagogue **16**
*Inner City Parish Church
pp124–5* **1**
Lutheran Church **11**
Serbian Church **26**
Servite Church **10**
University Church **28**

Museums
*Hungarian National Museum
pp130–33* **20**
*Museum of Applied Arts
pp136–7* **23**

Historic Buildings and Monuments
City Council Chamber **25**
Danube Fountain **12**
Ervin Szabó Library **21**
Franz Liszt Academy of Music **14**
Károlyi Palace **29**
Klotild Palaces **6**
Lóránd Eötvös University **27**
Municipal Council Offices **8**
New Theatre **13**
New York Palace **15**
Pest County Hall **7**
Turkish Bank **9**
University Library **30**
University of Economics **24**

Streets and Squares
Jewish Quarter **16**
József Nádor Square **3**
Mihály Pollack Square **19**
Mihály Vörösmarty Square **4**
Váci Street **5**
Vigadó Square **2**

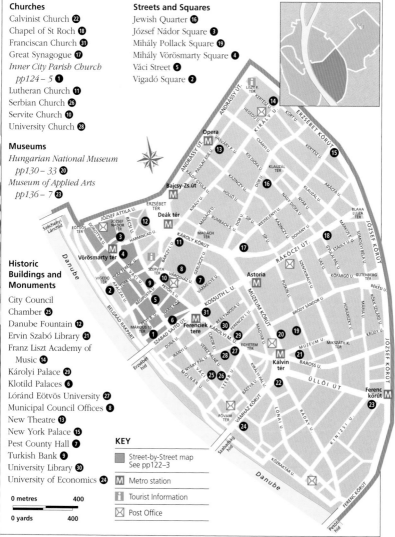

KEY
	Street-by-Street map See pp122–3
M	Metro station
i	Tourist Information
⊠	Post Office

0 metres 400
0 yards 400

◁ The well of Danaid, who was condemned to carry water to a leaking barrel, in Szomory Dezső tér

Street-by-Street: Around Váci Street

Váci Street has been Budapest's fashionable area for
walking, meeting in cafés and shopping in elegant
boutiques since the early 19th century. Its attractive
promenade is an enjoyable place for an evening stroll,
when it is stylishly illuminated.

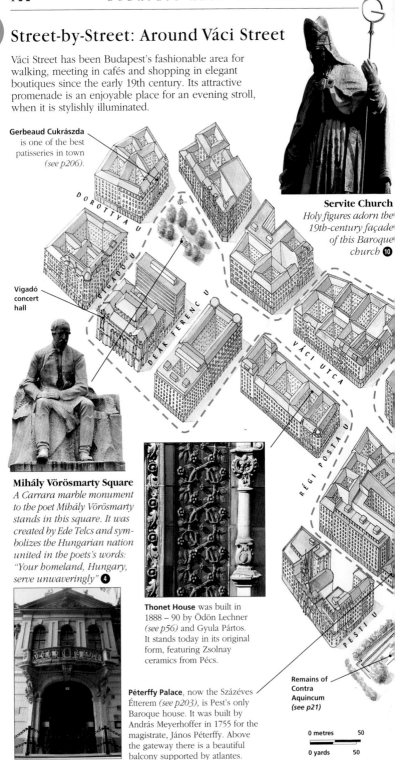

Gerbeaud Cukrászda
is one of the best
patisseries in town
(see p206).

Servite Church
*Holy figures adorn the
19th-century façade
of this Baroque
church* ❿

Vigadó
concert
hall

Mihály Vörösmarty Square
*A Carrara marble monument
to the poet Mihály Vörösmarty
stands in this square. It was
created by Ede Telcs and symbolizes the Hungarian nation
united in the poets's words:
"Your homeland, Hungary,
serve unwaveringly"* ❹

Thonet House was built in
1888 – 90 by Ödön Lechner
(see p56) and Gyula Pártos.
It stands today in its original
form, featuring Zsolnay
ceramics from Pécs.

Péterffy Palace, now the Százéves
Étterem *(see p203)*, is Pest's only
Baroque house. It was built by
András Meyerhoffer in 1755 for the
magistrate, János Péterffy. Above
the gateway there is a beautiful
balcony supported by atlantes.

Remains of
Contra
Aquincum
(see p21)

0 metres	50
0 yards	50

★ **Váci Street**
Budapest's most elegant promenade and shopping area is lined with fashion boutiques, cafés, fountains and statues. Off the street there are old courtyards and shopping arcades ❺

LOCATOR MAP
See Street Finder, maps 2, 7, 8, 10

Párizsi Udvar *(see p212)* is found on the corner of Kígyó utca and Petőfi Sándor utca. The arcade, which features shops, bookshops and a cafe, is decorated with beautiful wrought-iron work.

★ **Klotild Palaces**
This beautifully decorated block is one of two buildings, which together form a magnificent gateway to the Elizabeth Bridge ❻

KEY

— — — Suggested route

★ **Inner City Parish Church**
This white limestone and red marble tabernacle, in the church, dates from the early 16th century ❶

STAR SIGHTS

★ Inner City Parish Church

★ Klotild Palaces

★ Váci Street

Inner City Parish Church ❶

This church is the oldest building in Pest. It was first established during the reign of St István, the first king of Hungary *(see pp22–3)*, on the burial site of the martyred St Gellért. In the 14th century, a large Gothic church was built, which was used as a mosque under the Turks. Damaged by the Great Fire of 1723, the church was partly rebuilt in the Baroque style by György Pauer in 1725–39. The interior also features Neo-Classical elements by János Hild, as well as some 20th-century works.

The south tower includes one of the surviving walls of the Romanesque church.

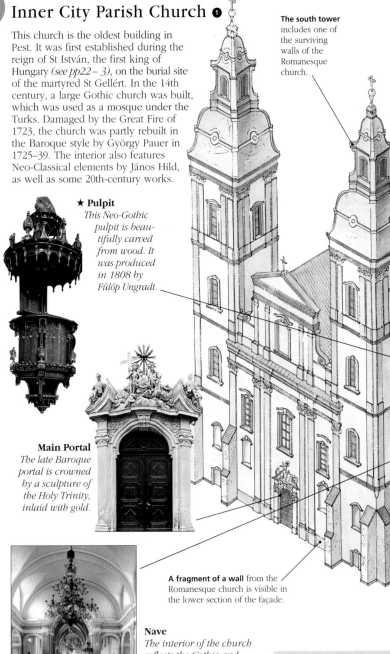

★ Pulpit
This Neo-Gothic pulpit is beautifully carved from wood. It was produced in 1808 by Fülöp Ungradt.

Main Portal
The late Baroque portal is crowned by a sculpture of the Holy Trinity, inlaid with gold.

A fragment of a wall from the Romanesque church is visible in the lower section of the façade.

Nave
The interior of the church reflects the Gothic and Baroque periods in which it was built. The nave, in the western section of the church, is Baroque in design.

STAR FEATURES

★ Fresco
★ Gothic Chapel
★ Pulpit

★ **Fresco**
This fragment of a 15th-century Italianate fresco depicts the crucifixion of Christ. It was transferred from the cloister to its current location in the choir.

VISITORS' CHECKLIST

Március 15 tér 2. **Map** 4 E1 (10 D5). *Tel* 318 31 08.
Ⓜ *Ferenciek tere.*
◯ 9am–7pm daily. ✝ daily.

Main Altar
The original altar was destroyed in World War II, and the current one, by Károly Antal and Pál C Molnár, dates from 1948.

Reconstructed Gothic tabernacle

Turkish Prayer Niche
One of the few remnants of the Turkish occupation (see pp26 – 7) is this mihrab, *or prayer niche, indicating the direction of Mecca.*

★ **Gothic Chapel**
This vaulted chapel is entered through a painted archway. It features recreated tracery windows.

Crest of Pest
The crest of Pest adorns the pedestal of a Renaissance tabernacle, which was commissioned by Pest's city council in 1507. It is the work of a 16th-century Italian artist.

HISTORICAL FLOORPLAN OF THE CHURCH

Nothing remains of the first church: the oldest sections date from the 12th-century Romanesque church.

KEY

▨ Romanesque church
▢ Gothic church
▢ Baroque church

The opulent façade of the Vigadó concert hall, decorated with figures and busts of statesmen, leaders and other prominent Hungarians

Inner City Parish Church ❶

Belvárosi Plébánia Templom

See pp124 – 5.

Vigadó Square ❷

Vigadó Tér

Map 4 D1 (10 D4). 🚊 2. **Tel** 354 37 55. 🚇 For refurbishment.

The Vigadó concert hall (closed until the end of 2009) dominates the square with its mix of eclectic forms. It was built by Frigyes Feszl in 1859–64 to replace a predecessor destroyed by fire during the uprising of 1848 – 9(see pp30 – 31). The façade includes features such as folk motifs, dancers on columns and busts of former monarchs, rulers and other Hungarian personalities. An old Hungarian coat of arms is also visible in the centre.

The Budapest Marriott Hotel (see p185), located on one side of the square, was designed by József Finta in 1969. It was one of the first modern hotels to be built in Budapest.

On the Danube promenade is a statue of a childlike figure on the railings: *Little Princess* (see p65), by László Marton. The square also has craft stalls, cafés and restaurants.

József Nádor Square ❸

József Nádor Tér

Map 2 E5 (10 D3). 🚇 Vörösmarty tér.

Archduke József, after whom this square is named, was appointed as the emperor's

Palatine for Hungary in 1796 at the age of 20. He ruled the country for 51 years until his death in 1847. One of the few Habsburgs sympathetic to the Hungarian people, he was instrumental in the development of Buda and Pest and, in 1808, he initiated the Embellishment Commission (see p30).

A statue of Archduke József, by Johann Halbig, stands in the middle of the square. It was erected in 1869.

Some of the houses on the square are worth individual mention. The Neo-Classical Gross Palace at No. 1 (see p48) was built in 1824 by József Hild. Once a café, it now houses a bank. The building at Nos. 5–6,

Sculpture in Vigadó Square

which overlooks the southern end of the square, dates from 1859 and was built by Hugó Máltás. At No. 11 is a shop run by the Herend company (see p212). Its factory has produced world-renowned porcelain for almost 200 years.

Mihály Vörösmarty Square ❹

Vörösmarty Mihály Tér

Map 2 E5 (10 D3). 🚇 Vörösmarty tér.

In the middle of the square stands a monument depicting the poet Mihály Vörösmarty (1800 – 55). Unveiled in 1908, it is the work of Ede Telcs.

Behind the monument, on the eastern side of the square, is the Luxus department store (see p213). It is located in a three-floor corner building dating from 1911 and designed by Kálmán Giergl and Flóris Korb.

On the northern side of the square there is a renowned pâtisserie, opened by Henrik Kugler in 1858. It was taken over by the Swiss *patissière* Emil Gerbeaud, who was responsible for the richly decorated interior which survives to this day.

The elegant interior of the Gerbeaud pâtisserie, on Mihály Vörösmarty Square

A tempting selection of coffee, cakes, pastries and desserts are on offer. In summer, these can be taken on a terrace overlooking the square.

Thonet House, decorated with Zsolnay tiles, at No. 11 Váci Street

Váci Street ❺

Váci Utca

Map 4 E1–F2 (10 E5). Ⓜ *Ferenciek tere.*

Once two separate streets, which were joined at the beginning of the 18th century, Váci Street still has two distinct characters. Today, part of the southern section is open to traffic, while the northern end is pedestrianized and has long been a popular commercial centre. Most of the buildings lining the street date from the 19th and early 20th centuries. More recently, however, modern department stores, banks and shopping arcades have sprung up among the older original buildings.

Philantia, a Secession style florist's shop opened in 1905, now occupies part of the Neo-Classical block at No. 9, built in 1840 by József Hild. No. 9 also houses the Pest Theatre, where classic plays by Anton Chekhov, among others, are staged. The building was once occupied by the Inn of the Seven Electors, which had a large ballroom-cum-concert hall. It was here that a 12-year-old Franz Liszt performed.

Thonet House, at No. 11, is most notable for the Zsolnay tiles *(see p56)* from Pécs, which decorate its façade.

No. 13 is the oldest building on Váci Street and was built in 1805. In contrast, the post-modern Fontana department store at No. 16, was built in 1984. Outside the store there is a bronze fountain with a figure of Hermes, dating from the mid-19th century.

The Nádor Hotel once stood at No. 20 and featured a statue of Archduke Palatine József in front of the entrance. Today the Taverna Hotel *(see p183)*, designed by József Finta and opened in 1987, stands here.

In a side street off Váci Street, at No. 13 Régiposta utca, is a building from the Modernist period. An unusual sight in Pest, this Bauhaus-influenced building dates from 1937 and is by Lajos Kozma.

Klotild Palaces ❻

Klotild Paloták

Szabadsajtó utca. **Map** 4 E1 (10 E5). Ⓜ *Ferenciek tere.*

Flanking Szabadsajtó utca, on the approach to the Elizabeth Bridge, stand two massive apartment blocks built in 1902. The buildings were commissioned by the daughter-in-law of Palatine József, Archduchess Klotild, after whom they were named.

They were designed by Flóris Korb and Kálmán Giergl in the Historicist style, with

One of the twin Klotild Palaces, from 1902, by the approach to the Elizabeth Bridge *(see p63)*

elements of Rococo decoration. The right Palace is under reconstruction as apartments and a hotel, due to open in 2009, and the left side houses the Casino Lido, a restaurant and a café.

Pest County Hall ❼

Pest Megyei Önkormányzat

Városház utca 7. **Map** 4 F1 (10 E4). **Tel** 485 68 00. Ⓜ *Ferenciek tere.* ⏰ *8am–4:30pm Mon–Thu, 8am–2pm Fri.*

Built in several stages, this is one of Pest's most beautiful, monumental Neo-Classical civic buildings. It was erected during the 19th century, as part of the plan for the city drawn up by the Embellishment Commission.

A seat of the Council of Pest has existed on this site since the end of the 17th century. By 1811, however, the building included two conference halls, a prison and a prison chapel. In 1829 – 32, a wing designed by József Hofrichter was added on Semmelweis utca, which was used to accommodate council employees.

In 1838 another redevelopment programme was begun, this time employing designs by Mátyás Zitterbarth Jr, a highly regarded exponent of Neo-Classical architecture. Completed in 1842, it included an impressive façade, which overlooks Városház utca. This features a portico with six Corinthian columns supporting a prominent tympanum.

Pest County Hall was destroyed in the course of World War II. During post-war rebuilding it was enlarged, with the addition of three internal courtyards, the first of which is surrounded by atmospheric cloisters. Due to the excellent acoustics, concerts are often held here during the summer.

Between Pest County Hall and the Municipal Council Offices building *(see p128)*, in the small Kamermayer Károly tér, there is a monument to the first mayor of Budapest. Károly Kamermayer (1829 – 97) took office in 1873 after the unification of Óbuda, Buda and Pest. The aluminium monument was designed in 1942 by Béla Szabados.

Municipal Council Offices ❽

Fővárosi Önkormányzat

Városház utca 9–11. **Map** 4 E1 & F1 (10 E4). **Tel** 327 10 00. Ⓜ *Ferenciek tere.* ⭘ *8am–4:30pm Mon–Thu, 8am–12:30pm Fri.* **www**.budapest.hu

The largest Baroque building in Budapest, this edifice was completed in 1735 to a design by the architect Anton Erhard Martinelli. It was originally a hospital for veterans of the war between the Christians and Turks at the end of the 17th century *(see pp26–7)*.

In 1894 the city authorities bought the building in order to convert it into council offices. Ármin Hegedűs was commissioned to refurbish the building.

Most notable are the bas-reliefs decorating the gates on the Városház utca side of the building. The scenes depicted in the bas-reliefs commemorate a victory of Charles III *(see p19)* and Prince Eugene of Savoy's role in the war against the Turks *(see p71)*. These are thought to be the work of the Viennese sculptor Johann Christoph Mader.

Turkish Bank ❾

Török Bankház

Szervita tér 3. **Map** 4 E1 (10 D4). Ⓜ *Deák Ferenc tér.*

Dating from 1906 and designed by Henrik Böhm and Ármin Hegedűs, the building that formerly housed the Turkish Bank is a wonderful example of the Secession style.

The exterior used modern construction methods to create the glass façade, which is set in reinforced concrete. Above the fenestration, in the gable, is a magnificent colourful mosaic by Miksa Róth. Entitled *Glory to Hungary*, it depicts Hungary paying homage to the Virgin Mary, or *Patrona Hungariae (see p117)*. Angels and shepherds surround the Virgin, along with figures of Hungarian political heroes, such as Prince Ferenc Rákóczi *(see p28)*, István Széchenyi *(see pp30–31)* and Lajos Kossuth *(see p106)*.

Glory to Hungary, the mosaic on the façade of the Turkish Bank

Servite Church ❿

Szervita Templom

Szervita tér 7. **Map** 4 E1 (10 D4). Ⓜ *Deák Ferenc tér.*

This Baroque church was built between 1725–32 to a design by János Hölbling and György Pauer. In 1871, the façade was rebuilt and the tower was covered with a new roof, designed by József Diescher.

Above the doorway there are figures of St Peregrin and St Anne, and above them sit St Philip and St Augustine. To the right of the entrance there is a bas-relief by János Istók, dating from 1930. It is dedicated to the heroes of the VIIth Wilhelm Hussar Regiment who gave their lives in World War I.

Lutheran Church ⓫

Evangélikus Templom

Deák tér 4. **Map** 2 E5 (10 E3). **Tel** 317 34 13. Ⓜ *Deák Ferenc tér.* ♿ **National Lutheran Museum Tel** 235 02 07. ⭘ *10am–6pm Tue – Sun.* 📷 📹 *by arrangement.*

Mihály Pollack designed this Neo-Classical church, built between 1799–1808. A portico, which features a tympanum supported by Doric columns, was added to the façade in 1856 by József Hild.

The church's simplicity is typical of early Neo-Classicism.

It also reflects the notion of minimal church decoration, which was upheld by this branch of Protestantism. Above the modest main altar is a copy of Raphael's *Transfiguration* by Franz Sales Lochbihler, made in 1811. Organ recitals are often held in the church, which has excellent acoustics.

Another Neo-Classical building by Mihály Pollack adjoins the church. Constructed as a Lutheran school, it is now the National Lutheran Museum. The museum illustrates the history of the Reformation in Hungary, with the most interesting exhibit being a copy of Martin Luther's last will and testament. The original document, dating from 1542, is held in the Lutheran Archives.

Neo-Classical main altar in the Lutheran Church

The Danube Fountain, built in 1880–83 by Miklós Ybl

Danube Fountain 🔟
Danubius Kút

Erzsébet tér. **Map** 2 E5 (10 D3).
Ⓜ *Deák Ferenc tér.*

This fountain, which once stood in Kálvin tér, was designed and built by Miklós Ybl (*see p94*) in 1880 – 83. It is decorated with copies by Dezső Győri of original sculptures, by Béla Brestyánszky and Leó Feszler, which were damaged in World War II.

The figure at the top of the fountain is Danubius, representing the Danube. The three female figures below symbolize Hungary's three principal rivers after the Danube: the Tisza, the Dráva and the Száva.

New Theatre 🔟
Új Színház

Paulay Ede utca 35. **Map** 2 F4 (10 E2). *Tel* 269 60 21. Ⓜ *Opera.*

Originally completed in 1909, this building has undergone many transformations. It was designed by Béla Lajta in the Secession style, and, as the home of the cabaret troupe Parisian Mulató, became a shrine to frivolity.

In 1921 it was completely restyled by László Vágó, who turned it into a theatre. After World War II, the theatre gained a glass-and-steel façade, and a children's theatre company was based here.

Between 1988 – 90 the building was returned to its original form using Lajta's plans. Gilding, stained glass and marble once more adorn this unusual building. Hungary's New Theatre is now in residence.

Franz Liszt Academy of Music 🔟
Liszt Ferenc Zeneakadémia

Liszt Ferenc tér 8. **Map** 7 A1 (10 F2). *Tel* 462 46 00. 🚊 *4, 6 to Király utca.*

The academy is housed in a late Historicist palace, built between 1904 – 7 by Kálmán Giergl and Flóris Korb. Above the main entrance there is a statue of Franz Liszt, by Alajos Stróbl. The six bas-reliefs above its base are by Ede Telcs, and depict the history of music.

The Secession interiors of this building have remained intact and deserve particular attention. The *Fount of Youth* fresco, in the first floor foyer, is by Aladár Körösfői-Kriesch, who was a member of the Gödöllő school. The academy has two auditoriums. The first seats 1,200 people and features allegories of musical movements. The second seats 400 and is used for chamber music.

New York Palace 🔟
New York Palota

Erzsébet körút 9–11. **Map** 7 B2. *Tel* 886 61 11. Ⓜ *Blaha Lujza tér.* 🅗 🖥 www.boscolohotels.com

Built between 1891–5 to a design by the architect Alajos Hauszmann, the building was initially the offices of an American insurance firm.

This five-floor edifice displays an eclectic mix of Neo-Baroque and Secession motifs. The decorative sculptures that animate the façade are the work of Károly Senyei.

On the ground floor is the renowned New York Café. The beautiful, richly gilded Neo-Baroque interior, with its chandeliers and marble pillars, now attracts tourists, just as it once attracted the literary and artistic circles in its heyday. Following refurbishment, the hotel reopened in 2006 with 107 rooms, a luxurious spa, and a restaurant serving international haute cuisine.

Statue of Franz Liszt above the entrance to the Academy of Music

Hungarian National Museum ⑳

Seal from Esztergom

The Hungarian National Museum is the country's richest source of art and artifacts relating to its own turbulent history. Founded in 1802, the museum owes its existence to Count Ferenc Széchényi, who offered his collection of coins, books and documents to the nation. The museum's constantly expanding collection of art and documents is exhibited in an impressive Neo-Classical edifice built by Mihály Pollack.

Placing the Cornerstone *(1864)*
This painting by Miklós Barabás shows the ceremony that marked the beginning of construction of the Chain Bridge (see p62) in 1842.

Campaign Chest
This carved Baroque campaign chest features the prince regent's decoration and the Hungarian crest. It dates from the insurrection led by Ferenc II Rákóczi (see p28).

Armchair
Adorned with multi-coloured fruit and floral ornamentation, this armchair dates from the early 18th century. It is the work of Ferenc II Rákóczi, who learnt carpentry during his exile in Turkey.

★ **Coronation Mantle**
This textile masterpiece, made of Byzantine silk, was donated to the church in Székesfehérvár by St Stephen in 1031. It became the Coronation Mantle in the 12th century.

KEY

- ☐ Coronation Mantle
- ☐ Archaeological exhibition
- ☐ 11th–17th-century exhibition
- ☐ 18th–19th-century exhibition
- ☐ 20th-century exhibition

MUSEUM GUIDE
On the first floor is the Coronation Mantle and the archaeological exhibition. Second floor exhibits comprise Hungarian artifacts from 11th–20th centuries. The Roman Lapidary is found in the basement.

Main entrance

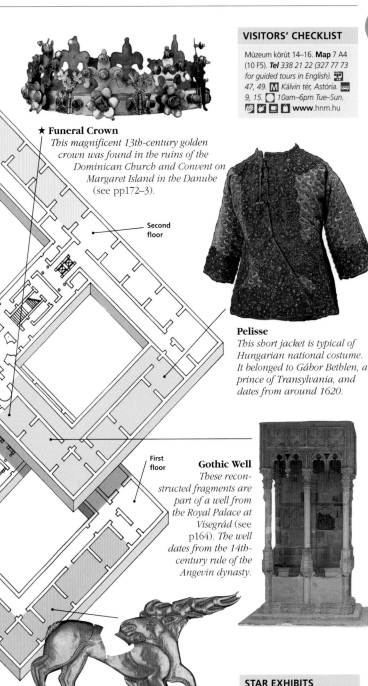

VISITORS' CHECKLIST

Múzeum körút 14–16. **Map** 7 A4
(10 F5). **Tel** 338 21 22 (327 77 73
for guided tours in English).
47, 49. Kálvin tér, Astória.
9, 15. 10am–6pm Tue–Sun.
www.hnm.hu

★ Funeral Crown
*This magnificent 13th-century golden
crown was found in the ruins of the
Dominican Church and Convent on
Margaret Island in the Danube
(see pp172–3).*

Second
floor

Pelisse
*This short jacket is typical of
Hungarian national costume.
It belonged to Gábor Bethlen, a
prince of Transylvania, and
dates from around 1620.*

First
floor

Gothic Well
*These recon-
structed fragments are
part of a well from
the Royal Palace at
Visegrád (see
p164). The well
dates from the 14th-
century rule of the
Angevin dynasty.*

★ Golden Stag
*This hand-forged Iron Age figure dates
from the 6th century BC. It was originally
part of a Scythian prince's shield.*

STAR EXHIBITS

★ Coronation Mantle

★ Funeral Crown

★ Golden Stag

Exploring the Museum's Collection

A 13th-century seal

The steps of the Hungarian National Museum were the scene of a major event in Hungary's history. It was from these steps that, in 1848, the poet Sándor Petőfi first read his *National Song*, which sparked the uprising against Habsburg rule *(see p30–31)*. This moment is commemorated each year on 15 March, when the museum is decorated in the national colours and a re-enactment is performed. Items from the museum's rich collection, including works of art and craft, historical documents and photographs, vividly illustrate this and other events from Hungary's varied and fascinating past.

Remarkably, the royal insignia, which includes a sceptre and golden crown, have survived Hungary's dramatic history. Discovered by the American forces during World War II, they were removed and stored in Fort Knox before being returned to Hungary in 1978.

In 2000, these other treasures of the royal insignia were transferred to the Domed Hall of Parliament *(see pp108–9)*, where they can also be visited.

ARCHAEOLOGICAL EXHIBITION

The archaeological display was opened in 2002 to celebrate the 200th anniversary of the museum's foundation. The visitor is taken through a display of Hungary's heritage, spanning the period between 400 BC and AD 804, from the first inhabitants of the country at Vértesszőlős until the end of the Early Medieval period, immediately preceeding the Hungarian Conquest.

The exhibition presents some of the latest and important archaeological finds, and abounds in authentic reconstructions of the past.

Monument to poet János Arany in front of the Neo-Classical façade

11TH–17TH-CENTURY EXHIBITION

The exhibition begins in the Árpád era and features one of the museum's most valuable exhibits, the crown of Constantine IX Monomachus, decorated with enamel work. Also on display in this section are the funeral decorations of

MUSEUM BUILDING

Built between 1837–47, according to a design by Mihály Pollack, this imposing Neo-Classical building is one of the finest manifestations of that architectural epoch.

The façade is preceded by a monumental portico, which is crowned by a tympanum designed by Raffael Ponti. The composition depicts the figure of Pannonia *(see p20)* among personifications of the arts and sciences.

In the gardens surrounding the museum there are a number of statues of prominent figures from the spheres of literature, science and art. A monument to the poet János Arany, author of the *Toldi Trilogy*, stands in front of the main entrance. This bronze

and limestone work dates from 1893 and is by Alajos Stróbl. The notable features of the interior include the magnificent paintings by Mór Than and Károly Lotz in the main staircase.

CORONATION MANTLE

One of the most important Hungarian treasures, the Coronation Mantle *(see pp22–3)*, is currently on display in a separate hall of its own in the museum. Made of Byzantine silk, it was originally donated to the church by St Stephen in 1031. The magnificent gown was then refashioned in the 13th century. The now much faded cloth features an intricate embroidered design of fine gold thread and pearls.

Carved base of a chalice dating from the 15th century

Béla III, Romanesque sacred vessels, weapons and an interesting collection of coins.

The period of Angevin rule *(see p18)* coincided with the birth of the Gothic style, which is represented here by some excellent examples of gold work. The next two halls explore the reign of Sigismund of Luxembourg *(see p24)* and the achievements of János Hunyadi *(see p24)*. On display here are copies of portraits of King Sigismund by Albrecht Dürer and a richly decorated ceremonial saddle. There are also several platinum and gold pieces, illuminated manuscripts and documents. The lifestyle of peasants from this era is illustrated, as well as the history of the royal court.

The reign of Mátyás Corvinus *(see pp24–5)* and the Jagiełło dynasty *(see p18)* marks the decline of the Gothic period and the birth of the Renaissance. Exhibits from this era include a 15th-century glass goblet belonging to King Mátyás, late Gothic pews from a church in Bártfa, armour and weapons, as well as a 16th-century dress belonging to Maria Habsburg.

Magnificent examples of sculpture, art and artifacts from the 16th and 17th centuries follow. Of interest are items that survived the Turkish occupation *(see pp26–7)*, especially the everyday objects and weapons.

A separate hall is dedicated to the Transylvanian principality and the important historical role that it played. Exhibited here are vessels and jewellery elaborately crafted in gold, 17th-century costumes, and original ceramics produced by the people of Haban, who settled there in the early 17th century. This last section of the exhibition ends in 1686, at the time of the liberation of Buda by the Christian armies after the Turkish occupation. In this part of the museum there are also portraits of influential Hungarians from the period, and an interesting exhibition of jewellery dating from the 17th century.

Printing press used in 1848 to print nationalist propaganda

18TH–19TH-CENTURY EXHIBITION

This part of the museum covers Habsburg rule, a period of great civil unrest. The exhibition begins with artifacts connected to the Rákóczi insurrection of 1703–11 *(see pp28–9)*. Weapons, as well as furniture from Ferenc II Rákóczi's palace, are exhibited here. One item of particular interest is the armchair produced by Rákóczi himself. The next hall is dedicated to 18th-century Hungarian art and culture.

Brooch from the 18th-century

The following rooms portray the Hungarian history of the first half of the 19th century. Artworks, including magnificent portraits and historic paintings, such as *Placing the Cornerstone of the Chain Bridge*, are assembled along with important documents and memoirs from that time.

The central section, dedicated to the uprising of 1848–9 *(see pp30–31)*, features a printing press on which were printed leaflets outlining the 12 demands in Hungary's fight for independence from Austria.

The exhibits from the second half of the 19th century include collections of masonic items, official decorations, coins and historic manuscripts. Items relating to the coronation of Franz Joseph in 1867 and the Millennium Celebrations of 1896 are also displayed here.

20TH-CENTURY EXHIBITION

Reflecting the technical developments of this century, Hungary's recent history is presented in a documentary style. Photographs, and documents are widely used to illustrate this period. Artifacts relating to World War I and the era of revolution between the wars, and shocking documents from World War II can be found here. The post-war history of Hungary is depicted mainly from a political perspective. Emphasis is placed on significant episodes, such as the uprising of 1956 and the events of 1989, which signalled the end of Communism in Eastern Europe *(see p35)*.

Guild chest from the 20th century

Jewish Quarter ⑯
Zsidó Negyed

Király utca, Rumbach Sebestyén utca,
Dohány utca & Akácfa utca. **Map** 2 F5
& 7 A2 (10 F3). Ⓜ *Deák Ferenc tér.*

Jews first came to Hungary in
the 13th century and settled in
Buda and Óbuda. In the 19th
century, a larger Jewish
community was established
outside the Pest city boundary,
in a small area of Erzsébetváros.
   In 1251, King Béla IV gave
the Jews of Buda certain privil-
iges, including freedom of

HOLOCAUST MEMORIAL

This sculpture of a weeping willow, designed by Imre
Varga, was unveiled in 1991 in memory of the 600,000
Hungarian Jews killed by the Nazis in World War II. It was
partly funded by the Hungarian-American actor Tony Curtis.

Window of the Orthodox Synagogue

religion. The Jewish community became well integrated
into Hungarian society, until
in 1941, a series of Nazi anti-
Semitic laws were passed and
the wearing of the Star of
David was made compulsory.
In 1944, a ghetto was created
in Pest and the deportation of
thousands of Jews to camps,
including Auschwitz, was imp-
lemented. After heavy fighting
between the Russian and German armies, the Soviet Red
Army liberated the ghetto on
18 January 1945. In total,
600,000 Hungarian Jews were

victims of the Holocaust. This
persecution is commemorated
by a plaque at the Orthodox
Synagogue on Rumbach utca.
   In the late 19th century, three
synagogues were built and
many Jewish shops and workshops were established. Kosher
establishments, such as the
Hanna Étterem *(see p200)* in
the courtyard of the Orthodox
Synagogue, and the butcher
at No. 41 Kazinczy utca, were
a common feature. Shops are
now being reconstructed to
recreate the pre-ghetto character of the Jewish Quarter.

Great Synagogue ⑰
Zsinagóga

Dohány utca 2. **Map** 4 F1 (10 F4).
Tel 342 89 49. Ⓜ *Astoria.* **Jewish
Museum** ⬜ *May–Oct: 10am–5pm
Sun–Thu, 10am–2pm Fri; Nov–Apr:
10am–4pm Sun–Thu, 10am–2pm Fri.*
🅿 🅲

This synagogue is the
largest in Europe. It was built
in a Byzantine-Moorish style
by the Viennese architect
Ludwig Förster between
1854–9. It has three naves
and, following orthodox
tradition, separate galleries for
women. Together the naves
and galleries can accommodate up to 3,000 worshippers.
Some features, such as the
position of the reading platform, reflect elements of
Judaic reform. The interior
has valuable decorative
fittings, particularly those on
the Ark of the Law, by
Frigyes Feszl. In 1931, a

museum was established; a
vast collection of historical
relics, Judaic devotional items
and everday objects, from
ancient Rome to the present

day, has been assembled. It
includes the book of Chevra
Kadisha from 1792. There is
also a moving Holocaust
Memorial Room.

A large rose window is the
façade's main ornamentation. It
is located between two richly
decorated towers crowned with
distinctive onion domes.

The façade is composed
of white and red brick
and intricately designed
ceramic friezes.

A Hebrew inscription from
the second book of Moses is
situated under the rose window.

Chapel of St Roch

Szent Rókus Kápolna

Gyulai Pál u 2. **Map** 7 A3. **Tel** *338 35 15.* Ⓜ *Astoria or Blaha Lujza tér.*

Pest town council built this chapel in what was then an uninhabited area. It was dedicated to St Roch and St Rosalie, who were believed to provide protection against the plague, which afflicted Pest in 1711.

In 1740 the chapel was extended to its present size, and a tower was added in 1797. The façade is decorated with Baroque figures of saints, although the originals were replaced with copies in 1908.

Inside, on the right-hand wall of the chapel's nave, is a painting of the Virgin Mary from 1740. A painting by Jakab Warsch, depicting the Great Flood of 1838, is in the oratory.

Mihály Pollack Square ⓲

Pollack Mihály Tér

Map 7 A4 (10 F5). Ⓜ *Kálvin tér.* **Festetics Palace Tel** *266 52 22.* 🖭 *by prior arrangement.*

At the rear of the Hungarian National Museum *(see pp130 – 33)* is a square named after Mihály Pollack, the architect of several Neo-Classical buildings such as the museum and Sándor Palace *(see p73)*.

In the late 19th century, three palaces were built side by side on this square for the aristocratic elite of Hungary: Prince Festetics, Prince Eszterházy and Count Károlyi. The beautiful façades makes this one of the city's most captivating squares.

Miklós Ybl *(see p94)* built the French-Renaissance style palace at No. 6 for Lajos Károlyi, in 1863 – 5. The façade is decorated with sculptures by Károly Schaffer. There is also a covered driveway for carriages. Next door, at No. 8, is a small palace, which was built in 1865 for the Eszterházy family by Alajos Baumgarten. At No. 10 is the palace built for the Festetics family in 1862, again by Miklós Ybl. The interior, especially the Neo-Baroque staircase, is splendid.

Magnificent staircase inside the Festetics Palace on Mihály Pollack Square

Hungarian National Museum ⓴

Nemzeti Múzeum

See pp130 – 33.

Ervin Szabó Library ㉑

Szabó Ervin Könyvtàr

Szabó Ervin tér 1. **Map** 7 A4 (10 F5). **Tel** *411 50 00.* Ⓜ *Kálvin tér.* ⏰ *10am–8pm Mon–Fri, 10am–4pm Sat.* **www.**fszek.hu

In 1887, the wealthy industrialist Wenckheim family commissioned the architect Artur Meining to build a Neo-Baroque and Rococo style palace. The result was the former Wenckheim Palace, regarded as one of the most beautiful palaces in Budapest. The magnificent wrought-iron

Spiral staircase in one of the rooms of the Ervin Szabó Library

gates, dating from 1897, are the work of Gyula Jungfer. Also worth particular attention are the richly gilded salons on the first floor, as well as the dome above an oval panel of reliefs.

In 1926, the city council acquired the building and converted it into a public lending library, whose collection focuses on the city itself and the social sciences.

The Ervin Szabó Library was named after the politician and social reformer Ervin Szabó (1877– 918), who was the library's first director. It has over a hundred branches throughout Budapest and some three million books.

Calvinist Church ㉒

Református Templom

Kálvin tér 7. **Map** 4 F2. **Tel** *217 67 69.* Ⓜ *Kálvin tér.* ⏰ *6pm Thu; 10am, 11:30am, 6pm Sun.*

This single nave church was designed by József Hofrichter and built between 1816 – 30. In 1848 József Hild designed the four-pillared façade and tympanum, and a spire was added in 1859. Inside the church, the pulpit and choir gallery were designed by Hild in 1831 and 1854 respectively. The stained-glass windows are the work of Miksa Róth. Sacred artefacts from the 17th and 18th centuries are kept in the church treasury.

Museum of Applied Arts ㉓

Opened in 1896 by Emperor Franz Joseph as part of the Millennium Celebrations, this collection is housed not within a Neo-Classical building, but within an outstanding Secession building designed by Gyula Pártos and Ödön Lechner *(see p56)*. The exterior incorporated elements inspired by the Orient as well as the Zsolnay ceramics characteristic of Lechner's work. Damaged in 1945 and again in 1956, the building only recently regained its original magnificence. The collection, founded in 1872, includes many examples of arts and crafts workmanship.

A Lalique pendant

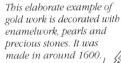

Pendant with Amphitrite and Triton
This elaborate example of gold work is decorated with enamelwork, pearls and precious stones. It was made in around 1600.

Silver Plate
This magnificent Baroque plate depicts the Battle of Vezekény. It was crafted in 1654 in Augsburg by Philip Jacob Drentwett.

Ground floor

Inner Courtyard
This courtyard, covered by a glazed roof, is surrounded by cloisters with arcades designed in an Indian-Oriental style.

MUSEUM GUIDE
The museum is home to various temporary exhibitions on both floors of the building. Examples of the types of items on show are illustrated here. The major exhibitions tend to change each year, whilst the smaller national and foreign displays change monthly. Recent exhibitions have included a wonderful display of glass and an exploration of clocks and time. The library, dating from 1872, is located on the first floor and contains around 50,000 books.

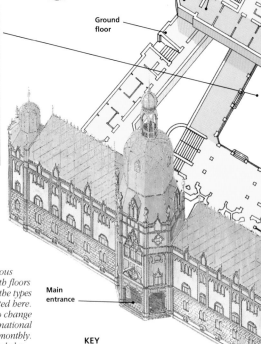

Main entrance

KEY

- ☐ Library
- ☐ Temporary exhibitions
- ☐ Non-exhibition space

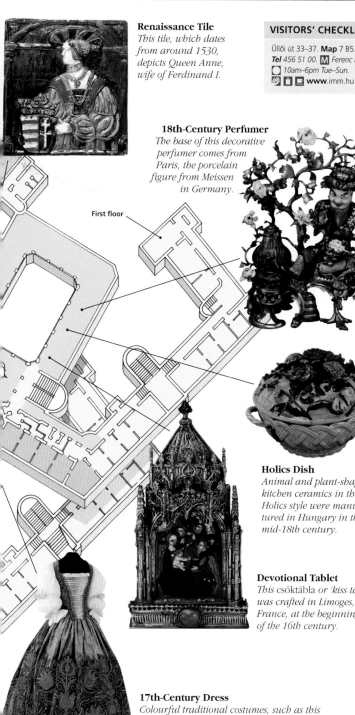

Renaissance Tile
This tile, which dates from around 1530, depicts Queen Anne, wife of Ferdinand I.

VISITORS' CHECKLIST

Üllői út 33–37. **Map** 7 B5.
Tel *456 51 00.* Ⓜ *Ferenc körút.*
🕐 *10am–6pm Tue–Sun.*
www.imm.hu

18th-Century Perfumer
The base of this decorative perfumer comes from Paris, the porcelain figure from Meissen in Germany.

First floor

Holics Dish
Animal and plant-shaped kitchen ceramics in the Holics style were manufactured in Hungary in the mid-18th century.

Devotional Tablet
This csóktábla or 'kiss tablet' was crafted in Limoges, France, at the beginning of the 16th century.

17th-Century Dress
Colourful traditional costumes, such as this richly embroidered dress, are often displayed in temporary exhibitions.

Central Market Hall ㉔

Központi Vásárcsarnok

Vámház körút 1-3. **Map** 4 F3.
Tel 366 33 00. 🚋 47, 49. Ⓜ Kálvin
tér. 🕒 6am–5pm Mon, 6am–6pm
Tue–Fri, 6am–2pm Sat. ● Sun.

Rebuilt in 1999, Budapest's
main produce market is a
great place to find local
delicacies such as spicy
kolbász salami and sheep's
cheese. There are numerous
farmers' stalls selling meat,
sausage, fruit, vegetables and
fish. The upper floor has a
dozen or so food booths and
souvenir stalls selling paprika,
caviar, Hungarian dolls, t-
shirts and chessboards. The
basement level has a small
grocery store and a cash
machine.

Sausages for sale at the Central Market Hall

**Decorative element on the façade
of the City Council Chamber**

City Council Chamber ㉕

Új Városháza

Váci utca 62–64. **Map** 4 F2 (10 E5).
Ⓜ Deák tér. **Tel** 235 17 00.
🕒 8am–noon Fri ✂ compulsory

This three-floor edifice was
built between 1870–75 as
offices for the newly unified
city of Budapest *(see p32)*. Its
architect, Imre Steindl, was
also responsible for designing
Parliament *(see pp108–9)*.
   The building is a mix of
styles. The exterior is a Neo-
Renaissance design in brick,
with grotesques between the

windows, while the interior
features cast-iron Neo-Gothic
motifs. The Great Debating
Hall is decorated with mosaics designed by Károly Lotz.
   Many antiquarian bookshops
and galleries have now opened
around here. Fashionable bars,
restaurants and cafés, and the
recent pedestrianization, make
this a very charming area.

Serbian Church ㉖

Szerb Templom

Szerb utca 2–4. **Map** 4 F2 (10 E5).
Ⓜ Kálvin tér. 🕒 8am–7pm daily.

Serbs settled in the now largely residential area around the
church as early as the 16th
century. The end of the 17th
century brought a new wave of
Serb immigrants, and by the
early 19th century Serbs com-
prised almost 25 per cent of
Pest's home-owners.
   In 1698, the Serb community replaced an earlier church
on the site with this Baroque
one. The church
gained its final
appearance after a
rebuilding project
that lasted until the
mid-18th century,
which was probably
undertaken by
András Meyerhoffer.
   The interior of
the church is
arranged acc-
ording to Greek
Orthodox practice.
A section of the
nave, which is entered from
the vestibule, is reserved for
women. This area is divided

**Ceramic tile from the
Serbian Church**

from the men's section by a
partition, and the division is
further emphasized by the
floor, which has been
lowered by 30 cm (1 ft). The
choir gallery is enclosed by an
iconostasis that divides it from
the sanctuary. This iconostasis
dates from around 1850. The
carving is by the Serb sculptor
Miahai Janich and the Italian
Renaissance-influenced paintings are the work of the Greek
artist Károly Sterio.

Lóránd Eötvös University ㉗

Eötvös Lóránd Tudomány
Egyetem Központja

Egyetem tér 1–3. **Map** 4 F2 (10 E5).
Ⓜ Ferenciek tere, Kálvin tér.
Tel 411 65 00. **www**.elte.hu

In 1635, Cardinal Péter
Pázmány, the leader of the
Counter-Reformation, established a university in Nagyszombat
(now Trnava in Slovakia). It
moved to Buda in 1777,
nearly a century af-
ter the end of the
Turkish occupa-
tion *(see pp26
–7)*, during the
reign of Maria
Theresa. Emperor
Joseph II trans-
ferred the university
to Pest, to the
environs of the
Pauline Church,
now called the
University Church.
It was not until
1889 that the university was
endowed with a permanent
home. This Neo-Baroque

building, now the Law Faculty, was designed by architects including Sándor Baumgarten and Fülöp Herzog.

The university is named after the noted physicist Lóránd Eötvös (1848 – 1919).

University Church 28

Egyetemi Templom

Papnövelde utca 9. **Map** 4 F2 (10 E5). *Tel* 318 05 55. M Kálvin tér. ⬤ 7am–7pm daily.

This single-nave church is considered one of the most impressive Baroque churches in the city. It was built for the Pauline Order in 1725–42, and was probably designed by András Meyerhoffer. The tower was added in 1771. The Pauline Order, founded in 1263 by Canon Euzebiusz, was the only religious order to be founded in Hungary.

The magnificent exterior features a tympanum and a row of pilasters that divide the façade. Figures of St Paul and St Anthony flank the emblem of the Pauline Order, which crowns the exterior. The carved-wood interior of the main vestibule is also worth particular mention.

Inside the church a row of side chapels stand behind unusual marble pilasters. In 1776 Johann Bergl painted the vaulted ceiling with frescoes depicting scenes from the life of Mary. Sadly, these frescoes are now in poor condition.

The main altar dates from 1746, and the carved statues behind it are the work of József Hebenstreit. Above it is a copy of the painting *The Black Madonna of Czestochowa,* which is thought to date from 1720. Much of the Baroque interior detail of the church is the work of the Pauline monks, for example the balustrade of the organ loft, the confessionals and the carved pulpit on the right.

Tympanum adorning the façade of the University Library

Károlyi Palace 29

Károlyi Palota

Károlyi Mihály utca 16. **Map** 4 F2 (10 E5). *Tel* 317 31 43. M Ferenciek tere, Kálvin tér. **Petőfi Exhibition** ⬤ 10am–6pm Tue–Sun. 📷 317 36 11.

In 1696 there was a small Baroque palace on this site, which was extended by András Mayerhoffer between 1759–68. Subsequent rebuilding, which gave the palace a Neo-Classical appearance, was undertaken between 1832–41 by Anton Riegl. It is named after Mihály Károlyi, leader of the 1918–19 Hungarian Republic *(see p34)*, who was born here in 1875.

The palace now houses the Hungarian Museum of Literature and the Petőfi Exhibition, which is dedicated to the poet Sándor Petőfi *(see p31)*. Other Hungarian poets remembered here include Atilla József, Endre Ady and Mór Jókai.

Sculptures decorating the pulpit in the University Church

University Library 30

Egyetemi Könyvtár

Ferenciek tere 6. **Map** 4 F1 (10 E5). *Tel* 266 58 66. M Ferenciek tere, Kálvin tér. ⬤ 9am–3:30pm Mon–Fri.

This Neo-Renaissance Edifice, by Antal Szkalniczky and Henrik Koch, was built from 1873–6. It is distinguished by the dome on the corner tower. The library's two million works include 11 *Corviniani (see p72)* and 160 medieval manuscripts and miniatures. The reading room has sgraffiti by Mór Than and frescoes by Károly Lotz.

Franciscan Church 31

Belvárosi Ferences Templom

Ferenciek tere 9. **Map** 4 F1 (10 E4). *Tel* 317 33 22. M Ferenciek tere. ⬤ 7am–8pm daily. 🎫 noon–4pm.

A Franciscan church and monastery have stood on this site, beyond the old city walls, since the 13th century. In 1541 the Turks rebuilt the church as the Mosque of Sinan, but after the liberation *(see pp26– 7)* the monks regained the building. Between 1727–43 they remodelled the church in the Baroque style, which it still retains today.

The façade features a magnificent portal incorporating sculptures of Franciscan saints, and the Franciscan emblem crowned by a figure of Mary being adored by angels.

The interior of the church is decorated with frescoes, dating from 1894–5, by Károly Lotz and paintings by Viktor Tardos Krenner from 1925–6. The jewel of this church is the Baroque main altar with sculptures that date from 1741 and 1851. The side altars and the pulpit date from 1851–2.

AROUND VÁROSLIGET

Városliget, or City Park, was once an area of marshland, which served as a royal hunting ground. Leopold I gave the land to the town of Pest, but it was in the mid-18th century, under Maria Theresa, that the area was drained and planted. Today's park was designed towards the end of the 19th century in the English style, which was the fashion of the

Statue of János Hunyadi

day. Városliget was chosen as the focus of the Millennium Celebrations in 1896 *(see p142)*, which marked the 1,000-year anniversary of the conquest of the Carpathian basin by the Magyars. A massive building programme was undertaken, which included the Museum of Fine Arts, Vajdahunyad Castle and the impressive monument in Heroes' Square.

SIGHTS AT A GLANCE

Museums
Ferenc Hopp Museum of Far Eastern Art ❻
Franz Liszt Museum ❷
House of Terror Museum ❶
Museum of Fine Arts pp146–9 ❾
Műcsarnok Art Gallery ❽
Kodály Memorial Museum ❹

Parks and Zoos
Funfair ⓬
Zoo ⓫

Streets and Monuments
Hermina Street ⓮
Millennium Monument ❼
Városligeti Avenue ❺

Historic Buildings
University of Fine Art ❸
Erkel Theatre ⓯
Széchenyi Baths ⓭
Vajdahunyad Castle ❿

GETTING THERE
The M1 metro line runs under Andrássy út from Bajcsy-Zs Út to Hősök tere, while bus 4 runs along the street above. Trams, buses and the metro operate in the south of the area, around Thököly út.

KEY
▢ Street-by-Street map
See pp142–3

Ⓜ Metro station

⊠ Post office

🚉 Train station

Street-by-Street: Around Heroes' Square

Árpád, leader of the Magyars

Heroes' Square is a relic of a proud era in Hungary's history. It was here that the Millennium Celebrations opened in 1896. A striking example of this national pride is the Millennium Monument. Its colonnades feature statues of renowned Hungarian leaders and politicians, and the grand central column is crowned by a figure of the Archangel Gabriel. Vajdahunyad Castle was built in Városliget, or City Park, adjacent to the square. Probably the most flamboyant expression of the celebrations, it is composed of elements of the finest architectural works found throughout Hungary.

★ Museum of Fine Arts
This monumental museum building has an eight-pillared portico supporting a tympanum ❾

Entrance to the Zoo

Millennium Monument
Dominating Heroes' Square, this monument includes a figure of Rydwan, the god of war, by György Zala.

Műcsarnok Art Gallery
The crest of Hungary decorates the façade of this building – the country's largest venue for artistic exhibitions ❽

Secession pavilion

THE HUNGARIAN MILLENNIUM CELEBRATIONS

The Millennium Celebrations in 1896 marked a high point in the development of Budapest and in the history of the Austro-Hungarian monarchy. The city underwent modernization on a scale unknown in Europe at that time. Hundreds of houses, palaces and civic buildings were constructed, gas lighting was introduced and continental Europe's first underground transport system was opened.

Archangel Gabriel

0 metres   200

0 yards   200

KEY

– – – Suggested route

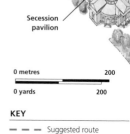

★ Széchenyi Baths
This is the largest complex of spa baths in Europe. Its hot springs, discovered in 1876, bubble up from a depth of 970 m (3,180 ft) and are reputed to have considerable healing properties **⑬**

Városliget

LOCATOR MAP
See Street Finder, maps 5 & 6

Ják Church
This church faithfully reproduces the portal of a Benedictine church, dating from 1214, which can be found in the area of Ják, near the border with Austria. It is part of the Vajdahunyad Castle complex.

Statue of Anonymous
Completed in 1903 by Miklós Ligeti, this is one of Budapest's most famous monuments.

★ Vajdahunyad Castle
This Baroque section of the castle houses the Museum of Agriculture **⑩**

STAR SIGHTS

★ Museum of Fine Arts

★ Széchenyi Baths

★ Vajdahunyad Castle

The former headquarters of the secret police on Andrássy Avenue

House of Terror Museum ①

Teror Háza Múzeum

Andrássy út 60. **Map** 2 F5 (10 E2). **Tel** 374 26 00. M Vörösmarty utca, 4,6 to Oktogon. 10am–6pm Tue–Fri, 10am–7:30pm Sat & Sun. **www**.terrorhaza.hu

The museum is located in the former headquarters of the secret police of both the Nazi and Communist governments. It records the grim events and practices of the "double occupation" of Hungary at the end of World War II.

Franz Liszt Museum ②

Liszt Ferenc Emlékmúzeum

Vörösmarty út 35. **Map** 5 A5. **Tel** 322 98 04. M Vörösmarty utca. 10am–6pm Mon– Fri, 9am–5pm Sat. **www**.lisztmuseum.hu

This Neo-Renaissance corner house was designed in 1877 by Adolf Lang. Above the windows of the second floor are bas-reliefs depicting famous composers – J S Bach, Wolfgang Amadeus Mozart, Joseph Haydn, Ferenc Erkel,

Ludwig van Beethoven, and Franz Liszt himself. Liszt not only lived in this house, but also established an Academy of Music in the city *(see p129)*.

In 1986, 100 years after Franz Liszt's death, this museum was established in his house. Various items were assembled here, including documents, furniture and two pianos on which he composed and practised his work.

University of Fine Art ③

KépzőműVészeti Egyetem

Andrássy út 69–71. **Map** 5 A5. **Tel** 342 17 38. M Vörösmarty utca. **Barcsay Gallery** 10am–6pm Mon–Fri, 10am–1pm Sat (seasonal). **www**.mke.hu

The university began as a drawing school, later becoming a Higher School of Art. Since 1876, it has occupied these adjacent buildings on Andrássy Street.

The two-floor Neo-Renaissance building at No. 71 was designed in 1875, by Lajos Rauscher. Its façade is decorated with sgrafitti by Robert Scholtz. The Italianate Renaissance exterior of No. 69, designed by Adolf Lang from 1875–7, is distinguished by Corinthian pilasters and a full-length balcony. The entrance hall and first-floor corridor feature frescoes by Károly Lotz. Only the Barcsay Gallery is open to visitors, but the interior can be glimpsed from here.

Sgrafitto by Robert Scholtz

Kodály Memorial Museum ④

Kodály Zoltán Emlékmúzeum

Kodály Körönd 1. **Map** 5 B5. **Tel** 342 84 48. M Kodály Körönd. 10am–4pm Wed, 10am–6pm Thu–Sat, 10am–2pm Sun. Mon, Tue. **www**.kodaly.hu

Zoltán Kodály (1881–1967) was one of the greatest Hungarian composers of the 20th century. His profound knowledge of Hungarian folk music allowed him to use elements of it in his compositions, which reflected the fashion for Impressionism and Neo-Romanticism in music.

This museum was established in 1990 and occupies the house where he lived and worked from 1924 until his death in 1967. A plaque set into one of the walls of the house bears testimony to this fact. The museum consists of three rooms that have been preserved in their original style, and a fourth room that is used for exhibitions. An archive has also been created here, for the composer's valuable handwritten music scores and correspondence.

Worthy of attention are the composer's piano in the salon and a number of folklore ceramics which Kodály collected in the course of his ethnographical studies. Portraits and busts of Kodály by Lajos Petri can also be viewed.

Városligeti Avenue ⑤

Városligeti Fasor

Map 5 C5. M Hősök tere.

This beautiful street, lined with plane trees, leads from Lövölde tér to Városliget.

At the beginning of the avenue is a Calvinist church built in 1912 – 13 by Aladár Árkay. This stark edifice is virtually bereft of any architectural features. However, stylized, geometric folk motifs

Original furnishings in the salon in the Franz Liszt Museum

Chinese gate at the Ráth György Museum on Városligeti Avenue

have been used as ornamentation and harmonize with the interior Secession decoration.

In front of the church is the Ráth György Museum, part of the Ferenc Hopp Museum of Far Eastern Art, displaying artifacts from China and Japan collected in the 19th century.

Further along the avenue is a Lutheran church. It was constructed between 1903–5 to a Neo-Gothic design by Samu Pecz, who also designed the interior detail. Worthy of note is the painting on the high altar, by Gyula Benczúr, entitled *The Adoration of the Magi*.

Ferenc Hopp Museum of Far Eastern Art ❻

Hopp Ferenc Kelet-ázsiai Művészeti Múzeum

Andrássy út 103. **Map** 5 B4.
Tel *322 84 76.* Ⓜ *Bajza utca.*
◐ *10am–6pm Tue–Sun.*
For guided tours call 456 51 00.
Ráth György Museum Városligeti
Fasor 12. ***Tel*** *342 39 16.* ◐
10am–6pm Tue–Sun. 📷

Ferenc Hopp (1833–1919), a wealthy merchant and the proprietor of an opthalmic shop, was the first great Hungarian traveller, amassing a collection of more than 20,000 items from countries such as India, China and Vietnam.

The collection's smaller examples of art and handicrafts can be seen in his former home, while its garden features large stone sculptures and architectural fragments.

The Chinese and Japanese collection is displayed in the **Ráth György Museum**.

Millennium Monument ❼

Milleniumi Emlékmű

Map 5 C4. Ⓜ *Hősök tere.*

This monument was designed by György Zala and Albert Schikedanz to commemorate Hungary's Millennium Celebrations in 1896, but was not completed until 1929.

At the centre of the monument is a 36-m (120-ft) high Corinthian column, upon which stands the Archangel Gabriel holding St István's crown and the apostolic cross. These objects signify Hungary's conversion to Christianity under King István *(see p22)*. At the base of the column there are equestrian statues of Prince Árpád and six of the conquering Magyar warriors.

A stone tile set in front of the column marks the Tomb of the Unknown Soldier.

The column is embraced by two curved colonnades, featuring allegorical compositions at both ends. Personifications of War and Peace are nearest the column, while Knowledge and Glory crown the far end of the right-hand colonnade, and Labour and Prosperity crown the far end of the left. Statues of great Hungarians, including statesmen and monarchs, are arranged within the colonnades.

The right-hand colonnade of the Millennium Monument on Heroes' Square, completed in 1929

Museum of Fine Arts ⑨

The origins of the Museum of Fine Arts' comprehensive collection date from 1870, when the state bought a magnificent collection of paintings from the artistocratic Esterházy family. The museum's collection was enriched by donations and acquisitions, and in 1906 it moved to its present location. The building, by Fülöp Herzog and Albert Schickedanz, is Neo-Classical with Italian-Renaissance influences. The tympanum crowning the portico is supported by eight Corinthian columns. It depicts the Battle of the Centaurs and Lapiths, and is copied from the Temple of Zeus at Olympia, Greece.

Grimani jug

First floor

The Water Carrier *(c. 1810)*
La Aquadora *demonstrates the full range of Francisco de Goya's artistic talent.*

Satyr and Peasants *(c. 1620)*
The Flemish artist, Jacob Jordaens, worked alongside van Dyck and was Rubens' principal associate.

★ **Esterházy Madonna** *(c. 1508)*
This unfinished picture by Raphael is so named because it became the property of the Esterházy family at the beginning of the 19th century.

Lower ground floor

St James Conquers the Moors *(1750)*
Giambattista Tiepolo portrayed the miraculous appearance of the saint during a battle at Clavijo in 844.

KEY

- ☐ Egyptian artefacts
- ☐ Classical artefacts
- ☐ German art
- ☐ Dutch and Flemish art
- ☐ Italian art
- ☐ Spanish art
- ☐ French and British art
- ▨ Drawings and graphic art
- ▨ 19th- and 20th-century works
- ☐ Temporary exhibitions

View of Amsterdam
(c. 1656)
*Jacob van Ruisdael was
a master of Dutch realist
landscape painting. He
greatly influenced the
development of European
landscape painting in
the 19th century.*

Second floor

Mother and Child
(1905)
*The rare subtlety
of this intensely
intimate picture,
by Pablo Picasso,
is achieved using
watercolour.*

Renaissance
Hall

Baroque
Hall

★ St John the Baptist's Sermon *(1566)*
*In this wonderful painting, Pieter Bruegel the Elder,
a renowned observer of daily life, depicts a preacher
addressing a group of peasants from Flanders.*

Ground floor

**These Women in the
Refectory** *(1894)*
*This pastel sketch by the artist
Henri de Toulouse-Lautrec,
an observer and protagonist
in the Parisian demi-monde,
depicts prostitutes in a bar.*

MUSEUM GUIDE
*As a result of restoration work on the museum,
begun in 1997, not all the rooms are currently
open to the public. The works displayed are being
moved as restoration work progresses.*

STAR PAINTINGS

★ Esterházy Madonna

★ St John the
Baptist's Sermon

Exploring the Museum of Fine Arts

Egyptian head (c. 1200 BC)

The museum's collection encompasses international art dating from antiquity to the 20th century. As well as Egyptian, Greek and Roman artifacts, the museum houses galleries dedicated to a variety of modern art. Alongside its interesting collection of sculptures, there are priceless drawings and works of graphic art. Over the next few years the museum will be undergoing a process of redevelopment. In spite of this, exhibits will continue to be open to the public throughout the duration of the restoration work. Individual collections will simply be moved to different locations as building work progresses.

Albrecht Dürer's simple yet beautiful *Portrait of a Young Man*

EGYPTIAN ARTEFACTS

Egyptian artefacts have been exhibited in the museum since 1939. Principally, they are the result of 19th-century excavations that involved Hungarian archaeologists.

The rich collection includes stone sculptures from each historic period, from the Old Kingdom to the Ptolemy dynasty. A nobleman's head of a votive statue dates from the New Kingdom and is a particularly beautiful example.

Also worthy of note is the collection of small bronze figures, which also date mainly from the New Kingdom, together with domestic objects that illustrate everyday life.

CLASSICAL ARTEFACTS

The collection of Classical artefacts is rather varied. It encompasses works of Greek, Etruscan, and Roman works.

Detail of a hunting scene on a 3rd-century AD Greek sarcophagus

The collection of Greek vases ranks as one of the best of its kind in Europe. A black-figure amphora by Exekias and a kylix from the studio of the painter Andokides are very fine examples of this work.

Bronze work, which dates from various epochs, including the famous Grimani jug from the 5th century BC, gold jewellery, and marble and terracotta sculptures are all exquisite artefacts from this era.

SCULPTURE

This collection is located throughout the museum. The most valuable element by far is a small bronze sculpture by Leonardo da Vinci (1452–1519). This is an unusually dynamic representation of King François I of France on his horse. Other superb examples of Italian sculpture, by masters such as Andrea Pisano of the Ronni family, can also be seen.

Leonardo da Vinci's figure of François I

GERMAN ART

Among the most valuable works in the collection are the *Portrait of a Young Man*, by Albrecht Dürer, and the carefully composed painting of *The Dormition of Mary*, by Hans Holbein. The work of such masters as Hans Baldung Grien and Lucas Cranach are worth seeing, as is the collection of German and Austrian Baroque painting, which includes work by Franz Anton Maulbertsch.

DUTCH AND FLEMISH ART

The museum's Dutch and Flemish collection features works by the finest masters, including influential landscape artist, Jacob van Ruisdael, with *View of Amsterdam (see p147)*. The subtle *Nativity* by Gerard David and Pieter Bruegel's detailed masterpiece *St John the Baptist's Sermon (see p147)*, depicting Flemish peasants listening to the saint's words, are exemplary exhibits.

The museum also boasts canvases attributed to Rembrandt, including *St Joseph's Dream*, portraits by Frans Hals and Jan Vermeer's *Portrait of a Lady*. Not to be missed are the magnificent 17th-century Dutch paintings by artists including Adrian van Ostade, Jacob Ruisdael, Jan Steen and others.

The highlight of the Flemish collection is the 17th-century *Mucius Scaevola before Porsenna* by Peter Rubens and his then assistant, Anthony van Dyck. The latter was responsible for the picture of St John the Evangelist, also on display.

Also important are the paintings of Adam and Eve and *Satyr with Peasants* by Jacob Jordaens, who also worked as an assistant to Rubens.

ITALIAN ART

This valuable collection of Italian art, which was the core of the Esterházy family's collection, is often considered the museum's biggest attraction. All the schools of Italian painting, from the 13th to the 18th centuries, are on display here. The Renaissance period is perhaps the best represented.

Of particular note is the captivating *Esterházy Madonna (see p146)*, an unfinished painting by Raphael. Another great work by this outstanding artist is the *Portrait of Pietro Bembo*.

There is no shortage of work by famous 16th-century Venetian artists among the paintings collected here. Important works by Titian, Bonifazio Veronese, Antonio Correggio, Jacopo Tintoretto, Giorgione and Giovanni Boltraffio are all exhibited here. An excellent example of Baroque art is Giambattista Tiepolo's vast late 18th-century painting, *St James Conquers the Moors (see p146)*.

Giovanni Boltraffio's *Madonna and Child* (c. 1506)

SPANISH ART

The most important features of this collection are seven paintings by El Greco, including *The Annunciation, Christ in the Garden of Gethsemane* and *The Penance of St Mary Magdalene*, a subtle though fully expressive work.

The dramatic *Martyrdom of St Andrew* by Jusepe de Ribera should not be missed, nor the work of artists such as Diego

El Greco's *The Penance of St Mary Magdelene* (c. 1576)

Velázquez, Bartolomé Murillo and Francisco Zurbarán. Francisco de Goya's observations of daily life produced paintings such as *The Water Carrier (see p146)*, which also deserves special attention.

FRENCH AND BRITISH ART

Works by French and British artists are not as numerous as Italian works, for example, but represent the various styles of the two countries.

French works include the well-composed *Resting on the Journey to Egypt* by Nicolas Poussin, *Villa in the Roman Countryside* by Claude Lorrain, and *Satyr and Peasants*, by the Flemish artist Jacob Jordaens *(see p146)*.

The collection of British paintings includes portraits by artists of the calibre of Joshua Reynolds, William Hogarth and Thomas Gainsborough.

DRAWINGS AND GRAPHIC ART

The collection of drawings and graphic art combines the work of old masters, including drawings by Leonard da Vinci, Raphael, Albrecht Dürer and Rembrandt, with pieces from artists of the 19th and 20th centuries. The collection is one of Europe's best.

19TH- AND 20TH-CENTURY WORKS

French painting makes up the largest constituent of the collection of 19th- and 20th-century art. The visitor can admire works by all the major painters of the time, including Pablo Picasso's *Mother and Child (see p147)*, Henri de Toulouse-Lautrec's *These Women in the Refectory (see p147)*, Gustave Courbet's *Wrestlers*, Edouard Manet's *Woman with a Fan* and Camille Pissarro's *Pont-Neuf*. Paul Gauguin's *Black Pigs*, one of his first Tahitian canvases, is also on display here. To complete the collection, the likes of Eugène Delacroix, Claude Monet, Pierre Bonnard, Pierre Renoir and Paul Cézanne are also represented.

Austrian and German 19th- and 20th-century art is represented with works by Waldmüller, Amerling, Lenbach, Leibl and Menzel.

Paul Cézanne's still life, *Credenza*, dating from 1874–7

The façade of the Palace of Art, featuring a six-columned portico

Műcsarnok Art Gallery ❽

Műcsarnok

Hősök tere. **Map** 5 C4. **Tel** 363 26 71. Ⓜ Hősök tere. ◯ 10am–6pm Tue–Sun noon–8pm Thu. 🎫 ♿ ✔

Situated on the southern side of Heroes' Square, opposite the Museum of Fine Arts (see pp146–9), is Hungary's largest exhibition space. Temporary exhibitions of mainly contemporary painting and sculpture are held here.

The imposing Neo-Classical building, which was designed by Albert Schickedanz and Fülöp Herzog in 1895, is fronted by a vast six-columned portico. The mosaic, depicting St István as the patron saint of fine art, was added to the tympanum between 1938 – 41. Behind the portico is a fresco in three parts by Lajos Deák Ébner: *The Beginning of Sculpture, The Source of Arts* and *The Origins of Painting*.

Museum of Fine Arts ❾

Szépművészeti Múzeum

See pp146–9.

Vajdahunyad Castle ❿

Vajdahunyad Vára

Városliget. **Map** 6 D4. **Tel** 363 19 73. **Museum of Agriculture Tel** 363 19 73. ◯ Mar–Oct: 10am–5pm Tue–Fri, 10am–6pm Sat & Sun; Nov–Mar: 10am–4pm Tue–Fri, 10am–5pm Sat & Sun. ⬤ Mon. 🎫 ♿ ✔ www.mmgm.hu

This fairytale-like building is located among the trees at the edge of the lake in Városliget. Not a genuine castle but a complex of buildings reflecting various architectural styles, it was designed by Ignác Alpár for the 1896 Millennium Celebrations (see p142).

Alpár's creation illustrated the history and evolution of architecture in Hungary. Originally intended as temporary exhibition pavilions, the castle proved so popular with the public that, between 1904– 6, it was rebuilt using brick to create a permanent structure.

The pavilions are grouped in chronological order of style: Romanesque is followed by Gothic, Renaissance, Baroque and so on. The individual styles were linked together to give the impression of a single, cohesive

design. Each of the pavilions use authentic details copied from Hungary's most important historic buildings or are a looser interpretation of a style inspired by a specific architect of that historic period.

The Romanesque complex features a copy of the portal from a church in Ják (see p143) as well as a monastic cloister and palace. The details on the Gothic pavilion have been taken from castles like those in Vajdahunyad and Segesvár (both now in Romania). The architect Fischer von Erlach was the inspiration for the Renaissance and Baroque complex. The façade copies part of the Bakócz chapel in the cathedral at Esztergom (see p164).

The Museum of Agriculture can be found in the Baroque section. It has exhibits on cattle breeding, wine-making, hunting and fishing.

The entire complex reflects more than 20 of Hungary's most renowned buildings. The medieval period, often considered the most glorious time in Hungary's history, is given greatest emphasis, while the controversial Habsburg era is pushed into the background.

Zoo ⓫

Fővárosi állat-és Növénykert

Állatkerti körút 6–12. **Map** 5 C3. **Tel** 363 37 10. Ⓜ Széchenyi fürdő. ◯ Daily, phone for opening hours. 🎫 www.zoobudapest.com

Budapest's zoo is one of the city's great attractions. It was established in 1866 by the Hungarian Academy of Sciences (see p114). In 1907 it was bought by the State and totally redeveloped, between 1909–11, by Károly

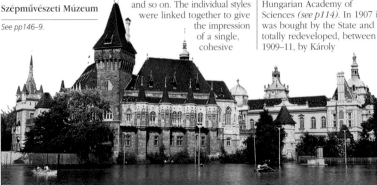

View across the lake of the Gothic (left) and Renaissance (right) sections of Vajdahunyad Castle

Kós and Dezső Zrumeczky.
The animals are housed in
enclosures, most of which
strive to mimic their natural
habitat. The elephant house,
however, by Kornél
Neuschloss-Knüsli, is a fine
example of Secession style.
Károly Kós, on the other hand,
adopted a folk style for the
aviary, in which a wide variety
of birds fly freely. There is also
a popular children's zoo.

One of the outdoor pools at the beautiful Széchenyi Baths

Funfair ⓲

Vidámpark

Állatkerti körút 14–16. **Map** 6 D2.
Tel 363 83 10. Ⓜ *Széchenyi fürdő.*
◯ Apr–Sep: 10am–8pm daily; Oct–
Mar: call for opening hours. 🚻

In 1878 there was already a
carousel here, along with
games and theatrical shows.
   Today it is a charmingly un-
sophisticated amusement park
with an assortment of old-
fashioned rides. Next door is
a smaller funfair for toddlers.
   There are numerous kiosks,
bars and restaurants serving
food, so it is easy to spend the
entire day here. The circus is
also close by (see p219).

Széchenyi Baths ⓭

Széchenyi Strandfürdő

Állatkerti körút 11. **Map** 6 D3.
Tel 363 32 10. Ⓜ *Széchenyi fürdő.*
◯ **Thermal Pool:** 6am–7pm daily.
**Swimming pool and group
thermal pool:** 6am–10pm daily. 🚻

A statue stands at the main
entrance to the Széchenyi
Baths depicting geologist
Vilmos Zsigmond, who dis-
covered a hot spring here
while drilling a well in 1879.
   The Széchenyi Baths are the
deepest and hottest baths in
Budapest – the water reaches
the surface at a temperature
of 74 – 5° C (180° F). The
springs, rich in minerals,
are distinguished by
their alleged healing
properties. They are
recommended for
treating rheumatism
and disorders of
the nervous system,
joints and muscles.
The spa, housed in a

Neo-Baroque building by
Győző Cziegler and Ede
Dvorzsák, was constructed in
1909–13. In 1926, three open-
air swimming pools were
added. The pools are popular
all year due to the high
temperature of the water.
Bathing caps are required.

Hermina Street ⓮

Hermina út

Map 6 E3, 6 E4 & 6 F4. 🚌 70.
Transport Museum *Tel* 273 38 40.
◯ May–Sep: 10am–5pm Tue–Fri,
10am–6pm Sat & Sun; Oct–Apr:
10am–4pm Tue–Fri, 10am–7pm Sat
& Sun. ⬤ Mon. 🚻 ♿ 🅿

This beautiful street is worth
walking along to experience
the romantic atmosphere of
the historic, elegant villas in
this area. Particularly notable
is the unusual Secession
building at No. 47, Sipeky
Balázs Villa (see p55), built in
1905 – 6 by architects Ödön
Lechner, Marcell Komor and
Dezső Jakab. The asymmetric
design of the villa's façade
includes features
such as a domed
glass conser-

Poster for a gala ballet
performance at the Erkel Theatre

vatory, an ironwork porch
and a tall, narrow side tower.
The villa's exterior decoration
is inspired by national folk art.
   Hermina Chapel at No. 23,
by József Hild, was built in
1842–6 in memory of Palatine
József's daughter, Hermina
Amália, who died in 1842.
   Backing onto Hermina Street,
at No. 11 Városligeti körút, is
the Transport Museum with
exhibits on the evolution of
air, sea, road and rail transport. Among the trains,
helicopters and aeroplanes
are some pre-World War II
right-hand-drive cars and the
first trams in Budapest.

Erkel Theatre ⓯

Erkel Színház

Köztarsaság ter 30. **Map** 7 C3.
Tel 333 01 08. Ⓜ *Keleti pu.*

An alternative venue of the
National Opera Company, this
is the largest theatre in
Hungary, seating 2,500 people.
Designed in 1911 by Marcell
Komor, Dezső Jakab and Géza
Márkus, its current form dates
from the 1950s. Concerts and
operas are performed here.

A steam train exhibited at the Transport
Museum, just off Hermina Street

FURTHER AFIELD

Budapest is a sprawling city and several sights on its periphery are well worth a visit. North from the centre of Buda are the fascinating ruins of Aquincum, a town founded by the Romans in approximately AD 100. To the west, the city is skirted by wooded hills, which offer walks around beautiful nature reserves and exciting cave visits. Out

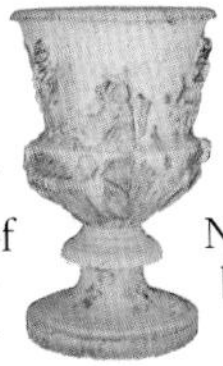

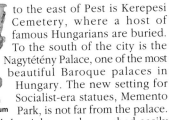

Roman urn from Aquincum

to the east of Pest is Kerepesi Cemetery, where a host of famous Hungarians are buried. To the south of the city is the Nagytétény Palace, one of the most beautiful Baroque palaces in Hungary. The new setting for Socialist-era statues, Memento Park, is not far from the palace. All the sights can be reached easily using public transport.

SIGHTS AT A GLANCE

Museums and Theatres
- Aquincum 27
- Gizi Bajor Theatre Museum 21
- Holocaust Memorial Center 10
- National Theatre 16
- Palace of Arts 11

Historic Buildings and Monuments
- Geology Institute 4
- Ludovika Academy 9
- Nagytétény Palace Museum 25
- Raoul Wallenberg Monument 1
- Memento Park 23
- Technical University 18
- Törley Mausoleum 24
- Wekerle Estate 17

Parks and Recreation Areas
- Buda Hills 26
- Congress and World Trade Centre 20
- Eagle Hill Nature Reserve 22
- Ferenc Puska's Stadium 5
- Railway History Park 12
- Szemlő-hegy and Pál-völgy Caves 2
- University Botanical Gardens 8

Cemeteries
- Jewish Cemetery 15
- Kerepesi Cemetery 6
- Municipal Cemetery 14

Churches
- Cistercian Church of St Imre 19
- Józsefváros Parish Church 7
- Kőbánya Parish Church 13
- Újlak Parish Church 3

KEY
- City centre
- Greater Budapest
- Airport
- Train station
- Motorway
- Under construction
- Main road
- Railway

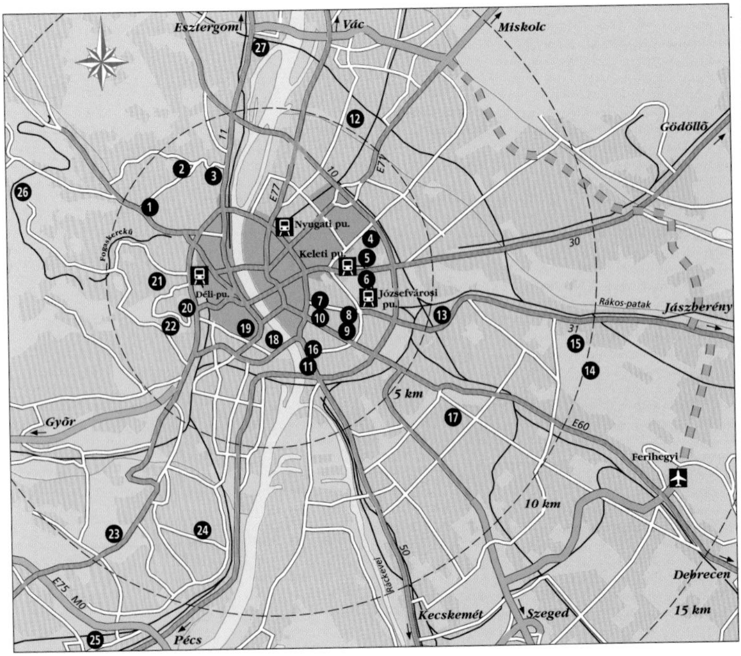

◁ **The huge 19th-century Catholic cathedral at Esztergom, overlooking the Danube** ***(see p164)***

Raoul Wallenberg Monument ❶

Raoul wallenberg szobor

Szilágyi Erzsébet fasor. 🚌 56.

Tucked away at the junction of Szilágyi Erzsébet fasor and Nagyajtai utca, is this monument to an heroic but little known figure of World War II. Raoul Wallenberg was a Swedish diplomat who used his position to save over 20,000 Hungarian Jews from the extermination camps. He set up safe houses in the city and obtained fake Swedish documents for them.

Following the liberation of Budapest by the Soviet army, Wallenberg disappeared. It is thought he was arrested by the KGB and sent to a prison camp where he died. The memorial, by sculptor Imre Varga, was erected in 1987.

Szemlő-hegy and Pál-völgy Caves ❷

Szemlő-hegyi-barlang és Pál-völgyi-cseppkőbarlang

Szemlő-hegy Cave Pusztaszeri út 35. **Tel** 325 60 01. 🚌 29. ⏱ 10am–4pm Wed–Mon. 🅿 ♿ 📷
Pál-völgy Cave Szépvölgyi út 162. **Tel** 325 95 05. 🚌 65. ⏱ 10am–4pm Tue–Sun. 🅿 📷

To the north of Budapest lies the Pilis mountain range, formed of limestone and dolomite. Natural geological processes which occur within these mountains have created some picturesque caves, two of which are unusual tourist attractions.

Szemlő-hegy Cave features extraordinary formations called "cave pearls", produced when hot spring waters penetrate its limestone walls. There are guided tours every hour.

In Pál-völgy Cave, strange formations protruding from the rock face resemble animals.

It is a good idea to wear warm clothes when visiting the caves as they are cold and damp. Some claim, however, that the atmosphere in the caves has a therapeutic effect on the respiratory system.

The Baroque interior of Újlak Parish Church, dating from 1756

Újlak Parish Church ❸

Újlaki plébániatemplom

Bécsi út 32. 🚌 17.

Bavarian settlers first built a small church here early in the 18th century. The present church, designed by Kristóf Hamon and Mátyás Nepauer, was finished in 1756. Its tower was added some years later.

In the Baroque interior there is a depiction of the Madonna, a gift from the inhabitants of Passau to the church. The main altar, dating from 1798, also includes

a painting entitled *The Visitation*, which was the work of Francis Falkoner.

Not far away, at Zsigmond tér, stands the Holy Trinity Column, built in 1691 as a memorial to the city's earliest plague epidemic. The Baroque monument was moved from central Buda to Újlak in 1712.

Geology Institute ❹

Földtani Intézet

Stefánia út 14. **Map** 8 F1. **Tel** 251 09 99. 🚌 75, 77. **Museum** ⏱ 10am–4pm Thu, Sat & Sun. 📷

This beautiful and unusual building, housing the Geology Institute, dates from 1898–9 and was designed by Ödön Lechner (see p56).

Lechner's very individual Secession style, also known as the Hungarian National Style, is on show here including motifs drawn from Hungarian Renaissance architecture.

On the picturesque elevations and gables of the building pale yellow plaster walls form a striking contrast to the brick-work quoins and window frames. Here and there Zsolnay blue glazed ceramic ornaments adorn the walls and harmonize with the blue roof tiles. The central pitched roof is topped by three human figures bent under the weight of a large globe.

Inside the Geology Institute is a small museum

The Geology Institute, with its stunning blue ceramic roof

with rock and mineral exhibits. Lechner's Secession interiors have been carefully preserved in their original condition. The central hall is particularly grand, and can be seen when visiting the museum or on its own with the caretaker's permission.

Ferenc Puskás Stadium ❺

Puskás Ferenc stadion

Istvánmezei u. 3–5. **Map** 8 F1. **Tel** 471 43 21. 🚇 23, 24, 36. 🕐 8am–2pm Mon–Thu, 8am–noon Fri.

Hungary's biggest sports stadium, named after a national football hero, was built between 1948–53 to a design by Károly Dávid. The roofless structure seats 78,000, but generally only fills to capacity for major events. The entrance is at the end of the "Avenue of Youth", which is lined with Stalinist-era statues, depicting various sports, by well-known Hungarian sculptors.

Kerepesi Cemetery ❻

Kerepesi temető

Fiumei út 16–20. **Map** 8 E3. 🚇 23, 24, 36.

Since 1847, the Kerepesi Cemetery has provided the resting place for many of Hungary's most prominent citizens. Fine tombstones mark the graves of some, while others were interred here inside large mausoleums.

The mausoleum of the leader of the 1848–9 uprising, Lajos Kossuth (see p106) and Lajos Batthyány, the first prime minister of Hungary (see p31) are found here. Ferenc Deák, who formulated the Compromise with Austria (see p32), is buried here.

Also at the cemetery are the graves of poets Endre Ady and Attila József (see p106), writers Kálmán Mikszáth Zsigmond Móricz and actors such as Lujza Blaha, whose tomb is particularly beautiful. Sculptors, painters and

composers are buried close to great architects.

Hungarian Communists who were sentenced to death in the show trials of 1949, were buried here. Their funerals inspired a revolutionary spirit which, a few years later, led to the 1956 Uprising (see p34).

Józsefváros Parish Church ❼

Józsefváros plébániatemplom

Horváth Mihály tér 7. **Map** 7 C4. **Tel** 313 61 26. 🚇 83. 🚋 9, 17.

Building work on this Baroque church began in 1797, but it was not completed until 1814. The main altar is by József Hild. A formidable architectural composition, it is based on a triumphal arch. This frames a magnificent painting, The Apotheosis of St Joseph, by Leopold Kupelwieser. The church also has two beautiful, late Baroque side altars.

University Botanical Gardens ❽

Egyetemi Botanikus kert

Illés utca 25. **Map** 8 D5. **Tel** 314 05 35. 🚇 Klinikák. **Garden** 🕐 Nov–Mar: 9am–4pm; Apr–Oct: 9am–5pm. **Glasshouses** 🕐 9am–noon, 1pm–3pm. 🖼️ 📷

Gardens were first established on this 3-ha (8-acre) site by the Festetics family. Their modest,

The late Baroque façade of Józsefváros Parish Church

early Neo-Classical villa is now the administration centre for the gardens. It was built in 1802–3, probably to a design by Mihály Pollack. The smoking room in the villa houses a huge collection of tropical plants, including the striking Victoria regia, which flowers once a year. The author Ferenc Molnár (1878–1952) used the gardens as a setting in his novel, The Paul Street Boys, although the lake mentioned in the book no longer exists. Not far away are Pál utca (Paul Street) and Mária utca, the scene of a battle the boys fought.

Ludovika Academy ❾

Ludovika Académia

Ludovika tér 2–6. 🚇 Klinikák. **Tel** 210 10 85. 🕐 10am–6pm Wed–Mon. **National History Museum** 🕐 10am–6pm Wed–Mon. 📷 ♿ www.nhmus.hu

The huge Ludovika Academy is in district IX, east of the city centre. It was designed in the 1830s by Mihály Pollack, the famous architect of the Hungarian National Museum (see pp130–33). A military academy until 1945, it is an impressive example of Neo-Classical style, with many original features intact. It is now the city's Natural History Museum, with a rich paleontological collection.

The tomb of actress Lujza Blaha at Kerepesi Cemetery

Holocaust Memorial Center ⑩
Holokauszt Emlékközpont

Pava út 39. Ⓜ Ferenc korut.
▦ 4, 6. **Tel** 455 33 33. ⏰ 10am–
6pm Tue–Sun. ▨ ♿ www.hdke.hu

The Center was founded in order to collect and study material relating to the history of the Holocaust, and to honour its victims. The building complex is a mix of classical and modern architecture, and its asymmetrical outline and dislocated walls all symbolize the distorted and twisted time of the Holocaust.

A permanent exhibition examines the history of the suffering of Hungarian Jews and Roma during the Holocaust.

The impressive open-space interior of the Palace of Arts, a cultural hub

Palace of Arts ⑪
Művészetek Palotája

Komor Marcell utca 1. ▦ 1, 2, 2A,
24. **Tel** 555 30 00, 333 33 01 or
555 33 00. ⏰ 10am–10pm daily.
www.mupa.hu **Ticket Office** (for
all events) ⏰ 1–6pm Mon–Sat,
10am–6pm Sun. www.jegyelado.hu

The Palace of Arts in the Millennium City Centre, located on the Pest side of the Danube between the Lágymányos bridge and the new National Theatre, brings together the different branches of the arts under one roof. Permanent residents include the Ludwig Museum of Contemporary Art, the National Philharmonic Orchestra and the National Dance Theatre.

Railway History Park ⑫
Vasúttörténeti Park

Tatai út 95. Ⓜ Klinikák. **Tel** 450 14
97. ⏰ Mid–end Mar: 10am–3pm
Tue–Sun; Apr–Sep: 10am–6pm;
Nov–Dec: 10am–3pm Tue–Sun.
● Mon, 19 Dec–mid-Mar. ▨ ♿
www.mavnosztalgia.hu

This open-air museum of railway history is one of Europe's largest. Set in a large park, it boasts around 100 locomotives – most fully functioning – dating from the early days of steam to modern times. Visitors have the opportunity to drive a steam train, play with a model railway and ride in a line-inspection car. Every year, the legendary *Orient Express* makes several visits here. The park is popular with families as well as enthusiasts, and there is a full programme of events for children.

Kőbánya Parish Church ⑬
Kőbányai Plébániatemplom

Szent László tér. ▦ 13, 28.
▦ 17, 32, 62, 185. ♿

An industrial suburb on the eastern side of Pest, Kőbánya is the unexpected home of the beautiful Kőbánya Parish Church. Designed by Ödön Lechner *(see p56)* in the 1890s, the church makes magnificent use of the architect's favourite materials, including vibrant roof tiles developed and produced at the now-famous Zsolnay factory in the town of Pécs. Like much of Lechner's work, including the Museum of Applied Arts *(see pp136–7)*, the church combines motifs and colours from Hungarian folk art with Neo-Gothic elements. Inside the church, both the altar and the pulpit are superb examples of early 20th-century wood

Gleaming ceramic tiles on the roof of Kőbánya Parish Church

carving. Somehow surviving heavy World War II bombing, a number of Miksa Roth's original stained-glass windows are still in place.

Municipal Cemetery ⑭
Rákoskeresztúr

See pp158–9.

Jewish Cemetery ⑮
Izraelita Temető

Kozma út. ▦ 37.

Next door to the Municipal Cemetery is the Jewish Cemetery, opened in 1893. The many grand tombs here are a vivid reminder of the vigour and success of Budapest's pre-war Jewish community. At the end of the 19th century, nearly a quarter of the city's inhabitants were Jewish. Tombs to look out for as you stroll among the graves include that of the Wellisch family, designed in 1903 by Arthur Wellisch, and that of Konrád Polnay, which

Schmidl family tomb at the Jewish Cemetry

was designed five years later by Gyula Fodor. Perhaps the most eyecatching of all belongs to the Schmidl family. The startlingly flamboyant tomb, designed in 1903 by architects Ödön Lechner and Béla Lajta, is covered in vivid turquoise ceramic tiles. The central mosaic in green and gold tiles represents the Tree of Life.

National Theatre ⑯

Nemzeti Színház

Bajor Gizi Park 1. **Tel** *476 68 68.* 🚋 *1, 2, 2A, 24.* **www**.nemzetiszinhaz.hu

The theatre, built in 2002, stands at the foot of Lágymányosi Bridge. The architect, Mária Siklós, designed a Neo-Eclectic building surrounded by a park containing statues of Hungary's best actors.

Wekerle Estate ⑰

Wekerle Telep

Kós Károly tér. Ⓜ *Határ út, then* 🚌 *194.*

Out in district XIX, the Wekerle Estate was built between 1909 and 1926, and represents a bold and successful experiment in 20th-century social planning. Named after Prime Minister Sándor Wekerle, the estate was

Façade of the Technical University, as seen from the Danube

originally known as the Kispest Workers and Clerks Settlement and was built to provide better housing for local workers.

Designed by a group of young architects, students of Ödön Lechner, the buildings have a uniquely Hungarian style. Other key influences were the English Arts and Crafts movement, and early English new towns such as Hampstead Garden Suburb in London.

Fanning out around Kós Károly tér, 16 types of family house and apartment block are separated by tree-lined streets. Wooden gables and balconies, and sharply pitched, brightly tiled roofs, contribute to the estate's lively and eclectic atmosphere.

Technical University ⑱

Budapesti Műszaki Egyetem

Műegyetem rakpart 3. **Map** *4 F4.* **Tel** *463 11 11.* 🚋 *4, 6, 18, 19, 47, 49.* 🚌 *7, 86.*

Founded in 1857, the city's Technical University moved to its present site in 1904. Built on reclaimed marshland, the imposing building over-looks the Danube just south of Gellért Hill *(see pp88–9)*. Extended at the end of World War II, it is now the largest higher education establishment in Hungary. Former students include Imre Steindl, the architect of the Parliament building *(see pp108–9)*, and the richest and most widely known graduate to date, Ernő Rubik, inventor of the Rubik Cube.

Cistercian Church of St Imre ⑲

Cisztercita Szent Imre Plébániatemplom

Villányi út 25. **Map** *3 C4.* 🚋 *61.* 🚌 *27, 40.* ♿

Not far from the Technical University is the Cistercian Church of St Imre. The vast Neo-Baroque structure with its double tower was built in 1938 and is typical of the grand and rather sombre architecture in vogue in Budapest during the inter-war years.

Inside the church are relics of St Imre, canonized at the end of the 11th century. Other patron saints of the Cistercian order are depicted above the church's main entrance.

A police station on the early 20th-century Wekerle Estate

Municipal Cemetery ⑭

A new, historic significance was gained
by the Municipal Cemetery following the
1956 Uprising *(see p35)*. Here, at
Budapest southeastern limits, the leaders
and victims of this bloody revolution
against the oppressive Stalinist government
were secretly buried in mass graves. During the 1970s, the country's democratic
opposition began placing flowers on the
site, at the far side of the cemetery. In
1990, after the fall of Communism, the
revolutionary heroes were given a ceremonial funeral and reburied, and several
memorials were set up to them.

View of Plot 300
*Until 1989, the state militia guarded
access to a thicket which covered the
communal graves of the heroes of
the 1956 Uprising.*

Campanile
*A wooden campanile is the type of decoration
often found in old Hungarian cemeteries.
It stands in front of panels listing the names
of over 400 victims of the 1956 Uprising,
giving the exact locations of their graves.*

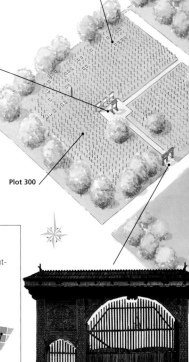

Plot 300

PLAN OF THE CEMETERY

In 1886, the city authorities opened a vast, new
municipal cemetery in Rákoskeresztúr, on the outskirts of town. It became the largest cemetery in
Budapest, occupying 30 sq km (12 sq miles).

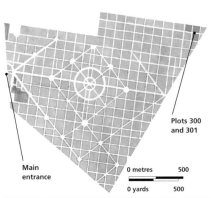

Plots 300
and 301

Main
entrance

0 metres   500
0 yards   500

★ Transylvanian Gate
*The 1956 Uprising Combatants'
Association erected the carved
Transylvanian Gate which stands
at the beginning of one of the paths
leading into plot 300. It is inscribed
with the words: "Only a Hungarian
soul may pass through this gate".*

★ **Imre Nagy's Grave**
A marble slab bears the modest inscription: "Imre Nagy, Prime Minister of Hungary, 1956". Arrested after the uprising, Nagy was interned and shot dead on 16 June 1956 in Budapest, following a bogus political trial.

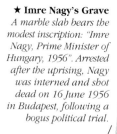

Plot 301

VISITORS' CHECKLIST

Kozma utca 8–10, Kőbánya.
📷 95 from Zalka Máté tér.
Plots 300 and 301 *30 mins walk from the main gate. Fee charged for cars.*

Christ the Sorrowful
A figure of Christ the Sorrowful is traditionally placed in a plot containing Protestant graves.

★ **Heroes' Monument**
This simple monument symbolizes the passage through purgatory. It was created by the leading modern Hungarian sculptor, György Jovánovics.

Protestant Graves
The tradition of Hungarian Protestants is to place a simple wooden post to mark each grave.

STAR SIGHTS

- ★ Heroes' Monument
- ★ Imre Nagy's Grave
- ★ Transylvanian Gate

View from Eagle Hill Nature Reserve, down across the smart residential quarter below

Congress & World Trade Centre ⓴

Kongresszusi és Világkereskedelmi Központ

Jagelló út 1–3. **Tel** 372 57 00. 🚌 61. ⭕ For events. **www**.bcwtc.hu.

Opened in 1975, this large arts complex houses a concert hall, a cinema, conference rooms and several restaurants. It host international conferences and events, as well as the annual Hungarian Film Festival (see p61). It was designed, with the neighbouring Novotel Budapest Congress (see p189), by the architect József Finta. The *Tree of Life* decorating the main wall of the Congress Hall is by József Király.

Gizi Bajor Theatre Museum ㉑

Bajor Gizi Színészmúzeum

Stromfeld Aurél út 16. **Tel** 356 42 94. 🚌 105. ⭕ 2–6pm Thu–Sun. 🖼 🎞

This museum was opened in 1952, in a garden villa which once belonged to Gizi Bajor, a leading Hungarian actress of her day. Its exhibits, which include furniture, portraits, theatrical props, fans and velvet gloves, transport visitors to the world of the theatre in the 19th century.

In 1990, the 200th anniversary of theatre in Hungary, the museum's collection was further extended, to include mementoes of well-known contemporary Hungarian

actors, after whom some of the museum's rooms are named.

The garden features the busts of several writers together with a number of other leading figures in Hungary's cultural history.

Eagle Hill Nature Reserve ㉒

Sashegy Természetvédemi Terület

Tájék utca 26. **Tel** 06 304 084 370. 🚌 8, 8A. ⭕ Mid-Mar–mid-June & Sep–mid-Oct: 10am–4pm Sat & Sun. 🖼 available.

A nature reserve more or less in the centre of a city of two million inhabitants is a remarkable phenomenon.

Access to the summit of this steep, 266-m (872-ft) high hill to the west of Gellért Hill (see pp88–9) is strictly regulated to protect the extremely rare animal and plant species found here. A smart residential quarter, which lies on the lower slope of Eagle Hill, extends almost to the fence of the reserve and the craggy 30-ha wilderness that it encloses.

It is well worth taking a guided walk, particularly in spring or early autumn. Only here is it possible to see *centaurea sadleriana*, a flower resembling a cornflower but much bigger. The reserve is also home to a type of spider not found anywhere else in the world, as well as to extraordinary, colourful butterflies and to *ablebbarus kitaibeli*, a rare lizard.

Memento Park ㉓

Memento Park

Balatoni út & Szabadkai utca. **Tel** 424 75 00. 🚌 50. ⭕ 10am–dusk daily. 🖼 **www**.mementopark.hu

In 1991, Budapest's City Council decided to gather in one place Communist monuments which had formerly occupied prestigious locations in the city.

The park, which has recently been enlarged and renamed, features gigantic monuments of the Communist regime. Statues of Karl Marx, Friedrich Engels, VI Lenin and Hungarian Communist heroes stand side by side, headed by the leader of the 1919 revolution in Hungary (see p34), Béla Kun.

Stalin's Tribune is a replica of the original grandstand from which Communist leaders greeted the crowds. Above the tribune stood an 8m- (26 ft-) high bronze of Stalin, but it was pulled down during the national Uprising in 1956 and only the boots remain.

The Barakk Museum has exhibitions on everyday life under the Communist regime, and a cinema has a screening of the special methods used by the Communist secret services.

Cubist-style statues of Marx and Engels in the Statue Park

The marble Törley Mausoleum

Törley Mausoleum ㉔

Törley Mauzoleum

Sarló utca 6. 3.

Until 1880 Budafok had a number of vineyards, but their cultivation was destroyed in that year by a plague of phylloxera (American aphid). It was then that József Törley, who had studied wine-making in Reims, started to produce sparkling wine in Budafok using the French model *(see p194)*. His wines sold well abroad and he quickly expanded his enterprise, storing the wines in the local cellars.

József Törley died in 1900 and was laid to rest in this monumental mausoleum designed by Rezső Vilmos Ray. Constructed of white marble, it is adorned with Eastern motifs and bas-reliefs by József Damkó.

Nagytétényi Palace Museum ㉕

Nagytétényi Kastély Múzeum

Kastélypark utca 9–11. **Tel** 207 00 05. 41. ○ Mar–Dec: 10am–6pm Tue–Sun Jan–Feb: 10am–6pm Fri–Sun. In period costume, by arrangement. **www**.nagytetenyi.hu

This is one of the best known Baroque palaces in Hungary. It was built in the mid-18th century, incorporating the remains of a 15th-century Gothic building. The work was started by György Száraz and completed by his son-in-law,

József Rudnyánszky, acquiring its final shape in 1766. Based on the typical Baroque layout, it includes a main block and side wings. The coping features the Száraz and Rudnyánszky family crests.

The palace suffered severe damage during World War II, but the original wall paintings and furnishings survived. In 1949, the palace was rebuilt and turned into an interior design museum. Now it is a department of the Museum of Applied Arts *(see pp136–7)*. On display are fine pieces of furniture from the 15th–18th centuries, early 19th-century paintings and more functional items, such as tiled stoves.

Standing close to the palace is an 18th-century Baroque church, built on the remains of a medieval church. Original Gothic features incorporated in it include the window openings in its tower and three supports on the outer wall of the presbytery. In 1760, the Austrian artist Johann Gfall created the painting in the dome which features illusory galleries. The altars, pulpit and baptistries also date back to the mid-18th century.

Buda Hills ㉖

Budai-hegység

Moszkva tér, then 56, then cog-wheel railway and chair lift.

To the west of the city centre are the wooded Buda Hills where Budapesters come to walk and relax.

The first station of a cog-wheel railway, built in 1874, is on Szilágyi Erzsébet fasor. This runs up Sváb Hill – named after the Germanic Swabians, who settled here under the Habsburgs *(see p28)* – and then Széchenyi Hill.

From the first station a narrow-gauge railway covers a 12-km (7-mile) route to the Hűvös Valley. As in the days of the Soviet Young Pioneers movement, the railway is entirely staffed by children, apart from the adult train drivers. At the top of János Hill stands the Erzsébet Look-Out Tower, designed by Frigyes Schulek in 1910. A chair lift also connects the summit of János Hill with Zugligeti út and is a good way of making the descent.

Aquincum ㉗

Aquincum

See pp162–3.

The Erzsébet Look-Out Tower at the summit of János Hill

Aquincum ㉗

The remains of the Roman town of Aquincum *(see p20–21)* were excavated at the end of the 19th century. Visitors are free to stroll along its streets, viewing the outlines of temples, shops, baths and houses, in what was once the centre of the town. This civilian town was founded at the beginning of the 2nd century AD, a couple of decades after a legionary fortress *(see pp170–71)* was established to its south. In the centre of the site there is a Neo-Classical museum displaying the most valuable Roman archaeological finds. On the other side of the road are the remains of an amphitheatre, where Aquincum's inhabitants once sought entertainment.

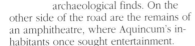

Roman Column

View Towards the Museum
The area opened to visitors is only a fragment of a much bigger town.

★ **Public Baths**
The walls of the thermal baths are immaculately preserved. Visiting the baths was a social event for the Romans.

Central Heating System
Archaeologists have here unearthed the Roman version of central heating, an under-floor system in which hot air was circulated under mosaic floors.

★ **Macellum**
This was the covered market hall. Having stalls positioned around a cool inner courtyard kept the produce fresh and made shopping comfortable all year round (see pp20–21).

STAR SIGHTS

★ Macellum

★ Museum

★ Public Baths

★ Museum
This Neo-Classical Lapidarium is part of the museum, which houses an exhibition of objects found at Aquincum and at other Roman sites nearby. These include weapons and inscribed stone monuments.

VISITORS' CHECKLIST

Szentendrei út 139. **Tel** 250 16 50.
🚉 Aquincum. 🕐 9am–5pm Tue–Sun 🎫 **Museum** 🕐 10am–5pm Tue–Sun ⬤ Mid-Oct–mid-Apr. 🎫 📷 www.aquincum.hu

Thoroughfare
Paving stones can still be seen on the network of streets that run across the town at right angles.

Double Baths
Built mainly of stone, the baths were once richly decorated. Traces of wall paintings and mosaics can still be seen in some places.

Drain Cover
Aquincum had a water supply system. Carefully crafted drain covers, such as this one, cut into the stone paving slabs, provided the required drainage.

Peristyle House
Surrounded by a colonnade, this courtyard once stood at the centre of a large town house.

Excursions from Budapest

Budapest is ten times bigger than any other Hungarian city. Sleepy and charming, the towns and villages on these pages are ideal for day or overnight trips. Coaches *(see p234)* and trains *(see p239)* are cheap and reliable. Esztergom, Visegrád and Szentendre to the north of the city can all be reached by boats *(see p235)*, which run throughout the summer along this beautiful stretch of the Danube. More off the beaten track, the towns and villages to the south offer a fascinating glimpse of traditional life.

Overlooking the Danube, the vast cathedral at Esztergom

Esztergom ❶

46 km (28 miles) NW of Budapest. 🚌 30,000. 🚉 from Árpád híd. 🚆 from Nyugati pu. 🚢 from Vigadó tér (summer only), take local buses 1-6 and get off at Béke tér stop. 🚏 ℹ Lőrinc utca **Cathedral** Szent István tér 1. **Tel** (0633) 41 18 95. ⬜ Daily 🏛 **Treasury Tel** (0633) 40 23 54. ⬜ Mar–Oct: 9am–4:30pm daily; Nov–Dec: 11am–3:30pm Tue–Sun. 🚫 📷 **Castle Tel** (0633) 41 59 86. ⬜ Daily 🚫 🏛 www.esztergom.hu

St István, Hungary's first Christian King, was baptized in Esztergom and crowned here on Christmas Day 1000 AD. Almost completely destroyed by the Mongol invasion 250 years later, the city was gradually rebuilt in the 18th and 19th centuries.

Esztergom today is still the country's most sacred city, the seat of the archbishop of Hungary. Dominating the skyline is the huge Catholic **cathedral**, built in the early 19th century. By the southern entrance, built by 16th-century Florentine craftsmen, is the red marble Bakócz burial chapel. On the northern side is the **treasury** containing a collection of ecclesiastical treasures rescued from the ruins of the 12th-century church that existed on the cathedral site.

Below the cathedral are the remains of the 10th-century **castle**, rebuilt several times. It features a 12th-century chapel. The picturesque old town is also well worth exploring. At its heart is the town square, home to several cafés.

SIGHTS AT A GLANCE

Esztergom ❶
Fót ❺
Gödöllő ❻
Kecskemét ❼
Kiskunfélegyháza ❽
Martonvásár ❿
Ráckeve ❾
Szentendre ❸
Vác ❹
Visegrád ❷

25 kilometres = 15 miles

KEY

▨ City centre
▨ Greater Budapest
━ Motorway
▪ ▪ Under construction
▬ Main road

Visegrád ❷

40 km (25 miles) N of Budapest.
🏛 1,800. 🚆 from Árpád híd.
🚢 from Vigadó tér (summer only).
🛈 Rév utca 15. Tel (0626) 39 81 60.
Castle Tel (0626) 39 81 01. ⏰ Mar–
Sep: 9:30am–6pm Mon–Sun; Oct–
Nov: 9:30am–4pm Mon–Sun; Dec–
Feb: 9:30am–4pm Sat & Sun. 🖼 🚻
Mátyás Museum & Visegrád Palace
Tel (0626) 39 80 26. ⏰ 9am–5pm
Tue–Sun. 🖼 🚻 by arrangement.
www.visegrad.hu

Set on the narrowest stretch
of the Danube, the village of
Visegrád is a popular tourist
destination, thanks to its
spectacular ruined **castle**.
A 25-minute walk, or a
short bus or taxi ride will take
you up to the castle from
Visegrád. Built in the 13th
century by King Béla IV, this
was once one of the finest
royal palaces ever built in
Hungary. The massive outer
walls are still intact, and offer
stunning views over the
surrounding countryside.
Halfway down the hill, in
the Salamon Tower, is the
Mátyás Museum, a collection
of items excavated from the
ruins of the **Visegrád Palace**.
Built by King Béla IV at the
same time as the castle, the
palace was renovated two
centuries later, in magnificent
Renaissance style, by King
Mátyás Corvinus (see pp24–5).
Destroyed in the 16th century
after the Turkish invasion, then
buried in a mud slide, the ruins
were not rediscovered until
1934, when the excavations
took place here.

Szentendre ❸

25 km (16 miles) N of Budapest.
🏛 20,000. 🚆 from Batthyány tér.
🚆 from Árpád híd. 🚢 from Vigadó
tér (summer only). 🛈 Dumtsa Jenő
utca 22. Tel (0626) 31 79 66.
Belgrade Cathedral Pátriárka utca 5.
Tel (0626) 31 23 99. ♿
Museum of Serbian Art Pátriárka
utca 5. Tel (0626) 31 23 99. ⏰ May–
Sep: 10am–6pm Tue–Sun; Oct–Apr:
10am–4pm Tue–Sun; Jan–Feb:
10am–4pm Fri–Sun. 🖼 🚻 **Margit
Kovács Museum** Vastag György út
1. Tel (0626) 31 07 90. ⏰ 10am–
6pm Mon–Sun. 🖼 🖉 🚻 by
arrangement. **Hungarian Open Air
Museum** Sztaravodai u. Pf 63. Tel
(0626) 50 25 11. ⏰ Apr–Nov: 9am–
5pm Tue–Sun.
www.skanzen.hu

Only 25 km (16 miles) outside Budapest, Szentendre is
a town built and inhabited by a

**Blagovestenska church in Fő tér,
Szentendre's main square**

succession of Serbian refugees. Most of Szentendre's
older buildings date from the
18th-century.
Orthodox religious tradition
lies at the heart of the town,
which contains many
Orthodox churches. The western European façades hide
Slavic interiors filled with
incense, icons and candlelight.
Blagovestenska Church on
Fő tér, is just one example.
Look out for the magnificent
iconostasis that separates the
sanctuary from the nave. Also
of interest is Sunday mass at
Belgrade Cathedral.
Next door is a **Museum of
Serbian Art**, full of icons and
other religious artefacts.
Since the 1920s, Szentendre

has been home to an ever
increasing number of artists
and the town contains many
galleries exhibiting the work
of local artists.
Margit Kovács Museum
shows the work of one of
Hungary's best-known
ceramic artists. Margit Kovács
(1902–77) drew inspiration
from Hungarian mythology
and folk traditions.
To the west of town is the
Hungarian Open Air Museum,
an ethnographical museum,
illustrating the different
Hungarian regions and their
rural architecture and culture
across the social groups, from
the 18th to the 20th century.
The museum is set in a
pleasant park.

Vác ❹

40 km (25 miles) N of Budapest.
🏛 36,000. 🚆 from Nyugati pu.
🚆 from Árpád híd. 🛈 Március 15
tér 17. Tel (0627) 31 61 60.

Vác has stood on the eastern
bank of the Danube since
1000 AD. Destroyed by war
in the late 17th century, the
town was rebuilt and today
its centre, built around four
squares, dates from the early
18th century. At its heart is
Marcius 15 tér, where the
Town Hall and **Fehérek
Church** are located. At the
northernmost end of the old
town, on Köztársaság út, is
Hungary's only **Arc de Triomph**. This was built in 1764,
after a visit from the Habsburg
Empress, Maria Theresa.

Arc de Triomph in Vác, built in
honour of Empress Maria Theresa

Exterior of Fót's Church of the Immaculate Conception

Fót ❺

25 km (15 miles) NE of Budapest.
🚗 16,000. 🚈 Nyugati pu. 🚌
Árpád híd. 🎫 Vörösmarty tér 3. **Tel**
(0627) 53 82 60. **Károlyi Palace
and park** Vörösmarty tér 2. ◯ by appt.
Tel *(0627) 35 80 22.* 🅿 & ground
floor only. 🎫 obligatory. **Church of
the Immaculate Conception**
Vörösmarty út 2. 🎫

Just outside Budapest is the
small town of Fót. Its main
attraction is the **Károlyi
Palace**, birthplace of the
country's first president, Mihály
Károlyi *(see p34).* The palace
was built in the 1830s, with a
pavilion added on each side a
decade later. Also worth a
visit is the town's attractive
19th-century **Church of the
Immaculate Conception**,
with its impressive many-
columned nave.

Gödöllő ❻

35km (20 miles) NE of Budapest.
🚈 Hév from Örs vezér tere.
Grassalkovich Mansion ◯
Apr–Oct: 10am–6pm daily; Nov–Mar:
10am–5pm Tue–Sun. ⬤ Jan.
Tel *(0628) 41 01 24.* 🅿 & 🎫

Gödöllő is most famous for its
restored Baroque palace, the
Grassalkovich Mansion. Built
in 1741, it was the favourite
residence of Queen Elizabeth,
wife of Franz Joseph. The
permanent exhibition in the
Royal Museum incorporates
the Ceremonial Hall and royal
suites, and details the life of the
Austro-Hungarian monarchy.

Kecskemét ❼

86km (52 miles) SE of Budapest.
🚗 110,000. 🚈 Nyugati pu.
🚌 Népstadion. 🎫 Kossuth tér 1.
Tel *(0676) 48 10 16.* **Town Hall**
Kossuth tér 1. **Tel** *(0676) 51 35 13.*
◯ 8am–4:30pm Mon– Thu, 8am–
2pm Fri. 🎫 by appointment. **Cifra
Palace** Rákóczi utca 1. **Tel** *(0676) 48
07 76.* ◯ 10am–5pm Tue–Sun. 🅿
& 🎫 www.kecskemet.hu

Spreading out in a vast sweep
around Budapest is the Great
Hungarian Plain, or *Alföld*,
which covers nearly half of
modern Hungary. For
hundreds of years, Kecskemét
has been the major market
town of the central-southern
plain. Distributing and pro-
cessing the products of the
surrounding rich farmland,
Kecskemét grew affluent, particularly towards the end of
the 19th century. As a result,
the town today boasts many
gracious squares and splendid
19th and early 20th century
buildings. The most famous is
Ödön Lechner's massive **Town
Hall**. Built between 1893–6,
the building is a combination
of both Renaissance and
Middle-Eastern influences.
The flamboyant **Cifra Palace**
(Ornamental Palace), built
as a casino in 1902, is a
uniquely Hungarian vari-
ation of the Secession
style *(see pp54– 7).*

Kecskemét Town Hall, designed
by Ödön Lechner

Kiskunfélegyháza ❽

110 km (66 miles) SE of Budapest. 🚗
40,000. 🎫 Szent János tér 2.
Tel *(0676) 56 14 20.* 🚈 Nyugati pu.
🚌 Népstadion. **House of Nature
Visitor Centre** Liszt Ferenc u. 19,
Kecskemét (for information on
Kiskunsági Park). **Tel** *(0676) 50 15 96.*
◯ 9am–4pm Tue–Fri, 10am–2pm Sat
🅿 **Kiskun Museum** Dr Holló Lajos
utca 9. **Tel** *(0676) 46 14 68.* ◯ late
Mar–Oct: 9am–5pm Wed–Sun. 🅿 🎫

Much of the Great Hungarian
Plain is now used to grow
maize and vines. Small areas,
however, have been preserved
as national parks. About 15 km
(9 miles) to the west of
Kiskunfélegyháza is the
Kiskunsági National Park.
Many rare native
animals and birds can

Detail of the ornate Town Hall façade at Kiskunfélegyháza

be seen here, as well as the traditional way of life of the plains herdsman. Visitors can also explore nature trails; information is available from the Visitor's Centre in Kecskemét.

The poet Sándor Petőfi was born in Kiskunfélegyháza, and his childhood home is now part of the **Kiskun Museum**. The **Town Hall** is a masterpiece, combining influences of the Secession style (see pp54–7) with motifs from folk art.

Ráckeve ❾

43 km (26 miles) SW of Budapest.
🚶 8,500. 🚌 Eötvös utca 11.
🚉 Stadion. 🛈 Kossuth Lajos
út 51. **Tel** (0624) 42 97 47.

The village of Ráckeve is built on Csepel Island, which extends 54 km (34 miles) south along the middle of the Danube from Budapest. Ráckeve (Rác means Serb in Hungarian) was founded in the 15th century by Serbs from Keve, who fled Serbia after the Turkish invasion (see pp26–7).

The oldest building in the village is the **Orthodox church**, built by some of the first of the Serbian refugees. Dating back to 1487, this is the oldest Orthodox church in Hungary. Its walls are covered in well-preserved frescos, the first telling the story of the Nativity and the last showing the Resurrection. The church also boasts a beautiful iconostasis separating the sanctuary from the nave.

Ráckeve's peaceful and convenient situation made it the country home of one of Europe's greatest military strategists, Prince Eugene of Savoy (see p26). Credited with the expulsion of the Turks from Hungary at the end of the 17th century, Prince Eugene built himself a country **mansion** on what is now Kossuth Lajos utca. Now used as a hotel, the interior of the house has been modernized, but the elegant façade has been preserved. The formal gardens can be seen from the river.

Well-preserved frescoes in the Orthodox church at Ráckeve

Martonvásár ❿

30 km (18 miles) SW of Budapest.
🚶 4,900. 🛈 Buda út 13. **Tel**
(0622) 46 00 16. 🚉 Déli pu.
Brunswick Palace Brunswick utca 2.
◯ 8am–dusk daily (park only). 🎫
Beethoven Museum ◯ 10am–
noon, 2–6pm Tue–Sun. In winter:
10am–noon, 2pm–4pm Tue–Sun. 🎫
🌐 www.martonvasar.hu

The village of Martonvásár has existed here since medieval times, but its principal tourist attraction is now the **Brunswick Palace**. Towards the end of the 18th century the whole village was bought by the German Brunswick family, and the original palace was built for Anton Brunswick in grand Baroque style. A century later, in 1875, the palace was totally rebuilt, this time in the Neo-Gothic style. Little evidence of the original palace remains today, among the flamboyant turrets and pinnacles. The magnificent parklands, however, are open to the public and are much as they always have been. The estate's church, built in 1775, also remains largely unaltered. The interior of the church is decorated with well-preserved frescoes.

Ludwig van Beethoven was a regular visitor to the original palace. He gave music lessons to the daughters of the house, Thérèse and Josephine, with whom he is said to have fallen in love. Some of the palace rooms have been converted into a small **Beethoven Museum**. The Beethoven festival is held in the gardens during the summer months.

The Neo-Gothic Brunswick Palace at Martonvásár

THREE GUIDED WALKS

Anchor at the
Vasmacska
restaurant

Budapest is a city made for exploring on foot. From Turkish bathhouses to Baroque palaces, evidence of the city's past is visible at every turn. These guided walks take you through three fascinating areas: Óbuda to the north of the city centre, once the site of a Roman garrison and now a residential district; Margaret Island, a park in the middle of the Danube; and the historic stretch that extends from Buda across Chain Bridge and into Pest. Óbuda has yielded some of the oldest archeological finds in Hungary. This walk takes in the ruins of a Roman amphitheatre, as well as more modern attractions. The walk around car-free Margaret Island includes an exotic landscaped garden. The third excursion encompasses the lovely old buildings of Buda's Castle District, an underground labyrinth and Pest's lively Central Market.

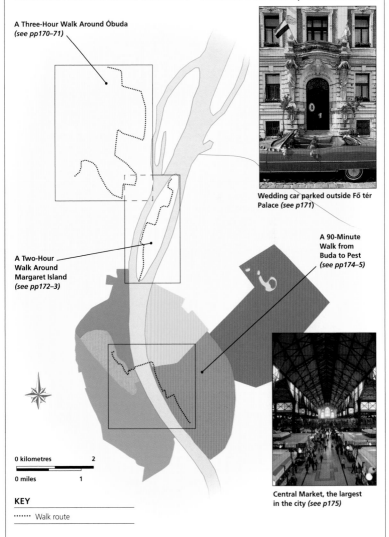

A Three-Hour Walk Around Óbuda
(see pp170–71)

Wedding car parked outside Fő tér
Palace *(see p171)*

**A 90-Minute
Walk from
Buda to Pest**
(see pp174–5)

**A Two-Hour
Walk Around
Margaret Island**
(see pp172–3)

Central Market, the largest
in the city *(see p175)*

0 kilometres   2

0 miles   1

KEY

······ Walk route

◁ **Statue of a young girl in Margaret Island's landscaped Japanese Garden** *(see p173)*

A Three-Hour Walk Around Óbuda

At first glance Óbuda today seems little more than a concrete jungle of tower blocks and flyovers. Behind the grey façade, however, there is a strong local identity and clues to the area's long and colourful past abound. Arriving here in AD 89, the Romans built a garrison in this district shortly before founding the civilian town of Aquincum *(see pp162–3)* to the north. After the departure of Romans in the 5th century AD, successive waves of invaders, including the Magyars *(see pp22–3)* all left their mark on Óbuda (literally "Old Buda"). By the end of the 16th century, Óbuda was a thriving market town, eventually forming part of the city of Budapest in 1873.

A section of Óbuda's impressive Roman amphitheatre ①

The elegant, Neo-Baroque Fő tér Palace with its sentry box ⑪

From the Roman Amphitheatre to the Roman Camp Museum

Begin the walk at the corner of Bécsi utca and Pacsirtamező út, which is dominated by the remains of a very fine Roman amphitheatre ①. The Romans arrived in the region soon after the time of Christ, building this impressive amphitheatre in the middle of the 2nd century AD, by which time Aquincum was the thriving capital of the province of Lower Pannonia *(see pp20–21)*. Originally used by the Roman soldiers from the nearby garrison, it became a fortress in the 9th century for the invading Magyar army. Not much remains of its once huge walls, but the scale of the theatre, which

was designed to seat 14,000, is still awe inspiring. From the amphitheatre, continue along Pacsirtamező út to No. 63, the Roman Camp (Táborváros) Museum ②. In the 1950s, this modern residential district, built on top of a Roman military camp complex, was found to be enormously rich in Roman artifacts. The museum (open Sundays and public holidays) houses Roman finds from the area, including ceramics, glassware and household tools.

Old Óbuda Synagogue to Flórián Tér

Retrace your steps and turn left down Perc utca, up Mókus utca, then Jós utca, turning left into Lajos utca. At No. 163 is the former Óbuda Synagogue ③, now a television studio. Built in the early 1820s to serve the area's growing Jewish community, this is a Neo-Classical building with a six-columned portico. Also on Lajos utca, at No. 168, is Óbuda Parish Church ④. Constructed in 1744–9 on the site of the Roman military camp, the church has survived since then largely unchanged. The interior includes a magnificently

carved pulpit showing the Good Shepherd and Mary Magdalene. Turning left up Óbudai utca, you will pass the house where the popular novelist, bon viveur and local character, Gyula Krúdy once lived ⑤. Writing in the early 20th century, much of

The former home of novelist and colourful local figure, Gyula Krúdy ⑤

Krúdy's work looks back at an idealized rural Hungary and is extremely popular in his country. From here, turn right along Tanuló utca and pass the ruins of the 14th-century St Clare's Nunnery ⑥. Then turn left towards Flórián tér. As you

Zichy Palace, built in the 18th century for an aristocratic family ⑩

pass Kálvin köz, on the left at No. 2 is the 18th-century Óbuda Calvinist Church ⑦. Next door is the presbytery, built in 1909 to a design by Károly Kós, better known for his work on the Wekerle Estate (see p157). No. 4 is home to a collection of folk crafts. Walk back up to busy Flórián tér, where in 1778 Roman thermal baths were discovered. Hidden in the underpasses beneath the square are the Roman Baths Museum and the Roman Settlement Museum ⑧.

Szentlélek Tér and Fő Tér

Tavasz utca, off to the the right from north of Flórián tér, leads to Szentlélek tér. In the south wing of the Zichy Palace, on Szentlélek tér, is the Vasarely Museum ⑨. The 20th-century artist Victor Vasarely is remembered as the founder of the Op-Art movement,

producing work full of bright colours and optical illusions. The crumbling Zichy Palace ⑩ itself was built for the Zichy family in 1757. Continue north up to Fő tér, one of the few areas of 18th- and 19th-century architecture remaining in Óbuda. On one side of the square stands the Neo-Baroque Fő tér Palace ⑪, its entrance still guarded by an 18th-century sentry box.

Imre Varga Gallery to the Hercules Villa

From Fő tér Palace walk up Laktanya utca, where there is a group of statues, Women with Umbrellas, by contemporary sculptor Imre Varga ⑫. At No. 7 Laktanya utca is the Imre Varga Gallery ⑬, where further examples of the sculptor's work can be seen. Finally, make your way up to Szentendrei út and cross it at an underpass. Turn right into Kerék ut (if you miss this, take the next right up Szél utca), then left into Herkules utca then onto Meggyfa utca to finish the walk at No. 21, the ruins of the Hercules Villa ⑭. Once a lavish Roman home, it takes its name from some stunning mosaics (see p21). Near the villa are the remains of the cella trichora, an early Christian chapel dating from the fourth century AD.

One of several Women with Umbrellas by Imre Varga ⑫

TIPS FOR WALKERS

Starting point: Pacsirtamező út.
Getting there: Bus 60 or tram 17.
Length: 3 km (1.8 miles).
Stops: The Kéhli Restaurant (see p199) on Mókus utca, or the Régi Sipos Étterem (see p199) on Lajos utca for the city's freshest fish.

A Two-Hour Walk Around Margaret Island

Historically inaccessible in the middle of the Danube, Margaret Island was a retreat for religious contemplation from at least the 11th century onwards. Relics of the island's past include the remains of two monastic churches and also the ruins of the convent home of Princess Margit, daughter of King Béla IV, who gave the island its name. Opened to the public in 1869, Margaret Island is today Budapest's most beautiful park, a car-free haven of greenery in the middle of the city and the ideal location for a peaceful stroll. On the western shore, the Palatinus Strand bathing complex makes use of the mineral-rich hot springs rising on the island.

The Water Tower ⑤

A relief of Archangel Michael on St Michael's Church ⑧

Centenary Monument to Palatinus Strand

The walk begins amid the peace and greenery of the southern tip of Margaret Island. Proceeding to the north, the first landmark is the Centenary Monument ① *(see p62)*, which stands in front of a sizable fountain. Designed by István Kiss, the monument was made in 1973, to commemorate the centenary of the unification of the towns of Buda, Óbuda and Pest *(see p32)*. At night the fountain is dramatically illuminated. You can also rent four-wheel family bikes here called *Bringóhintó*. Taking a left turn ahead, the Hajós Olympic Pool Complex *(see p53)* ② is soon reached. Built in 1930, the complex was designed by the multi-talented Alfréd Hajós. He won gold medals in swimming

events in the 1896 Olympic Games and was also a member of the Hungarian football team. Continuing northwards, there is a rose garden to the right before the ruins of the early 14th-century Franciscan Church ③ come into view. Constructed in the Gothic style of the time, the church was originally attached to a monastery. Visible in the west wall is the doorway which once led to the organ loft, as well as a spiral staircase and fine arched window. Further on is the busy Palatinus Strand ④ *(see p53)*. In front of the entrance to its pools stands a statue by French sculptor Emile Guilleaume.

Water Tower to St Michael's Church

Clearly visible to the northeast of Palatinus Strand, is the 57-m (187-ft) high Water Tower ⑤. Built in 1911 and now protected by UNESCO, this graceful tower is currently used as an exhibition space for a variety of previously unexhibited modern crafts and artworks, ranging from puppets to paintings. At the foot of the Water Tower is the Summer Theatre, a large modern amphi-theatre seating 3,500 people, which hosts a summer season of operatic performances. To the southeast of the Water Tower are the ruins of a 13th-century Dominican Church and Convent ⑥.

Ruins of the 14th-century Franciscan Church ③

Margit híd

Margit híd
250 metres / 300 yards

The latter was once home to Princess Margit, after whom the island is named. King Béla IV *(see p23)* swore that if he succeeded in repelling the Mongol invasion of 1241 that he would offer his daughter to God. He kept his oath, building the church and convent, to which the 9-year-old Princess Margit was sent in 1251. She led a godly and ascetic life and died here at the age of 29. Nearly 300 years later, in 1541, the nuns of the convent fled to Pozsony (now Bratislava, capital of the Slovak Republic) in the face of the Turkish invasion, *(see pp26–7)*, leaving the church and the convent to be destroyed. Severe floods in 1838 led to the discovery of the ruined church and its underground vaults. The tomb of the now-canonized Margit was also excavated here 20 years later. Just to the north of the Dominican Church and Convent, near to the Water Tower, is the beginning of Artists' Avenue ⑦. A collection of contemporary busts of Hungarian writers, painters and musicians lines this promenade leading up to the Grand Hotel Margitsziget. A little way before the hotel is

Stepped pathway through the lush foliage of the Japanese Garden ⑪

St Michael's Church ⑧. Originally built by members of the Premonstratensian Order, this is the oldest building on the island. In addition, the foundations of an 11th-century chapel have been excavated inside the 12th century church. Destroyed by the invading Turks in 1541, the church was eventually reconstructed in the 1930s, using materials from the original building. In the bell tower hangs a bell which, unusually, survived the Turkish invasion. Probably buried by the monks at the time of the invasion, the bell dates from the early 15th century. It was discovered in 1914 when its walnut-tree hiding place was uprooted during a violent storm.

Bust of Zsigmond Móricz on Artists' Avenue ⑦

Grand Hotel Margitsziget to Árpád Bridge

The Grand Hotel Margitsziget ⑨ *(see p185)* was designed in 1872 by Miklós Ybl *(see p119)*. For many years it was the most fashionable hotel in Budapest, known simply as "The Grand". After World War II, the hotel was modernized and called the Danubius Grand, and in the 1970s the luxurious Danubius Health Spa Resort Margitsziget ⑩ was built nearby. The two hotels are joined by an underground walkway and offer thermal baths and a variety of spa treatments *(see p52)*. Heading west from the latter hotel, the final stretch of the walk passes beside the Japanese Garden ⑪. A variety

of exotic plants, a rock garden, waterfalls and streams crossed on rustic bridges all add to the garden's atmosphere. The final stopping point on the walk is an unusual musical well, known as the Bodor Well ⑫. The original well was designed and constructed by Transylvanian Péter Bodor in 1820 and stood in the town of Marosvásárhely (modern-day Tirgu Mures, in Romania), which was then part of the Austro-Hungarian Empire. In 1936 this copy was built on Margaret Island. Continuing past the well, at the northern tip of Margaret Island the Árpád Bridge provides another link from the island to the city.

The musical Bodor Well ⑫

TIPS FOR WALKERS

Starting point: *Southern end of Margaret Island, reached from Margaret Bridge.*
Getting there: *Bus 26. Tram 4, 6.*
Length: *3.3 km (2 miles).*
Stops: *There are numerous take-away kiosks and cafés on the island, selling drinks, snacks and ice creams. The Danubius Grand Hotel and Danubius Health Spa Resort Margitsziget also have restaurants and cafés.*

KEY

• • • Walk route

River boat boarding point

HÉV railway station

0 metres	500
0 yards	500

A 90-Minute Walk from Buda to Pest

Buda and Pest were unified in 1873, an act made possible by the construction of the monumental Chain Bridge some 20 years earlier. Before that, the two areas had shared a relatively common history, but they always retained separate identities. Even today, Buda remains more regal and relaxed than commercial, dynamic Pest. This walk reveals such differences, while highlighting the bond that makes Budapest's whole greater even than the sum of its sublime parts.

views of the Royal Palace and the unmistakable Neo-Gothic silhouette of Mátyás Church.

Roosevelt tér to Váci utca
Facing the Pest side of the river there are rewarding vistas too: of Budapest's peerless Parliament building

The terrace and conical towers of Fishermen's Bastion ②

The Castle District
The walk begins at the 13th-century Mátyás Church ① (see pp82–3), one of the oldest buildings in Buda, and coronation church of the Hungarian kings. Directly behind are the ramparts of Fishermen's Bastion ② (see p80), from where there are famous views across the Danube to Pest. Return past the main portal of Mátyás Church and onto Tárnok utca, running the gauntlet of its myriad souvenir shops, before arriving at Dísz tér

(see page 73) and the Honvéd Monument ③. The monument was raised in honour of those who died in the Hungarian revolution of 1848–49.

Head south out of the square, along stately Színház utca to Sándor Palace ④ (see p73), one of Buda's finest buildings and the residence of the Hungarian president. Past the terminus of the Sikló, the funicular that links the Royal Palace to the embankment below, an extravagantly ornamental gateway ⑤ (see p70) leads from the Habsurg Steps to the Royal Palace. A wide path meanders in front of the palace and offers more fine views of Pest.

Across the Danube into Pest
The path leads down through well-kept terraces to Clark Ádám tér, named after the Scottish engineer Adam Clark, who built the awe-inspiring Chain Bridge and the Neo-Classical Alagút tunnel ⑥, which channels traffic underneath the Royal Palace. In the centre of the square is the Kilometre 0 Stone ⑦, from which the official distance from Budapest to Vienna is measured. Walk to the centre of Chain Bridge ⑧ (see p112) and look back towards the Castle District. On a clear day there are glorious

(see p106); and of the city's grandest hotel, the Four Seasons Gresham Palace ⑨ (see p114), on the far side of Roosevelt tér. The hotel's astonishingly opulent foyer is well worth a visit.

From Roosevelt tér, a walkway runs south alongside the tram lines on Belgrád Rakpart. After a short walk, the Budapest Marriott hotel ⑩, a modernist masterpiece, appears on the left. Nearby, on the right, perched on the railings next to the tram line, is László Marton's charming

View from Buda to the Parliament Building in Pest

TIPS FOR WALKERS

Starting point: Mátyás Church, Moszkva tér.
Getting there: Várbusz from Moszkva tér.
Length: 3.8km (2 miles).
Stops: Gresham Palace Kávéház on Roosevelt tér, Corso Etterem at Vigadó tér 2, or 1000 Tea at Váci utca 6 (see p199).

striking architecture of Vigadó Concert Hall on Vigadó tér ⑬

sculpture of a little boy, oddly entitled *Little Princess* ⑪. Passing the small pier at Vigadó tér ⑫ (*see p126*), you cannot miss the eclectic architecture of Vigadó Concert Hall ⑬ on the square's eastern side.

Continuing along the embankment, take a left turn just before Petőfi tér onto Régiposta utca. Next, a sharp right turn onto Apáczai utca leads to the Roman remains of Contra Aquincum ⑭ (*see p122*), and the Inner City Parish Church ⑮ (*see pp124–5*), now sadly hemmed in by the approach to the Elizabeth Bridge.

Turn left at the church, and, with the Danube at your back, head towards Váci utca to the point where it crosses the busy Szabadsajtó utca. Here, the Klotild Palaces ⑯ (*see p127*), massive twin apartment blocks built on either side of the road, provide a splendid gateway to the bridge.

Cafés and the Central Market

The southern part of Váci utca ⑰ (*see p127*) is less charming and more commercial than its northern counterpart, but on summer afternoons it is thronged with people, many of whom stop to enjoy coffee or something

Street tram and the *Little Princess* by László Marton ⑪

stronger on its many terraces. Halfway along on the right is the hapless St Michael City Church ⑱, built around 1230, devastated by the Turks in 1541, rebuilt in 1701, and finally completely renovated from 1964-8. Its unimpressive exterior belies a rich interior.

From here, more cafés and bars lead along a widening street to Central Market Hall ⑲ (*see p211*). The largest market in the city, its stalls sell fruit and vegetables, fish, meat and cheese, and Hungarian crafts.

Walk route	
Pedestrianized street	
Good viewing point	
Metro station	

0 metres 400

0 yards 400

The shops and busy terrace cafés of Váci utca ⑰

TRAVELLERS' NEEDS

WHERE TO STAY

Budapest has a broad range of accommodation from top-class hotels, some with spa facilities, and private apartments to campsites and hostels. The larger hotels often belong to well-known groups and meet international standards, but are more expensive. Cheaper accommodation can be found in hostels or bed and breakfasts, or outside the city centre.

Travel agents and tourist information offices *(see p181)* will provide information on these options. Of the 200 hotels and pensions we surveyed, over 80 have been selected from across the price catagories and are, in our opinion, the best on offer. Each of these is listed, along with a short description, on pages 182–9 to help you choose the right hotel.

The exterior of the Kempinski Corvinus Hotel *(see p186)*

WHERE TO LOOK

When deciding on accommodation, first choose the general location: Buda or Pest, or maybe even the picturesque suburbs further afield. In low-lying Pest, many hotels are literally only a few steps away from most of the major tourist attractions, while visitors who choose to stay in hilly Buda can enjoy cool, fresh air and quiet surroundings.

Good value for money can be found by renting a room in one of the small pensions or private hotels in and around Budapest. The more exclusive hotels offer a luxurious stay, but at a much greater price – as much as 40,000 Hungarian forints and above per night.

Most luxury hotels, such as the Sofitel Atrium Budapest *(see p184)*, are set along the eastern bank of the Danube. Others, such as the Marriott *(see p185)* or the Kempinski

Corvinus *(see p186)* are situated nearer to the centre of Pest, close to the theatres and shops. Those located further out of town are usually an easy journey from the city centre, particularly since hotels are often situated close to metro stations.

Tourinform *(see p181)* is a chain of tourist offices in Budapest that provide information (in Hungarian, English, French, German, Russian, Spanish and Italian) on accommodation and places to eat, as well as on tourist and cultural events. Maps can be found on sale here, as well as free booklets and pamphlets.

The offices are open daily, including during the winter months. Should visitors need information to supplement this guide, Tourinform offices can offer details on alternative accommodation – from hotels to campsites – car rental, sightseeing, and purchasing tickets to cultural and spectator sports events.

The Sofitel Atrium Budapest *(see p184)*, with suspended model plane

Reception desk at the Hilton Hotel *(see p182)* in the Castle District

HOTEL AND PENSION CLASSIFICATION

Hotels are classified in five categories from one to five stars and there are two categories of pension.

At the luxury end of the scale – the five-star and four-star hotels – all rooms have a bathroom, a telephone, a TV, a radio and a refrigerator, and many will be air-conditioned. The majority of these hotels will also offer business and fitness facilities. Three-star hotels have at least one restaurant and one bar, and staff are expected to speak at least one foreign language. Two thirds of the rooms in two-star hotels have their own shower or bath, while rooms in one-star hotels simply have wash-basins with hot and cold running water.

Pensions have a standard minimum room size, and every room has a shower or a bath. The accommodation is clean and simple, and all the necessary services and amenities should be provided by friendly and helpful staff.

The Radisson SAS Béke Hotel *(see p184)*, featuring a mosaic of György Szondi

HOTEL PRICES

Room tariffs reflect the hotel classification, but it is always wise to double check the price at the time of booking. A centrally located, higher category hotel will be much more expensive than in an out-of-town, lower category hotel. Relatively cheap rooms can be found in pensions and hostels. Hotel prices usually include breakfast, which in hotels with three stars or more typically means a self-service buffet. Pensions also offer good value, substantial meals.

Many luxury hotels, such as the Ramada Plaza *(see p189)*, offer substantial weekend reductions in the low season (mid-September to mid-March). During this period a three-night stay would cost the same as one-night stay during the high season.

In spa hotels, such as the Danubius Hotel Gellért *(see p183)*, which offer hydro-therapy, the fee for using the pools and sauna is included in the room price. However, any treatments, such as massage, will incur an extra charge. Check these details with the hotel in advance.

Prices in Budapest's hotels and pensions are invariably quoted in Euros.

HIDDEN EXTRAS

Both VAT and resort tax are included in the price of the room (resort tax is charged because Budapest is classed as a health resort), but there are often hidden surcharges that can greatly increase the overall cost of

a stay. For example, a number of hotels have currency ex-change desks, but these offer a poor rate of exchange. It is better to change money at a bank or *bureau de change* where rates tend to be much more favourable.

Telephone calls, particularly international calls, cost almost twice as much when made from hotel rooms as opposed to public telephones. There are plenty of these in Budapest, although it may be necessary to buy a phone card *(see p230)*.

Most hotels have their own car parks. Some, such as the Inter-Continental *(see p186)*,

the Sofitel Atrium Budapest *(see p184)* or the Victoria *(see p183)*, offer off-street or garage parking, for which a modest fee may be charged.

HOW TO BOOK

The Budapest tourist season starts in the middle of June and lasts until the end of September. During this period, as well as around New Year and the Hungarian Grand Prix weekend *(see p59)*, hotels become fully booked very quickly.

It is advisable to book at least two weeks ahead. Most hotels will accept bookings made by e-mail or fax and will reply in the same way. Guests should confirm their reservations with a follow-up phone call a few days before they arrive.

It is possible to find accom-modation without booking in advance, but rooms may be harder to come by, especially in the high season. Bookings can be made in the tourist offices at Ferihegy airports 1 and 2 *(see pp232–3)* and at Nyugati pu, the city's western train station *(see p234–5)*.

Stained-glass window in the Danubius Hotel Gellért *(see p183)*

The Danubius Grand Hotel Margitsziget *(see p189)*, **Margaret Island**

SERVICE

The services and amenities offered by each hotel will vary according to price. As in most other countries, hotel rooms are cleaned regularly, and most higher category hotels offer 24-hour service, including meals that can be brought to the room. This usually incurs an extra charge, but tips are always welcome.

Most reception personnel will speak some foreign languages, most commonly English and German. They are happy to help make sightseeing suggestions.

TRAVELLING WITH CHILDREN

Most hotels welcome children and offer free accommodation to those up to the age of four travelling with their parents. Additional beds can often be provided for older children in the parents' room for a small extra charge. Many hotels also offer a child-minding service.

DISABLED TRAVELLERS

Budapest is trying to make up for the neglect that disabled travellers to the city have suffered. Specialist facilities are gradually being introduced throughout the city. For example, most hotels have facilities enabling disabled guests to have as pleasant and easy a stay as able-bodied people. Such hotels will display information about their facilities for disabled guests. Further information can be obtained from tourist information offices and travel agents.

SELF-CATERING

A few hotels in Budapest, especially those in the embassy district, such as the Radio Inn *(see p186)*, offer accommodation in suites with kitchenettes. This type of accommodation is particularly good for families as it gives them the option of eating "at home", rather than taking every meal at a restaurant. Another advantage is, of course, the extra space, which allows greater freedom of movement; often hotel suites are equal in size to an apartment.

There are also some specially converted buildings that consist solely of self-catering apartments. The **Charles Apartment House** is a good example of this type of accommodation; the apartments are spacious and well equipped.

HOSTELS

Budapest has a few hostels that stay open all year. For visitors on a tight budget, these provide good, if basic, low-cost accommodation. **Travellers' Hostels Universitas** and the **Citadella** *(see p182)*, which is situated in the Citadel *(see pp92–3)* on Gellért Hill, are just some examples. Hostels often provide guests with a choice of staying in a dormitory or a single or double room.

SEASONAL HOSTELS

The closest thing to youth hostels that Budapest has are the college halls of residence, which are only available during the summer vacation in July and August. Many students' halls of residence are turned into hostels, adding approximately 4,000 beds to Budapest's accommodation list and providing tourists with a convenient and inexpensive place to stay.

Given their popularity, it is advisable to book a room in advance. This is best done on the Internet via the **Mellow Mood Travel Agency**, or via tourist offices and travel bureaux. International Youth Hostels Organisation membership will enable guests to get a discount on room rates.

The interior of the Danubius Astoria Hotel *(see p185)*

STAYING IN PRIVATE ROOMS AND APARTMENTS

Some visitors choose to stay in a private home. Accommodation usually consists of a separate bedroom and use of a kitchen and bathroom. The price depends on the facilities and the area, and varies from 5,000–10,000 Hungarian forints (€20-€40) per day for a double room and upwards of 5,000 forints (€20) for a single. **TO-MA Tour** and **Ibusz** are reputable agencies through which this type of accommodation can be booked.

Renting an apartment is economical for longer stays. As well as using agencies to find private apartments, it is worth checking the *albérlet* (to rent) advertisements in newspapers such as *Expressz* and *Hirdetés*.

CAMPING

Camping is only permitted at designated campsites. There are several of these situated on the outskirts of Budapest. The biggest and most picturesque of them all is **Római Camping**, which is located on the road leading from Óbuda to Szentendre. Campsites are open, in general, from May until the end of October. Some operations, such as the **EXPO**, are open only from 1 July to 31 August, while others are open throughout the year.

The restaurant of the Danubius Hotel Erzsébet *(see p185)*, in the city centre

DIRECTORY

INFORMATION

Hungarian National Tourist Office (UK)
Embassy of the Republic of Hungary, 46 Eaton Place, London SW1X 8AL.
Tel 020 7823 1032.
www.hungarywelcomes
britain.com

Hungarian National Tourist Office (US)
150 East 58th Street, 33rd Floor, New York, NY 10155-3398.
Tel 212 355 0240.
www.gotohungary.com

Tourinform Call Centre
24-hour Tel 438 80 80.
From abroad +36 30 30 30 600.
From Hungary 06 80 630 800.

Tourinform Buda Castle
1016 Budapest, Szentháromság tér.
Map 1 B4 (9 A2).
Tel 488 04 75.

Tourinform Ferihegy 2 Airport
1185 Budapest, Terminal 2A/B.
Tel 438 80 80.

Tourinform Liszt Ferenc tér
1061 Budapest, Liszt Ferenc tér 11.
Map 7 A1.
Tel 322 40 98.

Tourinform Nyugati Pu
Left wing of main station.
Map 2 F2.
Tel 302 85 80.

AGENCIES

Express Utazási Iroda
1052 Budapest, Semmelweis utca 4.
Map 4 F1 (10 E4).
Tel 327 70 93.
www.expresstravel.hu

Hungarian Youth Hostels Federation
1077 Budapest, Almássy tér 6.
Map 7 B2.
Tel 343 51 67.
www.youthhostels.hu

IBUSZ Travel Agency
1053 Budapest, Ferenciek tere 10.
Map 4 F1 (10 E4).
Tel 485 27 65/6.
www.ibusz.hu

SELF-CATERING

Charles Apartment House
1016 Budapest, Hegyalja út 23.
Map 3 B2 (9 B5).
Tel 212 91 69.
www.charleshotel.hu

HOSTELS

Citadella
1118 Budapest, Citadella sétány. Map 4 D3.
Tel 466 57 94.
www.citadella.hu

Marco Polo Hostel
1072 Budapest, Nyár utca 6.
Map 7 A3.
Tel 413 25 55.
www.marcopolohostel.com

Red Bus Hostel
V. Semmelweis utca 14.
Map 4 F1. *Tel 321 71 00.*
www.redbusbudapest.hu

Boat Hostel Fortuna
1137 Szent István Park, Alsó rakpart. Map 2 D1.
Tel 288 81 00.
www.fortunahajo.hu

Back Pack Guesthouse
XI, Takás Menyhért utca 33.
Map 3 B5. *Tel 209 84 06.*

SEASONAL HOSTELS

Mellow Mood Travel Agency
1077 Budapest, Baross tér 15. Map 7 C2.
Tel 411 23 90.
www.mellowmood.hu

PRIVATE ROOMS AND APARTMENTS

TO-MA Tour
1051 Budapest, Oktober 6 utca 22.
Map 2 E4. *Tel 353 08 19.*
www.tomatour.hu

IBUSZ Travel
1053 Budapest, Ferenciek tere 10. Map 4 F1 (10 E4).
Tel 485 27 70.
www.ibusz.hu

CAMPING

Csillebérc Autós Camping
1121 Budapest, Konkoly Thege út 21.
Tel 395 65 27.

Haller Camping
1096 Budapest, Haller utca 27. *Tel 215 47 75.*

Római Camping
1031 Budapest, Szentendrei út 189.
Tel 368 62 60.

Choosing a Hotel

Hotels have been selected across a wide price range for good value, facilities and location. They are listed by area of the city, in the same order as the rest of the guide. Within each area, they are listed alphabetically within each price category, from the least to the most expensive. Where breakfast is an optional extra, this is indicated.

PRICE CATEGORIES
For a standard double room with bathroom per night, including breakfast, service charges:

Ⓦ under 15,000 HUF
ⓌⓌ 15,000–25,000 HUF
ⓌⓌⓌ 25,000–35,000 HUF
ⓌⓌⓌⓌ 35,000–50,000 HUF
ⓌⓌⓌⓌⓌ over 50,000 HUF

CASTLE DISTRICT

Kulturinnov   P ⑪   ⓌⓌ
Szentháromság tér 6, 1014 **Tel** *355 01 22* **Fax** *375 18 86* **Rooms** *6*   **Map** *1 B4*

At the heart of Budapest's Castle district, the Kulturinov is a reasonably priced, simple hotel where location is paramount. Guests are not overwhelmed by luxury here, the rooms are all large, have ensuite facilities and offer peace and quiet. For serious sightseers it's a great choice, and the hotel building itself is a Neo-Gothic treat. **www.mka.hu**

Burg   P ⑪ ⚡   ⓌⓌⓌ
Szentháromság tér 7-8, 1014 **Tel** *212 02 69* **Fax** *212 39 70* **Rooms** *26*   **Map** *1 B4*

Located almost directly opposite the Mátyás Church in the heart of the Castle District, location is everything at the Burg. The rooms are comfortable, if a little spartan, and the bathrooms (all ensuite) are quite small. There is no extra charge for a room overlooking the church - ask for one when booking. **www.burghotelbudapest.com**

Carlton Hotel Budapest   🖥 P ⑪ ⚡ 📶 🔒   ⓌⓌⓌ
Apor Péter utca 3, 1011 **Tel** *224 09 99* **Fax** *224 09 90* **Rooms** *95*   **Map** *1 C5*

Despite its rather bleak exterior, this is a very comfortable hotel, situated beneath the Royal Palace just off Fő utca, close to Clark Ádám tér and handy for the Chain Bridge and Pest. It has good-sized, if slightly basic, single, double and triple rooms, all with large, bright bathrooms. A hearty buffet breakfast is available. **www.carltonhotel.hu**

Hilton   🖥 P ⑪ ⚡ 📶 🔒   ⓌⓌⓌⓌⓌ
Hess Andrástér 1–3, 1014 **Tel** *889 66 00* **Fax** *889 66 44* **Rooms** *322*   **Map** *1 B4*

The Hilton *(see p81)*, one of the most luxurious hotels in Budapest, is located in a remarkable old-new building in a great location. It offers three restaurants, serving Hungarian and international cuisine. With magnificent views over the Danube and the Pest cityscape, the high prices here are more than justified. **www.budapesthilton.hu**

GELLÉRT HILL AND TABÁN

Citadella   🖥 P   Ⓦ
Citadella sétány, 1118 **Tel** *466 57 94* **Fax** *386 05 05* **Rooms** *13*   **Map** *4 D3*

This hostel-style hotel occupies the casements of the Citadel *(see p92)*. It offers relatively inexpensive, neat and clean double and multiple-occupancy rooms, and there's no curfew. Getting back here late at night can be a trek, however. A popular wine bar, restaurant and nightclub are nearby in the Citadella complex. **www.citadella.hu**

Best Western Orion   P ⑪ ⚡ 📶 🔒   ⓌⓌ
Döbrentei utca 13, 1013 **Tel** *356 85 83* **Fax** *375 54 18* **Rooms** *30*   **Map** *4 D1*

Hidden in a secluded spot, this pleasant hotel offers clean, plainly decorated rooms with bathrooms, controlled air conditioning and colour TVs. A small restaurant serves a good range of inexpensive Hungarian and international cuisine. It recently became a Best Western hotel, and service has improved. **www.bestwestern.hu/orion**

Astra   P ⚡ 🔒   ⓌⓌⓌ
Vám utca 6, 1011 **Tel** *214 19 06* **Fax** *214 19 07* **Rooms** *9*   **Map** *1 C4*

A good-value hotel, set in a 300-year-old listed building. Recently renovated, it is small and cozy. The larger rooms – all set around a courtyard – need to be booked well in advance in high summer. A very good buffet breakfast is included in the price. There's a cellar bar and games room, too. **www.hotelastra.hu**

Danubius Hotel Flamenco   🖥 P ⑪ 📶 🔒   ⓌⓌⓌ
Tas vezér utca 3–7, 1113 **Tel** *889 56 00* **Fax** *889 56 51* **Rooms** *355*   **Map** *3 C5*

This good-value hotel is close to Buda's main sights. The interior depicts Spanish themes, and the Solero restaurant and La Bodega wine bar offer Spanish specialities. Rooms are large, well furnished and comfortable and the breakfast buffet is excellent. Popular with businessmen. **www.danubiusgroup.com/flamenco**

Key to Symbols *see back cover flap*

Buda Gold

Hegyalja út 14, 1016 **Tel** *209 47 75* **Fax** *209 54 31* **Rooms** *30*

Map *3 A2*

This wonderful, grand house in the Buda hills offers panoramic views – many including a view of the garden – and luxurious bathrooms. There's a very smart restaurant on site, and the buffet breakfast is hearty. Families should go for the good-value apartments, romantics for the tower rooms. **www.goldhotel.hu**

Danubius Hotel Gellért

Szent Gellért tér1, 1111 **Tel** *889 55 00* **Fax** *889 55 05* **Rooms** *234*

Map *4 D2*

This legendary spa hotel *(see pp90–91)* has both indoor and outdoor pools. Treatments such as massage are available. Other facilities include a restaurant, a bar, a nightclub and banqueting halls. The guests' rooms, it should be said, have probably seen grander days. **www.danubiusgroup.com/gellert**

NORTH OF THE CASTLE

Mercure Budapest Buda

Krisztina körút 41–3, 1013 **Tel** *488 81 00* **Fax** *488 81 78* **Rooms** *399*

Map *1 A4*

This 1950s hotel is close to the Vérmező park and has a large car park. Some of the rooms have beautiful views overlooking the Castle District, and there's no extra charge for these. The facilities include a swimming pool, a vegetarian restaurant, a bar and a beer bar. Dogs and children are welcome. **www.mercure-buda.hu**

Papillon

Rózsahegy utca 3/B, 1024 **Tel** *212 47 50* **Fax** *212 40 03* **Rooms** *30*

Map *1 B2*

Small, garishly decorated in pinks and purples but charming all the same, this is an unpretentious place where the family who own and run it make all guests feel very welcome. Rooms are small but acceptable, pets are allowed, and there's a garden with a paddling pool for children. Breakfast is included in the price.

Victoria

Bem rakpart 11, 1011 **Tel** *457 80 80* **Fax** *457 80 88* **Rooms** *27*

Map *1 C4 (9 B2)*

On the western bank of Danube, within easy reach of Buda's main tourist sights, this hotel provides big, comfortable air-conditioned rooms, many with views of the Chain Bridge, the Elizabeth Bridge and Pest. There is no restaurant, so breakfast is served in the bar. Facilities include a sauna and an in-house doctor. **www.victoria.hu**

art 'otel

Bem rkp. 16–19, 1011 **Tel** *487 94 87* **Fax** *487 94 88* **Rooms** *164*

Map *1 C4 (9 B2)*

Everything – from the artwork decorating the rooms and halls, to the design of the carpets and chinaware – is the work of American designer Donald Sultan. Rooms are large, with high ceilings, and are individually styled in the best taste. There's a trendy restaurant on site and a bar. A buffet breakfast is included. **www.artotel.de**

AROUND PARLIAMENT

City Hotel Ring

Szent István körút 22, 1137 **Tel** *340 54 50* **Fax** *340 48 84* **Rooms** *39*

Map *7 A1 (10 F1)*

The City Hotel is within easy reach of Parliament *(see pp108–9)*. All rooms are clean and subtly decorated in neutral shades. There are few facilities and services, and this is reflected in the reasonable prices. There is a cheerful breakfast room but no restaurant. There are, however, many places to eat nearby. **www.taverna.hu/ring**

Medosz

Jókai tér 9, 1061 **Tel** *374 30 01* **Fax** *332 43 16* **Rooms** *67*

Map *7 A1*

This former trade union hostel has been successfully converted into a basic hotel. Designed for communist comrades as opposed to courting couples, most of the modest rooms have beds arranged end-to-end. Such hardships are compensated for by its excellent location close to Liszt Ferenc tér and Oktogon tér. **www.medoszhotel.hu**

Andrássy Hotel

Andrássy út 111, 1063 **Tel** *462 21 00* **Fax** *322 94 45* **Rooms** *70*

Map *2 F4 (10 E2)*

Elegance and charm meet in this hotel on Andrássy Avenue, one of the most prestigious streets in Budapest. Luxury shops, trendy cafés and historical monuments are minutes away, while the hotel itself provides beautiful Mediterranean-style rooms. The hotel's Zebrano restaurant is one of the city's best. **www.andrassyhotel.com**

K + K Opera

Révay utca 24, 1065 **Tel** *269 02 22* **Fax** *269 02 30* **Rooms** *205*

Map *2 F4 (10 E2)*

This hotel belongs to the K + K group and is situated close to the State Opera House *(see pp118–19)*. Behind a splendid façade it offers guests comfortable accommodation in modern, clean and incredibly spacious rooms. There is also a café, a pub, a bar and secure car parking. Buffet breakfast included. **www.kkhotels.com**

Hilton Budapest WestEnd

Váci út 1–3: (inside WestEnd City Center), 1069 **Tel** *288 55 00* **Fax** *288 55 88* **Rooms** *230*   **Map** *2 F2*

This is the second Hilton to open in the city. It is sited next to the hubbub of the WestEnd shopping centre, yet the contrast between the two places could not be greater. The hotel is an oasis of calm – especially in the charming rooftop garden – and offers the usual Hilton mix of modernity, efficiency and service. **www.hilton.com**

Radisson SAS Béke

Terézkörút 43, 1067 **Tel** *889 39 00* **Fax** *889 39 15* **Rooms** *247*   **Map** *2 F3*

This old, magnificent hotel *(see p115)*, close to Nyugati pu metro station, has been restored and is now equipped with the latest facilities. The restaurants serve European and Hungarian delicacies, while the first-floor Zsolnay Café serves tea and coffee from Zsolnay porcelain *(see p56)*. **www.danubiusgroup.com/beke**

Four Seasons Gresham Palace

Roosevelt tér 5–6, 1051 **Tel** *268 60 00* **Fax** *268 50 00* **Rooms** *179*   **Map** *2 D5 (9 C3)*

After 50 years of neglect the Gresham Palace *(see p114)* has been magnificently restored, and now houses one of the best hotels in central Europe. The lobby is a tourist attraction in itself, the restaurants among the city's finest, and the staff impeccable. If you can afford it, look nowhere else. **www.fourseasons.com**

Sofitel Atrium Budapest

Roosevelt tér 2, 1051 **Tel** *266 12 34* **Fax** *266 91 01* **Rooms** *350*   **Map** *2 D5 (9 C3)*

Located close to the Danube, most of the Atrium's rooms have terrific views of the Castle District and Pest. There are stylish restaurants, serving international and Hungarian cuisine, terrace cafés and a cocktail bar. Souvenir boutiques and the Las Vegas Casino *(see p217)* are on the ground floor. **www.sofitel.com**

CENTRAL PEST

Anna

Gyulai Pál utca 14, 1085 **Tel** *327 20 00* **Fax** *327 20 01* **Rooms** *31*   **Map** *7 A3*

A small, charming hotel in the centre of the city. Standard rooms are on the small side, but are stuffed full of amenities, while the two apartments come with classic wooden furniture, including enormous beds, original wooden floors and an antique table and chairs. A good buffet breakfast is included. Parking in the courtyard costs 10 euros per day.

City Hotel Pilvax

Pilvax köz 1–3, 1052 **Tel** *266 76 60* **Fax** *317 63 96* **Rooms** *32*   **Map** *4 F1*

While far from being luxurious, this is a comfortable hotel. Only a lack of baths (rooms have showers only) lets it down. That apart, it is very well located for shops, service is excellent and breakfast very good. The on-site restaurant, the historic Pilvax, is famed for its inventive Hungarian cuisine. **www.taverna.hu/pilvax**

City Panzió Mátyás

Március 15 tér 8, 1056 **Tel** *338 47 11* **Fax** *317 90 86* **Rooms** *85*   **Map** *4 E1*

This small, neat pension offers basic rooms, all with showers (but no baths), at affordable prices. There is no bar or restaurant, but a very good buffet breakfast is available. The hotel is well located, and many of Budapest's attractions are within walking distance or are easily reached on public transport. **www.taverna.hu/matyas**

Club Hotel Ambra

Kisdiófa utca 13, 1077 **Tel** *321 15 33* **Fax** *321 15 40* **Rooms** *21*   **Map** *7 A2*

The exterior is starkly modern, but the interior is a real joy, made all the more homely by the friendly staff. Rooms are actually apartments, all individually air conditioned, with satellite TV and comfy sofas. There's a small fitness centre with a sauna, and buffet breakfast is included in the price. **www.hotelambra.hu**

Domina Inn Fiesta

Király utca 20, 1061 **Tel** *328 30 00* **Fax** *266 60 24* **Rooms** *112*   **Map** *2 F5*

It would be easy to walk past this hotel. The exterior is not out of the ordinary, with shops occupying most of the ground-floor frontage. Inside, however, the hotel comes into its own, with finely furnished 3-star rooms at a reasonable price. The hotel restaurant is good, and offers a range of vegetarian dishes. **www.dominafiesta.com**

Ibis Budapest Emke

Akácfa utca 1–3, 1072 **Tel** *478 30 50* **Fax** *478 30 55* **Rooms** *84*   **Map** *7 B3*

Situated in the city centre, in a quiet side street close to Blaha Lujza tér. Recently added to the Ibis chain of low-price, good-quality hotels, the Emke offers pleasant accommodation, including non-smoking rooms, and rooms that have been adapted for the needs of disabled visitors. Service is very friendly and breakfast is good. **www.ibis-emke.hu**

Ibis Centrum

Ráday utca 6, 1092 **Tel** *456 41 00* **Fax** *456 41 16* **Rooms** *126*   **Map** *7 A5*

This hotel is located close to the Hungarian National Museum *(see pp130–3)*, Kálvin tér and several restaurants. The less-than-luxurious but nevertheless comfortable rooms and friendly service ensure a restful stay, and, as with all Ibis hotels, the buffet breakfast is excellent. Four rooms have been adapted for disabled use. **www.ibis-centrum.hu**

Key to Price Guide *see p182* **Key to Symbols** *see back cover flap*

King's Hotel Kosher

🔢 🚹   ⓔⓔ

Nagy Diófa utca 25–27, 1072 **Tel** *352 76 75* **Fax** *352 76 17* **Rooms** *100*   **Map** *7 A2 (10 F3)*

Right in the heart of the Jewish Quarter *(see p134)*, this beautifully restored 19th-century building has been a hotel since 1995. The rooms are modern and plain, but many have small balconies overlooking the quiet residential street outside. The hotel's restaurant offers a tasty range of strictly Kosher meals. **www.kingshotel.hu**

Leo Panzio

🔃   ⓔⓔ

Kossuth Lajos utca 2/A, 1053 **Tel** *266 90 41* **Fax** *66 90 42* **Rooms** *14*   **Map** *4 F1*

In the very heart of Budapest, this is a superb little pension that offers good accommodation at a more than reasonable price. Rooms have private bathrooms (with shower and toilet), air conditioning and TVs. Some have great views of the lively streets below. A good buffet breakfast is included in the price. **www.leopanzio.hu**

Marco Polo Hostel

📃 🔃 🚹   ⓔⓔ

Nyár utca 6, 1072 **Tel** *413 25 55* **Fax** *413 60 58* **Rooms** *47*   **Map** *7 A3*

Excellent value backpacker hostel, right in the heart of the city and close to public transport, nightlife and sights. Dormitory rooms are partitioned into two-bed cubicles for a little extra privacy. There are also double, triple and quad rooms with en-suite facilities, a lively bar and an Internet café. Breakfast is included. **www.marcopolohostel.com**

Mercure Budapest Metropol

🔃 🅿 🍴 🚹 🔢   ⓔⓔ

Rákóczi út 58, 1074 **Tel** *462 81 00* **Fax** *462 81 81* **Rooms** *130*   **Map** *7 A3*

Located in the city centre, close to all amenities and transport links, the Mercure Budapest is a newly renovated hotel housed in a 19th-century building. It offers every modern convenience, including sound-proofing – much needed in this location – and Internet access in all rooms. It is popular with business travellers. **www.mercure-metropol.hu**

Cotton House

🔢 🚹 🔟   ⓔⓔⓔ

Jókai utca 26, 1066 **Tel** *354 26 00* **Fax** *354 13 41* **Rooms** *18*   **Map** *2 F3*

Upstairs at the Cotton Club bar is the Cotton House, offering some of the best decorated rooms in Hungary. Luxurious and classy, this is a great choice for couples or music fans – all the rooms are named and decorated in honour of a star of the stage or screen. This hotel offers incredible value for money. **www.cottonhouse.hu**

Danubius Hotel Astoria

🔃 🅿 🍴 🚹 🔢   ⓔⓔⓔ

Kossuth Lajos utca 19–21, 1053 **Tel** *889 60 00* **Fax** *889 60 91* **Rooms** *131*   **Map** *4 F1 (10 E4)*

This old hotel, designed in the Secession style *(see pp54–5)* but with a Neo-Baroque breakfast room, has been refurbished in its original style. Non-guests should visit the café just to admire the new interior. Guests can enjoy luxurious rooms that are now in tune with the rest of the building. **www.danubiusgroup.com/astoria**

Danubius Hotel Erzsébet

🔃 🅿 🍴 🚹 🔢   ⓔⓔⓔ

Károlyi Mihály utca 11–15, 1053 **Tel** *889 37 00* **Fax** *889 37 63* **Rooms** *123*   **Map** *10 E5*

Despite the rather awful façade, this hotel almost in the very heart of Budapest is tremendous value. There's been a hotel on this site since 1873, though the current building went up in 1976. Renovated entirely in 2002, it offers comfortable rooms, all with large bathrooms, pay TV and sound-proofed windows. **www.danubiushotels.com**

Mercure Nemzeti

🔃 🅿 🍴 🚹 🔢   ⓔⓔⓔ

József körút 4, 1088 **Tel** *477 20 00* **Fax** *477 20 01* **Rooms** *76*   **Map** *7 B3*

Built at the end of 19th century, this remarkable, almost Art Deco-style hotel features an impressive grand staircase. Other main attractions are a brightly coloured façade and a Secession-style restaurant, which offers good food. Rooms are comfortable; those facing the courtyard are particularly pleasant. **www.mercure-nemzeti.hu**

Marriott

🔃 🅿 🍴 🚹 🔟 🔢   ⓔⓔⓔⓔ

Apáczai Csere János utca 4, 1052 **Tel** *486 50 00* **Fax** *486 50 05* **Rooms** *362*   **Map** *4 E1*

The Marriott's excellent facilities include banqueting rooms, three restaurants, a business centre, and a fitness centre. The rooms are of a high standard and the staff provide an exemplary level of service. It was here, in 1991, that the decision was taken to dissolve the Warsaw Pact. **www.marriott.com/budhu**

Mercure Budapest City Center

🔃 🍴 🚹 🔢   ⓔⓔⓔⓔ

Váci utca 20, 1052 **Tel** *485 31 00* **Fax** *485 31 11* **Rooms** *227*   **Map** *4 E1 (10 D4)*

This is the most centrally located hotel in Budapest, situated right on Vaci utca, or Váci Street *(see p127)*. The sound-proofed, elegant rooms are oases of calm amid the noise and bustle of this busy commercial district. Suites come with jacuzzis and saunas. The Zsolnay Café on the ground floor is famous for its pastries. **www.mercure.hu**

Mercure Budapest Korona

🔃 🅿 🍴 🚹 🔟 🔢   ⓔⓔⓔⓔ

Kecskeméti utca 14, 1053 **Tel** *486 88 00* **Fax** *318 38 67* **Rooms** *424*   **Map** *4 F2*

Big, modern and sophisticated, the Mercure Korona is situated in a small street off Kálvin tér, close to cafés and restaurants. The hotel has a wide range of amenities, including its own swimming pool, gymnasium, sauna and solarium. Room rates are reasonable, but breakfast costs an extra 15 euros. **www.mercure-korona.hu**

Corinthia Grand Hotel Royal

🔃 🅿 🍴 🚹 🔟 🔢   ⓔⓔⓔⓔⓔ

Erzsébet körút 43–49, 1073 **Tel** *479 40 00* **Fax** *479 43 33* **Rooms** *414*   **Map** *7 A2*

Behind its distinguished façade, what was the Grand Hotel Royal has been transformed into the modern and elegant Corinthia Grand Hotel Royal. The lobby is a joy in itself, setting a luxurious scene even before guests reach their rooms, which are equally stunning. All are classically furnished in mahogany. **www.corinthiahotels.com**

InterContinental

Apáczai Csere János utca 12–14, 1052 **Tel** *327 63 33* **Fax** *327 63 57* **Rooms** *398*   **Map** *2 D5 (9 C3).*

This luxury hotel, situated close to Pest's riverside promenade, offers a magnificent view across the Danube to Buda's Castle District. Rooms are enormous with wonderful bathrooms. The facilities include a cocktail bar and a buffet restaurant. The beautifully decorated Viennese Café is on the first floor. **www.budapest.intercontinental.com**

Kempinski Corvinus

Erzsébettér 7–8, 1051 **Tel** *429 37 77* **Fax** *429 47 77* **Rooms** *365*   **Map** *2 E5 (10 D5)*

This exclusive hotel – all glass and class – often welcomes heads of state and other notable personalities among its guests. The large and expensively furnished rooms are enormously relaxing, and perfectly mix luxury with modernity. The hotel has excellent fitness facilities, two good restaurants, bars and a pub. **www.kempinski-budapest.com**

Le Meridien Budapest

Erzsébet tér 9–10, 1050 **Tel** *429 55 00* **Fax** *429 55 55* **Rooms** *218*   **Map** *2 E5 (10 D5)*

Housed in the centrally located and tastefully renovated Adria Palace, Le Meridien Budapest is an elegantly furnished hotel, where attention to detail is evident. Standard-size rooms are among the largest in Budapest. The fitness centre is one of the city's best, complete with an enchanting plunge-pool and jacuzzi. **www.budapest.lemeridien.com**

Marriott Millennium Court

Pesti Barnabás utca 4, 1052 **Tel** *235 18 00* **Fax** *235 19 00* **Rooms** *108*   **Map** *4 E1*

A luxury, centrally located executive apartment block, with individual apartments available for the night or for longer. All apartments are serviced and impeccably tasteful. The price is not cheap but, for a family, taking space in one of these apartments can actually work out to be highly economical. **www.execapartments.com**

AROUND VÁROSLIGET

Golden Park

Baross tér 10, 1087 **Tel** *477 47 77* **Fax** *477 47 70* **Rooms** *172*   **Map** *7 C2 (10 F5)*

The Golden Park Hotel is located in the heart of the business centre, and has good public transport links to the city's major sights. Newly reconstructed and refurbished, it serves a rich buffet-style breakfast and offers comfortable accommodation for individuals and group travellers alike. **www.goldenparkhotel.com**

Ibis Budapest Váci út

Dózsa György út 65, 1134 **Tel** *329 02 00* **Fax** *340 83 16* **Rooms** *322*   **Map** *5 A1*

Almost equidistant from Margaret Island and City Park, the Ibis Vaci út is a hotel that appeals to families looking for a good base away from the crowds. Rooms are far from large, but well furnished and equipped, and bathrooms are surprisingly spacious. As with all Ibis hotels, the buffet breakfast is very good. **www.ibis.hu**

Radio Inn

Benczúr utca 19, 1068 **Tel** *342 83 47* **Fax** *342 83 84* **Rooms** *34*   **Map** *5 C4*

This pension-style hotel is the official guesthouse of Hungarian National Radio and entertains many visiting personalities. Accommodation is in spacious suites with well-equipped kitchens. Facilities are quite basic, but the Inn is ideal for families as it is situated in the peaceful embassy quarter and there is a garden. **www.radioinn.hu**

Unio

Dob utca 73, 1077 **Tel** *479 04 00* **Fax** *479 04 01* **Rooms** *52*   **Map** *7 B1*

The rooms in this reasonably priced hotel are not spectacular, but they are nicely furnished with tasteful wooden beds, wardrobes and desks, and bright blue carpets (that might be a little garish for some). Bathrooms have a bath and a toilet. There is a good restaurant, and breakfast is included in the room rate. **www.uniohotel.hu**

Benczúr

Benczúr utca 35, 1068 **Tel** *479 56 50* **Fax** *342 15 58* **Rooms** *93*   **Map** *5 C4*

Situated in a quiet street close to Városliget *(see p142)*, this hotel offers small but comfortable rooms. In addition, there is a good restaurant, as well as a terrace and a garden. Guests are able to make use of the services of an in-house dentist. Prices are sometimes considerably reduced out of the high season. **www.hotelbenczur.hu**

Best Western Grand Hotel Hungaria

Rákóczi út 90, 1074 **Tel** *889 44 00* **Fax** *889 44 11* **Rooms** *499*   **Map** *7 C2*

Reputedly the largest hotel in the country, the Hungaria could feel dark and forbidding, but it doesn't because recent renovations have added life and colour to the warren-like corridors that lead visitors to their rooms. Rooms are comfortable, though not big, and the location is super. **www.danubiusgroup.com/grandhotel-hungaria**

Liget

Dózsa György út 106, 1068 **Tel** *269 53 00* **Fax** *269 53 29* **Rooms** *139*   **Map** *5 C3*

Situated on the edge of the Hösök tere or Heroes' Square *(see pp142–3)*, close to the Museum of Fine Arts *(see pp146–9)*, the bright, modern Liget offers pleasant rooms, a sauna, a solarium, wireless Internet and a rent-a-bike scheme. The buffet breakfast (included in the price) is excellent. **www.liget.hu**

Key to Price Guide *see p182* **Key to Symbols** *see back cover flap*

Residence Izabella

Izabella utca 61, 1064 **Tel** *475 59 00* **Fax** *475 59 02* **Rooms** *38* **Map** *5 A5*

An apartment hotel offering spacious, one-, two- and three-bedroom apartments just off Budapest's most exclusive street, Andrássy út. There's a 24-hour reception, security, parking, and a health club with sauna. Apartments have DVD and sound systems, and fitted kitchens. Rates exclude parking and breakfast. **www.residenceizabella.com**

FURTHER AFIELD

Agro

Normafa út 54, 1121 **Tel** *458 39 00* **Fax** *458 39 01* **Rooms** *145*

This out-of-town hotel, situated on Sváb Hill *(see p161)*, retains echoes of Budapest's communist past. However, relaxing surroundings and good food are matched by excellent sports and leisure facilities. There are also splendid views, and walking in the Buda Hills *(see p161)* is an enjoyable pastime. **www.hotelagropanorama.hu**

Charles Apartment Hotel

Hegyalja út 23, 1016 **Tel** *212 91 69* **Fax** *202 29 84* **Rooms** *66* **Map** *3 B2*

The studio apartments are a bit larger than hotel rooms and have a tiny kitchen. Standard rooms are unrenovated, business-class rooms were recently given a makeover. Rooms on the quiet side of the building do not suffer from traffic noise in the morning. The hotel's restaurant is very good, and breakfast is a real treat. **www.charleshotel.hu**

Nordic

Gyopár utca 6, 1028 **Tel** *274 62 92* **Fax** *274 62 92* **Rooms** *12*

Simple but clean and bright rooms await guests at this miniature castle in the Buda Hills *(see p161)*. The tower at the front is striking. A good breakfast is available, though at a small extra cost, and there is a sauna and plunge pool for guests' use (also for a small fee). To get here, take Bus 56 from Moszkva tér. **www.hotelnordic.hu**

Panda

Pasaréti út 133, 1026 **Tel** *394 19 32* **Fax** *394 10 02* **Rooms** *28*

This small hotel in the somewhat troubling shape of a step pyramid is situated in Pasarét, a quiet and exclusive residential district of Buda. Rooms are a little like boxes, but the hotel in general offers a family atmosphere and a substantial, tasty breakfast. Bus 5 provides quick transport to the centre. **www.budapesthotelpanda.hu**

Platánus

Könyves Kálmán körút 44, 1087 **Tel** *333 65 05* **Fax** *210 43 86* **Rooms** *128*

A comfortable, inexpensive hotel situated on the edge of the People's Park and close to the Népliget metro station. From the outside it looks like a suburban block of flats, but inside it has clean, functional rooms, and offers good food. Other facilities available include a sauna, a solarium and an in-house doctor. **www.hunguesthotels.hu**

Vadvirág Panzió

Nagybányai út 18., 1025 **Tel** *275 02 00* **Fax** *394 42 92* **Rooms** *16*

A homely, family owned and operated pension, located in a quiet, green district of the Buda Hills *(see p161)*. There are comfortable rooms with balconies, and a restaurant, terrace and sauna. To get there, take Bus 11 from Batthany tér to the end of the line. **www.hotelvadvirangpanzio.hu**

Villa Korda

Szikla utca 9, 1025 **Tel** *325 91 23* **Fax** *325 91 27* **Rooms** *21*

The popular Hungarian singer, György Korda, built this exclusive pension-style hotel in a smart residential district on the slopes of Mátyás Hill. It offers a high standard of service and exclusive company. There is no lift, and it is best reached by car due to its location and the steep road that leads to it. A genuine bargain. **www.villakorda.com**

Boat Hotel Fortuna

Szent István Park, Alsó rakpart, 1137 **Tel** *288 81 00* **Fax** *270 03 51* **Rooms** *60* **Map** *2 D1*

For something out of the ordinary, try this boat-hotel-cum-youth-hostel on the Danube, moored next to Margaret Bridge on the Pest side of the river. Some of the rooms are surprisingly large, though some are smaller than a cabin boy's quarters. There's a bar and restaurant, and a super lounge with classy leather sofas. **www.fortunahajo.hu**

Bobbio

Béla Király út 47, 1121 **Tel** *274 40 00* **Fax** *395 83 77* **Rooms** *22*

A bargain. One of the best kept secrets in Budapest. Find it by taking Bus 28 from Moszkva tér to the end of the line. Set in a small house, the rooms all have individual charms – from sloping ceilings to garden views from small balconies – and modern facilities such as wireless Internet access. The buffet breakfast is superb. **www.bobbio.hu**

Budapest

Szilágyi Erzsébet fasor 47, 1026 **Tel** *889 42 00* **Fax** *889 42 03* **Rooms** *289*

This establishment was built in the late 1960s and was the pride of the local hotel industry for many years. Its unique cylindrical shape makes it a landmark still. Its location in the Buda Hills *(see p161)*, and the magnificent view from the roof terrace remains unrivalled. There are two restaurants and a wine cellar. **www.danubiusgroup.com/budapest**

Classic

Zólyomi út 6, 1118 **Tel** *319 72 22* **Fax** *319 34 50* **Rooms** *32*   **Map** *3 A4*

A lovely, almost alpine villa in the Buda foothills, with basic but homely accommodation at a good price. Rooms are quite big, a little austere but very clean and well looked after. There's a restaurant and a sauna, as well as conference and meeting rooms. Classic is reached by Bus 139 from Deli station (Metro Line 3). **www.classichotel.hu**

Gerand Hotel Ventura

Fehérvári út 179, 1119 **Tel** *208 12 32* **Fax** *208 12 41* **Rooms** *149*

The façade is intended to be Neo-Classical but is in fact Neo-Socialist, but that shouldn't put anyone off this presentable and well-run hotel. Rooms (some are non-smoking) are a reasonable size and furnished in a modern style. There's a fitness centre, and a restaurant with a small terrace. Dogs are welcome. **www.gerandhotels.hu**

Gizella

Arató utca 42/B, 1121 **Tel** *249 02 01* **Fax** *249 22 81* **Rooms** *8*

A small pension high up in the Buda hills that may be difficult to get to without a car, but is well worth the effort. Rooms are tasteful and comfortable, all with ensuite bathrooms, and there is a superb garden, complete with a small pool. Take Bus 8 from Március 15 tér to Farkasréti tér, then follow the signs. **www.gizellapanzio.hu**

Gloria

Bláthy Ottó utca 22, 1089 **Tel** *210 41 20* **Fax** *210 41 29* **Rooms** *28*

On the edge of Nepliget, the Gloria is a good hotel at a great price. Looking like a little cottage in the forest, it is not luxurious (the rooms are a bit stuffy), but there is enough here to keep most guests happy. Staff are very friendly and speak all major languages. Breakfast is included in the price. **www.hotelgloria.com**

Griff

Bartók Béla út 152, 1113 **Tel** *204 00 44* **Fax** *204 00 62* **Rooms** *108*

Hardly welcoming from the outside, nevertheless this three-star hotel offers more than adequate facilities, including colour television in small but bright rooms, and child-minding. There's an excellent fitness centre, including a sauna, jacuzzi, solarium and squash courts. The restaurant features live Hungarian music. **www.hunguesthotels.hu**

Helios Hotel & Pension

Lidérc utca 5/A, 1121 **Tel** *246 46 58* **Fax** *246 46 58* **Rooms** *11*

Situated in the Buda Hills, but not too far from the centre by Bus 8, Helios Panzio offers peace and quiet. Rooms and apartments are comfortable and clean, and most have balconies that overlook the city. There's also a pleasant breakfast terrace and garden. Breakfast is included in the room rate. **www.heliospanzio.hu**

Ibis Budapest Aero

Ferde utca 1–3, 1091 **Tel** *347 97 00* **Fax** *280 64 03* **Rooms** *139*

By virtue of its situation close to Ferihegy airport, this hotel is particularly convenient for those making only a short visit to Budapest. The rooms are cosy and tastefully decorated, and there are suites for families and rooms for non-smokers. All rooms have balconies, and some are adapted for the use of disabled guests. **www.ibis-aero.hu**

Mediterran

Budaörsi út 20/A, 1118 **Tel** *372 70 20* **Fax** *372 70 21* **Rooms** *40*   **Map** *3 A2*

This bright hotel is a good choice for people who don't mind being a bus ride away from the city centre. Rooms are well sized and have modern facilities including wireless Internet, and bathrooms with both a bath and a shower. Bus 112 from Ferenciek tér reaches Mediterran in about 10 minutes. Children welcome. **www.hotelmediterran.hu**

Mohácsi Panzió

Bimbó út 25/A, 1022 **Tel** *326 77 41* **Fax** *326 7784* **Rooms** *9*

Small, pleasant and inexpensive, this pension is located just off Margit körút, in the Rózsadomb area of the Buda Hills *(see p161)*. Rooms are clean and have either a shower or a bath, and television. Those on the upper floor have marvellous views of Budapest. Underground parking costs 5 euros. **www.hotelmohacsipanzio.hu**

Molnár Panzió

Fodor utca 143, 1124 **Tel** *395 18 73* **Fax** *395 18 74* **Rooms** *23*

A mid-range pension in a residential district on the slopes of the Buda Hills *(see p161)*. Its green surroundings add to the homely atmosphere and offer guests complete peace. Family rooms are available. The amenities include a bar, fitness facilities and secure parking. There's also a restaurant with a bright, sunny terrace. **www.hotel-molnar.hu**

NH Budapest

Vígszínház utca 3, 1137 **Tel** *814 00 00* **Fax** *814 01 00* **Rooms** *160*

Smart and stylish hotel north of Nyugati station. Rooms are not large, but are well furnished, with many extras – including high-speed Internet access – and terrific bathrooms. A delicious breakfast is included in the price, and on-site dining is good. The bar is popular late in the evening. Fitness facilities include a sauna. **www.nh-hotels.com**

Normafa

Eötvösút 52–54, 1121 **Tel** *395 65 05* **Fax** *395 65 04* **Rooms** *62*

Guests have the option of indulging in complete relaxation at the Normafa, or exploring the beautiful scenery on foot. All rooms have terraces, and there is a large swimming pool, a sauna, tennis courts, a restaurant, a café and a beer bar. Rooms are not the biggest in the world, but represent terrific value for money. **www.normafahotel.com**

Key to Price Guide *see p182*   **Key to Symbols** *see back cover flap*

Rege

Pálos utca 2, 1021 **Tel** *391 51 00* **Fax** *200 88 24* **Rooms** *164*

An ugly glass and concrete high-rise building in the Buda Hills *(see p161)*, this hotel surprises by offering peace and quiet, beautiful views, and recreational facilities including a fitness centre with sauna. It is often patronized by actors. Rooms may be a little old fashioned, but they are more than adequate. **hunguesthotels.hu**

Veritas

Mogyoródi út 8, 1143 **Tel** *273 22 33* **Fax** *222 47 92* **Rooms** *54*

Yellow, orange and blue from the outside, the Veritas is no less garish inside. Rooms are well sized with large, comfortable beds and TV, though bathrooms are smallish – most have shower and toilet only. Breakfast is included in the room rate, and airport transfers are available at extra cost. **www.hotelveritas.hu**

Budai

Rácz Aladár út 45–47, 1121 **Tel** *249 02 08* **Fax** *249 21 86* **Rooms** *23*

Small but charming pension, well hidden from the city's bustle in the Buda Hills *(see p161)*. Some of the rooms have a great view, and some have balconies. (Not all do, so it is a good idea to ask when booking.) The best are loft rooms, with wooden beams and sloping ceilings. Tram 59 (from Moszkva tér) stops right outside. **www.hotelbudai.hu**

Danubius Grand Hotel Margitsziget

Margitsziget, 1138 **Tel** *889 47 00* **Fax** *889 49 39* **Rooms** *164*

This hotel on Margaret Island *(see pp172–3)* is linked by a tunnel to the Danubius Thermal Hotel, whose spa facilities guests at the Grand can use. Other attractions include shaded terrace cafés and restaurants, a swimming pool and tranquil walks. Bike hire is also available. **www.danubiusgroup.com/grandhotel**

Danubius Health Spa Resort Helia

Kárpátutca 62–64, 1133 **Tel** *889 58 00* **Fax** *889 58 01* **Rooms** *262*

One of the most modern spa hotels in Budapest. Light and airy, and located on the bank of the Danube with views of the boats on the river and Margaret Island *(see pp172–3)* . The Helia offers a full range of health and beauty facilities including massage, thermal waters and qualified medical advice. **www.danubiusgroup.com/helia**

Danubius Health Spa Resort Margitsziget

Margitsziget, 1138 **Tel** *889 47 00* **Fax** *889 49 88* **Rooms** *267*

The hotel hosts one of Europe's leading wellness centres, and sits on top of a natural spa that brings water to the surface at 70°C. It is then cooled to a range of temperatures and used for healing all sorts of ailments. The rooms are recently renovated, and offer comfort and luxury. Good restaurants. **www.danubiushotels.com/thermalhotel**.

Novotel Budapest Congress

Alkotásutca 63–67, 1123 **Tel** *372 54 00* **Fax** *466 56 36* **Rooms** *319*

Map *3 A2*

Situated in the immediate vicinity of the Congress and World Trade Centre *(see p160)*, the hotel offers modern rooms, swimming pool, sauna, bowling alley and cocktail bar. There is also a large car park. The reception rooms and banqueting halls can accommodate approximately 2,500 people. **www.novotel-bud-congress.hu**

Rubin Hotel & Business Center

Dayka Gábor utca 3, 1118 **Tel** *505 36 00* **Fax** *505 36 01* **Rooms** *85*

There are various relaxation and sporting facilities at this modern hotel, including sauna, swimming pool, tennis courts and bowling alley. In a quiet location close to the M1 and M7 motorways, the accommodation includes some suites with kitchenettes and some larger maisonettes for families. **www.hotelrubin.com**

Sissi

Angyal utca 33, 1094 **Tel** *215 00 82* **Fax** *216 60 63* **Rooms** *44*

Sissi was the affectionate name by which Hungarians referred to Empress Elizabeth, wife of Emperor Franz Joseph. She certainly did not stay in this modern and rather odd-looking hotel, but she might have enjoyed the luxury of the rooms, most of which have small balconies. There is a nice garden and terrace, too. **www.hotelsissi.hu**

Ramada Plaza Budapest

Árpádfejedelem utca 94, 1036 **Tel** *436 41 00* **Fax** *436 41 56* **Rooms** *310*

This hotel offers everything guests need to relax or to improve their health. Facilities include a swimming pool, hot- and warm-water spas, a jacuzzi and sauna, massage and a gymnasium. There is a resident doctor, and some staff are dedicated to the needs of disabled guests. Some rooms have views of the Danube. **www.corinthiahotels.com**

Adina Apartment Hotel Budapest

Hegedűs Gyula utca 52–54, 1133 **Tel** *236 88 88* **Tel** *236 88 99* **Rooms** *97*

Map *2 F1*

Total luxury. Modern, serviced apartments are set around an exclusive, leafy courtyard. There is an indoor swimming pool, jacuzzi, steam room, gym, parking and 24-hour security. The apartments and studios are huge, far bigger than any hotel room in the city. Prices are deservedly high. Long-term rentals are available. **www.adina.eu**

Hunguest Aparthotel Europa

Hárshegyi út 5–7, 1021 **Tel** *391 23 00* **Fax** *391 23 99* **Rooms** *91*

Modern, exclusive apartment-hotel in the Buda Hills *(see p161)*. Accommodation ranges from large apartments to studios. All rooms have a fully equipped kitchen, and upper floors have great views. Guests can use the facilities of the neighbouring Rege hotel *(see p189)* for an additional fee. Breakfast is included. **www.hunguesthotels.hu**

RESTAURANTS, CAFES AND BARS

Following a visit to Budapest, the Nobel Prize-winning Latin American writer Miguel Ángel Asturias said that "the exquisite taste of Hungarian cuisine is a language understood by all". The numerous restaurants, cafés and bars in Budapest give the visitor ample opportunity to sample the delights of this distinctive cuisine. The most typical examples of

Hungarian coffee

traditional Hungarian cooking can be seen on pages 192–3, while information on what to drink is given on pages 194–5. A detailed guide to the city's best restaurants, highlighting Hungarian specialities and covering a selection of price categories, is provided on pages 196–205. Cafés, wine bars, beer houses, pubs and clubs can be found on pages 206–9.

WHERE TO LOOK

There are a great many eating establishments in Budapest and the surrounding suburbs. Good traditional Hungarian dishes can be found within all price ranges in restaurants and inns, but in recent years Budapest has seen the arrival of cuisine from all over the world. Among the ethnic eating options now available are Italian, Greek, Chinese and Thai restaurants. American-style fast food chains are also appearing and are rapidly becoming popular.

The city's main tourist areas are well off for places to eat, but may not offer the best fare or prices. It is often worth looking off the main roads or away from popular areas to find establishments frequented by local Budapest residents. The restaurants, cafés and bars on Váci utca (Váci Street, *see p127*) are notorious for over-charging, especially at night.

Entrance to Ruszwurm Cukrászda (see p207), in the Castle District

TYPES OF RESTAURANTS, CAFES AND BARS

Budapest offers a variety of places to eat and a range of prices to suit most budgets. The differences between the types of establishments can be subtle, but they break down roughly into the following types. *Étterem* simply means restaurant – any type of cuisine may be served. A *csárda* comes in various forms. Most are folky restaurants typically offering interesting local specialities. A fisherman's *csárda*, known as a *halászcsárda*, will offer mainly fish dishes and soups. There are two types of inn, a *vendéglő*, which has an informal ambience, and a *kisvendéglő*, (literally a "small inn"), which is similar to a cosy pub. Cafés range from a *kávéház* (coffee house) to a *cukrászda* (patisserie), and types of bars include a *borozó*, a *söröző* and an *eszpresszó* (see pp206–9).

Lantern outside the Gerbeaud Cukrászda

WHAT TO ORDER

Ordering a Hungarian meal may not be as simple as it may first seem. There are many different varieties of Hungarian soups, some of which are a meal in themselves. *Bogrács*, which is often served in a kettle, and bean soups are the heartiest soups and would normally be followed by a light, hot pudding or pancakes. Hungarian fish soup is a particular speciality

and owes its red colour to paprika. This should be followed by delicate home-made noodles served with crackling, cheese and cream. There are also many light soups, or small portions of the more substantial soups, which can be eaten as a starter, thus leaving room for the main course.

The archetypal Hungarian main dish is goulash soup (*gulyás leves)* and there are several versions of the basic thick meat stew. Another Hungarian speciality is *pörkölt* (a paprika stew very similar to goulash). This stew is made with lean meat such as veal, poultry or fish, with sour cream added at the end of cooking. Almost all meals are eaten with bread; the white wheat variety is particularly delicious.

Food served in bars or bought from street kiosks is a different matter. More akin to fast food, it is often eaten standing up or on the move. Spicy sausages, liberally seasoned with paprika and garlic are served grilled or boiled. Grilled chicken and various smoked meats are also widely available. Another alternative is the delicious *lángos* (pronounced "langosh"), which is sold at markets. This flat, savoury, yeast cake is served with cream or cheese.

For more detailed information see *What to Eat* in Budapest on pages 192–3.

VEGETARIAN FOOD

Vegetarian cuisine *per se* is not found in abundance in Budapest. There are very few vegetarian restaurants, of which one, Govinda, is recommended in this guide *(see p198)*. Ethnic restaurants may offer a wider vegetarian choice.

Nevertheless, meat-free dishes can be found on most Hungarian menus. *Főzelék*, a vegetable dish that normally accompanies steak, sausage or a hamburger, can be ordered on its own or with egg. *Lecsó* is another popular vegetable side dish that makes a substantial meal by itself. Other specialities include *túrós csusza*, a pasta dish served with cottage cheese, sour cream and bacon. There are also many sweet and savoury *palacsinta* (pancakes).

RESERVING A TABLE

In Hungary it is customary to join other guests at a table, especially during the busy lunch period. To secure a private table, it is advisable to book in advance. This applies equally to Budapest's exclusive restaurants and cheaper establishments.

MENUS AND PRICES

All Hungarian restaurants display a menu by the entrance, and, as a rule, this is translated into English or German. The name of the dish is followed by a brief description. The day's "specials" – a set meal consisting of a soup, a main course and a dessert –

A charming outdoor café on Margaret Island

are listed at the head of the menu. Set menus are often very good value and provide an ideal opportunity to sample several Hungarian specialities.

The prices should also be displayed. If they are not, it is wise to go elsewhere or at least see the prices, including any surcharges, before ordering the meal. The introduction of printed and itemized bills has made it more difficult for hidden "extras" to be added to the final bill.

In most Hungarian restaurants the waiters tend to round up the bill, particularly when serving foreign customers. This practice led to a minor scandal in 1997 when several embassies, including the American and British delegations, compiled a blacklist of dishonest restaurants, after receiving numerous complaints, and published it on the Internet. The government closed the offending establishments and the situation has

now improved. Visitors should still be cautious, however. By selecting a restaurant from those listed in this guide *(see pp196–205)*, this problem should be easily avoided.

TIPPING

In some restaurants a service charge is included in the final bill, in others it is customary to tip. If a service charge is added, this should be stated on either the menu or the bill; this could be up to 15 per cent. However, if there is any doubt, it is courteous to leave a tip. In general, an acceptable tip is between 10–15 per cent of the cost of the meal.

CHILDREN

Children are welcomed in all restaurants without exception. If children's portions do not appear on the menu, the chef will prepare suitable dishes to order. These are usually charged at half price. The only exception is dessert, but this can often be shared. However, the desserts in Hungarian restaurants are so delicious that most children will happily eat a whole portion.

OUTDOOR EATING

Hungarian summers are long and dry, and eating *al fresco* has been popular throughout the country, and especially in the capital, since the early 1930s. Those who are looking for a quick lunch or to stop for coffee and watch the world go by during their city wanderings, should head for one of two recently redeveloped and fashionable locations on the Pest side of the Danube: Liszt Ferenc tér *(see p206)*, which runs off Andrássy út, not far from Oktogon metro station; or Ráday utca, which starts at Kálvin tér. Both areas are full of cosy restaurants, bars and cafés, and attract a youthful clientele. Every kind of restaurant can be found in these locations, too – from those serving traditional Hungarian food to Italian, Chinese and even Argentinian establishments.

The coffee shop at the Four Seasons Gresham Palace Hotel *(see p114)*

The Flavours of Budapest

The fusion of Magyar, Turkish, Balkan and even French influences has made Hungarian cuisine one of the most interesting and flavourful in central Europe. Hungary is a country where cooking know-how has always been a key aspect of the national culture. The improvised stews of nomadic Asiatic settlers survive as a delicacy to this day. Noted for its game, *foie gras* and rich meaty preparations, such as goulash and the legendary Debrecziner sausages, it is also a good place to enjoy freshwater fish and an array of delicious cakes and pastries.

Hungarian peppers

Sausages and cured meats on sale in the Central Market

MEAT

Beef is Hungary's favourite meat and, as a result, is produced in large quantities, usually to a very high standard. Cuts of beef are a regular feature on Hungarian tables and menus, especially in Budapest, and veal is becoming increasingly

popular too. Steak is widely dished up, often with a rich sauce as in *Budapest módra* (Budapest medallions). Beef is also used to make the many different types of goulash, although pork is another key ingredient in this dish, especially when it is prepared as *gulyásleves* (goulash soup). Pork is found in a wide range of other stews and sausages, and is eaten as bacon.

POULTRY & GAME

Geese are an important farmyard animal in Hungary, which is the world's second biggest producer of *foie gras* (after France). *Foie gras* is almost the national dish, usually cooked in its own fat and served warm. It is also found in pâtés and *confits*. Goose skin is widely enjoyed too, fried in its own fat and served with pickles.

Chestnut slice
Chocolate marzipan cake
Chocolate wafer cake
"Domino" cake
Apple slice
Poppy seed slice
Cheesecake

Selection of typical Hungarian cakes and pastries

LOCAL DISHES AND SPECIALITIES

Despite strong foreign influences, the classic dishes of Hungary dominate menus in the restaurants and cafés of Budapest. Many show their roots in one of the country's three historical regions. Goulash and its many variants, for example, is a dish of the Great Plain, the traditional method of cooking it in a kettle reflecting the nomadic past of the Plain's inhabitants. *Foie gras* may have been introduced into the country by the Austrian Habsburgs, but has become so popular

White asparagus that it is key to the cuisine of eastern Hungary, where most geese are now bred. The centre of the country, and the area around Budapest, has always had the sweetest tooth and nearly all the nation's favourite cakes and desserts originate from here.

Lángos *Crisp and golden, these deep-fried potato cakes make a popular, filling snack, served with soured cream.*

Market stall, laden with root vegetables and strings of dried peppers

Duck is another regular on Hungarian menus, frequently roasted with chestnuts or berries and served with red cabbage. Partridge may also be on offer, roasted with bacon and herbs. Rabbit, hare and venison are common as well, usually dished-up in spicy, goulash-style sauces.

FISH

Trout is probably the most widely eaten fish, although carp, perch, roach, zander and even eels can be found on most menus. A popular soup is *balászlé*, made with trout and carp and seasoned with a generous dash of paprika. Another favourite is *csuka teifölös tormával* (pike in horseradish sauce). Many Budapest restaurants offer a variety of imported fish, but these are usually expensive.

VEGETABLES

Potatoes, parsnips and cabbage are usually the main vegetables. But from May to July, fine white asparagus appears on market stalls, with many restaurants

Roasting chestnuts, a common sight on Budapest's winter streets

serving *spárgaleves*, a rich creamy soup made from asparagus and veal stock.

Paprika peppers are a culinary staple. They are either cooked as part of a dish – *töltött paprika* (peppers stuffed with meat and rice) are served up everywhere – or dried and ground up to be used as a spice. There are hundreds of different types of ground paprika, which vary in flavour and strength, but they all fit into seven broad categories: "special" (sweet and very mild); "mild" (faintly spicy); "delicatesse" (slightly hot); "sweet" (mild but fairly aromatic); "semi-sweet" (medium hot); "rose" (hot); and "hot" (fiery).

BEST LOCAL SNACKS

Sausages Street vendors everywhere offer the lightly smoked Debrecziner sausage, made from beef, pork, paprika and garlic. It is generally eaten with bread and mustard.

Chestnuts In winter, Budapest is crammed with stalls selling freshly roasted chestnuts.

Pancakes, fritters and doughnuts Snack bars all over the country serve tasty, fried, doughy snacks all day long. Try *alma pongyolában* (apple fritters).

Gingerbread Shops devoted to selling gingerbread are everywhere. At Christmas it is often highly decorated and given as a present.

Budapest Módra *Slices of fine sirloin steak are lightly cooked and served in a creamy, peppered sauce.*

Gulyásleves *A type of goulash, this pork, beef and vegetable soup is flavoured with garlic, caraway and paprika.*

Dobos torta *Fine slices of sponge cake are layered with chocolate cream and topped with chocolate icing.*

What to Drink in Budapest

Hungary is famous for its excellent wines and, although it is not a big country, it has as many as 22 wine regions. These regions produce all the characteristic wine styles, from *pezsgő* (sparkling wine) and light whites that come from Mátra, near Lake Balaton, to dry reds from Villány or Eger, as well as Tokaji, a distinctive sweet dessert wine. Many wines from different vineyards are matured in a maze of underground of cellars in Budafok. They are all widely available in Budapest's many restaurants, wine bars and wine shops. As well as being a prominent wine producer, Hungary also makes beer, *pálinka* (a drink distilled from different orchard fruits), several types of brandy and a bitter herb liqueur called Unicum.

American-style drinks cabinet

Light Hungarian beers

HUNGARIAN BEERS

In recent years Hungarians have been turning increasingly to beer as their chosen drink as it goes exceptionally well with many traditional, paprika-flavoured Hungarian dishes, goulash among them. There are three remaining authentic Hungarian breweries. These are Arany Ászok, Kőbányai (which was established in the Kőbánya district of Budapest some 150 years ago) and the excellent Dreher. Unfortunately, many other formerly Hungarian breweries have now been taken over by large foreign corporations. However, many of these brands are also well known and all are widely available in Budapest.

PÁLINKA

Kecskemét is the largest region that produces the alcoholic drink *pálinka,* which is distilled from fruit grown in the orchards situated on the Great Hungarian Plain, some 100 km (60 miles) southeast of Budapest. *Pálinka* is a spirit native to Hungary and comes in a variety of flavours including *barack* (apricot) and *cseresznye* (cherry). The best of them, however, is *szilva* (plum) which comes from the Szatmár district and is much favoured by the Hungarians. *Pálinka* is not the only spirit indigenous to Hungary. Other examples include Törköly, a spirit distilled from rape, which possesses a very delicate flavour, and Vilmos, a brandy made from Williams pears.

Barack pálinka

Pezsgő by Törley and Hungaria

the first production plant in Budafok, which continues to produce excellent sparkling wines over 100 years on. Today, Hungary has several other vineyards producing *pezsgő*, mainly concentrated around Budapest, in the Pannonia and Balatonboglár regions. As well as Törley, Hungaria is another good label to look out for.

SPARKLING WINES

Sparkling wine, called *pezsgő* (the Hungarian word for "sparkling"), enjoys a good reputation in Hungary. The classic method of producing these wines was introduced to Hungary from France by József Törley, in 1881. It was Törley (see p161) who built

HUNGARIAN WINES

The choice of good wine available in Hungary has increased dramatically over the past few years. This is thanks to the ever-improving wines being matured in private cellars. The styles currently

One of Budafok's cellars, where wines are aged in barrels

Egri Bikavér, "Bulls' Blood", a full-bodied red wine

A dry white wine from the Badacsony vineyards

SPRITZERS

On hot days, Hungarians enjoy drinking refreshing spritzers. The various types are differentiated by the proportion of white wine to soda water:

Quantity of wine	Quantity of water
Small spritzer (Kisfröccs)	
10 cl	10 cl
Large spritzer (Nagyfröccs)	
20 cl	10 cl
Long step (Hosszúlépés)	
10 cl	20 cl
Janitor (Házmester)	
30 cl	20 cl

favoured by the producers include dry white Chardonnay and Reisling, medium-dry Zödszilváni, Hárslevelű and Szürkebarát, medium-sweet Tramini and the aromatic Muskotály, which is produced in Badacsony, Balatonboglár, Csopak and Somló.

Among red wines, the dry Kékfrankos, Burgundi, Oportó, Cabernet and Pinot Noir are popular, as is the medium-dry Merlot, which is produced in Siklós, Sopron, Szekszárd, Tihány and Villány.

Another vine-growing district is Eger, which is famous for its aromatic, robust red Egri Leányka and the dry red Egri Bikavér, or "Bulls' Blood", which is produced from a combination of three grape varieties. Other Hungarian wines take their names from their place of origin or the variety of grape from which they are produced.

TOKAJI

The dessert wine Tokaji has a very different style. Its bouquet and flavour come from a mould that grows only in the fork of the Bodrog and Tisza rivers and the volcanic soil in which the vines grow.

Tokaji ranges from sweet to dry and is full-bodied and rich. Particularly worth sampling is Aszú, which is made with the addition of over-ripe grapes harvested after the first frost. The proportion of these grapes added to the must (grape juice) determines the wine's body and sweetness. The more of these grapes used, the sweeter and richer the Aszú.

Although cheap varieties of Tokaji do exist, they do not share the quality of the genuine article.

Unicum herb liqueur

UNICUM

For over 150 years, a blend of 40 Hungarian herbs has been used to create Unicum. The herbs, which are gathered in three separate areas, are combined to produce this bitter liqueur. Unicum can be drunk either as an apéritif before a meal or afterwards as a digestif with coffee.

The recipe has been held by the Zwack family, and remained a secret, since the reign of King Franz I (see p19). Originally, Unicum was prescribed as a remedy for the king by the court physician, who was himself a member of the Zwack family.

Sweet Tokaji Szamorodni

Dry Tokaji Szamorodni

Tokaji Aszú, a renowned golden dessert wine

Pear-flavoured Vilmos liqueur

Sisi, an apricot liqueur

Choosing a Restaurant

The restaurants in this section have been selected for their good value and exceptional food. Within each area, entries are listed alphabetically within each price category, from the least to the most expensive. For details of Budapest's best cafés and bars, beer halls, pubs and clubs, refer to pp206–09.

PRICE CATEGORIES
For a three-course meal for one with half a bottle of wine, including all unavoidable charges and service:

Ⓕ under 3,000 HUF
ⒻⒻ 3,000–4,000 HUF
ⒻⒻⒻ 4,000–5,000 HUF
ⒻⒻⒻⒻ 5,000–6,000 HUF
ⒻⒻⒻⒻⒻ over 6,000 HUF

CASTLE DISTRICT

Pierrot Café Restaurant
Fortuna utca 14, 1014 **Tel** 375 69 71   Map 1 B4

This popular place opened as a private café during socialist times when it was one of a kind. Though it now faces stiff competition, it still attracts a loyal crowd. The café has been redesigned but retains the original, elegant interior and a cosy café atmosphere. Live piano music in the evening, and all day at weekends. **www.pierrot.hu**

Pest Buda Vendéglő
Fortuna utca 3, 1014 **Tel** 212 58 80   Map 1 B4

Small, elegant restaurant with arcaded walls in a listed building. Part of an ancient system of underground caves, the restaurant provides space for a popular and extensive Hungarian and international wine cellar. The food menu itself is not all that extensive, but is interesting nevertheless, and everything is excellently prepared.

Alabárdos Étterem
Országház utca 2, 1014 **Tel** 356 08 51   Map 1 B4

A truly exclusive place in an outstanding Gothic building. Hungarian specialities of pre-paprika times are made to please today's taste buds. Everything from the service to the atmosphere reeks of class, though the prices are as expensive as anywhere in the city. Guitar music adds to the candle-lit medieval atmosphere. **www.alabardos.hu**

Rivalda Café & Restaurant
Színház utca 5–9, 1014 **Tel** 489 02 36   Map 1 C5

Next to the Castle Theatre, with tasteful theatre-inspired décor. Contemporary international cuisine with a frequently changing menu reflects the seasons, and most dishes are based on local, fresh ingredients. Many dishes are inventive, and all are superbly presented. There's pleasant jazz piano music in the evenings. **www.rivalda.net**

GELLÉRT & TABÁN

Siesta
Villányi út 4, 1114 **Tel** 466 24 05   Map 4 D5

Siesta is a small, family-friendly air-conditioned restaurant in the heart of Buda. The menu has mainly Mediterranean dishes, although it does include Hungarian specialities and a variety of international cuisine. Goose is featured on the menu on Mondays.

Beck's
Bartók Béla út 76, 1113 **Tel** 385 33 48   Map 3 C5

The rather unadventurous but reliable Beck's restaurant is located in the heart of Buda, and serves up Tex Mex food. There are salads, too, some pasta and loads of very sweet desserts, and this is a popular choice for the new Budapest rich who are making the surrounding area one of the city's most expensive.

Hemingway
Kosztolányi Dezső tér 2, (on Feneketlen Lake), 1113 **Tel** 381 05 22 ext 103   Map 3 C5

Papa Hemingway sure knew how to live large. He would have appreciated the spread-out, island-resort feel of this restaurant, set on a small lake. The terrace is one of Budapest's more impressive al fresco dining venues. The menu's flexible, and offers plenty of choice. Weekend lunchtime "playhouse" for children. **www.hemingway-etterem.hu**

Márványmenyasszony Étterem
Márvány utca 6, 1012 **Tel** 487 30 90   Map 3 A1

An old-style Hungarian restaurant with a fine gypsy band every night. Although hidden away, tourists tend to make the effort to find it, as tales of fine food, great prices and a relaxed atmosphere are legendary. Its many different rooms make it a great choice for groups, families or those wanting peace and quiet. **www.marvanymenyasszony.hu**

Key to Symbols see back cover flap

Szeged Étterem.

Bartók Béla út 1, 114 **Tel** *209 16 68*

Map *4 E3*

Next to the Gellért Hotel *(see pp90–91)*, this is a traditional Hungarian restaurant offering a good selection of specialities including several river fish dishes. The *Szegedi halászlé* (Szeged fish soup) is particularly tasty. A lively gypsy band belts out local popular favourites every evening. **www.szegedvendeglo.hu**

Citadella Étterem

Citadella sétány, 1118 **Tel** *386 48 02*

Map *4 D3*

The casements of the Citadel up above southern Buda have been turned into a restaurant of several rooms, all of which can suffer from disappearing wait staff. Once that problem is dealt with, the menu is a joy of traditional Hungarian food, though prices are steep. A gypsy band plays every night. **www.citadella.hu**

Marcello

Bartók Béla út 40, 1111 **Tel** *466 6231*

Map *4 E4*

A super little treat where all sorts of tourists, locals, expatriates and businessmen meet and become equals. Housed in a cellar accessed by a low staircase, Marcello is famed for its pasta and its great salad bar – there is a wide range of choice for vegetarians. Make a reservation if you want to get a table in the evening.

Búsuló Juhász Étterem

Kelenhegyi út 58, 1118 **Tel** *209 16 49*

Map *3 C3*

Traditional Hungarian restaurant on the western slopes of Gellért Hill, offering spectacular views and pleasant gypsy music. A wide choice of Hungarian specialities have been made lighter in the spirit of international gastronomy, but the often astronomically priced bill can leave a nasty aftertaste. **www.busulojuhasz.hu**

NORTH OF THE CASTLE

À la carte Kisétterem

Iskola utca 29, 1011 **Tel** *202 05 80*

Map *1 C3*

There is a small and really rather charming restaurant conveniently situated near Batthyány tér (on the red metro line). There is an unusually wide choice of fish dishes on the respectably long menu, and everything is given a homely, home-cooked touch by two caring chefs. Reservation is recommended for both lunch and dinner.

Csalogány Étterem és Kávézó

Csalogány utca 26, 1015 **Tel** *201 78 92*

Map *1 A3*

Popular and trendy restaurant/café with a modern, bright and breezy Mediterranean interior. Excellent poultry, fish and meat dishes are all grilled on lava stones for a real burst of flavour. For such a meat-orientated place, there's also a surprisingly good selection of vegetarian dishes and salads. A small selection of good wines. **www.csalogany26.hu**

Georgian Restaurant

Frankel Leó utca 30–34, 1015 **Tel** *326 04 06*

Map *1 B1*

A somewhat less than original name for a nevertheless super restaurant close to the Margaret Bridge. The food is impeccably authentic, featuring enormous shashlik kebabs cooked by Georgian chefs on a huge open grill. The decor is less Georgian, and far more contemporary. The homemade Georgian bread is great.

Arany Kaviár

Ostrom utca 19, 1015 **Tel** *201 67 37*

Map *1 A3*

Superb Russian seafood restaurant where, provided you do not over-indulge in caviar, you need not spend a fortune. Most dishes are based around fish and seafood, but there are Russian specialities on the menu, too, such as *pelmenyi* (Russian ravioli). Also, a surprisingly good vegetarian selection. **www.aranykaviar.hu**

Le Jardin de Paris

Fő utca 20, 1011 **Tel** *201 0047*

Map *1 C5*

This French restaurant is impressive in every aspect. The building is a national treasure, and protected as such, and the main dining room is a sparsely decorated, tasteful treat. The service is efficient and friendly without being pretentious, and live jazz softens the mood most evenings. The food is international-French, and there's a garden.

Fekete Hollo

Országház utca 10, 1014 **Tel** *356 2367*

Map *1 B4*

In a terrific location up on Castle Hill, this little gem is a traditional Hungarian restaurant where the kitsch medieval decor does little to detract from the excellent food. All Hungarian favourites are on the menu, though there is little for vegetarians. Service can be slow, but that's because the place is always full of happy diners.

Kacsa

Fő utca 75, 1027 **Tel** *201 99 92*

Map *1 C2*

Kasca serves some of the finest food in the country. The service is as ostentatious as the food is splendid, with dishes presented under silver serving domes, whisked away with great ceremony. Though duck dominates the menu, there is far more on offer, including inventive vegetarian options. Outstanding, but dreadfully expensive.

AROUND PARLIAMENT

Belvárosi Lugas Étterem
Bajcsy-Zsilinszky út 15/A, 1065 **Tel** *302 53 93*　　　　　　　　　　**Map** *2 E4*

Well-made, hearty dishes are served in a simple, appealing atmosphere. It's a favourite with locals, informal and relaxed. The food is great value, especially the daily specials that are chalked up on a blackboard. Great soups. In the summer a terrace is set up on the pavement, although constant traffic noise may disturb any conversation.

Govinda
Vigyázó Ferenc utca 4, 1051 **Tel** *473 13 10*　　　　　　　　　　**Map** *2 D4*

Popular at lunchtimes. this fast food-style restaurant serves vegetarian meals and salads. Here, no meat doesn't mean no flavour. In fact, some of the dishes are hotter than many people will ever have tasted – choose carefully. There's a shop attached, selling Eastern-style gifts and Krishna literature, and a meditation room.

Művész Vendéglő
Vígszínház utca 5, 1136 **Tel** *784 44 83*　　　　　　　　　　**Map** *2 E2*

Located behind the Vígszínház (Variety Theatre), this is an intimate, homely restaurant. The walls display photos of theatre personalities and, with its antique furniture, it looks like a grandmother's dining room. The cooking is also home-style and simple, but effortlessly tasty. A late breakfast is served.

Via Luna
Nagysándor József utca 1, 1054 **Tel** *312 80 58*　　　　　　　　　　**Map** *2 E4*

A truly Italian place, owned and operated by Italians, with an extensive menu of trattoria favourites. Excellent pasta is made on the premises, which is a rarity in Budapest, and so word has got out and the restaurant is always crowded. It is best to reserve a table. Both Hungarian and Italian wines are available.

Café Kör
Sas utca 17, 1051 **Tel** *311 00 53*　　　　　　　　　　**Map** *2 E4*

Popular bistro-style place, serving good salad plates and Hungarian/European-inspired dishes. None will win prizes, but all offer great value. Vegetarian food is made to order. A good selection of Hungarian wines offered by the glass betray the fact that this was once a wine bar. Reserving is recommended.

Cotton Club
Jókai utca 26, 1066 **Tel** *354 08 86*　　　　　　　　　　**Map** *2 F3*

Part of a three-part project on the same premises – with Cotton Club bar *(see p209)* and Cotton House hotel *(see p185)* – the restaurant is classy and clean, and serves unusual dishes in a unique atmosphere. It's a great place for a long evening: eat, then head downstairs for the live music. **www.cottonclub.hu**

Dzsungel
Jókai utca 30, 1065 **Tel** *302 40 03*　　　　　　　　　　**Map** *2 F3*

Children love Dzsungel (it means jungle), decorated as it is with parrots and monkeys and elephants, all making a vocal contribution at regular intervals. Most of the really rather original food is a little too fancy for some children, but there are more simple dishes on offer if you ask. A 10% service charge is imposed. **www.crazycafe.hu**

Marquis de Salade
Hajós utca 43, 1065 **Tel** *302 40 86*　　　　　　　　　　**Map** *2 F4*

This wonderfully named restaurant boasts an extensive menu featuring recipes from around the world, including interesting lamb dishes from Azerbaijan and Georgia. Basic Hungarian fare, such as *goulash*, is also on offer. Vegetarians have plenty to choose from, too. The reasonable prices are rare in this part of town.

Regös Vendéglö
Szófia u. 33, 1068. **Tel** *3271 19 21*　　　　　　　　　　**Map** *7 B1*

A small, authentic restaurant reminiscent of 1970s Hungary, offering traditional, delicious Hungarian food at extremely reasonable prices and in a warm and friendly atmosphere. There is a daily-changing menu and a popular lunch-time buffet.

Abszint
Andrássy út 34., 1061 **Tel** *332 49 93*　　　　　　　　　　**Map** *2 F4*

Abszint does serve a green absinthe, but without the wormwood. Still, it is the food that people flock here for: a French-inspired bistro menu that changes regularly, always features a good selection of game dishes, and never costs a great deal of money. A popular breakfast and lunchtime spot. **www.abszint.hu**

Belcanto
Dalszínház utca 8, 1061 **Tel** *269 27 86*　　　　　　　　　　**Map** *2 F4*

A legendary Hungarian restaurant, as famous for its good-time atmosphere as for its excellent food. In the evenings, diners enjoy favourite international and Hungarian dishes while waiters sing well-known operatic arias. Customers and visiting professional singers join in, and an orchestra plays dance music. **www.belcanto.hu**

Key to Price Guide *see p.196* **Key to Symbols** *see back cover flap*

Cactus Juice Pub and Restaurant

Jokái utca tér 5, 1061 **Tel** 302 2116

Map *7 A1*

The Cactus Juice has a fun, Western-themed decor and a lively atmosphere. After dinner, you are encouraged to move on to the bar, where there are over fifty kinds of whiskies on offer and an exclusive cocktail list. There is a DJ and dancing and large groups are catered for. **www.cactusjuice.hu**

Magdalena Merlo Étterem

1072, Kiraly u.59/b **Tel** 322 3278

Map *7 A1*

Cuisine at this family-friendly restaurant is based on Italian recipes, and Hungarian traditional dishes. The atmosphere is ideal for getting together with friends, accompanied by excellent food and refreshing beer. The weekly specials always take the seasons into consideration and there are often a few surprises.

Paris Budapest

Roosevelt tér 2, 1051 **Tel** 266 12 34

Map *2 D5 (9 C3)*

This establishment at the Sofitel Atrium Budapest has just about everything that is required in a fine restaurant: great food (French, Asian, Mediterranean and Hungarian), superb service and lovely views over the Danube. Diners are mostly regulars – locals and businessmen – who know their food. Exemplary wine list. **www.sofitel-budapest.com**

Sir Lancelot lovagi Étterem

Podmaniczky utca 14, 1065 **Tel** 302 44 56

Map *2 F3*

Excellent Renaissance-inspired dishes, brought to the table by waiters in period costume. Only knives and spoons are provided with the food, which is served in such substantial portions that diners rarely manage to finish. Renaissance music is played in the evenings. Reserving is advisable, especially at weekends. **www.sirlancelot.hu**

Arigato

Ó utca 3, 1066 **Tel** 353 35 49

Map *2 F4*

A good Japanese restaurant, where simple flavours are allowed to come to the fore and no expense has been spared to bring diners the best ingredients. As a result the food is good, but prices are very high. That doesn't stop people flocking here, though. Reservations are essential in the evenings.

Iguana

Zoltán utca 16, 1054 **Tel** 331 43 52

Map *2 D4*

Iguana is a perennial expatriate favourite. The food is standard Tex Mex fare, such as *chorizo*, *jalepeno* soup, *quesadillas* and *burritos*. On the menu a helpful green "Y" points the way to the many vegetarian choices, while a red chilli marks out the hot dishes. It is wise to reserve a table in the evening. **www.iguana.hu**

Mare Croaticum

Nagymező utca 49 (entrance on Weiner Leo utca), 1065 **Tel** 311 7345

Map *10 E1*

Croatia is famous for its fish, and this place does its homeland proud by offering only the freshest produce, along with tangy Croatian white wines. There is a wide selection of good, non-fish dishes too, but it's the the sea treats that keep this restaurant very busy. Reservations needed. **www.hbcetterem.hu**

Buena Vista Étterem

Liszt Ferenc tér 4–5, 1061. **Tel** 344 63 03

Map *7 A1*

This restaurant is an oasis of peace from the busy whirl of the street. The menu offers both Hungarian and international dishes, carefully prepared and beautifully served. There is an extensive wine list, making it easy to match your food to a wine.

Fausto's

Székely Mihály Street 2, 1061. **Tel** 877 62 10

Map *2 F5*

Opened in 1994, Fausto's offers sophisticated Mediterranean and international specialities. Choose from dishes such as wild salmon carpaccio with a caper sauce or home made spaghetti with duck ragout, or from a selection of beautifully prepared meat dishes. There is also an excellent Italian wine list. **www.fausto.hu**

Gresham Kávéház

Roosevelt Tér 5-6, 1051 **Tel** 268 51 10

Map *2 D5*

The more informal of the two restaurants at the Gresham Palace Four Seasons hotel (*see p114*) is the perfect place for a light lunch or early evening dinner. The stand-out choice on the menu is the exquisite "Three Foie Gras", the dessert menu is a real treat, and there is a wicked selection of freshly made cakes. **www.fourseasons.com**

Páva

Roosevelt Tér 5-6, 1051 **Tel** 268 51 00

Map *2 D5*

Doubts about the wisdom of dining at a hotel should be dispelled by the splendour of this restaurant. Pava is an establishment where fine food, fine wine and outstanding service combine with luxurious surroundings in a sophisticated, understated way. Not cheap, by any means, but still superb value for money. **www.fourseasons.com**

Trattoria Pomo D'oro

Arany János utca. 9, 1051 **Tel** 302 64 73

Map *2 D4*

Far too big to be a genuine Italian restaurant, this place is recommended nonetheless for its superb atmosphere, created by different dining levels and excellent staff, who ensure that everyone has a good time. There's little besides the usual tourist fare on the menu, but the fresh mussel dishes are exceptional. **www.pomodobudapest.com**

CENTRAL PEST

Alföldi Étterem
Kecskeméti utca 4, 1053 **Tel** *267 02 24*   **Map** *4 F2*

Popular, cheap and simple restaurant serving tasty Hungarian food in enormous portions. *Pogácsa* (savoury, heavy scones) are always fresh and on the table. It's tremendously crowded at lunchtime. The menu has been extended to include a choice of salads, though it must be said that this is not a great place for vegetarians.

BohémTanya
Paulay Ede utca 6, 1061 **Tel** *267 35 04*   **Map** *2 F5*

Reasonably priced, hearty Hungarian food in plain surroundings. (Bohém Tanya means Bohemian Farm.) Customers are allocated places in wooden cubicles big enough for eight, but when the place is busy they are often required to share the cubicle with other diners. **http://web.axelero.hu/bohemtanya**

Fatál
Váci utca 67, 1056 **Tel** *266 26 07*   **Map** *4 F2*

Often crowded, cellar restaurant serving enormous portions of standard Hungarian fare as made at home, with a huge quantity of beef and pork. It's a no-frills, all-comers-welcome type of place, where the cheap prices compensate for the often unreliable service. Little English is spoken.

Hanna Ortodoxkóser Étterem
Dob utca 35, 1074 **Tel** *342 10 72*   **Map** *7 A2*

A simple, Orthodox, kosher eating place in the courtyard of the Orthodox Synagogue on Kazinczy utca. Traditional Jewish dishes and kosher wines are served. Note that it is open from 8am–3:30pm, except on Friday and the Sabbath, when it opens in the evenings too. For Sabbath meals, customers pay the day before or after.

Két Szerecsen
Nagymez utca 14, 1065 **Tel** *343 19 84*   **Map** *2 F4*

A bright, friendly place with a pleasant atmosphere on Pest's "Broadway". It offers a good range of tasty salads, and Hungarian and French main courses. Most wines are available by the glass, keeping prices down, and food this good usually costs a lot more in Budapest. Booking is recommended, especially in the evening. **www.ketszerecsen.com**

Bangkok House
Só utca 3, 1056 **Tel** *266 05 84*   **Map** *4 F2*

The food served here may not be convincingly Thai, but it is certainly a good imitation, and about as authentic as you will find in this part of the world. The decor is great – all statuettes and funky South East Asian artwork – and the staff are extremely helpful. Prices aren't too bad, though portions can be a little small.

Baraka
Magyar utca 12–14, 1053 **Tel** *483 13 55*   **Map** *4 F1*

Here customers can enjoy fine French-inspired food, much of it genuinely inventive, in the centre of Budapest and at reasonable prices. As a result, Baraka is popular and it is necessary to reserve a table for dinner. A great wine list can encourage over-spending, but those who keep off the imported wines can eat here relatively cheaply.

Carmel Étterem.
Kazinczy utca 31, 1074 **Tel** *322 18 34*   **Map** *10 F3*

Legendary, non-kosher, Hungarian-Jewish cellar restaurant, always crowded with locals and tourists enjoying its famed *sólet (cholent)* with smoked goose. The food may not be entirely kosher but there are some super kosher wines available. Reservations recommended, especially at the weekend. **www.carmel.hu**

Club Verne
Váci utca 60, 1056 **Tel** *202 46 88*   **Map** *4 F2*

Rapidly becoming something of a Budapest legend, Club Verne is both a restaurant and a night-time venue for the city's hip crowd. Its dead-central location also makes it popular with visitors. The menu is based around American seafood favourites, though there is plenty for vegetarians too. The submarine decor may too much for some.

Columbus Pub
Vigadó tér, Port No. 4, 1051 **Tel** *266 75 14*   **Map** *4 D1*

All aboard for superb food and good times on probably the most kitsch theme boat in Europe. Nobody complains, however, as the prices are great, the views superb and the jazz mellow. Once on board, most people don't want to get off, and stay here long into the night. Reservations are essential for the restaurant.

Dionysos Taverna
Belgrád rakpart 16, 1056 **Tel** *318 12 22*   **Map** *4 F3*

Designed not entirely without success to recreate the atmosphere of a traditional Greek village, Dionysos is a good place for groups. The *meze* (of which there are at least 30), are great, and the main dishes authentic. The management deserves full marks for serving Italian not Greek olive oil, too. Reservations essential in the evenings.

Key to Price Guide *see p.196* **Key to Symbols** *see back cover flap*

Dupla

Kertész utca 48, 1073 **Tel** *321 91 19*   **Map** *7 A2*

This split-level restaurant has something of a pleasantly cluttered Bohemian feel, where the ensemble becomes more than the individual pieces. Enormous portions of less than original but tasty Hungarian food are on offer at terrific prices, and there's good live music most nights of the week, though not at weekends.

Fészek Klub

Kertész utca 36, 1073 **Tel** *322 60 43*   **Map** *7 A2*

People come here for two things: the sublime courtyard in summer, and the reasonable prices. The food is nothing special, but at these prices nobody complains. The staff are polite, professional and accommodating, and the menu even says that if you don't find your favourite dish, the house will make it for you. **www.feszeketterem.hu**

Kaltenberg Étterem

Kinizsi utca 30–36, 1092 **Tel** *215 97 92*   **Map** *7 A5*

Attractively furnished beer cellar close to the Museum of Applied Arts. Huge portions of simple Hungarian and Bavarian specialities (plenty of sausage and cabbage) are served by friendly staff and eaten by a friendly patronage. Beer is brewed in the restaurant's own, on-site brewery and several good wines are available. **www.kaltenberg.hu**

Kispipa Étterem

Akácfa utca 38, 1073 **Tel** *342 25 87*   **Map** *7 A2*

An establishment that hasn't changed in essence in 25 years that serves a wide choice of international and Hungarian dishes. Rezső Seres, composer of "Gloomy Sunday", no longer sits at the piano, but many of his songs are still played. Both the food and the service are as good now as they were in his day. **www.kisipa.hu**

Kulacs

Osvát utca 11, 1073 **Tel** *322 3611*   **Map** *7 B2*

This restaurant serves a very good selection of tasty Hungarian specialities, including some delicious and devilishly hot goulash soup. A gypsy band serenades the diners, many of whom don't appear to like being serenaded. Though entertaining for a while, the attention can become wearing. To encourage the band to ignore your table, tip them well.

Repetasarok Étterem

Curia utca 2, 1054 **Tel** *266 11 65*   **Map** *4 F1*

The word "repeta" means second helping in Hungarian. This interesting restaurant/ concert venue serves great food and drinks and hosts a wide variety of events. Particularly recommended are the English language comedy nights and parties; check the website calendar for more details. **www.repetasarok.hu**

Centrál Kávéház és Étterem

Károlyi Mihály utca 9, 1053 **Tel** *266 21 10*   **Map** *4 F1*

A recently revived, relaxed café-cum-restaurant with an authentic Central European, pre-War feel. Open for breakfast and late-night dinner. Good Hungarian and international cuisine with excellent cakes – betraying the fact that this place is as popular for coffee and cakes as it is for lunch and dinner. **www.central kavehaz.hu**

Cyrano

Kristóf tér 7, 1052 **Tel** *266 47 47*   **Map** *10 D4*

The central location of this chic eaterie keeps prices higher than they should be, but the food is never less than outstanding, and the ambience is hard to beat in this city. The fusion menu is inventive to the point of being extraordinary, but that's how most of the patrons like things to be. It is advisable to reserve a table for the evening.

Il Terzo Cerchio

Dohány utca 40, 1072 **Tel** *354 07 88*   **Map** *7 A3*

The Third Circle of the title is the third circle of Dante's Hell, but here it alludes not to the acid rain with which gluttons were punished in the original, but to the gluttonous portions of fantastic Italian food that are served in this restaurant. Prices are good if you avoid the Italian wines. **www.ilterzocerchio.hu**

Kárpátia Étterem és Söröz

Ferenciek tere 7–8, 1053 **Tel** *317 35 96*   **Map** *4 F1*

First opened in 1877, this is Hungarian cuisine, hospitality and imperial elegance at its best, set in an understated, beautifully ornamented interior. The beer hall on the premises serves the same dishes, but at cheaper prices and in a less formal atmosphere. Gypsy music is played in the evenings. Reservation recommended. **www.karpatia.hu**

Maharaja

Csengery utca 24, 1074 **Tel** *351 12 89*   **Map** *7 A1*

Run by a Punjabi family, Maharaja serves the best North Indian food in Budapest. Vegetarians in particular will be pleased by the wide vegetable selection. Decor is simple and stylish and the staff friendly and cheerful. There is a terrace as well as a private dining room. **www.maharaja.hu**

Matyas Pince

Március 15. tér 7, 1056 **Tel** *318 1693*   **Map** *10 D5*

This place is unquestionably touristy, and tour groups make getting a table a challenge, but it's great. The food is super – huge portions of Hungarian classics are served up by friendly waiters – and there's usually a gypsy band on hand to create a rollicking atmosphere. **www.taverna.hu/matyas**.

Pertu Station

Váci utca 41A, 1056 **Tel** *317 79 77*

Map *10 E5*

This basement diner is decorated exactly like one of the stations on Budapest's Millennium Metro. Indeed, bricks were brought from the metro to adorn the walls. The food is adequate – standard Hungarian fare at reasonable prices – and on Váci utca that's usually about all you can expect. **www.perturestaurant.com**

Soul Café & Restaurant

Ráday utca 11–13, 1092 **Tel** *217 69 86*

Map *7 A5*

An intimate restaurant with a pleasant and easy atmosphere on the once-gloomy but now thriving Ráday utca, which has filled with cafés, restaurants and shops. Well-prepared and tasty international cuisine vies for space on the menu with standard Hungarian dishes. It's all good, and there's plenty for vegetarians. **www.soulcafe.hu**

Vista Café and Restaurant

Paulay Ede utca 7, 1061 **Tel** *268 08 88*

Map *2 F5*

The vista referred to is the superb view from the enormous windows that overlook one of Budapest's busiest streets. A lively atmosphere is guaranteed here, and there is an extensive, delightfully designed menu of contemporary international cuisine. Also a large area for non-smokers. Live jazz some evenings. **www.vistacafe.hu**

Aranybárány

Harmincad utca 4, 1051 **Tel** *317 27 03*

Map *2 E5*

A legendary, traditional Transylvanian restaurant, where fine stews are served up in enormous portions. There is plenty of lamb on the menu (the title of the restaurant translates as "The Golden Lamb"), though lamb is certainly not a Hungarian speciality. Famous the world over, prices are high. **www.aranybaranyetterem.hu**

Bistro Jardin

Erzsébet tér 7–8, 1051 **Tel** *429 39 90*

Map *2 F2*

The flagship restaurant of the Kempinski Corvinus hotel. The hotel management has every right to be proud. From the jazz brunch on Sundays, which has become an expatriate institution, to the many theme weeks during which the menu is given over to a country or region, the food is never less than sensational. **www.kempinski-budapest.com**

Comme Chez Soi

Aranykéz utca 2, 1052 **Tel** *318 39 43*

Map *4 E1*

Not to be confused with the three-Michelin-starred Brussels establishment of the same name, nevertheless this Budapest restaurant does offer Belgian food, including the usual number of dishes cooked in beer, and mussels galore. Though some of the prices are high, there are less expensive choices on the menu.

Jazz Garden

Veres Pálné utca 44/A, 1053 **Tel** *266 73 64*

Map *4 F2*

A cellar, but it looks and feels like a garden, so the name is not entirely misleading. It's very popular among jazz fans, not only for the daily changing music, but also for its fine international cuisine featuring vegetarian options. Booking is recommended for the evening. Jazz usually kicks off around 9:30pm. **www.jazzgarden.hu**

Károlyi Étterem és Kávéház

Károlyi Mihály utca 16, 1053 **Tel** *328 02 40*

Map *4 F2*

An elegant restaurant in the lovely courtyard of the Károlyi Palace. Worth trying is the *borjúpaprikás lángosban* (veal paprika stew in potato pancake). The attractive gardens are uncommon in the city centre and therefore often booked for weddings. At weekends, it is worth phoning to check it is open. **www.karolyietterem.hu**

Lou Lou

Vigyázó Ferenc utca 4, 1051 **Tel** *312 45 05*

Map *2 D4*

A charming, intimate French restaurant where everything is perfect, from the tightly packed tables which are so good for eavesdropping, to the service and outstanding food. The sublime lighting should be *de rigeur* in all restaurants, but Lou Lou is one of a kind. Make a reservation or you will not get a table. **www.lou-lou.hu**

Avocado Restaurant and Music Cafe

Nyári Pál u.9 **Tel** *266 32 77*

Map *4 F2*

Stylish restaurant and bar in the heart of the city and near the shopping mile, and with a menu serving Hungarian, French, Italian and Far Eastern cuisine. The decor is discreet and understated, and in the evenings there is either a band or a DJ playing contemporary music. Menu available in Hungarian and English and friendly staff.

Empire

Kossuth Lajos utca 19–21, 1053 **Tel** *889 6022*

Map *10 E4*

The recently renovated Astoria hotel is the home of the Empire, which has fortunately retained its imperial charms, being all marble columns and fine-liveried, classically designed chairs. Male staff in immaculate attire serve traditional dishes to business people and travellers. Breakfast is served until 10am. **www.danubiusgroup.comm/astoria**

Múzeum Kávéház és Étterem

Múzeum körút 12, 1088 **Tel** *338 42 21*

Map *10 F5*

Next to the National Museum, this is a distinguished restaurant and café, established in 1855. It serves Hungarian specialities, though visitors should always be aware of what they are ordering, and how much it costs. Ostensibly friendly waiters often try to tempt the undecided with expensive items on the menu. **www.muzeumkavehz.hu**

Key to Price Guide *see p.196* **Key to Symbols** *see back cover flap*

Osteria

Dohány utca 5, 1072 **Tel** *269 68 06*

Map *10 F4*

Probably the best Italian restaurant in Budapest, indeed the country. It is popular with power-diners who like to impress clients, while well-to-do couples also enjoy its understated atmosphere. Try the duck *carpaccio*, followed by the black ravioli with cottage cheese. There isn't a pizza in sight. **www.osterio.hu**

Százéves Étterem.

Pesti Barnabás utca 2, 1052 **Tel** *266 52 40*

Map *4 E1*

This is apparently the oldest restaurant in Budapest. First opened in 1831, it is housed in a beautiful Baroque building furnished with antique pieces. It offers Hungarian and international cuisine, and gypsy music is played in the background. Desserts are outstanding. Expensive, but justifiably so.

AROUND VÁROSLIGET

HanKukGuan

Ilka utca 22, 1143 **Tel** *460 08 38*

Map *6 F4*

The food of Korea has never been as celebrated as that of its Chinese or Japanese neighbours, but a few more restaurants like HanKukGuan might change that. The menu is short, but everything on it is authentic, and some ingredients are clearly imported at great cost. It is astonishing then that prices are so reasonable.

Shalimar Indian Restaurant

Dob utca 50, 1072 **Tel** *352 03 05*

Map *7 A2*

This well-regarded North Indian restaurant offers Muglai cooking and friendly service at reasonable prices. All dishes are made fresh to order and can be spiced to your tastes. There are excellent luxurious seafood dishes, plenty of vegetarian choice and a selection of eight freshly baked Indian breads. **www.shalimar.hu/english**

Bagolyvár Étterem.

Állatkerti út 2, 1141 **Tel** *468 31 10*

Map *5 C3*

In the heart of Városliget (City Park), this enchanting restaurant whose name means "Owl's Castle" offers home-style cooking of a high standard – the chef and waiting staff are all female. There is gypsy music in the evenings. And, for those who have been inspired by their visit, cookery courses are available. **www.bagolyvar.com/angol**

Baraka Restaurant & Lounge

Andrássy út 111, 1063 **Tel** *462 21 00*

Map *5 C4*

If you are the kind of person who feels that food should be presented beautifully, by beautiful people and in beautiful surroundings, then Baraka, one of Budapest's trendiest restaurants, is just for you. The food is inventive, and there is a lovely garden for summer. You'll find it in the Andrássy hotel. **www.barakarestaurant.hu**

Haxen Kiraly

Király utca 100, 1068 **Tel** *351 67 93*

Map *7 B1*

This place serves up the classic Germanic experience of leather-trouser-wearing gentlemen playing accordion music as pretty waitresses serve up *bratwurst*, *sauerkraut* and huge mugs of beer – all to Budapest's friendliest patrons. It's raucous and not for the faint-hearted, but for an all-round good time it's hard to beat.

Oliva Restaurant

Lázár utca 1, 1065 **Tel** *312 00 80*

Map *2 F4*

Oliva is not as self-consciously authentic as other Italian restaurants in Budapest, but offers good, tasty, traditional food at reasonable prices. There are also some Hungarian specialities on offer, such as deer ragout with cranberries and homemade potato doughnuts. The wine list features many locally-produced wines.

1894 BorVendéglő

Állatkerti út 2, 1146 **Tel** *468 40 44*

Map *5 C3*

There is a stunning choice of over a hundred Hungarian wines in this cellar restaurant at the Gundel Palace in Vrosliget (City Park). Dishes are prepared by the kitchen that serves Gundel Étterem, but are less expensive. As with Gundel, the emphasis is on quality and Hungarian specialities. **www.gundel.hu**

Premier

Andrássy út 101, 1062 **Tel** *342 17 68*

Map *5 B4*

International cuisine and Hungarian specialities in an elegant restaurant in the villa of the Hungarian Journalists' Union. Daily specials at lunchtime. There are three dining rooms, one of which has a long table for formal occasions. The terrace, with its wrought-iron borders, is especially appealing in good weather. **www.premier-restaurant.hu**

Anonymus

1146 Vajdahunyad sétány (in the Vajdahunyad castle) **Tel** *363 59 05*

Map *6 D4*

The magical Vajdahunyad Castle is the home to this exclusive restaurant located next to the Városliget Lake. You can enjoy a romantic dinner while listening to live music from Hungarian stars. Excellent Hungarian cuisine and warm hospitality makes your stay unforgettable.

Gundel Étterem

Állatkerti út 2, 1146 **Tel** *468 40 40*   **Map** 5 C3

Probably Hungary's most famous restaurant. Not cheap, but no longer the most expensive. It features innovative Hungarian and international cuisine, including goose liver prepared in many different ways – warm, confit or paté. Gypsy music livens up the atmosphere and Sunday brunch is excellent value. Lovely gardens. **www.gundel.hu**

Robinson

Városligeti-tó, 1146 **Tel** *422 02 22*   **Map** 5 C3

This award-winning and stylish and restaurant has an unbeatable location - on its own island on City Lake. There is an outdoor terrace for summer dining and a fireplace in winter, and live guitar music in the evenings. The menu ranges from traditional classics to exotic seafood and vegetarian dishes. **www.robinsonrestaurant.hu**

FURTHER AFIELD

BioPont

Krúdy Gyula utca 8, 1088 **Tel** *266 46 01*   **Map** 7 B4

Here everything is natural and organic. There isn't a piece of meat, a dairy product or a fish in sight, and those who like what they eat can buy most of the ingredients in the shop attached. A bright café atmosphere attracts a student crowd, who flock here at lunchtimes. The whole restaurant is non-smoking.

Fenyőgyöngye Vendéglő

Szépvölgyi út 155, 1025 **Tel** *325 97 83*

Small, incredibly popular restaurant up in the Buda Hills, offering traditional Hungarian fare made in a lighter, healthier way. The garden area is perfect for families, and popular with Buda's middle classes on Sunday afternoons. Reserving a table is a good idea. Bus 65 runs to the door from Szépvölgyi út HEV station. **www.fenyogyongye.hu**

Jókai Étterem

Hollós út 5, 1121 **Tel** *395 36 58*

Relaxed restaurant in a lovely 19th-century villa in the hills near the Svábhegy cog-wheel station. Attentive service and well-prepared classic Hungarian dishes at incredibly good prices. The terrace is pleasant in the summer. For those who don't fancy the journey on the cog-wheel railway, Bus 21 from Moszkva tér runs close by.

Kerék Vendéglő

Bécsi út 103, 1034 **Tel** *250 42 61*

An authentic Old Buda restaurant from the 1960s, offering Hungarian cuisine to the music of an accordion player. It's not the most exclusive place in the city, nor will it win any design contests, but the garden is lovely and the food is great – both hearty and cheap. Tram 17 from Margaret Bridge gets you there. Booking is advised at weekends.

Náncsi Néni Vendéglője

Ördögárok út 80, 1029 **Tel** *398 71 27*

Customers are offered a wide choice of interesting, home-style interpretations of traditional Hungarian dishes. Giant *túrógombóc* (curd cheese dumplings) is a favourite dessert – with those who have remembered to save room. Booking is essential, especially for the popular garden area In summer. **www.nancsineni.hu**

Bajai Halászcsárda

Hollós út 2, 1121 **Tel** *275 52 45*

Located next to the Svábhegy cog-wheel stop. Traditional Hungarian dishes specializing in fresh river fish. A real treat is the Bajai fish soup with a huge portion of carp fillets served on the side. There is also *goulash*, and for dessert the fried doughnuts are worth trying. If you don't fancy the cog-rail, Bus 21 from Moskva tér runs close by.

Firkász Étterem

Tátra ú. 18, 1136 **Tel** *450 11 18*   **Map** 2 E1

The name means "scribbler", and this restaurant has a literary, quiet atmosphere, ideal for a sedate dinner after a long day sight-seeing. The menu is traditional Hungarian, with a wide selection of excellent wines. There is also live piano music. Booking is recommended. **www.firkaszetterem.hu**

Külvárosi Kávéház

István út 26, 1041 **Tel** *379 15 68*

A gem in the district of Újpest. International cuisine with excellent Hungarian dishes, including a three-course *betyárleves* (bone marrow on toast, golden soup with noodles and vegetables, beef cooked in soup). The absurdly cheap prices make this one of Budapest's most popular restaurants so reserve a table. Take metro M3 to Újpest-Központ.

Nefrit Chinese Restaurant

Apor Vilmos tér 4k, 1124 **Tel** *213 90 39*

Cantonese and Sechaun specialities in a pleasant restaurant in an old villa. Tasty *dim sum* are on offer, and prices are remarkably reasonable. Finding Chinese food in Budapest is easy; finding good Chinese food is tricky, so make your way here. You can do so on Bus 105 from Erszebet tér.

Key to Price Guide *see p.196* **Key to Symbols** *see back cover flap*

Öreghalász Étterem

Árpád út 20–22, 1042 **Tel** *231 08 00*

There's a homely atmosphere in this restaurant, where fresh river fish is the speciality. The decor is nautical but not over-the-top, and it enhances enjoyment of the super food. It is worth trying any fish soup from the wide range on offer, though non-fish dishes are also available. Booking recommended. **www.oreg-halasz.hu**

Arcade Bistro

Kiss János Altáb utca 38, 1126 **Tel** *225 19 69*

Map *3 A1*

Few restaurants in Budapest can match the outstanding patio that attracts the Budapest jet set to Arcade during the summer. The food here is excellent, too, contemporary and inventive, and beautifully presented. Prices are a little high but represent real value for money. **www.arcadebistro.hu**

Gotti Restaurant

Ráday utca 29, 1092 **Tel** *212 62 25*

Map *7 A5*

Popular new modern bar and restaurant in the buzzy café district of the city. There is a heated outdoor patio, weekend music performances and concerts and an excellent cocktail list. The food on offer ranges from traditional Hungarian to international cuisine. The desserts in particular are recommended.

Kisbuda Gyöngye Étterem

Kenyeres utca 34, 1043 **Tel** *368 64 02*

This restaurant has a natural, old-time drawing room atmosphere, where guests relax and enjoy excellent dishes from international and Hungarian cuisines to the soft music of a piano. A lunch here, where nothing should be hurried, usually turns into a long afternoon as the wine continues to flow. **www.remiz.hu**

Ristorante Krizia

Mozsár utca 12, 1066 **Tel** *331 87 11*

Krizia is a celebration of Mediterranean food and atmosphere. Elegance is balanced by hints of rusticity, from the terracotta pots to the overcrowded shelves of wine. The food is mainly Italian, and the pasta is made on the premises. There is a super wine list. Take the Millennium Metro to Oktagon to get here. **www.ristorantekrizia.hu**

Voros Postakocsi

Ráday utca 15, 1092 **Tel** *217 67 56*

It's worth eating here simply to gaze out of the enormous windows at the super-trendy people passing by on up-and-coming Ráday utca. The main dining room is large, but charmingly decorated. The food is good – mainly Hungarian but with an international and contemporary twist. The name means Red Post Wagon.

Chez Daniel

Szív utca 32, 1063 **Tel** *302 40 39*

Choose from the daily specials chalked up on the blackboard, then kick back and enjoy great food in one of Budapest's most relaxed restaurants. The food is mainly French, unfussy and accessible. The wine list is very good, and evenings here tend to be long. The small terrace-cum-courtyard is lovely. You'll need a reservation.

Jardinette

Németvölgyi út 136, 1112 **Tel** *248 16 52*

During the summer there are a number of tables in the garden, where chestnut trees provide shade from the sun, and the whole ambience is warm and Mediterranean. Sitting inside in winter, however, can feel a little like sitting in a greenhouse. Food is contemporary European – not fancy, but good. **www.jardinette.hu**

Kéhli Vendéglő

Mókus utca 22, 1036 **Tel** *250 42 41*

Excellent, long-forgotten tastes of Pest and Buda are served here in large portions. Established more than a century ago in Old Buda, this was the favourite eating place of Gyula Krúdy, the great Hungarian gourmet writer. Standards have not dropped a notch since he dined here. Reservations recommended. **www.kehli.hu**

Fuji Japan

Csatárka utca 54, 1025 **Tel** *325 71 11*

In a pagoda-style interior, Japanese food enthusiasts can watch the chef at work while enjoying dishes such as a beautifully presented selection of *sashimi*. There is more than raw fish on the menu, however. This is a real Japanese restaurant, with the high prices to prove it. **www.fujirestaurant.hu**

Rosenstein Restaurant

Mosonyi utca 3, 1087. **Tel** *333 34 92*

Situated near Keleti railway station, in an area not known for fine dining, is Rosenstein Restaurant. The wide menu features both international and Hungarian cuisine as well as traditional Jewish food. Meat-eaters are well-catered for, but vegetarian options are limited. **www.rosenstein.hu**

Vadrózsa Étterem

Pentelei Molnár utca 15, 1025 **Tel** *326 58 17*

Exclusive restaurant set in a beautiful Neo-Baroque villa and run by one family for 30 years. Soft piano music plays in the evenings. The gardens are lovely in summer. A taxi is required to get here, but the house will tell you when, at the end of the meal, it's time for carriages. The food? Outstanding, adventurous and expensive. **www.vadorzsa.hu**

Cafés and Wine Bars

To sample the true atmosphere of Hungary, it is essential to visit the smaller eating and drinking establishments that are scattered across the city and into the suburbs. Behind even the most ordinary of buildings, there could be hiding a timeless pocket of old Hungarian culture. Elsewhere, bright neon and loud music reflect the contemporary cultural interests of Budapest's youth. And between these extremes, visitors can still find a taste of 19th-century opulence in the old coffee houses and patisseries that once sat comfortably at the heart of the city's life.

CAFÉS & COFFEE HOUSES

Hungary has one of the oldest coffee-drinking traditions in Europe. Introduced by the Turks in the mid-16th century during their occupation *(see pp26–7)*, the coffee culture blossomed towards the end of the Habsburg era *(see pp32–3)*, when there were almost 600 *kávéház* (cafés) in the city.

The 19th-century café scene was a hotbed of intellectual activity dominated by literary and artistic circles. **New York Café** *(see p129)*, which opened in 1894, was for many years the centre of this creative scene; its walls adorned with frescoes painted by the leading artists of the day. **Centrál Kávéház** café saw a revival in the 1990s and gives an open and cheerful picture of past and present traditions.

Today's café scene is continually changing. *Eszpresszó* bars first appeared in the 1930s but were most popular in the 1960s. Much cheaper than their pre-decessors, they catered for teenagers with a taste for Western culture. These have subsequently been replaced by more modern cafés, such as **Moyo Café**, **Menza**, **Barokko**, **Paris Texas** and **Leroy**.

Almost every luxurious traditional *cukrászda* (cake shop) and *kávéház* closed down when *eszpresszó* bars became popular, but in recent years many have reopened again. A couple of old gems never closed: **Gerbeaud Cukrászda** serves the best coffee and cakes in the land, as it has done for well over a hundred years, while the **Gellért Eszpresszó** is a sublime recreation of a Habsburg-era coffee house, situated on the ground floor of the Gellért Hotel *(see p183)*. Both of these places offer the genuine Budapest coffee-house experience, complete with immaculately liveried wait-resses in pinafore dresses and a lady who insists on taking your coat. They are sublime reminders of a bygone age.

There are many styles of coffee in Budapest. A *kávé* is an espresso with milk and sugar, and a *dupla* is a double espresso. French-style milky coffee is called a *tejeskávé*, while cappuccinos are often served with whipped cream or in the Viennese-style – without either chocolate or cinnamon. For decaffeinated coffee, ask for *koffeinmentes*.

Tea houses are also popular now. **Big Ben** and **1000 Tea** are great choices in the downtown area.

WINE BARS

Wine and wine bars occupy a different position in the social hierarchy in Hungary than they do in, say, Britain or the United States. Whereas in these countries wine drinking is regarded as a somewhat middle-class pursuit, in Hungary it has traditionally been considered a workers' pastime. Despite the fact that young men are now starting to adopt beer as their drink of choice, the old ways of drinking wine are still to be found underground, in the *borozók* of Budapest.

A traditional *borozó* is an unglamorous, cheap wine cellar, where wine is served straight from the barrel and sold by the decilitre. The best example is **6:3 Borozó** or **Vidocq Borozó**. Few places have tables and chairs. In the city centre, besides the tradi-tional *borozós*, like **Villányi-Siklósi** or **Grinzingi**, there is the more stylish **Rondella Borozó**, where wine is drawn from barrels and served in curious jugs with a tap at the bottom.

Várfok Borozó, at No. 10 Várfok utca in the Castle District, is of the simple but authentic kind. At the other end of the spectrum, there are places like the **House of Hungarian Wines** *(see p180)*, where you can taste wines from each wine region in Hungary, or the **Hilton Hotel** *(see p182)*, which houses a stylish wine bar in a medieval cellar. Such establishments tend to serve expensive wines in bottles, rather than straight from the barrel.

The popular, full-bodied range of dessert wines called Tokaji *(see p195)* also has a number of wine bars dedicated to it. The best is **Tokaji Borozó**, in central Pest, where most customers drink standing up.

Other good choices are the **Bor La Bor Pince** or the **Borpiac étterem**, which operate as wine bars and restaurants in one.

COCKTAIL BARS

Budapest is currently alive with trendy cocktail bars that buzz from the early evening onwards with a young crowd, enjoying after-work drinks in the Italian fashion (*aperitivo*).

There are cocktail bars all over the city, but the trendiest establishments tend to be found on "the tér" (Liszt Ferenc tér). Indeed, Liszt Ferenc tér is quite simply the social heart and soul of Budapest during the spring and summer months. Favourite places nearby include **Incognito** and **Karma**.

On the other side of the Danube, a hip crowd meets every evening at **Oscar's American Bar**, famous for its selection of more than 200 cocktails. The lucky few for whom money is no object head for the **Four Seasons Bar**, in the Gresham Palace hotel. Visitors to the city may like to follow suite, not least to enjoy the hotel's splendid interiors.

FOOD AND CUSTOMS

Wine bars, where people can pop in for a glass of wine or a spritzer *(see p195)* at any time of day, do not generally serve food. Occasionally, however, light snacks are available. Typically, these consist of a slice of bread and dripping garnished with raw onion and sprinkled with paprika; or *pogácsa*, a yeast pan-bread, served with crackling, cheese, caraway seeds or paprika. Wine bars with tables sometimes serve frankfurters or knuckle.

Visitors should take note of the following warning. In Hungary, unlike most other Europeans countries, it is not done to clink beer glasses together with fellow drinkers. This apparently innocent gesture was adopted by the Austrians as they executed Hungarian generals after the uprising of 1848–9, and can still cause great offence.

DIRECTORY

CAFÉS

Alkoholos Filc Kávézó
Várfok utca 15/B. **Map 1** A3. **Tel** 213 51 55. **Open** 9am–10pm Mon–Sat. **Closed** Sun.

Anna Café
Váci utca 7. **Map 4** E1. **Tel** 266 90 80. **Open** 8:30am–midnight daily.

Auguszt Cukrászda
Kossuth Lajos utca 14–16. **Map 4** F1. **Tel** 337 63 79. **Open** Mon–Sun daily.

Barokko Club and Lounge
Liszt Ferenc tér 5. **Map 7** A1. **Tel** 322 07 00. **Open** 11am–1am Sun–Tue, 11am–2am Wed-Sat.

Big Ben Teaház
Veres Pálné utca 10. **Map 4** F2. **Tel** 344 43 81. **Open** 10am–10pm daily.

Café Firenze
Szalay utca 5a. **Map 2** E3. **Tel** 331 83 99. **Open** 9am–6pm daily.

Centrál Kávéház and Restaurant
Károlyi Mihály u.9. **Map 4** F1. **Tel** 266 21 10. **Open** 7am–midnight Mon–Fri, 8am–midnight Sat–Sun.

Gerbeaud Cukrászda
Vörösmarty tér 7. **Map 2** E5. **Tel** 429 90 00. **Open** 9am–9pm daily.

Hattyú Kávézó
Hattyú utca 14.
Map 1 A3.
Tel 202 77 77.
Open 24 hours daily.

Leroy Café
Ráday utca 11.
Map 10 F5. **Tel** 219 54 51. **Open** noon–midnight daily.

Lukács Café
Andrássy út 70. **Map 5** A5. **Tel** 373 04 07.
Open 8:30am–7pm Mon–Fri, 9:30am–7pm Sat & Sun.

Menza
Liszt Ferenc tér 2. **Map 7** A1. **Tel** 413 14 83. **Open** 11am–midnight daily.

Moyo Café
Liszt Ferenc tér 10.
Map 7 A1. **Tel** 342 44 57. **Open** 11am–midnight.

Mozart Café
Erzsébet körút 36. **Map 7** B2. **Tel** 352 06 64. **Open** 9am–11pm Mon–Sun daily.

Müvész Café
Andrássy út 29.
Map 2 F4 (10 E2).
Tel 352 13 37. **Open** 9am–midnight daily.

New York Café
Erzsébet körút 9–11.
Map 7 B2. **Tel** 886 61 67. **Open** 10am–midnight daily.

1000 Tea
Váci utca 65. **Map 4** F2. **Tel** 337 82 17.
Open noon–9pm Mon–Sat.

Paris Texas
Ráday utca 22.
Map 10 F5. **Tel** 218 05 70. **Open** noon–3am daily.

"R" Café
Károlyi Mihály utca 19.
Map 4 F2 (10 E5).
Tel 328 01 17. **Open** 11am– midnight daily.

Ruszwurm Cukrászda
Szentháromság utca 7.
Map B4 (9 A2).
Tel 375 52 84.
Open 10am–7pm daily.

WINE BARS

6:3 Borozó
Lónyai utca 60.
Map 4 F2. **Tel** 217 07 48. **Open** 8am–midnight Mon–Sat.

Borpiac Étterem
Török utca 1. **Map 1** B1.
Tel 212 45 08. **Open** 3pm–11pm Mon–Sat.

Bor La Bor Pince
Veres Pálné utca 7. **Map 4** F2 (10 ES). **Tel** 328 03 82. **Open** noon–midnight daily.

Grinzingi Borozó
Veres Pálné utca 10.
Map 4 F2 (10 E5).
Tel 317 46 24. **Open** 9am–1am Mon–Sat, 3pm–11pm Sun.

House of Hungarian Wines
Szentháromság tér 6.
Map 1 B4. **Tel** 212 10 31. **Open** 12pm–8pm daily.

Móri Borozó
Fiáth János utca 16.
Map 1 A3. **Tel** 214 92 16. **Open** 2–11pm Mon–Sat, 4–9pm Sat & Sun.

Rondella Borozó
Régiposta utca 4.
Map 4 E1.
Tel 483 08 30.
Open 5pm–2am Tue–Sun.

Tokaji Borozó
Falk Miksa utca 32.
Map 2 D2. **Tel** 269 31 43.
Open noon–9pm Mon–Fri.

Várfok Borozó
Várfok u.10. **Map 1** A3.
Tel 214 30 77. **Open** 11am–8pm Mon–Fri, 10am–6pm Sat, Sun.

Vidocq Borozó
Lajos utca 98.
Tel 240 39 37.
Open noon–11pm Mon–Sun.

Villányi-Siklósi Borozó
Gerlóczy utca 13.
Map 4 F1 (10 E4).
Tel 267 02 41. **Open** 8am–11pm Mon–Fri, 9am–10pm Sat & Sun.

Vincellér Borszaküzlet
Erd utca 10.
Map 1 B3.
Tel 201 15 61. **Open** 10am–6pm Tue–Fri, 8pm–midnight Sat & Sun.

COCKTAIL BARS

Four Seasons Bar
Four Seasons Gresham Palace Hotel. Roosevelt tér 5–6. **Map 2** D5.
Tel 268 60 00 **Open** 11am–1am daily

Incognito
Liszt Ferenc tér 3.
Map 7 A1. **Tel** 342 14 71. **Open** 2pm–midnight daily.

Karma
Liszt Ferenc tér 11.
Map 7 A1. **Tel** 413 67 64 **Open** 11am–2am daily.

Oscar's American Bar
Ostrom utca 14.
Map 1 A3.
Tel 212 80 17.
Open 5pm–4am Fri & Sat, Mon–Thu 5pm–2am. Closed Sun.

Beer Halls, Pubs and Clubs

There are drinking establishments in Budapest to suit practically every taste, from traditional Hungarian beer halls to high-tech nightclubs, and many stay open late. The most recent developments on the scene – themed Irish, English or sports bars – cater to crowds of English ruffians who visit the city on "stag" weekends. It is still possible, however, simply to stroll around the city and drop into the places frequented by locals. You will find Budapest a very friendly and informal place to drink; if you sit at an empty table, others will probably join you. Note that in traditional pubs a waiter will automatically bring more beer as soon as you appear to be close to finishing your glass, unless you indicate otherwise.

TRADITIONAL BEER HALLS

In recent years, beer has started to take over from wine as Hungary's favourite drink. Driven by this fashion, in Budapest many wine bars have been turned into *sörözs* (beer halls), and several new establishments modelled on the German *bierstube* and the English pub have opened. As a result, beer-drinking has become an aspirational pastime, and prices in the *sörözs* and pubs are much higher than in the *borozós* (traditional wine bars, *see p206*). This price difference is particularly noticeable in the popular tourist areas.

The cost of drinking beer is, however, reflected in the relative sophistication of the pastime; it is possible to buy almost all the major brands in the city, as well as Hungarian *világos* (light) and *barna* (dark) beers (*see p194*).

Beer is measured by the *korsó*, the equivalent of a pint, and the *pohár*, a smaller glass. A variety of good and moderately priced snacks and hot dishes, including smoked knuckle, is available in *sörözs*, as, indeed, is wine. By contrast, the *borozós* rarely offer food, and never beer.

The best of the old-style beer halls is probably historic **Fortuna Mátyás**, located in the Castle District. A more mainstream drinking experience can be had in the **Jam Pub** in the Mammut Shopping Centre, which even has live music most nights of the week, at 9pm.

IRISH PUBS & THEME BARS

Like many Eastern European cities, Budapest has been invaded by theme bars and pubs, notably Irish pubs. Some are friendlier than others, some are more Irish than others, but all have Guinness at the usual, extortionate prices. **Becketts** was the first Irish pub in Budapest and it remains popular with tourists, locals and expatriates. There's great pub food on offer, and good music at weekends. Equally celebrated is **Fregatt**, a hybrid Irish-English-Hungarian pub decked out in bizarre naval style. **Janis' Pub** is named after Janis Joplin and is a gem – with a bright blue exterior and live music at weekends. The small but enjoyable **Zappa Café** pays homage to another great legend of rock, Frank Zappa.

Budapest also has many easy-going venues where the music is less important than the atmosphere. For example, the **Cotton Club**, where sultry female singers croon to a trendy, upmarket crowd; and the **Old Man's Music Pub**, where a range of performers from Irish fiddlers to Hungarian punk bands entertain happy, drunk crowds from 9–11pm daily.

For Hungarian "oompah" music, complete with floor show, head for the peerless **Kalamajka Dance House**. It is touristy and expensive, but great. **Alcatraz**, where clients sit behind bars in their own private cells and staff wear prison warden's costumes, takes the theme pub concept perhaps too far; but it is still around after years on the scene, is more popular than ever, and has good live music most nights.

BOHEMIAN HANGOUTS

Though not in the same league as Prague, Budapest has nevertheless long been a haven for individualists looking for something a little different. Many are attracted by its glut of unusual places to eat and drink, such as the **Red Lion Tea House**, an Eastern-style retreat from modern life, where the serving of tea is an art form. Another favourite hangout is **Piaf**, a superbly decadent dive reminiscent of a speakeasy.

NIGHTCLUBS & DISCOS

Nightlife in Budapest is on its way to competing with that of other European capitals and new clubs open daily. Among the most recent arrivals on the scene is **Trafo Bar Tango**, a cultural centre for young, alternative artists housed in a renovated power station. It's also the setting for numerous exhibitions and literary events, and music styles range from reggae to classical Indian music.

The biggest and probably the most popular club in the city is **Bahnhof**, which is found, predictably enough, behind Nyugati train station and is frequented by a terrific mix of locals, expatriates and tourists, attracted by the relatively cheap drinks and mainstream dance music. It's open on Thursday, Friday and Saturday. Also popular is the disco boat **A38 Ship**, moored just past Petőfi bridge on the Buda side of the river. It is a cultural centre with a restaurant, bars and a concert hall, and hosts numerous national and international cultural events, exhibitions and festivals.

Older clubs are often centered around student venues. **Petőfi Csarnok**, a cavernous youth entertainment centre built in 1984 during the

Communist era, is a stage and disco complex that hosts local and international rock bands. **E-Klub** is open on Fridays and Saturdays and is always crowded with Technical University students. **Közgáz Pince Klub** is a really vibrant student club held in the huge hall of the University of Corvinus (*see p138*).

GAY VENUES

Budapest's trendy gay crowd usually heads for **Angyal Bár**, which always has great disco music from all eras and a friendly atmosphere. Friday nights are male-only, but at other times there is a mixed crowd. Also good is **Upside Down**, which attracts all sorts

to its celebrated karaoke nights on Mondays and Wednesdays. Weekends are for hardcore techno fans and almost exclusively male. **Coxx**, a massive men-only complex with bar, disco, restaurant, internet café and gallery is famous for its theme nights – anything from fancy dress to no dress at all.

DIRECTORY

BEER HALLS

Astoria Café Mirror
Kossuth Lajos utca 19.
Map 4 F1.
Tel 889 60 22.
Open 7am–11pm daily.

Fortuna Mátyás
Fortuna Spaten, Hess András tér 4. **Map** 1 B5.
Tel 375 61 75.
Open 11am–midnight daily.

Gerbeaud Pub
Vörösmarty 7. **Map** 10 D3. **Tel** *429 90 22.*
Open 12am–11pm daily.

Gösser Söröző
Régiposta utca 4.
Map 4 E1 (10 D4).
Tel 318 26 08. **Open** 10am–midnight daily.

Jam Pub
Lövöhaz utca 1–3, Mammut II. **Map** 1 A3.
Open 9am–4am Sun–Wed, 9am–6am Thu–Sat.

Kaltenberg Royal Bavarian Brasserie
Kinizsi utca 30–36. **Map** 7 A5. **Tel** *215 9792.* **Open** noon–11pm daily.

Tóth Kocsma
Falk Miksa utca 17.
Map 2 D2.
Tel 302 64 43.
Open 3pm–midnight Mon–Fri, 5pm–midnight Sat & Sun.

IRISH PUBS & THEME BARS

Alcatraz
Nyár utca 1. **Map** 7 A3.
Tel 478 60 10. **Open** 4pm–2am Sun–Thu, 4pm–2am Fri & Sat.
www.alcatraz.hu

Becketts Irish Pub
Bajcsy Zsilinszky út 72.
Map 2 E3 (10 E1).
Tel 311 10 35. **Open** noon–1am Mon–Thu, noon–3am Fri, Sat.

Cotton Club
Jókai utca 26.
Map 2 F3.
Tel 354 08 86.
Open noon–1am daily.
www.cottonclub.hu

Fregatt
Molnár utca 26.
Map 4 E2 (10 D5).
Tel 318 99 97.
Open 5pm–2am daily.

Janis' Pub
Királyi Pál utca 8.
Map 4 F2.
Tel 266 26 19.
Open 4pm–3am Mon–Sat, 6pm–midnight Sun.

John Bull Pub
Apáczai Csere János utca 17. **Map** 2 D5.
Tel 338 21 68.
Open 11am–1am daily.

Kalamajka Dance House
Arany Idnos utca 10, Budapest V. **Map** 4 E2.
Tel 266 78 66.
Open 5pm–2am Sat.

Morrison's Music Pub
Révay utca 25. **Map** 2 F4.
Tel 269 40 60.
Open 7pm–4am Mon–Wed. www.morrisons.hu

Old Man's Music Pub
Akácfa utca 13.
Map 7 A2.
Tel 322 76 45.
Open 3pm–4am daily.

Zappa Café
Mikszáth Kálmán tér 2
Map 7 A4.
Tel 0620 972 17 11.
Open 10am–2am Mon–Fri, noon–4am Sat & Sun.

BOHEMIAN HANGOUTS

Piaf
Nagymezö utca 25.
Map 2 F3.
Tel 312 38 23. **Open** 10pm–5am Sun–Thu, 10pm–7am Fri–Sat.

Red Lion Tea House
Jókai tér 8. **Map** 10 F1.
Tel 269 05 79.
Open 11am–11pm Mon–Sat, 3pm–11pm Sun.

NIGHTCLUBS & DISCOS

A38 Ship
Pázmány Pétér sétány, Petöfi híd.
Tel 464 39 40.
Open 11am–4am on programme days.
www.a38.hu

Bahnhof
Váci út 1. **Map** 2 F2.
Tel 302 47 51.
Open 9pm–4am Thu–Sat.

D3 Music Club
Kossuth Lajos utca 20.
Map 4 F1. **Tel** *317 51 80.*
Open 4pm–2am Tue–Fri, 8pm–4am Sat. .

E–Klub
Népliget út 2.
Tel 263 16 14.
Open 10pm–5am Fri & Sat.

Fat Mo's Music Club
Nyári Pál utca 11.
Map 4 F2.
Tel 267 31 99.
Open 6pm–2am Sun–Wed, 6pm–4am Thu–Sat.

Közgáz Pince Klub
Fvám tér 8. **Map** 4 F3.
Tel 215 43 59. **Open** 10pm–5am Tue–Sat.
Closed Sun & Mon.

Petöfi Csarnok
Zichy Mihály utca 14.
Map 6 E4. **Tel** *363 37 30.*
Open Times vary with events.

Trafo Bar Tango
Liliom utca 41, IX District, Ferencváros.
Tel 456 20 53.
Open 6pm–4am daily.
www.trafo.hu

GAY VENUES

Angyal Bár
Szövetség utca 33.
Map 7 B1.
Tel 356 86 40.
Open 10pm–5am daily.

Coxx
Dohány utca 38.
Map 7 A3.
Tel 344 48 84.
Open 9pm–4am daily.
www.coxx.hu

Upside Down
Podmaniczky Tér 1.
Map 2 F3.
Tel 0670 367 96 22.
Open 10pm–5am daily.

SHOPS AND MARKETS

Shopping in Budapest has changed dramatically since the more spartan days of Communism. A huge variety of consumer goods, both foreign and home produced, are now available here. Major shopping streets include the pedestrianized and fashionable Váci utca (Váci Street, *see p127*) good for folk art and Zsolnay porcelain, and the less fashionable, but much cheaper

String of paprika peppers

Nagykörút, where locals come to do their shopping. For a more traditional shopping experience, don't miss a visit to some of Budapest's many markets. These range from stunning 19th-century food halls such as the Great Market Hall (Nagy Vásárcsarnok), to flea markets such as the huge and lively Ecseri Flea Market, for everything from bric-a-brac to furniture and antiques.

OPENING HOURS

Most shops in Budapest open from 9am to 5:30 or 6pm Monday to Friday, and from 9am to 1pm on Saturday. Greengrocers, bakeries and supermarkets are open from 7am until 8pm. Shopping centres, department stores and plazas open at 10am and close at 9pm except Sundays, when they close at 6pm. Indoor markets are open on Sunday, and most cafés sell milk and bread on Sunday morning. One result of the increase in private enterprise since 1989 is a large number of small shops which open 24 hours a day and sell groceries, cigarettes and alcohol.

Westend City Center shopping mall

HOW TO PAY

Credit cards and Eurocheques can be used to pay for goods and services in many of the more touristy parts of Budapest. Outside these areas it is best to carry plenty of cash in Hungarian forints.

VAT EXEMPTION

The price of all goods in Hungary includes a value-added tax of 20% (ÁFA). With the exception of works of art and antiques, it is possible for non-EU citizens to claim back the value-added tax on anything costing more than 50,000 forints. First, present your goods at customs within 90 days of purchase to receive your customs certification and a refund claim form. You will need your sales receipt and currency exchange or credit card receipt, plus the customs certification, to apply for your refund within 183 days of your return home.

DEPARTMENT STORES AND MALLS

There are a number of department stores in the city, many housed in spectacular old buildings.

Traditional folk crafts, on sale around Váci utca

More of a mall than a department store, the **Duna Plaza** on Váci út is smart but not centrally located. A store worth a look is **Skála Metro** on Nyugati tér opposite the railway station in Pest.

Many large stores are clustered in the old buildings of Váci utca, such as C&A and Zara, but most of these brands can be found in one place in the modern shopping centres.

Over the past decade more than 10 major shopping malls have opened and have proved popular with both locals and visitors. The most centrally-located mall is **Westend City Center**. Central Europe's largest, it has over 350 stores, including Armani, Benetton and Marks & Spencer, in addition to a 14-screen cinema and a food court.

The huge and stylish **Mammut** on Moszkva tér is frequented by the better off inhabitants of Buda, and is easily accessible for those who do not have the good fortune to live nearby.

Recently opened is the modern **Arena Plaza**, with more than 200 shops.

Delicate lace, an example of traditional Hungarian folk art

MARKETS

Markets of all sorts are an essential part of life in Budapest, and offer a delightfully traditional shopping experience to visitors. Perhaps the most spectacular are the five cavernous market halls which dot the city. All were built in the late 19th

Fruit and vegetable stalls at Central Market Hall

century and several are still used as markets. The three-level Great Market Hall (Nagy Vásárcsarnok) known officially as the **Central Market Hall** (Központi Vásárcsarnok) on Fővám tér is the largest of all. More than 180 stalls display a huge variety of vegetables, fruit, meat and cheese, under a gleaming roof of brightly-coloured Zsolnay tiles. The market opens from 6am–5pm Mon–Fri and 6am–2pm Sat (see p138).

In addition to the covered market halls, there are open-air food markets in every Budapest neighbourhood. In many you will see country women in traditional costumes selling fruit and vegetables, as well as local cheeses, honey and sausages. Some of the best markets are at Lehel tér (district XIII), Bosnyák tér (XIV) and Fehérvári út (IX). Delicious hot sausages with mustard and fresh bread, or *lángos*, a flat bread served with cream or grated cheese, are traditional and widely available market snacks.

Beginning at 156 Nagykőrösi út in district XIX, is the **Ecseri Flea Market**, open on

weekends. Outside, a maze of wooden tables is covered in Communist artifacts, second-hand clothes and all sorts of bric-a-brac, while from tiny cubicles inside the market, serious antique dealers sell porcelain, icons, silverware, jewellery and much more. It is necessary to obtain per-mission from the Museum of Applied Arts (see pp136–7) before you can take antiques out of the country.

Another market well worth a visit is the extremely busy **Józsefvárosi Market**, situated close to Józsefváros pu on Kőbányai út and open 7am–6pm daily. Many of the traders here are Chinese, using the Trans-Siberian railway to transport a huge variety of new goods from China, southeast Asia, the former Soviet Union and eastern Europe, all sold at knock-down prices. Look out for all sorts of entertaining and obvious southeast Asian fashion fakes, as well as electronic goods, Chinese silks, Russian caviar and vodka, and Stalinist memorabilia.

Marks & Spencer, a branch of the British department store

What to Buy in Budapest

Despite price rises since the return to a free-market economy, many Hungarian goods are still great bargains. Embroidered peasant blouses and wooden carvings make unique souvenirs, as does the distinctive porcelain produced at the world-famous Zsolnay and Herend factories. Cheap, good quality CDs and records are widely available, and Hungarian wines, salamis and other foodstuffs can be bought in the city's many lively markets. Clothes and shoes made to your specifications represent one of the city's most luxurious bargains.

FOLK ART

Hungarian folk culture is still alive and well in many parts of rural Hungary. You can buy textiles, ceramics and woodwork from flea markets *(see p211)* and from street vendors around Moszkva tér and Parliament *(see pp108–9)*. Folk art shops such as **Folkart Centrum**, sell machine-made products, and, for genuine Transylvanian textiles there is the **Judit Kézműves** hand-made shop. For the cheapest authentic folk costumes, head for the **Central Market Hall** (Nagy Vásárcsarnok).

ANTIQUES

Dominated by 18th- and 19th-century pieces in the Habsburg style, the Budapest antiques scene is concentrated in the Castle District, around Falk Miksa utca and on Váci utca (Váci Street, *see p127*). **Moró Antik** is a tiny shop specializing in 18th-century weapons, while the huge **Nagyházi Gallery** sells everything from jewellery to furniture. The **Ecseri Flea Market** *(see p211)* is also a good place for antiques.

PORCELAIN

There are two major porcelain manufacturors in Hungary, **Herend** and **Zsolnay**. Herend enjoys a reputation as the producer of the country's finest porcelain, while Zsolnay's brightly glazed tiles can be seen on many of the city's notable buildings. Second-hand porcelain can be bought in antiques shops and markets. Both companies have shops selling new pieces.

CLOTHES AND SHOES

Made-to-measure clothes and shoes, and ready-made designer clothes offer some of the best deals to be had by visitors to Budapest. Many people have clothes made up in their choice of fabric by a local designer – who is likely to be happy to oblige for a fairly modest fee.
At the smart end of the market, there is **Naray Tamás Boutique**, the showcase for one of the most famous designers in Hungary. **Dáriusz Ekszerstudió**, which opened in 2004, is already one of the country's most exclusive jewellers. Shoemakers in Budapest tend to make only men's shoes. **Vass** will make you a one-off pair of dress shoes in about a month. They will cost around 130,000 Hungarian forints.

FOOD AND WINE

Food and wine in Hungary are great value and make excellent souvenirs for you to take home after your stay. Sausage is a national passion and can be bought in shops and markets all over the city. Some of the most popular types include spicy sausages from Debrecen, smoked sausages from Gyulai and a whole range of world-famous salamis. Also worth bringing home are dried mushrooms, *paté de foie gras*, a string of paprika or some fresh sheep's cheese. All these can be bought in Budapest's markets and in major supermarkets like **Pick**. Hungary's national beverage is wine *(see pp194–5)* and there are

various top-quality bottles to look out for. These include fine desert wines from the Tokaji region, Muscats from Kiskunhalas on the central plain, and Chardonnays from Mátraalja. Also popular are the herbal liqueur Unicum, and the strong, fiery *pálinka*, which is made from plums, cherries or apricots. Wines and spirits are available in supermarkets and in specialist shops such as the **House of Hungarian Wines**, **Borház** and the **House of Pálinka**.

MUSIC

Hungary's rich folk and classical music traditions make low-priced CDs, tapes and vinyl a tempting purchase in Budapest. For Hungarian folk music, from traditional Roma (Gypsy) music to recordings of village folk music, the old-style **Rózsavölgyi Zeneműbolt** is a good choice. In nearby Dob utca, **Concerto Records** offers a selection of new and second-hand vinyl and CDs, specializing in classical and opera, with some jazz, folk and funk. The state label, **Hungaroton**, has a shop in Rottenbiller utca that sells a wide range of classical music as well as some pop.

BOOKS

For illustrated books and English-language guidebooks, try the **Litea Bookstore and Café**, where you can brouse through the books while enjoying coffee and cakes at tables set among the shelves. The large **Studium Libri** stocks many books in English. A wide range of English-language newspapers, magazines and novels are available at **Bestsellers**. **Írók Boltja** sells art books and some English-language books, while **Pendragon** stocks a varied assortment of fiction in English. One of the best places for maps and English-language guide books is **Párizsi Udvar**. **Librotrade-Kodex** stocks books in English, French and German. For antique books, etchings and maps a good place to try is **Központi Antikvárium**.

DIRECTORY

DEPARTMENT STORES

Arena Plaza
Kerepesi út.
Map 8 E2. *Open 10am–9pm Mon–Sat, 10am–7pm Sun.*
Tel 061 880 70 00.

Duna Plaza
Váci út 178.
Tel 465 16 66.

Mammut I–II Mall
Lövőház utca 3.
Map 1 A2.
Open 10am–9pm Mon–Sat, 10am–6pm Sun.
Tel 345 80 20.
www.mammut.hu

Westend City Center
Váci út 1–3.
Map 2 F2.
Tel 238 77 77.
www.westendcity center.hu

MARKETS

Central Market Hall (Központi Vásárcsarnok)
Vámház Körút 1–3 (Fővám tér).
Map 4 F3.
Open 6am–5pm Mon, 6am–6pm Tue–Fri, 6am–2pm Sat.
Tel 217 60 67.

Ecseri Flea Market
Nagykőrösi út 156.
Open Sat & Sun.
Tel 282 95 63.

Fehérvári út Market
Fehérvári út 20.
Map 4 D5.

Fény utca Market
Near Moszkva tér.
Map 1 A3.

Józsefvárosi Market
Kőbányai út.
Map 8 F4.

Lehel tér Market
Lehel tér.
Map 2 F1.

FOLK ART

Folkart Centrum
Váci utca 58.
Map 4 E1 (10 D3). *Open 10am–7pm daily.*
Tel 318 58 40.

Judit Kézműves
Szentháromság utca 5.
Map 1 B4.
Tel 212 76 40.

ANTIQUES

Moró Antik
Falk Miksa utca 13.
Map 2 D2.
Tel 311 08 14.

Nagyházi Gallery
Balaton utca 8.
Map 2 D2.
Tel 475 60 00.

PORCELAIN

Herend Shops
József Nádor tér 11.
Map 2 E5 (10 D3).
Tel 317 26 22.
Szentháromság utca 5.
Tel 225 10 50.
Andrássy út 16. **Map** 2 F4
Tel 374 00 06.
Váci útca 19-21. **Map** 4 E1 *Tel 266 63 05.*

Zsolnay Shops
Kossuth Lajos u.10.
Map 4 F1 *Tel 328 08 44.*
József krt. 59–61. **Map** 7 B4 *Tel 318 70 93.*
Kecskeméti u.14. **Map** 4 F2 *Tel 318 26 43.*
Bajcsy Zs.u.23. **Map** 2 F3 *Tel 311 40 94.*
www.porcelan.hu

CLOTHES AND ACCESSORIES

Dáriusz Ekszerstúdió
Wesselényi utca 36.
Map 7 B2.
Tel 328 05 98.
www.brilians.hu

Naray Tamás Boutique
Károlyi Mihály utca 12.
Map 10 E5.
Tel 266 24 73.

Vass Cipőbolt
Haris köz 2.
Map 4 E1.
Tel 318 23 75.
www.vasshoe.hu

FOOD AND DRINK

Borház
Jókai tér 7.
Map 2 F3 (10 F1).
Tel 353 48 49.

La Boutique des Vins
József Attila utca 12.
Map 2 E5 (10 D3).
Tel 317 59 19.

House of Hungarian Wines
Szentháromság tér 6.
Map 9 A2.
Open noon–8pm.
Tel 212 10 32.
www.winehouse.hu

House of Pálinka
Rákóczi út 17.
Map 7 A3. *Open 9am–7pm Mon–Sat. Free tasting: Fri.*
www.magyarpalinkaha za.hu

Pick
Kossuth Lajos tér 9.
Map 2 D3 (9 C1).
Tel 331 77 83.

MUSIC

Concerto Records
Dob utca 33.
Map 2 F5 (10 F3).
Open noon–7pm Mon–Fri.
Tel 268 96 31.

Hungaroton Records
Rottenbiller utca 47.
Map 7 C1. *Open 8am–3pm Mon–Fri.*
Tel 322 88 39.

Liszt Ferenc Zeneműboltja
Andrássy út 45.
Map 2 F5 (10 E2).
Tel 352 7314.

Rózsavölgyi Zeneműbolt
Szervita tér 5.
Map 4 E1 (10 D4).
Open 9:30am–7pm Mon–Fri, 10am–5pm Sat.
Tel 318 35 00.

BOOKS

Bestsellers
Október 6 utca 11.
Map 2 E4 (10 D2).
Tel 312 12 95.
www.bestsellers.hu

Írók Boltja
Andrássy út 45.
Map 2 F4 (10 E2).
Tel 322 16 45.

Központi Antikvárium
Múzeum Körút 13–15.
Map 4 F1 (10 E4).
Tel 317 35 14.

Librotrade-Kodex
Honvéd utca 5.
Map 7 C3.
Tel 428 10 10.

Litea Bookstore and Café
Hess András tér 4.
Map 1 B4 (9 A2).
Open 10am–6pm.
Tel 375 69 87.

Párizsi Udvar
Petőfi Sándor utca 2.
Map 4 E1 (10 E4).
Tel 235 03 79.
www.parisiudvar.hu

Pendragon
Pozsonyi út 21–23.
Map 2 F1.
Open 10am–6pm Mon–Fri, 10am–2pm Sat. Closed Sun.
Tel 340 44 26.

Pendragon at CU
Zrínyi utca 12. **Map** 2 D4.
Tel 327 30 96.
Open 10am–6pm Mon–Fri, 10am–2pm Sat.

Studium Libri
Váci utca 22 (main pedestrian precinct).
Map 4 E1 (10 D4).
Tel 318 56 80.
www.libri.hu

ENTERTAINMENT IN BUDAPEST

Budapest has been known as a city of entertainment since the late 19th century, when people would travel here from Vienna in search of a good time. Its buzzing nightclubs were frequented for their electric atmosphere and the beautiful girls that danced the spirited *csárdás* and the cancan. Nowhere else did fiddlers play such heartrending music or were the gambling casinos wit-

Street performer

ness to such staggering losses as in Budapest. Between the wars the city was as famous for its glittering society balls as for its libertine delights. The half-century of Communist rule dampened the revelry, but since 1990 the music scene has flourished and theatres, cabarets, festivals, cinemas and discotheques are all buzzing. Above all, renowned nightclubs have risen convincingly from their ashes.

ENTERTAINMENT HIGHLIGHTS

Budapest has two opera houses, an orchestral concert hall at the **Franz Liszt Academy of Music** (*see p208*), several other concert halls including the new **National Concert Hall** at the Palace of Arts (*see p156*), an operetta theatre, numerous cabarets and more than 50 theatres, including the fringe. Among them is the **Merlin Theatre** (*see p217*), which performs only in English.

The greatest concentration of theatres is in district V, in Nagymező utca, which has been nicknamed "Budapest's Broadway". Along this 100-m (328-ft) stretch there are two theatres, the **Operetta Theatre** (*see p216*), the satirical cabaret **Mikroszkóp Színpad** (*see p217*), reputed to be the best in Hungary, and the **Moulin Rouge** (*see p217*) revue theatre. Film-lovers are

spoilt for choice, as Budapest boasts many **cinemas**.

Városliget (*see pp142–3*) offers a permanent circus, funfair and zoo, with bars and beer tents in the summer.

The youth entertainment centre, **Petőfi Csarnok** (*see p217*), hosts rock concerts and the largest disco in town. **A38 Ship** is a music club in a converted ship and **Millenáris** is a relatively new concert venue and cultural centre with a varied programme. The **Budapest Arena** holds 12,000 spectators, and stages a range of cultural events. Casinos and striptease clubs are the latest addition to the city's nightlife.

FREE ENTERTAINMENT

It is not difficult to find excellent, free entertainment in Budapest. During the summer, there always seem to be street entertainers and musicians wandering around the **Castle District**, often in elaborate period costume, playing instruments or acting out scenes from Hungarian history. During the **Budapesti Búcsú** in June (*see page 59*), all entertainments, from singing and dancing to theatre, are staged by the city council for free. In July, the **Danube Water Carnival** offers most of its thrills without charge, and the **Summer on the Chain Bridge**, Budapest's largest summer festival, offers a series of events every weekend, from mid-July to September. Hungarian culture, handicrafts, music and folklore are celebrated. Guided tours of Budapest's leading

sight, **Parliament**, are now free for citizens of the EU.

Entry to Budapest's museums is no longer free, although permanent exhibitions are usually cheaper than temporary ones.

BUYING TICKETS

Tickets for all plays and concerts can be purchased in advance, either at a booking office or by telephoning the venue direct. Addresses and telephone

Lavishly staged opera at the State Opera House (see p216)

numbers are listed in the directory on pages 216–17. The most difficult to obtain are tickets to the **Franz Liszt Academy of Music** concerts, as these tend to be sold many days in advance. Similarly, seats at opera and operetta performances sell out quickly. The best way of securing a seat, particularly for summer performances, is via **Rózsavölgyi Fegyirodá** or **Ticket Express**, which are

Actors in satirical cabaret at Mikroszkóp Színpad *(see p217)*

located right in the centre of town, close to Vörösmarty tér. In Budapest, like anywhere else, you can risk it and try buying returned tickets at the last minute. A cheap alternative, but not for the weary, is to buy a standing-room pass.

LATE NIGHT TRANSPORT

Budapest's metro (see p238) runs until just after 11pm. Buses marked with black numbers and the letter 'E' provide the night transport on busy routes. There are also night trams running on some routes, though their frequency varies from between one and three an hour. Night buses should be boarded through the front door, and tickets shown to the driver. The stop-request button is situated above the exit door.

The HÉV train (see p239) that connects Budapest with its suburbs stops running at about 11:30pm.

DISABLED ACCESS

Much work has been done since Hungary joined the European Union to make the country's venues accessible to as wide a range of people as possible. However, a lot of Budapest's older venues are far from wheelchair-friendly. Places which are equipped for

Poster pillar

disabled visitors include the **Mátyás Church** (see pp82–3), the **State Opera House** (see pp118–19) and the **Franz Liszt Academy** (see p1129). The pedestrianized **Liszt Ferenc tér**, with its preponderance of outdoor cafés and terraces is also perfect for disabled travellers. The bars and pubs of Central Pest, many of which are located in basements, are not. Note that many venues (including the State Opera House) offer small reductions for disabled visitors.

The Hungarian Disabled Association
San Marco utca 76. **Tel** 250 90 13. **www**.meosz.hu

LISTINGS MAGAZINES

The best Budapest listings publication is the free weekly *Pesti Est*, which, though published almost entirely in Hungarian, is comprehensible to most people. It is available in bars, restaurants, hotels and shops. Visitors should also try the *Budapest Times* and the *Budapest Sun*, English-language free weekly newspapers that list the best current events as well as comprehensive English-language cinema screening times, theatre, opera and classical music listings. Both newspapers, and *Pesti Est*, are also available online.

The dramatic entrance to the Moulin Rouge theatre (see p217)

Other cultural bulletins include *Exit* and *Programme*, which are published in English and German, and *Budapest Panorama*, which is published in English, German, Russian, Italian and French.

LATE-NIGHT SCAMS

Budapest is generally a very safe city, but it is not without its dangers, especially late at night. Tourists are seen as easy prey by fraudsters, and it is important to stay alert at all times. Attractive peroxide-blondes promenading Váci utca and introducing themselves to single men may appear friendly and genuine at first sight, but, alas, they are not. It they insist you join them for a drink in a bar of their choice, you should refrain from doing so. They are not prostitutes, but "consumption girls", employed by bars to bring in foreign men to buy them drinks – which, as will become apparent only after the bill arrives, cost thousands of Hungarian forints.

Although a number of bars that carry out this practice have been closed by the authorities, it still goes on. Always check how much you are paying for a drink and be wary of instant female friends.

Late nights are also the delight of unscrupulous taxi drivers, eager to make a killing from tipsy tourists. Never get into a taxi that does not clearly state it belongs to a reputable taxi company, or which does not display its tariffs on the side of the driver's door. Always ask for a rough estimate of the cost before getting in.

The elegant interior of the Franz Liszt Music Academy (see p216)

Music

Thanks to great composers such as Liszt, Bartók and Kodály *(see p144)*, and the wealth of its folk tradition, Hungary is famous for its music. Hungarians have always been a nation of music lovers; in addition to performances by national artists, Budapest is frequently visited by revered musicians from around the world.

OPERA AND OPERETTA

The standard of opera in Budapest is high. Performances are at either the **State Opera House** *(see pp118–9)* or the **Erkel Theatre** *(see p151)*. At both there is a mainly classical repertoire, sung in Italian. The secondary focus is on Hungarian works. The **Operetta Theatre** *(see p115)* stages Hungarian operettas.

CLASSICAL MUSIC

The **Franz Liszt Academy of Music** *(see p129)* is the leading venue for classical music. The city's largest venue is the new **National Concert Hall** *(see p156)*. Concerts are sometimes held in the domed hall of **Parliament** *(see pp108–9)*, which has excellent acoustics, and at the **Congress Centre** *(see p160)*. Budapest also has a strong tradition of music festivals, *(see pp58–61)*.

SACRED MUSIC

Concerts of organ music are held between March and December in the magnificent setting of the **Mátyás Church** *(see pp82–3)*. Among the composers whose works are featured, Bach is the most popular. **St Stephen's Basilica** *(see pp116–7)* serves sporadically as the venue for concerts of choral music. Between March and October the Musica Sacra Agency organizes concerts in the **Great Synagogue** *(see p134)*.

FOLK & GYPSY MUSIC

Performances of folk and gypsy music are held at the **Duna Palota** and **Hungarian Heritage House**. Watch out for shows by the Hungarian State Song and Dance Ensemble and a Gypsy band that is part of the ensemble but also stages independent concerts.

During July and August the city is visited by folk troupes from all over the country.

From October to May, the city's dance houses rock to the sounds of fiddles and flutes. One of the most renowned is **Fonó Budai Zeneház**, which stages peasant and gypsy bands from Transylvania. The popular **Marcibányi téri** cultural centre stages folk and gypsy music events, and house music, as well as playing host to various other arts events and shows.

JAZZ

Jazz was very late in reaching Hungary. The best known and revered Hungarian jazz band is the Benkó Dixieland Band, which during Spring Festivals *(see p58)* plays in various theatres and large halls. The best place for jazz-lovers to congregate is **Columbus Jazz Club**, where Hungary's best players perform from 8:30pm every evening. The club boasts views of the Danube and it is a good idea to reserve a table. The **Cotton Club** *(see p198)* is also very popular.

DIRECTORY

TICKETS

Rózsavölgyi Jegyiroda
Szervita tér 5. **Map** 4 E1.
Tel 266 83 37.

Ticket Express
Andrássy út 18.
Map 10 E2. *Tel* 312 00 00.
Deák Ferenc út 19.
Map 4 E1. *Tel* 266 70 70.

OPERA AND OPERETTA

Erkel Theatre
Köztársaság tér 30.
Map 7 C3. *Tel* 333 05 40.

Operetta Theatre
Nagymező utca 17.
Map 2 F3.
Tel 472 20 30.

State Opera House
Andrássy út 22.
Map 2 F4. *Tel* 331 25 50.

CLASSICAL MUSIC

Congress Centre
Jagelló út 1–3.
Tel 372 57 00.

Franz Liszt Academy of Music
Liszt Ferenc tér 8.
Map 7 A1. *Tel* 462 46 79.

National Concert Hall
Palace of Arts
Komor Marcell utca 1.
Tel 555 30 00.

Parliament
Kossuth Lajos tér. **Map** 2
D3 (9 C1). *Tel* 441 49 04.

SACRED MUSIC

Great Synagogue
Dohány utca 2–8. **Map** 7
A3. *Tel* 342 89 49.

Mátyás Church
Szentháromság tér 2.
Map 1 B4 (9 A2).
Tel 355 56 57.

St Stephen's Basilica
Szent István tér.
Map 2 E4 (10 D2).
Tel 403 53 70.

FOLK AND GYPSY MUSIC

Hungarian Heritage House
Corvin tér 8. **Map** 1 C4 (9 A2). *Tel* 201 50 17.

Duna Palota
Zrínyi utca 5. **Map** 2 E5
(10 D2). *Tel* 317 13 77.

Fonó Budai Zeneház
Sztregova utca 3. **Map** 2
E5 (10 D3). *Tel* 206 53 00.

Marczibányi téri
Művelődesi Központ
Marczibányi tér 5/A.
Tel 212 28 20.

JAZZ

Columbus Jazz Club
Vigadó tér, Dock 4.
Map 4 D1. *Tel* 223 53 95.

Cotton Club
Jókai utca 26. **Map** 2 F3.
Tel 354 08 86.

Theatre, Cinema and Casinos

Budapest has many theatres, which are worth visiting not only for their impressive repertoires, but also because they are invariably located in beautiful, historic buildings. Cinemas show the latest films, although few retain the original soundtrack. For late-night dancing, the city has a wealth of popular clubs to choose from.

THEATRE

The first theatre to stage plays in Hungary was the **National Dance Theatre** *(see p73)*. Other established theatres include the **Madách Theatre, Nemzeti Theatre, Pesti Theatre** and **Laser Theatre**. The **Merlin Theatre** performs in English. **Trafó** is an exciting showcase for all the contemporary arts.

Budapest has over 30 drama and cabaret theatres including **Mikroszkóp Színpad**, which hosts satirical cabaret shows *(see p214)*, and the **Moulin Rouge**. The most prestigious is the **József Katona Theatre**, which became famous following performances in Paris and London. The **Vígszínház**, meaning "comedy theatre", specializes in musicals (as does the Madách Theatre). In summer rock-operas are staged on Margaret Island. These shows are remarkable both for the quality of the production and the magnificent island setting.

CINEMA

Many of Budapest's cinemas were built during the 1920s and 1930s and, despite renovations, have been superceded by modern multiplexes such as those in the shopping malls **Duna Plaza, Westend City Center**, and **Corvin Filmpalota**.

Most foreign films in Hungary are now both dubbed and subtitled into Hungarian, leaving cinema-goers free to choose which version they prefer. Those who do not understand Hungarian should choose the *angyol nelvü* (English soundtrack) version of the film. For films in English with no subtitles at all, look out for the words, *angol nyelvü, felirat nélkül.*

Apart from foreign films, the cinemas also show native Hungarian films. The range covers both the latest releases and vintage films from a time of Hungarian cinematic glory, notably

when Miklós Jancsó and István Szabó received international awards for directing. The renovated, Moorish style **Uránia Filmsínház** film palace dates from this time.

All cinema tickets can be bought a few hours in advance. Some cinemas will sell tickets for showings the next day.

CASINOS

Budapest has several casinos. Most occupy historical buildings next to smart hotels.

Casino Várkert, for example, occupies one of the city's finest Secession-era buildings, built to a design by Miklós Ybl *(see p119)*. It originally functioned as the engine room of the water supply system of the Royal Palace. For the past 40 years it has operated as an elegant restaurant and, since 1992, as both a casino and a restaurant.

At any of the casinos listed below, players can try their hand at roulette, Black Jack, poker and the wheel of fortune. All are open 24 hours a day and, with the exception of the **Las Vegas Casino**, require evening dress. Passports are also universally required.

DIRECTORY

THEATRE

National Dance Theatre
Színház 1-3. **Map** 9 A3.
Tel 356 40 85.

József Katona Theatre
Petőfi Sándor utca 6.
Map 4 E1 (10 D4).
Tel 318 37 25.

Laser Theatre
Népliget, Planetárium.
Tel 263 08 71.

Madách Theatre
Erzsébet körút 29–33.
Map 7 A2. **Tel** 478 20 41.

Merlin Theatre
Gerlóczy utca 4.
Map 4 F1 (10 E4).
Tel 317 93 38.

Mikroszkóp Színpad
Nagymező utca 22–24.
Map 2 F3 (10 E1).
Tel 332 53 22.

Moulin Rouge
Nagymező utca 17.
Map 2 F3. (10 E1.)
Tel 434 99 95.

Nemzeti Theatre
Bajor Gizi Park 1.
Map 7 B1. **Tel** 476 68 68.

Pesti Theatre
Váci utca 9.
Map 4 E1 (10 D4).
Tel 266 52 45.

Trafó
Lilom utca 41.
Map 7 B5.
Tel 215 16 00.

Vígszínház
Pannónia utca 1.
Map 2 E1. **Tel** 340 46 50.

CINEMA

Corvin Filmpalota
Corvin köz 1.
Tel 459 50 50.

Palace Duna Plaza
Váci út 178.
Tel 999 61 61.

Palace West End
Váci út 1–3.
Map 2 F2. **Tel** 999 61 61.

Uránia Nemzeti Filmsínház
Rákóczi út 21
Map 7 A3.
Tel 486 34 13.

CASINOS

Casino Tropicana
Vigadó utca 2.
Map 4 D1.
Tel 327 72 50.

Casino Várkert
Ybl Miklós tér 9.
Map 9 C4.
Tel 202 42 44.

Grand Casino Budapest
Deak Ferenc tér 13.
Map 2 E5.
Tel 483 01 70.

Las Vegas Casino
Roosevelt tér 2
(Sofitel Atrium Hotel).
Map 2 D5.
Tel 317 60 22.

Sports

Hungarians are fine athletes, as is testified by their consistently outstanding performances at competitive events, such as the Olympic Games. Budapest's world-class sports facilities serve as venues for many of these international events, including European and World championships. Sporting opportunities for visitors to the city are both varied and accessible.

SPECTATOR SPORTS

Most competitive sporting events are held either in the magnificent **Ferenc Puskás Stadium** (see p155), which seats 80,000 spectators, or in the modern, indoor **Budapest Aréna**.

Soccer remains the most popular spectator sport, although Hungarian fans can only look wistfully back to the time when their national side was highly successful. In the 1950s, for instance, Hungary beat England 6:3 at Wembley. League matches in Budapest attract big crowds. The atmosphere is particularly electric when local favourites Ferenc-város, FTC, take to the pitch.

Two of the three great events regularly held in Budapest are the Welcom Marathon Hungary and the Budapest Marathon. These are run on the last Sundays of April and September, respectively. The third big sporting event of the year is the Hungarian Grand Prix (see p59), which takes place during August at the Mogyoród racing circuit.

Hungarians achieve impressive results in boxing, canoeing, swimming, water polo and fencing, which are all widely supported.

HORSE RACING AND RIDING

As a nation of former nomads, the Hungarians have retained a great love of horses. In Budapest this passion finds its expression in horse racing, which is enormously popular. A few hours spent at a racetrack can be a cheap and fun way of soaking up the local atmosphere. Near the Albertirsai út (see p234) is the Trotters' Racecourse, at the **Kincsem Park**.

Those wishing to be rather more energetic and ride instead of watch horses, should contact the **National Riding School**, the **Petneházy School**, the **Kincsem Horsepark** or the **Budapest Riding Club**.

SPORTING ACTIVITIES

Practising sport for fitness and pleasure is both cheap and popular in Budapest.

Strolling through the city's parks, particularly on Margaret Island, you will encounter scores of eager joggers, both young and not so young. The indoor and outdoor swimming pools are also full of regular visitors, who come here for an hour or so of healthy exercise. Particularly popular is the **Hajós Olympic Pool** on Margaret Island, which is named after Hungary's first Olympic gold winner for swimming, who was also the pool's architect. Busy open-air swimming options include **Komjádi Pool** (see p52) and the neighbouring **Lukács Baths** (see p101), both of which can be enjoyed even in winter as the hot spring water creates a steamy atmosphere over the water's surface. For the hottest spa water in the city, head to the **Széchenyi Baths** (see p151), which is the largest bathing complex in Europe. However, the most atmospheric and beautiful baths are undoubtedly the 16th-century Turkish **Rudas Baths** (see p93).

Cycling is also gaining in popularity, particularly since the introduction of cycling lanes to the city's roads (see p229). If you want to play tennis, there are numerous courts available, but these tend to be monopolized by local Hungarians. Your best bet for a game is to befriend a local tennis player, or find a hotel that has its own court.

Despite the moderate climate, it is also possible to undertake winter sports in Budapest. From December until March the **Városliget Lake** (see pp142–3) is turned into a skating ring and many people take to the ice. **Sváb Hill** (see p161) is generally snow-covered from December to March and has several ski runs and ski lifts.

DIRECTORY

STADIA

Papp László Budapest Aréna
Stefánia út 2.
Map 8 F1. **Tel** 422 26 00.

Ferenc Puskás Stadium
Istvánmezei út 3–5.
Map 8 F1.
Tel 471 43 21.

HORSE RACING AND RIDING

Budapest Riding Club
Kerepesi út 7.
Tel 0630 221 28 64.

Kincsem Horsepark
Söregi út 1.
Tel 0629 423 056.

National Riding School
Kerepesi út 7. **Tel** 0630 301 83 44.

Petneházy School
Feketefej utca 2–4.
Tel 397 12 08.

Kincsem Park
Albertirsai út 2–4.

SWIMMING POOLS

Császár Komjádi Uszoda
Frankel Leó út 55.
Map 1 B1. **Tel** 212 27 50.

Lukács Baths
Frankel Leó utca 25–29.
Map 1 C1. **Tel** 326 16 95.

Hajós Olympic Pool
Margitsziget. **Tel** 450 42 20.

Rudas Baths
Döbrentei tér 9. **Map** 4 D2.
Tel 356 13 22.

Széchenyi Baths
Allatkerti körút 11.
Map 6 D3. **Tel** 363 32 10.

Children's Budapest

Visiting Budapest can be made great fun for children. There are several choices of energetic outdoor pursuits, including a funfair, a terrific zoo and, of course, a range of glorious of swimming venues. If the weather is poor, the city's historic buildings, museums and art galleries will entertain and inform. In addition, a handful of puppet theatres cater specifically for younger audiences.

youngsters occupied. Shows, which often star international artists, take place daily.

At **Vidám Park Funfair** (see p151) in Városliget, there are merry-go-rounds, a railway, shooting galleries and games machines.

SIGHTSEEING FOR KIDS

Busy Pest is a difficult area in which to entertain kids, but the **Postal Museum**, set in an opulent 19th-century mansion, is well worth a morning's visit.

In Buda's **Royal Palace** (see pp70–1) and **Castle District** (see pp68–85), the city's long history can be understood instinctively just by wandering round the ancient and lovely buildings. The **Hungarian National Gallery** (see pp74–7) feeds young imaginations, as does the fabulous *turul,* the statue of a mythical giant bird that stands in the Palace Courtyard. The magnificently carved **Mátyás Fountain** (see pp72–3) is also worth a look.

In the Old Town, the **Labyrinth of Buda Castle** (see p85) on Lords' Street is a bizarre underground exhibition that fascinates kids, and there are displays of armour and weapons in the **Museum of Military History** (see p85) . A final "must" is a ride on the **Budavári Sikló** funicular railway (see p239).

SWIMMING

The most suitable complex for young families is the seasonal **Palatinus Strand** (see p53) on Margaret Island, where there are pools of varying temperatures, water slides and artificial waves. Numerous kiosks sell snacks, ice cream and fruit.

During the winter season, the **Gellért Hotel and Baths Complex** (see pp90–1) is a better alternative. Here, the large swimming pool has artificial waves, and the paddling pool's warm water is wonderful for toddlers. **Széchnyi Baths** (see p151) also welcome children.

CIRCUS, FUNFAIR & ZOO

People of all ages love the Budapest **Zoo** (see pp150-51), which is one of the best in Europe. Attractions include a large sea-water aquarium, a terrarium with splendid snakes, and an impressive aviary.

A visit to the **Great Capital Circus** is an easy way to keep

INDOOR ATTRACTIONS

Budapest Bábszínház and **Kolibri Színház** are two of several puppet theatres that stage international favourites, such as *The Jungle Book, Cinderella* and *Snow White,* as well as Hungarian classics.

In People's Park, the **Planetárium** is known for its special entertainment shows – remarkable compositions of laser effects, pictorial projections and music, staged under an impressively large dome.

SCENIC RAILWAYS

Children love the trip up into the **Buda Hills** (see p161). The first stage is a ride on the cogwheel railway that runs up Széchényi Hill. At the top, there is a playground and the start of the Children's Railway, which follows the ridge of the hills to the Hvös Valley. The way back down is on the Libeg chair-lift that runs from the top of János Hill to Zugliget (linked by bus 158 to Moszkva tér). Young railway enthusiasts also enjoy the **Railway History Park** (see p156).

DIRECTORY

SIGHTSEEING

Budavári Sikló
Clark Ádám tér,
Szent György tér.
Map 1 C5 (9 B3).

Hungarian National Gallery
Szent György tér 2.
Map 3 C5. **Tel** 375 55 67.

Labyrinth of Buda Castle
Úri utca 9.
Map 1 A4 (9 A2).
Tel 212 02 07.

Postal Museum
Andrássy út 3.
Map 2 F4 (10 E2).
Tel 268 19 97.

Mátyás Fountain
Royal Palace.
Map 1 C5 (9 B3).

Museum of Military History
Tóth Árpád Sétany 40.
Map 1 A4. **Tel** 325 16 00.

Railway History Park
Tatai út 95. **Tel** 450 14 97.

Royal Palace
Map 1 5C (9 4B).

SWIMMING

Gellért Hotel and Baths Complex
Kelenhegyi út 4. **Map** 3 C3. **Tel** 466 61 66.

Palatinus Strand
Margitsziget.
Tel 340 45 05.

Széchnyi Baths
Állatkerti körút 11.
Map 6 D3.
Tel 363 32 10.

RECREATION

Great Capital Circus
Állatkerti körút 7.
Map 5 C3.
Tel 344 60 08.

Vidám Park Funfair
Állatkerti körut 14–16.
Map 5 C3.
Tel 363 83 10.

Zoo
Állatkerti körút 6–12.
Tel 273 49 01.
Map 5 C3.

INDOOR ATTRACTIONS

Budapest Bábszínház
Andrássy út 69.
Map 5 A5 (10 E2).
Tel 342 83 41.

Kolibri Színház
Jókai tér 10.
Map 2 F3 (10 F1).
Tel 311 08 70.

Planetárium
Népliget.
Tel 263 18 11.

SURVIVAL GUIDE

PRACTICAL INFORMATION

Tourist
information
sign

Budapest was always famous for its hospitality and the Hungarians, particularly in recent years, have been emphasizing tourism as an important part of the national economy. The biggest problem in its development is the formidable barrier posed by the Hungarian language, which hinders access to information. The Hungarians are therefore trying hard to learn foreign languages. In all tourist offices, bigger hotels and most restaurants either English or German is spoken. Information brochures and tourist pamphlets are now published in several languages. It is difficult to get lost in Budapest as the road sign system is easy to follow. The historic monuments in the city centre are best visited on foot, while the more distant sights can be easily reached by public transport *(see pp236–41).*

TOURIST INFORMATION

Prior to your arrival in Budapest it is worthwhile getting in touch with your nearest **Hungarian National Tourist Office**, who can supply useful information and put you in touch with reputable tour operators.

Many agencies specialize in organizing individual trips and tours to Hungary including **Travellers Cities Ltd, Kirker Holidays** and **Page & Moy.** They can all provide you with detailed information on meals and accommodation and help you to make reservations.

Official tourist information centres (Tourinform) in Budapest can be found at a number of locations, including **Liszt Ferenc tér, Sütő utca** at **Deák tér, Buda Castle** and **Ferihegy 1 and 2** airports.

General tourist information in a variety of languages is provided by these centres. They also sell the Budapest Card *(see p224)* – which enables unlimited travel around the city – as well as souvenirs, guide books and maps. Brown tourist signs can be found at all the important points of the city to help visitors find their way around.

ADVICE FOR VISITORS

Budapest has a favourable climate year round, but the best time to visit is between March and the end of June, and from the middle of August until October. July is generally very hot.

Various festivals and cultural programmes take place throughout the year. The end of the year is a fun time, when visitors can experience the Christmas Fair and the New Year's Eve street party.

On arriving in Budapest it is a good idea to get hold of the foreign language information booklets. The *Budapest Panorama*, the *Budapest Guide* and the *Dining Guide* each contain a calendar of cultural and tourist events for the month. They are free and are easily available from tourist centres and hotel reception desks. They all contain maps of Budapest, and free city maps are also published by the Tourism Office of Budapest.

It is also worth investing in the Budapest Card *(see p224)*, which can be bought for 48- or 72-hour periods. As well as entitling cardholders to unlimited use of public transport and free admission to museums, gives reductions on the price of tickets for various cultural events.

OPENING HOURS

Museums and galleries are open all year round. Opening times for specific venues are given under their individual entries.

One of several tourist information offices in Budapest

Horses on a tourist carriage

As a general rule, the winter season from November until March sees museums offering shorter opening hours. In the summer, from April until October, they tend to stay open a couple of hours longer, typically from 10am until 6pm. Museums remain closed on Monday, except for the National Jewish Museum *(see p134)*, which is closed on Saturday instead. Most museums, both state and private tend to charge an entrance fee, though it is worth checking to see if there are any applicable discounts.

Shopping centres in Budapest are open each day of the week, grocery stores are open from 7am to 7pm and other shops from 10am until 6pm during the week. On Saturdays shops close at 1pm, while on Sundays some department stores and market halls are open, often until 2pm. Detailed information on the opening hours of particular shops and markets can be found on pages 202–5 of this guide. Hungarians tend to take lunch early, between noon and 1pm.

ENTRY TICKETS

Tickets to museums and historical monuments can be purchased on the spot.

Average prices vary from 700 to 1,500 forints per person, but some can be as much as 2,000 forints. Nevertheless, students and school children are always entitled to reductions. Opera, concert and other tickets can be bought at ticket agencies *(see pp214–15)*. Theatre and opera tickets are also sold at individual box offices, either for shows on the same day or in advance. Ticket prices can vary from 1,500 to 10,000 forints, depending on the show.

ETIQUETTE

Casual clothes are often worn to the theatre, particularly during summer. By comparison classical music concerts and operas are much smarter affairs and even tourists will feel more comfortable wearing evening dress. Traditionally, Hungarians attach great importance to being properly dressed when going to an opera or concert hall.

DIRECTORY

TOURIST OFFICES IN BUDAPEST

Tourinform Call Centre
24-hour Tel 438 80 80.

Tourinform Buda Castle
1016 Budapest,
Szentháromság tér.
Map 1 B4 (9 A2).
Tel 488 04 75.
www.budapestinfo.hu

Tourinform Ferihegy Airport
1185 Budapest,
Ferihegy 1.
Tel 296 57 94.
Ferihegy 2, Terminal A.
Tel 296 54 94.
Ferihegy 2, Terminal B.
Tel 296 54 95.
www.budapestinfo.hu

Tourinform Hotline
Tel from abroad
+36 30 30 30 600.0.

Tourinform Hotline
Tel from Hungary
06 80 630 800.

Tourinform Liszt Ferenc tér
1061 Budapest, Liszt Ferenc tér 11.
Map 7 A1.
Tel 322 40 98.
www.budapestinfo.hu

Tourinform Sütő Street
1052 Budapest
Sütő utca 2
(Deák Ferenc tér).
Map 2 E5 (10 D3).
Tel 438 80 80.
www.budapestinfo.hu

TOURIST OFFICES ABROAD

United Kingdom
Hungarian National Tourist Office
Embassy of Hungary
46 Eaton Place
London SW1X 8AL.
Tel 020 7823 04 11.
www.hungary welcomesbritain.com

United States
Hungarian National Tourist Office
350 Fifth Ave
Suite 7107, New York
NY 10118
Tel 212 695 12 21.
www.gotohungary.com

TRAVEL AGENTS ABROAD

Kirker Holidays
4 Waterloo Court, 10 Theed St, London SE1 8ST, United Kingdom.
Tel 020 7593 22 88.
www.kirkerholidays.com

Page & Moy
Compass House,
Rockingham Road,
Market Harborough,
Leicestershire LE16 7QD,
United Kingdom.
Tel 0116 217 80 10.
www.pageandmoy.com

Travellers Cities Ltd.
203 Main Road,
Biggin Hill, Kent TN16 3JU, United Kingdom. *Tel* 01959 54 07 00.
www.travellerscities.com

USEFUL WEBSITES

Hungarian National Tourist Office
www.hungarytourism.hu

Tourinform
www.tourinform.hu

Tourism Office of Budapest
www.budapestinfo.hu

Additional Information

Tourists in Szentháromság tér

and a 10 to 20 per cent discount in recommended restaurants.

The card costs about 6,500 Hungarian forints for 48 hours and 8,000 forints for 72 hours. Cards can be purchased at tourist offices, hotel reception desks, museums and at the ticket offices of the majority of the larger metro stations.

Enclosed with the card is an information pamphlet, in four languages, listing its benefits.

Budapest Card

PASSPORT AND CUSTOMS REGULATIONS

Citizens of the US, Canada, and Australia need a valid passport to visit Hungary for up to 90 days. EU visitors may stay as long as they please. Visitors from other countries require a visa which can be obtained from any Hungarian embassy. All visitors should check their requirements prior to travelling. Only visitors on long-term visas can apply for and obtain a residency permit.

The loss or theft of a passport should be reported to the appropriate consulate or embassy as soon as possible. Carry your passport or a copy of it to identify yourself. For safety reasons, keep a copy in your hotel. As well as personal belongings, visitors can bring the following items into the country tax-free (fees up to 175 Euros): 200 cigarettes, 2 litres wine, 1 litre liqueur, 500 g coffee or 100 g tea.

Signs showing facilitites and major tourist attractions in Budapest

TAX-FREE GOODS

Non-EU residents can apply for the refund of VAT (ÁFA in Hungarian) charged on goods purchased in Hungary. To reclaim it, visitors need to present the ÁFA invoice at the border. This only applies to sums in excess of 50,000 Hungarian forints (175 Euros), and does not apply to works of art. The exported goods must be new and not previously used in Hungary. They must also have been bought within the last 90 days.

BUDAPEST CARD

This splendid new facility, introduced in 1997, is designed for tourists visiting the city for two or three days.

The Budapest Card entitles a visitor, together with one child under 14, to use all city transport – metro, bus, tram, trolley bus, funicular and HÉV – free of charge, as well as providing free entry to 60 museums, the zoo and the funfair. It also entitles the holder to a 50 per cent discount on guided tours of the city, a 10 to 20 per cent discount on tickets to selected spas and cultural events,

PRESS, RADIO AND TV

In Budapest all the world's top newspapers and magazines are easily accessible at hotels. A number of the larger news stands maintain a constant stock of international newspapers and magazines. The largest number of these can be found at the underpasses near Nyugati and Keleti stations. As well as these, there are also various shops around town which specialize in English-language newspapers, books and maps (see pp212–3).

Bear in mind that the foreign daily newspapers on sale tend to be yesterday's editions, but even so they often sell out by lunchtime. For English-speaking tourists there are also quite a few magazines, including *Budapest in your Pocket*, *The Budapest Sun* and *NLG*. These provide the most comprehensive information on local and, in some cases, world events as well as full entertainment guides.

The city's larger hotels are geared up for the needs of the international traveller and, in addition to the state and independent Hungarian television channels, most offer tens of satellite TV channels in English and other European languages.

English language magazines, published in Budapest

DISABLED TRAVELLERS

Budapest is becoming more accessible for disabled visitors, although it is best to call ahead to the sights or obtain specialist information prior to your visit to ensure it is as hassle free as possible. Many buses are now equipped for boarding and some metro stations have special lifts. For advice and help, contact the **Hungarian Disabled Association**. Many museums and monuments present difficulties for the disabled, although increasingly they are being renovated to be wheelchair-friendly.

BUDAPEST TIME

Budapest uses Central European time, in keeping with the rest of mainland Europe, which means it is two hours ahead of Greenwich Mean Time (GMT) in the summer and one hour ahead in the winter.

Examples of the winter time differences between Budapest and other major cities are as follows: London: -1 hour; New York: -6 hours; Dallas: -7 hours; Los Angeles: -9 hours; Perth: +7 hours; Sydney: +9 hours; Auckland: +11 hours; Tokyo: +8 hours.

PUBLIC TOILETS

There are not many public toilets in Budapest, and most require a small fee for their use. It is worth carrying some small change if you anticipate having to use them.

The cubicle type is found in some squares and parks and these are usually free. In cafés and restaurants there are toilet attendants and the price for using the facility is usually clearly displayed.

There are no public toilets in metro stations, except for Batthyány tér.

Sign for the ladies' toilet

Sign for the gentlemen's toilet

Apart from the generally understood picture symbols, the toilets are signed in Hungarian: *Hölgyek* (ladies) and *Urak* (gentlemen), or *Nők* (women) and *Férfiak* (men).

ELECTRICAL AND GAS APPLIANCES

Hungarian electricity supply is 220 V and the plugs needed are the standard continental type. Adapters can be purchased in most countries. Since sockets are generally earthed, the most commonly used plugs are the flat type.

Hungarian gas cookers are equipped with a bimetal safety device, which means that after lighting the knob should be held down until the burner warms up. This is an effective means of preventing the escape of any unlit gas.

Hungarian plug with two pins

DIRECTORY

FOREIGN EMBASSIES AND CONSULATES IN BUDAPEST

Australia
Királyhágó tér 8–9.
Tel 457 9777.
Fax 201 97 92.
www.ausembbp.hu

Canada
Ganz ú. 12–14.
Map 1 B2.
Tel 392 33 60.
Fax 392 33 90.

New Zealand
Teréz körút 38.
Map 2 F3.
Tel 428 2208.
Fax 428 2208.

South Africa
Gárdonyi Géza utca 17.
Tel 392 09 99.
Tel 200 72 77.
@ dha@axelero.hu

United Kingdom
Harmincad utca 6.
Map 2 E5.
Tel 266 28 88.
Fax 266 09 07.
@ info@britemb.hu
www.britishembassy.hu

United States
Szabadság tér 12.
Map 2 E4. *Tel* 475 44 00.
Fax 475 47 64.
@ usconsular.budapest
@state.gov
www.usembassy.hu

HUNGARIAN EMBASSIES

United Kingdom
35 Eaton Place,
London SW1X 8BY.
Tel 020 7235 5218.
www.huemblon. org.uk

United States
3910 Shoemakers Street
NW, Washington DC,
20008.
Tel 202 362 6730.
www.huembwas.org

INTERNATIONAL NEWSPAPERS

A Világsajtó Háza
V. Városház utca 3–5.

Map 10 E4. *Tel* 317 13
11. **Open** 7am–7pm
Mon–Fri, 7am–2pm Sat,
8am–12 noon Sun.

Bestsellers
V. Október 6 utca 11.
Map 10 D2. *Tel* 312 12 95.
Open 9am–6.30pm
Mon–Fri, 10am–5pm Sat,
10am–4pm Sun.
www.bestsellers.hu

DISABLED TRAVELLERS

Hungarian Disabled Association
San Marco utca 76.
Tel 250 9013.
Fax 454 1144.
www.meosz.hu.

Security and Health

Police Symbol

Budapest is not just a beautiful city, it is also one with efficient and well-maintained services which help to ensure the safety and well-being of its residents. The public telephones generally work, the bus and tram stops display timetables and public transport is both clean and reliable. Nevertheless, as with all other central European countries, there are a growing number of negative social phenomena. Local people are increasingly complaining about rising crime rates, the plague of pickpockets and incidences of car theft. Visitors to Budapest will also be sadly aware of the growing numbers of homeless people living on the streets.

Police car

ADVICE TO VISITORS

Documents and money should be carried in a secure inside pocket or in a money belt. Traveller's cheques are widely accepted, so there is no need to carry much cash on you.

Money should be exchanged at a bank, your hotel or an exchange bureau, never on the black market. Do not leave valuables in your car.

There are four multistorey car parks in the city centre: at Nos. 4–6 Aranykéz utca, No. 20 Nyár utca, and on Erzsébet tér and Szervita tér. A lot of the larger hotels have an underground garage. Cars parked improperly may be clamped or towed away to a car park outside the centre. To find out where a car has been taken, call the **Removed Cars Information** line. Fines of up to 30,000 HUF can also be imposed for parking

Police badge

offences. Pickpockets operate during rush hours, targeting people in crowded metro stations, buses and shopping centres. They also operate at all the main tourist sights, and on nearby public transport. When working as a group, they may surround unsuspecting tourists and jostle or distract them. For this reason it is a good idea to have a photocopy of your passport and your travel insurance. If a passport is lost call the police in Szalay utca

Road policeman on a motorbike

11–13 (373 10 00), where English is spoken. Once the appropriate police certificate is obtained, report the loss to your embassy (see p225).

SECURITY

Hungarian police are frequently seen patrolling the streets on motorbikes, on foot or in cars. In addition, every district has its own police station. The Hungarian word for police is *rendőrség*. In the event of anything going missing, because of loss or theft, a report should be made immediately to the police. In the event of a lost passport, see the section under the heading *Advice to Visitors.*

All visitors should check their visa requirements prior to travelling. Australian tourists will need a visa, but Europeans and Americans can stay for three to six months without one. However, after one month make sure to check the registration requirements at a local police station. In reality, this applies mainly to tourists staying in private accommodation or with friends, since all hotels, hostels and pensions automatically register foreign guests. For more information, see the Hungarian Ministry of Foreign Affairs' website (www.mfa.gov.hu).

Tourists coming to Budapest by car are obliged to have the green insurance card, while those hiring a car need only present their driving licences. Hitchhiking, although not against the law, is not a recommended way of travelling in Hungary.

Women should not walk unaccompanied late at night in poorly lit areas and should avoid deserted streets. Rákóczi tér and Mátyás tér, in district VIII, have been infamous for their brothels since the 19th century and have a long-standing tradition as hangouts for prostitutes. Prostitution has been officially outlawed in Hungary since 1950. In recent years, however, it has been tolerated more.

MEDICAL MATTERS

When travelling to Hungary it is highly recommended that visitors take out travel insurance.

Foreign nationals are only entitled to free medical help in emergencies, such as accidents or a sudden illness requiring immediate medical intervention. Any other medical care, including hospitalization, must be paid for. The cost depends on the type of insurance policy held and the relevant agreement between Hungary and the visitor's home country. Most insurance companies expect policy holders to pay for their treatment as they receive it and then apply for a refund on their return home. All the relevant bills and police reports must be submitted with any insurance claim. Remember that, where applicable, a report must be made to the police within seven days of any incident.

Budapest's pharmacies (*Gyógyszertár or Patika*) are well stocked and, in case of a minor ailment, the chemist will be able to recommend a suitable treatment. Some drugs require a prescription, while others can be sold over

Pharmacy sign

the counter. If your nearest pharmacy is closed, there should be a list displayed, either on the door or in the window, of all the local chemists and it will indicate which ones are on 24-hour emergency duty.

No special vaccinations are required for Hungary and the general standard of hygiene in the country is reasonably good. That said, allergy sufferers and people with breathing difficulties should take account of the summer smog conditions, which are particularly acute in the crowded streets of Pest. Those susceptible should consider staying in the Castle District, from which cars are banned, or retreating to the wooded Buda Hills (*see p161*)

Pharmacy shop front

or the greenery of Margaret Island (*see pp170–71*).

The water in Budapest is of good quality. It is generally considered safe to drink water straight from the tap. There are also numerous thermal baths (*see pp50–53*) which are an excellent way to relax.

Ambulance

DIRECTORY

EMERGENCY SERVICES

Ambulance
Tel 104 (also 311 16 66).

Fire
Tel 105.

Police
Tel 107.

Metropolitan Police
Tel 443 50 00.

Electricity Emergency Service
Tel 06 40 38 38 38 (ask for number of local service) or for emergency maintenance Tel 06 40 38 39 40.

Gas Emergency Service
Tel 477 13 33 (24 hours)

Water Emergency Service
Tel 06 40 24 77 42.

HELPLINES

Aids Helpline
Tel 338 24 19 (8am–4pm Mon–Thu, 8am–1pm Fri).

Alcoholics Anonymous
Tel 251 00 51.

BKV Lost Property
Tel 461 66 88, choose 3 on the menu.

Fönix SOS Medical Service
1125 Budapest,
Diós drok utca 1–3
Tel 200 01 00.
www.fonixsos.hu

Foreigners' Registry Office
Budafoki utca 60.
Tel 463 91 00. Open 8am–noon Mon–Wed & Fri, 8am–6pm Thu.

International Vehicle Insurance
Tel 061 209 07 30.

Removed Cars Information
Tel 107 (Police) or 307 51 07.

SOS Non-Stop Dental Service
Kiraly Utca 14. **Map** 2 F5.
Tel 267 96 02 (24 hours).

Telefon-doktor
Tel 317 21 11.

Vehicle Assistance & Breakdown Emergency Service
Tel 188.

Mak-Magyar Autóklub
Tel 188 for information. Headquarters Tel 345 16 87.

PHARMACIES

Déli Gyógyszertár
Alkotás u.1/b. **Tel** 355 46 91.

Teréz Patika
Teréz krt. 41. **Map** 10 F1.
Tel 311 44 39

Local Currency and Banking

Bureau de change sign

The Hungarian currency system is rapidly approaching the European standard. Budapest now boasts many modern banks, both Hungarian and foreign, which are located in smart and spacious buildings. The service is efficient and courteous. There are many automatic cash dispensers and bureaux de change in the town centre and around the railway stations. An increasing number of shops and restaurants now accept credit cards, but it is still more common in Budapest to pay for goods and services in cash. Most banks will now also advance money on a credit card.

Cash dispenser

CURRENCY REGULATIONS

Foreigners are allowed to bring 350,000 Hungarian forints into Hungary, which at the beginning of 2000 was equal to about US $1,400 (890 pounds sterling). The same amount of money can be taken out of the country. There are no restrictions concerning the denominations of the Hungarian currency brought in or taken out.

Tourists who bring in foreign currencies totalling in excess of 100,000 Hungarian forints should declare them on arrival and ask the customs official for a receipt. This can then be presented when leaving the country, as the same limit applies to foreign currencies brought in and taken out of the country, without the need for an additional licence.

Foreign currencies can be easily exchanged into forints in banks, bureaux de change and hotels, but there is a limit of 20,000 Hungarian forints per day. To exchange any unspent forints back into a convertible currency, visitors have to present the proof of purchase. So keep all the exchange receipts until the end of the visit. Otherwise, tourists will find themselves at home with forints that devalue quite rapidly, at a rate of 10–15 per cent relative to the major foreign currencies.

BANKS AND BUREAUX DE CHANGE

For the best rate of exchange, take foreign currency to a bank or bureau de change, which are generally run by Hungarian banks. Before changing money, check the rate of exchange, as they do tend to vary quite widely. The rates quoted by some exchange offices can be misleading as they could apply only to sums in excess of 200,000 forints, which is stated in a very small print.

The least favourable rates are in hotels and at the airport, while the best are offered by the bureaux de change near the railway stations and in the city centre, in Petőfi Sándor utca. A reasonable, average rate can usually be found at Hungarian banks.

The branches of **Budapest Bank** are open Monday till Friday, from 10:30am until 2pm. Merchant banks, such as **K & H Bank**, are open Monday till Thursday, between 8am and 3pm, and on Friday between 8am and 1pm. Most banks are closed on Saturdays and Sundays, but the bureaux de change and automatic cash dispensers remain open.

Exchanging money is only permitted in licensed, designated places. Transactions on the street are illegal, and those who enter into such transactions are likely to receive counterfeit money.

Most hotels, stores and restaurants accept credit cards. The most widely accepted are VISA, American Express, MasterCard and Diners Club. The logos of accepted credit cards are usually on display.

DIRECTORY

BANKS

Budapest Bank

Váci út 188.

Tel 450 60 00.

CIB Bank

Medve út 4-14.

Tel 457 68 00.

K & H Bank

Vigadó tér 1.

Tel 300 00 00.

Magyar Külkereskedelmi Bank Rt

Váci utca 38.

Tel 0640 333 666.

OTP Bank

Deák F. utca 7–9.

Tel 366 63 88.

Erste Bank

Népfürdö út 24-26.

Tel 0640 555 444.

Entrance to a branch of the Budapest Bank, in Váci utca

Hungarian currency

The Hungarian currency unit is the forint (HUF or Ft). Banknotes are issued in denominations of 200, 500, 1,000, 2,000, 5,000, 10,000 and 20,000 forints. Both an old and a new style of some notes are currently legal tender, but an older version of the 5,000 than the one shown here is no longer accepted.

200 HUF

500 HUF

1,000 HUF

2,000 HUF

5,000 HUF

10,000 HUF

20,000 HUF

Coins

Currently in circulation are coins of 5, 10, 20, 50 and 100 forints. As with the bank-notes, new coins are gradually being phased in – the new 100 forint coin, with a brass disc inside a nickel ring, is now the only legal version.

10 HUF

5 HUF

20 HUF

50 HUF

100 HUF

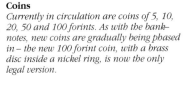

Communications

Telephone symbol

The Hungarian telephone operating system has undergone enormous changes in the last few years. Nowadays, you can easily access the telephone number you require. There are many telephone boxes throughout the city, although card-operated telephones are much more widespread than coin-operated ones. Most telephone boxes no longer contain a telephone directory. However, by dialling 198, the telephone information system provides a directory enquiry service.

Telephone box

USING THE TELEPHONE

Telephone cards are the best option, and can be obtained in units of 800, 1,800 or 5,000 forints. They are widely available from tobacconist shops, post offices, street vendors and some newspaper kiosks. Alternatively, coin phone boxes accept 10, 20 50 and 100 forint coins and also €1 and €2 coins. The minimum rate for a local call is 20 forints, and 100 for an international call. To make an international call dial 00,

wait for the dialing signal and then dial the country code, followed by the rest of the number.

Budapest telephone numbers consist of seven digits (when combined with the dialing code there are eight digits). There is really no advantage in using the services of a hotel operator, as this only adds to the length of the call and makes the call very much more expensive.

Cheaper off-peak rates apply throughout the night and on public holidays.

USING A CARD TELEPHONE

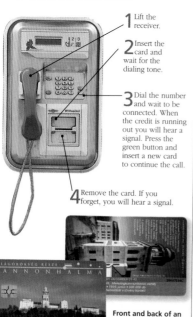

1 Lift the receiver.

2 Insert the card and wait for the dialing tone.

3 Dial the number and wait to be connected. When the credit is running out you will hear a signal. Press the green button and insert a new card to continue the call.

4 Remove the card. If you forget, you will hear a signal.

Front and back of an 800 forint plastic telephone card

USING A COIN TELEPHONE

1 Lift the receiver.

2 Insert coins and wait for the dialling tone.

3 Dial the number and wait to be connected. When the credit is running out you will hear a signal and should then insert more coins.

4 When you have finished speaking, replace the receiver. Wait for any unused coins to be returned.

10 HUF   **20 HUF**   **50 HUF**

Budapest's Districts

Budapest is divided into 23 districts. Streets of the same name may appear in several different districts, so it is important when addressing a letter to quote the four-digit postal code.

INTERNET CAFES

Email is a popular way to communicate from abroad. Budapest has several internet cafés offering coffee and snacks while you check your emails or search the internet.

Internet Galéria & Café
VI Szondi utca 79. **Map** 5 A5. **Tel** 269 00 73. **Open** 8am–midnight daily.

Kávészünet Internet Café
XIII Tátra utca 12/b. **Map** 2 E3. **Tel** 236 08 53. **Open** 8am–10pm Mon–Fri, 10am–8pm Sat–Sun.

Siesta Netcafé
VI Izabella utca 85. **Map** 7 B1. **Tel** 312 32 59. **Open** 10am–2am Mon–Fri, noon–2am Sat, noon–midnight Sun.

POSTAL SERVICES

When going to a post office in Budapest, you must be prepared to spend some time there. Postage stamps cost between 70 to 190 Hungarian forints for sending a postcard. Apart from ordinary stamps, all post offices sell various special issues that are very pretty. Ask the cashier if you can see the different designs.

On weekdays, most post offices are open from 8am until 6pm, and they usually close at 2pm on Saturday and are closed all day Sunday. If you know the values of the stamps you require, it is easier to buy them from a *trafik* (a tobacconist shop or a newspaper kiosk), as often there are long queues at post offices.

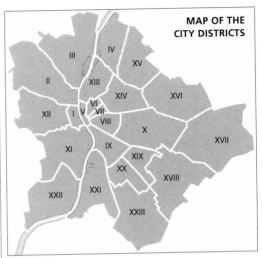

MAP OF THE CITY DISTRICTS

Post office logo

Post offices cannot be avoided, however. Airmail (*légiposta*) or registered letters have to be posted at a post office and poste restante mail has to be collected there. Telegrams can also be sent by telephone from post offices. Public fax machines can be found at most post offices.

Budapest postal codes are four-digit numbers. The first digit refers to Budapest, the second and third digits refer to the district number and the fourth digit defines the postal area within the district.

Post boxes are emptied daily at the times indicated on the front of the box.

POST OFFICE ADDRESSES

Bajcsy-Zsilinszky út 16. **Map** 10 E1. **Open** 8am–8pm Mon–Fri.

Baross tér 11. **Map** 8 D2. **Open** 7am–8pm Mon–Fri, 7am–2pm Sat.

Krisztina körút. **Map** 3 C1. **Open** 7am–8pm Mon–Fri, 7am–2pm Sat.

Teréz körút 51. **Map** 10 F1. **Open** 7am–8pm Mon–Fri, 8am–6pm Sat.

Városház utca 18. **Map** 10 E4. 8am–8pm Mon–Fri, 8am–2pm Sat.

Red post box for national and international mail

USEFUL TELEPHONE NUMBERS AND DIALLING CODES

- Sending telegrams: 192
- International operator calls: 190
- Inland operator calls: 191
- Inland information: 198
- International information: 199
- SDC for international calls: 00
- SDC from Budapest to other Hungarian towns: 06
- SDC from Budapest to Australia: 00 61
- SDC from Budapest to France: 00 33
- SDC from Budapest to New Zealand: 00 64
- SDC from Budapest to South Africa: 00 27
- SDC from Budapest to the UK: 00 44
- SDC from Budapest to the US: 00 1
- For Budapest from UK and most of Europe: 00 361
- For Budapest from US and Australia: 00 11 361

GETTING TO BUDAPEST

Hungarians like to boast that Budapest is the heart of central Europe – a claim with some justification, as the city acts as a major crossroads linking north to south and west to east. It has excellent rail links with the whole of Europe and its two largest railway stations, Keleti and Nyugati (*see p235*) are conveniently situated in the centre of town. The country's motorway network has undergone improvements in recent years, making up for decades of neglect.

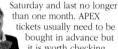

A plane owned by the Hungarian airline, Malév

Budapest can now be reached by motorway from all directions but the north. Travelling down by car from Slovakia and Poland, via Vác, is not recommended. The poorly maintained, narrow road makes for a very tedious journey, particularly at peak travelling times. For convenience, it is better to make use of the air links Budapest has with major cities throughout Europe. The journey from London to Budapest, for example, takes just two and a half hours.

ARRIVING BY AIR

Airlines from around 60 towns and cities, in 30 different countries, now fly to Budapest. The city's Ferihegy airport is used by many major international airlines, including **Air France, British Airways, Northwest, Lufthansa**, the Hungarian national carrier **Malév**, and the major low-cost airlines. Between them, British Airways, Malév and the low-cost airlines operate eight flights daily between Budapest and London's international airports.

It is possible to fly to Budapest from other airports in the UK, including Manchester, only by taking a connecting flight from another European city, such as Brussels or Frankfurt. Consequently, flight times and costs are greater.

Northwest airline's flights

from the United States involve a transfer or touchdown in Frankfurt or Zurich, but there is a daily direct code-share flight from New York's JFK airport with Northwest reservations on a Malév-owned plane. The flight takes around ten hours.

A direct flight service now operates between Beijing and Budapest.

TICKETS AND CONCESSIONS

When planning to travel to Budapest by air, bear in mind that substantial savings can be made by purchasing APEX tickets, although they do carry certain conditions. The tickets require fixed dates for departure and return, and the stay must include at least one

Malév stewardess

Saturday and last no longer than one month. APEX tickets usually need to be bought in advance but it is worth checking purchasing arrangements with individual airlines. For those aged 2–24, British Airways offer youth fares to Budapest which, although nominally higher than the lowest APEX fare, carry none of the normal restrictions. Low-cost airlines offer good deals year-round. The low autumn-winter season is a good time to look for special offers from the major carriers. Look out also for low-price weekend flight-plus-hotel deals between September and March.

FERIHEGY AIRPORT

Budapest's international airport terminals, Ferihegy 1 and Ferihegy 2, are 16 km (10 miles) from the city centre. Ferihegy 2, built in 1985, was extended to accommodate more flights in 1997–8 and, in 1999 took on all Budapest's passenger services. Ferihegy 1, an older terminal, has been modernised and now mainly handles low-cost airlines. Terminal 2a deals with the arrivals and departures of the Hungarian carrier, Malév; Terminal 2b handles those of all foreign airlines.

Both terminals offer good amenities to passengers.

Check-in desk at Budapest's modern Ferihegy 2

A Malév aircraft parked outside Ferihegy 2

Catering facilities include bars, cafés and restaurants, and there are numerous boutiques and shops. Both airports have tourist offices and currency exchange facilities. All the major car rental firms have desks in the arrivals halls of Ferihegy 1, Ferihegy 2a and Ferihegy 2b. The main names to look out for are Avis, Budget and Europcar (see p236).

For departing travellers, there are several duty-free shops selling all kinds of goods – not only Hungarian products.

Airport taxi company logo

Malév airlines' logo

GETTING TO THE CENTRE

For around 2,500 Hungarian forints (4,400 forints return) the **Airport Minibus Shuttle** takes passengers from either terminal to any address in the city centre. Minibuses have wheelchair access and can pick up returning passengers. (Call 24 hours before departure.) Bus no 200 runs to Kőbánya-Kispest metro station, followed by the blue M3 metro line, and trains to Western Railway station leave from Ferihegy Terminal 1. The airport taxi, **Zóna Taxi,** charges 3,600–4,400 forints depending on which zone in Budapest you are travelling to.

DIRECTORY

AIRPORT AND AIRLINES

Ferihegy Airport
Tel 296 96 96 (general info).
Tel 296 70 00 (flight info).

Air France
Rákóczi út 1–3.
Map 10 F4.
Tel 483 88 00.

British Airways
Rákócz út 1–3.
Map 10 F4.
Tel 411 55 55.

Lufthansa
Lechner Ödön
Fasor 6
Tel 411 99 00.

Malév Airlines
Könyves Kálmán Krt. 12/14
Tel 0640 212 121

Northwest (KLM)
East West Business Centre,
Rákóczi út 1–3.
Map 10 F4.
Tel 373 7737.

AIRPORT MINIBUS

Airport Minibus Shuttle
Tel 296 85 55.
(Phone booking 6am–10pm daily.)

AIRPORT TAXI

Zóna Taxi
Tel 365 55 55.

BUDAPEST'S AIR LINKS WITH EUROPE

Budapest has air links with major cities in every European country. From each of the locations marked on the map you can travel to Budapest in under three hours.

Ticket offices at a main railway station in Budapest

RAIL TRAVEL

Budapest has direct rail links with 25 other capital cities. Every day, more than 50 international trains, many of them express services, arrive and depart from the city's four railway stations. Some trains terminate here, while others enable passengers to join connecting services. Hungarian trains are widely considered to be a very efficient means of getting around, and their reputation is well deserved. Most importantly, they invariably depart and arrive at the right time.

Trains from Budapest to Vienna, the main communication hub for western Europe, depart approximately every three hours. The fastest trains run at top speeds of 140–160 km/h (85–100 mph). The travelling time is an efficient 2 hours 50 minutes. The "Transbalkan" train, which also has car carriages, runs from Keleti pu to Thessaloníki in Greece every day.

Detailed information on all domestic and international rail travel running to and from Budapest can be obtained from either Keleti pu or the MÁV (Hungarian Railways) ticket sales office, which is centrally located at No. 35 Andrássy út.

It is worth knowing that there are several concessionary fares available. Foreign visitors to Hungary can buy a season ticket that is valid for between seven and ten days

and offers unlimited travel throughout the country. There are also a number of Europe-wide passes that allow you to travel cheaply on trains throughout Europe and Hungary.

Local trains can be either "slow" *(személy)* or "speedy" *(sebes),* but both invariably make frequent stops. A much better option if time is tight is for you to take the fast *(gyors)* train. There are also modern Intercity trains, which take passengers to Pécs, Miskolc, Debrecen, Szeged, Békéscsaba and all the larger cities in Hungary in around 1–3 hours. Seat reservations, costing a small extra charge, are required on these clean and comfortable trains.

Railwayman

RAILWAY STATIONS

There are three main railway stations in Budapest – Keleti pu (East), Nyugati pu (West) and Déli pu (South). A fourth station, Józsefváros pu, handles mainly domestic

traffic, although it does cater for a handful of longer routes. Most international trains run from Keleti pu. The express train to Croatia ("Maestral") and trains to the Lake Balaton resorts leave from Déli pu, almost hourly in high season. The easiest way to get to Keleti pu is by the M2 metro. The same line connects Keleti pu with Déli pu. For Nyugati pu take the M3 metro line, or trams 4 or 6. A special minibus runs between the various railway stations.

Rail information
Tel *371 94 49.*
Tel *0640 49 49 49.*
www.elvira.hu
Central Ticket Office
József Attila u.16. **Open** daily.

COACH TRAVEL

Budapest has one international coach station, called Népliget (Üllői út 131), which can easily be accessed by the M3 metro line. There are three national coach stations: Népliget (to Western Hungary), Stadionok (to Eastern Hungary), and Árpád Bridge (to Northern Hungary and the Danube Bend). Népstadion station can be reached by the M2 metro line, while Árpád Bridge is served by the M3 line. The international routes are served by luxury coaches, which have all the usual facilities. The domestic and main international traffic is served by Volánbusz coaches, which operate routes to most of the major towns throughout Hungary.

Coach information
Tel *382 08 88 or 219 80 86.*

The imposing exterior of the Nyugati Railway Station

Luxury air-conditioned tourist coach

TRAVELLING BY BOAT

From April until October hydrofoils cruise the Danube from Vienna to Budapest, via Bratislava. It is also possible to take a hydrofoil or pleasure boat along to the Danube bend, to towns such as Esztergom and Visegrád (*see p164*). See the timetable at the departure point at Vigadó tér for details.

Cruise companies
Mahart Passnave *Tel 484 40 13.*
Legenda Ltd *Tel 317 22 03.*

TRAVELLING BY CAR

Note that parking in Budapest is extremely difficult.

Motorways are marked "M" and international highways "E". The speed limit is 130 km/h (80 mph). Seven main roads lead out of Budapest and one, the A8, starts in Székésfehérvár. The M1 stretches from Budapest to the Hegyeshalom border crossing, where it joins the Austrian motorway network. Tolls are payable on all motorways. The M3 links Budapest to Polgár and is being extended to join up with the Slovak road network. From Budapest the M5 leads to Kecskemét (*see p166*), while the M7 links to the Balaton resorts.

Minor roads have three or four digits, with the first digit indicating the number of the connecting main road.

Traffic regulations include: driving with the headlights on, wearing seatbelts in the back and keeping to the speed limit of 50 km/h (30 mph) in built-up areas.

Drivers must purchase an electronic motorway sticker for all motorways except M0, bought at petrol stations near or on the motorway.

Vehicle assistance
Tel 188 (for breakdowns).
Tel 0640 40 50 60 (for information).

A road sign directing traffic to Margaret Bridge and the M3

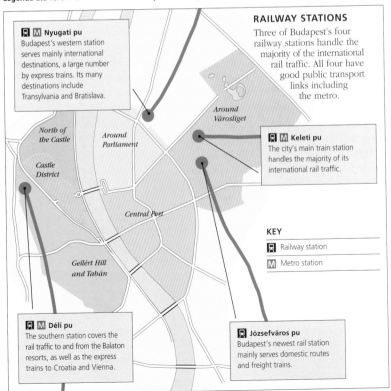

RAILWAY STATIONS

Three of Budapest's four railway stations handle the majority of the international rail traffic. All four have good public transport links including the metro.

🚊 Ⓜ **Nyugati pu**
Budapest's western station serves mainly international destinations, a large number by express trains. Its many destinations include Transylvania and Bratislava.

Around Városliget

North of the Castle

Around Parliament

🚊 Ⓜ **Keleti pu**
The city's main train station handles the majority of its international rail traffic.

Castle District

Central Pest

KEY
🚊 Railway station
Ⓜ Metro station

Gellért Hill and Tabán

🚊 Ⓜ **Déli pu**
The southern station covers the rail traffic to and from the Balaton resorts, as well as the express trains to Croatia and Vienna.

🚊 **Józsefváros pu**
Budapest's newest rail station mainly serves domestic routes and freight trains.

GETTING AROUND BUDAPEST

Budapest is a sprawling city with many suburban districts. However, most of its main tourist attractions are centrally located and can be easily reached by the city's public transport system, or on foot. The many choices of transport by rail, road and even water provide the visitor to Budapest with ample opportunity to travel through and around the city to reach their chosen

One of Budapest's environmentally friendly city buses

destinations. The infrastructure of Budapest is chiefly determined by the *körúts* (ring roads), which radiate out from the city centre and into the city's suburbs. The metro system mainly operates in Pest, although the red M2 line crosses the Danube at Batthyány tér and runs just north of the Castle District. The overland HÉV train provides a service from the city centre to the suburbs.

DRIVING IN BUDAPEST

The large number of one-way streets in Budapest make it a very difficult city for visitors to navigate by car. The many changes of direction often result in unfamiliar drivers becoming lost. Any confusion brought about by the complex system of roads is further aggravated by the heavy rush-hour traffic. There are also few places to park in the city, so it is much better to sightsee on foot or by public transport.

In Hungary it is strictly forbidden to drive following

One-way traffic in direction indicated

Stop sign at road junction

End of pedestrian and cycle zone

any alcohol consumption. If any trace of alcohol is found in the bloodstream, the fine for drink-driving can be as high as 50,000 Hungarian forints (approximately US $220) and is only payable in forints.

All car occupants, both in the front and the back seats, are required by law to wear seat belts. Motorcycle drivers and passengers must wear helmets at all times.

In built-up areas the speed limit is 50 km/h (30 mph), and most of the road signs follow the European pattern. In towns the use of the horn is legally restricted to cases of imminent danger. Despite this, Hungarian drivers hoot loudly and often at both pedestrians and other drivers.

New regulations permit the use of mobile telephones by drivers only when the car is fitted with a hands-free system. Otherwise, it is advisable to pull over and stop if you wish to make or receive a call.

BUDAPEST ON FOOT

Budapest is a city in which every pedestrian will find something of interest. Visitors who enjoy rambling along leafy trails should take the railway or bus 21 from Moszkva tér to the Buda Hills (*see p161*). Those who prefer to stroll through picturesque streets and alleyways should go to Buda's Castle District, which is closed to traffic. Váci utca (Váci Street, *see p127*) is fully pedestrianized and has seats where weary walkers can rest and watch the bustle. The promenade along the Danube is one of the most pleasant walks in Budapest.

Pedestrian zone

V. Kerület, Lipótváros
Báthori utca
2 ——— 2

New street name plate

OKTÓBER 6. UTCA

Old street name plate

Pedestrian crossing

Walk signal at a pedestrian crossing

HIRING A CAR

Cars can be hired from the airport on arrival in Budapest (*see p233*), or from one of several car hire offices, such as **Avalon Rent Kft, Avis, Budget Hungary** or **World Wide Rent A Car**. Be prepared to leave a credit card deposit ranging between 100,000 forints and 800,000 forints and to pay US $80–240 per day for unlimited mileage.

PARKING

Budapest's car parks, indicated by a blue "P", reduce the problem of on-street parking (and also relieve traffic congestion). There are more covered car parks in the centre, for example at Nyár utca, Aranykéz utca, Osvát utca and Szervita tér. There are attended and unattended car parks situated in other busy parts of the city as well. Several hotels also have car parks, and may offer spare parking spaces to non-guests. Parking charges vary from 120 to 400 Hungarian forints per hour. Parking cards for use in meters can be bought from outlets in the city.

Parking at the main tourist attractions, for example, near Hősök tere (Heroes' Square, *see pp142 – 3*) or the Citadel *(see pp92 – 3)*, is free for the duration of the visit. These car parks cannot be used by people not visiting the particular sight.

When parking in a metered parking bay, the length of stay must be specified in advance. Parking without a valid ticket or overstaying the allocated time can lead to either a parking fine or wheel-clamping.

CLAMPING AND TOWING

Wheel-clamping is growing in Budapest; all illegally parked vehicles are subject to clamping. As well as paying a fine, it costs around 7,000 forints (US $34) to release a car from a clamp, and around 9,300 forints (US $45) if a car has been towed away – usually to a car park outside the city. Parking meters often display the telephone number to contact in the event of wheel-clamping. It is also worth asking a car park attendant for advice. If the car has been towed away, details on its whereabouts and retrieval can be obtained by telephoning 383 07 00.

Stopping and parking prohibited

FIZETŐ ÖVEZET
H–P: 08.00–18.00
Szo : 08.00–12.00
MAXIMUM 2 óra
Fizetés a jegykiadó automatánál.

Parking of cars allowed in this zone for a maximum of two hours

A wheel-clamped car

CYCLING

Cycling in Budapest is difficult and fairly dangerous. Cyclists have to be careful of the tram rails and the uneven, cobble-stoned surface of some roads.

Budapest's main roads are closed to cyclists and designated cycle lanes continue to be in short supply. Until recently, Szentendrei út was the only road with a cycle lane. However, the provision of other new cycle routes in Budapest has made cycling an increasingly popular pastime.

The best way to see some of Budapest is by taking a cycling trip around Margaret Island *(see pp172 – 3)*. Several bike-hire shops on the island can provide everything needed for a day's cycling. Bicycles available include children's bikes, thus enabling family groups to explore the paths.

USING A PARKING METER

2 The display panel shows the maximum and minimum parking charges. If you are using a parking card it indicates the value remaining on the card.

1 Insert coins to the value of your ticket, or insert a parking card.

3 When the display shows the correct amount of time you require, press the green button to request a ticket.

4 When using a parking card, each time the blue button is pressed, the machine deducts a fee equal to 15 minutes of parking time.

5 Turn the red button to abhort the process at any time.

6 Ticket appears here.

Getting Around by Metro

Budapest has three metro lines *(see inside back cover)*, which intersect only at Deák tér station. Here passengers can change trains (stamping their tickets once again), by following the clearly marked passageways. The oldest line, the yellow M1 line, runs just beneath the surface of the city. Built in 1894, it is known as the Millennium Line after the celebrations that took place two years later *(see p142)*. Recently it has been modernized and extended. Two more lines – the red M2 and blue M3 lines – have been added since 1970, serving the rest of the city.

Sign over the entrance to the M1 metro line at Oktogon tér station

Signs for the M2 and M3 lines

THE METRO SYSTEM

A journey on the Millennium Line (M1) is an event in itself, with beautifully preserved late-19th century stations and wooden carriages *(see p10)*.

Two words to remember when using the metro system are *bejárat*, meaning entrance and *kijárat*, meaning exit, both of which are always clearly marked.

To plan a journey, consult the map at the back of this guide. Most metro stations display maps of the local area. A recorded voice message announces when the door is closing and gives the name of the next station. Smoking and eating are not permitted on the trains, and music can only be listened to through headphones. Dogs are allowed to travel on the metro, but only when muzzled. They are required to have a franked ticket for the normal fare on all forms of public transport.

The metro service runs from 4:30am until just after 11pm. Up-to-date information is available on www.bkv.hu.

A typical station on the original M1 metro line

USING A TICKET

Tickets are bought in advance and need to be franked in a machine before a journey is made. On the metro, the machines are located outside the platforms. Tickets are checked frequently, and there is a fine of 6,000 forints to be paid on the spot for travelling without a valid ticket.

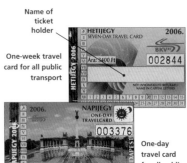

Name of ticket holder

One-week travel card for all public transport

One-day travel card for all public transport

TRAVEL CARDS AND SEASON TICKETS

Travel cards are available for 1, 3 or 7 days; and season tickets (for which a photo is needed), for 14 or 30 days, or one calendar month. Prices change constantly. A Budapest Card *(see p224)*, entitles the holder to free city transport and entry to many sights for 6,500 or 8,000 forints for 2 or 3 days, respectively.

SINGLE TICKETS

These can be purchased separately, or more economically in booklets, for journeys with or without transfers on public transport. There are cheaper tickets for metro journeys of 3 stops (no transfers), 5 stops (with transfers) and unrestricted travel. When changing metro lines a new single ticket must be validated.

Single ticket for all public transport

Travelling on the HÉV

The suburban railway logo

The overland HÉV railway provides an essential means of transport that connects Budapest with its suburban districts. It carries residents to and from work and tourists to attractions located 20 – 30 km (10 – 20 miles) away from the city centre. The standard tickets *(see p238)* used on other forms of transport can be used to travel to the central destinations on the HÉV line, but additional fares are payable to more distant destinations. Tickets can either be bought at stations before travelling or from the conductor while on the train.

A standard HÉV train carriage

SUBURBAN RAIL LINES

The HÉV line most commonly used by tourists runs north from Batthyány tér *(see p100)* towards Szentendre *(see p165)*, taking in such sights as Aquincum *(see pp162 – 3)* along the way. Many of the trains on this line terminate at Békásmegyer rather than running on to Szentendre. Check the destination on the front of the train before boarding. Another line runs from Örs vezér tere (at the eastern terminus of the M2 metro line)

to Gödöllő, passing the *Hungororing* Grand Prix race track *(see p59)* near Mogyoród en route. Gödöllő, a small Baroque town, was once the summer residence of the Habsburgs *(see pp28 – 9)*.

The third HÉV line begins at Közvágóhíd and terminates at Ráckeve *(see p167)* . Tourists who make this long journey can enjoy a visit to the palace of Prince Eugene of Savoy.

The HÉV service between Boráros tér and Csepel Island is the longest at approximately 50 km (30 miles).

OTHER TOWN TRANSPORT

The Budavári Sikló is an old funicular railway, which takes passengers from the head of the Chain Bridge in Buda to the top of Castle Hill.

Several modes of transport operate in the Buda Hills *(see p161)*. A cog-wheel railway connects Szilágyi Erszébet fasor with Széchenyi Hill, with its picturesque walking trails, while the Children's Railway runs from there to the Hűvös Valley. A chair lift, or *libegő*, descends from the top of János Hill down onto Zugligeti út.

Getting Around by Taxi

Taxi sign

It has always been easy to find a taxi in Budapest, and now, with over 15,000 registered cabs, the competition for passengers is fierce. Nevertheless, not all taxi drivers read the meter correctly and they have been known to exploit foreign visitors, especially those unfamiliar with Budapest who are travelling to the city centre from airports or railway stations. To reduce this risk, choose a taxi whose tariffs and meters are clearly displayed.

USEFUL TAXI NUMBERS:

Budataxi 233 33 33.
City Taxi 211 11 11.
Főtaxi 222 22 22.
Budapest Taxi 433 33 33.
Rádiótaxi 777 77 77.
Taxi 2000 200 00 00.
Tele5 355 55 55.
6x6 Taxi 466 66 66.

A typical taxi meter

FARES

Taxi ranks can be found throughout Budapest and are seldom empty. Taxis can also be hailed on the street but it is often better to book one from your hotel. Before getting in to the taxi, ask

what the fare will be. Ensure that the meter is set at the beginning of the journey and get a receipt for the fare. Fares increase from year to

year but can be negotiated with unlicenced taxis. This price should always be agreed in advance. The total charge is made up of three parts; a basic charge, a per-kilometer charge, and a waiting charge.

A licenced taxi in Budapest

Getting Around by Tram

There are over 30 tram lines in Budapest, which extend to practically every part of the city. These yellow trams are an efficient and speedy means of getting around Budapest, as they avoid traffic and run very frequently. Services start early in the morning, at around 4:30am, and run regularly throughout the day until 11pm or midnight, depending on the route. Night trams operate only on certain routes, at an average of four trams per hour. Timetables are displayed at each stop. It is worth knowing that *utolsó indul* means "last tram".

THE TRAM SYSTEM

Tickets for trams can be bought at metro stations, tobacconist shops *(trafiks)* and some newspaper kiosks. Passes valid for a week or more require a photograph and can only be bought at metro stations. When ticket

Yellow Budapest tram

offices are closed, tickets can be bought from vending machines. Tickets should be franked in a machine found inside the tram. Each ticket is valid for a single journey without changes, and can be used on any form of public transport. It can be cheaper and more convenient to buy books of 20 tickets.

When a tram line is closed for maintenance, replacement buses are provided. These display the tram number preceded by the letter "V".

TRAVELLING WITH LUGGAGE

Every passenger on the tram, just as on the bus or trolley bus, is entitled to carry two pieces of luggage. These should not exceed 40 by 50 by 80 cm (16 by 20 by 30 inches) or 20 by 20 by 200 cm (8 by 8 by 80 inches) in

TRAM STOP

Every tram stop displays the appropriate tram numbers and the timetable.

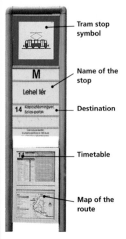

Tram stop symbol

Name of the stop

Destination

Timetable

Map of the route

size. You can also carry one pair of ice skates and one pair of skis, providing they are clean, as well as a child's buggy. If you need to transport a bicycle or a larger item of luggage, up to 100 by 100 by 200 cm (40 by 40 by 80 inches) in size, then the rack railway or the designated carriages of the HÉV trains should be used. Any items left on public transport can be traced at the Lost Property Office, at No. 18 Akácfa utca *(see p227)*.

USEFUL TRAM ROUTES

Budapest trams are possibly the most convenient form of public transport for tourists. Particularly valuable sightseeing routes are trams 18, 19 and 61 on the Buda side of town and trams 2, 4 and 6 on the Pest side.

KEY

○   Interchange tram stop

▬▬▬   Line 2

▬▬▬   Line 4

▬▬▬   Line 6

▬▬▬   Line 18

▬▬▬   Line 19

▬▬▬   Line 61

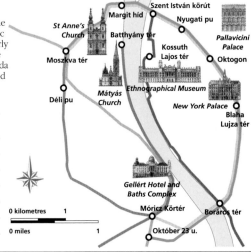

0 kilometres   1

0 miles   1

Getting Around by Bus

Budapest has about 200 different bus routes, which altogether cover most of the city. The blue Ikarus and new Volvo buses generally run from 4:30am until 11pm, with departures on most routes every 10–20 minutes. Times and a list of destinations are on display at most stops. Ordinary buses are indicated by black numbers and stop at every stop. Buses with red numbers follow express routes and omit a number of stops.

THE BUS SYSTEM

Budapest's bus transport is extremely efficient and makes exploring the city easy, even for first-time visitors. Tickets can be purchased at metro stations and from tobacconist shops *(trafiks)*. They must be punched upon entering the bus.

The driver always announces the next stop, often informing the passengers about any interchanges. To ensure that the bus stops, passengers should press the button located by the door before their required stop, otherwise the bus may carry on. Most drivers will welcome or bid farewell to passengers. Remember that Budapest's bus drivers tend to drive fast and that the streets, particularly in Buda, can be steep. This combination makes it advisable to hang on tightly

A clean and efficient bus in Budapest

BUS STOP

The layout of bus stops is very similar to that of trams and trolley bus stops.

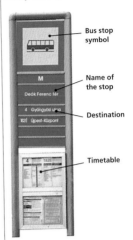

Bus stop symbol

Name of the stop

Destination

Timetable

to the hand grips when standing on a bus.

It is advisable to avoid buses in the centre of town during rush hours, when traffic becomes congested. At these times it is best to take the metro or even to walk.

Getting Around by Trolley Bus

Trolley buses serve mainly the suburbs and as such are little used by tourists. They are a particularly uncomfortable form of transport, as they move slowly along narrow streets. In addition, their pantographs often get dislodged, causing short breaks in the journey.

Trolley bus stop symbol

THE TROLLEY BUS SYSTEM

The same rules apply to travelling on a trolley bus as to travelling on a bus. Again, remember to signal to the driver by pressing the button located above the door when approaching your stop. Otherwise, if there are no passengers waiting at the stop, the driver will not automatically come to a halt.

Trolley buses are numbered from 70 upwards and there are about 15 different routes in Budapest. Tickets must be punched upon entering the bus, and are the same type as for other forms of public transport. Failure to punch the ticket may result in an on-the-spot fine of 2,000 forints. A particularly pleasant route is trolley bus 70, which runs between Kossuth Lajos tér and Erzsébet Királyné útja.

TICKET VENDING MACHINE

Tickets are sold at tobacconist shops (trafiks), *metro stations and the vending machines at major transport junctions and HÉV railway stations. (These are often out of order.)*

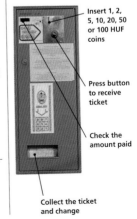

Insert 1, 2, 5, 10, 20, 50 or 100 HUF coins

Press button to receive ticket

Check the amount paid

Collect the ticket and change

STREET FINDER

The map references for all the sights, hotels, bars, restaurants, shops and entertainment venues described in this book refer to the maps in this section. A complete index of street names marked on the maps appears on pages 254–6. The map below shows the area of Budapest covered by the *Street Finder* and is colour-coded by area. The *Street Finder* also includes bus and tram routes, major sights and places of interest together with other useful information listed in the key below. As an aid to navigation, all street names, both on the *Street Finder* and in the index, are in Hungarian. Slightly confusing are the terms *utca* (often abbreviated to *u*), which means street, and *út* meaning avenue, a term mainly applied to wide, busy roads. Other commonly used terms are *körút* (ring road), *tér* (square), *köz* (lane), *körtér* (circus) and *híd* (bridge).

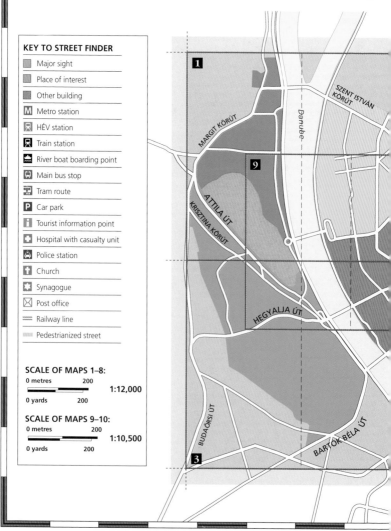

KEY TO STREET FINDER

- ▪ Major sight
- ▪ Place of interest
- ▪ Other building
- Ⓜ Metro station
- 🚇 HÉV station
- 🚉 Train station
- 🚢 River boat boarding point
- 🚌 Main bus stop
- 🚊 Tram route
- 🅿 Car park
- ℹ Tourist information point
- ✚ Hospital with casualty unit
- 🚔 Police station
- ✝ Church
- ✡ Synagogue
- ⊠ Post office
- ══ Railway line
- ▬ Pedestrianized street

SCALE OF MAPS 1–8:

0 metres	200	
0 yards	200	1:12,000

SCALE OF MAPS 9–10:

0 metres	200	
0 yards	200	1:10,500

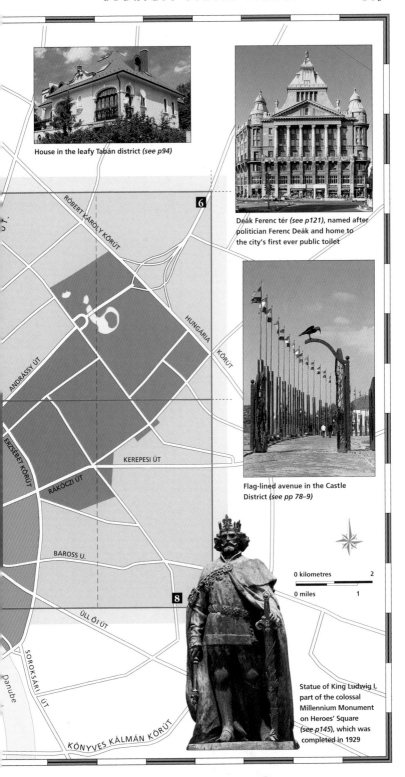

House in the leafy Tabán district *(see p94)*

Deák Ferenc tér *(see p121)*, named after politician Ferenc Deák and home to the city's first ever public toilet

Flag-lined avenue in the Castle District *(see pp 78–9)*

0 kilometres 2

0 miles 1

Statue of King Ludwig I, part of the colossal Millennium Monument on Heroes' Square *(see p145)*, which was completed in 1929

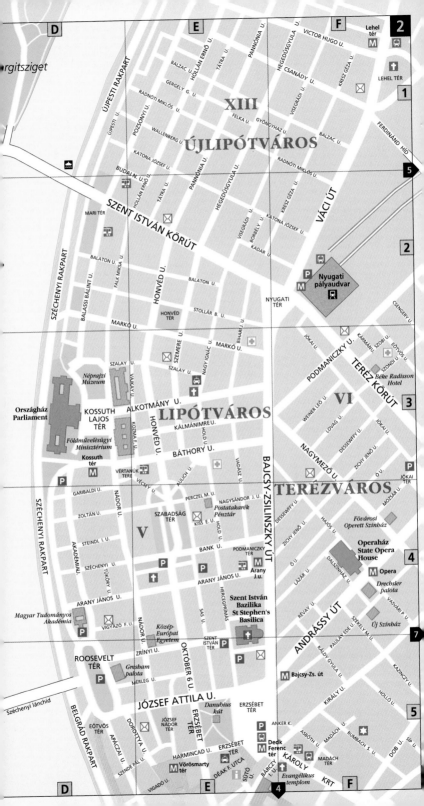

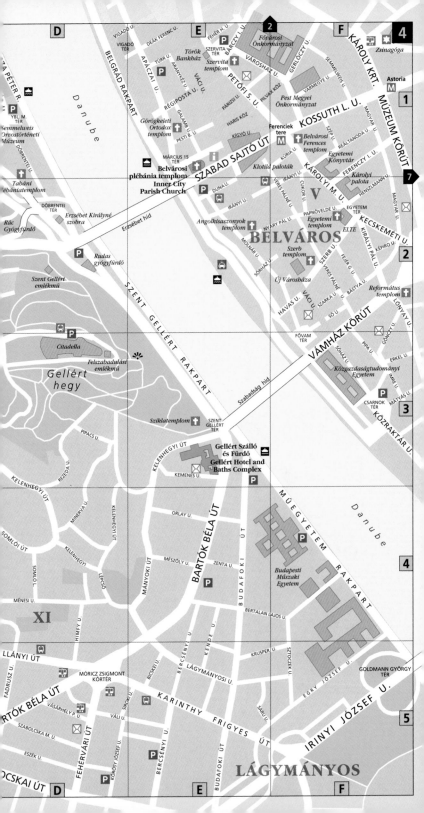

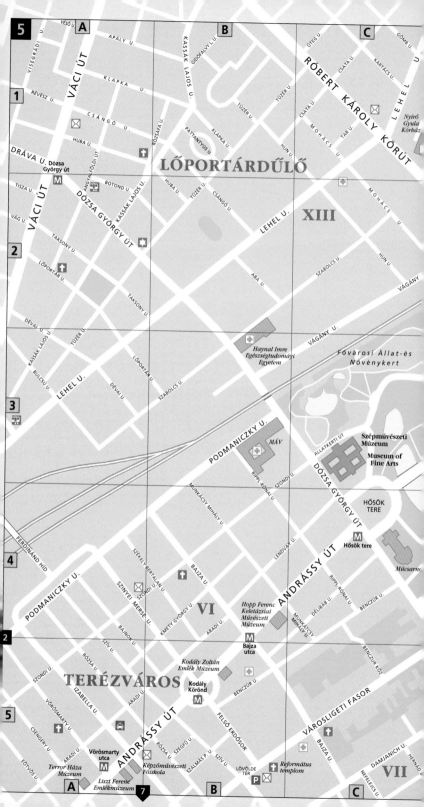

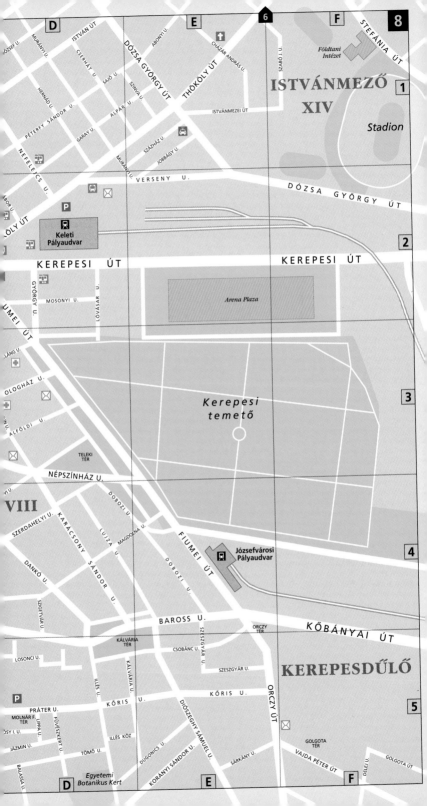

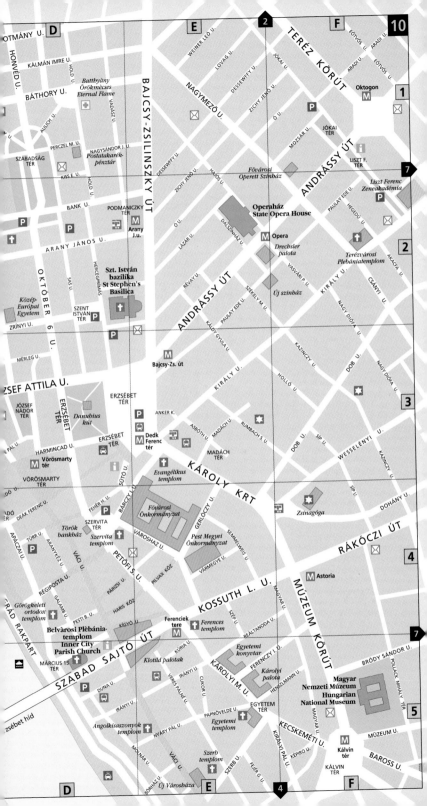

Street Finder Index

Index

Acknowledgments

Dorling Kindersley would like to thank the following people whose contributions and assistance have made this book possible:

Main Contributor
Tadeusz Olszanski was born in 1929 in Poland. During World War II, he fled with his parents to Hungary, where he attended a Polish school in Balatonboglar. He has since visited Hungary many times as a journalist and is the author of five books about the country. These include a volume of articles, Budapesztanskié ABC. In addition, he has translated over 30 Hungarian novels and dramas into Polish. From 1986 to 1994, he lived in Hungary, working both as the manager of the Institute of Polish Culture and as a correspondent for Polish Radio and TV. In recognition of his activities in promoting Hungarian literature and culture, he was awarded the Pro-Hungarian Culture Award and the Tibor Derye Literary Prize.

Additional Contributors
Sławomir Fangrat, Mariusz Jarymowicz, Iza Mo cicka, Barbara Olszanska, Ágnes Ördög, Ewa Roguska, Craig Turp.

Editorial and Design
SENIOR MANAGING EDITOR Vivien Crump
DEPUTY ART DIRECTOR Gillian Allan
PRODUCTION Jo Blackmore, David Proffit
DTP DESIGNERS Lee Redmond, Ingrid Vienings
MAPS Maria Wojciechowska, Dariusz Osuch
(D Osuch i Spółka)
Elizabeth Atherton, Lydia Baillie, Claire Baranowski, Arwen Burnett, Lucinda Cooke, Mariana Evmolpidou, Fay Franklin, Anna Freiberger, Rhiannon Furbear, Vicki Ingle, Maite Lantaron, Catherine Palmi, Rebecca Milner, Amir Reuveni, Rachel Symons, Anna Streiffert, Ellen Root, Andrew Szudek, Ros Walford, Sophie Warne.

Researchers
Julia Bennett, Javier Espinosa de los Monteros.

Indexer
Hilary Bird.

Additional Photography
Demetrio Carrasco, Ian O'Leary.

Special Assistance
The Publisher would like to thank the staff at shops, museums, hotels, restaurants and other organizations in Budapest for their invaluable help. Particular thanks go to: the Ambassador for the Republic of Hungary in Warsaw; the Ambassador for the Republic of Poland in Budapest; Gábor Bányai; Katalin Bara and the rest of the staff at the Hungarian airline, Malév; Beatrix Basics, Tibor Kovács, Izabella Bősze and Péter Gaál at the Hungarian National Museum; Éva Benkő and Judit Füredi Hamvasné at the Museum of Fine Arts; Zoltan Fejős and Endre Stefana Szemkeő at the Ethnographical Museum; Béla Juszel and Éva Orosz at the Hungarian National Bank; the staff of the Kiscelli Museum; Imre Kiss, Zsuzsa Mátyus and Tivadar Mihalkovics at the State Opera House; Konrad Adenauer Stifung; the staff of the Franz Liszt Museum; Zsuzsa Lovag at the Museum of Applied Arts; the Meteorological Office of the Republic of Hungary; the staff at the Hungarian Post Office; Katalin Neray at the Ludwig Museum; Anita Obrotfa at the Budapesti Turisztikai Hivatal; Csilla Pataky at Cartographia Ltd; Géza Szabó; Mária Vida at the Semmelweis Museum of Medical History; Annamária Vigh at the Budapest History Museum. Ágnes Ördög and Judit Mihalcsik at the Tourism Office of Budapest, 1056 Március 15 tér 7, for sourcing pictures and providing new information.

Photography Permissions
Dorling Kindersley would like to thank the following for their kind permission to photograph at their establishments: Ágnes Bakos, Margit Bakos and Bence Tihanyi at the Budapest History Museum; the staff of the Budapesti Turisztikai Hivatal; Eszter Gordon; István Gordon at the Kurir Archive; Astoria Hotel; Dénes Józsa at the Museum of Fine Arts; Ágnes Kolozs at the Museum of Applied Arts; the Ludwig Museum; the Hungarian National Museum; the Hungarian Academy of Sciences; Tibor Mester at the Hungarian National Gallery; Béla Mezey; the Imre Varga Gallery; András Rázsó at the Museum of Fine Arts; the Semmelweis Museum of Medical History; Judit Szalatnyay at the Kiscelli Museum; Ágnes Szél; Ferenc Tobias and Erzsébet Winter at the Ethnographical Museum; Richard Wagner at the Museum of Applied Arts; the Hungarian airline, Malév.

Dorling Kindersley would also like to thank all the shops, restaurants, cafés, hotels, churches and public services who aided us with our photography. These are too numerous to mention individually.

Particular thanks are due to Marta Zámbó at the Gundel Étterem, who provided the Hungarian cuisine photographed for this guidebook.

Picture Credits
t=top; tc=top centre; tr=top right; tl=top left; cla=centre left above; ca=centre above; cra=centre right above; cl=centre left; c=centre; cr=centre right; clb=centre left below; cb=centre below; crb=centre right below; bl=bottom left; bc=bottom centre; br=bottom right; b=bottom.

The publisher is grateful to the following individuals, companies and picture libraries for permission to reproduce their photographs:

Alamy Images: Tibor Bognar 175tl; Kevin Foy

10cla; 47tr; Chris Fredriksson 232bl; Peter Horree 126br; Michael Jenner 190tc; INSADCO Photography/ Martin Bobrovski 193c; Jon Arnold Images/Doug Pearson 192cl; nagelestock.com 80cr; Sergio Pitamitz 41bc, 79c; Travelog Picture Library 11br; Westend61/Johannes Simon 174cla; Astoria Hotel: 180b.

BKV Zrt: 241c; WWW.BRIDGEMAN.CO.UK: Bibliotheque Polonaise, Paris, Aleksander Lesser (1814-84) *Grand Duke of Lithuania* (engraving) 25br; Magyar Nemzeti Galeria, Budapest 77tr; Budapest Festival Centre: 58ca; Budapest History Museum: 32c, 33c, 38cb, 38b, 72t; Budapest Spa LLC: 51tc, 53tr, 143tc; Budapesti Turisztikai Hivatal: 50cr, 50clb, 50br, 51b, 58t, 59b, 60b, 156b.

Corbis: Jon Hicks 175cr, Barry Lewis 91tl, 193tl.

Danubius Hotel Group: 180b.

Europress Fotougynokseg: 11tr, 25crb, 27crb, 51crb, 83cr, 95cl, 122bl, 140, 152, 156cl, 166tl, 166tr, 214bl; Darnay Katalin 93tr, Szabu Tibor 123crb.

Eszter Gordon: 35ca.

Robert Harding Picture Library: Gavin Hellier 174bl; House of Terror: 144tl; Hungarian National Gallery: 16, 23b, 24cb, 26ca, 38ca, 54cla, 56cl, 74tl, 74tr, 75ca, 75cr, 75cra, 75b, 76t, 76c, 76b, 77t, 77c, 77b; Hungarian National Museum: 8, 20t, 20ca, 20cr, 20cb, 20b, 21t, 21cra, 21c, 21crb, 22t, 22c, 22cl, 22br, 23t, 23c, 23cra, 23crb, 23b, 24cl, 24c, 25t, 25c, 26t, 26b, 27t, 27cra, 27crb, 27cla, 28t, 28ca, 28c, 28cb, 29t, 29c, 29cra, 29crb, 30cl, 31tr, 32t, 32cra, 32cl, 32crb, 33cr, 37cl, 40tl, 130tr, 130tl, 130ca, 130cb, 131t, 131ca, 131cb, 131bc, 133t, 133c, 133b; Hungarian National Tourist Office: 226t.

Jewish Museum: 39cr.

Kurir Archive: 34tr, 34br, 35br.

Leonardo MediaBank: 180tl; Ludwig Museum: 40b, 73b.

Béla Mezey 34ca; Museum of Applied Arts: Ágnes Kolozs 5br, 56tr, 57bl, 136tr, 136tl, 136c, 137tl, 137cra, 137cr, 137crb, 137b; Museum of Fine Arts: 39tr, 146tl, 146tr, 146ca, 146cb, 146b, 147t, 147ca, 147cb, 147b, 148tl, 148tr, 148c, 148bl, 149t, 149c, 149b.

Office of the President of the Republic: 19tr.

Red Dot, Budapest: 50t, 85tr; Serenc Isza 51cra, 190cla, 190br, 190t, 191cb, 191bl, 222bl, 216bl; Reuters:STR 59cr.

Széchenyi National Gallery: 39tl, 126tr, 110t; Széchenyi National Library: 24c, 25c, 26c, 27c, 72b; Ágnes Szél: 34tl, 37br, 41c, 78bc, 84b, 160b.

Tourism Office of Budapest: 10tc, 10br, 45tr, 50br, 65tl, 78clb, 114tl, 151tr, 175br, 215tr.

WestEnd City Center: 210cra.

Zona Taxi: 233c.

Front Endpaper: Europress Fotougynokseg: crb.

Jacket
Front - Alamy Images: Jon Arnold Images/Doug Pearson main; Hungarian National Museum: bl. Back - Alamy Images: Peter Horree bl; DK Images: Demetrio Carrasco cla; Dorota and Mariusz Jarymowiczowie tl, clb. Spine - Alamy Images: Jon Arnold Images/Doug Pearson t; DK Images: b.

All other images © Dorling Kindersley. For further information see: www.dkimages.com

DORLING KINDERSLEY SPECIAL EDITIONS

DK Travel Guides can be purchased in bulk quantities at discounted prices for use in promotions or as premiums. We are also able to offer special editions and personalized jackets, corporate imprints, and excerpts from all of our books, tailored specifically to meet your own needs.

To find out more, please contact: (in the United States) **SpecialSales@dk.com** (in the UK) **Sarah.Burgess@dk.com** (in Canada) DK Special Sales at **general@tourmaline.ca** (in Australia) **business.development@pearson.com.au**

Phrase Book

Pronunciation

When reading the literal pronunciation given in the right-hand column of this phrase book, pronounce each syllable as if it formed part of an English word. Remember the points below, and your pronunciation will be even closer to correct Hungarian. The first syllable of each word should be stressed (and is shown in bold). When asking a question the pitch should be raised on the penultimate syllable. "R"s in Hungarian words are rolled.

a	as the long 'a' in father
ay	as in 'pay'
e	as in 'Ted'
ew	similar to the sound in 'hew'
g	always as in 'goat'
i	as in 'bit'
o	as in the 'ou' in 'ought'
u	as in 'tuck'
y	always as in 'yes' (except as in ay above)
yub	as the 'yo' in 'canyon'
zb	like the 's' in leisure

In Emergency

Help!	Segítség!	shegeetshayg
Stop!	Stop!	shtop
Look out!	Tessék vigyázni	teshayk vidyahzni
Call a doctor	Hívjon orvost!	heevyon orvosht
Call an ambulance	Hívjon mentőt!	heevyon menturt
Call the police	Hívja a rendőrséget	heevya a rendur shayget
Call the fire department	Hívja a tűzoltókat!	heevya a tewzoltowkot
Where is the nearest telephone?	Hol van a legközelebbi telefon?	hol von a legkurze-lebbi telefon
Where is the nearest hospital?	Hol van a legközelebbi kórház?	hol von a legkurze bbi koorhahz

Communications Essentials

Yes/No	Igen/Nem	igen/nem
Please (offering)	Tessék	teshayk
Please (asking)	Kérem	kayrem
Thank you	Köszönöm	kurssurnurm
No, thank you	Köszönöm nem	kurssurnurm nem
Excuse me, please	Bocsánatot kérek	bochanutot kayrek
Hello	Jó napot	yow nopot
Goodbye	Viszontlátásra	vissontlatashruh
Good night	Jó éjszakát/jó éjt	yaw-ayssukat/yaw-ayt
morning (4-9 am)	reggel	reggel
morning (9am-noon)	délelőtt	daylelurt
morning (midnight-4am)	éjjel	ay-ye l
afternoon	délután	daylootan
evening	este	eshteh
yesterday	tegnap	tegnup
today	ma	muh
tomorrow	holnap	holnup
here	itt	it
there	ott	ot
What?	mi	mi
When?	mikor	mikor
Why?	miért	miayrt
Where?	hol	hol

Useful Phrases

How are you?	Hogy van?	hod-yuh vun
Very well, thank you	köszönöm nagyon jól	kurssurnurm nojjon yowl
Pleased to meet you	Örülök hogy megismerhettem	ur-rewlurk hod-yuh megishmerhettem
See you soon	Szia!	seeyuh
Excellent!	Nagyszerű!	nud-yusserew
Is there ... here?	Van itt ... ?	vun itt
Where can I get ...?	Hol kaphatok ...-t?	hol kuphutok ...-t
How do you get to?	Hogy lehet ...-ba eljutni?	hod-yuh lehet ...-buh el-yootni
How far is ...?	milyen messze van ...	meeyen messeh van ...
Do you speak English?	Beszél angolul?	bessayl ungolool
I can't speak Hungarian	Nem beszélek magyarul	nem bessaylek mud-yarool
I don't understand	Nem értem	nem ayrtem
Can you help me?	Kérhetem a segítségét?	kayrhetem uh shegeechaygayt
Please speak slowly	Tessék lassabban beszélni	teshayk lushubbun bessaylni
Sorry!	Elnézést!	elnayzaysht

Useful Words

big	nagy	noj
small	kicsi	kichi
hot	forró	meleg
cold	hideg	hideg
good	jó	yow
bad	rossz	ross
enough	elég	elayg
well	jól	yowl
open	nyitva	nyitva
closed	zárva	zarva
left	bal	bol
right	jobb	yob
straight on	egyenesen	ejeneshen
near	közel	kurzel
far	messze	messeh
up	fel	fel
down	le	leh
early	korán	koran
late	késő	kayshur
entrance	bejárat	beh-yarut
exit	kijárat	ki-yarut
toilet	WC	vaytsay
free/unoccupied	szabad	sobbod
free/no charge	ingyen	injen

Making a Telephone Call

Can I call abroad from here?	Telefonálhatok innen külföldre?	telefonalhutok inen kewlfurldreh
I would like to call collect	Szeretnék egy R-beszélgetést lebonyolítani	seretnayk ed-yuh er-bessaylgetaysht lebon-yoleetuni
local call	helyi beszélgetés	hayee bessaylgetaysht
I'll ring back later	Visszahívom később	vissuh-heevom kayshurb
Could I leave a message?	Hagyhatnék egy üzenetet?	hud-yuhutnayk ed-yuh ewzenetet
Hold on	Várjon!	vahr-yon
Could you speak up a little please?	kicsit hangosabban, kérem!	kichit hungosh-shob-bon kayrem

Shopping

How much is this?	Ez mennyibe kerül?	ez menn-yibeh kerewl
I would like ...	Szeretnék egy ...-t	seretnayk ed-yuh ...-t
Do you have ...?	Kapható önöknél ...?	kuphutaw urnurknayl
I'm just looking	Csak körülnézek	chuk kur-rewlnayzek
Do you take credit cards?	Elfogadják a hitelkártyákat?	elfogud-yak uh hitelkart-yakut
What time do you open?	Hány kor nyitnak?	Hahn kor nyitnak?
What time do you close?	Hány kor zárnak?	Hahn kor zárnak
this one	ez	ez
that one	az	oz
expensive	drága	drahga
cheap	olcsó	olchow
size	méret	mayret
white	fehér	feheer
black	fekete	feketeh
red	piros	pirosh
yellow	sárga	sharga
green	zöld	zurld
blue	kék	cake
brown	barna	borna

Types of Shop

antique dealer	antikvárius	ontikvahrioosh
baker's	pékség	paykshayg
bank	bank	bonk
bookshop	könyvesbolt	kurn-yuveshbolt
cake shop	cukrászda	tsookrassduh
chemist	patika	putikuh
department store	áruház	aroo-haz
florist	virágüzlet	vi rag-ewzlet
greengrocer	zöldséges	zurld-shaygesh
market	piac	pi-uts
newsagent	újságos	oo-yushagosh
post office	postahivatal	poshta-hivatal
shoe shop	cipőbolt	tsipurbolt
souvenir shop	ajándékbolt	uy-yandaykbolt
supermarket	ábécé/ABC	abaytsay
travel agent	utazási iroda	ootuzashi iroduh

Staying in a Hotel

Have you any vacancies?	Van kiadó szobájuk?	vun ki-udaw soba-yook
double room with double bed	francia-ágyas szoba	frontsia-ahjosh sobuh
twin room	kétágyas szoba	kaytad-yush sobuh
single room	egyágyas szoba	ed-yad-yush sobuh
room with a bath/shower	fürdőszobás/ zuhanyzós szoba	fewrdur-sobahsh/ zoohonzahsh soba
porter	portás	portahsh
key	kulcs	koolch
I have a reservation	Foglaltam egy szobát	foglultum ed-yuh sobat

Sightseeing

bus	autóbusz	owtawbooss
tram	villamos	villumosh
trolley bus	troli(busz)	troli(booss)
train	vonat	vonut
underground	metró	metraw
bus stop	buszmegálló	boossmegallaw
tram stop	villamosmegálló	villomosh-megahllaw
art gallery	képcsarnok	kayp-chornok
palace	palota	polola
cathedral	székesegyház	saykesh-ejhajz
church	templom	templom
garden	kert	kert
library	könyvtár	kurnvtar
museum	múzeum	moozayoom
tourist information	turista információ	toorishta informatzeeo
train station	vasútállomás	vashootallawmash
closed for public holiday	ünnepnap zárva	ewn-nepnap zarva

Eating Out

A table for ... please	Egy asztalt szeretnék... személyre	ed-yuh usstult seretnayk ... semayreh
I want to reserve a table	Szeretnék egy asztalt foglalni	seretnayk ed-yuh usstultfoglolni
The bill please	Kérem a szamlát	kayrem uh samlat
I am a vegetarian	Vegetáriánnus vagyok	vegetari-ahnoosh vojok
I'd like ...	Szeret nék egy ...-t	seret nayk ed-yuh ...-t
waiter/waitress	pincér/pincérnő	pintsayr/pintsayrnur
menu	étlap	aytlup
wine list	itallap	itullup
chef's special	konyhafőnök ajánlata	konha-furnurt oyahu-lotta
tip	borravaló	borovolo
glass	pohár	pohar
bottle	üveg	ewveg
knife	kés	kaysh
fork	villa	villuh
spoon	kanál	kunal
breakfast	reggeli	reg-geli
lunch	ebéd	ebayd
dinner	vacsora	vochora
main courses	főételek	fur-aytelek
starters	előételek	elur-aytelek
vegetables	zöldség	zurld-shayg
desserts	édességek	aydesh-shaydek
rare	angolosan	ongoloshan
well done	átsütve	ahtshewtveh

Menu Decoder

alma	olma	apple
ásványvíz	ahshvahnveez	mineral water
bab	bob	beans
banán	bonahn	banana
barack	borotsk	apricot
bárány	bahrahn	lamb
bors	borsh	pepper
csirke	cheerkeh	chicken
csokoládé	chokolahday	chocolate
cukor	tsookor	sugar
ecet	etset	vinegar
fagylalt	fodyuhloot	ice cream
fehérbor	feheerbor	white wine
fokhagyma	fokhodyuhma	garlic
főtt	furt	boiled
gomba	gomba	mushrooms
gulyás	gooyahsh	goulash
gyümölcs	dyewmurlch	fruit
gyümölcslé	dyewmurlch-lay	fruit juice
hagyma	hojma	onions
hal	hol	fish
hús	hoosh	meat

Hungarian	Pronunciation	English
kávé	kavay	coffee
kenyér	ken-yeer	bread
krumpli	kroompli	potatoes
kolbász	kolbahss	sausage
leves	levesh	soup
máj	my	liver
marha	marha	beef
mustár	mooshtahr	mustard
narancs	noronch	orange
olaj	oloy	oil
paradicsom	porodichom	tomatoes
párolt	pahrolt	steamed
pite	piteh	pie
sertéshús	shertaysh-hoosh	pork
rántott	rahntsott	fried in batter
rizs	rizh	rice
rostélyos szelet	bifstek	steak
roston	roshton-	grilled
sajt	shoyt	cheese
saláta	sholahta	salad
só	shaw	salt
sonka	shonka	ham
sör	shur	beer
sült	shewlt	fried/roasted
sült burgonya	shewlt boorgonya	chips
sütemény	shewtemayn-yuh	cake, pastry
szendvics	sendvich	sandwich
szósz	sowss	sauce
tea	tay-uh	tea
tej	tay	milk
tejszín	taysseen	cream
tengeri hal	tengeri hol	seafood
tojás	toyahsh	egg
töltött	turlurt	stuffed
vörösbor	vur-rurshbor	red wine
zsemle	zhemleh	roll
zsemlegombóc	zhemleh-gombowts	dumplings

Numbers

0	nulla	noolluh
1	egy	ed-yuh
2	kettő, két	kettur, kayt
3	három	harom
4	négy	nayd-yuh
5	öt	urt
6	hat	hut
7	hét	hayt
8	nyolc	n-yolts
9	kilenc	kilents
10	tíz	teez
11	tizenegy	tizened-yuh
12	tizenkettő	tizenkettur
13	tizenhárom	tizenharom
14	tizennégy	tizen-nayd-yuh
15	tizenöt	tizenurt
16	tizenhat	tizenhut
17	tizenhét	tizenhayt
18	tizennyolc	tizenn-yolts
19	tizenkilenc	tizenkilents
20	húsz	hooss
21	huszonegy	hoossoned-yuh
22	huszonkettő	hoossonkettur
30	harminc	hurmints
31	harmincegy	hurmintsed-yuh
32	harminckettő	hurmintskettur
40	negyven	ned-yuven
50	ötven	urtven
60	hatvan	hutvun
70	hetven	hetven
80	nyolcvan	n-yoltsvun
90	kilencven	kilentsven
100	száz	saz
110	száztiz	sazteez
200	kétszáz	kayt-saz
300	háromszáz	haromssaz
1000	ezer	ezer
10,000	tízezer	teezezer
1,000,000	millió	milliaw

Time

one minute	egy perc	ed-yuh perts
hour	óra	awruh
half an hour	félóra	faylawruh
Sunday	vasárnap	vushamup
Monday	hétfő	haytfur
Tuesday	kedd	kedd
Wednesday	szerda	serduh
Thursday	csütörtök	chewturturk
Friday	péntek	payntek

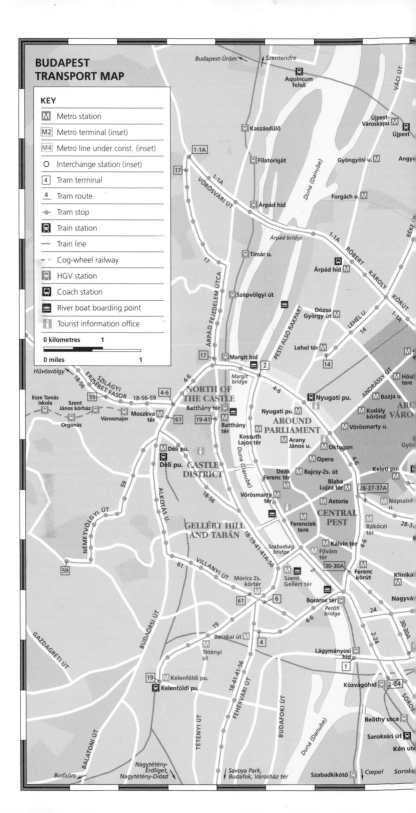